THE

Lazarus Rumba

THE

Lazarus Rumba

Ernesto Mestre

PICADOR USA

New York

Picador® is a U.S. registered trademark and is used by
St. Martin's Press under license from Pan Books Limited.

Part of chapter 8 was originally published in *The James White
Review* and in *Best American Gay Fiction 1996.*

The epigraph is from *The Selected Poetry of Rainer Maria Rilke,* edited
and translated by Stephen Mitchell, copyright © 1982 by Stephen
Mitchell, and reprinted by permission of Random House, Inc.

The lyrics of "La fiesta no es para los feos" by Walfredo de Guevara
(pages 425, 426, 427, and 429) are reprinted by permission of the
author.

The extract by Pablo Neruda (page 448) is from *Selected Poems,*
edited by Nathaniel Tarn, originally published by Jonathan Cape,
and is reprinted by permission of Random House UK Ltd.

BOOK DESIGN BY JENNIFER ANN DADDIO

Library of Congress Cataloging-in-Publication Data

Mestre, Ernesto.
    The Lazarus rumba / Ernesto Mestre.—1st ed.
        p.   cm.
    ISBN 0-312-19907-4
    1. Cuba—History—1959—Fiction.   I. Title.
PS3563.E8135L39   1999
813'.54—dc21   99-21857
                                                                      CIP

First Edition: June 1999

10   9   8   7   6   5   4   3   2   1

To Andrew,
without you I'll lose
my way — a gray crane adrift
on a broken branch

& to my beautiful brothers

ACKNOWLEDGMENTS

This book was a long time in writing, and I am very grateful to the many without whose assistance and generosity I could not have finished it: for fellowships awarded during the time of writing, the New York Foundation for the Arts, the MacDowell Colony, and the Blue Mountain Center; for aid in establishing the cultural and historical background of Cuba, Tad Szulc's *Fidel: A Critical Portrait* (1986), Manuel Prieres's *Senderos de Rocío y Sal* (1991), Luis Manuel Núñez's *Santería* (1992), Gabriel García Márquez's essay, "Fidel—The Craft of the Word" (1991), and the works of Heberto Padilla, Reinaldo Arenas, and Guillermo Cabrera Infante; for their devotion to this novel, and their tireless efforts on its behalf, my agent Harold Schmidt, who read the bulky manuscript first and took it on, my old-fashioned editor Michael Denneny (there are few left like him), his assistants Sarah Rutigliano and Christina Prestia, also Robert Cloud, Lisa Shea, and Tom and Elaine Colchie.

A different kind of gratitude is reserved for my parents and the rest of my family, for their loving support, especially tía Cucha, for the bold example of her life, and Angela, because her name is so fitting; and for Bill Dante, whose love, kindness, and understanding during the writing of this novel are not forgotten.

I have my dead, and I have let them go,
and was amazed to see them so contented,
so soon at home in being dead, so cheerful,
so unlike their reputation.

— *RAINER MARIA RILKE*

CONTENTS

Book One: *A Widow's Grief: An Old Tale*

GENEALOGIES

Renata, la Blanquita ~ Teodoro Lucientes = doña Adela   doña Edith = Juanito Daluz

Marta

Elena Mulé   Yolanda Mulé

Julio César Cruz = Alicia ~ Héctor ~Triste   Juanito
(lovers)

Teresita

Atila Paco Fortunato
(cocks)

El Rubio

Tomás de Aquino
(a bullmastiff)

(rumored)
Maruja ~ Fidel Castro

Joshua

(many illegitimate offspring)

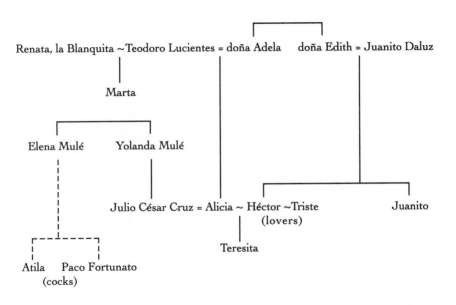

CHARACTERS

Doña Adela, mother to Alicia Lucientes
Alfonso, a bodega manager
Anita, servant at St. Catalina de Ricis Church, doer of spiders
Atila, a blue-feathered fighting cock, a resurrector
Barba Roja, rebel comandante, captured Guantánamo
Mr. Blank, or *Mr. Dash,* a yanqui businessman, surname stolen
Carmen Canastas, lover of the rebel Barba Roja, teller of tangled tales
Fidel Castro, a university student, later el Líder
Charo, captain of a leaky trawler
Doña Álvara Clarón, a gallega, madam of the orange whorehouse
Miguel Córtez, a mail carrier
Doña Paca Córtez, a postmaster
Julio César Cruz, rebel comandante, husband to Alicia Lucientes
Teresita Cruz, daughter to Alicia Lucientes, illegitimate
Cuco, la Loca, servant of Federico Sánchez
Luisito Cuzco, a bartender and rumbero
Héctor Daluz, an acrobat at the gypsy circus, cousin to Alicia Lucientes
Juanito Daluz, his brother, also an acrobat
Juanito Daluz, their father, husband to doña Edith Oregón
Gianni Denti, an Italian journalist
Tomás de Aquino, a bullmastiff
Father Jacinto de la Serna, a professor at the Belén school, caretaker of the
    young Julio César
Father, a comandante in a labor camp, a torture artist
Plácido Flores, an undertaker
Paco Fortunato, a blue-feathered cock, a hunk
Georgina the Manwoman, a performer at the gypsy circus
Father Gonzalo, monsignor of St. Catalina de Ricis Church
Pío Gorras, an apothecary, rumored thief of organs
Delfina Gutiérrez, the heroine of an introduced story, thief of bridal
    gowns

Richard Hadley, a yanqui trawler captain

Humberto, an architectural student, murdered

Maruja Irigoyen, Joshua's mother, banisher of clocks

Brother Joaquín, keeper of a Marist house

Josefa, a madrina in the Valley of the Nightingales

Duchess Josefina, a suicide, mother of four suicides

Joshua, founder of the Colony of the Newer Man, rumored bastard child of Fidel Castro

Alicia Lucientes, widow of Julio César Cruz, later a dissident

Marta Lucientes, half sister of Alicia Lucientes through father's mistress, later a dissident

Teodoro Lucientes, their father, husband to doña Adela, lover to Renata, la Blanquita

Luis el Catorce, a tomcat

Margaret MacDougal, a charitable yanqui

Marcos, reformed counterrevolutionary in the Valley of the Nightingales

Mercedes and *Beba,* brainy, bespectacled twins

Dr. Isidoro Antonio Mestre, a well-meaning physician

Mingo, a finquero

Elena Mulé, a breeder of cocks

Yolanda Mulé, her sister, mother to Julio César Cruz

Ñaña, a halfwit

Doña Edith Oregón, mother to Héctor and Juanito, wife of Juanito Daluz

Perdita, a laundress

Mongo Pérez, last survivor of the village of suicides, maker of snow

Pucha, leader of CDR in Guantánamo, later a dissident

Armando Quiñón, a photographer

Renata, la Blanquita, mistress to Teodoro, mother of Marta Lucientes

Federico Sánchez, a comandante in a labor camp, admirer of Héctor

Doña Sánchez, his mother

Roque San Martín, a bakery administrator

Yéyé San Martín, his wife

Benicia San Martín, their daughter, la reina de los quince

Señor Sariel, an old master at the gypsy circus, later master to Héctor and Juanito

Camilo Suarez, el Rubio, police chief of Guantánamo, gourmand

Triste, contortionist at the gypsy circus, lover of Héctor

La Vieja, leader of CDR in Los Baños

Sara Zimmerman, a Jewish doctor

THE

Lazarus Rumba

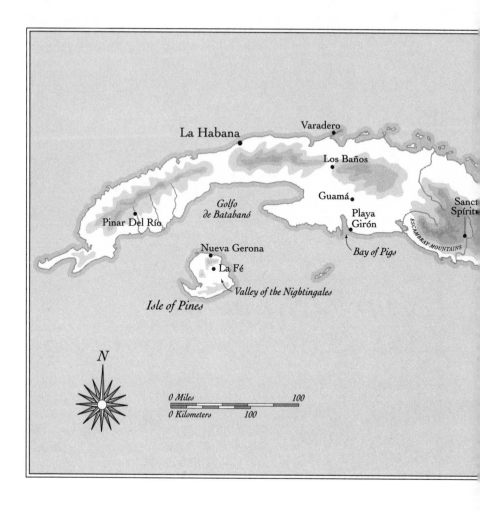

La Habana

Varadero

Los Baños

Guamá

Playa
Girón

Sanct
Spírit

Pinar Del Río

*Golfo
de Batabanó*

Nueva Gerona

• La Fé

Valley of the Nightingales

Bay of Pigs

ESCAMBRAY MOUNTAINS

Isle of Pines

N

0 Miles   100
0 Kilometers   100

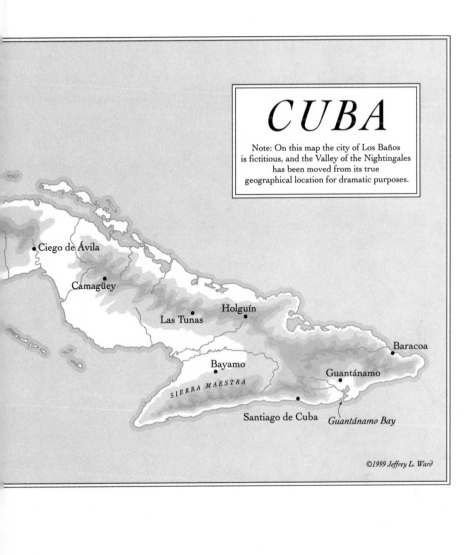

CUBA

Note: On this map the city of Los Baños
is fictitious, and the Valley of the Nightingales
has been moved from its true
geographical location for dramatic purposes.

Ciego de Ávila

Camagüey

Holguín

Las Tunas

Baracoa

Bayamo

Guantánamo

SIERRA MAESTRA

Santiago de Cuba   Guantánamo Bay

PROLOGUE

One Dance

"Do me spiders."

And she would, before his coffee, as he murmured his morning prayers. She would do him spiders. First one and then two and then a few more and soon hundreds upon hundreds. (She was that good with spiders.) Up and down his back, up and down his hairless legs and especially around and around the hardened dried soles of his feet.

He had confessed to her the joy of spiders.

Spiders had begun long ago, in the days of the hepatitis epidemic, when he had been sedentary for so long that spiders were the only way to get his blood to circulate a bit. Spiders probably helped him survive, though the doctors in their summer linen suits would never admit that. Back in the days when his stool was white-on-white like the heavily sugar-powdered guava pastelitos, those overrich pastries that had always been his favorite, and his urine was the color of plum juice. Spiders had saved him then, so now he could not wake without them.

"Do me spiders."

And she would, every morning daintily defying propriety. She would do him spiders.

What would his congregation say if they knew about spiders? What does the Lord say?—since He does know. It's only spiders. They saved him long ago. Where would he be without them? Where would they all be without them? Sheep without a pastor.

"Do me spiders."

And she would, always nervous at the feel of his leatherback skin.

After the first time, the spiders had a tendency to disappear. They would jimjam and jitterbug flirtatiously up and around the bump in his lower nape and behind the ridge of his ear for a minute or two, and then as if yanked up and away by some resentful mother spider disappear until the next day or the day after when they would dance just a little bit longer than the time before—until he found he could almost command their presence.

"Do me spiders."

And she would, more and more often, for longer and longer periods, till her hands tired and the spiders could no longer dance, for he would never ask her to stop.

Her sister had been the genius. She had invented spiders and saved her from her unthinkable thoughts of Francisco, the boy who worked the coffee fields shirtless, his field pants rolled up to his knees, the sap from the beans smudged on his belly. On a muggy pillow-shifting night they came in battalions to soothe her, the spiders her sister said were spiders from God's garden, dancing on her shivering back and bare butt and on her tickly soles. They had saved her the nights the ghost of Francisco's limber torso demanded her dreamy attention.

"Do me spiders."

And she would, always telling him where they came from. She would do him spiders from God's garden. Because she had done it to her sister in the last days of her fevers, turned her own creation on her, done her spiders before she had gone forever to God's garden. That's how she paid farewell. Doing her spiders. And she never thought of spiders again until they had brought him home from the hospital—he insisting a man should die in his own bed, the doctors in their guayaberas (for it was a Sunday) insisting he wasn't going to die. She cared for him as always. She washed his listless limbs with a warm damp cloth, and even washed in and around his privates. He was too weak for shame. She wondered who would give him his last rites. He couldn't do it for himself, she was sure of that. The morning he prophesied would be his last, she remembered her sister's last morning and she remembered the spiders. How could she resist giving his poor bereaved soul one last bit of pleasure. Down came the spiders from God's garden. Up and down his back, scurrying on the fallen flesh of the too prominent ribcage, up and down his hairless legs, till the skin became bumpy, and especially around and around the hardened dried soles of his feet. She did him spiders for the first time. From then on he would hardly need to ask.

"Do me spiders."

And she would, though it was months till she could work up the vigor with which she had done it that first time. Till it became a ritual like morning Mass. She would do him spiders.

BOOK ONE

A Widow's Grief:
An Old Tale

ONE

The Rumbas in Beethoven's Violin Concerto

In the middle of morning Mass, as Father Gonzalo led the sparse congregation into the Apostles' Creed, fragments of memories, heavy and sudden as summer raindrops, began to tincture the familiar fabric of the prayer. He remembered the seawater that was green, its foamy crests soapsuds white. He remembered the riverwater that was brown, its ripply hiccups piss yellow. Sometimes the sea flows into the river. In the sea he is moved by the hands of the Lord. In the river he must swim. The river is crowded with barges. The revelers on the barges are dressed in elegant costumes. They are celebrating a once-in-a-lifetime victory. They dance a rumba. Their waste is flushed into the river. He swims by unnoticed, his lips pursed, trying not to taste the water.

It was silent. The drone of the Creed had lifted and melted in the air like incense. He hurried the rest of the service. After Communion, he muttered for the faithful to go in peace and snuck out a side door near the altar. The congregation—less than twenty faithful—remained inside the church. Father Gonzalo knew they were not waiting for him. They always did this, extending their stay inside the cool dark home of the Lord to avoid the rainy-season mugginess.

He passed through a covered archway into the rectory. He removed his robes as he walked. Anita, his servant, had left the screen door to the rectory kitchen open again. Father Gonzalo slammed it shut and sat at the square wooden table set for one. She was at the stove, her back to him. She ignored the noise of the door. He scratched a mosquito bite on his neck.

"Los mosquitos nos comen," he said. "I've told you to keep that door shut."

Anita came to him, bent his head forward, and examined the bite. "I'll put something on it later. Eat your breakfast first."

She placed a cup of cafecito negro in front of him first and then his eggs lightly scrambled with the buttered and sugared toast. Father Gonzalo ate quietly. Anita drank her coffee standing behind him.

"Don't forget you have to go see doña Adela's daughter."

"¡Sí, ya sé! How can I forget? It's early yet; I told her I'd be there at one."

He finished breakfast and went upstairs to his room and removed all his clothes except for the pair of baggy cotton undergarments that covered half his slight, brown frame from above the navel to just below the knees. He washed his face in the basin by the window. He grabbed his cherry-wood rosary from the top drawer of his dresser, went to his bed, threw aside the tattered mosquitero and lay facedown with his hands crossed under his chin.

Anita knocked and without waiting for an answer entered his room. She sat by the bed.

"Ay, Virgencita, it looks like a demon was pricking you with his fingernails last night! Quédate ahí, I'll be right back."

He did not notice her go and return.

She set a pan on his night table and wrung a cloth over it. She passed it over his upper back. It felt cool and soothing till she pressed it to one of the bites. He lost his place on the rosary and began anew with the second decade of Hail Marys.

"Magnesian salt," she said. "It disinfects them."

"Sí, ya sé," he said. "Do me spiders."

She pressed the cloth to a few more bites. He pinched hard, between his index finger and thumb, the fourth bead of the second decade of the rosary till it left its imprint on his flesh.

"Do me spiders," he repeated.

She put down the cloth and did him spiders with both hands, all ten fingers wiggling and just barely grazing his flesh. The spiders danced nimbly around each bite, like celebrants around a fire, tickling the surrounding skin with their thready steps, then they moved downward on his back single file through the ridge on the right side, spreading again and dancing more freely on the soft field just north of his boxer waistband. As she moved down his legs, past his swollen ankles to the bottom of his tender toes, he felt an excruciating bliss that had nothing to do with the prayers he was murmuring; he sighed, he hummed to the joy of the spider dance and lost his place on the rosary again.

"I too have known sorrow," doña Adela said to him as she let him into the parlor and took his thick-woven straw hat. She pressed her cheek to his and Father Gonzalo smelled her breath of desolation. She wore a loose printed housedress and slippers. Her hair was tied back in a tight bun so that the gray roots were accentuated and the many frizzled strands that had come loose set her face in a shadowy ruff apart from her small body, which moved in quick little bursts like a squirrel or a nervous child. Father Gonzalo followed a few steps behind her into the kitchen and doña Adela latched together the shuttered door and pushed open the window over the sink.

"Todo igual, coño. It's been two weeks and nothing has changed—all day locked in my room and wrapped in that musty old shawl she found the devil knows where. I think it was my mother's (la pobre, que en paz descanse). Y lo peor, now she has stopped eating altogether. She says the world smells too much of the dead and that it ruins her appetite. Imagínate, cosas de locos."

She searched the pockets of her printed housedress, till she came across a folded envelope, worn with handling. She handed it to Father Gonzalo, informing him that the police captain had brought it to her the afternoon before. Father Gonzalo examined the contents of the envelope and shook his head and muttered that something had definitely gone awry when they could no longer properly bury their dead.

"A number. That is all the consolation we get for their murder . . . a number. 'For obvious reasons, and in the interest of national security, the revolutionary authorities reserve the right to bury its traitors.' Imagínate, when was that law passed? I have not shown it to her. I can't."

She offered him something to eat. Father Gonzalo shook his head. He was not hungry. "Un cafecito nada más, por favor, Adela. Then I'll go see her. Maybe she'll talk to me today. Maybe the fasting has awakened her spirit."

"She talks to no one except her cousin. He returned to town as soon as he heard what had happened. He spends hours with her. Pero no sé . . . how much good can he do when he is as faithless as a gypsy, behaves more like a child than she does."

"Adela, she is not a child. She is twenty-six."

"She is behaving like a child. She is not the first woman to lose a husband."

"Sí, verdad, Adela," Father Gonzalo shook the letter in his hand, "but the manner in which she lost him—"

"What about the manner in which I lost mine! You of all people know too well. It was enough to have buried myself with him, wrapped in a shroud of shame! But I endured (pues gracias a tí y a la Virgencita) and I will not have my daughter go mad. She too will endure. ¿No es así, Gonzalo? Won't she? Ay, no sé cuanto más puedo. Estoy completamente desesperada." She tried to hide her tears as she set the coffee down for her guest. Her hands had grown bonier and the veins were thick, bulging out like termite trails. Her fingernails were dull and bitten.

Father Gonzalo reached out and held her damp hands. He felt the sting of the cured mosquito bites on his back. "No seas boba, coño, you have to take care of yourself. Without you what will become of her? These days of doubt will nurture her faith when it grows again. La duda es pura mierda, Adela, but no other fertilizer can so richly nurture our faith."

Music came from Adela's room. Father Gonzalo recognized it and went silent and lowered his eyes and held a tight smile.

"Ay, esa música," doña Adela said, snatching her hands from his. "Como si esto fuera un manicomio. All day long with the same music and the stupid puzzles in that dark room where she can't even see at high day. I'm going to lose her, tan jovencita, mi única hija, and I'm going to lose. . . . No! No! Coño, I won't lose her. I'll take that old shawl and the phonograph and all the scratched records and every piece of her silly jigsaws and build a bonfire in the patio, see what she does then!"

Father Gonzalo had his eyes closed and was listening with pleasure to the intruding melody. "You'd burn Beethoven?" he said, unable to sweeten the harsh tone of sanctimony.

"Que Dios me perdone, Gonzalo, but I'd burn Santa Victoria's handkerchief and Santa Teresa's heart a million times if it meant saving my daughter! What is it with her? I too have known sorrow. ¡Perdóname, Virgencita, perdóname!"

Father Gonzalo opened his eyes.

She now wept openly and folded her hands over her belly and finally her floating suffering face seemed to fuse into her body and her torso curled inward like the stalk of a rainstruck infant flower. From Adela's room, Beethoven's violin concerto reached a swollen pause. Father Gonzalo told Adela she had not done anything to deserve any of this. He told her that the Lord does not act like a scripted judge, meeting out specific judgment for each sin.

"She is not the first," doña Adela said between sob-breaths. "The well of my patience is running dry, Gonzalo. Bien sabes, I too lost a husband."

A few days before the death of her husband, doña Adela had spoken the same words to Father Gonzalo. A director in a sugar mill, and then a renowned diplomat for the three elected governments before the 1952 coup d'état directed by the handsome indian sergeant Fulgencio Batista, Teodoro Lucientes had been, in the eyes of the townsfolk in Guantánamo, a devoted father and a loving husband most of his life. Yet fate, as Father Gonzalo liked to say in his homilies, lives in a hovel near the foothills of tragedy. On the third week of his retired life (a career choice enforced by the new military regime that had many favors to dole out to those who helped undermine the elected governments) Teodoro suffered a coronary, and faced with such drastic evidence of his mortality, decided to turn his life inside-out, upside-down, blowing into the chasm of death, that is, ass-backwards, so that he could face for the first time, in those few moments left, all those days, months, and years of shrouded desires. So Teodoro Lucientes' public life became his secret one, and his secret life his public one. (Indeed, his life had been no secret at all, for every thing that the eyes of the townsfolk of Guantánamo knew, their tongues, their blind tongues, knew two or three things better—and what tongue has never been stained with the ruby dye of gossip?) To put it plainly, sin pena ninguna, with the bluntness of the blindest rubiest tongue, his wife and daughter became his mistress and bastard and his mistress and bastard became his wife and daughter.

After he returned from the hospital, he shuffled through the house wearing only a nightgown, his feet like giant eggplants. The doctors had prescribed that he move around the house and even take walks outside, but his ankles felt as if arrows were lodged there and he could not make it up and down the porch steps unless he had had a few drinks, which doña Adela (and the doctors) strictly forbade. One madrugada, after breaking the glass in the liquor cabinet and drinking half a bottle of rum, he discarded his nightgown and went out to the porch and swung on the blue porchswing, keeping rhythm as he stroked his semierect penis. The tender skin became chafed and bloody and he grew so tired that his forearms burned. He broke into tears, yearning for his other life. Shaken from her dream, in which she heard the screeches of the porchswing as the cries of a horde of hungry seagulls, doña Adela hurried outside and wrapped her husband in a colcha and cured him and guided him to bed, taping his penis to his stomach so that it would not stain the bedsheets. Teodoro, groggy with rum, looked at his organs distended with serous fluids. "Qué pena," he said, "so huge and so useless."

Doña Adela resisted the urge to slap him.

Two days later, after his siesta, Teodoro untaped his penis and discarded the nightgown again, but this time he threw on a wrinkled gray linen suit, and stuffed a blue-tongued bird-of-paradise freshly plucked from his wife's garden into the breast pocket and covered his rumpled mane of gray with a stylish Panama and stiffened his sagging mustache with labored curling motions and shuffled out to the terrace barefoot. He glanced only for a second at his wife sitting there, enjoying the afternoon breezes while rocking herself on the rickety porchswing, in and out of her own siesta.

"I am going to the sea," Teodoro said, his left eye flickering, "to walk in the sands of my youth."

Doña Adela could not muster up the strength to stop him, though she knew he was not going anywhere near the sea; and the first few times he did this, she regarded him with an understanding and scrupulous pity, bemoaning to anyone who might listen how her poor man had gone soft in the head, loco loquito de la cabeza. Yet with each tiny embarrassment of each afternoon departure, and with each further humiliation on his return, sometimes way past dinnertime, six or seven hours later, sometimes way past the following dinnertime, and the following, two or three days later, rosy-faced and drunk with a long-deferred joy, proclaiming how wonderful and soothing the sea air was, her pity began to break down like sugar in a still and ferment into a harsh intolerance. At early Mass on Sundays, she heard the ruby whispering behind her, and from the pulpit Father Gonzalo noticed the tightening of her jaw muscles as she whispered the Prayer of Contrition. One Sunday, she approached Father Gonzalo outside the church, amidst the entire congregation, and pressed her lips so close to his ears that they tickled him, and she whispered: "The well of my patience is running dry, Gonzalo. My husband is very ill. ¿A quién le rezo ahora? What kind of God listens to our prayers, anyway? What kind of God takes a man from his wife and lets him die in the bed of his whore?"

Because he had no answer to any of these questions, Father Gonzalo assured doña Adela that when the time came, Teodoro would die in her hands, but he warned her that it was a sin to so bluntly judge God by the manner in which He lets us stray from Him. Much better to judge Him, Father Gonzalo said, by the manner in which He guides us back towards His Bosom. Many years later, seated at her kitchen table, attempting to console her for the reclusive rebelliousness of her recently widowed daughter, he would use this very same logic, almost these very same words, though they had not proved very useful then and he doubted whether they would prove very useful this time. But it was the only way Father Gonzalo knew how to apply his faith, through a tenacious adherence to dictums that seemed to fly in the face of all common sense. But isn't that what faith is, the most uncommon sense?

And like all men of such uncommon sense, he had heavy doubts.

Why not judge God by the manner in which He lets us stray from Him? Would not any other father be judged by the way he turns from a wayward child, the rashness with which he shuts the front door of the house, then the kitchen door, then the servants' entrance, the conceit with which he stiffens his neck and covers his ears and sews tight his lips and draws the window shutters, so there is no passage through which grief can escape or the vanquished child can call to him, no passage through which he (the father) can answer? Isn't the manner in which He lets us stray, in fact, one and the same manner in which He calls us back? Is not His well-known silence God's greatest sin against His children? Sí, coño, for even the most benevolent father sins.

Why not Him?

———

Father Gonzalo knew that if Teodoro died in doña Adela's arms it would be mere chance, and completely against his will, such was the course of his madness, his inside-out last days, and the shameful details of these days that doña Adela whispered to Father Gonzalo and his servant Anita in the rectory kitchen after Mass on Sundays, they already knew. For who, even among the holy, can resist the ticklish prodding caresses of blind rubied tongues? How does a confessor interrupt a confession that has become a litany of another's sins?

Things were known.

On the eve of his retirement, Teodoro had bought for his mistress-that-was-now-like-his-wife a black Ford convertible, a thing so shiny with darkness that its too obviously symbolic color could be discerned better in the soft moonlight than in the garish sunlight. (It was the shame of the moon to be so enamored of this horrid machine that proved where no proof was needed Teodoro's infidelity—silky rays caressing its shiny coat, its leather seats, its buffed chrome, its glassy orbs, its dormant gauges. Le ronca, does the moon have nothing better on this earth to caress?) The thing—the yanqui machine—was conspicuously parked on the gravel, atop the hill, in front of the two-tiered olive house near the Bano River, the house that belonged to his mistress-that-was-now-like-his-wife's mother.

And her name? Or must the rubied tongues, out of sheer cowardice (for heaven forbid that their names ever be attached to their tongues), always speak this hyphen-happy slashy-sure anti-brevity margin-hugging speak? Her name for the soul of wit? (And these questions themselves asked without words, with the pursing of lips that first touch the hot cafecito, with a disquieting shift behind the confessional screen.)

Está bien . . . la Blanquita. That was her name, or at least that is what she was called.

That is all the rubied tongues offer for now; and with that, pursed lips and disquieting shifts are answered and they make do, and that they call her, as she was called: la Blanquita—she whose skin was veined and translucent as a yanqui's. Like rare Italian marble, some would say, or the face of the moon on a crisp blueblack night (in the ruby tales the moon is a crucial symbol, of light purloined, nature half-hidden). Like a varicose ankle, others claimed, or a rat fetus (dead, or better yet, unborn animals are also crucial symbols in these tales). Fine marble, a pretty moon. A tattooed ankle, a womb-plucked rat. A question of taste, or of situation.

Teodoro loved la Blanquita, and had loved her for many years, and had known her before he knew the woman he married, and about a year after impregnating his wife, impregnated her, so that his daughters numbered two, one aged fourteen, the other one almost thirteen, one named and called Alicia, the other one named one thing and called another—these two sisters almost strangers to each other, *almost* because Father Gonzalo knew that they sometimes—no, not sometimes, once a week exactly, on Tuesday afternoons—unknown to doña Adela, saw each other.

Things un-known were, claro (as is the nature of these tales), over-known.

Long before he had bought the black Ford convertible for la Blanquita, Teodoro had been extravagant in other ways, in ways the sun knew better than the moon. Under the pretext that a sister and a sister must know each other, every Tuesday afternoon he left early from his post at the mill and picked up his daughters at their separate schools and walked them hand in hand to the olive house on a hill near the Bano River. There, on the breezy veranda, they would enjoy the afternoon merienda with la Blanquita and her mother, who, when her daughter and her daughter's lover retired upstairs, entertained the sisters with wicked tales of demons and witches that lived among them. As time passed, Teodoro grew bolder and he would wander into town hand in hand with la Blanquita, flanked by his two daughters, and to those he ran into, at the barbershop, in the gardens of Parque Martí, at the movie theater, on the front steps of the yellow church, he would remain the gentleman he always was and lower his head and lift his Panama and greet with a simple "Pues buenas," and move on.

On Tuesday afternoons doña Adela had no husband, and for many years she let that be, taking her longest siestas on that day, and warning the servants, on pain of dismissal, that no one, for no reason, should raise his voice above a whisper, and much less disturb her, till her husband returned with her daughter from the beach, where they went each Tuesday afternoon. Only once was her long Tuesday siesta interrupted, and once proved enough. A young indian girl, the daughter of one of the cooks, had snuck into the kitchen and, playing with the butcher knives, had sliced her hand open betwixt thumb and index finger and at the sight of her gushing blood began to wail, and neither her father nor the other servants, with cupped hands over her mouth and whispery consolations into her ears and kitchen rags around her hand, could get her to stop. Doña Adela appeared at the kitchen doorway, a long leather belt at her side, like a whip. The cook stepped away from his whimpering daughter as doña Adela approached, and he did nothing as he watched his employer beat his injured child with such venom that the rags came loose from her wounded hand and spread her blood in splashes all over, on the yellow walls, on the refrigerator doors, on the shiny countertops, on her father's apron, and on the dress and face of the woman who was so mercilessly administering uncounted lashes on his daughter's legs. When the beating was done, doña Adela, gasping for air, the drops of blood commingling with the sweat on her brow, told her cook that there was no need to worry, that he still had his job, and that he should get his poor daughter to a hospital. When

Teodoro came home that evening, he diligently washed every drop of blood from the kitchen, and that night did not sleep, re-covering the stained walls with a shiny coat of yellow. He never asked what had happened, and when the old cook tried to relate to him the story, he silenced him, assuring him that his gentle wife had never once laid a violent hand on her own daughter, much less on anybody else's daughter. And from then on, on the cook's daughter's birthday, year after year, Teodoro secretly gave her gifts as lavish and extravagant as the ones he gave Alicia on her own birthday.

With no other option, seemingly satisfied, the cook behaved as if the bright yellow walls had never been stained with his daughter's blood, and doña Adela was never again disturbed from her long Tuesday siesta, her patience long as Penelope's, till the day she approached Father Gonzalo and put her lips to his ears and asked him, befuddled as a three-year-old: "What kind of a God takes a man from his wife and lets him die in the bed of his whore?"

God, chided for His silence, answers Father Gonzalo.

When?

When He sees fit, when His servant is least in the mood for answers, most caught in the horridness of domesticity—in those crusty-eyed moments between dreams and the morning rays filtering through the mosquitero—there God is, too clever to come in dreams (that is only the stuff of stories), where his servant may defend himself with all the skill and wile of the beastly unconscious—for how often is He called to ease suffering, and He comes instead to prove that gouty joints are a mere inconvenience, a heresy, an affront to His imagination to say: "I am now at the worst. I am replete with morbid humors." For whosoever can mouth those words, the worst is yet to come.

Pero vaya, at least He answers. Digan lo que digan, He always returns His calls. Just that He is working in a different time scheme, and sometimes His servant forgets this, and unwarrantedly accuses Him of an unholy silence. His servant could not be more wrong. He is the chattiest god there ever was. All His servant has to do is open His Book and read the stories therein: the Lord answers!

He starts and ends with His most finished law, a law that no god before him dared conceive (much less put into practice), a law so revolutionary that it is the first law mock-revolutionaries cast aside. Did not Fidel, almost from the morning he rode into the capital—(Is that the Virgin on his breast? The glow of the tyrant on his cheeks?)—did not he cast it aside almost immediately?

God, chided for His silence, answers Father Gonzalo:

Every man's soul is his own, to it he answers before he answers to his Lord, so it must be; in his own heart he must fashion a likeness of that silent greatness. So it must be. Else the Lord go mad and the world be left Fatherless. What if a man begot twenty children and had to answer, under law, for each and all of their wrongs, and what if the children each begot twenty more and the man had to answer, under law, for all the wrongs of his children's children and, in time, for those of his children's children's children? Would there be any escape from damnation for this poor soul burdened by all his wrongful brood? So is the fate of your wretched Lord. Think of all My children, think of the awful generations of My brood. I am sick. Worse in being worshiped than you in worshiping. I can command the prayer's knee, but not that selfish heart that feels nothing beyond its own wringing, that with a set of woeful susurrations thinks he can, like a lazy tenant, transfer over the caring of his house to Me. Am I a handyman? Is that what your Lord has become: someone to tighten every leaky tearduct, unstop every clogged heart, straighten every crossed nerve, dig up every weed in the garden of your dreams, plug up every hole in the flesh of those houses I gave you, free of charge, a gift? And am I to be blamed when that house goes up in flames or is eaten by termites through your own negligence? No other creature is as ungrateful as My own children. And you have the gall to wonder why I so often go silent. Silence is my resting place. The only place in My own world where I find peace.

I am sick of this. Your house is your own. See to it, damn it!

On those days, Father Gonzalo listened to God cuss in a voice sophisticated and savage, understood and not understood as the cry of birds, not in his dreams (for as a sleeper he was almost dreamless) but during the course of the wakeful day; it passed through the holes of his tattered mosquitero as he rejoiced at the end of another sleepless night, wandered out from the sacristy as he most absently said morning Mass, buzzed along with the mosquitoes and black flies as he walked to the rectory to have his breakfast, creeped into his flesh when Anita did him spiders, burned at the tip of his one daily cigarette as he performed his egestions, flicked ashes at the urgings in his loins, cut in slivers of light through the brim of his straw hat as he daily visited the many in the parish who sought condolence, cuddled with him at the siesta hour, hissed from behind the voices of the few who came to afternoon confession, stewed in the okra broth Anita prepared for dinner, and then after dusk, just when Father Gonzalo's joints began their most honest ache, God abandoned him. He cursed no more. He went silent.

Not that He was not there, Father Gonzalo knew that God was always there, just that sometimes, like one in a dreamless sleep, or one who is replete with words but will not mouth them, He says nothing.

In the worst of his bedtime hours, when no position can bring comfort to his flaring joints, Father Gonzalo wonders if God dreams during the day, and if he, as his minister, somehow manages, unwittingly, to infiltrate himself into all of God's tempestuous nightmares.

What kind of God suffers more than those who pray to Him?

On a September afternoon when the pelican skies threatened to disgorge themselves, doña Adela waited for her dotard husband on the rickety porchswing. He appeared an hour before dusk.

"I am going to the sea—"

"The sea will swallow you today!" his wife said.

Teodoro's pearly eyes jumped from their sockets, the left one opening as wide as the right one for the first time since the heart attack, and he stared at her as if he were conscious of her for the first time since he had felt the imminence of his death.

"Good, then let there be no mourning!"

With that, he lifted his hat and departed barefoot into the lightning-bleached twilight. Doña Adela lost no time, she grabbed her daughter, suited her in her rubber mango-yellow raincoat and black galoshes and instructed her to grab the plastic bag with her father's new unused shoes, bought three sizes too big because his feet were so swollen.

"Ya basta," doña Adela said, as she threw on a raincoat the color of guava flesh. "I've lost all patience. Not a good thing, mijita, but that's the way it is. Vamos."

The sea, as they both knew, as the rubied tongues had it all over town, was not his destination, though the two-tiered house whose sun-bleached porchsteps Teodoro had stained with his muddied feet was olive, like the sea often is on blustery afternoons. The old woman (la Blanquita's mother) was sitting out on the white-railed veranda, rocking in her chair, oblivious to the rain that had already begun to slant its way in and slap at her cheeks. She wore a lavender dress that came down to her black lace anklets and a gray woolen shawl, which she held tightly wrapped around her shoulders. Her skin was wrinkled and as offensively white as her daughter's. She squinted her clear eyes at the two figures standing out in the rain.

"Qué bueno, you have come, maybe you can talk some sense into her. She has hidden your sister in the attic. The old man has left one daughter to come and die with the other one and Renata hides her from it. As if death were such a bad thing! Qué bueno, you have come, now he can die with the whole family together, two wives, two daughters. Yo no me meto, I'll stay out here in the storm. I am old, I have seen enough people die."

Doña Adela let the raindrops pelt her face. She welcomed them, a drumbeat to the fury in her: "Where is my husband?"

"Ay, Alicia, que bella sigues, I have not seen you in such a long time. Why don't you ever come by alone, without him, to see your sister? Because you are going to lose a father does not mean that you will lose your sister. You have a most beautiful daughter, señora. I remember you once were beautiful too. . . . Así son las cosas de la vida, you stole him from her then, now she steals him from you. Who's to say what's better?"

"Your daughter is a whore! Where is my husband?"

"No, no, chica, the whores are others. If you knew how my poor Renata suffers. I will tell you about the whores if you want me to (many wicked tongues speak into this shriveled ear), but not my daughter, not my poor daughter. She too suffers like an abandoned wife. In another world maybe you would have been friends, partners against him, for that man, handsome as he is (even now, even after all these years—what god makes women wither and men bloom in their old age?), is a demon, a beautiful demon, but a demon nonetheless."

Doña Adela grabbed her daughter's hand and followed her husband's muddy footsteps up the sun-bleached porchsteps and through the front door of the house.

"Come, mijita," she said, "and you will see what a desgraciado you have for a father."

"Second floor, first door on your right," the old woman called to them, then she tightened her shawl around her and murmured to herself: "Yo no, yo me quedo aquí. I don't care how wet I get. This is one story I do not want to know."

Doña Adela hurled that first door open with a violence that startled her more than it did the petite woman in the light blue peignoir sitting on the edge of the iron and brass bed where Teodoro was lying, except for the bareness of his feet (the toes like black grapes), fully dressed. He stirred and raised his head: "Alicia . . . Adela, my pink and yellow sunflowers. How did you get so wet? Have you been to the sea? Come, come, sit by me on this side, hold my other hand. Don't fight, por favor, don't fight, for me, for the father of your daughters."

Renata la Blanquita did not move, her eyes fixed on the wife whose life she had in so many prayers cursed. Her skin was like a smoked glass through which doña Adela imagined she could see the gross fist of her heart, and when she spoke her voice fluttered like a trapped moth: "He always talks to me about you and your daughter. I hate when he does that. But I never once let him know. Es un hombre bueno."

Doña Adela said nothing as she moved towards the bed and began to lift her husband up. When Renata resisted, holding him down, saying that this bed is where he wanted to die, Teodoro waved his hand at her and told her to have some respect for his wife, to be quiet.

"Don't fight. I am going now. Así es, a man dies in his own home, with his own wife and his own daughter. ¿Qué voy a hacer?"

Renata said nothing more. She let go of him and with measured steps backed off into a far corner of the room, her hands over her mouth, her eyes brimming with a flood of tears that no levee of pride could hold back, and watched her lover stumble out of the room with his arm around his wife, watched and said nothing more.

When they got to the door, Teodoro leaned heavily on his wife and turned to face his mistress: "Why are you weeping, woman? Is it for yourself or for me? I can't tell. If it's for me, don't bother, don't waste your tears. I don't deserve them. . . . Do you want to come? Then come. We can all be together at last. What law have I broken in loving more than once? Why all this grief for someone who loved twice? Go, woman, find your daughter and come."

Renata did not move, did not answer.

Doña Adela fixed a hold on her husband's arms. She spoke (like the Lord on certain afternoons) in hisses: "No one is coming, you crazy old man, except you. Solo, solo morirás si sigues así."

Teodoro nodded and turned around. When he spoke again, his back to his mistress, still leaning heavily on his wife, both women thought that he was speaking to her *and* the other at the same time. "That's right . . . that's right, this is how it must end. (What was I thinking?) In your own bed, with your own wife and your own daughter. I love you, woman, let my life be a proof of that and not this my errant death. I am stuck. I am stuck. Only one step more."

And they were out of the room. In her rage, doña Adela had not noticed that Alicia had gone from her, and when she went to ask her for her husband's shoes, there was no one there. She left Teodoro standing with a tight grip on the banister, warning him not to go back into that room. He mumbled to her of the need for a man to die in his own bed, in his own home. She climbed a narrow staircase to the attic and pushed the half-open door slowly and peered in.

Two girls were sitting on the dusty floor, cross-legged, holding hands. They had been waiting, staring wide-eyed, brows furrowed, at the half-open door, as if expecting one of the witches from the old woman's stories to burst through. One wore a rubber raincoat with the hood thrown back and galoshes, the other a knee-length white summer dress and leather sandals. Aside from that, they were unimaginably similar; both had the black-black hair that had once been the color of their father's. (It was not until the year of doña Adela's pregnancy that his hair and his eyebrows went from the color of coal in January to the color of cigarette ashes on the day his daughter arrived—though Renata had surmised that it was the dire knowledge that with the birth of his daughter he could never leave his wife that made his shock of hair turn gray just like that.) Both had fair skin (though not pale like a yanqui's, but colored, colored in subtle peach-blossom primrose tones), dark eyes and little noses, and thick lips that looked as if they had been wet with the juice of a strawberry, a face like his, his, the father's—(Where was the mark of the wife or the mistress in these frightened angelic faces? Had both loved the father so much that they were unwilling to leave any mark on their own daughters?)—whom doña Adela's mother had warned about on the day of her engagement, proclaiming that it was a dangerous thing when the groom was more beautiful than the bride, when his unpainted face put to shame any beauty mask the bride would wear (*Not even a pansy's face,* the old bitter woman had said from behind the shadow of her mosquitero, on that day that, up to that point near midnight, before she burst into her mother's room with the news, had been the happiest of the young Adela's life, *is as naturally gorgeous as the face of that hunk of man who has asked you to marry him. Cuidado, mijita, such beautiful men end up either as absent husbands, o bueno, que Dios te proteja . . . maricones*). And though one girl, doña Adela knew, was a year older, they seemed no more than hours apart in age, as if one had stalled and the other hurried her journey to womanhood, a journey almost ended now, with the sisters hand in hand, sitting cross-legged in an attic, terrified of the sounds beyond a half-opened door, of the grief they knew, one day, as women would be theirs, two girls, so alike they could have been sisters born of the same woman.

"Buenas," the one girl that was not her daughter said. "I am Marta."

"I know," doña Adela would have liked to say, and take her, this child that haunted her Tuesday siestas (that in those nightmares sometimes became her husband, sometimes her own daughter, sometimes herself, lying expectant of torment), in her arms and hold her tight, till she melded into her own body, but she didn't, she remained cordial, stern: "Buenas," she answered and then turned to her daughter. "Alicia, we are leaving now, grab your father's shoes and come."

Alicia obeyed, and when she got to the half-opened door she turned and waved to her sister, who remained cross-legged, alone in the attic and could not wave back.

When they tried to put the shoes on Teodoro he became agitated and kicked his legs and almost fell over the banister: "No, no, damn it! I will go barefoot. I have always hated shoes and now I hate them even more. What good are shoes where I am going?" Doña Adela relented. She took off her raincoat and put it on him and they slowly made it down the stairs, out the front door, and down the porchsteps. Teodoro turned and spoke to the old woman still sitting in her rocking chair, her hair hanging over her face, wet and loosened by the rain, her lavender dress sticking to her bony shins: "Adios, vieja," he said. "You have been kind to me."

"Adios, hombre," the old woman answered, her voice shivery, "how could I not be kind? Coño, I was half in love with you myself. You're going to make a beautiful corpse! Women are going to start wanting to make love to the dead."

Doña Adela pulled her husband away. She grumbled to the dark heavens, begged to know what kind of God lets the whole world go mad, just like that, quicker than the graying of a hair.

The following morning Teodoro awoke before dawn. He stumbled out of bed by himself, stepped out of his pajamas and underpants and, naked, shuffled to the bathroom.

"What are you doing?" doña Adela said, following him, weary-eyed, for she had not slept at all, listening to his heavy breathing (gasping for air at each take), expecting it at any moment to cease, especially when it became most desperate, his neck clenching, the veins in his brow deepening, his vocal chords plucked by a boding air like the heightened last notes of a symphony.

"Voy a cagar and then I am running a bath and then going out."

"Out where? You can't even walk. We practically had to carry you here last night."

"Not to the sea, that's for sure."

"You're not going anywhere. Gonzalo is coming at eight."

"For what?"

"To . . . to give you your last rites."

"How pleasant." Teodoro sat on the toilet. He farted loudly. He looked down and shook his head. "So big and so useless . . . *not* to the sea that's for sure." He hawked and spit on the tile floor, then looked up at his wife cautiously as if he were a child that had just committed a grievous wrong. "Adela . . . Adela, when I die throw me into the sea. I want to ride the white dolphins, the ones we saw in Varadero. Remember how in love we were there, Adela. Bury me there." He grimaced and bit his thumbs and began to weep. "My feet hurt, Adela, my feet hurt so much, how am I going to go out if my feet won't take me."

"No seas dramático. Call me when you are ready," doña Adela said. "I'll have Alicia bathe you. Gonzalo will be here soon." She shut the door and went to the kitchen to make coffee. Her daughter was already there, in the half-morning shadows, at one corner of the long kitchen table, drinking a glass of milk.

"He's going to make it, isn't he, mamá?"

"Yes, mija, for now. But he is very ill." She set the cafetera on the flame and just when the first thick black spurts of coffee came bubbling up, they heard the loud thud in the bathroom.

"Dios santo," doña Adela said and grabbed her daughter's hand and led her from the kitchen. The bathroom door was jammed, Teodoro's fallen body behind it. They pushed without overdue force, as if in respect for the corpse they knew blocked their way. Teodoro's body lay sprawled and naked on the bathroom floor, a razor blade in one hand, half his face shaven, the other half still foamy with suds. Doña Adela put two fingers to her husband's neck, then she unrolled some toilet paper and wiped her husband's still-soiled bottom. And as she did she spoke to him with the assuredness that he could still hear her: "Qué pena, mi bello, none of them will ever see you again." She grabbed the razor from his hand and handed it to her daughter. "Finish shaving your father, I don't want Gonzalo finding him like this. I am going to go call him."

"Mamá, I am only a girl," Alicia protested.

"Not any more, mi cielo, not any more."

"Sí, no lo digo por decirlo," doña Adela said. "I too have known sorrow. I remember many an afternoon after he died sitting out there on that porch-swing, literally gurgling up this greenish-yellow bile (I could never digest el almuerzo, no matter how lightly I ate), and like a fool I collected this bile, day by day, and set it in a closed jar on my nightstand, as if I could measure to the exact quarter ounce the amount of venom I had been forced to swallow. Yes, I too almost went mad. But when I could not fight it anymore, I let it in me. Sea lo que sea, Gonzalo, we have to teach my daughter to do the same."

"In time we will. I'll go and see her now. Is there anything I can offer her to eat?"

"Ay, mijo, you can try. I baked her favorite this morning, guava and cheese pastelitos. I brought them to her fresh from the oven. Ni lo miró, didn't even lift her head from the jigsaw. They sat there on the escritoire and got cold."

"Bueno, de todas formas, heat some up, bring them in to me later. Let me talk to her a bit first." He grunted as he stood up from the table and walked out of the kitchen down the hallway to the glass-paned doors of Adela's room. He tried to listen to his God, but the Lord was usually silent when Gonzalo was performing his duties. He knocked lightly.

"Alicia, soy yo, Gonzalo. May I come in?"

No answer. Only a scratchy lonely, lovely Beethoven violin.

"Alicia?"

"Para que tocas coño. You're going to come in even though I don't want you to."

Father Gonzalo turned the knob and opened the door only about a foot, wedged himself inside the room, and shut the door. The smell of open storage trunks and old wet paper hit him instantly. The damask drapes over both windows that faced the patio were drawn. Father Gonzalo waited for his eyes to adjust, listening to the concerto and saying a Hail Mary in his head. He saw her shadow emerge out of the darkness and instinctively he tightened the muscles in his belly. She jabbed him with four fused fingers of her right hand about an inch above the navel.

"Aquí," she said.

Father Gonzalo did not move. He waited, holding his breath. She jabbed him again, under the left side of the ribcage and to the right of the sternum, and higher up more to the right, and just beneath the right nipple: "Y aquí . . . y aquí . . . y aquí . . . y aquí . . ."

Father Gonzalo grabbed her hand. He heard her laugh.

"Don't listen to mamá, I am not mad, Gonzalo. You *are* a priest after all. We both know where the other two bullets struck. They blew off his huevos. They sought to shame him even as they murdered him. Poor Julio. They were so beautiful, his huevitos."

The sparse afternoon light squeezing its way through the drawn curtains and the yearning notes of Beethoven's concerto created a marriage of shadow and sound in the room so that at first, it seemed to Father Gonzalo, one was competing with the other in trying to engage his senses, till he noticed that they had no awareness of him at all and were rather involved in an intricate ritual of seducing each other—the violin whine cutting its way into space and carving shapes with the clay-thick dimness and the shapes, in turn, throwing themselves behind the music and giving it depth and width, making it a thing of dimensions.

Alicia shuffled away from him and crouched on the floor in front of a giant, half-finished jigsaw puzzle. She picked up a few pieces from one of the three unused piles and put them in place.

"How can you see which shapes match which in this darkness?" Father Gonzalo said.

"They are all with us now," Alicia said. "They have migrated back to this Island like flocks of sparrows after a hurricane. I have not seen *him* yet though . . . I have not seen Julio."

At a crescendo the record skipped. Alicia did not move to fix it.

"Can't you hear it?" she said. "The drums inside the violins. There are many rumbas inside this beautiful concerto, ahí, escondiditas, just like the dead hide in the lives of the living . . . but you have to listen without your ears. Do you know how to do that? Listen with your hips. Can't you hear it? They've returned by the bunches."

The skipping continued, irritable at first, but then Father Gonzalo noticed that through the unappreciated abracadabra of monotony, the violins did become drums, with their own liberated rhythm, their own wake-the-bones song. O, if Beethoven knew what a marvelous rumba he had wedged in between two notes! There must be others (think of all the notes), thousands of other rumbas just as beautiful.

Alicia held one piece of the jigsaw aloft: "Two thousand one hundred and forty-three pieces. I've done it four times already. It is the white castle of a mad king."

Father Gonzalo walked farther into the room, his eyes slowly becoming more adjusted, his hands groping the edge of the bed for guidance.

Alicia resumed working on the jigsaw puzzle, jiggling on her sitting bones, dancing with no legs. Father Gonzalo made it to the phonograph and moved the needle, the rumba vanished with a screech, the violin resurged like a bird flying out of a well.

"Don't bother," Alicia said, "it'll get stuck again, it is an old record."

"Perdóname," Father Gonzalo said, "but I don't understand all this. Seré bobo, but I just don't understand this method of mourning."

Alicia said she was *not* in mourning. She stood up, took a ball of yarn from one of her drawers and sat on the rocking chair at the far end of the room under the two large draped windows. She rocked herself vigorously, in and out of the slivers of orange light that glistened off her cheekbones and cast unforgiving shadows over her face. On her lap, she knit a tangle of unrepentant knots.

"I had a horrible dream. My cousin Héctor, the one who was once going to be my husband, saw his brother die. They were playing together and then they were separated and his brother rode a bike over a hose in the gas station and it exploded. I made Héctor watch the explosion again and again and I held him as he wept."

"'*Even in our sleep,*'" Father Gonzalo said as if reading a script from his mind, "'*pain that cannot forget falls drop by drop upon the heart, and in our own despair, against our will, comes wisdom to us by the awful grace of God.*' A pagan wrote that."

"Es verdad, no entiendes . . . Héctor is coming later today, he understands. I will not share my grief with any other, only him, not with you, not with mamá, not even with Marta (she has already shared in too much grief), although I have to say for a young woman, she is wiser than the lot of you. . . . My husband is dead. My husband was murdered. His dignity stripped from him. And what do *you* want me to do about it. Say a few Padre Nuestros? A few Santa Marías? And you think that that will make this mad widow sane and quiet her husband's troubled spirit?"

"I don't want to steal your grief from you. But I do want to make sure it doesn't destroy you. You haven't eaten in two days. ¿Por qué? Will that bring your husband back? Will that *ease* his spirit? And this boy Héctor, I know he is your cousin, but what can he understand about your grief. He is half a child, half a savage."

"Héctor *loves* me, which is more than I can say for you or mamá."

"That's neither fair nor just."

"Go, Gonzalo, go murmur your rosaries, that is the only thing you know how to do."

"Alicia, mi vida, I did not come here to argue."

"Why did you come here? To save me? To guide me painlessly into the wonders of widowhood, like you did with mamá? Mil gracias, pero no, Gonzalo. Just leave me alone. Héctor will be here soon. I am fine. Bien, requetebién."

There was a knock at the door. No one answered and doña Adela waited for a moment before she entered with a trayful of reheated guava pastelitos. She set them on the escritoire. The steam from the pastries became invisible as doña Adela passed from the light of the hallway into the darkness of the room.

"Who asked for those?" Alicia said.

"No seas atrevida. Gonzalo wanted some. They're not for you." She set the tray down and walked out.

One strike against them, their wispy steam that was their opening act unseen (the first veil dropped in their besieging dance on the senses, the only lure needed for many who would engorge themselves on the promise of such curvy exhalations), the pastelitos turned to the bravura of their odor. Father Gonzalo was silent. He waited till the room was filled with their mollifying aroma, the air particles coated with their lurid sweetness.

Alicia stood and violently drew open the curtains behind her, as if in hope that the light from the patio would consume the smell of the reheated pastries. She walked across the room to her vanity and stared hard into the mirror, not looking at herself but at the room behind her.

Immediately, she knew it was him. She remembered the two long groove-deep wrinkles that sped off from the bridge of his nose, and rode just under the ridge of his eyebrows, all the way along, and stretched out over his temples and finally curled back and in on themselves, like drawn seawaves. His cheeks were slashed with other wrinkles (these, she did not remember), deep and short and butchered, as if carved by a hurried sculptor with a small dull chisel. Alicia did not know if worms had teeth, but if they did, she suspected they were responsible for these wrinkle-scars on her father's cheeks (after they had bored through the cherry coffin that Plácido Flores, the undertaker, had promised them would protect the body for forty-six years— *¡mentiroso!*). But aside from this, the grave, so famed for its feast on earthly beauty, had done little damage to his dear head in eleven years. His hair was a bit rumpled but still as full, his lips as flushed, his eyes as dark, as on the morning when Alicia had shaved half his still-warm face. (When Alicia was four, her abuelita had taken her aside, lulled her near to the bed where a cancer was eating at the inside of her mouth, pulled aside the mosquitero and warned her—the old bitter woman was full of warnings—*Never look at your father straight in those shit-colored eyes, he'll hypnotize you, make you want to love no other man. It almost happened with me once. His own mother-in-law he tried to bewitch. Listen to me, child, I am a dead woman.* And as if to prove it, she grabbed her lower lip with her bony fingers and folded it back and showed Alicia the patch of little white tumors growing there like mushrooms. *So listen to me, your life will be much the wiser if you always heed the voices of the dead.* She wrapped around her the black shawl that Alicia would wear many years later and said nothing more.) Teodoro was sitting on the floor overlooking the construction of the mad king's castle like a foreman, the gray linen suit he had been buried in wrinkled and splotched with mud, eating a guava pastelito and letting crumbs spill on the floor, something he very well knew annoyed doña Adela. Alicia noticed his feet were bare and muddied again, even though doña Adela had spent a whole afternoon washing them and digging out dirt from under the toenails before his body was sent to the coroner.

"Papá, what did you do with the nice crocodile skin shoes mamá buried you in!"

"Ay chica, I gave them to Ernesto Hemingway," her father responded. He added a few pieces to the right tower of the white castle, before he stood. "It's been two years since his death and the poor man is still moaning about migraines. It's forcing him to drink again. The wretch still mad and sullied as ever. But at least now he's got a nice pair of shoes to wander the night in, same size and all, imagínate! Bueno, he was a big man and after the swelling in my feet went down they didn't even fit me anymore. I'm glad he came back. This Island is the only place that's ever made him happy. He haunts the Finca Vigía, driving the staff who takes care of it up the wall; he was not very pleased that his pleasant home was made into a museum. And he doesn't write anymore; says its a moot endeavor in this world, *este mundo lleno de pobre sombritas,* just like that, he says it in a perfect unaccented Spanish: *este mundo lleno de pobre sombritas!*"

"Papá, you shouldn't have given your shoes away."

Teodoro had been loitering in the room with his daughter ever since the death of her husband, and only now with the thick aroma of the pastelitos was he forced out into view. He said their redolence stirred the wild white porpoises of his nostalgia, who rode him back to the white-blossomed orchard where he had first stolen a kiss from Alicia's mother. (*There's not too much color in this first world beyond yours, not many subtleties in the glaring brightness,* he complained to his daughter. *That's a problem. I'm going blind with all the whiteness. No one ever thinks to furnish the dead with a nice pair of sunglasses, but all this glorious light does really get annoying after a while.*) He searched and searched for his wife to kiss her anew, relenting only when the flowers dropped and the fruit ripened and rotted on the branches. Disheartened, he returned to his daughter, no longer willing to hide from her.

"Never mind me and those gaudy shoes, ya te dije, they didn't fit me anymore" he now insisted, and stared at her till Alicia looked back into his eyes "What about you, mijita? I am here now. *I* love you too. I remember how you bathed me when I was ill, cleansed me when my own wife wouldn't. Are you better?"

"No," Alicia answered, "the same. . . ."

Father Gonzalo did not dare disturb Alicia. The next day, at confession, she would recount her shoeless father's visit word for word, how since the day of his death he had been searching for a way to apologize to doña Adela, to take her back to the perfumy guava groves of their youth, how she resisted all his advances, barring him from her sleepworld with a dream netting that kept away the spirit of her late husband as one keeps away mosquitoes, how he had been at Alicia's wedding and only a year later mounted the car with her husband on his attempt to flee into the yanqui naval base and been with him as he was shot down near la Cerca Peerless, *y los pendejos yanquis, they saw everything from their jeeps and their flying devils, the mighty marines with their rifles and their Colt pistols shoved up their culos (¡así son los yanquis!),* how he had watched Hurricane Flora devastate their town, helpless against the uprooting powers of nature that too often reach beyond death, how he had called to the wounded Julio, uncared for in the revolutionary hospital, left to die, whose only answer had been *that he was thirsty and that he needed to go see his old friend,* and how her father ate and ate the wondrous guava pastelito that kept remaking itself in his very hands, the crumbs under him growing into an irritating pile.

Father Gonzalo allowed for some truth to all this. It was known then that unenlightened spirits do populate the indiscriminate air; and besides, if anything, the old man's ghost, real or not, had helped the widow take the first wary steps back to the bosom of the Lord, though Father Gonzalo knew there were many sins that she could not yet confess.

Time, the Lord hisses, *give it time.*

A Serpent's Spit

Later, after Oscar began to ram his head into the flimsy metal fence in the center ring, after he broke it down and battered his way into the crowd, after he deftly picked up Jorge the Ringmaster and gave him the flight of his life, spared only because he landed on the acrobats' netting in the first ring, after Oscar rushed out of the big top trampling over the fleeing panicstricken mob, Gorgeous Georgina the Manwoman from the fleshy streets of New Orleans still perched on him, after he overturned the four-door Soviet-made jeep with two barbudos and a tribunal consul still in it, after they tried to curb his madness by barring his way with the heavier Felicia, who was on her way from the menagerie to perform and after they saw no choice but to shoot Oscar dead, the blood from his skull spouting over Georgina in her white sequin suit, its gory warmth abolishing forever the delicate side of her nature, many in the know said it was the avenging spirit of comandante Julio César Cruz that made Oscar, the genial Indian elephant, go berserk. The poor beast had been possessed and four members of the crowd never returned home from the winter circus on that balmy Christmas day of 1963.

Except for the appalling presence of the empty convertible, the day had begun well enough. Many heads were pounding from riotous noche buena celebrations, but the preliminary parade proceeded early from Parque Martí in the center of the city, each caravan receiving the customary Christmas blessing from Father Gonzalo in the front courtyard of St. Catalina de Ricis Church. He blessed the flustered lions and the trapped tigers and the trained monkeys, approaching their cages with a crafty calm, and he blessed the troupe of macaws and cockatoos and budgies that as a sideshow had been trained to recite scenes from *Hamlet* in perfectly florid Elizabethan English, and he blessed the sad clowns and the half-naked acrobats (though Héctor, the lead acrobat, would not kneel before him to be sprinkled with holy water), and he blessed all the geeks and all the freaks twice (for these were his favorite performers in the carnival), and he even kissed Rodolfo the Strongman's rough-hewn horns, tugging at them slightly and from then on never doubting the story that his mother had been raped by a moose while visiting the state of Florida in los Estados Unidos. Then they were off, towards the bay, to the big top on the rocky ground of Manatí Point. Some who were there say that Father Gonzalo had gotten too caught up in the festivities, that towards the end of the parade, as the last float with yet more clowns passed by him, he joined the crowd and began to follow the performers towards the bay, forgetting to bless Oscar and Felicia the Indian elephants, and more important, forgetting to bless the old black Ford convertible pulled by two spotted mules that traditionally brought up the end of the parade (yes, the same one that the moon had once so adulterously caressed), a rusty hollow carriage of state, un cacharro, for the previous four years occupied by the town's most powerful circus supporter, this year empty, and with a Cuban flag draped across the hood in honor of his recent death. What could have prompted Father Gonzalo's flagrant oversight in not blessing the cacharro? Was he so fearful of the Fidelistas, the armed soldiers of the regime who had made their presence felt through the parade route, their disapproval graven in their stern guarded faces as if insisting even now, in the middle of this Christmas fiesta: *¡Hay caña que cortar! La Revolución needs you in the fields, not here!* Or worse, was Father Gonzalo in cahoots with them? These were the questions certain factions were asking after the tragedy that Christmas night, not daring to promulgate answers.

On that day of tribulations and extravagance, Alicia was conspicuous in her plainness. Yet only a few noticed her pacing twelve steps behind the empty mule-drawn cacharro. Her sister, Marta, was by her side. They held hands, two women who would be later well remembered on this day, a day marked by all the future tribunals as the birth date of their sorcerous conspiracy against the revolutionary government, but who were, for the moment, mostly ignored.

Two women, who after the stormy afternoon in which they had fallen in love—in the manner of any two people who are forced to see each other on a daily basis, and know that they are supposed to feel some sort of disdain for the other, yet feel nothing but the dull ache of indifference, and tolerate each other, and look forward to the six hours they must spend together each Tuesday afternoon, not with exhilaration nor with dread, but with the patient anticipation that precedes all those collected hours they must simply get through, since the Tuesday afternoons led by their cheerful father are carefree, undaunting, there is nothing special about them, all the same, these placid Tuesday afternoons, for two girls who for years felt nothing, no hate, no jealousy, no fondness, no substance in each other, who one stormy afternoon find themselves alone in a dusty attic, and because they know they must, because they know there is no other thing to do (as they have never in all their Tuesdays together chitchatted, played games, not as much as once looked each other directly in the eyes) sit and hold hands, and with a most natural ease, forced by the moment, begin to realize that all the woes that have befallen one have befallen the other, and if they just sit here in this room and hold hands, no harm will ever come to them through the half-open door on the other side of the dusty attic—behaved as sisters for the first time in their lives.

After Teodoro's death, Alicia went each Tuesday afternoon to the olive house near the Bano River to see her sister, and though the old woman welcomed her visits, Renata was less hospitable. She had lost her voice on the stormy afternoon on which her lover, leaning heavily on his wife, abandoned her, but she had learned to scream in the words she scribbled on the notepad that she carried tied to a leather bracelet on her wrist.

"GET OUT OF HERE! YOU ARE NOT WELCOME IN THIS HOUSE!"

Alicia handed the note back to her and said: "I have come to see my sister, not you."

"YOU HAVE NO SISTER. DO YOU THINK YOUR BASTARD OF A FATHER IS THE ONLY MAN I EVER LOVED!"

Alicia again handed the note back to Renata and turned her back to her and sat on the sun-bleached porchsteps for the six hours she was accustomed to spending with her sister on Tuesday afternoons. She read no more of the capitalized insults to the memory of her father that blew over her shoulder like a leaf storm. At dusk, she stood and said her good-byes to the old woman on the veranda and walked home. When her mother asked her where she had been, she answered that she had gone to the beach as she had gone with her father every Tuesday afternoon since she was five.

For over fifty weeks, she persisted with her Tuesday love like a most obstinate unrequited lover. The old woman entertained her with stories of her daughter's mounting madness, which were much more interesting, she prologued, than stories of any witch or demon: "You are brave, señorita Alicia. I wish my daughter were so . . . she has lost it, gone off the deep end, as if there were only one man in this world. Vaya, he was beautiful, romantic . . . and a great lover (oh, señorita Alicia, the things Renata has told me about your naked father, phrases I had imagined a daughter could never whisper to a mother), pero coño, al fin y al cabo, only a man, what do *they* know of the misery of this world? What dignity is there in going mad over them?"

A window screeched open behind the old woman and a hand reached out and handed her a note; the old woman pushed it off at arm's length, read it and laughed. "She says, in capitals, that I should shut up, that at least she had a man to go mad over. Does she not think I had men too? Does she think some angel came down and made *her*? Well, I won't shut up, carajo. I am her mother. This is my house, which I bought with my own money (I had men, but I did not need them to supply for me), and I am sick of these little notes . . . do you know what she does? She pastes them all over the house with children's glue, these not capitalized, but in a very tidy, minuscule, whispery script, as if the memory were too fragile to support the weight of the heavy block letters: in the parlor, *here, where the bastard-of-a-father could barely wait to get into the house, where he lifted my ankle-length skirt, wrestled me to the floor, and did not even bother as much as to pull his pants below the beltline;* on the kitchen table, *here, where the bastard-of-a-father, in the middle of his merienda, sticks his hand under my blouse and begins rubbing chocolate frosting on my nipple and spitting warm lemonade in my belly button;* under the dining room table, *here, where the bastard-of-a-father laid out a linen bedsheet and we sat naked and drank straight from a bottle of Bordeaux;* on the toilet seat, *here, where the bastard-of-a-father walked in on me in the middle of my necessities and stood by me with his groin pressed to my face and said he loved no sound better in the world than the gush of my urine;* on the third step of the attic stairways, *here, one afternoon long ago, where the bastard-of-a-father toiled so long, for so many hours, that his head split open and out of it was born a girl;* and of course, in every corner of her bed, so many notes that they would fill a thousand-page manuscript, piled so deep that cockroaches have begun to nest in them, and my mad daughter is forced to sleep on a cot in the attic, the one room in the house where not a note is pasted, for even in the headboard of her own daughter's little bed a most chilling note was pasted (which I quickly removed before Martica saw it), *here, where the bastard-of-a-father forced me to whisper things into his ear pretending I was his own.* (Imagínate, a demon, that's what your father was. He possessed her.) I'm surprised she has not yet caught up with her daughter, mi pobre Martica, and pasted a note on her forehead, *here, the bastard the bastard-of-a-father fathered.*"

One Tuesday, Alicia arrived and the old woman informed her that Renata had expanded her installation of noted memory. She pointed to the little notes pasted to the hood of the already rust-spotted yanqui convertible, to the railing of the veranda, to the begonias in the flower garden, to the trunk of the almond tree, to the tiles on the roof, and even one (and the old woman lifted her haunch to prove it) to the seat of her rocking chair. Looking at all the notes, their edges stirred by the breeze so that they seemed like insects caught in a web, Alicia realized for the first time that her father had not restricted his visits to this house merely to Tuesdays, had loved his mistress more, much more than on those afternoons when she and her sister sat on the veranda and listened to the old woman's tales. She felt for the first time a stab of shame for her abandoned mother (alone in that room where Alicia would later hide from her own grief), thinking Teodoro at work late, in the capital on business, out with yanqui buyers, when the desperate wings of these webbed insects told Alicia where Teodoro had been all the while: *here . . . here . . . here . . .* and she could not find the dignity with which to sit on the sun-bleached porch-steps and wait for her sister any longer. So she stood under the small attic window and called to her: "Mi hermana, coño, it has been a whole year, this is my last Tuesday. Either you come down now, or we will never see each other again." She waited and there was no answer and just as she was about to turn and leave, her fate as an only daughter sealed, the lace curtain was parted and the window cracked open and a piece of paper flew out like a butterfly and fluttered down to her and rested on her palm and opened its wings to a script as small and delicate as any Alicia had ever seen: *Meet me tonight at eleven, after the two witches have gone to sleep, in the backseat of the convertible. I will tell you all, my lovely sister, and for every hour you have waited, for every day we have behaved as perfect strangers, I will kiss you a hundred times.*

That night, Alicia found her sister curled in the backseat of the convertible. She had a ball of her mother's notes crumpled in her hand. She had removed them from the hood of the car. "These are lies," she said to her sister. "I followed her out every night. I know exactly every place they've done it. Most of them are true—" she pointed to the note that glimmered with the moonlight on the roof tiles, "even that one . . . but these are lies. She has begun to invent some things that never happened. Not like she doesn't have enough true places. If she goes crazy enough then we're in for it . . . there'll be little notes pasted all over town. I know, I followed her, to Parque Martí (under the poinciana trees), to the papaya gardens of the Jewess doctor Sara Zimmerman (where the old lady was said to watch joyously from a second-story window at all the illicit lovers who went there for refuge), to the hills overlooking the naval base (the roar of yanqui warplanes drowning out their moans), to the empty stalls of the farmers' market (the nectar from yesterday's fruit smudging their skin), and even, once, to the front steps of the yellow church (where she made him, since he was a little drunk, swear a wedding vow before she'd let him do it). Where haven't I gone in this town following my crazy mamacita and her beautiful lover?" She jumped out of the car and kissed Alicia on both cheeks. "He *was* beautiful, wasn't he? Beautiful as you, mi hermanita."

She jumped into the driver's seat and shifted the gear, then threw her shoulder to the trunk of the convertible and Alicia was surprised at how easily the tires began to move on the gravel. "Come on, help me, once we get it going it's mostly downhill to the river." The car was just a hull with tires now, she explained. Her mother had always hated it, even when Teodoro was alive and they would ride in it on Tuesday afternoons (their nightly adventures were all done on foot). Renata had never driven the car. After Teodoro died, and their financial situation had become a little more desperate, the old woman began selling the innards of the car to those in the neighborhood, yelled outrageous prices right from her rocking chair, till the car was nothing but a rusty frame and bucket seats on rubber. (She figured that piece by piece she would get more than if she sold the whole thing at once; and besides, she knew she could never convince Renata to get rid of it, for it had become a too-obvious symbol of her capitalized hatred for the bastard of a father. The more its hull rusted, the happier she grew. Though she would never know, till the day of her death some two years after her lover's death, the venomous silence finally choking her, how much more powerful a symbol it might have been—for it was hollow on the inside, as she came to know her lover's passion had always been.)

"Come on, my beautiful hermanita," Marta called, "help me here!"

When they got the car to the edge of the hill and it began to roll on its own, Marta ran to the driver's seat and Alicia hopped into the passenger side. They rode down to the shore of the river as if there were a most powerful yanqui engine in that rusty hull of a thing. They listened to the current and sat in the backseat and held hands again and Alicia let her sister kiss her, on the cheeks, on her hands, on the soles of her feet, as many times a hundred as the hours Alicia had waited through leafstorms on sun-bleached porchsteps, as many times a hundred as the days when they had behaved as perfect strangers. It was near dawn when the sisters had pushed the car back up the hill, Marta's white summer dress soiled with sweat and wrinkled with yearning, and parked it on the exact spot where Teodoro had parked it last.

Some years later, when Alicia's future husband would take a liking to that empty hull of a car, and figured out a more efficient way to start the ghost of an engine, hitching two spotted mules to the front fender, and passing a steering strap through the glassless windshield, the yanqui thing was driven again around town, to Mass, to the circus, to the market, the retired comandante in the driver's seat, his rooster perched on his shoulder, the two sisters holding hands in the backseat, as joyously and carefree as Teodoro had once driven it, though the old woman railed at them from her rocking chair on the veranda that every time the car was moved from its spot on the gravel in front of the olive house, Renata's ghost would take to littering the house with crumpled notes, which the old woman opened, hoping to find some message from the beyond, but never found as much as one word, one exclamation point, one capital, the little sheets full of nothing, like the insides of the black Ford convertible.

Though she still fingered the same ebony rosary she had held tight since reopening her heart to the Lord, on that Christmas morning 1963, that day of tribulations and extravagance, Alicia had forsaken the black trappings of mourning. She wore a light cotton tawny dress that was soberly tailored at the neckline and hugged the waist with a modest assurance. Its hem toyingly revealed and then hid her knees as she paced. Only her face betrayed her simplicity. In less than a month, it had regained its irresistible fullness and her fair skin accented her black straight hair that fell down to her collarbones. She matched again the beauty of her sister, who wore, as usual, a white summer dress and leather sandals. Some of the handful who noticed them called out prayers of endurance. Others suggested they mount the mule-drawn convertible as an affront to the unwelcome soldiers. Alicia shook her head and continued to walk serenely just twelve steps behind. Soon she was forgotten. The revels proved too attractive for anyone to dwell on the rueful widow and her condolent sister for long. Only the soldiers kept a judicious eye on them and only they noticed when the sisters entered the big top and took their place in their customary seats (the husband's seat, between them, empty), in the fourth row facing the center ring. Only they saw Héctor, the lead acrobat dressed in a blue robe, come to Alicia and take her hand and plant three quick kisses. So only they could later testify that while Oscar made havoc of that day's performance, literally rampaging over life and limb, while others were darting for the exits like rats from thunder, Alicia remained in her seat, holding hands with her sister, indestructible, her head bowed, whispering to her ebony rosary.

So? Is divine composure a crime? Can the healing power of ultimate renascent faith be judged subversive?

The 83rd Neighborhood Committee for the Defense of the Revolution set up a separate subcommittee to investigate the *accident* at the circus; as chairman it appointed one of its most vocal officers, Ana Josefa Risientes, known to everyone in Guantánamo as Pucha. Six days after the accident, on New Year's Eve morning 1963, Pucha paid a visit to doña Adela. She was out rocking on the porchswing. When she saw Pucha approaching, she closed her eyes and tilted her head back.

"Buenas," Pucha said, still on the sidewalk. "I am looking for Alicia Lucientes."

Doña Adela did not open her eyes. Pucha tapped her key on the curled iron railing of the balustrade.

"Señora, this is important. I am here as a minister of la Revolución. I know that you are her mother."

Doña Adela opened her eyes and sat up. Her visitor was wearing a straw hat and round dark-tinted sunglasses and pants rolled up at the hem and an untucked oversized man's shirt. Her face was bony and her nose sharp. Her skin was orange and she wore no paint.

"Don't you animals ever take a holiday from your revolution?"

"No seas bruta, señora, we have made arrests and we plan to make more. I just want to speak to your daughter."

Doña Adela began to swing, the rusty chains creating a naughty metallic symphony of protest. "My daughter is not here."

"May I come into your house? I will talk to you then."

"No, you may not. I have nothing to say to you. Besides, I don't let your *gente* into my house."

"Mire, whatever that means, I am not disrespecting you."

"Ni yo a tí. And we both know what it means."

"Very well then, let me just say that we are investigating the unfortunate events at the circus last week. We need to speak to Alicia Lucientes. We know she was there. And let me say more, that you have not been any help, neither to us nor to her. I repeat, arrests have been made. Buen día y feliz año, señora." She turned and walked away, the flapping of her plastic sandals a vulgar answer, doña Adela thought, to the magnificent caterwauling of her porchswing.

In the chapel of St. Catalina de Ricis Church, Father Gonzalo's book club was in the middle of a seemingly unlearned uproar.

"This is outrageous," one member muttered. Alicia knew her as a schoolmate of her mother.

"We won't have it, Gonzalo," another member said, a finquero with hairy ripply forearms who had lost most of his lands to the Second Agrarian Reform Act. He waved a thin paperback with scripted red lettering. "¿Pero cómo vamos a aceptar esto? How dare you propose as the next book on our agenda a work written by an admitted socialist! ¡Esto es basura!

¡Propaganda! Can't you see what thinking like this has done to our country? What tyrants it has bred! Don't you know that this author, this damnable atheist, this Peruvian pig, supported the godless revolution, and *to this day* still speaks well of our besotted Líder!"

Father Gonzalo, seated on the steps of the altar, face down, shook his balding brown head. He too was holding a copy of the paperback he had hand-delivered to each of the members' houses a few days before. He began to finger through the pages gently, cautiously, as one might approach an insulted lover. He spoke without raising his head.

"Mi amigo Mingo, I don't suppose you have read this work and thus I can't accept your condemnation as valid. Sí, es verdad, the author is a socialist, an atheist, some say even a Marxist-Leninist. But you will find in this great short novel, *when you do read it,* that he condemns tyranny twice as heartily as you. Así que, next Monday when we meet again we will talk about *La ciudad y los perros,* forgetting about the author, and certainly forgetting about the author's politics, for writers, poor souls, are only themselves in the worlds of their fancy."

"No, Gonzalo, no puede ser," Mingo said. He walked up to Father Gonzalo and tossed the book on his lap. "You are offending us, offending especially that woman there who less than three months ago had her husband brutally murdered by a regime this author openly praises. Why? Because her husband had grown tired of being lied to. And now you want us to read this garbage!"

All looked to Alicia and her sister, Marta, seated together in the second pew, ready to follow her out, leaving the suspect Father Gonzalo with a book club of one. But Alicia did not move. She put on her silver-plated reading glasses, which made her look incongruously older and slowly leafed through the thin novel. She removed her glasses and looked up towards the altar. "I will read this," she said. "You are not offending me, Gonzalo. I will read this and we will discuss it next Monday." She grasped her sister's hand.

Mingo threw up his arms. "No lo creo. Well, *I* won't read it. I'll be back when you pick something more appropriate." He pointed a finger at Father Gonzalo. "What about your promise to find a good translation of Proust? Or wasn't he as important a writer as this Peruvian comunista?" Without waiting for an answer, he exited the chapel.

"Too bad," Father Gonzalo said, "Mingo is a good reader. . . . He would have liked this novel. Maybe he'll repent and return next week."

As they were dispersing, a light tapping was heard on the chapel door, which was then hesitantly pushed open. Father Gonzalo half expected it to be Mingo, already repented, and he was about to proclaim, as a conciliatory gesture, his resolve to definitely find Proust the next time he visited Santiago. Instead Father Gonzalo saw a diminutive figure enter his chapel, comically dressed in a campesino's outfit, the straw hat and the workshirt and the canvas pants.

"Father Gonzalo, pardon me for intruding," she said. "I am looking for Alicia Lucientes. I was told she was here."

Alicia continued gathering her things, her back to the door, as if she had not heard.

"I am Pucha, an officer of the local CDR," she extended her hand to Father Gonzalo. "I think I have met you before."

Before he took her hand, Father Gonzalo tapped his forehead where a hat would sit. "Please, you are in the house of our Lord."

Pucha withdrew her hand and removed her hat and bowed her head gawkishly towards the altar. "Discúlpame. . . . I went to see her mother first—"

"What?" Alicia turned. "What do you want? Why are you pestering mamá?"

"Señora Alicia, mucho gusto," Pucha said extending her hand and again it was unreceived. "The CDR has appointed me to head an investigation of the accident at the circus last week. May we go somewhere to talk?"

"No, we'll talk here. I have nothing to hide." She gestured for everyone to stay in the chapel. Father Gonzalo sat again on the marble steps of the altar, and tucked the two pirated thin paperbacks under one leg.

"Fine. Were you at the circus Christmas day?"

"You know I was. There were five or six soldiers constantly watching me."

"Yes, well, I need to ask you some questions."

"I need to ask *you* some questions. Where's my cousin Héctor? That's why I went to the circus. I went to see Héctor perform. And after all the commotion I find out that he was arrested, as if he and not the elephant had caused all the damage!"

"Señora Alicia, Héctor *was* arrested. Many performers were. He will have a just trial."

"A trial for what?"

"Por favor, I need to ask *you* some questions."

"¡No! ¡Al carajo! No answers till you tell me why Héctor was arrested."

"Pues bien. Héctor was arrested for crimes classified under *la dolce vita*. There were rumors . . . no, mejor dicho, documentations. He was arrested for antisocial behavior, antirevolutionary behavior—"

"You can arrest the whole circus—no, half the country—for that crime!"

"Deviant sexual behavior, if you'd like to know specifically, señora Alicia. Your cousin Héctor was arrested because he is a homosexual, un maricón. He enjoys throwing up his legs and getting topped by other men!—which is against the laws of nature, not to mention the laws of la Revolución!"

Marta swallowed a tiny gasp and Father Gonzalo grimaced and shook his head as if such conversation were better kept out of his chapel. Alicia noticed both these gestures and dismissed them. *"¿La dolce vita?"* she said. "Isn't that the same *classification* under which you arrested Julio?"

"Señora Alicia, maybe we'd better go somewhere else to talk."

"Are you arresting me?"

"No, not at all. I have no power to arrest you. But please do come with me." She pointed towards the door with her hat. "Por favor, we just need to ask you some questions."

Alicia complied, for Father Gonzalo's sake, for her sister's sake, although she knew in the long run she could protect neither of them from what was to come. They questioned her for three hours at the makeshift investigative offices el Rubio, the pale blond police captain of the revolutionary police, had set up near the site of the shut-down circus, in the airless lobby of an abandoned hotel, which smelled like a dog pound, due to the unwashed drooling obese bullmastiff that dozed there in one corner of the room. When Alicia entered, it raised its massive skull and examined her with indifference and promptly shut its jaundiced eyes and fell back asleep. Alicia's answers were curt and as uninformative as possible; she told el Rubio that she did not know in advance of the convertible draped with a flag in honor of her husband, and she told him that she followed it on impulse, a matter of respect, of honor, and not one of subversion. She had been going to the circus anyway, to see Héctor. He was the greatest acrobat on the Island. And who cared if he was a homosexual? That was a matter between him and God.

Before they let her go, they went through her handbag in front of her, they wrote down the name of the novel with the red-scripted title in three different notebooks, and they warned her that they might be needing her for further questioning, and that they might be calling on her sister. "Though she is not your *full* sister, I understand," el Rubio added sarcastically. And he assured her she could see her cousin Héctor soon, when everything was cleared up and those arrested were given fair trials. The circus, though, he vowed, was shut down forever, for it was a breeding ground for the licentiousness la Revolución had fought long and hard to eliminate. Alicia tried not to show any signs of caring one way or the other, though it was impossible to keep her face and manners moodfree when they spoke of Héctor, or mentioned her sister.

"Madness in animals is not a good thing, y'all," Georgina the Manwoman concluded during her own interrogation, speaking in her beguiling singsong tongue, so that not even the yanqui-looking blond police captain understood her, ". . . means that madness in people is only a serpent's spit away."

The Widow's Bathwater

It was only after she walked out, knowing el Rubio's eyes were fixed on her through the large grimy bay window of the abandoned hotel, that Alicia began to feel the weight of his vigilance like a heavy plank strapped across her shoulders. Dusk had fallen and already the air was aflicker with New Year's celebrations. Explosives rattled and cabcomed creating contorted serpents of sound, and from the open windows of the city tenements on Oriente Street sultry ballads of that melted year's sad loves blared. Alicia was heading for her mother's house to fall into a deep sleep before midnight, for she never again wanted to feel that bubbly New Year's joy that makes even the most alienated lovers hug each other strangely and hope for better things to come. She would sleep and never again waste the smiles of her heart flirting with those wily first minutes and first hours all dressed in gossamer mañanas. What made her change her path and head for the abandoned house she had shared with her husband she would never know, but once she was there, having entered through the patio in the back, sighing at the withered brown tentacles of the hanging coconut plant, at the corpse of her husband's rooster rotting in the fountain, and passed through the outer courtyard into the main dining room, she knew she would not leave, not that night and not for many nights to come.

That same evening, she set out to restore the house from the abundant damage caused first by Hurricane Flora and later by irreverent looters. She stacked all the mangled furniture left behind into an absurd colossus of lost riches in the backyard. Then right after midnight she sprinkled it with some gasoline she had found in the work shed and tossed a lit match into it. The splintered French country table and the wobbly Moroccan chairs were the first to disappear, wisping heavenward towards the new moon. The hand-painted bombe commode and the Louis XVI-style duchesse that had enjoyed each other's presence side by side in the master bedroom held out longer, bristling with renewed elegance in their final minutes. The shattered mahogany mirror recorded the glow of their glorious struggle a thousandfold jagged times as it too disappeared with the old year. At the height of the fire, she fetched the corpse of her husband's rooster, said a quick prayer, and tossed it in. A single high muffled note, like that of a boxed violin, escaped from its lungs.

After she was finished, all that remained in the house, all that survived of these riches that had so often embarrassed her, that Julio had brought from his farm in Bayamo, long ago bequeathed to him by the one-eyed Jesuit professor who had been his guardian, was two undamaged serapi carpets, which neither the looters nor the storm recognized as treasure worthy of their rage (except for one small water stain), a ceramic figure of the crucified Christ made by Spanish monks, the goose-feather mattress from their marriage bed, a photographic portrait of her husband in full guerrilla regalia, defaced by a black unkind scripture shaped like a noose around his neck, and in the bathroom an antique tub, its legs the sculpted bronze talons of a falcon, full of water tinged the color of ink from a drowned squid by a monstrous decomposing piece of waste.

"Qué desgracia," Alicia mouthed, leaving the shit in the tub as a monument to the memory of what had been done to her husband.

On the morning of New Year's Day, having slept not a wink from looking for the ghost of her departed husband, reputed to have been spotted the week after his murder meandering about that house, she changed into a faded flowery housedress she had found in one of the upstairs closets, wrapped an old perfumy scarf around her head, kicked off her shoes, broke open all the shuttered windows and with the new air at her back, bleached the graffitoed stucco walls, polished the parquet floors, and wiped clean any windowpanes that had not been shattered. When she was finished, she dragged the goose-feather mattress out onto the front porch, and thinking of him as she might have seen him in the darkened room of her widowhood, a discomfited phantom full of holes, Alicia waited for the spirit of her husband.

For six days she refused to accept visits from her mother and did not bathe or change her faded flowery housedress or remove the old perfumy scarf from her head. When she awoke each morning she went to the bathroom and stared at the insult in her husband's falcon-legged bathtub, then walked to the kitchen and threw up in the sink. On Sunday, the fifth day, when Father Gonzalo came (at doña Adela's request) to hear confession and administer a private holy service, even he was taken aback when she opened her mouth to receive the communion wafer and her breath reminded him of the rotted airs of those receiving their last rites. He decided to shame her into cleanliness. He would bring the entire congregation of the book club to meet at her house the following day.

"Bien," Alicia said, "I shall receive you."

That night she did not sleep. She aborted any pass her mind made at memory. She read the novel by gaslamp light on the front porch. By dawn, the gaslamp flame flickered with abandon. Alicia, having turned the last page, took up her ebony rosary and lay back on the goose-feather mattress. In her delirium, brought on by both the viciousness in the novel and her sleeplessness, she heard the music of days past, the exultant strings she had heard with him when they had sneaked to the west side of Berlin. She remembered him nude when he had shed his military garb in the monkish hotel on the east side, not one bit tired after a whole day of meetings and secret conferences, his body more fleshy now than on that afternoon she had first seen him when he burst into her classroom and disrupted the multiplication lessons—as a retired soldier, his body had suddenly taken the look of the warriors in the ancient mosaics, taut and supple, as if reined together by the wine-dark scar on his left side that ran from the side of his belly, under the ribcage and up the sternum and then near his throat dipped downward again towards his nipple so that it looked like a palm twisted and cut in half by a thunderbolt.

"Vamos, mi cielo, enough of these dried-ass comunistas. Tonight we enjoy life. Tonight we listen to Beethoven."

He trimmed close his unruly beard, the dark hairs falling like iron shavings on the stained sink, and eagerly donned an Italian suit and a stylish fedora she had never seen before, its brim dipped so low that it met his puckish wink. He laughed as he grabbed her.

"In the *other* Berlin, claro."

She never asked what he had given the guard at the gate who patted him on the back as if they were old friends and chuckled: "*Viel Spaß,* comandante." She assumed it was yanqui dollars, for her husband had always had access to them, especially when he was abroad. And it must have been yanqui dollars that paid for a private box at the concert hall. Alicia could then think of no curses on yanqui dollars. They listened to the famous Lithuanian violinist lead the Berlin Philharmonic through a redemptive version of Beethoven's violin concerto. During the last movement coruscant tears streaked down his gaunt cheeks and mingled with the sweat falling from his brow. At intermission, the comandante brought two glasses of champagne into their box, and they kissed and toasted this their honeymoon, six months late.

And six months later, comandante Julio César Cruz was dead. Alicia thought that maybe that venture into West Berlin at a time when he was visiting the other side of the city as an ambassador for the revolutionary government (*Even your honeymoon,* doña Adela had taunted her daughter, *he smears with his maldita Revolución!*) was on the long list of charges at the secret military trial in La Habana. Maybe it was then that he had cemented the plot he had been accused of masterminding under supervision of la CIA. Alicia never asked, not when he left her alone in the balcony during the second half of the performance, the Seventh Symphony, having capriciously turned angry about a champagne stain on the pleats of his trousers, and not when they made love later that evening, the melancholic grandeur of the weeping Lithuanian still fresh in their ears, her husband's warmth pizzling all the folds of her innards, and not on the night that the revolutionary police twisted apart the wrought-iron door of the inner courtyard and burst into their home on B. Street, dragging him out of their bed and cuffing his wrists and taking him naked as he was, and not on the evening he returned from his trial in La Habana, stripped of his military titles but supposedly a free citizen and el Rubio had him arrested again, so that their reunion took place in a visitor's room for common criminals, and not on the day Che himself came to Guantánamo, on the six o'clock from Santiago, and forced el Rubio to release her husband, and not when he came home that evening and she met him at the twisted wrought-iron door and went to kiss him and he turned his head so that her kiss landed on the grizzle of his beard, and not on those few nights when she attempted to revive his lost flesh, for nothing, nothing: *Leave me alone, mi vida,* he muttered, *I have no dignity with which to love you. Por favor,* and not on the eve of her birthday, some weeks later, when he informed her that he was leaving, headed for the yanqui naval base that very night, his birthday gift a light dry kiss on the lips, the only passion he was able to muster after his trial, and a promise that he would see her soon again, maybe in Madrid, maybe in Miami: *Te veré pronto . . . donde sea,* and not two days later, when she and Marta visited him at the revolutionary hospital, his wounds uncared for, his mind woozy with morphine, the nurses deaf to Marta's demands to change his bandages, checking on the patient only to see if he had died yet. Alicia did not want to know. Not then and certainly not now. Lying back on the goose-feather mattress, all she remembered were those moments during intermission when they had drunk champagne and he had licked her teeth with his tongue, and for a moment she had forgotten what she had long known: that sooner or later, the guerrillero she had fallen in love with when he burst into the tiny wistaria-covered schoolhouse in the mountains to retrieve hidden arms would make her a much too young widow. She had forgotten that he was anything else but *hers.*

She laid her head back on the wedding mattress and shut her eyes and tried to conjure him as he had been in those brief moments. The morning bay breeze stiffened and whirled about the porch, drying the sweat on her unshaven legs and causing the faded flowery dress to flop about and blow up like a sail so that all her body was exposed to the fresh eddies of sea air. Her skin bristled, but not with the memory of him, her husband, nor with the sounds of a long-ago faded concerto, nor with the memory of that scar like a thunderstruck half-palm, nor with the silver tears of a gaunt Lithuanian, but with the soft steps of a more recent memory, with the sweep of a naked foot, with a more lovely voice than any Lithuanian could tease out of horsehair and taut string: *primita, mi pobre primita bella.* He, the last visitor, even after the father, had also been barefoot. He too hated shoes. "What good are shoes in the air, primita?"

"Primito, thank you for coming again. I know they must be very disappointed that you abandoned them so early in the autumn tour. Mi pobre primito bello, how *is* the circus?"

"You already asked me that. I told you the circus is nothing without me. But for you, for you, I would abandon the world."

With this, his voice, which he had used to take from her the musty old shawl, to lift her into the bed behind her, to tease her into unbuttoning his shirt and showing him (poking him) where they had shot her husband, aquí y aquí y aquí, she was pleased and pleased herself, not summoning that moment when she went to kiss him, as he eased her mourning in a manner the mother and the priest, the sister and the ghost, could not, and he too turned his face, even as he, the cousin (who could be nothing else to her *but* cousin), cemented their love.

What sin when so many others have done it?

"Alicia. Alicia, mi amor," a soft unalarmed voice shook her from her lost worlds.

The hand she brought out from under the old housedress had such a tight grip on the ebony rosary that when she released the pressure the stony beads laced around the three middle fingers left deep livid notches on the lowest knuckles. Alicia sat up and hid her legs under the flow of her dress. She did not look at Father Gonzalo, who stood under the porch-steps, when she told him to go, to come back in a few hours with the members of the book club, for she had been up all night reading the novel and she needed some time to collect herself.

Father Gonzalo left without saying a word.

There had not been running hot water in the abandoned house since after the hurricane, so Alicia went into the kitchen and began to boil water in two large tin pots over four flames. She then went to the bathroom, fished the flaky serpent of shit from the antique tub with a pair of rusty tongs she had found in the kitchen and, finally removing the faded flowery housedress and the old perfumy scarf, submerged herself in the cold tainted water, remaining under as long as her lungs could stand it. When she came up for air her panting turned naturally into a relentless outflow of tears. It was the first time she had been strong enough to weep since her husband's death, and she continued to weep as she pulled the drainplug and felt the foul water sliding off and away from her, like a mantle of drool, clinging for a moment longer to her softer parts and she tasted the water's pungency as it dripped on her lips. Then, as she was, she returned to the kitchen and added five teaspoons of lye powder to the first pot of boiled water and pail by pail carried it to the bathroom to disinfect and scour and whiten the antique tub. Then she filled the tub, again bringing the hot water pail by pail, running some cold water from the faucet. On her last trip she grabbed a sharp ivory-handle stiletto she had once claimed from her husband and many times used to gut chickens and suckling pigs. In the bathroom, she opened a cabinet that had miraculously been left untouched by the vandals, six separate shelves of jars and vials of countless shapes and sizes full of salts and powders and extracts of over fifty varieties of flowers, herbs and fruitseeds, some imported all the way from the mountains of Nepal, some acquired in the fruit market not far from her mother's house. To this morning's bath she added some Dead Sea salts, two pinches of the gummy pollen from the fuchsia flower, which was said to promote tolerance of mankind's vainglory, four drops of the clear viscous liquid from the leaves of the nettle weed, which jolted one from morning drowsiness as forcefully as four cups of cafecito cubano, a gush of coconut oil, and two handfuls of the dried ragged pink strips of the cuckooflower, because these were said to open your senses to the least obvious side of beauty. Alicia stepped in slowly, the skin on her feet and lower legs stunned by the immediate heat but soon adapting to the soothing warmth so that her whole body yearned to drown in the same gratification. She realized she had not yet stopped crying, although her whimpers were now more in delicate staccato instead of the arioso lamentations of moments before. The bath she knew would ease her sorrow further. She lowered herself in. With a soap bar made with almond flesh she washed her hair and her face and right at the surface of the water her breasts and under her arms and then she reached under the water and washed her unseen parts and her lower extremities. When she put the bar down and reached for the stiletto sitting on the soapdish her crying had stopped and she felt an easiness in her actions she had not felt in many months. She guided the knife underneath the lip of her navel. Her husband had always doted on the chestnut down that trickled up from her pubes to her navel like wisps of smoke from a smoldering bonfire, found them bewitching. She thought them repulsive, but to please him she had let them grow during the year of their marriage. Now they would go. She lifted her hip up and slicked her lower belly with the soap bar and pushed the stiletto through. The hair readily gave way to the blade and scattered on the surface of the water, some clinging, like insect legs, to the twisted petals of the cuckooflower. Alicia continued to shave until her lower body was as smooth as it had been on her wedding night. She then guided the knife again under her navel and repeatedly rubbed the blade against her skin, up and down and up and down in dexterous flicks, like a sculptor detailing stone. When she nicked herself and saw the red patiently thread out of the cut and retain its shape against the bathwater, she accepted what she had known. It was the first time she had seen any blood since her sister Marta had tried to change the soiled bandages on her husband. Alarmed, as if in fear she might now hurt a better part of herself, she dropped the knife. The ivory handle created a dull compressed thud as it landed on the porcelain of the filled tub.

"Dios mío," she said, as if speaking to one that was there with her. "What have we done?"

She tied her hair back in a tail, wrapped herself in a white unsoiled sheet and, cross-legged on the serapi carpet in the living room, waited for the members of the book club. Father Gonzalo arrived first. When he saw Alicia, recently bathed and calmly seated on the carpet, he waved the others in.

"Perdónenme," Alicia said, "but they took all the furniture."

They sat cross-legged like her, in a circle on the serapi carpet. There were fewer of them than there had been at the church, although Mingo, the finca owner, had returned, apparently having rethought his position, or having been promised Proust, sin fallo, next. They were also joined by doña Paca, the town's old postmaster, who because of her age had great trouble crouching down on the carpet, Plácido Flores, the undertaker with leathery brown skin, Mercedes and Beba, the brainy bespectacled twins who between them many supposed had read all of this world's great literature from the ancient Greeks to the latest South American novel, the handsome young Rafael, one of Father Gonzalo's altar boys, and Marta, who sat by her sister Alicia and kissed her softly on the lips and held her hand. The others remained distantly cordial until they were just about to begin the discussion. The members were leafing through the novel, some rereading notes they had scribbled in the margins, when Alicia dropped from her shoulders the sheet she was wearing to reveal her surprise. Plácido Flores smiled with his eyes, Mingo stared with his, Rafael blushed and like the ladies quickly averted his glance. Marta was fumbling with the sheet in an effort to cover her sister when Alicia spoke firmly: "Look, are you blind?" Her hands were caressing the yet unpronounced fullness of her belly. "It will be born in the torrid days of June. I shall name him Julio César."

"What if it's a girl?" Rafael said, his eyes now fixed each to each on the chocolate nipples of the half-naked widow.

"How can it be a girl," doña Paca said, "when it will be named Julio César!"

The child was a girl. She was born on a hot rainy afternoon in mid-June, exactly nine months and fourteen days after comandante Julio César Cruz's death. Alicia named her Teresa Julia. She would have to live up to the comandante's tenacious noblesse and to the unrotted idealism of the Spanish saint.

TWO

Swimming Without Getting Wet

The skies were uncooperative with the official demands for mourning. The heroic guerrillero Che Guevara was dead, his body mutilated by Bolivian government rangers, but the skies paid no respects, summer lingered festively into the second week of October and warmed the sands and the waters as if it were still August. The most important eulogy had begun, grated its way into a Strauss waltz during the Sunday classical hour. Fidel's voice was raspy as he reminisced about his revolutionary companion, and it would get raspier hour after get-on-with-it hour, at times stooping to sotto voce and near the end, two or three hours past dinnertime, peaking with a frothy fury.

Father Gonzalo shut off the battery-powered radio at his side. It would be useless to search through other stations, el Comandante-en-Jefe commanded the airwaves. Lately, attendance had been plummeting at the early afternoon Sunday Mass. Fidel's radio speeches were certainly to blame. Father Gonzalo could not compete with such tireless sermonizing.

The Jesuits should have nabbed Fidel, kept him, made him a bishop or something. Sent him to Rome even.

Every Sunday as soon as the Speech began, Father Gonzalo shut off the radio. He did not want the coming sunset ruined. He did not want the girl's mind polluted. Although it would be eventually, if not this year then the next or the next, whenever it was she started school. They would tie a flag-colored hanky around her neck and don her with a star-pinched tilted beret and call her "pionera," a five-year-old a pioneer for the principles of la Revolución. Still, now she was innocent and Father Gonzalo enjoyed spending the late afternoons with her after her grandmother doña Adela had dropped her off at late Mass.

"Teresita," he called to the girl. "What are you making, mi vida?"

"Castillos, bobo," the girl at the edge of the shore answered, dumping yellow plastic bucketfuls of moist sand upside down, surrounded by makeshift towers and flooded moats.

"Who lives in the castles?"

"The king and the queen, claro." Of course. "And the princess," she added. She spoke into the sea and Father Gonzalo could just barely make out her tiny precious voice.

"Claro," he assured her. He sat back in the canvas beach chair, tilted his head to the light and dug his bare feet deeper into the sand.

He had met the heroic guerrillero once, had received him at the rectory some months after the rebel landing. Che was sneaking into towns asking for help from the pulpit.

"Simpático, simpatiquísimo," Father Gonzalo had always said. "Say what you will, the man was a charmer, almost convinced me to help. Almost . . . to help *again,* but by then I had already grown disillusioned."

People had always confused the girl's father with Che. Same look. The only physical trait the girl had inherited from her father was her curled and cigar-dark hair (though darker, almost black). The burnt caramel eyes were not his, the round face not his, the light cinnamon skin not his.

Father Gonzalo eyed her again before he tilted his head back to the sunlight and dug his right foot deeper into the sand. He wished she would turn around and face him instead of the sea. But she was too busy chattering to herself, creating stories to support her ever-crumbling towers, and it was the sea and not him that demanded her attention as it began to surround her and soak her sundress and with each touch of its foamy slippery fingers steal layer upon layer of the castle walls.

Father Gonzalo read a bit and dozed off and watched the girl and read some more, phrase by phrase from a smuggled fraying copy of William James's *The Varieties of Religious Experience* in the original English; tediously and methodically over three months, he had made his way to the last chapter, James's "Conclusions." It would be the first book in English he would read from cover to cover. Though he would never dare speak the twisted tongue, except sometimes, alone in his room, after he was sure that Anita had retired to her sleeping quarters, when he would recite portions of the King James Bible out loud, especially the more apocalyptic parts of the Old Testament—Daniel or Isaiah. Now he came upon a phrase in this text that stopped him and forced him to stare at the girl as he mouthed it—*"a preponderance of loving affections"*—as he watched her glistening, slightly reddening back protected by the aloe lotion he had so inattentively put on her, rubbed into her tiny shoulders and dashed quickly across her breast that would not be breasts for ages yet, before he strapped on the lace-adorned swimsuit her grandmother had knit for her and rubbed the lotion on her still baby puffy legs and on her rosy feet and in between her stubby toes—*"a preponderance of loving affections"*—even as he swiped her longish dark curls behind her wee round ears just to dab them a bit on the inside and on the ridges, though she pulled away laughing, mouth agape, because it tickled her so, even as she pulled away laughing. And then the dismay of putting the lotion on himself, rolling up his pants above the knees and covering his bald legs and taking off his shoes and socks to expose the monstrosity of his swollen right big toe (this dropping disease was his heaviest cross), so tender his heart beat down there with more vigor than anywhere else, its heavy measure now buried in the sand above the ankle (for though it was painful at first, as if he had stuck his foot into a nest of scorpions, eventually, if he did not weaken, the pain subsided—or it so much crossed the threshold that it came full circle—and the stinging sand became an anodyne, so it felt as if his feet were sunk in a pail of ice water; and having conquered for a moment his debility he could read or nap peacefully).

When he dozed off he dreamt of a gargantuan forest-green elephant mounted by the girl's father, comandante Julio César Cruz, riding into some unknown village and scaring the natives away. The comandante's laughter, sweet as a child's, as he trampled and trampled over villagers awoke Father Gonzalo. He stared away at the empty shore for lidless moments before he noticed the sea had taken the girl, her fortress of towers and moats washed to an inconsequential lump. How long had he slept? He turned on the radio. Fidel was still raving. He ran into the sea and saw her sundress riding on the sheen of some distant wave. He waded in knee-deep and then waist-deep and then chest-deep, though he could not find her and in every foamy spurt of this or that or that-one-there wave was her lacy swimsuit spit out by the fussy sea and he would not be able to chase her into the deep for he could not swim, or had not swum in years, since the rivers of his youth—had never swum in the sea—though he kept on going in till he was up to the last point of his bulging toe, stretching like some desperately out-of-shape ballerino yearning to fly, on his toe that no longer ached for his heart was now beating prominently behind his ears, and though he leapt, he failed to clear the cusp of the bigger waves that seemed to have forgotten about the swallowed girl and shifted their onslaught to him. With every try at breath he gulped in briny hot seablood, till he felt the so-often promised peace of the last seconds; though just as he gave in to it, as his limbs ceased their entangling epilepsies that if anything had helped to tighten the chords of the sea current around him, just as his marrow longed no more for air, as his heartbeat escaped him and headed for the surface, his tingling toe brushed the sea bottom and he regained footing and the peace abandoned him and his struggles began anew and he forgot about the girl until he had made it to the shore. There, he heard the comandante's girlish laughter again and followed it, dragged himself to a shady spot underneath a royal palm where one of Neptune's unfathomed beauties slept, naked, her upper body face down, her legs on their side, wriggled into a semipose, her dry locks spread out on the sand like a coronet of kelp, as if she had fallen asleep waiting for a portraitist. Beside her was the lacy swimsuit partly stained with urine the sand had already drunk. Father Gonzalo crawled towards the sleeping child.

"Carajo, mi cielo," he said. "How you remind me of your father. Already you swim without getting wet!" He pressed his pallid cheeks to hers and waited for the kiss of life.

Invisible Butterflies

On the way out to the terminal, Alicia felt so grungy she yearned to drown in one of her morning baths. She wondered how she had gone so many days without them. The taxi rumbled past a rusty iron bridge and turned into a dusty road. The windows were only partly cracked and it was stuffy inside the car. Summer had gone on for too long, she thought, and made the mistake of looking at her watch, as if there the seasons instead of the hours were kept. It was one-thirty in the afternoon.

"Casi, casi," the driver said, catching her in the rearview mirror. "We'll be there in no time, señora Alicia."

"Sí, gracias," she said. She had no idea who he was or how he knew her name, although she supposed he did not really drive a taxi for a living. She twisted the watch on her wrist so that it rested face down on her lap and promised herself not to please the driver by looking at it again. To soothe her skittishness, she took a piece of homemade rock candy from a paper bag in her purse and sucked on it. Soon, she was calmer. The candies made her think of home. She thought of her daughter's late-night neckpecks, light and lighter with her guppy lips, cuddled beside her belly to breast, still kissing even as she breathed sleep. Alicia shifted in her seat and rolled her window down a bit.

"Just up ahead a few miles. Soon. No se preocupe, you'll make the train!"

She was getting sick of his head of unwashed hair, of the cigarette dangling in his ear, and especially of the strip of his face visible in the rearview mirror, his bushy eyebrows and reddened eyes and grooved, bark-like forehead twisting into masks of mock kindness. She lowered her eyes and pulled out from her handbag a leatherbound notebook she had once used as a marriage diary. There had been six entries, one on each page, some long and some short, all joyous from what she remembered, for now the notebook was blank, the remnants of the six pages poking out of the binding like shorn weed-flowers. She brought it with her to record what she saw. But seeing, she had been too nervous to pull out the notebook and write, or perhaps she was just able to trust her memory more than she had imagined she would. As astounding as it might sound, her cousin Héctor seemed happy. How could she write that down! For over three years she had been trying to visit him, imagining the most dire conditions. Why else would they be stalling her visit? And now she had seen him; yes, he was upset that his mother had condemned his behavior publicly and taken to writing demeaning letters about him to *Granma* from her asylum in Santiago de Cuba, letters that the paper published and signed with "La madre desconsolada," *but not you, mi primita bella, I knew you would never abandon me, and some day they'll let us out, after they are finished with all their cruel games, after all, they must know we are not criminals.* He spoke to her through a chainlink fence as he took a break from a soccer match with the other prisoners. They had shaved off his shock of black curled woolly hair. He only wore a pair of shorts so Alicia could see that he was field-burned and thinner, but not as thin as she had feared. In fact, aside from the thick slit of a scar underneath his left nipple, which looked like a rosy worm trying to push its way out of his breast (and reminded Alicia of her husband's darker longer scar), Héctor was still very much himself; though sinewy, he had always been thin—how else to perform those heretofore unseen acrobatic feats, how else to outwit death every time he braved the Lazarus rumba.

"Do you miss the circus?"

"Claro, como no, I miss it. But there are some pleasures here." And he smiled. Alicia felt a blush and lowered her eyes and loved him again as when she had been a child.

"Mira, Héctor, I am not going to let them keep you in here!"

"Tranquila, primita, no promises," he said and smiled again. "There is very little you or anyone can do. Now let me kiss that beautiful face."

She pressed her cheek to the fence that in the unrelenting heat somehow retained the night-before chill and Héctor planted seven quick kisses on her.

He kisses like our daughter, Alicia wrote in the notebook as the taxi rumbled into a main road. She breathed easier a few minutes later when she saw the main building of the train terminal. When they arrived she tried to pay the driver with two crumbled pesos but he refused, almost shouting at her: "¡En nombre de la Revolución!" He helped her with her luggage all the way up to the ticket counter and then disappeared without the slightest farewell. Alicia fumbled with the two bills and the notebook she still held in her hand as she pulled out more money to buy her ticket home. She had been gone for almost a week, a day up and five days of waiting before the authorities at the labor camp had let her meet with Héctor. She had stayed with distant kin of her father, a second or third cousin and his wife and children who lived in the province of Camagüey not far from the labor camp. They had been cordial but forced her to sleep and tidy up in a moldy three-wall lean-to in the back of the house, that from the smell ingrained in the wood, Alicia figured, had once served as an outhouse. Her father's kin thus made it clear to her that though they would never deny family lodging, they were in no way in support of gusanos or counterrevolutionaries. Alicia had been arrested twice since the death of her husband for meeting with intent to defame la Revolución. Twice they had to let her go without pressing charges, for after all, it was just a book club. Every morning Alicia had a silent breakfast with the family and walked over to the labor camp about four miles away, or to the Military Unit for Aid to Production as it was officially called. On the fifth morning one of the daughters broke the silence at breakfast.

"Why don't they let you see him, so you can go?" she asked.

Alicia honored the silence and the girl was frightened away from the table by the father's castigating looks. That morning Alicia finally saw Héctor. Their meeting lasted less than five minutes, a cold fence between them. A guard came by and dragged Héctor back to the soccer game.

"Vamos, cabrón," he said, grabbing him by the arm. "I've got some good money on you maricas today. We gotta finish this game before evening call." Héctor resisted a bit, kissing his hand and waving it Alicia's way. The guard pulled him again and his rifle slid off his shoulder and to the ground as they were turning. Héctor went for it and hesitated and waited for the guard to signal his approval with a nod of his head. He then picked up the rifle and handed it back to him. "Tus cojones son míos," the guard said. Héctor laughed and looked away from Alicia. The other guards, sitting up against one of the barracks, their weapons lying unmenacingly beside them or bouncing in between their legs, watched this scene without interest. One last time, Héctor turned, planted a kiss on his hand and sent it Alicia's way.

"¡Te quiero, primita! Come again soon."

"I will," Alicia said, pretending to catch the fluttering gift and waved as if she were saying good-bye to a child at a recreational camp.

That was Saturday, conscript relaxation day. Sunday she was told the camp was off-limits: conscript education day. Weekdays the conscripts were out in the fields dawn to dusk. Fidel had promised the world the largest sugar harvest in history and because of the heat, harvesting had begun a few weeks early and every hand available was put to the task.

When she made it back to the house, the taxi was waiting for her, the driver napping on the hood, momentarily lifting his head and grumbling that he had been called to go to the train station. There was no one inside the house, the parents and even the children were volunteering in the field that day. Alicia wrote a note of gratitude and she realized when addressing it that she had never learned any of the children's names. Before leaving, she pulled out three pieces of rock candy from her purse and left them on top of the note, one for each of the nameless children.

On the train she passed the cane fields and looked for the children among the hundreds of volunteers inexpertly swinging their machetes, just barely having worked their way into an interminable field, even as the afternoon sun dipped so low that their wide-brimmed straw hats proved useless and heat gleamed off their sweat-masked faces. At what age would they force her daughter to come out and work in these fields? How long before they would teach her the basics: *Slash it down-and-close to the ground, compañerita, for all of the sweetness sits low on the stalk, like sugar that sinks to the bottom of the coffee cup, like love that sticks to the underbelly of a little girl's heart.* How long? Lazy, sharp-beaked birds treaded behind the army of macheteros, pecking bugs and caterpillars from the exposed part of the field. *The harvest is theirs,* Alicia wrote on the second page of her leather notebook. *These fortunate birds are the only ones who should thank Fidel.*

And she continued to write, looking up suspiciously every now and then at the tilted heads of the few other passengers in the coach, and shutting the notebook when the conductor came along, because she knew how gallingly she was defaming la Revolución in those just-written pages. Though at one point during the ride, in the province of Oriente, at about the time the train traversed the northern foothills of the mountains that had nurtured the rebels not long ago, her river of words, like the many twisty streams in those mountains, meandered away from its bilious fountainhead. She called for her daughter. *Teresita, ven, besa a mamá,* she scribbled horizontally and diagonally and in the shapes of kisses themselves, which she had always told her daughter were invisible butterflies. So on the page Alicia fashioned inky butterflies—like wet kisses, she thought, not *so* invisible—with enormous wings that she hoped would hasten her journey home, all beckoning in their flight with the same phrase: come Teresita, kiss your mamá.

In Santiago de Cuba the train was delayed overnight. Alicia put away her notebook and slept in her seat. Near dawn a few Fidelista soldiers mounted the train and walked down the aisles from end to end, making a lot of noise with their boots so that most of the passengers woke up. Alicia did not look into their faces. She thought of what Fidel had said once when an American journalist asked him why trains never ran on time in Cuba, insinuating that this could be considered a sign of failure in the process of the revolution. Fidel answered that trains always ran on time in Nazi Germany—there was never a delay—that trains running on time are no measure of the moral and historical stature of a nation. Alicia went out to the station and bought coffee. She had not eaten in over a day but she was not hungry. The train finally departed in the afternoon. The Fidelistas stayed on and paced the aisles. When she arrived in Guantánamo late that evening, she began to make her way on foot from the station to her mother's house, lugging her bags. No one offered to help, no one even greeted her, not the few passersby on the street, not the driver of the horse carriage that served as one of the three cabs in town and not the young folk loitering on the porchsteps of her mother's house, unlucky ones with nowhere to go and nothing to do, who had not yet been summoned to the cane fields and who had not figured out where the rum was that evening. Alicia left her belongings on the porch and hurried inside, barely acknowledging doña Adela when she opened the door, who went to hug her but was left waiting for the embrace, her arms outspread.

"Where is she?" Alicia asked wild-eyed, dashing past her mother.

"¿Pero estás loca? Say hello at least. Do you think I have forgotten how to care for children?" Doña Adela shut the door and smoothed her hair back with both hands, a gesture she often used to express disbelief.

"I just want to see her. Did she miss me? A whole week."

"She's sleeping in my bed."

Alicia smiled and headed for her mother's room.

"Don't wake her," doña Adela called. "She got burned a bit at the beach today. She just fell asleep."

The child slept on her back, the sheet tossed aside, her pajama top pulled off and held in one hand. The slow rise and fall of her belly measured her quiet sleep. Alicia lay beside her, her head resting close to her daughter's belly. She did not want to wake her but she was not able to resist touching her after so long, gingerly placing her hand on her belly, feeling the heat of her sunburn rising from her like a light fever.

"Did you miss me?" Alicia whispered. "Ven, besa a tu mamá."

The girl opened her eyes and nudged her mother's face away with the hand that held the pajama top and whimpered that she was burning and just as quickly fell back into her quiet sleep, her belly rising and falling.

Monday Cola

She looked in both refrigerators and there was no milk. She stepped out on the patio and called for her mother, but doña Adela had not yet returned from la bodega.

"Sorry," she said to her guest. "You'll have to take your coffee black."

"That's fine, perfectly fine, dear," Father Gonzalo said. "So tell me, tell me of your trip."

Alicia scooped two careful teaspoons full of raw sugar into the cafetera and sighed.

"Sabes, their coffee tasted like ink water," she said. "These miserable folk live right by the largest sugar-producing fields in the world and their coffee goes unsweetened, as if they were saving every little scoopful to be weighed in at the record harvest. ¡Viva Fidel! they seem to be screaming, as they pucker their faces and sip the bitter stuff." She poured Father Gonzalo a bountiful cup and then herself the little that was left in the cafetera.

"¿Y Adela?" Father Gonzalo asked.

"She'll drink from mine . . . if she ever shows up."

Father Gonzalo swirled the coffee and took a long whiff from his cup as if he were taking in sea air. He took two small sips. They were seated at one end of the long kitchen table where Alicia remembered Father Gonzalo spending many a long afternoon with her mother as doña Adela rolled out cookie dough or prepared dinner the nights Julio, the indian cook, was off. Even then, as a little girl, Alicia had made coffee for him. First poured the blond sugar into a measuring cup, then waited till the first thick spurts of coffee dribbled out into the cafetera, and poured out just enough to wet the sugar, barely staining it, and then beat and beat the sugar with a tablespoon till it was a thick caramely foam and the muscle between her thumb and index finger hurt. Only then did she pour the rest of the coffee into the measuring cup (and a touch of boiling milk, which her mother had ready for her), so that the sugary foam was doubly thick on top. "Perfecto, delicioso," Father Gonzalo always said, taking the first sip so that the foam would stick to his upper lip and he licked it off with his tongue before he smiled. Alicia would then be allowed to have some of the coffee herself and sit for a while with Father Gonzalo and her mother. She tried to remember what Father Gonzalo looked like back then, but she could only see him as she saw him now. Had he not aged, or were her memories of that time simply vanishing, the grievous present like a pool of black oil over the waters of her past? Still the same slicked-back thin black hair, still only slightly balding, still the smooth orange-brown skin that would never wrinkle (when Alicia had asked her mother if Father Gonzalo was an indio, doña Adela had crossed herself and hushed Alicia as if she had just spoken a sin), still the eyes the same color of the sugary foam, the whites mapped with stringy vessels, because as doña Adela told her daughter all of the sins of his congregation were on Father Gonzalo's head and he could not sleep (Alicia forced herself to stay up for two nights in penance for having asked if Father Gonzalo was an indio, pinching herself in the palms of her hands when she got sleepy), and still the stooped shoulders, because—Alicia supposed—the sins of so many weighed heavy on him as well. Maybe Father Gonzalo had not aged because he had looked old ever since Alicia knew him.

"So, tell me," he said.

"There isn't much to tell," Alicia said, sipping only a bit of her coffee and putting the rest aside for her mother when she returned. She grimaced. "I don't make it like I used to, eh?"

"It's fine, perfecto, delicioso. At the rectory, Anita makes it so watery that when you add milk it turns the color of old newspapers. I've since stopped adding milk. Who would have guessed it? La Revolución has forced us to drink coffee thinner than the yanquis'!"

"If that were all," Alicia said and reached for the cup again and sipped some more coffee and dropped her eyes. She had not slept much, worried over her daughter's sunburn, rubbing different lotions from her mother's bath closet on the child every hour or so during the night. By daylight, the girl's skin felt fresh and she awoke without complaining. Alicia ran a cool bath and they bathed together, playing the splashing game for so long that when doña Adela walked into the bathroom and saw the puddles of water on the floor outside of the tub, she rebuked both of them. Alicia complained that her mother's tub wasn't big enough and doña Adela said then go to her own house to make such a mess, as she brought out the mop and started soaking up the water and Alicia said, fine we will and winked at her daughter and wrapped her in a fresh towel, though she was shaking from a fit of giggles and not from the chills.

"Mamá's bath is so big, Aunt Marta even jumps in with us sometimes," the girl said.

Doña Adela ceased her busy mopping when she heard the name of Alicia's half sister, as if she were allowing a phantom to pass through her before she resumed her task.

"Teresita, cállate," her mother said, and led her away from the bathroom as doña Adela was beginning to go over their bare feet with the mop.

"You're going to ruin that girl by bringing her up so loosely," doña Adela called to Alicia. "Dress her nice; I'm taking her to morning Mass and then to the market."

They had only been at the poorly attended Monday morning Mass for the opening minutes, Father Gonzalo said, had left after the Prayer of Contrition, much earlier than other Mondays (they usually left after Communion); Teresita had waved at him on the way out and he waved back from behind the serpentine, marble altar, his dissimulating finger wiggling on the hand he still held to his chest from the last *mea culpa*. Doña Adela took Teresita to the market because she knew what power the girl had over Alfonso, the bodega's manager, how he would call them up from the back of the Monday cola (others lined up from before sunrise) just so he could play with Teresita for a while, how he would stuff one or two more liters of milk in doña Adela's bag than the rations mandated, and a few extra scoops of coffee beans, and three chunks of fresh guava paste, how he would give her the freshest bread and the choicest portions of paticas de puerco, even calling Teresita back behind the butcher counter because he knew how fascinated the girl was with the blood juice and with the cleavers, though they stood far enough from the butchers, Alfonso putting her down and keeping her back so that the blood wouldn't splatter on her white dress. Once he even showed her a freshly gutted pig that was to be prepared for the wedding of a certain elite comandante. "If I'm still around," Alfonso said to the girl, "you will have a much bigger *machón* than that for your wedding."

Doña Adela never objected to the old man's increasing infatuation with her granddaughter because she knew it meant her granddaughter would eat better during the week. So every Monday she made sure she took Teresita to morning Mass and then to see Alfonso. She watched them closely but she never interfered with his affections. Though not without reservations, Alicia accepted all this.

"Just keep a good eye on them and make sure the old bastard doesn't get any ideas."

"Ay Alicia, no seas dramática; he's a good honest man."

"Keep an eye out anyway. Que al fin y al cabo, he's not one of us."

"What does that mean?"

"It means he's on the inside. It means he fills with pride when you call him compañero. It means you cross him and he'll make sure our ration cards are all used up by the second week of the month."

"Mija, sometimes I think you should have left this country long ago."

"We're not talking about this country, we're talking about your granddaughter!"

At this doña Adela said nothing more. And Alicia said nothing when they left for Mass and then the market on Monday mornings, Teresita looking overly angelic in one of her white linen dresses that her grandmother had sewn for her. This Monday they had taken much too long. They had been gone for three hours. Alicia sipped the last of the coffee she had been saving for her mother.

"She'll bring more," she said.

"Are you going to tell me of your trip or not?"

Alicia was silent. She went for the coffee cup again, knowing there was no coffee in it, and pretended to drink from it, tilting it all the way back so that the grainy sugar syrup touched her lips.

"She'll bring more," Father Gonzalo said. "Tell me."

"He's in a camp, like a prisoner of war camp almost, or a labor camp. *They* call it a military camp, but all the conscripts do is work in the fields. I saw him for less than five minutes."

"Concentration camps, Fidel's enemies call them. Certain pamphlets have passed through the rectory detailing this or that atrocity, especially with cases like Héctor, attempts to cure their sexual deviance. I would be more vocal about it, but it's a difficult subject to approach from the pulpit."

"He didn't *seem* tortured . . . seemed almost healthy. That in itself is more frightening than anything, that they make believers out of them, so much so that he is happy there!"

"You should speak at the church about your trip, speak about Héctor."

"What would that do?"

"I can't do it, but you can."

"What would it do?"

"It might bring people in, for one! Put some life back into the services."

"It might also get you arrested," Alicia said and reached for the empty coffee cup again. "El Rubio has his hackles up."

Father Gonzalo put both his hands over hers. "You can be the guest homilist. Two Sundays from yesterday," he said. "It'll give you time to prepare a sermon and me time to get the word out, make sure there are people there to hear it."

"¿Qué sé yo de sermones?"

She tried to lift the cup to her lips but Father Gonzalo held tight to her hand.

"There is nothing to know. Just say what you saw. Say what you suspect. Say what we all know but are too afraid to tell each other. Do you want to get Héctor out of that camp?"

Alicia thought of Héctor's kisses through the cold fence and tried to convince herself that el Rubio would not dare harm Father Gonzalo. "Yes," she answered quietly but assuredly, "I want to keep Héctor alive. I want to get him out of there."

"Then it's set." Father Gonzalo seemed very pleased. "Two weeks from yesterday. The early afternoon Mass, the one your mother goes to."

There was a sound towards the front of the house and Alicia went to the kitchen doorway and looked out and turned back into the kitchen and put her index finger to her lips. Father Gonzalo nodded. "I'll talk to her about it later," Alicia said. Father Gonzalo nodded again.

The girl ran into the kitchen first, ahead of her grandmother. She went to Father Gonzalo's side. The priest lowered his head to her and the girl kissed him on the cheeks.

"We left early," she said.

"I know," Father Gonzalo said. "I saw you."

The girl put out both her arms in front of her and then she pulled down on the collar of her dress. "I'm not burned anymore."

Father Gonzalo kissed her hands. "Good," he said.

Doña Adela walked into the kitchen carrying a small bag. She put it down on the table. Beadlets of sweat gathered on her forehead. She took out of the bag one liter of milk, a small bag of coffee beans, a bag of bread rolls, and half a stick of butter.

"You'll talk to me about *what* later?" doña Adela said.

Alicia was silent. She stared at the meager groceries.

"They're out of meat for the month," doña Adela said. "Alfonso has taken ill. Some woman is in charge of the store for now. ¡Sinvergüenza!"

"Shall I make you some coffee, mamá?"

"No. I'll wait till tonight."

The girl took one of the bread rolls out of its plastic bag and bit into it. It was crunchy. Doña Adela promised to steam them and rebake them. They all agreed it was the best thing to do. Father Gonzalo soon excused himself. While he was hugging doña Adela he made the victory sign to Alicia with his hand around the old lady's back. The girl, by her mother, mocked him, waving the victory sign back and chanting, *dos dos dos*. Two weeks, Alicia knew. She would start to work on her sermon that night and perhaps pick an appropriate verse from the Gospel for Father Gonzalo to read beforehand.

The Sermon of the Seven Kisses

It was Christmas Eve. It had been over two weeks, in fact well over two months, since Alicia had promised Father Gonzalo to deliver her sermon at his late afternoon Sunday Mass. Now, at Midnight Mass, almost ten weeks late, Alicia was ready, her sermon handwritten on five sheets from her daughter's drawing pad, folded twice and held in her lap as the congregation waited for Father Gonzalo and the celebrants to enter the church. She was seated on the fourth pew from the altar, her mother and daughter beside her, the young girl asleep with her head resting on her grandmother's lap. The church was teeming with people, many faces Alicia did not recognize, out-of-towners certainly. How had they heard? There were even five uniformed soldiers, barbudos, lined up along the back wall beside the life-size porcelain statue of St. Lazarus of the Wounds, their weapons pressed respectfully to their side, their berets tucked neatly in their back pockets. Next to them, his hand wrapped around one of St. Lazarus's lesioned ankles, his black beret disrespectfully covering his blond crown, was Camilo Suarez, the captain of the revolutionary police force, el Rubio. Alicia had seen him conferring with Father Gonzalo out in the courtyard when she arrived, had watched him tie his gray bullmastiff, heretically named Tomás de Aquino, to the left railing of the church steps. She was going to talk to Father Gonzalo before the service, but instead she hurried past them and Father Gonzalo did not try to stop her. Now everyone else tried to ignore the soldiers and the pale police captain. Though the windows were cracked and the ceiling fans were whirring, a dead air inhabited the church and the many people were busy fanning their faces with the available missals or with their fanciest, hand-woven abanicos brought out for this one evening of the year. It was almost midnight. The congregation waited for Father Gonzalo. Alicia passed her hands through her daughter's hair. It was moist with sweat. She opened up the folded sheets of the sermon once and began to fan her. Doña Adela did the same with her missal. The girl turned her head over, wiping her face on her grandmother's lap.

Finally the old organ groaned a well-worn carol and Father Gonzalo and his procession entered. As he passed by Alicia, Father Gonzalo eased his pace, turned his head and sent her a cryptic smile, an almost imperceptible arching of his lips, and he shook his head discreetly. When he reached the altar he was handed a silver incense burner and he swung it, circling the altar and approaching the first few pews till the whole church smelled of prayers. There were readings and singing and more incense-swinging and the congregation stood and sat accordingly. Doña Adela remained seated till her granddaughter awoke just as Father Gonzalo was haltingly introducing the guest homilist, then the girl and the grandmother stood, and then because the girl started it, they all did something they were unaccustomed to doing in church, they all stood and clapped and when Alicia had reached the pulpit they all sat and listened.

This is what Alicia said in those brief moments, this is what they called at her trial the Sermon of the Seven Kisses.

> Cristianos, today we come together in the Child's name to celebrate His birth, and though we celebrate, we must also mourn; for once there was a woman heavy with Child, and the Child was the Light of the world, and the Child was born and the Light spread over the world. Now, this was

during the time of the Blind King, and the Blind King was envious of the Light and he called his seven wisest councilors and threw a feast and they all became drunk with wine. And then he said to them: "Who is this Child that the people call the Prince of Light?" And the wise councilors answered: "He was born of a peasant woman, and a star shines over His birth." Then the Blind King flew into a rage and screamed at his councilors: "Go! Go and find Him!" And the wise councilors became frightened and they stopped eating and drinking and the Blind King composed himself and then spoke softly: "Go, and when you have found Him send me word, for I would like to pay homage to this Prince born of a peasant woman." And early the next morning the seven wise councilors left and followed a star that shone even in the noonday sky. And they traveled for many days, huddling close together at night for warmth, for the desert winds were cold and harsh. When they came to the town of Bethlehem, in the province of Judea, they found the Child and His Parents in the home of a poor smith, for it was census time and the inn was full. And they paid homage with gifts of gold, frankincense, and myrrh. And the mother of the Child said: "What do you ask in return?" And each of the Blind King's councilors said: "Only that we may kiss the Child." And they kissed the Child seven times, on each temple, on each hand, on each foot, and on His soft belly, and after such adoration they warned the parents about the Blind King and of his rage and told them to flee to the land of the tall pyramids. And the parents bore the Child away that same day. When the wise councilors left, they continued to travel north, to Spain and then to England and Scotland, to serve there as foreign wizards and never to serve the Blind King again. Now, the Blind King felt betrayed and he mounted his horse and called his soldiers and ordered every child under the age of two in and around Bethlehem to be beheaded. So it was done. And when the soldiers returned to the palace drenched in the children's blood, the Blind King asked them to smear it on his face, for he needed proof and he could not see them. And one by one, each soldier smeared the Blind King's cheeks and the Blind King's beard with the blood of the murdered children, till the Blind King smelled the blood and he laughed and laughed and he convinced himself that there had been no Prince of Light born of a peasant woman, the blood drying and cracking on his face. So tonight, though we celebrate the escaped Child, we also mourn for this Blind King and for his kingdom that night, which was full of weeping and loud lamentations.

There was no applause when Alicia stepped down from the pulpit. It was so silent that she imagined you could hear the rustle of her dress all the way in the back of the church, just as she could hear the growls of the tethered Tomás de Aquino from the church steps. And though Christmas morning was supposed to bring with it cool winds from the North, it had gotten stuffier inside the church during the few minutes that Alicia spoke. The five barbudos in the back had not moved, though their olive uniforms were stained with sweat now, under the arms and around the collars. El Rubio, however, looked unshaken, his short-sleeved black shirt dry, his eyes studying the open scabs of St. Lazarus's foot. Father Gonzalo hesitated a bit, his head bowed as if in private prayer, before he approached the pulpit and asked the congregation to join him in praying the creed of their faith. He forgot to thank Alicia. When Communion time came everyone approached the altar to receive the host—except for the five soldiers, el Rubio, and a handful in the congregation—and when the service was ended and Father Gonzalo led the celebrants and the congregation out, the soldiers remained pressed to the back wall, el Rubio grown more infatuated with the figure of St. Lazarus, having moved his attention up the statue's leg to the rags that covered his shame like a diaper, caressing its surface with the ends of his fingertips as if he were a curator vetting a priceless piece. Alicia did not look at them as she stepped outside and headed for the group around Father Gonzalo, her daughter's hand held on one side, her mother's on the other. The group dispersed as soon as Alicia approached, many glancing at her and nodding their heads and smiling gently and saying farewell to Father Gonzalo—who stood on the opposite side of the steps from where Tomás de Aquino was tied—tapping on his forearm. One of them, an elegant gentleman in a straw hat, did not go away so quickly. He waited for Alicia and closed his hand on her shoulder. "Wonderful," he said in a loud whisper, "a beautiful parable, mi niña. ¡Eres una gran filósofa!" and quickly, he hurried off. Father Gonzalo's face shone in the dying moonlight and Alicia could not miss the pit of disillusion in his eyes. When he spoke to her he did not look at her, instead he looked at her daughter and held her daughter's face and kissed her daughter's hands. The girl yawned. It was late.

"I promised them you would not insult their blessed revolution," Father Gonzalo said. "I had to. They said they would cancel the service if I didn't. Perdóname, Alicia. I had to. I wish you would have let me see that . . . that sermon beforehand."

Doña Adela grunted, picked up her granddaughter and tried to pull Alicia away. "Vámonos. . . rápido," she said. "Vámonos, coño."

"And where shall we go hide?" Alicia said, resisting. "And where shall I hide my daughter? Do you think they'll leave us alone if we escape from them now?"

"I had to," Father Gonzalo repeated. "It'll be all right. I'll talk to him."

"No es culpa de nadie," Alicia said. "I would have read it anyway, even if you had said not to."

When the five soldiers stepped out onto the church steps they simultaneously retrieved their berets from their back pockets, shaped them one-handed and placed them gingerly on their heads, with a slight tug at the right side for the appropriate tilt. They remained at the top of the steps, patiently waiting for the congregation to disperse. El Rubio did not appear and the five soldiers walked towards Father Gonzalo. Although two were in front and three behind, no one seemed to lead the other, their stride casual and unmilitary. They moved as with a purpose so primitive and so intuited that there was no need for rank-and-order. They did not surround them as doña Adela expected. They stood like bowling pins in front of them and stared at Alicia, their eyes burnished more with boredom than conviction. They said nothing. El Rubio appeared at the church entrance, he glanced at Tomás de Aquino, who had fallen asleep in a puddle of his own urine, and shook his head. As he approached them he removed his beret and retucked his long blond curls behind his ears and put the beret back on. He apologized to Father Gonzalo for his dog's accident. He smiled as if embarrassed, revealing a row of alternately yellow and brown teeth, with two or three holes in the bottom row, and in the corners the dull glint of gold caps. He was gorged and thick-bellied as his dog and wide-hipped as a matron, but his arms were slender and his fingers long and his shoulders narrow and his neck curvy and smooth as any virgin's, so that he seemed a man molded from two discrepant sets of clay.

He spoke to the monsignor: "It is strange, no, Father? that he has lesions scattered all over his body, but that his skin is erubescent, healthy almost. What do the lesions symbolize? Do they mean that the flesh must suffer infection before it is deemed holy?"

Father Gonzalo had learned how to remain silent when confronted by el Rubio.

"Or . . . is the flesh infected by nature, and therefore holy by nature, which therefore explains the fiction of this glowing-skinned lesioned old saint . . . hmmm . . . but perhaps this is not the proper time for such musings. . . . Father, it is with regret that I must do this."

"Do not seek for my permission, hijo mío. You will not get it. I will watch what you do and I will pray for you tonight."

El Rubio thanked Father Gonzalo. His blue eyes floated in a mesh of ropy burst vessels, like twin gems seined from an incarnadine sea. He said he would need many more than one night of prayers. He turned to Alicia.

"Señora Alicia Lucientes-Cruz, you are under arrest for malicious intent to defame la Revolución and for mocking el Comandante-en-Jefe. You will have the right to counsel and you will be judged by your own Neighborhood Committee for the Defense of the Revolution."

The girl had been shaken out of her drowsiness and had begun to whimper. Doña Adela put her down and motioned for Father Gonzalo to take her away. She put her arm around Alicia and held her tight.

"Ven, ven Teresita," Father Gonzalo said to the girl, leading her into the garden in the church's courtyard. "Vamos a ver las flores." The girl went. Father Gonzalo picked her up and she rested her head on his shoulder. He walked towards the church garden. At the iron gate, he stopped and turned around to face el Rubio and the five soldiers. Doña Adela gestured at him with her hand to go into the garden, then she turned to Alicia. "I'm not letting them take you."

"Mamá, por favor, go with Teresita. I will be fine. No harm will come to me."

"I can assure you of that, señora Alicia," el Rubio said. "It saddens me greatly to do this. I knew comandante Cruz. I fought alongside your—"

"Don't you dare conjure his name for your base purposes!"

"Muy bien entonces, señora, you are under State arrest. Do come with us."

"¡Malditos son todos!" doña Adela screamed as the five soldiers separated her from Alicia. "Here lies the greatness of your maldita Revolución! Taking away a daughter from her mother on Christmas morning. Get your hands off *me*! ¡No me toquen carajo!"

"May I remind you that the charge against your daughter is a serious one." El Rubio had waved the barbudos away from doña Adela. His face had grown stern, and his movement, as he walked towards her with his hands clamped behind his back, formal. Their eyes locked and doña Adela felt as if their faces were coming continually and continually closer till el Rubio's nidorous breath broke the spell. "Just a word of warning, vieja," he said in a voice so low that doña Adela knew that the five soldiers and Alicia, having stepped back, could not hear him.

"¡Capitán Suarez! Por favor," Father Gonzalo said. He had made his way back with the girl asleep in his arms and was standing to the side of el Rubio. "I will not have you speaking that way to any of my parishioners. I know too well of the glories of your Revolución, and it certainly does not entail speaking so to proper ladies. Así que por el amor the Dios Santo, if you have any business to do here, proceed with it and please leave the church grounds . . . or . . . or I shall call the mayor."

El Rubio laughed. He walked away from doña Adela towards the soldiers. "You take heed as well, padrecito. We will not tolerate too much more insurgence from your banished class. Take her. Alicia Lucientes-Cruz is under arrest. Now! We have worn out our welcome here. The padrecito is going to sic the mayor on us." He went to Tomás de Aquino and awoke him by planting a swift kick to the midriff (punishment for having desecrated the church steps, which he announced to Father Gonzalo), then he untethered the bullmastiff, keeping him on a short leash, and walked a pace ahead of the five soldiers and Alicia.

Alicia went without resistance, kissing her sleeping daughter once. Doña Adela broke into tears and put her arms around Father Gonzalo. The girl awoke, lifted her head from Father Gonzalo's shoulder, looked around and caught a glimpse of her mother in the distance and yawned.

"¿Dónde va mami, abuelita?"

"She's going to look for the Child Jesus who was born today," Father Gonzalo answered for the speechless doña Adela. "And when she finds Him, she promised she would kiss Him once for all of us."

"On his head, on his hands, on his feet, and on his belly," the girl said, yawning and resting her head again on the monsignor's shoulder. "Just like the story."

"That's right, just like the story."

Doña Adela cried harder and crumpled tight in one of her dress pockets the five sheets of drawing paper Alicia had handed to her on the way out of the church. She would burn them as soon as she got home.

THREE

Berta His Beloved

Now, huddled with his tomcat under five fourteen-pound sacks of raw coffee beans in the makeshift cellar where the girl Teresita used to hide, he thought back to the first time he saw the milk twirled with red. It happened seven days before, very early on a Friday morning, almost two weeks to the day after the forbidden hunting expedition. As he squeezed left and right, left and right, left and right on the monumentally swollen nipples of Niña, his most productive cow, he became, as usual, entranced by the perfect whiteness rising in the tin bucket. After Niña had filled one bucket and was halfway up the second bucket, she emitted a jet of crimson milk from her left nipple that whirled and sunk into that unforgiving whiteness. Mingo stopped. His first thought was that his hand was bleeding and he cursed himself for ruining half a bucket of good milk. But his hand was fine. His second thought was that he had been hallucinating; so he took a wooden stick and stirred the milk in the bucket and it turned the rosy color of a newborn calf's bottom. "Te mato," he grumbled to his most productive cow. He put aside the bucket with the pink milk and put under her an empty bucket and began anew. Again, Niña filled it about halfway, and again she ruined it by the nineteenth or twentieth squeeze of her left nipple that squirted blood. Mingo slapped his cow on the side. Niña responded with a flip of her tail that knocked off Mingo's frayed-brim straw hat and brushed the bristles of his unshaven face. "Puta barata," Mingo said, standing from his stool and backing off, suddenly afraid of his most productive cow. He turned to his other cows. And one by one they all disappointed him in the same way: the young and small Berta staining her milk on the fourteenth squeeze, María on the twenty-second, Isabela on the ninth, and Carmela on the twelfth. When he milked them again, he felt that they were conspiring against him for they shuffled the order of their transgression: this time Carmela ruining her milk on the fourteenth squirt, Berta on the twenty-second, María on the ninth, and Isabela on the twelfth. Mingo hurried away from the barn as if fleeing from a bad dream. When he stepped outside, he fully expected the skies to be gathering with thunderclouds as if the day of justice were at hand. But it was a pleasant morning like any other—only in the late afternoons did the spring become torrential—and whoever resided in the placid skies had no idea (it would seem) that Mingo's cows were producing milk stained with blood.

On the next four mornings, he awoke an hour or so earlier than usual, before the hazy ruddiness of dawn, as if somehow he could fool his cows back to health, catch them in the innocent moments after waking, when perhaps whatever beast was churning inside them and making their milk bloody was still asleep. But morning after morning, even as he awoke progressively earlier and earlier, so that at one point, he was barely asleep for an hour, his cows gave him buckets and buckets of useless pink milk. After a few days, the store owner in town and the milkman who delivered to the elite military families and to the yanquis in the naval base became impatient, threatening to find another source if the matter was not taken care of soon. Mingo offered weak excuses for his lack of produce and promised that soon, very soon he would have the finest, richest-tasting milk in the Western world again available. He called the famous Jewish doctor, Sara Zimmerman, who treated both humans and animals with the miraculous juice of papaya leaves. Doctora Zimmerman tasted the milk (something Mingo had not dared do). She grimaced and spit it back out. She told Mingo she would treat his cows if he wanted her to, but if she were the farmer and these were her cows she would sell them right away for whatever paltry sum anyone would offer, for though they might live, never again would they produce clean milk. These cows were doomed. Doctora Sara Zimmerman rarely gave such a dire prognosis, even when the patient was already dead.

Mingo walked down into town to visit Father Gonzalo, for he was beginning to suspect the meddling, dropsical saints had something to do with all of this. On the first morning, Father Gonzalo did not answer Mingo's call, though Mingo banged tirelessly on the rectory door, went around back and pressed his face against the grimy kitchen window, which Anita refused to clean because a devout parishioner once swore she

saw in the grime the headless torso of the Baptist, and even tried to speak
to Anita, who was weeding the garden and assured him that *no, no, the Father is not in, and will not be in, not for now, not for a while and will you please
go then, please go, señor Mingo.* With this, chased away like a demon, Mingo
returned up the mountain to his finca, his farm. When he got there, he
fashioned a rattan from the stem of a palm frond and savagely rattled and
whipped his five useless cows. Afterwards, stained with the blood that had
splattered from their backs in penance for the blood that had stolen into
their milk, Mingo sat in a rocking chair in the living room of his six-room
bohío, staring at the yellowy discolored photographic portrait of Lydia,
his escaped wife, letting his monumental black tomcat Luis el Catorce
climb on him and lick the vestiges of his rage from his cheeks. He leafed
through his unreadable French edition of *Du côté de chez Swann* and waited
for the following dawn. By then, his next-to-smallest cow Carmela had
died from her wounds, one eye open, one shut by a plumlike bruise.
Mingo did not milk his cows that morning; rather he dug a wide hole in
the soft soil not far from the cabbage patch and there he dragged Carmela
by her horns and buried her. As he pushed her into her resting hole,
Carmela simultaneously let out a long hiss from her relaxed sphincter and
pissed wine-dark blood from her enlarged and welted glands.

During the next few days, the cabbages turned brown, mangoes
dropped half-grown and contaminated the air with an effluvial sourness,
avocados too dropped, exploding in midair like ill-fashioned grenades,
watermelons broke open at their own will to reveal flesh darker than
Carmela's wine-dark nipplepiss, with worms disappearing and reappear-
ing into each other, and even the pigs grew earth-shy, cowering by the
wooden fences of their pens, afraid to wallow in the mud. Only the guava
grove at the far end of the finca remained unscathed. Mingo went to visit
Father Gonzalo again. This time he caught a peep of him sneaking out of
the side door and headed towards the chapel. "Wait, coño! Wait!" Mingo
yelled. Father Gonzalo stopped. He looked back. When Mingo reached
him, Father Gonzalo summoned all his angels of pity, put a gentle hand
on Mingo's shoulder and smiled. "What troubles are you drowning in?"
the priest offered, knowing well the gist of the story he was about to hear.
Mingo recounted everything up to that morning, when after bathing in
the river, he had sliced a giant water scorpion in half with his machete and
was sure to have seen both parts scurrying away, one growing a head, the
other a tail. Father Gonzalo shook his head all the meanwhile: "That hunt.
That hunt . . . it was said—"

"Ay, por favor, padre, I'll not hear anything about the *forbidden* hunt,"
Mingo said, "as if we were living in the days of the witches; that's water
under the bridge, done for. Those birds were threatening my crops. They
were interfering with my planting. I got rid of them. It's what any farmer
would have done. Something else is at work here."

"Yet, those people warned you."

"Those people who? . . . los santeros de Alicia. Father, you and I know very well that those people are religious and political fanatics. Blind as the moon at high day!"

"Pero con respeto, Alicia Lucientes and her family are no such—"

"She's the worst! ¡Esa viuda está jodía de la cabeza! But she's wily. ¡La espuela del diablo! It's a shame that she's taking the whole town for a ride—*even you!* . . . unless . . ." Mingo stared beyond Father Gonzalo searching everywhere for the agents of the widow-bitchwitch's wicked jealousies. And there they were, sprinkling seeds of sanguineous poison into the fodder pit and blowing hot breath over the cabbage heads and injecting the mango trees with the yellow virus and spreading on the avocado trees with flat wooden ladles, like butter on toast, the germs of the bloating disease and poking stiff zombied worms into each and every watermelon and even tainting the pigs' mud with the smell of the sea! He left Father Gonzalo. That evening he locked Luis el Catorce in the makeshift cellar, stripped, and with only a shotgun as dress gear, four shells full, strapped on by a musky leather band, he buried himself head-deep in the fodder pit, crushing his way under until only the muzzle and the left side of his face were protruding. He waited for the intruders. At one o'clock that morning, he blew to feathery puffs a white chicken that had the misfortune to stray into the edge of the pit while fleeing from an overeager insomniac rooster. At three-thirty the same fate befell the rooster, still awake and goatish, and wondering, just wondering if his love had not staged her dramatic disappearance and was now hiding in the pit. And just before milking time, when light was barely beginning to divide the shadows, Mingo saw the demon of his troubles. First the horns, inching ever so slowly into his firing range, as if the demon had been warned that a trap might be set, slowly, slowly, into firing range. Mingo could not see its face, but the harsh self-propagating morning light, now directly behind it, created a halo that with its very brightness darkened the demonface. Slowly, slowly, into firing range, lazy, as if without its inimical purpose, till it noticed something twitching in the pit (maybe the left side of Mingo's face that was rebelling against the long night stillness). Something twitching—and the demon, curious, raised its head, extended its neck, and moved directly into pointblank firing range. Then Mingo, realizing that his hand had wandered off the trigger, worked his way down the barrel, through coarse fodder, down, down and squeezed it, blowing away the right side of the demon's face. The demon groaned like an earthly beast, doubled over and fell into the pit. It was a heavy demon, so heavy that when it landed on the left side of Mingo's face, the left side of Mingo's face did not twitch anymore. Soon, Mingo could not breathe; and he was sure he was destined to die a twin death with the demon of his last days. But he wasn't so sure that he didn't struggle to get out, straining his neck and pushing out with his no longer twitching cheek as if it were not a minor face muscle destined only to control the delicate subtlety of face gestures, but a power muscle like the thighs or the pectorals, pushed and pushed against the demon's breathless ribcage to no avail, for it was forcing him down on its death journey to join with the likes of it. So he blew his last shell, muffled by the downpouring, already rotting demon-guts, so that after its stilled blood and its not quite yet ripe shit and its not aged enough piss streamed down Mingo's cheek and what felt like the demon's liver or kidney or whatever dangled on his forehead like a twisted beret, Mingo spotted through the demon hole, beyond a splintered protruding rib, a gibbous piece of the blue-white sky. He reached for the rib and used it to pull himself up through the tunnel the blast had created, till he was out, naked, except for a gummy variegated placental coat, birthed of a demon. Except it wasn't a demon at all. He could tell by the wide peachy rump that many a tortuous dawn after his wife had fled (and some *indeed* before she had fled) had been his only solace, that with the furry end of its tail reached back and tickled his inflamed sac and later grew a body and a face and a mouth that groaned for *all of it, coño por favor, todo todo digo, even those monstrous tennis balls.* That rump Mingo would know anywhere. He had murdered and been born of Berta, his second most productive and by far his most gorgeous cow. Pobre Berta, who, forgetting her beauty, he had beaten like a dog a few days back. Pobre Berta, who had wandered early out of the barn.

Flummoxed somewhat by his misdeed—but more so by the urges that were sneaking up on him as he relished in the memory of having been once and for all, all inside her—Mingo ran to the river. He washed himself of her liquid flesh and, when clean, relieved himself of his sordid memories. He then walked back through the finca to his cottage, as he was, in newborn undressed flesh, pulled out a bottle of moonshine rum from a hidden stash in the closet under the stairway and sat by the fodder pit till evening, singing hymns of mourning for his beloved Berta, till the bottle was finished and he wished that he and all his lands would vanish forever from the face of the earth. *¡Maldita la Revolución!* he had always said. But now he found no comfort in that. So he added some curses: *¡Maldita la viuda de mierda! ¡Maldita esa bruja! Damn the widow-bitchwitch and all the shadows of her offspring!* And he passed out by the death-stunk fodder pit, reciting his favorite phrase from his favorite writer, that he at once understood and did not understand . . . *à contre coeur* . . . *à contre coeur* . . . a soul stripped of allegiance.

He would fix it. He would not go broke. He still had three cows; welted, hobbling, and terrified, but still alive, still producing milk, which had always been the finest milk in the province, not the thin bitter goat's milk of the mountains and not the compromising pap you could drain from a mother's tit, long ago, in the days of innocence. This was heaven's milk, what they served to the legions of angels before dawn to give them strength to lift the sun and hurl it through its diurnal path. And it still would be so! Even if it had lost its chasteness, if it could no longer be gowned in white and was now dressed for the honeymoon, the color of a blushing mango. For Mingo was thinking about mangoes when he awoke the following dawn in the fodder pit that was now the grave of his beloved Berta, thinking about mangoes because the sky was streaked like a horny ripe-for-fun mango—the pinks and reds of expectation below, from where the perilous, hot-for-a-little-morning-joy ball broke the curled night, jolting it into poses more receptive, into moods more seductive, and then espaliering from the reds bands of yellow on a latticework of greens and blue-grays, till there, far beyond, across the arc of the oyster-shell sky, the night remained the night, dull-gray, dormant and frigid.

He followed his usual morning rituals, bathing in the crisp river water, and then urinating in a dry coconut shell and mixing it with fresh guava pulp before drinking it, because he had read in an Eastern handbook on the matter that drinking a bit of one's own urine in the morning increased sexual power. Never bothering to dress, he fed his remaining cows, gave them food enough to last a week, though they cowered in a corner of the barn when they saw him. He buried Berta's mutilated carcass in a secluded field beyond the mango grove, carried it over his shoulder after he had finished digging a hole wide and deep enough to accommodate in eternal comfort her wide rump and in soil rich enough that her peachy hide would remain fresh for generations and generations. When he shoveled the warm earth over Berta, he prayed for shelter against the curses of the widow-bitchwitch. Then he knelt on the burial mound, threw his head back into the noon light and full of tears honored the memory of his beloved one last time, dreaming of those secret peachy-rump dawns, baptizing the innocent dead, so entranced he never heard the commotion behind him, the mob gathering in the mango grove, nor did he hear the first few rotten mangoes that whizzed by him, landing on the riverbank, and even tried to ignore the pulpy missile that hit him square in the buttocks just as he had squeezed them tight and was surging into the final gestures of his pining. Here they came, hundreds and hundreds of them, mostly women, the more reverent followers of the widow-bitchwitch.

"¡Diablo! ¡Bestia! ¡Ateo!" they screamed, chasing him into the river and leaving him for drowned, after pegging him in the head a few times with dry mango pits.

Mingo survived as he always had, through his wits and through the surprising ability of his pudgy body to perform under duress. He knew every inch of his finca as well as any man knows his own body, even the riverbed—where it was pebbly white, where it was shifty and sandy, where it dipped, where it twisted. So when he made it to the river, with the mob and their flying mangoes not so far behind, he knew he was safe. At least for the time being. He swam about a quarter of a mile underwater, thinking not of his safety, but of Berta and how the mob was sure to desecrate her grave, and came up at the bend of the river not far from his cottage. He waited for dusk before he made his move into the house, heading for the makeshift cellar and hiding with Luis el Catorce under five heavy bags of coffee beans.

He stayed in the cellar for four days, eating the coffee beans and drinking coconut juice—there was a pile of recently picked coconuts in storage—and his own urine, without guava pulp, straight from nature, warm still, for sustenance, till he was sure the mob had quitted him and dispersed. He thought he was ready for anything when he went to the grave site, till he saw the smoldering heap of ashes that had served as their cooking fire, and got a whiff of the rich smell of seared meat that still lingered in the air. They had eaten his beloved, feasted for three days and gorged themselves on Berta's flesh, even chopped the horns from her discarded skull that lay by the riverbank and used them as drinking vessels. As Luis el Catorce sniffed at the carcass, and unnoticed by his master took a few bites, Mingo knelt over the empty hole that had been her grave and began to plan his revenge. He would get the widow-bitchwitch. He would get her just as surely as he once had saved her. "They are all the same. ¡Comen santos y cagan diablos!"

Nothing More or Less

When Alicia Lucientes was arrested on Christmas morning 1967, Mingo, Father Gonzalo, Alicia's sister Marta, and other members of their weekly book club had organized to come to her aid, forgetting about literature altogether and using the time allotted for their weekly meetings to set a strategy for defense. *They* would represent her in the revolutionary mock court and not some government-appointed doltish comunista. But even getting that far was a monumental task. On New Year's Day, Mingo and Father Gonzalo went to the leader of the local Committee for the Defense of the Revolution, or el Comité, as they succinctly referred to themselves, the group that would initially sit in judgment of Alicia. Her name was Pucha she said when they introduced themselves and added that she had much more on her mind than that upcoming trial. "So you want to represent Alicia Lucientes in court? You, a finquero? And you, un curita?"

In the sparse room where she conducted the business of el Comité there was a scratched wooden table scattered with papers on one end and domino pieces stacked neatly on the other, surrounded by six schoolboy chairs; there was also a splintery filing cabinet and an old bicycle, with a well-oiled chain but in need of a paint job, that leaned up against the back wall, and on one side wall hung a portrait of José Martí, yellowed by time and wrinkled by the heat, and on the other one of Fidel surrounded by adoring crowds during one of his speeches, his finger wagging at the heavens. Pucha sat in a swiveling oak chair. She tapped the tabletop with a pencil.

"Carajo, Padre . . . *you* at least should know better. Why? Why is it that you want to do this? Do you think you will help her? Do you think you will convince the tribunal of her *obvious* innocence, when she goes up there to the pulpit and tells her little story that virtually dared el Rubio to arrest her! You know the rules, Padre. Muy fácil. La Revolución does not need your God. You stay out of our business, we'll stay out of yours. Señora Alicia broke that rule. Señora Alicia wants to infect our people with her lies just because she cannot face the shame of what her husband did. And you want to represent her in court? You want to associate with her publicly?"

Pucha put the pencil behind her ear, leaned back and waited for an answer. Her auburn hair was tied back in a bun. Her face was bony and the skin hung on it like an ill-suited garment, burned brown. Blood leaked into the whites of her eyes and her pupils were a coruscant urine color. She wore an oversized men's button-down. "I have things to do, señores," she said, pointing their attention to the multitude of papers heaped on the tabletop. "¿Sí o no?"

"Yes, of course, yes," Father Gonzalo said. "That's why we came, so that we may represent her. Thank you . . . Pucha."

"Bueno entonces, if el Rubio agrees—claro, only if *he* agrees, quién sabe, my cousin is very strict when it comes to these official matters—then it is settled, you will represent her in court. I will give you documents concerning her trial as soon as I receive them."

"May we see her?"

"That matter you will have to take up with el Rubio . . . mañana. Hoy es día de fiesta. Now, sit down for a second, gentlemen. There's actually something *you* can do to help me." She gave Mingo and Father Gonzalo each a list of scribbled addresses and placed in front of them a stack of fancy cotton-fiber peach-colored envelopes. Father Gonzalo marveled at their quality.

"Where did you get these?"

"Never mind that, just get busy and print those addresses on them."

Pucha handed each of them a fine-tipped pen. Mingo and Father Gonzalo worked quietly while Pucha stuffed the envelopes and stamped them. Some of them were going as far away as the capital. Father Gonzalo stopped every third or fourth envelope to further admire its quality. When it began to get unbearably warm inside the room, so warm that sweat from their palms was staining the fancy envelopes, Pucha pushed open the door to let in the afternoon breeze and from the splintery cabinet pulled out a bottle of rum and three shot glasses.

"Chispa de tren, I call it. El Rubio himself makes it—O bueno, his shorn-headed indian servant makes it, but he likes to take credit." She poured them each a shot and then herself one. Mingo and Father Gonzalo looked at each other and then at their shots of moonshine and not wanting to offend their influential host raised their glasses and drank.

"To Alicia!" Mingo said.

"Pues, to Alicia," Father Gonzalo said after a moment's hesitation.

"Feliz año and good luck, señores." Their glasses clinked. "You're going to need it."

They went back to writing the addresses on the envelopes, Pucha complimenting their handwriting, especially Mingo's, and when they were finished, they helped her with placing the invitations inside and stamping them. It was for a wedding to be held in the spring. Father Gonzalo knew the bride. "I baptized her. Sometimes I still see her grandmother at Mass."

"Esa vieja está senil," Pucha muttered. "¡Gusana! She wont be at the wedding."

"Why?"

"There is no invitation for her."

"To her own granddaughter's wedding!" Mingo said.

"She speaks ill of the groom." Pucha's tone stiffened. "Speaks ill of his whole family. A lieutenant colonel and not yet thirty. A veteran of Playa Girón. A hero."

"Aah," Father Gonzalo said. "Un militar. I see."

Mingo grumbled as he sealed the last of the envelopes. Pucha took all the envelopes, dropped them in a sack, bundled them tight, and tied the sack on the rack behind the seat of the old bicycle. "Muchas gracias." She poured them each another shot of her cousin's homemade rum against their mild protests. She raised her glass and before either of the men could toast to Alicia again, she blurted, "To the bride and groom."

"To the wedding," Father Gonzalo said.

"To her grandmother being there," Mingo said.

They clinked glasses again.

Outside, Pucha carried the bicycle herself down the steps of the veranda, though Mingo and Father Gonzalo twice offered to help. She threw on a Che-style beret and hopped on the bicycle. When she took off her moccasins and tied them down with the mail bag, Father Gonzalo noticed that her feet were badly in need of a pedicure, the toes twisted one on the other like neighboring vines, the nails blackened, the skin dry and veined with cracks as if she had walked the distance of the Island barefoot.

"Come see me early tomorrow. I will put you in touch with el Rubio and I am sure he will let you see señora Alicia then. The other matter . . .

that's up to him. Bueno, me voy, have to get these invitations out. This is what my job is all about, building new families to grow under la Revolución . . . los veo tempranito mañana."

They nodded and the leader of the 83rd Neighborhood Committee for Defense of the Revolution pedaled off. Mingo and Father Gonzalo were left on the dusty road to make their way back on foot. Mingo pulled out from his pocket a crumpled wedding invitation. He laughed and handed it to Father Gonzalo. "For the grandmother . . . when you see her at Mass!"

In his office at the Department of State Security, el Rubio picked at his rotted teeth with a long sewing needle. He did not offer his visitors a seat. He grimaced when the sharp end of the needle found tender gum, as he insisted he had Alicia Lucientes' best interests in mind.

"No matter how repugnant her crime may have been, caballeros, she needs someone who will be able to defend her properly, someone trained in the law. We will appoint her the finest attorney available. I hope your dismay with la Revolución does not go as far as to accuse us of cheating your friend of justice. She will have that, eso se lo juro. Tell la vieja . . . the mother, she may see her daughter after the trial. We will move expeditiously. I assure you, caballeros."

When Father Gonzalo protested, el Rubio insisted he had no time. Tomás de Aquino was suffering from a bad case of colic and needed to be escorted to the revolutionary hospital.

Alicia Lucientes was handed to the revolutionary tribunal by the 83rd Neighborhood Committee for the Defense of the Revolution and tried and sentenced in justice, in less than an hour, to six months' confinement in Villa Brown, a dilapidating row of houses on the hills overlooking the bay that had once served as a private school for the children of the personnel at the yanqui naval base, now encircled by billowing rolls of concertina wire and used as a retraining center for political discontents. Of the seventy-six detainees then present, Alicia was one of four women. Mercedes and Beba, the brainy bespectacled twins who had once belonged to Father Gonzalo's book club, were there serving time for distributing counterrevolutionary literature. They had translated many of Lewis Carroll's stories and printed them in pamphlets to distribute among schoolchildren. They had been sentenced to two years' confinement. Their trial also had been expeditious. Alicia was pleased to see them. Beba, the more contumacious of the two, pushed a rolled-up tattered manuscript into Alicia's hand. Her translation of the first chapters of *Through the Looking-Glass*.

"You get out before us," she said, her lenses magnifying the conviction in her pale gray eyes. "Make sure this gets out with you, make sure it is copied and distributed throughout the schools and the libraries, and make sure only *my* name stays on it; porque aunque Mercedes helped, I will take all the blame when the time comes."

"Ay, Beba, estás loca," her sister said.

Alicia folded the manuscript and stuffed it in the side pocket of the simple gray dress they had given her to wear.

"Be careful," Beba said, "no one here is who they say they are. ¡Curiosísimo!" She grabbed her sister by the arm and led her away. Mercedes turned, waved to Alicia, and shook her head as if offering an apology. Alicia waved back. No apologies necessary.

On Alicia's fourth day there, her mother was allowed to visit; and as Alicia requested, doña Adela did not bring Teresita. Her mother told her of plans to release her soon. Mingo and Father Gonzalo were working out a deal with el Rubio.

"If it requires my silence," Alicia said, "if it requires forgetting about Héctor, I'll be part of no deal. I'll serve the time the court has mandated."

"I don't know what it requires. Y coño, stop being so stubborn. You have a daughter—that should be your first concern. Where do I tell her her mamita has gone for six months?"

"She *is* my first concern. That is why I have done all this, why I am here. So that she never doubts who her father was and why he died. Tell her the truth, that is what you tell her!"

"Bueno, tranquila mijita."

They sat on the veranda of the fanciest house in the complex, glaringly the only one that had been given a paint job since the yanquis left, twice a year, a crisp sunny yellow, coated on so thick now that the grain on the wood sidings was invisible, drowned by the unbearable yellow, the only one with a garden, blossoming with begonias and oleanders and black-eyed susans, the one nearest the bay, where the comandante in charge of the camp lived with his wife and son, where Alicia had already been interviewed by him seven times in three days, about her beliefs, about the depth of her will to disturb the process of la Revolución.

"We do not want to crush any of our citizens," he said, sucking on a panatela. "We want to show them what benefits, what progress la Revolución has brought to our Island, a never-ending event unprecedented in human history. No reign of terror here. *But* those too self-involved, too heavy with pride to rise with us, we will not save from drowning. ¿No es así?"

"It is exactly what *you* choose it to be. Isn't it, comandante? Nothing more or less."

"No. No." The comandante laughed. "If I can assure you of anything, it is that it will be you and only you who will choose your fate."

The breeze blew in from the bay and comforted Alicia, so that she was thinking little about her fate when she handed her mother the folded manuscript of Beba's translation. Doña Adela opened the papers and squinted, trying to make out some of the words.

"I need my glasses. What is it?"

"Put it away before the guard comes back. Read it to Teresita tonight and then store it someplace safe till I get out of here, with the copy of my sermon. You still have that, don't you?"

"Yes." Doña Adela had not found the courage to burn it the night Alicia was arrested.

The guard was seated outside the gates by the bayshore, his back to them, his weapon at his side, his head thrown back to the dying afternoon sun. It was Sunday and the comandante and his wife and son had gone to Santiago for the day. Still, Alicia was not comfortable with her mother visiting, sitting there on the veranda of his house.

"Someplace safe," she repeated. Then there was silence and doña Adela refolded the manuscript and stuffed it down her breast so that it was held in place by the lower strap of her brassiere. She loosened her blouse. After a while, the guard came, his face flushed from the sun, and politely led doña Adela away. Alicia kissed her mother on both cheeks.

"Don't stop talking to her about me. Don't let my daughter forget me." Doña Adela nodded. The guard waited as they kissed again, then he grabbed doña Adela by the forearm.

When her mother was gone, Alicia made her way back on her own to the beaten-up tin shack at the other end of the complex where she was housed with the other three women. When the guard was out of sight, she picked a black-eyed susan for each of them. Four days later, she was released, no conditions set down, serving only a week of her six-month sentence. Mingo, she heard from her mother, had struck a deal with el Rubio.

"Acuérdese, señora Alicia," the comandante of the too-yellow house said on her last day there. "You choose."

When one of the hand-scripted copies of *Through the Looking-Glass* was confiscated by the government some weeks later, reported by a twelve-year-old pionero to his neighborhood CDR, the teacher was arrested and the twins Mercedes and Beba had their sentences extended by five years, even though only one of their names appeared on the manuscript. Credited with the translation, they had chosen, and they had chosen *together*. El Comité was still looking for other culprits based on the handwriting sample from the manuscript.

Guava Milk

For the first time in eight nights, he slept in the bright and airy bedroom of his cottage, on the wide four-post bed his wife had insisted on buying in Santiago long ago, before the revolution, wrapped in the linen sheets that had been a wedding present from his mother, except the room wasn't bright or airy anymore, for he had boarded up all the windows of the house and bolted shut all the doors as if its tenant had fled forever, and the bed didn't seem so wide anymore for his magnificent dreams tossed him to and fro, and the sheets smelled not of spring air as they had once, but of stuck sweat and dried urine. When he awoke the first day from a dream of him and Berta alone in a gleaning guava grove beyond the world's reach, the room was still dark and the plywood shutters had been nailed in so well and sealed in so close that not one sliver of morning penetrated the hostage night. So Mingo dreamt on, repeating the questions that had dominated his dream out loud. "¿Cuánto me quieres, mi vida? Yo que te adoro. ¿Cuánto me quieres de veras?" And he imagined the answer in-wrought in the sweet blanket of her breath, as he rubbed his cheeks against her furry dewlap and when he leaned under her and drank her milk it tasted like the juice of the guava fruit.

The following day, through dreaming, he went to work. He exited the house through the trapdoor in the cellar, dressed like a finquero for the first time in over a week, in his veal-hide boots and rumply canvas pants and baggy workshirt, neatly tucked, and signature wide-brimmed straw hat. "I hope you're ready, girls," he said to María, Isabela, and Niña as he entered the barn. He fed them and when he milked them they gave him their stained milk without reserve, as if they had forgotten the lesson of the beating a week back, gave him eighteen and a quarter bucketfuls of milk the color of rose tears. By noon, he was on his way to the northern end of his finca, a fifteen-minute walk across the twisty brook and down the side of the mountain, to a miniature less-productive version of the guava grove he had dreamt about. Years ago, before the land reform acts, it would have taken him over eight hours to walk from one end of his lands to the other, now it was a matter of minutes. But his shrinking universe no longer bothered him. He filled three baskets with ripe guayabas and headed back to the cottage. In the cellar, he ripped the goatskin off his homemade drum, cleaned out the oak cask and turned it upside down. When it was dry, he poured into it four sackfuls of raw sugar he had purchased through la bolsa negra, the moist hiss of the sugar coursing to the cask bottom encouraging Mingo in his purpose. He then added all the fruit pulp and stirred it with a long wooden oar till his shoulders burned and the mixture was a stiff paste. To this, he added the stained milk, stirring it again and letting it sit overnight.

He bathed in the river before he went to bed, swimming over to the site of Berta's desecrated grave and back and over and back and so on till he was so tired his powerful limbs were barely cracking the surface of the dark waters and then he dog-paddled to shore and crawled out of the river and slept in the sealed house. First thing in the morning, he went down to the cellar and stacked three splintery cola crates on top of each other, grabbed half a dry coconut shell, climbed up and stood over the cask of guava milk. Belly thrust forward, he smiled and urinated into the cask, catching the last squirts in the coconut shell and chugging it down.

The urine collected like a sheet of tinted glass at the top of the mixture, above the cream that had risen to which clung bits of guava pulp with tiny sand-colored seeds that looked like shredded flesh and bits of bone. Mingo stepped down and stirred the now finished, last-secret-ingredient-added concoction with the wooden oar. In half an hour it was ready to be bottled. He washed his entire stock of liter-sized bottles in the river. That very afternoon he would go down to town and begin to sell his new product.

On a wooden board, he made a sign with red paint:

Leche de guayaba. ¡Barata y muy rica!

He sealed the liter bottles, loaded up a creaky wooden cart, hitched it to Roberto, his strongest mule, and down the mountain he went, the bottles clinking against each other like a festival of bells. He set up shop from the back of his cart, just outside the town limits, not far from the yanqui naval base. His first sale was to a Cuban worker from the base who lived in town. Less than an hour later, he was back with his wife and two daughters to buy four more liters of guava milk. He paid in yanqui dollars, let his wife carry the goods, grabbed each of his daughters by the wrist and hurried away. His daughters broke loose from his grip and jumped around their mother like dogs before mealtime. Mingo stuffed the illegal currency deep into his pockets. Thus it was with that day's sales, usually paid in dollars—some worker from the base or from the purlieus of town would wander past and buy one liter of Mingo's guava milk and less than an hour or two later, return to buy three or more liters. One woman, whom Mingo recognized from the days of Father Gonzalo's services up in his finca, bought as many as ten liters on her return trip. By the time the moon had risen, Mingo was on his way back to his finca, his pockets full of illegal money and his heart tipsy after the first few swigs from the grog of vengeance.

The following day Mingo made more guava milk and the day after, early in the morning, he was on his way back down the mountain to set up shop again. He only made it about halfway down. A throng of people, mostly women, many of whom Mingo knew were members of the widow-bitchwitch's cabal, some men, including the one who had bought the first liter, with his wife and two young daughters again with him, were marching up towards his finca. The one leading them was a milk-skinned redhead with a full handsome figure, a sharp nose, and a stony chin. The early light reveled in her flowing hair, pushing its way in and out of the wavy strands and leaving behind little pearls of brilliance, like droplets on a shored swimmer's back.

"Soy Margaret," she said, making it a point to speak in her heavily accented Spanish, "la esposa del coronel MacDougal, el americano que dirige la base naval."

Mingo extended his hand. "Mucho gusto, Margaret."

Margaret forced a smile. Her teeth were crooked and they gave an incongruous air of humility to her expression. "We want some more of your milk," she said.

Mingo went to the back of his cart, opened it, and stuck his sign up. He searched in one of the leather sacks hanging on Roberto the mule and pulled out a piece of charcoal. He made two dark X's on the sign. This is how it now read:

Leche de guayaba. ¡Baxataxy muy rica!

The mob gathered around the cart, Margaret's orders to stay back having no effect.

"How much milk do you want, Margaret?" Mingo said, as if implying he was only going to sell to her. The mob moved in closer around the cart. Margaret pulled out a roll of American money, and others behind her tried to follow suit, though they pulled out single crumpled worthless pesos from their pockets instead.

"La yanqui primera," Mingo said.

"I want to buy for all of them," Margaret said. "I'll take the whole cart, mule and all." She started counting the roll of money. "How much do you want?"

"Roberto too, entonces. . . ." Mingo proposed a preposterous amount, more money than perhaps his present lands were worth and Margaret asked how many liters there were and Mingo told her and Margaret proposed half the amount and, without waiting for Mingo to answer yes or no or to haggle further, she counted out the money and handed it to him. She signaled for two of the women to grab hold of the mule. "¡La repartimos esta noche, dos litros para cada familia!" As they left Mingo behind, many voiced their objections to only two liters a family.

"The day after tomorrow," Mingo yelled. "I'll have even more milk. Bring back the empty liters and I'll give you a discount!" He had never seen or felt an American twenty-dollar bill. Now, he was the foolhardy owner of not only a wad of twenties, but of a few fifties and hundreds. He thought that the serious man pictured on the fifty looked a lot like himself when he let his beard grow. He laughed at this, at his own knurly countenance on a piece of American money.

So it was that Mingo got to know Margaret MacDougal and her charitable ways, every other day as she bought his entire stock of guava milk, no matter how much he made and always cutting the price to just under half of what Mingo asked. Although many Cubans worked in the naval base and traveled back and forth from yanqui territory to Cuban land, Margaret was the only American allowed free passage in and out by the Cuban government—because of her strong record as a good yanqui liberal, and to the chagrin of her husband the colonel, a vocal decade-long supporter of la Revolución. Margaret MacDougal, la peliroja con el corazón de oro, as the Guantanameros knew her, with her husband's American money, bought all the guava milk Mingo produced during the late days of that spring. And with her wont kindness, except for the three liters she kept for herself, distributed it to all the needy in the town of Guantánamo.

From the porch of her mother's house, Alicia Lucientes watched the people hurry for the distribution of guava milk. "Comunistas," she grumbled, though she said nothing when her mother brought back two liters to feed Teresita.

Soon, only the women of Guantánamo and a few at the naval base, the wives and daughters of officers, were drinking guava milk. The men began to find it distasteful, sour as spoiled wine, though they accompanied their women, their own wives and mothers and daughters, on the every-other-day trek to stock up with more of the concoction that they could not bare to whiff but their women chugged like starved wolf cubs. It became so that every other day was not enough, that by the time each family had brought back its two liters, or sometimes three—for though demand increased, at the height of production Mingo was most effective—by the time they had set the liters down on the kitchen table, the men disappearing into the pantry or back out into the patio, the brave ones who stayed to watch gagging as soon as the first of their women put their lips to the first bottle, too eager to pour it out into a glass, passing it around the table like a chalice, and the other bottle and the third, so that by noon of the day they had brought home their guava milk, it was gone. And what to do but go out and search for more, gathering in the foothills of the mountain in droves, as if by instinct, to journey to the source. Why wait till the day after tomorrow? Why depend on the yanqui redhead? Though she was gracious and kind, unlike any yanqui they had ever known, still this hunger would not depend on charity for long.

A band of seven of the most desperate women went up to the finca that very night and broke into Mingo's cottage through an unshuttered window on a rooftop gallery. They found Mingo in the makeshift basement. He was wearing only an old peasant smock stained with the pink juices of the guava pulp. He stirred the contents of the large wooden cask with a long oarlike stick. His tomcat expertly balanced his hefty frame on the edge of the cask and curled his nose at the mixture. One of the women giggled at the sight of Mingo's muscle-bound hairy legs and at his crooked toes grasping the dirt floor, firmly dug in by the long-hook toenails, so as not to lose leverage while stirring; the others were too hungry to giggle or find any comedy in him who was at once both their savior, because he had invented the guava milk, and their tormentor, because from now on he could never make enough to satisfy all of them. When Mingo saw them peering in through the trapdoor, scratching over each other for position, he pulled out the wooden oar from the guava milk and waved it over his head like a scimitar as he chased them out, up the creaky pine staircase to the gallery window from which they flew to the ground. As the last one jumped out, Mingo caught her on the bottom with a swing of the oar and when she fell to the ground, the others began to lick her where the oar had left traces of sticky guava cream on her skin and she yelped and begged to let her taste their mouths after they had licked her ass-skin sore. Then they fled like thieves towards the guava grove on the other side of the mountain.

Two days later, when Mingo sold his guava milk to Margaret, meeting her halfway down the mountain as had become the habit, he did not see the seven who had broken into his cottage. He told Margaret about it and made her promise to exclude these seven hounds from any future distribution list. Margaret handed him a roll of yanqui money, more fifties and hundreds than ever before, and promised Mingo she would take care of it, punish the greedy ones who could not wait the required two days for their ration of guava milk. That night, some women broke into Mingo's cottage again, this time busting in through one of the downstairs windows and making off with some twelve liters and the guava-milk-dipped oar that one of the braver ones grabbed from Mingo as he swung it at her. Their group had grown to more than twenty. By now, they had shed most of their clothing, and were caked with the black mountain earth. Before they fled, they surrounded the captured oar and danced around it and then licked it dry and let it drop and fled singing:

> *To the mountain! To the mountain!*
> *From where the saints can rule the world.*

Mingo went to retrieve the oar and decided he had made enough money from the red-headed yanqui, decided to stop production of guava milk after this last batch.

The Meat of Castrated Goats

The morning after she was released, Alicia took a long bath in dissolved Dead Sea salts and later rode up the mountain in a horse-pulled coach to Mingo's finca, accompanied by Father Gonzalo, Teresita, and Marta. Mingo was out back by the leaning barn milking one of the cows when he saw the group approaching, Teresita in the lead running towards him; he tugged out one of the cow's nipples, aimed it at the girl, and squeezed out a long squirt that flew in a low arc some thirty feet through the air and landed on the girl's face. Teresita stopped, her eyes closed, unsure of what had just hit her. Mingo spattered her again. The girl shivered, though the liquid that had just hit her face again was warm as the sea on a late summer afternoon.

"Mingo, no jodas," her mother called, "le vas a manchar su ropita." Mingo laughed. Teresita wiped her face and opened her eyes just as he was readying to shoot her again. This time she ducked out of the way and ran in a frenzy towards him, her arms dancing in front of her, scooting this way and that as to avoid the enemy milk-fire. Later that day, Mingo would show her how to milk the cow and how to squirt anybody who dared approach her. And Teresita got each of them before they left that afternoon, her mother, her aunt, Father Gonzalo and Mingo himself, right on the butt while he was bent over inside the chicken coop feeding the gray hens. Each time her mother returned to the finca during the next few weeks, Teresita insisted on accompanying her—she needed to practice milking.

"You stain your mother's or your aunt's dress one more time, señorita," doña Adela told her one morning as they left, "and I'll make you scrub it yourself. It's a waste, a terrible waste!"

"Up there in the mountain," Teresita said to her mother, "la leche es buena, and everybody laughs when I spray it around. Down here it makes abuela mad because it stains our dresses and because the woman at the bodega only gives her so much."

Part of the deal Mingo had agreed to with el Rubio for the immediate release of Alicia was the further communization of his little-remaining lands and their produce, less than a third of which he was now allowed to keep for sustenance and black market profit, the rest going to the revolutionary government; or more likely to el Rubio and his cohorts. Alicia learned the details of the agreement through Father Gonzalo, though he made her promise never to thank Mingo or even to let on that she knew anything about it. It was the way Mingo had wanted it. "It was a true act of charity," Father Gonzalo said. "Of kindness, which is a greater thing." So when Teresita laughed and sprayed milk around, Mingo let her, imagining it was el Rubio's portion of the milk she was wasting.

Mingo's finca became the place for them to gather as a group. *Dissidents with their hearts buried en la mierda de vacas,* Pucha said of them. Doña Adela rarely went up to the finca, complaining to Mingo that the ride up the mountain was too grueling, though the truth was that Alicia simply would not allow it, would not risk having the entire family gathered up and charged with conspiracy to disrupt la Revolución. At first, it was just the five of them—Mingo, Alicia, Marta, Father Gonzalo, and the girl. Every morning, they would arrive about eleven and help Mingo finish his morning chores and prepare el almuerzo—usually chicken with rice and fried plantains, or white-peppered quinbombó with a side of corn frituritas—then Mingo and Father Gonzalo would take their siestas in the rope hammocks hanging from the dead trunks of royal palms. Alicia and her sister would talk through the early afternoon and before nightfall Ernesto, the coach driver, was back to give them a ride home. It went like this till Father Gonzalo decided to hold the Maundy Thursday services of that year by the river near Mingo's cottage. That morning Alicia heard from her relatives in Camagüey that her cousin Héctor had died in the labor camp from a serious case of hepatitis. His mother had been contacted at the asylum in Santiago and she had refused to accept his remains. During the Maundy Thursday service, as they stood in line to have Father Gonzalo wash their feet in the river, Alicia asked Mingo if she could bury Héctor in his lands.

"That boy ate the meat of castrated goats," Mingo said.

"What?" Alicia nearly shouted, and many with their feet dunked in the cool whispering river glared at her.

"That's how it happens, the meat of castrated goats, one has to be very careful not to feed it to the young."

"That's how *what* happens?"

"His problem, why he was put away—his lust for other men."

"Does that mean I can't use your land?"

"Pues no, of course you can bury him here. He has to be buried somewhere, no? His flesh can't be left out there for the birds to pick at. I meant no offense. That's just how it happens, the meat of castrated goats."

When Alicia asked the revolutionary authorities for Héctor's body to be sent her, they said it had been cremated for fear of spreading the hepatitis. She went to Santiago and waited for the six o'clock train nicknamed the Death Express. It was the train on which each day the remains of the dead were brought home to the province from other parts of the Island. An old crooked man exited the last coach and handed her a glass jar full of gray dust labeled with a small neat script: *Héctor Daluz.* The jar was heavy but to Alicia it still seemed such a paltry thing. "This is it?" she said. "This is all of him?" He said, "I am sorry," and it sounded more like an apology than a condolence. Alicia spread the ashes by the river shore in

Mingo's finca and asked Father Gonzalo to hold a service there for Héctor on each of the seven Fridays following. On the first Friday, a rose-chested pigeon descended from the heavens as they were reciting el Padre Nuestro, resting on Father Gonzalo's makeshift dried palm-frond altar, picking at the already parted and consecrated Host. Luis el Catorce climbed up on the altar and leapt at it, but the bird had made off with the wafer. The following Friday there were six of them, this time distracting Father Gonzalo enough, and taunting Luis el Catorce till he was hopping up and down with his paws outstretched so that it looked as if he had been possessed by a vulgar saint, so that they got away with most of the Communion wafers. The following Friday, Mingo brought his shotgun.

"No," Marta said to him. "You must not shoot them. They are Héctor's spirits come to celebrate his own Mass, come to enjoy the body of Christ."

"¡Mierda! They're hungry vermin is what they are!" Mingo pointed his shotgun to the empty skies. "I *will* shoot them. They are desecrating the Mass and they'll eat all my crops."

"You must not harm them!"

That Friday they came late, after Communion, perhaps because they were gathering in such massive numbers, because somehow they knew this time they would need the protection of the many. A rosy wind that snuffed the morning light blew them in; Father Gonzalo had returned to the altar and was brushing the few crumbs of the Host from a silver plate into the chalice—a mile-wide mantle of birds approaching almost without noise. Father Gonzalo lifted the golden chalice skyward with both hands as if consecrating its contents again. The birds swooped, and in a moment the flutter of the wings was deafening and Father Gonzalo could not see his congregation and could not call out for help, hypnotized by their eurhythmic attack song that now could be heard and felt beyond the ceaseless beatings of their wings, stilled by the vibrant color-spin of salmon-melon torsos and gray-white bellies and fire-marble eyes, in front of him and to the side of him and below him and above him as if drowning in a fathomless warm sea of feathers.

When the birds finally lifted, Father Gonzalo's hands were empty. He crouched down on the ground below the altar and began to search frantically, like a man who has lost his spectacles. He must have dropped it; he simply would not believe that the birds had taken the chalice with the blood-wine and the Corpus Christi crumbs.

In her dreams, Marta saw the birds transformed into bare-chested barely winged angel boys and when they descended around her, she would grab this one or that one (they were not that much different from each other) and peck light kisses on their soft necks—joyful that all of them were secretly hers—and release them as soon as they began to wriggle. Later, after the hunt, she had other dreams, that they returned to earth louder than a plague of locusts, their beaks agape, their thin tongues lashing at her, wailing their untimely deaths.

When Mingo insisted on hunting the birds for the sake of his crops, Marta convinced Alicia and Father Gonzalo to dissociate themselves from him, and holy services up in the finca were canceled by Father Gonzalo (as much due to the great scare the pigeons gave him as to please Marta), though the birds kept returning in larger and larger numbers to the site where Héctor's ashes had been sprinkled by the river. At first, Mingo was dissuaded enough from the hunt that he tried to frighten the birds away. He fashioned a drum made from the single-piece skin of a giant castrated mountain goat, soaked for three days and then spread just loose enough over the mouth of an oak cask and fastened to its side. He let the skin dry for another three days, till the morning he saw the cloud of birds gathering in the horizon. He strapped the large drum to his back and carried it out to the riverside. He played with the sureness of a practiced tribesman, in a rhythm so seductive that the rushing water listened to it and the flow of the river seemed to slow down to keep pace with it, rolling by two steps forward and one back with the forgetfulness and ease of a salsa dancer. The first day, when the birds heard the drum music, the whole flock changed course, veering southerly towards the sea and Mingo kept on beating on the goatskin drum till long after they had disappeared and his palms were raw and his finger joints pulsed and the river was tired of dancing. The day after, the same; but the day after that, a few birds wandered away from the flock and hovered in the air above Mingo for a while before they rejoined their brethren. And so it was that more and more of the birds joined in the primitive drum dance by the river. (Pigeon gossip.) In a week's time, the drum beckoned the flock more than frightened them and Mingo played on, under the noon darkness of their feathery mantle, the bird's waste matter falling on him like rain, making slick the goatskin, his arms numb to his elbows. He played on, he played on, till he made sure that the call of the drum was ingrained in each and every one of the birds, that they were so bewitched by the goatskin-music that he could command them forth at any time and to any place, even to their deaths. He fantasized about leading the vermin to the sea like a latter-day Cuban San Patricio and tossing the drum into the firm grip of the waves and watching the crests reach up like silver fingers and grab each and all of the bedeviled flock. But these were fantasies. He knew the truth of their deaths lay in the pellets of his shotgun; and the more he played his drums, the more the birds trusted him, their masses lowering down closer and closer, till their rainstorm of waste matter muffled the cry of Mingo's goatskin drum. And as he played on, as the pungent mushy yellow and gray shit splattered from the drowning goatskin onto his face and into his wide-open snarl of a mouth, rapt and yelling like a rabid dog, he tasted them and he knew they were his unto death.

To the Mountain!

Alicia Lucientes had tried to resist the richness of guava milk, even though every other day when doña Adela came back from Margaret's distribution line on the hills by the yanqui base, her daughter had a glass and her sister—whom doña Adela had slowly allowed to be received at their breakfast table, and relenting, had learned to care for, to hold (as she had wanted to do on that rainy afternoon when she first met her), to treat, as if she were her own—had a glass and her mother herself had a glass and she offered to pour Alicia some, and at first Alicia waved her off but after a moment she said: "Bueno, un poquito, dos deditos nada más." And her mother poured her un poquito, just a bit, two fingers' worth in her glass and Alicia swirled it as they eyed her and took it all down in one gulp. After she got up and left, straightening her skirt, hiding all outward signs that that one simple tasting, ese poquito, had left her yearning for bucketfuls of more guava milk, her daughter, her mother, and her sister had one more glass, finishing off the first liter. "El resto para mañana." Doña Adela put away the guava milk in one of the two barren refrigerators, and Marta and Teresita could hardly wait for tomorrow.

Those nights, Alicia stayed over to sleep at her mother's house. Before dawn she went to the refrigerator and carefully pulled apart the tinfoil seal in one of the two remaining liters, pinching it right under the lip of the bottle and lifting it slowly, to have un poquito más and fill the gap in the liter with cold water and reseal it and shake it, no harm done. Once, her mother caught her putting back the liter in the wrong refrigerator. "¿Qué haces mi vida?"

"Nada. I can't sleep." Alicia kissed her mother and walked out of the kitchen. After that, doña Adela overpoured when her daughter asked for un poquito, dos deditos nada más. She would pour six or seven fingers' worth, and Alicia would drink it, pretending not to notice.

When production of guava milk stopped in the second week of August, because it was rumored that a band of wild women was threatening Mingo's life, Alicia also pretended not to miss it. And when her mother and Marta came back from the bodega on Mondays with their ration of a half-liter of regular white milk for each adult and the one weekly liter allotted to the child, and she poured Teresita a glass and Marta a glass and herself a glass, Alicia refused.

"¡No, que va, que voy a tomar esa mierda!" Then her daughter began to follow her example and refuse the white milk, so Alicia forced herself to drink half a glass, as they all forced themselves to drink it for its nutritional value, though this stuff was watery and probably nutrient-free and milk would never taste like milk again.

One morning, Marta did not show up for breakfast, and when Alicia arrived with her daughter from her house, fresh from a morning bath, in crispy-ironed summer dresses, doña Adela sat alone at the kitchen table, her head propped up on her hands, her eyes bleary, her ash-colored hair sprouting every which way, like the ghosts of weeds.

"Se ha ido," she said. "I couldn't stop her. She told me that she doesn't belong in this house anyway. She is right you know . . . I never should have learned to love her."

"No hables boberías, mamá. Gone? Gone where?"

"Where all the young women are going, mija, to the mountain, where they can feed themselves."

"A ver a Mingo," Teresita chanted, "a ver a Mingo. To the mountain!"

"Don't let this one out of your sight." Alicia led her daughter by her hand to her grandmother.

"I didn't *let* Marta go . . . and what power did I have over her anyway. She was never mine. And where are *you* going?"

"To find my sister."

"Yo quiero ir, mamita!" the girl shouted. "To the mountain. ¡A ver a Mingo!"

"No." The grandmother put her hand over the child's mouth. "¡No, por el amor de Dios!"

Alicia left that very morning for Mingo's finca, packing only a change of clothes, the ivory-handled stiletto she had once taken from her husband, and an army canteen (also her late husband's) full of fresh water and a dash of sugarcane juice. It was overcast and the hot and the gray-green sky seemed to be slowly descending on the earth. The trek up the mountain on the gravelly dirt road that led directly to Mingo's finca took over three hours. She stopped twice to pick mangoes off the pregnant boughs, salmon- and lavender- and yellow-skinned, tempting as the fruit that never falls in paradise. Easily they were tugged off the branches, as if in a moment their own weight would have detached them. The first time, Alicia peeled the skin off with her teeth and bit into the mango and tasted not the firm fibry sweet pulp that the skin of such fruit promised, but rather an acid mush so strong and foul that it had corroded the pit and crumbled it to small pieces. She spit it out and gargled with water and washed her chin furiously. The second time, about an hour later up the mountain, having spit out the last trace of the first fruit and too hungry to resist, Alicia picked another heavy-with-promise mango, now more careful, peeling the skin back with the ivory-handled stiletto, holding it at arm's reach. This time, the mango's flesh was tender and it was the right hue of orange-yellow and it was sweet. Before moving on up the mountain, Alicia ate three mangoes off the same branch with so much relish that she stained her summer dress with the juices dripping from her chin. The fruits gave her strength and in less than half an hour Mingo's finca cottage was within sight. She waited, resting under the shade of a royal palm and sipping her sweetened water, not knowing yet how to proceed, how to confront Mingo, where to begin looking for her sister. At three in the afternoon, her stomach began to turn. At four, she heaved up chunks of unchewed, undigested mango flesh coated with a grainy crimson gravy. She heaved till her stomach was squeezing on itself like an empty clenched fist. She covered the mess with dirt and she washed her mouth with the sweet water and she napped on a rope hammock that was stretched out not far from Mingo's cottage, lulling herself to sleep with deep breaths that eased her nausea.

When she awoke it was dark and there was a sealed liter bottle full of guava milk resting on her belly. She cracked the seal and drank half of it. It lent her back some strength. She wandered away from the vicinity of the cottage—which was sealed from the inside with plywood shutters—down to the rivershore. She heard water splashing and giggles and when she moved closer, not bothering to hide her approach, she saw shadows in the water, some nearer to her, waist-deep, others beyond these, with only their heads poking out of the silver water, the moonbeams gleaming off their wet hair, and beyond them, on the far shore, there was a shadow wider and heavier than all the others around which the smaller shadows danced like so many happy moons around Jupiter, their legs kicking up above the surface of the water and crashing back down with a fountainlike splattering, around and around the roly-poly gyrating center shadow, a tropical mazurka.

"Marta . . . Martica," Alicia called out in a voice just above a whisper. One of the figures on the nearer shore turned its head and then signaled towards the others and swam towards them. "¡Vámonos! ¡Vámonos de aquí!"

All of the lithe figures scattered to the far shore and ran from the river, leaving the heavy shadow with his arms waving, imagining himself a conductor, still turning and turning on its own axis, not ceasing till he noticed his sudden solitude and then he froze and, with his arms still extended, dove in and swam to the near shore of the river. Alicia did not move as the heavy shadow crawled out of the river and approached her. With her right hand behind her she clutched tight the ivory handle of her husband's stiletto. By its walk, she knew who the shadow was. When he got close enough, she saw that Mingo was naked, his legs covered with wet fur, still barrel-chested but his legs grown more monumental since she last saw him, his penis half-blooming, horizontal, his arms thicker knit with muscle than she remembered. Alicia did not move. She could not see the old Mingo's face in the moonlight for it was masked with a classic scowl, like the villain's in yanqui cartoons, the brow furrowed, the eyebrows bent downward towards each other, his lips flat and the whole face pushing outward. "What are you doing on my land?"

Before Alicia could answer, Mingo raised his hand and swung it down, heavy as a bearpaw, and knocked from Alicia's left hand the half-liter of guava milk she had yet to drink. As the milk spilled, Alicia reached for it and Mingo kicked it away with his bare foot, his knee catching Alicia on the left side of the face and knocking her over. When he saw the knife, Mingo leaned down to her and stuck his tongue out, which was long and hoary, and he bleated like a dueling ram and his head trembled and then, backing off, he left her there. After the numbness on her cheeks eased, Alicia went and picked up the glass liter and drank the little bit of guava milk that had not spilled and spit out bits of stone and grass that had fallen into the bottle. She then followed Mingo and watched him enter his cottage through a trapdoor on the west side. When the mountain winds began to blow, Alicia knew it was late and she went into the barn and fashioned a bed of dry hay and slept, hoping she would awake before Mingo.

Morning came without Mingo. Alicia awoke late, her face stinging, shocked to see slats of high morning light slicing through the barn walls. The cows in their stalls were restless. Holding at bay the thought that she was being watched, Alicia changed quickly into her other dress, lifting up her slip and smelling it to make sure it was not too offensive, and she tied her hair back and exited the barn. Outside, on the shadowed side of the building, nestled neatly on tufts of wild grass one by the other as if left there by a very assiduous milkman, were three liters of fresh guava milk. Starved, she sat down in the morning shadows and leaned back against the barn wall and sip by sip finished most of one liter, putting it down only when she heard a rustling on the other side of the barn. She circled the barn once and twice, but she saw no one. The third time around, she saw the barn door had been cracked open. She went inside.

"You slept here? ¿Estás loca? That man wants you dead! He thinks you responsible for everything." A bony woman, barefoot and in a white linen tunic tied at her waist by a thin, weathered rope stood over her makeshift bed. Alicia reconized her. She crossed over to Alicia with an innate stealth, her bare steps light and low as a cat. She grabbed Alicia by the forearm, and shut the barn door. "Qué bien, I see you've enjoyed some of the breakfast I left for you."

Alicia thanked her in a low mumble and then took a deep breath.

"No te preocupes," the woman told her, patting her on the shoulder. "Your sister is with us. She is fine. Here, have some more." She took from Alicia the second liter of guava milk and broke open the seal and took a small sip and moaned with pleasure and offered it to Alicia, who took two big gulps.

"Can I go see her?"

"She's sleeping. You'll see her tonight."

"I know you."

"You should. I recommended to the tribunal your sentence of six months."

"Coño, Pucha, la del Comité."

A thin sardonic smile on Pucha's face grew into a chuckling assent. "La misma."

"What have you done with Martica?"

"Your sister wants to be up here. She came to us, we did not go to her."

"Who is 'us'? Why can't I see her?"

"You will see her. You'll see her tonight. I told you that she's asleep now. They're all asleep. Now let's get out of here before this idiota Mingo wakes up. . . . I see he got you a bit." She touched the left side of Alicia's face, under where it had begun to bruise. "No, it's nothing."

Pucha put her arm around her and led her out of the barn. Mingo's massive tomcat came to them and rubbed up against their legs. He was hungry. Pucha found a discarded coconut shell and poured some guava milk for him, but Luis el Catorce wrinkled his nose at it. They waded across the river. Pucha held the two liters of guava milk aloft. The water never reached higher than their breasts. On the far shore they lay in the morning sun and let their clothes dry out. Pucha took off her tunic and spread it on a flat boulder. She wore only a set of frilly panties, which when wet, were as if she wore nothing at all. There was so little flesh on her body that Alicia could see the sharp points of her hip bone protruding on both sides and she could count each and all of her ribs and she had pointy bitch's teats with nipples the color of indian clay.

"It'll dry faster like this."

Alicia ignored her and remained dressed and soon Pucha had fallen asleep beside her, the dark color of her skin and the infinitesimal rhythm of her belly the only evidence that she was not a wasted corpse. Alicia got up and wandered away from the rivershore, following a dirt road that turned pebbly and soon became no road at all. She crossed the coffee fields, the bean fruits on the vine large and red as cherries. When she came to a small orchard of mamey trees she picked one of the thick-skinned fruits and cut it open with her stiletto, which she now kept slipped in the drawstring of her dress, and she flicked off the large black seed and cut long slices of the ruddy flesh and guided them to her mouth with the blade. She walked on, all the way to a glen crowded with royal palms and still capped with a late morning mist. Then, thinking she must have strayed off Mingo's land, she turned and headed back to the rivershore. Pucha was dressed and awake when she returned, sitting cross-legged on the flat boulder where her tunic had been drying. Alicia moved quickly to the riverbank and bent over and threw up the fruit she had eaten on her journey. She washed her face, stood up and examined herself. There was reddish spittle running down the front of her dress and the hem at the knees was muddied.

"Nothing in this finca is edible," Pucha said, as if she had known this for many years. "No matter how good it looks or how sweet it tastes, it'll rot your insides. Claro, except for the guava milk that *he* makes. On that we must subsist. Remember that, it'll make your stay here much more pleasant."

"I am not staying. I am taking Martica and we are going home."

"Lo que quieras. I'm just telling you for your own welfare."

Alicia turned away from Pucha. She took off her leather moccasins, pulled the light dress off over her head, and went to the river to wash vomit and mud off it. When she came back, wearing only her satin slip, with the wrung-out dress drooped over her arm, Pucha jumped off the flat boulder. "Put it here."

Alicia spread the dress over the boulder.

"Eres una muchacha muy hermosa."

Alicia ignored this and pretended to concentrate on spreading out her dress so it would dry quickly. Then Pucha moved towards her and Alicia clumsily moved away.

"Very pretty dress," Pucha said, feeling the wet fabric of Alicia's dress. "I do not mean to make you uncomfortable, señorita."

"You do not make me uncomfortable; and it's señora not señorita."

"Sí, verdad."

There was a moment of silence as if Pucha meant to pay homage to the husband she had a second ago forgotten had existed. Alicia wiped the mud off her feet and put on the leather moccasins. Then she went to the riverbank and picked up the stiletto and canteen she had left there. She filled the canteen with riverwater.

"Did it bother you when I called you beautiful?"

"As soon as my dress dries I want to go find my sister."

"She is also a beauty. Were you twins?"

"¿Cómo te atreves?"

"Call your sister beautiful . . ."

"Call her so in such tones."

"*Señora* Alicia, have you ever thought of la Revolución as anything else besides the process that ended your husband's life?"

"That murdered my husband . . . no, that is exactly how I have always thought of it."

". . . since his death?"

"His murder."

"And before that?"

"Before that I was happily married."

"Yes, that beautiful daughter would prove it."

Alicia stared hard at Pucha for the first time and said nothing.

"You're too bright to have been forever the lovely wife of comandante Julio César Cruz, the old soldier who wanted nothing else to do with la Revolución. In a queer way his death gave you a chance to become your own woman, a chance of which I may say you took full advantage."

"I really don't know what you're talking about. And whatever insults you intend are missing their mark."

"No, al contrario, I mean no offense. I think you are precious, no matter how much no jodes y no jodes a nosotros, el Comité, the folks of la Revolución. . . . See, it's what la Revolución has done for all women, lifted us out of centuries de vivir en las sombras, beside husbands and fathers and sons. It is the legacy of the Spaniard, a repugnant legacy, but at least the Spaniard had a noble heart, no matter how wrongheaded his ideas may have been he would bleed and die for them. The Spaniard is never an opportunist like the yanqui, who takes this idea and borrows that one and steals another, whatever suits him; as long as the balance of power is never tilted against him, he is happy. And the only thing these two cultures have in common, these two people—the Catholic and the Protestant—who had dominated our land for centuries before la Revolución, stained into the fabric of each society like blood, is the out-in-the-open oppression of women. La Revolución promised to change that. And it has. What was I under yanqui rule? A lavandera in Santiago. I washed clothes for the rich families of that town, not because I couldn't do anything else, but because I couldn't aspire to anything else. Luckily I had the strength to run away from that. I ran to the mountain. I fought in the war alongside other women. Never in the history of warfare have women played such an integral part in the gritty process of victory, in the bloodrivers of the battlefield."

"What battlefields?" Alicia said, regretting instantly that she had been drawn into a conversation. "You had a cockroach tyrant in the capital who fled after his Rural Guard had lost a few skirmishes! Battlefields? Do you not think husbands whisper stories to their wives? Do you not think I know what a sham the great Cuban revolutionary war was? Or (and now it's my turn to insult you) have you never been in bed with a man, do you not know the many shameful truths told through a pillow at the end of the day?"

"Regardless . . . la Revolución *has* rewarded us, and we have cast off the shame of the Spaniard and the shallowness of the yanqui forever. Is this not something we should prize? A thing so worthy it will inspire poets to invent a thousand battlefields that never existed."

Alicia walked away from her to the riverbank. She sat there peering through the clear unhurried current into the riverbed, the afternoon light turning the pebbly bottom yellow. She felt calm for the first time since she had arrived on the mountain. She was glad she had insulted Pucha, glad she had not dishonored the memory of her husband and she yearned for him as she had not since receiving the news of Héctor's death, to be prick-led by his beard and giddied by the tracing of his long violet scar with her index finger and drenched in his sweat and even suffocated by the gami-ness in between his legs when he came to her unwashed from these very mountains. She saw the sun sculpt with its jointless gilded fingers a figure in the pebbles of the riverbottom, and she was both horrified and exhila-rated when she noticed that the figure was of the other one, not her hus-band. She stirred the waters with her hand, blurring the image.

"Here, you're going to need strength. We still have some climbing to do."

She felt Pucha's fingers on her bare thigh. She moved her leg away. Pucha reached her one of the two remaining liters of guava milk.

"No quiero," Alicia said, though she was very hungry.

Pucha cracked open the seal and offered her the liter bottle again. Ali-cia ignored her.

"Do you always work so hard to alienate people trying to help you?"

"Please, I just want to find my sister."

"We'll go as soon as the sun begins to fade." She pushed the liter of milk under Alicia's nose. Alicia took it and waited till she had stepped away before she took a sip and another sip.

When her dress had dried, she put it on. It felt gauzy and warm as if woven from the thin rays of the late afternoon light. She went to find Pucha, who had gone back across the river and was resting on Mingo's rope hammock, again having discarded her tunic, caressing Mingo's tom-cat who was napping on her belly.

"The sun is almost set," Alicia yelled.

"Soon," Pucha yelled back. She did not move from the hammock till night began to fall. Alicia wondered if Pucha was waiting for Mingo and she paced restlessly on the opposite rivershore, every once in a while glancing across towards the darkening shape of Mingo's finca cottage and listening to the drawn plaintive moan of his hungry cows. When Pucha recrossed the river, she held her white tunic aloft like a banner; and though at one point her body sunk under the dark surface, the tunic remained above in her outstretched hand, swaying in the breeze. When she emerged in front of Alicia, her dark skin was bumpy and her nipples enlarged.

"Qué rápido se enfría el río."

She wrung the water out of her hair and threw on her dry tunic.

Alicia followed Pucha three steps behind, the first mile or so climbing close to the riverbank and then veering towards a forest where Alicia pulled closer because it got so dark she could just barely make out the shapes in front of her, till it became so impossibly dark and the ground so covered with overgrowth that she had to grab hold of Pucha's tunic so as not to lose her, and she dropped her ivory-handled stiletto, not even paus-ing to look for it; and the strap of her canteen got caught by the reach of a branch and it was stripped from her, water spilling like urine down her leg. She could not tell for sure whether her eyes were opened or closed though they must have been closed for the brilliance broke in front of her at first in a flash of orange and red, like predawn desert lightning, and she found herself in an oasis of light. Alicia stopped and breathed like a diver who has found a pocket of air in an undersea cave and she let go of Pucha's tunic though Pucha was motioning her to follow her further.

"Come, come see the beauty of your hermanita."

As she moved further, into a clearing just beyond, Alicia saw that the light was coming from twenty-five torches set in groups of five, spaced like the points of a pentagon and each pentagon then becoming a point in a larger pentagon around a gigantic statue of a dark-faced lady in regal robes. Figures danced around each smaller pentagon, barefoot and dressed in unsashed caftans (much like Pucha's) and draped with yellow shawls that became wings when they spread their arms out in unison. On their necks were many strands of glass-bead necklaces that flickered golden in the torchlight and clinked and clinked. Each group chanted its own music and danced at its own pace. But all kept the beat of one god. In the background, at the fraying of the light, a drummer, black-skinned and gleaming like polished stone, with arms thick as boas provided rhythm for all five groups, his head thrown back so that it was engulfed by the woody darkness and his neck and torso streaming with sweat so that it looked as if he were headless. His bare torso and legs had the contours of a man but his breasts and nipples were enlarged like a pregnant woman's. As Alicia looked for her sister among the dancers, her foot began to tap to a song she had heard many times and among all the chanting she could listen to it above all else:

. . . y si vas al Cobre, quiero que me traigas . . .

The group that sang it was the one farthest from her, across the way from the statue, and because she could not make out the faces of the dancers, she moved away from Pucha, going counterclockwise around the perimeter of the larger pentagon. She saw her sister smiling and dancing like a coquette, spreading her yellow wings as if threatening to fly away. Her smile reminded Alicia of Héctor's smile when she had seen him in the labor camp, and she was troubled at the thought that joy could be found in the wrongest places. But the instinct to protect her sister, to take her home, had disappeared and Alicia gave in to the song and began to chant along, at first meekly, but soon clapping her hands and stomping her feet.

Her sister held out her hand to her and somebody threw on her back the parrot-wing shawl and glass-bead necklaces fell on her as if having dropped from the moonless sky and before she could protest she was inside the pentagon of torches dancing on a bed of rotted bark around half a giant coconut shell filled with honey and with pebbles from the riverbed. She danced till sweat made her gauzy dress stick to her skin. And when she felt the rhythm of the headless drummer as real as the very beat her blood obeyed, she opened her parrot wings and danced alone as the drummer played on and her limbs began to find a range of motion that had been previously unknown. She thought of herself as one of the circus contortionists Héctor used to perform with and she found joy in this and she shook and twisted some more as if this could lull him (the beloved cousin) somehow back to her and when his presence brushed her cheeks and then fled from her she began to hop violently on one foot and then the other and she imagined she grew a tail, long and hairless like an opossum's, coiled at the end and stiff enough to bounce on, and she swung her arms about, still moving as one with the pounding of the headless negro. When she fell exhausted to the ground, she heard someone say that this new initiate definitely belonged to one of the warrior gods, to the god of mischief: "She belongs to Elegua."

"Like Fidel," someone answered.

Pucha reappeared, carrying a wicker basket full of the fruit she had warned Alicia against eating, behind her three other women, dragging in Mingo's old mulecart a gigantic birdcage with spires and domes and swings made of shaved cane reeds, so thin that it seemed impossible that the cage could serve its purpose, that the three rose-chested pigeons flying around in circles inside could not at any time they desired burst through the fragile skeleton and free themselves. But why flee from such a beautiful home? They did not come out until Pucha had the cage lowered to the ground and entered through its gate, so wide and so high that all she had to do was slightly lower her head, and as she danced the pigeons descended on her, one on each shoulder, the other on her outstretched hand. She came out of the cage. She began to juggle the pigeons so that they folded in on themselves and became rosy blurs of feather. The other women approached Alicia, carrying the basket of fruit to where she was crouching and they rained the fruit on her head and it did not hurt for the fruit was soft and overripe and then they smashed the fruit over her body and spread the sticky pulp on her face and in her hair and using mango pits they scrubbed her legs and under her dress and Alicia stood and again began to move with the rhythm of the drummer and the possessed women danced around her and then converged on her and licked the fruit pulp off her skin. When they spread out again, Pucha approached Alicia, still juggling her feather balls, and she threw one around Alicia so that it circled her head and the other and the other; the pigeons began to go around her so fast that all Alicia could see was the blur of their colors and all she could hear was the whirr of their wings, till she saw Pucha's bony hands again, and in one quick flip of her wrists the three pigeons hung headless on her forearm, three rivers of blood becoming one, as she caught the flow in the cup of her other hand and drank from it and fed the other women, then poured the river over Alicia's head and the women ripped her dress down to her waist and spread the blood over her body, falling on her and rubbing against her with their slick torsos, their smiles lined with strings of blood. Her sister plucked feathers off the pigeons and stuck them to Alicia's face and arms and legs, so that it was then, in those moments when she knew she would not be conscious for too much longer, that she felt Héctor plant kisses all over her, and sing their childhood song in a quivery voice, as if he were going from this earth forever.

> *Besitos besitos, en los labios labios,*
> *Besitos besitos, saben a mar a mar,*
> *Besitos besitos, somos diablos diablos,*
> *Besitos besitos, te voy a dar a dar.*

She tried to follow him, convinced that with all these feathers she could now plumb or surge into any world after him.

Mingo's Dreams Before Dying

In the mountains there are women. They whisper dire curses. They dance to end his life. They know the rhythm of his blood.

His blood beat best in the river, underwater, halo-hearts rippling from the thumps on his chest, which he swam through and swam through with the joy of a circus animal till his shoulders burned and his lungs clenched for air. He slept whenever and wherever he tired, dreamless, hiss-snoring short and loud as if unpracticed with breath, in the hemp-rope hammock that hung between the two stumps of royal palm or on the packed-mud floor of his finca cottage, or, his favorite, on the warm round pebbles of the riverbank, which massaged his every muscle and every limb as he rolled on them and frottaged his figure on his blanket of green fronds. At first, he ate nothing but the petals of cannonball flowers, crouching on all fours and gnawing at the entire bush until only the pistils remained, and when he had gone through the entire patch, he ate with his cows, knocking heads with them and establishing position at the trough, long enough so that they would accept him as one of them, but then he ran from there and jumped into the river and became some other creature. Since he was always naked and since he often fell asleep in the midday sun, his skin soon began to suffer from exposure and he would remain in the riverwater longer and longer to cool the sting (though the waters magnified the light and burned him all the more). He began to peel and shed like a serpent, first behind his neck and on his shoulders and then along his back and his arms and his buttocks and his legs. The skin peeled off in gauzy toast-colored leaves and he layered one skin-leaf over the other and the other and he could still see through it. After the first layer had sloughed off at the palm-side of his fingers and at the back of his feet where the Achilles meets the sole and at the end of his penis (where it dangled like the skin-dress of a shorn banana and obstructed his urine that night), the second layer began to peel off at the back of the neck and at the shoulders. Again it was see-through thin, though rosier, every pockmark and follicle imprinted a bit less clearly, and after the second coat had been carried away by the mountain winds and he jumped in the riverwater he felt its coolness nearer to him.

When he shed a third coat and a fourth coat he searched out for the daggerlike, toothy leaves of the aloe plant and he plucked them and squeezed out their clear jelly insides and covered himself with it, even between his toes and around and around the irritated folds of his anus, which was coming undone. At night, he covered his blankets of palm fronds with the aloe gel and wrapped himself in it head to toe and wriggled within like an unborn lizard in its egg. But his skin sucked up nature's moisture and no sooner had he thicked on aloe gel on one part of his body than it was as dry or drier than before and still peeling, as if something underneath his skin was thirstier than all the desert sands. He shed a fifth coat and his nipples began to blend into his flesh, which was now all the color and the texture of the end of his penis with the skin pulled back. When he touched himself at night with the memory of his most beloved cow, the underskin tore and the whole shaft of his penis bled. And he shed a sixth coat and all his body hair began to fall out and on the seventh the hair on his scalp and his eyebrows and his skin was then all the color and the texture of the inside of his lips. It hurt to swim but it hurt more to walk or to crawl or to lie down to sleep, so he spent all his hours floating in the cool river where his skin came off not in leaves but as slime under his fingernails when he scratched himself, which he did, all over, because down to its nerve layer his skin itched and itched. And when he lost count of how many coats he had shed, when he saw one of his raw testicles bobbing on the surface of the river, free of its sac but still linked to his loins by its thin chord, and he looked for the other one and it too had escaped, though heavier, it had sunk, he dared not move and he knew the women of the mountain had cursed him and he knew that they worshiped the child with the crooked staff and the river goddess and he knew that he was now a creature of their making.

After the current tore off his testicles, and more and more skin shed from his hands, the skin from one finger became entangled with the neighboring finger so that soon his hands were webbed and the same happened with the toes and his eyes bulged out of their sockets and spread nearer to his ears, though these were disappearing with every coat he shed, and he began to hear by wagging his tongue and his lungs longed less and less for air and he became an expert fisherman and darted to catch a minnow or a trout, clenching it in his teeth and then gulping it whole. Down to its core, his skin toughened and it was white with measlelike speckles and the currents of the water encrusted the end of one section over the other so that on certain mornings when he wandered into a quiet pool he heard his own skin and he felt as if he were wearing one of his ex-wife's tight-fitting sequin dresses. He was glad he had stopped shedding and he was happy to be a river thing.

One morning, he saw his gluttonous tomcat Luis el Catorce perched on a thrusting jagged rock on the riverbank, grown much bigger than he knew cats could grow. He was postured for the hunt, his back legs coiled for the leap, his front paws lightly set on the rock, the left one lifted a bit, his neck thrust out, his upper lip curled and his mouth lightly parted so that his fangs were visible and the slits in his eyes thin and sharp as needles. Maybe it was a trick of the water, but Luis el Catorce had grown much too large, larger than a tomcat, larger than his cousins in the jungle. As the river thing surfaced to investigate, the cat waited just till the muzzle of the rose-speckled fish had broken the clear glass of the surface of a pool away from the current and he dashed at it with his left paw, just-just missing it, and the surprised fish disappeared back into the current. His loving Luis el Catorce, who had purred away many a night stretched out on his belly or curled up beside him, his head nuzzled into his armpit, whom he had fed religiously six and seven times a day, anything, mango pits, scorpion's tail, cornhusks, withered bull testicles, turkey gizzards, pigeon breast, and (his favorite) shrimp heads, anything, for there was nothing Luis el Catorce would not eat, had just tried to murder him, to eat *him,* which he could certainly do now, with one swing, for it was no trick of the water, his omnivorous tomcat had grown into a giant.

So the river thing grew fearful of being a river thing, and he dreamed of being a bird so that he could fly away from that river, away from his murderous tomcat. When a pair of sparrow lovers sat on a branch that leaned over the river, the river thing leapt out of the water and at them, not to eat them as they must have feared for they darted off, but to ride on their feathery backs away from there. And he tried this with every bird that approached the water, repulsed by the other things in the river as if he were not one of them, even when he became so hungry that his vision blurred and his arms and legs felt for the first time as if they were missing and he could swim only very short distances with the help of the current. Eventually, he became so weak that he could no longer leap out at birds and he would have died in the river if the current had not maneuvered him into a whirlpool by the riverbank that had him swimming in circles till he saw the snarl of Luis el Catorce under the water and felt his fangs pierce into the small of his back.

He was there and not there at the same time. There, he passed a slimy shoot and was squeezed out into a cave of shallow firewater that melted his flesh and turned it into something else, and not there, he had been gnawed down to his dry bones, right down to the spiny cage in which drummed his heart, and although he could no longer see or hear or feel, he remembered the women of the mountain laughing to the rhythm of its last beats, laughing at the plight of Luis el Catorce, who keeled over and fell into the river, a hooklike fishbone lodged in his wind canal.

BOOK TWO

How the Dead Come Back: The Tale as Rumba

FOUR

The Camarita Flirts with Eternity

"Think about la foto before and after," his French master Henri had told him, "*never* during, for when the moment comes the moment goes, and you must be very quick. But if you miss it . . . so what? Moments are infinite. Acuérdate, la camarita flirts with eternity."

At first, Armando Quiñón owned only two cameras, one battered Leica for candid shots and a secondhand Rolleiflex for his studio, and like his master, technique and equipment were less important to him than intuition, knowing the moment and cabining it in the black box to make it eternal. He had been taught to hide his Leica, to cover the chrome with black tape, and he wore a loose, wide black leather belt so that when he needed, he could tuck the camera behind it, because in candid shots the subject must not be aware of the photographer or the pictures will lose their mysterious immediacy. "La foto can be art," his master had said, "only if it is honest to reality. If you stage a foto, la jodiste ahí mismo. This is true even in the studio. Paintings are made. Fotos are captured. Thus as fotógrafo you must make yourself and your camarita invisible, even, no, *especially* when pursuing the inanimate!"

In 1942 the city of Guantánamo was changing. "Oye sabes, ya casi no metemos a yanquis," as some Guantanameros put it. In the years between the world wars, the Americans had undertaken a massive expansion of the naval base established there in 1903. They leased new lands from this or that regime on the hilly promontories on both sides of the channel that flows into the uterine Guantánamo Bay. They rebuilt the landing strip and called it Aeropuerto Tres Piedras, because it was said that the day they dug the first dirt, a hailstorm surprised the half-naked penny-hired campesinos, many who had never seen hail of such size, and they screamed that the three thrones of Dios Santo were falling from the heavens. When they finished the landing strip they erected new barracks with tin roofs for the stock and rank and handsome wooden cabins with tropical gardens for the officers and their families, and built an aqueduct near the Yateras River north of the city, whose channels would bypass Guantánamo entirely and feed the naval base exclusively, and they refurbished the hospital and even set aside a new plot of land to serve as a cemetery.

Armando Quiñón's cousin worked as an assistant to a commander in the naval base, and since he dropped her off every morning before walking to the studio, he got to know the young guards at the entrance gates and brought them rum and flattered them and offered to photograph them for they looked like the staunch warriors in American movies, chisel-faced and bright-eyed and broad-shouldered, and he brought them the developed shots handsomely mounted on black cardboard foldouts so they could send their likenesses to their noviecitas back home. Soon, in this manner, he was able to gain admission into the base, wandering freely with the worker's pass the guards had given him. On the way out, after he had clandestinely taken five or six rolls of pictures, they would pull out their billfolds and show him crinkled yellowed pictures of their girlfriends, crude compared to the ones he had taken of them, the women's youth dueling with the wrinkliness of the photographs, and Armando Quiñón promised them he would make new and wonderful portraits of them if he ever made it to Cleveland, Ohio, or to St. Augustine, Florida, or to wherever the other girls were from.

Armando Quiñón took so many pictures inside the naval base that in the spring of 1942 he was able to mount a show in his studio exclusively on this subject. He photographed the campesinos fleeing from the famous hailstorm, their arms wrapped around their heads, their mouths open in ceaseless terror as the sky fell in a blur of stones around them. He photographed the beautiful row of officers' cabins, and even some of the inner gardens. He photographed off-duty sailors with their fishing lines cast in impressive symmetry at el Punto de los Pescadores, and these same men wading nude in the shark-infested bay, their bodies gleamy with youth and lean with labor, splashing water on each other and frolicking like boys. (This last photograph he did not exhibit, but kept locked in an oak chest in the cellar of his studio.)

Doña Edith Oregón, a light-skinned mulata with roily blue lapis-dense eyes, attended the exhibit at Armando Quiñón's studio on Narciso López Street and bought three of his photographs. She said it was the work of a true artist. It was hot inside the studio and the two metal fans Armando Quiñón had whirring on opposite corners did little and doña Edith was heavy with child, but she stayed for three-quarters of an hour, surveying each photo, waddling from here to there, returning to one she had already examined, and wiping the sweat off her brow with a lace handkerchief till it dripped from her hand and left dark blood-brown spots on the studio's dusty wooden floor. When she wanted a picture, she pointed to it and wagged her swollen finger and Armando Quiñón took it off the wall and wrapped it in brown paper for her. She bought the hailstone picture and two pictures of the blond prepubescent daughter of the colonel in charge of the base. "Joven," she said, "de veras que eres un artistazo, un monstruo. I want you to be the photographer at our child's baptism. My husband will pay anything!"

Doña Edith had twins. The first had odd-colored eyes, one opaque blue like his mother, the other chocolate-brown like his father señor Juanito Daluz, the renowned hatmaker. This one they named after his father. The other had eyes like toasted almonds. Him they called Héctor. They were both born with a head of shoeshine-black tight-curled hair and skin the color of their mother's, de cafe con bastante leche. Señor Daluz cried when he held them and kissed their heads, calling them "mis ositos pardo." The boys held tight to each other's hands and when the mother tried to separate them to put them each in his bassinet they wailed and wailed till they were joined again. Señor Daluz bought two cribs and dismantled them and refashioned it as one large crib so that his boys could sleep together.

Only a handful were invited to the baptism at St. Catalina de Ricis Church: doña Edith's half sister doña Adela, and her husband Teodoro, and their daughter Alicia, and a few other close friends and respected clients of the hat shop. Armando Quiñón, hidden behind a torrent of lilies from the week before's Easter service, made sure to take a few shots of each group as they entered the church. By the baptismal font, Father Gonzalo called forth the parents and the children. Señor Daluz held the son that was his namesake and doña Edith held Héctor and both of the children held on to each other's hands. When Father Gonzalo trickled the waters of the Spirit on the first, both children giggled, and when he did it to the second, both broke out in tears, and when the parents tore their grasp trying to console them, they wept louder. The child Alicia had made her way under the baptismal font to Father Gonzalo's side to get a priest's-eye view of the ceremony and was grasping the edge of the baptismal font and standing on the tip of her toes, the ends of her fingers grazing the surface of the holy water. When the children started to weep, she suddenly pulled her hands from the font as if the water were boiling and lost her balance and fell back and might have hurt herself had Father Gonzalo not caught her. After untangling herself from his robe, she snuck under the font and went to the child Héctor and passed her hand over his forehead, still wet with the Spirit: "No llores mi nenito bello." Héctor stopped crying and at once so did his brother and the waters of the Spirit dried unto their brows.

They were now children of Christ. So proclaimed Father Gonzalo and everyone cheered.

Armando Quiñón was delighted. They had mostly forgotten about him even though he had been among them almost as a celebrant, close enough for portraits that would certainly be deemed priceless by doña Edith and her generous husband. That very evening he went into his darkroom to develop the pictures, though first he spent some time sipping spicy rum and admiring some of the pictures locked away in his oak chest, till he had to force himself away from his reveries for he had promised doña Edith that the very next morning he would have some samples. He developed the shots of the celebrants entering the church first and they were exquisite. Doña Edith's pride showed in the shadows that darkened everything around her, even the child Héctor cradled in her arms, but would not dare obscure her face. She had known where Armando Quiñón was and had turned to the lilies and beamed a smile. Armando Quiñón tried different methods of development, shielding her face so that the background and the bundle in her arms would be equally lit with life, but still her face and smile were the only resplendent orb of the photograph, like an early autumn moon on a dark horizon; and so Armando Quiñón let it be. Señor Daluz, carrying the other child, was overcome with an excruciating joy, because he was old and had wanted children all his life and this was almost a miracle, since doña Edith was nearing forty and the doctors had assured him, less than a year before, that there would be no children, that his wife's ovaries had shrunk to the size of a ciruela, and all this you could read in the photograph, in his defiant dark eyes, in the stooped posture with which he held his son, his arms fully wrapped around him like the European war pictures of village women carrying their babies away during the air raids; then doña Adela in an overflowing silk crepe dress and her husband in his customary over-wrinkled ash-colored linen suit and in between them, holding to each of their hands, their daughter Alicia, her face and her shiny black hair, tailed on each side, the center of the photograph; and Father Gonzalo, vested white-on-white, his arms outspread, welcoming the celebrants, behind him the serpentine marble altar and the crossed legs and half torso of the porcelain Crucified, right up to the pierce on His left side. Although he was still young, Father Gonzalo's deep brow was outlined with fissures of doubt, marks that gave him a precocious dignity and inspired in others an ultimate faith in the Faith. This last one is the only known photograph to have survived Armando Quiñón's days. Doña Adela kept it handsomely framed in mahogany and on her death, many years later, bequeathed it to her granddaughter.

All the other photographs from that day, Armando Quiñón would never show anyone. He did not take doña Edith's calls for two weeks, and when she sent her housemaid to his studio to see if ese loco está vivo o muerto, Armando Quiñón shook his head and said that he must see la señora in person.

"Pero bueno, que defachate es esto. It's been two weeks. Where are my pictures?"

"Señora, con mucha pena, but there are no pictures."

"¿Cómo?"

"The camera was faulty. It leaked fluid into the film."

"On all the film?"

"All."

"¡Qué desastre! My husband will not be happy."

"No, señora, he won't."

"Joven, I said not long ago that you were a great artist, but I was sadly mistaken. En la hora de los mameyes, you are nothing. Un miserable. You have ruined one of the happiest moments of our lives."

The following morning Armando Quiñón found the three photographs that doña Edith had bought wrapped in a paper garbage bag and leaning against the front door of his studio. An angry charcoal script proclaimed: BASURA DE BASURA. He sat on the curb and pulled out his Leica from behind his belt and photographed each passerby who stopped to inquire about the package. He answered only one thing, that the Spirit is invisible and will always be invisible, that man will never know It through his primitive means, and this cryptoanswer enticed a young seminarian to ask the price of this "garbage from garbage" trinity of photographs and Armando Quiñón said he could have them for nothing, for it would be wrong to charge twice for the same pictures.

As doña Edith's twins grew they remained inseparable. Sleep could not break them apart for their dreams seemed to be shared, and in the morning when they recounted them to señor Daluz, one would correct the other one on a certain detail and the other one would remember: "Sí, sí, verdad, así fué," and go on. And even their necessities were done together, for they had been potty trained side by side, and now when one had to go he would nudge the other one who knew that he also had to go, and they urinated crossways, and that was the Cross of the Savior, and when the streams touched each other and splashed on them, that was the Blood of the Savior, so they said a Padre Nuestro before they buttoned up. Before they got too big, they sat on the same toilet and defecated together and after they got too big, one would just sit on the edge of the bathtub and watch the other and, if they were sure doña Edith wasn't going to interrupt them, they wiped each other. These times they would say no prayers.

When they were six, doña Edith threw a large feast for her husband's sixtieth birthday and she invited family and many friends and many other acquaintances. The only person of notability that was not invited was the photographer Armando Quiñón, although many are sure that he must have been there for they saw the gruesome photographs that he took that night. Since there was so much beer and rum drunk, it is entirely possible that he snuck in unnoticed after the festivities were well under way, and doña Edith was either too busy playing hostess or, vaya, ya un poco jumada, for she was known now and then to indulge, to behave too much like a chusma, the surest sign (aside from the shade of her skin) that the man that had been her father had not been her sister's father.

The twins were sent to bed early, after they sang and their father blew out the sixty candles on the coconut meringue cake. They were not heard from for three hours, when doña Adela silenced all the merriment with her miraculous keen-pitched wails. She had gone to check on the twins and taken her daughter, because Alicia wanted to kiss her cousins good night, and found Juanito with his head on a pillow on Héctor's lap and the pillow was soaked with blood and Héctor's pajama bottom was soaked with blood and it was patiently dripping on the floor, and his pajama top was wrapped around his brother's head, also sopped in blood.

"No pasó nada, ti-íta," Héctor said. "He's going to be fine. The blood is stopping. No pasó nada, ti-íta."

Doña Adela screamed till the room was filled with people and they had taken the injured boy from his brother and then she took the soaked pillow and pressed it to her face to muffle her screams and her face was the color of the child's blood and when they took her out to the cobblestone patio to get some fresh air she got on her knees under the giant fig tree and screamed some more, like a great diva whose breath seems to be spiraling through her from the center of the earth, and it was late and those who had not been invited to the fiesta were well asleep and they awoke from dreams of tortures and stake burnings only to find that the screams were as real as the sweat on their sheets and doña Adela screamed till her voice had gone and she could not as much as whisper for two weeks and her voice lost its gauzy delicacy forever.

The boy Juanito lost his blue eye. The two surgeons in town had been at the party and were too inebriated, so an intern had to operate and could not stop the hemorrhaging and could not save the eye. While they made the boy a glass eye, he wore a black eyepatch and his father told him that he was now a pirate named Zorro, and he bought him a cape with a white "Z" emblazoned on it and made him a droopy-brimmed black hat to match; though when the boy asked for a play sword so that he could duel with his brother, doña Edith forbade it. In fact, she had not allowed her two sons a moment alone since the accident, and she would always blame Héctor for this and other misfortunes in the other boy's life. They had just been playing, as Héctor was forced to recount again and again, just for a while, because they had been sent to bed muy tempranito. The twins' ornate iron beds were a fanciful work of art that señor Daluz had shipped from Macy's in Nueva York as part of a deal that had given that famous store exclusive rights to many of his straw hat designs. They were set perpendicular to each other (though most nights the twins used only one bed, sleeping head to toe and tickling each other to sleep) and their frames were exquisite examples of the human will to bend and twist what would seem unbendable and untwistable, thick beams of iron crossed and intersected and wove around each other, and everywhere they touched they were strapped and braced by delicately looped laces of thinner iron, knots unknottable, its loose ends twisted downward. "A masterpiece," señor Daluz had proclaimed when he finished assembling the boxed parts, after hours of botched attempts. "Es verdad, that when it comes to this, no one knows better than the maldito yanquis."

Doña Edith had stared hard at the finished product and answered that it looked more like the bed of a whore than the bed of a child. She did not notice her husband's error, in her contempt she did not see that he had mistakenly assembled one of the headboards (the one on Héctor's bed) downside up and outside in, so that the ends of the looped knots pointed dangerously heavenward, like the horns of a demon, whose shadows the boys expertly used in the stories they told each other after the lights had been turned off.

The night of the accident the lights remained on (or rather were turned on after they had been turned off). Héctor began doing somersaults on his bed. It was hot and he began to sweat, so he took off his pajama top. Soon his brother joined him; but Juanito was not as good yet, so Héctor taught him, and Juanito also began to sweat and took his top off. Héctor grabbed him by his belly and by his back and flipped him this way and that as if he were a giant puppet.

"Sí, mamacita, como un titeresón; but then I lost him. I don't know what happened, pero se me fue. Maybe it was the sweat, maybe I was just getting sleepy, but when I lost him, his face went right into one of the horns of the demons that grow out of the bed. And I thought that he was dead, porque at first he did not move. But then he started to cry and I told him that it would be all right porque I didn't want to scare him. I told him that the blood would stop, but it didn't mamacita (I used his pajama, the pillow, my leg, but it didn't stop mamacita), it didn't stop and that's when ti-íta came in and that's when they took him from me."

Doña Edith looked at her second-born as if he had never been inside her womb: "From now on when I turn the lights off, they will remain off." Héctor could not bear to look back at her, and he mumbled with his chin pressed to his chest: "Sí, mamacita."

When the glass eye arrived, doña Edith would not allow the surgeons to put it in. It was not the right color. They had made it the color of the boy's other eye and not its original color.

"Look very closely," doña Edith said to the surgeon and she opened her eyes wide, pressing down with her fingers underneath, so that the surgeon could not mistake their color. "*That* was the color of my boy's eye. That's the color I want the glass eye to be."

"Señora, this is a very expensive process."

"Mi esposo paga lo que sea, carajo. Just do it right this time!"

The eye came back and the pupil was made of amethyst and it was still not the right color, but doña Edith accepted it because she was tired of seeing her son with a black patch. When he returned from the hospital the boy was more striking than ever, because now one of his eyes was the color of violets and the other one had turned almost black.

"Una belleza," his mother said, holding Juanito's face in both her hands, and his father agreed and his brother agreed also. Though when the boy reached for something, it wasn't there. He was still not used to his eye that did not work.

That winter, señor Daluz abandoned his marriage bed. He slept in a pallet out in the cobblestone patio, wrapped head-to-toe in a thick woollen blanket to hide his flesh from the mosquitoes, cuddled up between the pulpy row of banana trees and the brick wall to shield himself from the north wind. One morning he awoke with his head poking out of his woollen cocoon, fresh droppings covering his eyes from the pigeons that roosted up on the wall. That afternoon he ran high fevers and flaky scales grew on his eyelashes and by the following morning the lashes had fallen off altogether and by the fourth day señor Daluz said that he could not see. Specialists came from Santiago de Cuba and they put patches soaked in sulfonamide ointment on his eyes and they said it was only temporary, a common infection, though usually occurring in children. They quelled his fevers with cool baths and when his eyelids healed, they shone their little instruments into his eyes and found no corneal damage, no invisible ulcers, pupils that reacted normally, and they shrugged their shoulders and adopted that half-glazed look (that far-gone expression that seems a concentrated effort at forgetting a lifetime of little defeats), common to poets but rare in scientists (except when the nature of a thing has utterly eluded them), and they admitted they could not understand why the old man still could not see. Doña Edith said that she understood and sent the doctors away.

Señor Daluz sold his hat shop for an extravagant price, and the rights to all his most precious hat designs he auctioned off to the fancy stores of la Quinta Avenida in Nueva York, and set his wife in charge of the family's finances and assured her he would spend the remainder of his life caring for his sons. He said he could see things now, but not as he had seen them before, but in their true nature. He saw only halos of light, the flame burning in each animate and inanimate thing. And so he set to work with his new life's sole task. So that the twins could play together, he took apart the iron beds with the aid of giant vice-grip pliers, he undid the iron knots and pounded flat the demons' horns and stretched and molded the iron beams in brickoven flames and stitched together straps of leather that would never become hats and gathered powerful springs from abandoned yanqui cars and forgotten Swiss grandfather clocks and built for them a trampoline all around the majestic fig tree in the cobblestone patio. And the trampoline was good, and it was wide and spacious as the earth itself.

"¿Qué carajo has hecho con mi patio?" doña Edith said when she saw it.

"Now, no one will get hurt," señor Daluz answered his wife and hopped up on the trampoline and began to bounce on it head over heels like a happy child. The banana trees that encircled the cobblestone patio now encircled the trampoline and their languid leaves hung over its edges and they warned señor Daluz when he brushed up against them that he was near falling off so he would hop back towards the aroma of the heavy figs and propel himself so high up above the red-brick patio wall that, with his halo-vision, he saw the bluish glow of the mountains on one side of the city and the olive glimmer of the sea on the other.

Since the invention of the camera some have believed that it is a soul-stealer, an instrument of sorcery, that the lenses and mirrors that magnify and reflect one off the other like glass lovers demand a price for their concession to the vanity of the photographed; that is, they will leave you this, the picture, the record of what was and will never be more, but also take that, a morsel of the spirit that should know that what is is on its own and that those odious glass lovers *can* never, and *will* never, change that. This is one superstition. Another one is that what the camera cannot see and capture, the camera is simply too weak to know, vampires and ghosts and so on; or if it does capture them at all, it captures them in the manner that señor Daluz got used to seeing the world, as fuzzy halos of light. And one more superstition (this one arising from the scientific fact that the camera is useless in pitch darkness, that the glass lovers need some meager or fragile thread of light before they can even begin to show affection for each other; and thus follows): that something so unfeeling in the darkness must be unholy indeed.

So how can there have been pictures of the night of the accident, when only a high gibbous moon shone? What light struck doña Edith's patio to make her sister's twisted face of screams visible to Armando Quiñón's black-taped Leica? For certainly some swore they saw those pictures . . . and of the boy being carried into Ñico's station-wagon ambulance, which was late because Ñico also doubled as a cab driver and had to hurry back from a faraway fare to the yanqui naval base, and even of the socket where the eye had been, *after* the operation and before the pirate's patch. No puede ser. They would have never let Armando Quiñón into the operating room, for even his parents were forbidden to enter there and only saw the child the morning after . . . *with the eyepatch!*

Whatever the truth of the existence of these pictures, and as mentioned already, some swear to have seen them and can describe in detail the shape of the bloodstains on the viscose dress doña Adela wore, one like a lizard and another like a giant horsefly . . . and how the tinted goose feathers from the torn pillow stuck to her necklace of pearls . . . and more ghoulishly, the shape and depth of the scoop in the boy's right eye, as if dug by a spoon with teeth.

But whatever the truth of *any* of this, it is clear that Armando Quiñón's interest in photographing the twins was renewed for some also swear that they saw the pictures of the baptism, and they saw why Armando Quiñón had had to lie to doña Edith, for there it all was: the resplendent orb of doña Edith's face, señor Daluz's defiant stooped gait, the stubborn joy with which the child Alicia joined her elegantly dressed parents, and Father Gonzalo, always appearing the most handsome, the most inspiring when he was vested white-on-white; only one thing was missing from *every* photograph, the children, the children of Christ: doña Edith and her husband held bundles of darkness as they entered the church, the child Alicia smiled over twin shimmering hazes of gray smudged light, Father Gonzalo dribbled the waters of the Spirit over . . . over no child, no thing, nothing but a bundle of swaddling cloth; Armando Quiñón's mounted Rolleiflex, hidden behind the lilies, his black-taped Leica held expertly behind the wrist, had both failed to *see* the children . . . sí, sí, how right had he been with his cryptoanswer, *that the Spirit is invisible and will always be invisible, that man will never know It through his primitive means*: the twins, on that day, lent not a morsel of their spirit to the camera; though this was to change—they appeared in many photographs later, beginning with the accident, which dates from this period; there are rumored pictures (among all those that were destroyed at the end), of the boy Juanito, of the boy Héctor, of their proud and blind father and of their monumentally misshapen instructor (whose tale is forthcoming), all taken atop the trampoline, under the giant fig tree (certainly while doña Edith was away—there are no words of any pictures of her—which she was often because the new owner of the hat shop had hired her as day-to-day manager of the store to insure continued profits). Thus, there was a rather well-documented record of Héctor and Juanito's rise to fame, all found on the third day after the triumph of la Revolución, when they blew open the twin locks of Armando Quiñón's cellar room and oak chest. In the name of decency though, the record was destroyed, burned in a public bonfire on Narciso López Street, along with everything else in that studio except for the body of the artist himself.

Señor Sariel

He had not been a boy for a long time. He had lost both his parents many years before and had also lost a few brothers and sisters and lost a son and lost six wives. Very few people addressed him as anything but señor Sariel. He was just under five feet tall, was shiny-bald, and his face was round and puffy, like one of Da Vinci's scowling infants. His eyes were black and bulbous and his eyebrows were white and shaped like the cap of a seawave; and though his skin was brown, his nose was crisscrossed with so many burst capillaries that it was the color of a fresh bruise. He could shape his hands into claws by dislocating his fat thumb so that a short flat tarsal from the inner hand became the smaller pincer, and the other four digits curled and fused together the larger pincer. He limped and sometimes used a wheelchair for he had fallen from a high trapeze during a tour of the southern states of los Estados Unidos and had shattered most of the right side of his pelvis, so that it was now held together with pins and screws. He said that his ancestry line could be traced all the way back to the last great Moor of Spain and that he himself was born in Granada, under the shadows of the Alhambra, over a hundred years ago, and that as a boy he had lived and performed as an acrobat in Algiers. Some believed him. Some didn't. He *did* look like a moro, but aside from his limp, he was too nimble-bodied to be any older than forty.

When the gypsy circus came to the city of Guantánamo in the winter of 1955, señor Sariel was at the height of his second career. Before anyone saw the clowns or the acrobats or the caged animals, or even Georgina the Manwoman (in front of whose tent there was a sign in red paint proclaiming that mothers and children under thirteen were not allowed in), they lined up to watch señor Sariel perform his awesome feats of strength with his fantastic claws and work miracles with his carnivorous white-winged horseflies. He performed almost in the nude, in a tiny pair of black trunks, and his torso was tattooed with orange and red and black eyeless pythons that wrapped around him, so that it seemed that his skin was a shell and that his great round head belonged to someone else entirely. His back was rounded and bulky and ridged down the spine. His shoulders were so wide that his clavicles seemed two misplaced bones (of the thighs perhaps) and his chest was monumental, textured with twisted ropes of muscles. There was a long rosy zipper-scar down his right thigh, and his calves were like twin baseballs. His toenails were painted black and, aside from his eyebrows and the cotton puff on the point of his chin, not a strand of hair grew on him. Those that dared look as he rocked on his round back to do his tricks said that the package inside his briefs was as impressive as any other thing about the man.

Héctor and his brother told their blind father what they saw. His hands were like mittens of missculpted flesh and they were so mighty that he could crush stones to bits and open giant oysters with great pearls inside them the size of iguana eggs and, lying on his back, he could bend two steel rods at once, yet his hands were also so delicate that he could handle his white-winged horseflies by their antennae. At one point, he pulled from out of his ear a yellow butterfly, and from out his other ear another one, and from out of his nose a third, and the butterflies danced in a fluttery circle around him. He proclaimed that these were the sugary butterflies of sappy romance novels. *They always appear,* he said, *when some character has fallen tragically in love with another. They surround the lovers, inhabit their lives in ways that they themselves cannot do with each other. They usually come by the hundreds, but alas, I have only three. But three is a good number, you know, you look like a well-schooled group . . . your holy trinity and all that.* Señor Sariel let the yellow butterflies dance, and seemed even to draw joy from their circle. Then he picked up his bongo drums and rapped on them, softly at first, almost inaudibly, as if not to swallow the lightness of the butterfly dance. But as the rapping became louder, his white-winged horseflies emerged, from the folds of the tent, from under the platform stage, from the very drums he was using to summon them, and even, it seemed, from the noses and ears of the audience members. Señor Sariel laughed. "Here they come," he chanted. "Here they come." And the tent grew dense with them, and their tireless opaque wings swallowed light and spit it back out in pieces, so that señor Sariel's hands, rapping on the drums, seemed to be moving with the jittery gestures of a silent film character, and the butterfly dance lost all its grace, as the white-winged horseflies surrounded the trio and tightened and tightened their circle, till it was a yellow knot, and just like that the butterflies disappeared into the mouth of the buzzing white cloud.

"Love gone wrong!" señor Sariel screamed and laughed, his drums culminating a crescendo. "Love in the ruins!" He grabbed his crotch. "There to your clever poet! There to your fancy symbols! There to your *RO-mance*! There to your fairy tale!"

After the show, on his wheelchair and dressed in his customary sackcloth burnoose and leather-strap sandals, señor Sariel followed the boys home. All night he sat under the marquee of the abandoned theater across the street and drank Kentucky bourbon and tapped his bongoes and watched the boys' shadows rise and fall over the red-brick patio wall. The following morning, he wheeled himself up to the porch steps of doña Edith's home, using the butt-end of his long curved machete to propel himself, and began to shout that if her sons had an instructor they could become great circus stars. When there was no answer, he rattled the blade of his machete against the balustrade. Undaunted, doña Edith came out and smelled him and wheeled him away to the edge of the city not far from the circus tents and turned over his wheelchair so that he almost fell on the blade of his instrument. "¡Ahí está, perverso!"

"Maldita," señor Sariel drooled, "harming a harmless invalid." That night he went back to the theater and watched the twin shadows again and read out loud from the wooden handle of his machete, on which were carved in Arabic, twirling around it like a serpent of eyes and tails, the twenty-one questions without answers. Then he drank bourbon till he passed out. The day before the circus left town, he noticed their blind father at his show again, and he hobbled down from the stage into the crowd and he made two white-winged horseflies fly around and around the old man's head till the old man smiled. His teeth were yellow in the middle, then brown, then black at the edges. Señor Sariel could tell that the old man did not expose them much, that he always hid his smiles with his lips and that this time he had simply forgotten to do so. And in the dirty smile señor Sariel saw the old man's sorrow, in spite of or, more likely, due to the great beauty of his twin sons. And he asked him: "When can I best see them?"

And the old man, still smiling with all his rotted teeth answered: "They bathe in the laundry pail after they jump. Their mother makes them bathe so they can sleep clean."

The night the circus left town, señor Sariel was on the rotted wood rooftop of the abandoned theatre and after Héctor and Juanito had finished practicing their jumps on the trampoline, they stripped down and filled a laundry pail with a garden hose and washed each other with a white block of soap, under the arms and behind the ears as their mother had taught them, then they climbed up on the giant fig tree and twisted themselves on the stronger branches till the moonlight dried their gecko-brown bodies. Señor Sariel had them with his eyes. He did not rejoin the circus. All his possessions, his worn leather suitcase and the petrified stump of royal palm in which lived his battalion of white-winged horseflies and his bongoes and his flying sandals and his curved machete, were left under a chestnut tree in the empty lot where the circus had stood. Señor Sariel tied everything to the back of his wheelchair and dragged it back to the abandoned theatre where he set up house behind the torn water-stained screen. In the projector room he found sixteen reels, but only one was undamaged, an Italian movie about a circus strongman who does not recognize his love until it is too late. In the afternoons señor Sariel watched it without sound, since the speakers had been stolen. Every evening, he hobbled up to the roof through a back stairwell—though Ñaña, the halfwit of la plaza, said she saw someone fly up there once, with many wings, boned and leathery like a bat—and he watched the boys jump and bathe and dry off. He began to perform under the shattered marquee, and many people who had missed the circus and did not know who he was dismissed him as a charlatan. So one night, upside down from the roof, clinging to a rusty pipe with his legs, señor Sariel scribbled on the marquee with a piece of tar. He proclaimed his return.

¡Señor Sariel! ¡Aquí! ¡Hoy Mismo!
¡Más Bárbaro Que Nunca!

The crowds came, blocking traffic on Perdido Street and spilling into the porch of doña Edith's home. The twins peered over the patio wall from behind the broken cola bottles mortared there and when he knew they were watching, señor Sariel undid himself, became less and less human and more and more a creature other, tunneling through the concrete sidewalk with his claws as if he were digging through sand and coming up on the other side of the street. And the more the twins' fascination grew, their heads lilting higher and higher above the patio walls, the more señor Sariel's resolve grew.

One evening, as he was preparing to rest behind the tattered screen of the abandoned theatre, half-heartedly tapping on his bongoes, lost in longing, señor Sariel felt a hundred streams of light unveil him. Someone had turned on the ancient projector and its light burst through each and every tear on the screen, concentrating into dense lasery beams that he felt certain would burn holes in him. He threw on his sackcloth burnoose and flipped the hood over his head.

"Who's there?"

"Ahí está, papito," a boy said. "¡Ahí! ¡Míralo qué cabezón!"

Señor Sariel peered through one of the larger tears on the screen but the light burned his eyes and blinded him momentarily.

"¡Ahí! ¡Ahí!"

The child's voice was making his limbs weak. He hobbled to his wheelchair and set the bongoes on his lap and wheeled himself to the side of the stage, to the fringes of the projector light. The Italian movie was playing.

"Mira, papito. ¡Salió! He came out!"

The old man tapped his son on the shoulder. "Go on, tell him."

"My papito says that my mamita says that you should go back to wherever you came from and that if you dig out the sidewalk anymore she's going to call the police."

Señor Sariel had his hood pulled so low over his great head that he was sure the boy could not see the hunger in his eyes. "And what do you say, hombrecito?"

The young man raised his chin and his amethyst-eye caught a glint reflected from the screen and it glittered. He looked at his father, but the old man stared away into a dead space.

"Héctor says we want to be acrobats! She didn't let him come. But that's what he says."

The old man grabbed his son by the arm. "What will your mamita say?"

Señor Sariel could not resist. With a fervent syncopated conjuration from his drums, he released his battalion of white-winged horseflies from their night-spell and they poured forth from the dead palm stump where they had been pegged and burst through the holes in the screen in gushes (through the massive torso of the strongman and from the silenced trumpet of his sad love), wrestling with each other (many losing their buoyant miniscule triangular heads in the battle) for position to dance first around the amethyst-eyed boy. The old theatre became so full of white-winged horseflies that their wing shadows overcame the projector light and the lives of the strongman and his neglected love were snuffed and señor Sariel could not see through the whirring cloud. "Ahora, what says your papito that says your mamita?"

There was no answer. The old man had dragged the boy out.

Over the next two weeks, doña Edith filled sixteen garbage bags with dead white-winged horseflies and crushed larvae and aborted pupae and still it seemed that they were more in number than they had ever been, a pestilence brought on from the night of the visit to the abandoned theatre. The morning after, a few had appeared in her sons' room and a few more in the folds of her husband's discarded guayabera. From then on, as the spring wore on, inspired with the heat, they doubled and redoubled their numbers, and wherever the boys were, and wherever the boys had been, there the white-winged horseflies would be. In the morning, drawn by the sweat of their night sheets, they covered their bed in such great numbers that it seemed as if they were trying to invade the fortress of their dreams, and they followed them into the bathroom where the boys performed their ritual as ever, one assisting the other, and there the horseflies tarried longer than anywhere, grazing with their wings the soiled discarded tissues and sipping on the drops that had splattered from the toilet and rubbing their spindly legs on the moist towelettes the twins had used to scrub each other's faces and dipping their antennae into the spilled fake teardrop from the bottle one boy applied to the other's glass eye. They rubbed clean their used breakfast utensils and drank the last ring of milk from their glasses and followed them out to the patio and imitated their motions on the trampoline as if they too were wingless and unused to floating on air. At night, they disappeared during the moonbath and waited for them in their rooms, thickening the bedposts and the dresser and the doorframe, their fragile frames fluttering one upon the other till all things inanimate in that room buzzed with life.

When doña Edith became pregnant again it was said the horseflies had

had her, for their number was so great in that house that it would have been impossible to avoid them in whatever weak moment she had turned again into the arms of her unforgiven husband. And although the greater number of them certainly had an avid infatuation with the twins, a good number of them didn't, braver ones, for these put their lives in extreme danger and they pursued doña Edith at her every task, even though she was armed with three swatters, held in place at her hips by the sash of her housedress like toy swords, and a few tamer, nobler ones even reserved their interest for the old blind father, enough so that soon he was letting them direct him to and fro as if they were his forty thousand eyes. At the third month of her pregnancy, tired of killing horseflies and filling bags, doña Edith left to finish out her term at her mother's house in Santiago and she promised that when she returned she would fumigate the house with so many poisons that anyone not wanting to be more dead than the Christ at six in the afternoon either better run miles from that house or get on that maldito trampoline and jump till he reached the outer boroughs of heaven.

A week after she left, señor Sariel was invited into the cobblestone patio to teach the boys how to become great acrobats and the white-winged horseflies little by little disappeared.

Armando Quiñón had become well acquainted with many of the circus stars through the years. Every winter he was there with his hidden Leica and his mounted Rolleiflex and every spring he presented a "circus" show in his studio. Only one performer never allowed photographs to be taken of him, he a firm believer of the first superstition, that the camera stole the soul of the photographed. So on the day doña Edith abandoned her home, Armando Quiñón was immediately suspicious of the man wrapped in a black sackcloth burnoose who wheeled himself into his studio, claiming to be the famous señor Sariel and asking him to record the next few months of his life in photographs. "Ya sé, ya sé that I have never let you photograph me. So you doubt. Pero, my soul is not *in* me anymore; it is escaped somewhere into that house full of horseflies. So I need not fear your little instrument now." He lowered his melonball head and pressed his bandaged hands to his chest. Armando Quiñón put his hand on his visitor's shoulder, a gesture more of camaraderie than sympathy.

"So what need have you of my camera?"

"Bueno, now that the lady has left the house, I will be invited in there to teach those boys how to fly, make them into great acrobats, and I want you to record every moment of it, for though I am an old man, I will live to be much older, and in a thousand years, when those boys are long gone from this earth, I will be able to look at your pictures and relive my joy."

"Estás jodío, viejo," Armando Quiñón muttered, turning away. "You come in here blabbering nonsense and you expect me to drop everything and come with you."

Señor Sariel pulled out a plump fig from one of his pockets and ate it whole; then he undid the bandage around his right hand and pulled from his other pocket a leather sack and spread his legs as to create a hammock in his lap with the skirt of his burnoose and emptied the contents of the sack, bars and coins of gold and silver carved with yanqui writing.

"These are from los Estados Unidos. Long ago, we toured there. A man who owned a bourbon distillery in Kentucky bought my third wife from me . . . a beautiful woman, descendant of both Cleopatra of Egypt and Queen Isabela of Spain . . . mira, mira esto." He held up one large coin, "A twenty-dollar gold piece made, by executive order, for presidente Teddy Roosevelt. Claro, my wife was very beautiful, she sold for much more than all this, but this is quite enough, no crees?" He refilled the sack and handed it to Armando Quiñón. "Y más que eso, you'll have the pleasure of being with the boys, whom I hear you've photographed before and whom you have grown quite fond of . . . from a distance. ¿Sí o no?"

Armando Quiñón blushed. He did not know the dwarf with the great bald head could also read minds and he agreed to señor Sariel's deal, though, as he took the heavy bag of yanquí gold and silver, he felt as if something precious had just been stolen from him.

The late summer days arrived like conquerors from the center of the earth, unleashing all their tropical fury so that by August not a breeze was felt that didn't feel like an oven's breath and not a night lasted long enough to mitigate the harsh memory of the sun. During the day, little could be done. The heat paralyzed all things that aspired to motion. Production at the sugar mill was down five- and then ten- and then twenty-fold, till it finally shut down temporarily because so many of the grinding wheels melted one into the other's grooves, like lovers who kiss too long. The mail was not delivered for weeks. None dared assume the task after Jacinto, the giant West Indian who had been the postman since el año de la cometa, dropped to his knees one afternoon and threw aside his olive-green mailbag and then took off his boots and stepped out of his drenched uniform and peeled off his undergear, and none could believe that a man who must have been close to sixty or sixty-five, *yes at least that, for it was he, on his first day, who hand-delivered all of the invitations for abuelita's wedding,* still had the body of a young bull, with muscles ripply as the river-current, and none could believe when he crisscrossed town as he was, waving his massive arms in the air, and kicking his feet up and about as if in a mad and primitive rain dance, his skin-bagged organ keeping rhythm, slapping against his thighs this way and that like a marvelous rubber pendulum. He made his way past the town towards the bay screaming with all his lungs: "¡Qué calor! ¡Qué calor, cojones!" It was said that after he jumped into the bay he wrestled sharks for six days and did not lose once, but on the seventh he met his match and his severed head washed up on the beach at the yanqui naval base, his fantastic body a grand feast for some unknown water fiend.

The twins Héctor and Juanito never felt the heat. When their father welcomed into his house the dwarf and his friend the photographer, the house was still so replete with white-winged horseflies that they served as an armor against the rogue heatwave. On the outside, they shielded the house from the sun, entwined by their spindly legs, covering the exterior walls like live shingles, and many died there, and their dried corpses sticking to the house walls served as the most poignant memory of the hot spell for many summers after and those that didn't remember would pass by the house and see the great mass of fossils scorched and bent into the walls in attitudes of torment and would break into an intolerable sweat as if their bodies were suddenly reliving that dreadful summer. On the inside of the house, the white-winged horseflies served as colorful overflowing curtains and puffy canopies against the midday, the great multitude of their delicate wings creating unimagined gestalts; and even on the worst days, when the temperature jumped so far above the thermometer's range that the orange groves to the east of the city whispered their agony as all the fruit sizzled from inside the rind and the sea was placid as a pond, too fatigued to pound the shore, inside the house and even in the cobblestone patio, horsefly breezes blew gauzy as an autumn dusk and señor Sariel was most comfortable in his sackcloth burnoose and señor Daluz even once donned his only wool sweater, whose collar was beginning to fray.

In the cobblestone patio, the giant fig tree grew wild with fruit and even at high day the sun gazed through the horsefly canopies as adoringly on the twins as their two visitors did, undaring to unleash on them all its frenzy. Héctor and Juanito jumped on the trampoline and picked fruit and with these señor Sariel taught them how to juggle. *Es fácil, facilísimo,* though the amethyst-eyed boy had trouble at first because of his lack of depth perception; but once he learned that what was there was not there but here and what was here was not here but there, he could juggle five and even six figs at once. The real task though, or at least the reason señor Sariel had been let into the cobblestone patio, was to teach the boys how to fly, and to this señor Sariel set his mind and Armando Quiñón set on them his Leica to record it for posterity, or as señor Sariel put it, for his later self, *porque coño, ya te dije: I am my own posterity!*

"Ahora, quítense todo," he said to the twins one day while playing them a rumba. "It's too hot for clothes. Los hacemos como los griegos." And the boys immediately obeyed and took off their tattered T-shirts and their knee-length shorts and Héctor continued shaking his hips to señor Sariel's drums but the amethyst-eyed boy stopped and crossed his hands over his bare chest and looked at his brother. "¡Todo, coño!" señor Sariel said from his wheelchair. "Do you want to learn how to be acrobats or not? La ropa will weigh you down, keep you from flying."

So Héctor pulled down his briefs and he kicked them up so that they hung from a branch of the fig tree and then he helped his brother out of his and when they were completely nude, they jumped up on the trampoline and hopped onto a branch of the fig tree and held on to each other.

"Muy bien," señor Sariel said and forced his eyes off the boys, off their prune-brown genitals and glanced at Armando Quiñón who just stood there with his mouth half-open and was not doing what he had been paid to do, not using his wrapped-in-black-tape camarita. "Oye animal, se te sale la baba," he said to him and Armando Quiñón recovered his senses and began to take pictures of the boys on the fig tree. Señor Sariel shook his head and chuckled and then he pulled down his hood and wriggled his way out of his burnoose and put aside his drums and with his teeth unwrapped the bandages around his hands. Armando Quiñón helped him up on the trampoline and señor Sariel warmed up, landing alternately on his back and on his chest and all he was wearing was his black performing trunks.

"You too, like the Greeks," Héctor urged from the fig tree.

Señor Sariel smiled. His teeth were tiny yellow squares and they had huge gaps between them. He pulled off his trunks and threw them at Armando Quiñón who was still looking through his Leica at the boys and did not get out of the way so that the trunks landed on his head. Héctor laughed but the amethyst-eyed boy couldn't and he pressed his groin to his brother's thigh.

Señor Sariel worked up a sweat on the trampoline. He moved in the air with the grace of a winged thing and when he tired he attached himself to one of the stronger branches of the fig tree and hung upside down by his legs. Héctor picked a ripe fig and tossed it to him. Señor Sariel had his eyes closed, but he reached out and snatched the fig. The thing in between his legs also hung upside down and it reached his belly button and it was fleshy and folded in layers of painted skin that drooped over the head and gathered at the end, pursed like a spinster's kiss. Héctor had to tilt his head to know the story that was etched there and he whispered it in his brother's ear for his brother would not look.

Once there was a jealous man with a wife whose beauty was the envy of all. Her hair was like a silky midnight, her eyes like violet pools, her lips like nectar, her cheeks like the twin halves of the pomegranate and her breast like twin fawns. The man was a merchant, pues mira, mira, those are the beautiful Persian carpets that he sells. Héctor leaned over to the branch where señor Sariel was hanging and pointed at them, almost touched them, and at the sense of his nearness the story unfolded for him, the carpets unweaving themselves and exposing their hidden images. *But this man dared not travel lest his wife take another man and he sold carpets only from his home so that he could always keep an eye on her. The wife spent her husband's money as fast as he could make it, on herself and on all her twelve maids, whom she lavished with expensive perfumes and embroidered dresses.*

"Why do you treat the servants as if they were royalty!" the husband demanded.

"Because they are good to me."

Eventually, the merchant found that he must journey to other towns if he was to make enough money to keep her satisfied. So he went to the bazaar and bought a parrot that spoke all the world's languages and was said to have been cross-bred with a falcon a few generations back so that his sight was infallible, and this parrot he set loose in his house before he went on his journey. When he came back, he asked the parrot: "How has my beautiful wife kept busy?" And the parrot told him all, todo todito, how those twelve maids that were always with her were not maids at all, but young boys in wigs and dresses and how before the merchant's carriage was less than a mile out of his estate, the boys had taken off their wigs and their dresses and they were more beautiful as boys than as girls, dark and lean and armed with such unmelting purposes that they formed a circle around her in the garden and had her one by one, and then again and a third and fourth time, and when she was too weak with joy, sprawled and useless, they had each other, keeping their circle around her, so that none was undone and none was undoing.

Héctor leaned further towards señor Sariel and traced the circle of boys with his index finger and the painted boys were warm with rushing blood and Héctor wanted to linger there with them. But the story continued.

At hearing this, the merchant began to pluck the hairs from his thick beard in clumps and scream in such rage that the parrot found the nearest window and flew out of the house. That night, the merchant hired some thugs and the twelve maids were tied up and made into true maids and the removed parts were ground and fed to the goats and the merchant beat his wife across her lovely round nalgas with the flat end of his scimitar. This way it was painful but she would not be scarred.

So that the parrot wouldn't fly away again, the merchant had a fantastic gilded cage made and he hung it high on the inside terrace so that from there the bird could still watch every spot of his property. And when he journeyed again he commanded: "Watch all and tell all."

The parrot agreed, though he was insulted at being imprisoned when all he had done was tell the truth.

When the beautiful wife found out it was the parrot who had blabbed on her, she rounded up her maids that were now truly maids and she ordered them: "You four, take your grinding stones and grind under the parrot's cage all night; you four, take your flowering pitchers and from the roof water the cage till dawn; and you four, ay que pena, my strongest, my rock-built, how I dread to know that you'll soon grow soft as I, take the shields you once used as warriors and shine them in the moonlight and wave them back and forth around the cage till your limbs are weak." And since they still loved her, though they could not have her, they planted kisses on her cheeks and obeyed her.

So when the merchant returned and he asked the parrot: "How has my beautiful wife kept busy?" The parrot answered: "My good lord, pardon me, but last night I was able to see or hear nothing, for the driving rain and the thunder and the lightning distracted me all night."

"¡Mentira!" the merchant bellowed. "We're smack in the middle of the dry season."

"No, no, my lord, I swear, rain and thunder and lightning all night long."

The merchant, concluding that it was this damnable bird who had had his wife this time, grabbed the parrot by the scruff of the neck and drove a tent pike through his heart and drove it deep into the ground so that his soul would never flee its rightful torture and the parrot's blood tainted all his plumage.

When the wife heard, she was delighted and now every time the merchant traveled there were enough lovers from the king's army not only for her but for all her maids that were now truly maids. They had plucked twelve crimson feathers from the corpse of the honest parrot and they used them to tickle each other in their injured parts before their lovers arrived.

There were other stories, for every time señor Sariel revealed himself, a new one was painted on and the older one had vanished, as if the folds of his foreskin panted for the colored images like the brittle North African earth for rain. On the branch of the fig tree, Héctor whispered all the stories in his brother's ear and his brother understood only through him. Though after the stories, after señor Sariel meditated upside down from the fig tree and he began to teach them the art of flying, it was Héctor who had to keep up with his brother and at times even contend with him for their teacher's attention.

"An acrobat is like a ballet dancer with wings," señor Sariel said falling from his branch onto the trampoline. "He walks on his tiptoes first and then he walks on air. Así." After two light hops, señor Sariel threw himself to the air and he pressed his head to his knees and he was a wind-wheel and he pushed himself higher and rolled in on himself faster so that his painted thing shot out like a loose spoke or like the squiggle of a runamok "Q." Whatever he taught Héctor and Juanito, he taught them while hovering in the air or hanging upside down from the fig tree.

"The word literally means to walk on tiptoes," he said, hanging again from the branch. "In Greek." At this last word the boys remembered their nakedness and they remembered their teacher's nakedness and the amethyst-eyed boy stood behind his brother.

To put them again at ease, señor Sariel undid himself from the fig tree and landed on the trampoline on his globular head and bounced on it a while, balancing himself perfectly with his four outstretched limbs.

Héctor laughed and his brother tried to mimic him, though still holding his cover behind him and now putting his arms around Héctor's shoulders; and even Armando Quiñón, whom they had mostly forgotten about, put down his Leica and broke the mold of his melancholy with an uncontrollable fit of carcajadas.

"Bueno, ya de boberías," señor Sariel said and he bounced on the trampoline so that a rumble passed from one side to the other and the twins were soon in the air. Señor Sariel hovered near them and he touched lightly the back of Héctor's head and Héctor went head over heels for the first time and señor Sariel did the same with the amethyst-eyed boy.

"¡Ahora, miren, miren!" he screamed in the air. "Press your head in between your knees as if you want to know yourself worse than you ever wanted to know anybody." He grabbed his knees and tucked his head in so deep that his thin lips were grazing the stories of his painted thing and he began to twist and twirl in the air with such speed that soon the only thing the twins could see was the color of his python-tattoos, orange and red and black swirled into each other like a hypnotist's tool. When he straightened himself, he looked at them: "¿Bueno, qué esperan?" The twins did as he had done and that night when they had finished—their frames clung to some lower branches of the fig tree like galleon wrecks on a reef—they could not wash, so señor Sariel had to wash them. He dressed them in their linen pajamas and put them to sleep, blowing in their ears with his fig breath so that they would dream about the circus and about flying together to some faraway island, as alone as they had been in the womb and as they will be again in a later larger solitude and there entwined they would know each other's love as the only worthy thing on this earth.

Señor Sariel slept in a windowless square-box room to the side of the patio with a thin tin door that he never latched shut. The room had been used by the laundress Perdita. It was furnished only with a thin foam mattress thrown on the floor and a wobbly chair, which Perdita used more than the mattress because she suffered from insomnia. On the wall was attached a gas lamp, which Perdita also made much use of at night. When doña Edith fled she had taken Perdita with her under the tacit threat that if she did not accompany her she would never work again for any mistress in all of Cuba. Perdita cried when she said good-bye to the twins and white-winged horseflies stuck to the globby tears on her charcoal cheeks and left their imprint there. Perhaps this is why señor Sariel was sure he had once known the previous occupant of his room and was sure she had died of longing, for he felt the fingers of her spirits graze the back of his neck just after he shut off the gaslamp towards the early hours of the morning. He slept for an hour, or at most two, till he welcomed Armando

Quiñón back through the side door and readied himself for his students again. One night, he heard the tin door creak open and since he was sure it was the wandering ghost of Perdita, having lost track of living time and come a bit too early, he did not look up and continued seated on the foam mattress, naked, his legs spread wide, the folds of his foreskin spread out before him like a wide canvas, to his left, a half-full uncapped bottle of bourbon and a pile of ripe figs, to his right, laid out in a fan, needles of various shapes and sharpnesses, which he dipped into three different ink jars of turquoise blue, magenta, and yellow ink and pierced into the un-der-hull of his skin, etching there, point by point, a new tale from his far-away land.

"¿Qué haces?" The voice teetered between boy and man with a huski-ness that refuted the notion of a phantom. Startled, señor Sariel pierced too deep into his skin and the blood took a while in coming but when it did it flooded the scene he was working on as Jullanar of the Sea told her king of fighting off the old fisherman who had wanted to deflower her many years before and señor Sariel's blood was now the blood of the old man as Jullanar beat him over the head with the empty husk of a lobster and señor Sariel folded the skin over it and let it dry and let it remain part of the tale before he looked up. He gestured for the boy to step in and the boy did. He looked into his eyes. They were the color of fresh honey. They brimmed with curiosity. He gestured again for the boy to shut the tin door and the boy did and asked if he should hook the latch. Señor Sariel answered him that no that there was no need for secrecy.

"¿Qué haces?" the boy repeated. He was wearing only the pants of his linen pajamas and the hardness of his enthused youth was so evident in the gaslamp shadows that the loose-fit cloth of his pant leg fell like a sail from a twisted mast. Señor Sariel called him closer and he unfolded his skin-canvas and showed him the scene of Jullanar and the old fisherman and the blood was encrusted there as if it really had poured from the old man's head. The boy looked at the scene and saw the hoary beard of Jullanar's king and the wrinkled and spotted hands of the one who had tried to have her chasteness and he was sad for her.

"Poor Jullanar," he said. "She lives in a country of old men."

"No es pobre, Héctor," señor Sariel said. "No es pobre nada." He rounded up the fan of his needles and inserted them by size and shape into the sheaths of their leather case and he shut tight the three ink jars and put them aside. He offered Héctor the bourbon bottle and the boy took it and swigged back a shot and could not assume (though he tried) a straight face to hide the burning inside him. Since señor Sariel could not finish etching Jullanar's tale he told Héctor of it and as he told him he showed him where each scene would develop—as Jullanar gave the old king a son who was born feet first, which meant, the court magician said mournfully, that he would die by water, and as the son grew and learned of horses and of archery and of the Koran and stayed away from the yellow river as his mother demanded. Héctor listened till he himself was transformed into the young prince and when he reached the age of manhood, Jullanar's brother, who was a great sultan of the sea, visited and bathed the new man in the juice of oysters and smeared his eyes with the ink of squids and rubbed on his loins the sperm of porpoises. "Now your son cannot die by water," the sultan-brother said to the king. "For just as you rule the earth, we rule the sea and the rain and the river."

Héctor took another shot of bourbon and sat on the opposite end of the mattress and stretched his legs towards señor Sariel. "My muscles hurt," he said.

"Which ones?"

"Todos."

"It means they're growing. It means you're getting stronger."

Señor Sariel grabbed Héctor's foot and massaged it with his strong hands. The gaslamp flickered in the boy's eyes and untoasted them to a lighter shade. He let out a low soft hum. Señor Sariel offered him the bottle and Héctor took one last long shot and he let señor Sariel pull off his pajama pants. His body was sunburned evenly throughout and smooth except for the soft down of his legs and the dark bramble out of which his pinga shot out like a tuber inverted. Señor Sariel kissed the high arches of Héctor's feet and the boy lay back. Señor Sariel was good throughout. When at first the pain was too much and the boy grew frightened, señor Sariel retreated and he touched the boy's genitals and fingered his culo with the same delicacy he used when handling his white-winged horse-flies; and all night he whispered other stories in a changed voice to better teach Héctor how simply pain is converted to pleasure and terror to rapture.

Héctor awoke the next morning on his belly in the foam mattress, his arms folded under his head. On his skin he smelled what he thought was Perdita's cleaning water and he smelled nodded-off flowers. Before señor Sariel left him alone, he kissed both his nalgas and hovered over him so that Héctor smelled figs behind his ears and he felt the skin of the painted thing dragging over his back (though it wasn't pleasant anymore).

"You will not die by air tampoco," his teacher said.

With the help of the photographer, señor Sariel had a pair of trapezes sewn together with shafts of caña brava and hemp rope and he hung them from opposite branches of the giant fig tree above the trampoline.

"El trapecio is the high art of the acrobat," he proclaimed and he hung from one trapeze and swung his body till he was moving in great arches and Armando Quiñón grabbed the bar of the other trapeze (as told) and climbed up on the ridge of the garden wall, breaking off a few cola

bottles and when señor Sariel screamed: "¡Ahora! ¡Ahora carajo!" Armando
Quiñón threw the trapeze towards him and señor Sariel swung towards it
and let go and twirled himself in the air so that his body seemed horned
and svelte (like a winged chameleon), tinted orange and red and black;
and when he was himself again he was swinging from the other trapeze
towards Armando Quiñón, whom he snatched with his legs and swung
back with him. The photographer wriggled and screeched like a mouse
caught by a nightowl and wet himself in the air. All this, to the great
pandereteo of the twins who watched from below and pointed to the
spreading stain on the photographer's trousers and asserted: "Mira, se
meó . . . mira, se cagó." Their merriment, however, quickly ceased when
señor Sariel dropped Armando Quiñón onto the trampoline and asked the
twins to get into their Greek *uniformes* and come join him up on the
trapeze. The photographer stumbled down from the trampoline and disappeared into the house. Héctor stripped and helped his brother strip as
he always did and when they were on the higher branches of the giant fig
tree señor Sariel pointed Héctor away to the opposite trapeze so that only
the amethyst-eyed boy joined him on the one he was hanging from. After
they got swinging well, señor Sariel dropped down to the trampoline so
the amethyst-eyed boy was alone on the moving trapeze. Héctor, on the
opposite trapeze, hung still as a cat before a leap.

"You're going to hang there all day like a corpse," señor Sariel
screamed at him. "Mueve el culo y las patas and you'll see how you'll fly."
So Héctor shook his ass and his legs and soon he was swinging in arches as
high as his brother, so that when they converged the soft ends of their toes
grazed each other. In less than an hour, señor Sariel taught them how to
swing up and stand on the bar and how to hang upside down with the
knees bent over the bar and how to bend their feet like knees so they could
hang upside down by them and they would have learned much more than
that the first day had Armando Quiñón not interrupted them. He came
out of the house with his linen coat and his baggy trousers and his underwear and even his leather sandals hanging on his forearm, dripping and
washed, he himself wearing just a towel around his pointy girlish hips and
with a look deeper than embarrassment on his face. "Oye, me parece que
quedó el viejo," he muttered. "I went into his room to look for something
to put on and though his eyes are still open and he's still shedding tears,
his body has turned to stone."

They had not seen señor Daluz in two and a half weeks. And they had
not missed him. In his worsening blindness, the old man had turned into
a ghost. After his wife fled and after the white-winged horseflies that had
guided him for a while (and whom perhaps he had relied on much too
much, neglecting the gift of his halo-vision for the sheer pleasure of their
white-winged breezes) disappeared, the halos had darkened and he lost all
sense of time. He had his breakfast at midnight and his supper at noon

and would reprimand the boys for staying up so late at two in the afternoon and shed furious tears in the hours of la madrugada (spinning the radio dial this way and that at the wrong times when all actors were still in
their own beds on their sixth dream of fortune and stardom) for all his favorite radio-novelas had been cancelled and all he could get was static.
Soon, all that his sons knew of him was the murmuring jeremiad from his
room as he replayed all the plots of the most famous novelas, raising his
voice an octave to play the heroine and lowering two or three to play the
villain. (Once—it seemed so long ago—his son Héctor and his niece Alicia had lent themselves for the parts, but now they had gone and to señor
Daluz it was as if they existed no more.) When the voices ceased from his
room, no one noticed. Armando Quiñón found him with his ear pressed to
the radio speaker, and even in his chagrin the photographer did not forget
his art, for a last picture of señor Daluz, his flesh the color of light marble,
was said to have been thrown into the bonfire along with all the other indecent ones of that period, found in the cellar room of Armando Quiñón's
studio on the artist's last day.

That night, when Héctor came to señor Sariel's windowless room, he
did not take off his pajamas and señor Sariel etched no tale into his foreskin and did not take off his sackcloth burnoose nor unpeel the bandages
around his hands. After they had a few shots of Kentucky bourbon, señor
Sariel told Héctor to go back to his brother, that it was a bad time to leave
him alone, and that in the morning they would telegram doña Edith in
Santiago de Cuba.

Two days later, doña Edith arrived in a heavier pregnancy than her first
one. She was appalled that the disfigured dwarf was living under her roof,
but when she announced her plans of grabbing him por el cabezón ese de
muchacho retardado and throwing him out on the street (this time making sure that he landed on the blade of his machete), Héctor responded in
all seriousness (for the first time since the night of the accident looking
straight into his mother's eyes) that he would follow señor Sariel and then
nudged his brother beside him and the amethyst-eyed boy said that *sí, sí,
yo también*.

"Qué malagradecidos son los dos," doña Edith said and she sat back
and caressed the fullness of her belly. "Gracias a Dios that there will be
more. These will be different. These will love their mamacita."

Señor Sariel stayed, on the condition that he never set foot inside the
main house and that he sleep and even do all his necessities in Perdita's old
room, and for this doña Edith threw him out a rusty bucket. "Ahí mea y
caga si quieres, desgraciado, en el cuartico de la negra (may she rest in
peace), for that's where you belong!"

She did not send him any food, but he was content solely with eating
the mango-sized figs from their tree; and though she could not stop her
sons from training on the trapeze and trampoline with him, like the

Greeks, as they always had (*If we can't practice with him, we'll leave, ma-macita. The naked body is a wholesome thing, así nos enseñó él, así nos dejaba papito*), she barred the photographer from the cobblestone patio, still unforgiven for his great sin thirteen years past, and at night she padlocked all the doors of the main house and drew the storm shutters on every window, so that señor Sariel did not see Héctor in his linen pajamas for three weeks. During this time, doña Edith did everything to rid herself of the disfigured dwarf. At night she whispered bedtime stories to her twins of monsters so like him that Héctor would immediately catch on and correct this detail or that of the monster's physiognomy and veer the story away from doña Edith's insidious course down a raunchier road, stealing scenes from señor Sariel's painted thing, till the amethyst-eyed boy blushed and doña Edith huffed that story time was over and tucked them in hastily and put out the lights. One morning, during one of their long training sessions on the trapeze, she stole into señor Sariel's windowless room and took the sackcloth burnoose and the bandages that he wrapped around his hands. She threw the load into her hurdy-gurdy washing machine and washed it with the blood of hens, spoiled rum, the crushed leaves of poisonous tobacco, and bits of the wings from his own horseflies, which she chiselled off the outer walls. She cranked the machine with all her strength so that the hen blood turned bubbly, as if over a flame. Afterwards, she put the burnoose and the bandages through the ringer nine times, each time chanting a curse that her father's mother had taught her, in a language she had never understood. She hung it to dry and replaced it all in his room before they finished training, none the worse for the wash, except for an almost imperceptible rosy tint, like the light of dawn before it is dawn. But nothing changed. Day after day the boys were as happy with him as he was with them. So, fearing that she would go into labor soon and have to leave the boys all to him, she decided on one last drastic measure. Laden as she was with child, one night, after she had padlocked all the doors and closed tight all the storm shutters, she climbed on the trampoline and up the wooden side-steps the boys had nailed to the trunk of the giant fig tree, and leaning from one of the sturdier branches picked every one of the ripe figs she could reach. The next morning, she awoke the boys before dawn and asked them to go out to the cow field in Mingo's finca near the mountains and pick out the one mushroom she had always told them never even to step on. And the twins knew exactly which one it was, the one with the parasol-shaped yellow cap, the one frizzled like a ballerina's dress three quarters of the way up the pale stalk.

"A whole basket," doña Edith commanded. "Y no se atrevan a meterse uno en la boca." The twins rubbed their eyes and did their necessities together and set out for the grazing field.

Armando Quiñón saw them that morning, for there were photographs thrown into the bonfire of his last day of the twins frolicking with each other on their way to the field, and photographs of the twins throwing off their clothes, and photographs of the twins climbing on the back of Mingo's morning-dazed cows and supposedly (surely these must have gone into the bonfire first) of Héctor teaching his brother what señor Sariel had taught him, on the back of the monumental and doomed Niña, Mingo's most productive cow. They returned late in the afternoon and señor Sariel refused to see them, berating them that discipline was the first and last virtue of the artist, that without it one remained a mere dabbler, a dilettante. It was the first and only time that the twins saw him lose his temper. They spent the rest of the afternoon watching their mother crush and muddle all the mushrooms they had brought her and add a tad of honey and the pulp of the figs and crush and muddle some more.

"¿Qué es eso, mamacita?"

"Pan con queso." She shooed them away with an upside-down wave of her hand.

It was early evening. Héctor and Juanito had disobeyed their mother, they had each eaten a bit of the parasol off the frizzly dressed mushrooms. They began to feel light as the crisp dusk breeze. They wanted to practice and they were sure, in their gathering euphoria, that their master would forgive them. They went through the cobblestone patio to señor Sariel's windowless room. The tin door was unlatched and in the darkness of the room they could only make out shadows though they heard something fluttering like a wounded bird attempting flight. Héctor lit the gas lantern on the wall. Señor Sariel was naked and belly-down on the foam mattress, the muscles underneath his turtle-shell back quivering as if on the brink of convulsions, a tipped empty bottle of bourbon on one side of the mattress, his arms used as pillows underneath his great bald head. On his feet he wore a pair of brown leather talaria that strapped all the way up to his twin baseball calves. The wings of these marvelous sandals were colored, like the leather, in variegated shades of worn brown, attached down near the Achilles tendon, and as they beat the air they succeeded only in lifting señor Sariel's legs so that his knees barely rose off the surface of the mattress, and when the wings tired and folded his legs flopped down. In these moments, when the tiny wings rested, Héctor began to undo the talaria, strap by strap, from señor Sariel's feet. They were on so tight that after he removed the first one there were roundabout welts on the skin around his ankles. Héctor kissed his hand and passed it over the marks. The sandal took off and batted itself against the ceiling and against the walls as if searching for a window. Héctor grabbed one of its hanging straps and wrapped it around his brother's hand while he undid the other sandal. This one he grabbed himself and forced down with his bare foot, crushing one wing a bit, and strapped around his foot and lower leg as tightly as señor Sariel had worn it. Then he grabbed the other one from his brother and did the same on his other foot and leg. At first, the wings dragged on the floor and nothing happened. Héctor paced from end to end of the narrow room, stomping hard as if to awaken them. Señor Sariel grunted and Héctor stopped. A moment later, the wings began to beat and Héctor was casually lifted off the floor so that his head brushed against the ceiling. He reached his hand down to his older brother and pulled him up. The amethyst-eyed boy, crazy with joy, wrapped his legs around his brother's waist and his arms around his neck, the force of his leap twirling them round and round.

"¡Volamos! ¡Volamos!" the amethyst-eyed boy screamed.

"Ssshhh. You'll wake him."

The wings soon tired and they could only support the weight of the brothers a few inches above the ground. They left señor Sariel's room and snuck past their busy mother in the kitchen. Héctor threw his brother up on his shoulders and they left the house towards Parque Martí. They were flying so close to the ground that those who saw them in the early evening shadows thought nothing unusual of it, merely that the boy was on fast skates. In the park, there were lovers snuggling by the dry fountain who ignored them, and there were bachelors out for a walk after having dined alone, too consumed with solitude to pay any mind, and there were mujeres who lived in the green house by the bayshore, who were just awaking and whistled at them from their breakfast tables and called them pollitos ricos. They took La Calle Doce Norte out of the park and went to where the railroad tracks crossed over the Bano River. Héctor took the talaria off his feet and strapped them to his waist, buckling one with the other, and they went underneath the track and counted the cars on the trains that passed. They jumped into the river. The wings of the sandals around Héctor's waist beat the waters and acted as fins. The amethyst-eyed boy found the water was so shallow that if he stood on his tiptoes his head would bob just above the surface of the slow-moving river. Héctor swam in circles around him and poked him in the belly. The amethyst-eyed boy laughed and swallowed water. It tasted like the railroad track smelled, of old iron and rust. When the current picked up, Héctor swam to the opposite shore and took off his drenched shorts and his pullover shirt and his briefs and spread them on the round pebbles to dry, leaving only the talaria around his waist, and then he jumped back into the river. The amethyst-eyed boy did as his brother had done, and when Héctor swam towards him the water swirled as the wings beat about his waist. They searched for each other's warmth in the cold water, Héctor's hips pushing back and forth against his brother as if obeying the beat of a feverish rumba, and soon his brother pushing back as if moving also with the earth's heartbeat. Héctor pulled him close, and with one hand on the back of his head, and with his mouth half-opened, kissed him. The amethyst-eyed boy had never tasted his brother's tongue: it was tender and wet like the flesh of a freshly picked mango and it tasted of plums and oranges. All that they did they did under the cold dark water and before they were finished three trains had roared by, though they had not counted the cars and they had not noticed that the current had taken them about two hundred meters downriver. They swam back to search for their clothes. It had been so long that the moon had disappeared, so at first they could not find them and they were sure that somebody had stolen them, that someone had watched them play, for they found their clothes neatly folded and laid out under the knurly trunk of a chestnut tree whose over-reaching branches hung over the dark river and grazed the sides of the trains as they passed. Héctor strapped the talaria back on his feet. When the amethyst-eyed boy climbed on Héctor's shoulders, Héctor could feel the bulge of him squashed against his neck. As they flew home, the amethyst-eyed boy pulled out his penis and rested it on the upper ridge of his brother's ear and shot out an impressive stream—powerful as that of any incontinent fountain-boy, as if the river itself had lent him its infinite waters—part of which splashed against Héctor's temple and ran down his cheek, salty like tears. They fell into a fit of carcajadas when they sprayed Ñaña the Halfwit as she laid curled under newspapers and torn books underneath a store awning on the corner of José Martí and Narciso López Streets.

"¡Lluvia! ¡Huracán!" they screamed between the ebb and flow of their laughter.

Ñaña the Halfwit cursed them and waved her rag-wrapped fists at them and before she fell asleep again murmured prayers to her gods that both those mariconcitos die young, prayers that were almost answered that very night, for after they turned the corner, the talaria's wings got beating so fervently (as if fleeing from the madwoman's curses) that they carried the boys away with a horse's fury and as they approached the brick wall of the cobblestone patio they were headed straight for it and the amethyst-eyed boy's piss-manic thing went limp on Héctor's ear and dribbled on his shoulder and they both covered their heads with their arms and screamed for their lives, so that they never knew if they went straight through the wall or at the last minute veered over it, just missing the sharp edges of the broken-off cola bottles. They ended up hung by their limbs on one of the larger branches of the fig tree, both the talaria's wings cracked on Héctor's ankles, struck with a fatal susurration. Below them, sitting on the trampoline, his back resting on the trunk of the giant fig tree, his belly blown out like a starving child's, his hands wrapped around his painted thing, was señor Sariel. He had been hungover and had eaten the whole basket of fresh figs he had thought the twins had left for him as a conciliatory gesture, twice-giant figs like he had never seen on the giant tree before, that tasted of rain and earth and dung. He was passed out again and the twins dropped from the tree and snuck past him. They buried the talaria in a small plot of earth where the banana trees grew on the outskirts of the cobblestone patio and they bathed each other in the laundry pail and slept early that night, without their pajamas.

They never saw their master again.

In the Room Lit with a Red Bulb

On the evening of January 3rd, 1959, when the rebel Barba Roja and his men, already staggering from two whole days of celebration (the country was theirs), broke into Armando Quiñón's studio and found him hanged in the cellar room with one of his own wide black leather belts, blood-dark drool still slipping from his chin and puddling on the dusty floor beneath him, he (Barba Roja) immediately sealed the room, placed two drunk guards at front door of the main studio, and let only one other man examine the evidence with him.

"¡Coño," his companion said, looking around, "qué puta ha pasao aquí!"

The room was lit by a single red bulb. There were black and white, 20-by-26 centimeter pictures spilling from an oak chest in the corner of the room and spread all over the floor beneath the suicide, as if when he had opened the chest the innumerable pictures had been packed in so tight that the chest spewed its contents all over the room. There was one slit rectangular window near the ceiling (at street level) whose panes had been covered with black paint. There was a long wooden table running along the right wall. The three developing trays sitting on it were still filled with developing chemicals. Pinned to the wall above them was perhaps the last picture Armando Quiñón had developed, of the rebels that very morning, descending like gods from the mountains, Barba Roja in front and directly to his left, his half-naked companion, wet curls down to his shoulders and clamped down by a pushed-back beret, a full dark beard, around his neck a black ebony rosary whose cross dangled around his belly button, a Belgian rifle thrown over one shoulder and a magnificent broad-chested rooster perched on the other, its neck craned, crowing in the glory of a new age, behind them a defocused army of other half-naked deified barbudos.

"Qué pena," comandante Julio César Cruz said, examining the picture, caressing the mute blue rooster on his shoulder. "How pictures lie."

"No te preocupes, compadre," Barba Roja said. "Atila is mute but he is as brave as a lion." He too caressed the silent rooster and Atila, suddenly moved by so much affection, stretched his neck out as if to crow and the muscles in his chest tightened and his beak opened but he produced no sound. Both men cast their looks away from him as not to embarrass him.

They found a shadeless lamp and plugged it in and switched it on. The bulb was bright and it annihilated the red light. They examined the pictures spilled all over the room and Barba Roja shook his head and looked at the suicide. He had meager limbs with long skeletal fingers and toes whose untrimmed nails had now turned purplish. His ribs were countable and his long dank hair and clumps of his beard stuck to the leather loop around his neck. The only sign of health was the tenacious dignity that he maintained, even now, in the arch of his eyebrows, the outer ends tilted minutely upward, as one who is sorrowfully watching what he already knows too well. Barba Roja was suspicious. A chair had been kicked away too far from the hanged man. Barba Roja picked up one face-down picture that seemed out of sync with the big-bang explosion of the oak chest, placed exactly as if it had floated to the other side of the room from the hands of the dying man. It was a picture of a naked boy in his late adolescence, getting out of a pail-tub where he had been bathing, reaching for something, a towel perhaps, outside of the scope of the picture. He's in some sort of house . . . no, no, a tent, for the walls have folds. The boy's arms and shoulders and back are those of a man, and so is the half-aroused thing hanging from the cross of his thighs. Barba Roja handed the picture to Julio César.

"That's him? That's Héctor, the famous acrobat?"

"Sí, creo . . . his face is a bit out of focus."

"Bueno, it's not the face the artist was after."

Barba Roja moved the chair under the suicide and climbed on it and examined the noose around the neck, then he stepped down and examined the hands and the genitals, carefully pulling the skin of the engorged penis back and feeling it for moisture. He took the picture back from Julio César and raised it to the drooling chin of the suicide and let it go. It landed almost exactly on the spot where he had picked it up from, but this time face up.

"Pobre," he said, as he took out a handkerchief and wiped the dead man's chin, "it must have taken him quite a while to die. . . . And the traitors who murdered him would have us believe that he died, well, jerking off to a picture of his beloved." He felt again the dead man's genitals. "But they did not have the gall to fake that."

"Murder?"

"Sí, exactly like Carmencita told us. They caught up with him." He pointed to the picture. "And now that boy has one more of the dead in love with him."

Carmen Canastas's Tangled New Year's Tale

It was said that Carmen Canastas was not Barba Roja's mistress, that she was not his girlfriend, and that she was certainly not his wife, that she was rather his *querida,* his beloved. It was also said in meaner and lower tones that he shared her, that when she snuck out to the foothills of the Sierra Mountains to meet him at an abandoned schoolhouse every Friday at dusk, he had her right there, smearing the fallen unerased blackboards with their sweat, that then he took her up to La Plata, the rebels' head-quarters in the Sierra, and let other comandantes enjoy her. And in an almost inaudible whisper it was said moreover that once, while drunk, el Comandante-en-Jefe had had her and proclaimed her más dulce que el jugo de caña, for which *his* lover Celia had Carmen Canastas banished from La Plata. She in turn, it was said, had told her mother doña Ana, in whom she confided like a sister, that while el Líder was having her, she reached down there to tug on his huevos, because that's the way Barba Roja himself liked it, and grabbed one, bigger than a hen's egg, and searched and searched for the other one that wasn't there until he asked her: "¿Qué buscas?" And she answered: "Nothing, mi vida," and tugged hard on the single one to which he yelped with joy and pushed into her anew. But of course, el chisme, the pastime of rubied tongues, grows out of envy, and Carmen Canastas was a creature that inspired envy with the innocence that water and light inspire weeds.

She was not stunning of figure, nor angelic of face, a bit plump with acne scars on her cheeks. Her eyes were a common muddy brown and her brow was too deep. Her voice was her only beauty. Her conversations were punctuated here and there with certain immeasurable suspirations, tiny puffs of sorrow, and when she spoke of her beloved, there seemed to be a light drizzle falling at the back of her throat, a curtain of mountain mist that she spoke through. Sometimes her voice, soft and worn and wrinkled, as if someone had used it in a lifetime previous and in it were woven all the lessons of a journey already taken, became her and she wore it as a linen mantle to hide all her defects, for she wore no paint and used no hairspray or talcum powder or perfume and in some humid days she smelled nothing like a woman (for the hair grew moist and bushy in her armpits). She had studied opera. She had gone to the first year of law school at the University of Havana, but her mother became ill and she returned to care for her. When she met Barba Roja, she was near thirty. From the start he called her mi guajirita Guantanamera, she called him mi viquingo.

Almost two years later she welcomed him and his band of rebels as saviors. She prepared a large Año Nuevo feast (two days late) in her mother's house, setting up a long dining table in the patio and using old wooden cola boxes as chairs and starched bedsheets as tablecloths. She slaughtered and roasted twelve suckling pigs and served them with rice and black beans and malanga fritters and fried ripe plantains. They drank rum and burgundy straight from the bottles for there weren't enough glasses and they toasted the new age of hope and the end of tyranny in fifty-nine different ways and in six different languages, including Latin, which Barba Roja had learned as a child in the seminary. He sat at the head of the table, to the left of him comandante Julio César Cruz and his mute rooster and to the right of him Carmen Canastas. When the guerrilleros began to get rowdy, shouting curses at the yanquis who had spent the last two days spreading rolls of concertina wire around the perimeter of their naval base, Barba Roja pointed to the empty rocking chair near the table and asked them to calm down, to have some consideration for Carmen Canastas's mother who was ill and resting in her room. And because he knew her voice would soothe them, he asked Carmen Canastas to tell them some inspiring story of herself, of how she taught the peasant children to read. Carmen Canastas surprised him and told a story he had never heard. It wasn't about the campesino children but about the time she was hired as a tutor for the children performers of the traveling gypsy circus. And that's how she came to tell Barba Roja and his men of the tragedy of the young acrobat Héctor Daluz and his brother, the amethyst-eyed boy, the most popular stars in all that circus's long history.

"Pues mira," Carmen Canastas said, "it was their cousin who convinced me to do it. You know her, comandante Cruz, esa Alicia Lucientes. We taught together for a year or so. Una muchacha bella, but intelligent also. She taught mathematics; I taught languages. In the summers, she traveled with the circus as a tutor. Two summers ago, I went with her. We toured from Baracoa, where the circus is based, all the way to La Habana, setting up tents in a finca near Bayamo, by the airport in Camagüey, right next to the railroad tracks in Sancti Spíritus, in a forest near Santa Clara, and even on the sands of Varadero along the way. From town to town word spread about the twins, about the mystery of their disappeared master, and about their marvelous and sensual act that made one feel as if anything in this life were possible. The sandwich men that traveled ahead of the circus walking the streets of the westward towns and announcing with their huge placards and monumental voices the day and time the circus would arrive were hardly needed. People already knew. And they traveled miles and miles in buggy carts loaded with entire families (grandmothers and uncles, nieces and bastards, first and second cousins) and gladly paid a week's wages just to see the twins perform. There was never an empty seat in the main tent during their act, which was often performed two and three times a day just to satisfy the horde. So that every morning, when it came time for their lessons, the twins were tired and sleepy-eyed and paid little attention to Alicia or me, except, I found, when I read to them from a tattered book of stories that had, since I was a child, been one of my favorites, the tales of Shahrazad. Héctor's interest always perked, and he would grab the book from me and turn to his brother and read out loud, trepidatiously, for he seemed to have only a child's grasp of the art of reading, then he would tire and close his eyes and lift his head and recite the story as if he were reading from a text inside his head, sticking closely to the plot, but adding here and there such prurient details that I, at first, could only attribute it to the fact that he was fifteen and his hormones were raging.

"'Niño, no seas chusma,' I said to him, feigning shock, although the details were never coarse or vulgar and seemed to sprout very naturally from the deeper layers of the story. 'No, así es,' he answered, 'así es como el cuento cuenta.' Then he would shut the book, as if the printed pages were somehow an affront to his version of the story, and continue to recite to his brother. And, by correcting a phrase here and there, and adding my somewhat less flourishing touches to his tales, I was able to open their minds to the beautiful simplicity of our language. Alicia, however, was not so successful, unable to teach them anything at all about Euclid and his dreams. '¿Para qué sirven todas estas figuritas, todos estos numeritos?' they asked her.

"'Because figures and numbers are everywhere,' she answered, reddening somewhat, 'and because even those little flights you do from the trapeze are controlled by numbers, and by angles (which are the mothers of figures), how many twists you can do around each other, how many seconds you can stay airborne before you start falling, at how many degrees should you let go of the bar, at how many should you grab it on the swing back? So that if it wasn't for numbers and angles you'd be nothing but a couple of snot-nosed kids? Do you think you fly through the air by magic?' It was the wrong way to put it. From then on, the twins learned their mathematics lessons simply because they were scared of her. (Though Héctor suspected that she was angry not about the lessons but because he could never love her like she loved him.)"

At hearing this Julio César stood from the table, took the blue feathered rooster off his shoulder and placed him gently on the seat and walked to a far corner of the patio. Everyone at the table pretended not to hear the gush of his urine against the brick wall.

Barba Roja leaned toward his lover and whispered in her ear: "Cuidadito, mi guajirita. Some things are better left beautifully unsaid."

"Bueno, the truth is the truth, mi viquingo."

Julio César returned to the table, sat down, and reperched Atila on his left shoulder. He slapped Barba Roja on the thigh and a thin grim smile crossed his face. "Don't listen to him, Carmencita. Sigue—with the truth, if you are able."

"Pues así fue, the twins were so in love with the danger and beauty of their act and with the adoration the masses heaped on them, that all our lessons, eventually even the Arabian tales, seemed to them the very core of boredom. They became so distant that I would have learned nothing else about them had it not been for the photographer that was following them around and who, many in the circus had whispered to me, had become their legal guardian, had adopted them when their mother had abandoned them. (Alicia, however, assured me that doña Edith—their mother and her aunt—had never abandoned them, that they had run away from home two years before, when their master disappeared, and joined this circus and that in her grief doña Edith had lost the girl she was carrying and almost died herself.) I began to question the photographer. I brought spicy rum to his sleeping cart at night and he gladly received me. We talked as one talks late at night with an old friend; and from the compartment just beyond we could hear Héctor and Juanito's innocent snores. 'They sleep together as they always have,' the photographer said. His name was Armando Quiñón. He had known the twins since their birth, had been the hired photographer at their baptism and, from the photographs he showed by the gaslamp light, had kept a detailed record of their youth as if he were a parent. Though I never saw any pictures of the baptism. He claimed that these were locked away in his studio. When I asked him why, he became cryptic: 'These boys have been marked from the beginning.' I left it at this. He had had too much rum. I bid him good night.

"I saw other pictures. While at Varadero, he walked with me in the first morning hours along a deserted part of the beach. He was dressed as always in a brown linen baggy suit that looked like a set of expensive pajamas and sandals and a wide belt wrapped tight around his narrow waist so that he looked like an emaciated Eastern warrior. He carried under his arm a black leather album. We sat under a royal palm that leaned contortedly into the shore as if yearning for sea travel. He handed me the album and I opened it. 'This was their master,' he said. 'I have never showed you these pictures at night for fear of disturbing your dreams.' He said nothing more and as I leafed through the album all I could hear was the click-clack of the seashells as the morning tide aroused them from their sleep.

"¡Qué horror! Let me just be brief enough to say, sin ser muy melodramática, that this man, their master, was so inhuman in shape and feature—with his giant hairless head that seemed to be carved from lard and his rounded back and barrel chest and his disfigured limbs and folds of painted skin that drooped from his groin—that you could not guess whether he crawled out from a nest under the sands of the earth or was dropped here from a distant planet. When I had leafed through the album twice, forgetting for a moment that I was not alone, Armando Quiñón spoke as if reading my mind: 'His name was señor Sariel. There are two stories of his end.' He paused and let me examine the last few pictures in the album. 'I believe both of them, no matter how contradictory they may seem. Mira ahí, that's the headless shell of his painted body. It was found washed up on a beach at the American naval base four days after he disappeared. And the yanquis being yanquis made a spectacle of it. They put it on display in the naval base museum, alongside the relics of their predecessors, and said it was the suit of the devil shed before he burrowed back to his home by digging through the bottom of Guantánamo Bay. They opened the base to the natives and for a dollar one could view the exoskeleton of the devil and for a dollar more step inside the shell and assume this costume of the dark prince. People lined up for days. This was the fall of 1955 and the city government and Batista's Rural Guard feared rumors floating about the populace that it was Fidel returned from his exile in Méjico to brew his rebellion from under the folds of the earth. But the yanquis were right, o mejor digo, half-right, although that shell almost certainly belonged to the disappeared master—see the turtle back, the monstrous barrel chest, the hands twisted into claws—and he might have certainly crawled back to his home from a hole at the bottom of the bay, but señor Sariel was no devil, not in that sense. If he had been, he would not have fled.' Armando Quiñón stopped. He pulled a silver flask from an inside pocket of his suit and took two long swigs, then he stood and brushed the sand from his pants and took the black leather album from me and reached out a hand to help me up. 'Fled from what?' I asked. 'It's time for their lessons,' he said. 'The teacher should never be late.'

"I didn't see him again until we had arrived in La Habana, setting up our tents in an empty lot less than a mile from the presidential palace, close enough so we could see the back windows in the residential floor flicker on and off and make out the tiny shadows of the tyrant's lavandera-whores and pale-skinned henchmen. The first few nights I could not find Armando Quiñón in his sleeping cart or anywhere else. He disappeared after he put the twins to sleep and returned many hours later under the pink haze of the late summer aurora, disheveled, drunk, and one time even with a bruise on his left cheek. When I confronted him he threatened me with having the twins pulled from under my tutelage and telling me nothing more of their disappeared master, a story he knew I was eager to hear: *Fled from what?* So I quickly backed down. That evening, after Alicia had fallen asleep, he came to our cart with a bundle in his arms, which he handed to me. 'Póntelo,' he said, 'I'll wait for you out here.' It was one of his linen suits (this one sand-colored) and an oversized straw hat that I had to push back so that it wouldn't sink under my eyes, even with my hair all bundled up under it. There was also a long leather black belt, which I wrapped three times around my waist and knotted instead of buckled, as he himself did with his own. I wore my own sandals, for the ones in the package were four or five sizes too big.

"'You look like a scarecrow,' he said when he saw me. We walked silently for an hour, through the side streets in the old city where no one approached us. I kept pace two or three steps behind him and never during our journey did he look back at me. We hit a main road in the outskirts of the city and walked inland, then veered and followed a winding dirt road through a burnt field. The mountains were black in the horizon and our way soon became steep. I was tiring and I let Armando Quiñón know and his only answer was to quicken his pace. We climbed and descended and climbed and descended and the plant life thickened around us till it seemed we were in the middle of some forest and the wind took voice through the trees and the road narrowed. Finally I saw some torches shining in a distant vale, their light cut a wide tunnel through the misty darkness. As we approached I saw the shadows of figures and heard their raucous voices. A thick canvas circus tent was set up in a clearing and there were two military trucks, a new black Cadillac and a circus truck parked to one side. A Bengal tiger was tied by his neck to the trunk of a banyan tree and it slept amidst all the noise. Armando Quiñón told me to lower my hat a bit and to tuck some strands of hair that had come loose back under my hat and that I was a man now, or a boy at least, and to speak and act like one. We were greeted at the tent flap by a large hairy man whom I recognized as one of the workers that traveled in the circus. He was drunk and welcomed us effusively, hugging Armando Quiñón and grabbing my face with both his thick hands and proclaiming: '¡Qué lindo, coño! Te felicito, Armando. . . . But where are the twins?'"

"Es verdad," Barba Roja said, interrupting Carmen Canastas, "you would be beautiful, even as a boy." Every one at the table agreed, even the three guerrilleras who looked more like boys than Carmen Canastas ever could, but when they raised their bottles to toast there was no wine left in them. Carmen Canastas apologized and quickly disappeared into the house. She returned with three bottles of red wine in each hand; she was followed by her aging ill mother who was dressed in a faded houserobe and shuffled operosely with the aid of two oak canes, but refused any help when Barba Roja and two other guerrilleros stood up to lend her support.

"Déjenme coño," she grumbled. "Llego sola." Carmen Canastas smiled and Barba Roja persisted and guided the old woman to her rocking chair, which he slid near the head of the table, without touching her. She sat and smoothed her tangled hair with her twisted hands and breathed deeply. "These are they, hija? These are the liberators then? I can already tell which one is yours. El grandón, the one with the red beard."

"Sí, mamá."

"A rowdy bunch . . . eso es bueno." She looked at comandante Cruz

and at his rooster and then at the barbudos and then at the three guerrilleras, who from the grime on their faces seemed as if they too were bar-
bu*das*, all still smelling of their long months in the mountains.

"Maybe after they bathe," the old woman said, "I can pick mine."

Everyone laughed.

"No estoy jugando," she said and they laughed harder, a few of the
men offering their services.

"Mucho gusto. I am doña Ana. Pero ahora creo que voy a tener que de-
jar eso de doña and simply be Ana, or señora Anita. Good. Good. Pues mijita, forgive me. Go on with your story. I was straining to hear from my
room. I know this man, this photographer, and I once knew the twins'
mother, an arrogant woman. There is someone who will never give up her
petty bourgeois title. She is in an asylum in Santiago now. And even there,
they say, she must be addressed as doña. Go on, mijita, sin pena."

"You were going inside the tent," comandante Cruz reminded Carmen
Canastas. He leaned back and petted his rooster. Atila leaned his head into
his master's hand like a loyal hound.

"Inside the tent," Carmen Canastas said, "there were three minirings
and some bleachers set up. It was warm and it smelled of torch fumes.
There were many boys aged early to late adolescence, mostly mulatos,
whom I recognized as sons of the laborers and minor performers in the circus, some of whom were performers in their own right, though I could not
know them for these children were offered no tutoring, no formal education at all, and there were three or four yanqui-looking rubios whom I had
never seen, milling about, wearing either nothing or thin white trunks
that revealed everything. Some were sprawled on the bald dirt ground,
breathing heavily and covered with sweat and sometimes blood. One boy
came up to Armando Quiñón and kissed him on the cheek. 'I'm on next,'
he said proudly. Armando Quiñón returned the kiss and told him he
would watch. The boy glared at me as he passed. I held on to Armando
Quiñón now as he made his way to the shadows sitting up on the bleachers. Other boys also saluted him on the way. Up four rows in the bleachers was a stout bearded man in military garb. The torchlight shone off the
medals on the breast of his open coat and off the golden medallion of the
Virgin hanging from his neck and shadows deepened the pockmarks on
his cheeks. In his lap he held the youngest boy in the group, no older than
nine or ten, wearing nothing, who had fallen asleep, or had been drugged
más probable, and rested his head on the man's meaty thigh. He stroked
the boy's hair. 'Armandito,' he said, 'you come at a good time as always,
the late late show, el hombre tarántula is about to appear. You know him,
sometimes he works with that bitch Georgina inside her tent. Pero carajo,
Armandito, where are the twins?' Armando Quiñón went up and sat on
the bleachers next to the man and gestured for me to join them. He also
stroked the nude boy's long hair. He put his other hand on my knee. 'This

here is Guillermo,' he said to the ogre. 'I bring him straight from the mountains. He will help us do it.' Do what, I thought, and it was then that I looked closely at the ogre's face and recognized him immediately. He was one of the indio tyrant's top generals, rumored to be his main henchman and in control of the secret police. 'Mucho gusto, Guillermito,' the ogre said, extending his left hand faceup to me. 'But why do you wear so many clothes? I can see nothing of you.' Armando Quiñón stood and brushed his hand away from me. 'Mi general, con mil perdones, but this boy is not a whore. ¡Es un revolucionario! You promised you would deliver Batista to us if we gave you what you asked. And here we have given you all, staged your vilest fantasies in the flesh and still nothing from you!' The ogre was silent for a moment and when he spoke it was with the utmost serenity: 'Not all, Armandito. The twins, Armandito, remember them. That was part of the deal. Give me those lovely twins and I will give you el idiota Fulgencio with a pear in his mouth and a stake up his ass, ready for roasting!'"

"A plot to assassinate Batista while we were still in Méjico?" Comandante Cruz stood up suddenly as he spoke and Atila opened wide his wings to maintain balance on his master's shoulders. "Where is this photographer? Can we go see him?"

"Wait, Julio. No, this was the early summer of '57. You were already well entrenched in the mountains. But listen me out, then we'll go see him. Colorín sin colorado, este cuento no se ha acabado."

"There's much more," doña Ana said and motioned with her palsied hand for comandante Cruz to sit.

"Torches came on all around the middle ring and the boy who had greeted Armando Quiñón appeared, led by the circus medicine man (a quack with potions was all this man was really). The medicine man examined the boy's eyes and the boy's throat then stripped him and fondled the boy's genitals, as if this was merely the process of the examination, until the boy became aroused. The ogre chuckled beside us. Finally, the medicine man fastened a rubber band on the boy's genitals near the base and took a small glass container from his coat pocket and with a dropper under the boy's tongue gave him whatever potion he saw fit for the upcoming match. He then gave the boy a pat on the ass and pushed him into the center ring. The boy, now evidently more aroused, crouched into a wrestling stance and started shuffling in circles and looking wildly about. From the shadows there emerged to meet him a tiny-headed man that looked like a giant virus, with four disfigured arms growing out of his shoulders and the stump of a third leg growing out of his right hip and a short tail out of his coccyx. He too was naked, though his genitals were hardly visible, and bristly hairs, tinted orange and yellow twirling in concentric circles, covered all his body, even the extremities. The opponents circled each other, the boy growing more and more aroused and his eyes assuming the distant look of a battler. The young boy in the ogre's lap opened his eyes and looked up. The ogre lowered his head and whispered into the boy's ear: 'Es el hombre tarántula. He was once a beautiful young man, but the gods turned him into that for disobeying his grown-ups.' The boy's eyes widened. In the ring, the opponents still circled each other, the boy undaring to make a move. The tarantula, who was one of the touring circus's most popular freaks, emitted a tiny spittle from the center of his tiny head but the boy ducked and it missed him. The second one too missed, but the third hit the boy on his right shoulder and he dropped. When he stood he could not move his right arm and as he continued circling his opponent, trying to avoid any further hits, it flopped beside him like a dying fish. When he slowed, another spittle hit him above the knee and again he dropped as if struck by a blow. When he tried to stand his leg gave out from under him and, now frightened, he pushed himself away with his other leg. Then this one too was hit and the other arm, so the boy was soon helpless and almost completely paralyzed. The tarantula approached his opponent and clumsily turned him over and picked him up and folded him over and huddled him close and surrounded him with all his limbs and pressed his tiny head into the boy's nape and began to rock against him till one's groan of pleasure was indistinguishable from the other's whine of pain.

"The ogre too now was rocking on his hips against the drugged child, whispering gnarled obscenities and cupping his thick hand over the child's groin and when I caught Armando Quiñón's eyes, he gestured me with his head to move away. I headed from the bleachers to the entrance flap, for the first time afraid, repentant that I had left my sleeping cart that night. When the tarantula was finished with the boy he dropped him with a thud and shuffled over to the medicine man at the other end of the ring, his *cosita* now visible all wet and skinny and fleshy pink like a goat's. He patted the medicine man on the shoulder. The medicine man grumbled something back and went over to the boy and turned him over and checked his pupils and unwrapped the band from the base of his crotch and again placed the dropper under the boy's tongue and gave him whatever poison he saw fit.

"Armando Quiñón walked into the ring and I think I saw him take his black taped camarita from under the flap of his belt and click a couple of quick pictures at waist level, his instrument hidden from the ogre, of the sodomized boy and the kneeling medicine man. He stood by them and turned to face the shadow of the ogre. 'You'll never see my twins, you grán mariconsón,' he said. 'Armandito, no seas bobo,' was the quiet answer, 'a man does not go back on his word. We had a deal, un acuerdo entre hombres: the twins for the tyrant.' Then the voice descended back into its filthy murmurs. Armando Quiñón joined me and led me outside. A few of the ogre's bodyguards were taunting the tiger tied to the banyan tree.

They dangled from a branch just out of the beast's reach a barely alive pigeon tied to the end of a leather thong. The tiger too seemed drugged and its heavy paws inexpertly swiped the air and tripped on the falling roots of the banyan branches as if he were a cub just learning how to move. Armando Quiñón grabbed me and took me away from there.

"Then, as if to avoid any questions I might pose about what we had just seen, he repeated the question he had left his story dangling on a few days earlier. 'Fled from what? you ask,' he said as we moved into the woody path. 'He never told me, though from the condition I saw him in on the last night and from what I heard later from the twins, it seems doña Edith tried to murder him. She prepared for him a whole basket of poisoned sweet figs—made it seem she had picked them right from the tree. It was his weakness. He ate them all. But señor Sariel was strong as an ox; and vengeful as a wronged woman (as you will see). I found him that last night curled up in an alleyway near my studio on Narciso López Street, puking on himself. He was wearing only his black performing trunks and had all his belongings wrapped in his sackcloth burnoose and tied to the handle of his machete like a beggar's luggage. His winged sandals had been stolen. His drums he told me had been pierced open by a kitchen knife and he buried them in a plot of earth inside the cobblestone patio as if they had once lived and were now dead. 'I'm going,' were his last words to me, a grainy drool easing its way down his chin to the cotton-puff goatee at the point. 'Maldita vieja, me voy pal carajo.' Though the streetlight was dim, I took out my Leica and snapped a couple of quick pictures. He gave me a look of disgust, which he reserved for special occasions such as when he had not wanted me to photograph the twins, but he said nothing; then he grabbed his machete with one hand and rested the other hand on my shoulder for support. As he stood, a hot dry wind, as if from a fresh fire, stung my cheeks and I smelled his reeking insides and everything darkened. I dropped my Leica. For a moment I was blind and my blood cooled, as when something unknown and unseen passes right behind you. And then, though I knew he was already far away, I heard him speak to me as if he were still right beside me, whispering in my ear: 'Don't let anyone add to the life I have given them, and don't let anyone take it away else monstrous woes damn them and their own.' I now was dreaming, and I remained so convinced till I heard Ñaña the Halfwit, who also must have been spending the night in the alleyway, scream: 'Mira, mira pa eso, the angel with nine wings. ¡Ahí va!' She pointed into the night sky with her draggled trembling paper-wrapped hands. I looked up and saw the shadows of the beast fleeing from us, nine featherless reptile wings, two sets of four as wide as three times himself and flapping in unison, and one long thin one running down the ridge of his back, not a wing really, but taut skin on a bow-bent bone, which caught the breezes and seemed to function as a jib. This is the last I saw of our señor Sariel.

"'Ñaña the Halfwit was wise enough to pick up my camarita and hand it to me. But I was wise enough to simply tuck it behind my belt, there was no light and there would be no pictures. Ñaña the Halfwit crossed herself and went back to her bundle of papers muttering that the time of judgment was at hand for she had slept in the same sheets as the angel with nine wings and that blessed are those invited to do so.' Armando Quiñón paused, as if to let me absorb all this or to give me a chance to express my disbelief. We were already making our way out of the wood and heading towards the burnt fields. 'As if I had been dreaming,' he said, 'that's how I felt about it later, how else to feel about such events. Though whenever I saw Ñaña the Halfwit at the plaza, she stared at me until I looked back into her eyes, and in that brief look we shared our secret and she would smile.'

"We veered off the road and crossed diagonally across one of the burnt fields. When Armando Quiñón spoke again, it was almost morning. 'Two days later, doña Edith suffered a stillbirth. She went mad, blaming and beating her two sons, screaming at them how señor Sariel had stolen into her womb and with his twisted hands grabbed their sister by the neck and choked her to death before any life was given to her, and if this weren't enough, el maldito diablo, he crunches all her not-yet-hardened bones, even the tiny nailless toes, and tears her open from the slit of her sex to the base of her neck so that your sister is born inside out and in several pieces. This she screams at them as she beats them with their dead father's belts, wielding five or six at a time, so that it seemed to the twins that she was a fiend with many arms.'"

"Coño, it's a good thing that we finished eating a while ago," Barba Roja said. "More wine, for this story is running longer and gorier than expected."

"Así es," doña Ana said, nodding her head, "her stories go on for days. Y olvídate, you can't miss a thing, for they are more tangled than Ñaña the Halfwit's hair!"

Barba Roja brought more rum and more wine. Carmen Canastas cut and served the guava cobblers that had been cooling all this time, and as she walked around the table, scooping a piece of dessert to each, she continued: "Anyway, who knows the truth of all of this, who knows if doña Edith simply suffered a stillbirth like so many other women and in her grief began inventing stories about the poor circus master, stories that Armando Quiñón, in his own kind of grief, was eager to pass on. But when their mother lost it, that's when the twins fled to Baracoa, that's when they joined the circus. They brought nothing with them except the clothes on their back, but with their master's spirit guiding them they soon became great trapeze stars, so that when I joined the circus as a tutor a year and a half later, they were the lead act. Armando Quiñón followed them to Baracoa and became their self-proclaimed protector and guardian, and as he toured the countryside with the circus, he picked up on the discontent of the masses and a true revolutionary zeal began to grow in him. I never learned anything else about the plot against Batista or where it originated. During the next days after we spoke events overcame my curiosity. The plot was apparently disclosed to the tyrant. That same weekend, during the Sunday afternoon performances, the tyrant showed up with his entourage of thugs and whores, and even a few priests and a bishop, catered to by four nuns, followed him (they must have come from Mass) and the first five aisles were all cleared, the people holding tickets simply escorted out so that the tyrant and his entourage could sit.

"The ogre sat on the tyrant's right and the bishop on his left and the tyrant leaned over to one side and then the other and talked to them in hushes as if they were paramours. The whole party seemed bored with the animal acts and with the clowns and with the freaks, and the bishop even shook his mitered head at some of the more raunchy shenanigans of the brothers Adolfo and Claudio, the Italian clown duo who portrayed the bedroom lives of the more famous opera characters, the bearded Adolfo the tenor and the androgynous Claudio the soprano, and closed his eyes and joined his hands at his pursed lips as if in rageful prayer during the performance of Triste the Contortionist, el negro, who twisted himself into an upside-down wooden cross, so that his arms were his legs and vice-versa and his head wasn't sitting on his shoulders but grew out from under his groin, then his own twenty nails, shiny white and long as spikes pierced his flesh and bit into the cross, which prevented him not a bit from further unshaping himself till he was free and arms were arms and legs were legs and his head above and his feet below, and the tyrant put his hand on the bishop's thigh and tapped it lightly as if to assure him that it was all right, just games and tricks, though I am sure the tyrant knows nothing of opera or of Triste's black magic, and their interest only piqued when Jorge the Ringmaster announced the twins.

"They appeared from the tunnels leading out of one of the bleachers, holding hands and prancing in unison like forgetful gazelles. The people broke into instantaneous applause. The twins wore only a pair of close-fitting dancer tights that stretched down to their knees. They were barefoot. Their torsos were sunburned and smooth except for the tuft of hair around their belly buttons. They each wore a strip of sackcloth as a headband. (Armando Quiñón had told me once that it was part of the fabric of the burnoose their master always wore.) As they reached the center ring and bowed in unison, a gleam of reddish violet light shot out like a beam from inside one of the boy's heads. The tyrant rubbed his eyes with his thumb and index finger and turned to look at the bishop. The bishop pretended to have seen nothing and acknowledged the tyrant's inquisitive look only by returning his own previous gesture. He put his heavy-ringed hand on the tyrant's knee and drummed it placatingly with his long skeleton fingers. The twins took a while before they let go of each other, and when they did separate they bowed to each other like gallant enemies about to do combat. This was the most marvelous thing in their act, why people came (I suspect—no mejor digo, I know, lo sé clarísimo), beyond their obvious talent, the heart-skipping leaps from one trapeze to the other that wasn't there and then it was, caught by a brother's upside-down knee-hanging grip at the last segundito (a collected gasp from the bleachers) and in the same instant let go again, thrown upward into somersaults and twists and twirls, so that now the beam of amethyst light was a spinning halo, because one boy, the glass-eyed one was lighter than the other one and he was usually the one thrown, but beyond all this, the one thing that made them marvellous, lo milagroso that caused them to come from all over to witness, even the tyrant, even the bishop and his four nuns, was their obvious and terrible affection for each other, which manifested its wonderful peccancy in every over-brotherly gaze, every touch, every grip that almost wasn't, every knee interlocked with an elbow or a bare foot clenching another bare foot, handlike as an ape's. That is what they all came to see, that great sin that hung like a blush-colored mist about them, as visible almost as the ring of light around the airborne amethyst-eyed boy's head."

"¿Incesto?" comandante Cruz said. "Between brothers? Did Alicia know?"

"Yes," Carmen said. "She must have known, for at the beginning of that summer she had met with Héctor and their illusive wedding was forever called off, a great relief to doña Adela, Alicia's mother (though she wasn't supposed to know, pero esa vieja lo sabe todo), though her daughter's heart was broken. She made me accompany her that summer (that's really why I too became a tutor) and confided in me about many things. She has never told me what she spoke about with Héctor, and I doubt she will ever tell you, comandante, no matter how close you get."

"They have been close enough to rub bellies already," Barba Roja said nudging his friend.

Comandante Cruz dismissed him: "No hables tonterías."

"That's hardly any of our business anyway," doña Ana said. "No sean metíos, this is a new age of freedom, in politics *and* in love. Down with the old hipócrita morality of the eunuchs of Christ!" She raised both her oak canes and brandished them like swords. The guerrilleros cheered her with their drinks. "Al diablo, if two brothers want to love each other and make love to each other with their eyes, their looks, then so be it. Isn't that why you got rid of the tyrant? Isn't that kind of freedom the purpose of all revolutions?"

Some guerrilleros cheered, some put their drinks down. Carmen grabbed her mother's arms and made her lower her canes. "Mamita, por favor, you shouldn't be getting so excited."

"Digo lo que creo. That is one of the few advantages of being as old and as sick as I am. That I can speak my mind and no one is going to put my head in a guillotine."

"This revolución will never have any use for the guillotine, señora Ana," comandante Cruz said solemnly.

"I hope not, comandante, but even if it does, I will not live to see it. So I am worried for you and for my daughter, not for me. I will not live much longer."

"¡Mamá!"

"I repeat: no need to worry for us, señora Ana."

Barba Roja put his hand on his comrade's empty shoulder. "Basta," he said.

"Tomorrow is the sage of history," doña Ana said.

"Mamá, por favor, enough."

"Go on, Carmen. Go on with your story. Es verdad, I have said enough. And please, comandante, do not pay much attention to me. Soy una vieja loca pal carajo."

"The tyrant had the rope nets pulled out from under the twins," Carmen said. "When they came out for their second performance later that afternoon and they climbed the rope ladders, the rope net was never spread under them. When they jumped on the trapeze an old campesina stood up and cupped her hands to her lips and screamed at them: '¡No! ¡No! ¡Que no hay malla!' Then Jorge the Ringmaster announced in his booming voice, as the twins swung above him, that that's the way the twins wanted it, without a net, for never had they fallen onto a net except to dismount, so what was the use of it. They began their act, hurling themselves from one trapeze to the other, the little puffs of cloud from the chalk in their hands now more visible each time they clasped the bar or each other and their little grunts of effort as they peeled off into the air or as they landed, audible even in the furthest bleachers."

"Where was Armando Quiñón?" doña Ana asked. "Why did he permit it?"

"Because Jorge had not been lying. The twins had asked for the net to be removed."

"Why? To impress the tyrant?"

"No, but to keep him and the ogre glued to their seats, to give Armando Quiñón plenty of time to flee."

"Sí, sí, the tyrant knew," doña Ana said, banging her cane for emphasis.

"Then the drums began to beat," Carmen Canastas said, "and this signaled the finale of their act, what had then become known as the air rumba. I did not think they would dare try it without a net. It involved four trapezes, all swinging in and out into a common point directly above the center ring, the two acrobats crossing each other as they kept the opposite trapeze moving. They met in the middle, in the air, letting go and hurling themselves upward as high as the canvas ceiling, then open-armed, at the zenith of their leap, they approached each other and on the way down they listened to the drums and shook and twisted around each other with such force and speed that before they fell onto the returning trapeze and separated, you could not tell them apart or say who was what, for all you saw was a blurry ball of amethyst light, and for those few seconds (maybe less than seconds) this ball of light seemed to shake to the sounds of the drums, as if it had hips, as if it borrowed its rhythm from the deepest folds of the mountainous earth, then the twins separated and the drums stopped and their act was over. They listened to the applause from their opposite perches and saluted and bowed to each other across the way and you could feel their affection course through the vacant air like an electrical storm. It was the first time they had done the air rumba without a net. They never used a net again that summer.

"That year, after the summer tour, the amethyst-eyed boy disappeared. They were living near Baracoa, in the one-hut bohío of Triste the Contortionist's grandmother. One dawn, in December, Héctor awoke and found his brother gone. He went out with Triste and searched the guava groves where the amethyst-eyed boy liked to sit under the aromatic trees and indulge in his new pastime of smoking Romeo y Julietas, which Triste's abuelita had taught him how to suck.

"No sign of him. They searched the coffee fields, the giant mango trees where he liked to climb and leap from branch to branch, under the white sheets of the tobacco fields where sometimes he went off to snooze. After two days, they called the local sheriff and he chuckled at these gypsies worried that one of their own had gone wandering and disappeared. 'Isn't that what you do best,' he said. 'Roam away from here, away from there, unnoticed? Isn't that your famous curse? Your roaming?' But he promised he would have the Rural Guard alerted. Héctor came to Guantánamo and told Alicia and me of his brother's disappearance, and we accompanied him to Santiago de Cuba to see his mother. She had been checked into an asylum by her own mother. We visited doña Edith there, a freshly painted white turn-of-the-century monastery with many rooms, sparsely furnished. Doña Edith did not recognize Héctor and we did not tell her of the disappearance of her other son. As we were leaving, Héctor kissed her on both cheeks, as she massaged her engorged belly: 'Pues carajo, why haven't you congratulated me. I'm due again any day now. Twins, the doctors say. ¡Hijos del gran diablo!' She laughed. Héctor kissed her again. She was not expecting, but every year, the doctors said, her belly grew for nine months as if she were, then one day she let out whatever phantoms were breeding in there and her belly shrank. She had given birth to three invisible sets of twins, which she cared for and breast-fed as if they really existed. We left her there with all her invisible brood and returned to Guantánamo.

"We went to visit Armando Quiñón the following morning. His cheeks were sunken and his dark eyes pressed into their sockets and he grew a gray unkempt beard, thick as Spanish moss. He wore his baggy suit, but the top was unbuttoned and he wore no belt, so his pants slipped down his hips. He squinted when he opened the door to his studio. At first he looked at us as if he did not recognize any of us, but then he stared hard at Héctor and life seemed to return to him for a mere moment. His eyes shot forward like the lens of a camera. 'Querido,' he said, and caressed the back of Héctor's head. He welcomed us into his studio. The shutters were drawn in the front room and whatever light broke through did so in slats of trembling dust. There were empty tin cans thrown all around and it smelled of rancid pork. When we told him about Héctor's brother, Armando Quiñón broke into a fit of tears. He sat on the floor in one corner of the room and bowed his head and put both his slender hands over his face and continued to sob until we left. He blubbered to Héctor that in the days nearest his destruction, Satan's crimes become the most heinous. 'Salvation must be at hand.' He sounded like Ñaña the Halfwit. He then asked if we had found a body, as if he knew for a fact that the amethyst-eyed boy had been murdered.

"No body was ever found. That Christmas, at the beginning of the circus's winter tour, a gift arrived for Héctor in a small leather pouch—the amethyst eye, washed and polished. Héctor cut a slit into the flesh above his left nipple and stitched the glass eye into the wound, the amethyst facing out. When it became infected, and pus poured out from all around the sewn-in gem like milky tears, he refused to have it removed and suffered through three weeks of fevers and vomiting till his body adopted to his third eye and the pink flesh grew around the edges like a newborn's eyes, and thick black hair around it like lashes. That year, in the latter shows of the winter tour, when the circus reached the outskirts of La Habana again, Jorge the Ringmaster began introducing Héctor as the acrobat with three eyes, and no one knew what he was talking about till they saw the shimmering halo of amethyst light when he was performing the air rumba by himself, using all four trapezes and keeping them all going as if there were two acrobats still and his amethyst-eyed brother had never disappeared. From then on they began to call his act the Lazarus Rumba, because for those few moments he was in the air he showed not just his brother—who was inside him now, his amethyst eye peeking out of Héctor's heart-hole—but all the dead how to come back. In that trembling halo the people in the bleachers would see the mother who died at childbirth just last month, or the husband who was trampled by one of his oxen while working the fields, or the pretty brown-eyed girl who went blind and was taken by the meningitis epidemic, and even the sweetheart who had died long ago during the Spanish Civil War and whose photograph had obstinately sat by the bed slept in by three different husbands, all the dead shaking their hips side by side with the half-naked Héctor as he leaped and twirled from trapeze to trapeze and summoned the dead with his beacon of amethyst light from the fields that border forgetfulness. And to this day, those who know how to best long for a lost loved one go not to the cemetery to kneel by a marble tomb, or to the cathedral to play with beads, but to the gypsy circus, to munch on cotton candy and watch Héctor perform his air dance with the dead, his Lazarus Rumba."

"¡Qué pollo!" doña Ana said. "I can't wait to pass on and shake my hips with that young thing."

"Mamá, no seas bruta!"

"Bruta no. I hope you'll be there, hope you'll all be there. Then you'll see how well this dead mamacita can rumba!"

A Shroud of Papaya Leaves

At dusk, when the bonfire was its most intense, the flames stretching their blue-nailed orange fingers twelve feet in the air, Barba Roja stood at the front door of Armando Quiñón's studio, shoulder to shoulder with comandante Julio César Cruz, their telescopic rifles cocked in front of them and the mute blue rooster Atila perched between them, one talon on each separate shoulder, digging in with his nails like the two comandantes had dug themselves in with their boots. The mob wanted more. It wanted the body. That, Barba Roja could not permit. They had taken all the black and white photographs and the antique oak chest (trampled it to pieces) and the countless wooden frames and even the suicide's trademark linen baggy suits and fed them all to the fire. Bare-torsoed children ran around the perimeter of the flames and sang, and they used emptied upturned rum barrels as drums:

> *Manteca, más manteca,*
> *o este fuego se seca.*

A redheaded yanqui woman, who had been a supporter of la Revolución and abandoned her husband and deserted the naval base a few days prior, when a rebel victory seemed imminent, watched with her wide-eyed freckle-faced children as if looking on at a primitive ritual.

> *Azucar o manteca,*
> *al fuego pal que peca!*

One of the children had a bottle of rum and he drank from it and passed it on to the others. Some drank the rum, some spit it back out at the fire and the flames jumped and hissed at the squirt of liquor. The adults around them laughed and they too spit at the fire.

Barba Roja was disturbed. Even some of his own men were now joining in. But he had a plan. He would wait till the fire died out and then disperse the mob. He would let them enjoy themselves. This gross excitement was the normal process of victory. He would not, however, relinquish Armando Quiñón's body, nor let any harm come to Ñaña the Halfwit, who was now also trapped inside with the cleansed corpse, not even if he had to fight off his own men or use force against the rum-tipsy children.

Things had gotten out of control too easily. Just a few hours before, he had been in the cellar room alone with comandante Cruz. He had sent word to Carmen Canastas with one of his men and she was going to come identify the body and then they were going to take it down and give it a proper burial. As the commander in charge of the victorious rebel troops Barba Roja was now interim mayor, police captain, and fire marshall of Guantánamo. (Although he would appoint someone else to each of these positions soon.) They waited. They sifted through the pictures of the photographer's beloved Héctor, in many poses and at many ages, here hanging by his legs from a tree branch beside the gross creature that was their maestro, naked, his lips parted into an almost audible sigh and his eyes closed and his hair much longer then, dangling below his head in thick curls like an indian headdress woven from the coarse wool ringlets of black sheep, and other pictures as he grew older and his upper body began to broaden and take on the contours of a man, and almost always in the pictures, Héctor wore nothing, as if in this life he had never known such displeasures as the toe-clamp of wrong-sized shoes or the hangrope of a shirt's top button, or the thousand-mosquito-bite itchiness of a wool sweater and had simply gone about as he was made, never embarrassed by a moment of it. And there were just as many pictures of the amethyst-eyed boy, though he was obviously more hesitant about discarding his clothes and more wary of the shadow of their maestro, which was cast in every picture, obvious as the light, even the ones where he was not there, outside the frame, or further even, outside of their lives, before he had turned up and after he had vanished. As in the scoop of the boy's eye—the picture that Armando Quiñón somehow took in the hospital, the one where it looks as if the eye had been dug out by a spoon with fangs—in the shadows of that wound, Barba Roja clearly saw the puffy-chin profile of their maestro, the great melonball head and the bulbous nose etched in the gray and black and blacker of the boy's eye socket; and in the blood the boy had left behind, Barba Roja saw the shape of the white-winged horseflies that would infest the house many years later, as if their maestro had not come from the outside world at all, but had always been in them and at a certain point in their lives had been given the freedom to exist.

Both men saw the obvious worth of the photographs, not just as records of lives lived, but as telling pieces of art. Even prophecy, Barba Roja insisted as he began to arrange the pictures and realized how the shadowlands of these black and white frozen images told time backwards and forwards and his esteem for the gaunt naked man hanging behind him grew by the minute. He looked at the last picture Armando Quiñón had taken of the rebels descending from the mountains that morning, and he stared hard and squinted his eyes with the picture at arm's length and flipped it slowly all the way around, though he remained blind to the script of time to come. The events that were forecoming that night would tell him more than any picture could.

There was a boot-knock at the trapdoor. Barba Roja climbed the wobbly wooden stairs slowly and threw the door upward with a push of his left arm, his right hand on the butt of his pistol. It was the town's deposed chief of police. He backed away, both his hands sticking out to show that he was unarmed as he had been when he surrendered to the rebels that morning. Except now, he wore a crisp uniform, the kind officers wear to parades or before they shoot themselves in the temple, and his mustache was waxed and shaped and his hair slicked back. A few of the townspeople stood behind him, having made their way into the front of the studio.

"With all respects, comandante," the former chief of police said to Barba Roja, "the people want to see el muerto. There is a whole crowd outside."

"Is Carmen Canastas out there? Tell her I need to see her."

"I do not see your . . . la señorita Canastas. But there's a whole mess of other curious folks outside, comandante, and they want to see the body, o mejor dicho, they actually want the body. You see the man hanging down there was a devotee of Satan, one of the women folk in our town actually saw him conversing with one of the fallen angels, and ritual says his body must be burned to dust so that we may rid ourselves of his sins. With all respect, comandante, for you are an intelligent man, and you well know how revoluciones, no matter how worthy, as yours, sin duda ninguna, is worthy, can never, o mejor dicho, should never change the holy rites of the people. They have started a bonfire. They demand the body of the photographer, so that his devil-flesh will never infect the earth that feeds us."

"And you were the chief of police in this town?" Barba Roja said. "Pobre gente." He heard the drums and the chanting outside. He stepped back down the stairs and without saying a word motioned with his hand for comandante Cruz to take down Armando Quiñón's body. The former chief of police got down on his knees and poked his head into the cellar room, the blood running down to his head and expanding the veins that stretched on his brow, thick as tentacles.

"It's a suicide, comandante, *and* the man was denounced as a pederast. His body must not contaminate the earth, else we all be poisoned with the filth of his sins."

"¿No me digas? You have sins of your own to worry about. And I am afraid that your penance has been much too brief. For your sake, I hope that this man's death was a suicide. There will be an investigation. So go out and tell the people that they cannot and that they will not have the body. Clear the way for us. We are removing it from here. And pray on your head, viejo, that no harm comes to any of us or to this body as we are taking it out, lest you suffer the same fate as this wretched soul."

"Comandante, por el amor de Dios, you cannot hold me responsible for the actions of that mob out there. Están revueltos, nothing and no one will sway them for their purpose."

"Come dije ya, viejo, pray that you can. . . . And take off that silly costume."

Barba Roja slammed shut the trapdoor.

Comandante Julio César Cruz had taken off his olive jacket and tied it around the body of the suicide, or alleged suicide, as Barba Roja told him to refer to the corpse. The blue rooster Atila was perched on the corpse's sunken chest, attempting again to crow, but all he could manage was a gurgly wheeze. Comandante Cruz consoled him and threw the body of the photographer over his right shoulder and perched the rooster on his left, where the flesh was uncallused (the rooster always traveled on the right shoulder, where Armando Quiñón's body now hung, it seeming disrespectful to the comandante to carry a dead man on his left) so he was uncomfortable at first, shifting and digging in with his talons till he cut past the undershirt and into flesh and blood drooled down his master's back and down his master's arm and stained the band of his Swiss watch and climbed on one of the veins in the back of his hand and rode it down to his ring finger and split at the nail and met again at the tip and dripped on the concrete floor and continued to drip in measured time all that day, for the corpse stayed on the right shoulder and the rooster on the left digging into an unfamiliar roost, so that many years later, after comandante Julio César Cruz's own death, after Barba Roja had forgotten that he was once a rebel and had once loved Carmen Canastas and fled in his own air force jet to Miami, any one in the town who was not blind could show you, step by step, where the two men had gone that day with the body of the photographer. The blood of comandante Julio César Cruz, falling with the rhythm of an English poem from his ring finger, every five or six steps, marked the trail of their journey. And after his death, when this or that revolutionary committee tried to wipe out all the traces of his rebel existence, and they repaved all of Perdido Street (because that was the longest part of the journey with the body, to the cemetery and to Sara Zimmerman's garden), covering the blood spots with rocky sand and cement and fresh tar, only to find less than a week later that spots had reappeared, spreading open like ink on tissue paper, they accused his widow and her group of painting the spots on the street. They repaved again with heavier sand and two more layers of cement and the blackest coal tar from Wales and left guards at every corner from the house with the white-winged horsefly shingles to the above-ground cemetery near the Jaibo river, to no avail, for the spots reappeared again, grown to the size and shape of sunburst medallions, as if the spots had splashed down from many miles above the earth. This time they could not blame the widow, so they blamed the guards and had them all arrested and charged with counterrevolutionary activities. They repaved Perdido Street again and again with so many layers of sand and cement and tar that eventually passersby had to climb *up* on Perdido Street from the sidewalk and mockers of the revolutionary committees began to refer to the street as Perdido Hill. All again to no avail, for the blood that dripped from comandante Julio César Cruz's ring finger as he carried the body of Armando Quiñón on the day of his alleged suicide, the same day the rebels had proclaimed their victory to the world, is still seen there, and so many pilgrims still follow the path up and down Perdido Hill that it has become famous for its outlaw vendors at every corner (where the guards had once stood), selling everything from black market sugar and coffee beans to clusters of the small white flowers called baby's breath that the pilgrims scatter on the street because they were said to be a favorite of the photographer and a small cluster of them in a hand-blown vase was the only living thing found in his studio on the day of his alleged suicide.

Barba Roja took the flowers as he led the way out of Armando Quiñón's studio and held them pressed to his solar plexus and that's why Ñaña the Halfwit later told them her story. She caught up with the two rebel comandantes and the corpse and the rooster after they had made it unharmed past the mob outside, after they had passed by the house of Carmen Canastas, whose mother had been suddenly struck by a fever in whose shadows she saw the three-eyed acrobat, and she became enamored with the long bones of his feet and the shape of his hips and the curves of his shoulders and the breath of his dream in the flutter of his eyes, as he danced around her and with his hips summoned her from this earth. Together, they said a prayer for doña Ana and carried the photographer's body away from there to the house with the white-winged horsefly shingles on Perdido Street.

Ñaña the Halfwit was waiting for them there. Her cheeks were painted deep cherry, like a ceramic doll, her eyelids morning blue and she wore a papier maché wedding dress she had constructed for herself out of old newspapers soaked in cane juice. She liked it because it was different, not white but gray and yellow and runny black. Her slippers were made from old tin cans. She had polished them and they glittered. When she saw the cluster of baby's breath and the suicide with the olive skirt hanging on comandante Julio César Cruz's right shoulder, she broke into her story, following the two men and the corpse and the rooster towards the cemetery.

"You will not bury him!" she called to them, the hem of her paper dress splitting and revealing the lesions on her patchy-haired leg. "Don't bother going to Campo Santo. His bones will sing till the end of time. It is written. His father was a poor laborer in the fields, un machetero. His mother was devout. ¡Pero coño!, she could not do without it for one night. So soon they had eighteen children, and no matter how hard the man worked, he could not feed his family. His wife blamed him and screamed at him when he got home, so tired from swinging his machete that he could not lift his arms; though later at night she made up with him and kissed his swollen feet and got what she needed. The man cried with his sons and daughters for he was as hungry and as weary as they were. One day, he came home from the cane fields and there was a roast at the table and it smelled like lamb. The man screamed at his wife. He asked her where she had gotten the money for such an expensive meal and he spit at her and called her putísima and desgraciada. She assured him all this was not so and said she would prove it was not so later in the bedroom. And she did. Meanwhile, the man sat and ate with his children. The meat was sweet and melted in their mouths, though when they offered the mother some, she said she had already eaten. Every so often, from then on, there was meat on the table that smelled like lamb and melted in their mouths."

Ñaña the Halfwit's feet hurt and she fell behind the two comandantes and their corpse and their rooster, all who seemed untouched by her story: "Aguanten, carajo. Listen! Pues soon the machetero noticed some of his children were missing. He questioned his wife. She said they were gone to visit their grandmother in the capital and the man believed her because he wanted to believe her. More meat was served. More children were missing. The wife glared at the husband when he ate and said she had already eaten and sent more of his children to the capital. One night, while crossing a field of flowers after sixteen hours of cane cutting, the man heard a song in the cluster of the flowers that were colored like doves and shaped like miniscule suns. Florecitas como ésas, comandante. He recognized the voices of his missing children chanting all at once:

> *Mamacita kills us,*
> *Papacito eats us,*
> *and our bones are food for flowers.*

He ran home and beat his wife with the blunt end of his machete in front of his remaining offspring, beat her till she was dead, and cut her up and fed her flesh to the wild hogs and charred her remains at the pit. And for the sins of the mother and the father all the remaining children were cursed and they must never lie on holy ground. So don't bother. Put him down and let the birds of death feast. It is his fate. Wait! Wait! ¡Espérenme, coño!"

The inside of her tin slippers now cut at the side of her feet and the two comandantes with the corpse and the rooster far outpaced her, out of hearing range, so she murmured the last part of the story to no one. She could not take off her shoes; they were essential to the beauty of the outfit; but she stopped talking and concentrated hard on catching up with them, clanking along bow-legged to ease the bite of her slippers. By the time she caught up, the two comandantes with the corpse and the rooster were on their way back from the front gate of the cemetery, having been forbidden entrance by Plácido Flores, the undertaker with skin like a workhorse's hide.

"Pero, comandante," Ñaña the Halfwit said to Barba Roja, not meaning to mock, "you conquered this town, it is yours to rule."

"Muchachona," Barba Roja spoke to her for the first time, "I cannot kill one man for the sake of burying another, and that is what I would be forced to do."

"Then you understand. It was written that you would. Pero vengan, I will bring you to someone who will help you."

Tired and unwilling to return to Armando Quiñón's studio and face the mob, the two comandantes followed Ñaña the Halfwit back past the house with the white-winged horsefly shingles, all the way to the opposite end of Perdido Street to the papaya gardens of the Jewess doctor, Sara Zimmerman. She came out to greet them, her hands smeared with the blood juice from the pomegranate she was picking at. She was a dwarfish woman, a whole head shorter than Ñaña the Halfwit, with fair skin stained all over with mud-colored spots shaped like amoebas. Her hair was faded red and it was short, unkempt, and receded halfway back her skull. She wore no jewelry except for a band of seven gold rings on her marriage finger, extending past her knuckle all the way up to her fingernail so that the finger stuck out and she could not bend it. She wore a white doctor's smock and rope-soled sandals. The nails of her feet were discolored and eaten away with fungus. She kissed Ñaña the Halfwit on the crown of her head and commended her on her beautiful dress that was now coming apart at the top, revealing her bone-marked breasts. Sara Zimmerman then approached comandante Julio César Cruz and grabbed the cross of the ebony rosary that was hanging around his neck and tugged at it slightly and then kissed the crucifix and kissed the comandante on the

ball of his right shoulder and the corpse on the sole of its bare left foot and
Barba Roja on the palm of his hand. Only the rooster she did not kiss.

"Buenas," she said. "I have been expecting you. Ñaña said that she
would bring you." The two comandantes stared in surprise at Ñaña the
Halfwit and Sara Zimmerman broke into a fit of laughter and because she
wore quality dentures she looked much younger, though she seemed disturbed by her merriment and covered her mouth and apologized, and is if
in conciliation, offered them some of her pomegranate. When the two comandantes declined she laughed again, covering her glamorous teeth with
her stained hands and apologizing all the while. "I don't mean to disre-
spect el muerto," she said between chortles. "Bring him in. I will prepare
him."

"Prepare him for what?"

"For his flight from this world. Vengan." She opened the wrought-iron
gates to her gardens and pinched herself on both cheeks as if to suppress
any further attacks of laughter.

"She looks ill," Barba Roja whispered to Ñaña the Halfwit.

"En la casa del herrero," Ñaña the Halfwit answered, loud enough for
Sara Zimmerman to hear, "cuchillos de palo."

Within grew papaya trees in every season, and of every type, as if her
gardens were a little world unto itself: in the larger south end, three-story
stalks with giant loose-wristed seven-fingered leaves and fruit like elephant testicles; in the north section tinier parasol trees with fruit like
grapes; in the west side trees with leaves gold and red and orange as if they
had filched the light of many a dusk; and in the east a field of black mountain soil with spindle shoots just breaking to the surface in groups of six,
like the legs of buried grasshoppers. In the center of the gardens was a
mossy fountain, at whose edge Sara Zimmerman asked comandante Julio
César Cruz to lay down the body of Armando Quiñón, though when he
put it down the corpse remained frozen in the position it had been
drooped over the comandante's shoulder, so it sat with his arms and his
torso stretching down to his toes like a yogi. Sara Zimmerman undid his
olive skirt and returned with a basket of leaves from the south end of the
gardens and a pail of milky fluid. With the juice, she washed the body and
then dunked the giant leaves in the pail and, beginning with the feet,
wrapped Armando Quiñón's body in them. Like an expert masseur, the
green-fingered leaves took hold of the stiff toes and immediately loosened
them, so that they went slack and it seemed that the blood had begun to
course again. Patiently, she wrapped Armando Quiñón's entire body and
while doing it told them about the sadness of her relentless laughter.

She was a Pole. She had had six brothers, all who perished in concentration camps along with her parents and most of her family. She recited
her brother's names by counting the six gold rings of her wedding finger.
Luckily, a prescient and politically zealous aunt smuggled Sara Zimmer-

man to a kibbutz in Palestine before the Nazi monsters began the work of undoing their world. She became a woman in the holy land. She fell in love and married a poet named Emu. She touched the last gold ring on her finger when she said his name. It was her wedding band. They had been happy. Emu's great-great-grandmother taught her the art of healing. She was a holy woman and had lived in the land for more than a century and a half, a descendant of the rabbis driven from Spain. In her room, she carried on long conversations with the prophet Elijah that would last till dawn. She drank plum wine with him. Then, it was said, the prophet made love to the old woman and whispered in her ear the secrets of nature and disappeared. From her room, passing her hand over Emu's back, Sara Zimmerman could hear the torrential horse-hose gush of the prophet Elijah's urine in the outhouse. He was a vulgar and mean old man, Sara had heard, who had once set a bear on two boys who made fun of his baldness. "Qué va, I am not a real doctor," Sara Zimmerman said, "my skills are from a more ancient science."

At about the same time she became pregnant, Sara Zimmerman was struck with malaria. She was ill for many weeks. The girl was born with only one leg and three eyes—though none of them could see—and she could barely breathe for she had lungs the size of a bird's. They named her Rachel and she only lived into her third week. Emu died that same month of grief.

"In our time it is said you cannot die of such things." Sara Zimmerman touched her last ring again and could not help but laugh. "He had bought wedding rings for all my dead brothers, because he was sure that one day I would find them and they would marry his sisters and his cousins. The day we buried Emu I became infected with the laughing sickness. The doctors in Jerusalem said it was from a lesion I had suffered in the right part of my brain during the highest fevers of the malaria. The holy woman said it was the spirit of her great-great-grandson fighting against my sorrow and forcing me to laugh. I believe *her*. I am still infected with the laughing sickness . . . but don't worry I don't think it is contagious."

Sara Zimmerman then laughed. As she finished wrapping Armando Quiñón's body, she said that she had fled to Cuba because after the state of Israel was finally established, there was too much joy in the streets, and she could not stand the noise of the rejoicing and the noise of her laughter. It made her grief intolerable. Cuba was far away and it was romantic and she had read in a story once that Cubans were the most skilled laughers in the world, so maybe someone there would show her how to master her laughter. She began to grow papayas to sustain herself, but found that in the milky juice of their stems lay hidden many of the secrets that the prophet Elijah had discussed with the old holy woman. Sara Zimmerman said that the juice was so rich with the life-giving minerals of the land that it cured everything from hepatitis to baldness—though apparently

not her own, nor the prophet Elijah's. Armando Quiñón's body had softened and it was now completely wrapped in the giant wet papaya leaves so
that it looked like a fish ready to roast.

"My garden has also provided many a joy for the children of this
town." She pointed out the holes in many of the chameleon-horny but
soft-stemmed papaya trunks. "When they are finding out about being
men, they hop the gate after midnight (when they think I am asleep) and
cut holes into the trees and make them the receptacles of all their desires.
At first I tried to stop them, but I found that far from being damaged, the
violated trees seemed to prosper and deliver sweeter fruit. Now rarely a
night goes by when I don't hear the caterwauling of the neighborhood's
not-yet-men." Sara Zimmerman laughed—but not it seemed from her
laughing sickness. She knew some of the holes were too high up on the
stem and too thick and deep to have been made by any boy.

"I knew him," Sara Zimmerman said. "I have seen him in this garden
before. Sometimes . . . mostly . . . he just came to watch, to take pictures
with his little camarita. Now take him back to his home and the angels of
Tobias will guide him away from all our ills."

They thanked Sara Zimmerman—although they weren't sure exactly
what it was she had done—and comandante Julio César Cruz carefully
placed the softened and warmed body over his shoulder and held to it, for
it was slippery and felt alive. Atila opened his blue wings and balanced
himself on the other shoulder, again drawing blood, but this time on purpose, as if in revenge, for his master had not asked Sara Zimmerman to
cure his muteness.

Ñaña the Halfwit led them back to Armando Quiñón's studio and
through the growing mob, acting as a shield for the two comandantes
with the corpse and the rooster, taking on the mob's first insults. Two
sparks from the bonfire on Narciso López Street, willful as hungry fleas,
hopped onto the tail of her papier maché wedding dress and set it afire. As
Barba Roja stomped out the flames, and Ñaña the Halfwit, her head
turned, watched—more amazed than frightened, as if her predictions of
the apocalypse, of the earth catching fire from underneath, had come to
be—the bottom half of the disintegrating dress tore off, completely exposing her hairy violet-lesioned legs and the thick tangled mound of her
sex from where she had hung seven tiny red Christmas tree ornaments.

"She has balls," the boys in the mob screamed, reaching for her. "¡Ñaña
la loca tiene siete cojonecitos rojos!" These same boys grew scared when
they saw that she was willing to give herself to them, thrusting her hips
forward and back so that the Christmas tree ornaments clinked against
each other, signaling like wedding bells to other joys, till Barba Roja
grabbed her and carried her—also over his shoulder—into Armando
Quiñón's studio.

The studio and the cellar had been emptied of everything—even the artist's expensive cameras had been used as fire food—and, with the developing chemicals, the bonfire thrived. Barba Roja felt a wave of grief quickly gel into anger at losing the picture of him and his men descending from the mountains, but he could not reprimand the guerrilleros that he had left in charge (they were celebrating, it was their day of victory). For three hours he and comandante Julio César Cruz and Atila stood on guard at the front door of the studio on Narciso López Street. It was long past dark and most of the mob, along with the children and many of Barba Roja's own men, was drunk. So perhaps it wasn't a north wind (as many later recounted) that began to whirl and arouse the flames, not the wind at all that picked up the child—a heavy boy of thirteen or more, who had fought and survived in the mountains (as if the wind had more arms and was more wicked than Batista's Rural Guard), who was for a moment a kid again and was prancing and singing of Ñaña the Halfwit's seven red balls—and threw him into the bonfire. The flames ceased their twirl dances and seized the boy with their thousand tongues that changed colors as they tasted him. What was orange was now sharp crimson and what was blue a fierce violet.

The two comandantes jumped at once from their post at the door, Atila the rooster stitching them together by their shoulders, and ran in unison towards the commotion. Barba Roja put down his rifle and broke free from Atila's left talon and threw himself into the fire, bringing out the burning boy in a bearhug and smothering him on the ground with his own body. For a moment the revelries continued, the singing, the banging on the rum-barrel drums, and the dancing and the drinking, as if this accident was in no way going to deter the mob from its purpose, from burning him that deserved to be burned, the pederast, the suicide, to whose long tally of sins would later be added (seeing you could not very well blame the wind) the death of this boy. Once the fire on the boy was out, Barba Roja stood up and backed away. He could not feel his own burns, many of which were serious, for he saw the child's bald black skull. The eyelids were missing and the lips were melted together in a flat pout. Barba Roja picked up his rifle and fired it in the air, once, twice, and again till there was silence, and the bonfire, as if in penance (or satiated), began to quiver and undo itself. It was then that they heard the glass break. Though it wasn't the usual noise of glass breaking, no intimation of violence in the sound. It was the melody, they imagined later, of a heavy snowfall, of the clumpy crystally flakes crumbling one on top of the other.

Still ignoring his burns, Barba Roja traced the sound to the cellar of Armando Quiñón's studio. He reappeared cradling the half-dressed Ñaña the Halfwit as she played with her Christmas ornaments and told him how Armando Quiñón's papaya-leaf embalmed body had turned into a flock of green butterflies and with their many winged caresses seduced the black glass of the window near the ceiling to give way and escaped.

"Where is the body?" Barba Roja kept repeating, his right cheek already blistering.

"Gone, gone now with the angels of Tobias!" Ñaña the Halfwit answered.

As they cured his burns later that night, Barba Roja assured himself that during the disturbance someone had snuck into Armando Quiñón's studio, perhaps the same men that had murdered him, stolen the body, and threatened Ñaña the Halfwit, who concocted the ludicrous tale of the butterflies in order to appease her fears. Such things only happen in stories, a cliché of unimaginative novelists. That's where she got it from. (Ñaña the Halfwit was known to be an avid reader, and she collected torn discarded books and put different works together, one story seamlessly ending another.) They murdered the photographer, Barba Roja said. They murdered the boy. He firmly held to this version, even after comandante Julio César Cruz recounted to him, while visiting him at the hospital, how some days after they had buried the scorched boy in a pauper's cemetery outside the city and placed a heavy boulder as a tombstone over the grave, a flock of butterflies in all shades of green—like the olive and the avocado, like a meadow or a sea, like hope and envy—descended on the boulder and covered it, trying to lift it. Atila, inspired by their effort, regained his magnificent operatic voice, and forced his master to take him to that far-away cemetery every Wednesday at dawn, to fuel his inner strength from watching those butterflies that might or might not have been the spirit of Armando Quiñón, relentlessly attempt to do the undoable, to lift the set-in boulder and take the sacrificed boy with them, and in failing day in and day out became enamored with failure, and the sunlight scorched their wings into the boulder and blended them one into the other till no movement was discernible and it seemed that the boulder was covered merely by moss.

And though through his bandaged lips Barba Roja called him a dreamer, and warned him that such dreams and their dreamers are dangerous to la Revolución, comandante Julio César Cruz said that the suicidal butterflies had reminded his rooster, who would soon be sixty, of the fairy tale days of his youth.

FIVE

Atila and His Resurrected

As the deer pants for streams of water, as the saint for rectitude, as the drunk for wine, as the demon for tortuousness . . . as the cock for hens (or, as we shall see, for its own like), so we yearn for the grace of a savior. And here comes he, his coral comb long as a horse's mane, rested to the left, strutting and posing beyond his own will, but no pansy-nancy he, no, for the dames quiver.

Who? Who will be chosen today?

"¡Atila!"—a voice resounding in its clammy and guttural nakedness. "¡Atila! ¡Venga! ¡Venga! It's not what you think."

What does a cock think? For one, that the time has come again to please the madre-mistress. For another, that he's not in the mood. Wasn't it just yesterday? Or the day before? Has she grown that love-hungry? I must be good.

How good? To this lover friction often proves a primitive, outmoded form of arousal. Melody, music, chico. Es la honda del futuro. Orgies in concert halls!

So, Atila, you, once the bluest-feathered of all cocks, with a tail of rain-bow blues, like the beaches in Varadero, mount the rosy dimply belly of your amorphously reclined madre-mistress and you crow, timidly at first, for it is late afternoon and cocks, even one as infidel as you, have a dog-matic sense of time and the habits it enforces; but the mound on which you are poised flutters with minute delight, so you crow a bit louder, chal-lenging the dying sun, though it will pay no attention to heretics like you and continue to die; still you crow louder, longer, enthused by the convic-tion that east is now west and west east, your song makes it so; and the belly underneath you begins to tremble with pleasure—what can explain these rumbling folds of flushed flesh? what does your song do? where does it go? is it that you now see your song, Atila, as if in a painting, stretch-ing forth in airy skydyed banners from your beak? featherlike, they tickle the roundness of your madre-mistress, floating in the air, no, swimming rather, for they have a purpose, however slowly, they are heading to that somewhere where their tickle is even better received, that unique pleasure vessel bound to break and break, there to that eternally inchoate wee-wee

whose very raison d'être is to be tickled, there, the aeolian banners of your
song head; but now you sue for privacy, your gossamer banners cover the
entire painting and as they thicken, one behind the other, we are left only
with shadows of shadows; still, even in our adumbral ignorance we can
guess what's going on (taking an old fool's advice we see with our ears),
and your song puffs us with a giddy enlightenment, bringing us, like your
madre-mistress, under your spell; we too are now round-bellied and su-
pine, and . . . and . . . cosquillitas, ay sí, ay Atila sí, ay mi querido trum-
petero, now we too have rose petals strewn in our hair like the girls from
Andalusia, qué bárbaro, qué monstruo, qué rico, sícoño, sísícoño, sísísí!

   "Atila, no, not that, not now. ¡Salga de aquí! I just bathed! Get off me
you dirty elf!" Elfish in all things but in his will to please, Atila does not
get off his freshly-bathed, starchily dressed, perfume-laden mistress.
"Now look what you've done, you've torn my dress, you horny weather
vane. Get off me! Save your energy. For today you will test the true power
of your art. But not on me! Off! Vaya, vaya, off! It must be so simple for
you to arouse the living, for we the living are fraught with ticklish parts,
even the most somber one of us is full of funny bones, delighted with
cosquillitas. But can you stir the dead, Atila? Does your magic go that far?"

   What does a cock now think? One, she has lost it. Se jodió la vieja. My
madre-mistress has gone cuckoo. In fact, I can hear her marbles spilling
one by one from the hole in her temple; and I can see the bats entering,
through that same hole, into her belfry.

   What else does a cock think? What if she's serious? What does she
know? What if she's sane as death itself?

   "Can you quicken the dead, Atila? Is your song that good?" But hasn't
Atila already quickened the dead? Is the madre-mistress playing dumb?
Or do animals not count?

Elena Mulé, an Egyptian with chartreuse eyes and skin clay-tinted by the
artless light of her birthland, owned a finca (a tiny acre-and-a-half rectan-
gle of rock and sand and dirt actually, willed to her by the old woman who
had adopted her) near the town of Holguín, in the province of Oriente.
There, she raised her infamous flock of blue-feather fighting roosters,
which she sold to gamblers for prices so outrageous that it would take
them two or three years of heavy betting to recoup, for prices that, had the
soil of her land been mountain-rich, so full of minerals and spirits that it
would have been harmless to eat it (as she had once done as a girl after the
voyage from her land), it would have taken the sale of a whole year's harvest (coffee beans and zapotes and mangoes and nísperos and cabbages) to
equal it. Though it was worth it, for Elena Mulé's blue roosters were the
best fighters on the Island. So much so, that when by chance two of them
were pitted against each other, no one laid down apuestos. No one had the

patience or the strength to watch the entire match. The blue roosters would fight for hours, sometimes into dawn and through the almuerzo and the siesta hours and into the following night. It got to be that in order to speed things up, when two of Elena Mulé's cocks happened to meet, the owners had to tie them up by their puffed-out breasts to a wooden stake, which they would drive into the ground so that the roosters would be beak to beak and unable to duck away from each other's talon-swipes. This still didn't speed things up enough, so owners got to adjusting tiny unseen blades—navajitas—on their rooster's talons; but Elena Mulé had raised them under such a strict code of chivalry that the blue cock would as soon bite off whatever appendage the blade was fixed to as swing it at an opponent. Eventually the board of regulations for the Island's cockfights outlawed any match involving two or more of Elena Mulé's blue roosters. The gamblers, being what they are, then took to dying their prized roosters, partly to avoid this regulation, but also to hustle other owners, who soon grew so fearful of any of Elena Mulé's cocks that they refused to schedule matches against them. The chemicals in the dye killed hundreds of roosters from toxicosis. When Elena Mulé found out about this she shut down her business, and she had plenty of money left over from her sales, neatly ordered in a boxy leather suitcase, to live out the rest of her days.

At about this time, a few years after the turn of the twentieth century, what proved to be her longest-living rooster was hatched. She named the puff of blue smoke chickball Atila, after the king of the Huns, the scourge of the gods, for she felt that the coming hundred years would need such a character. Atila did not live up to his barbarous namesake until his twentieth year. Careful not to plant ever again in her roosters' hearts the seed of violence, Elena Mulé raised them as aesthetes. As chicks, she set them on the pianola and sang them arias from all the great operas, avoiding the more furious works, especially the one that was all the rage in Europe then, *Tosca*. As youngsters, she read to them from the lyric poets, emphasizing the most tender verses of José Martí. And she taught them how to peck at corn and gargle water in such a manner that they would not seem like animals at all, and they dined at the kitchen table with her, each rooster with his own hand-painted china. She even taught them how to properly seduce the white-feathered ladies of the henhouse (who indeed suffered from the prejudice of the times and were taught no manners, thus remaining hens, animals), so that even at the time of coupling there would not be a hint of aggression (except that some of the more cackle-free white-feathered ladies made up with their noise what the blue roosters lacked in brute force).

This all worked well enough till Paco Fortunato was hatched. He was a distant cousin of Atila, and Elena Mulé named him so because the luck of the genes had furnished him with an unrenowned beauty. Whereas the feathers on Atila's tail were the five different hues of the waters at Varadero Beach, the feathers on Paco Fortunato's tail were seven-colored, of all the seas on the earth; whereas the down on Atila's belly was soft as cotton, the down on Paco Fortunato's underside seemed to have been recently woven by a battalion of silkworms; whereas Atila was broad-breasted and the way his coral comb hung to the left gave him a princely playboyish air, when Paco Fortunato passed by, gorgeous even to the nails in his talons, which Elena Mulé trimmed and polished every other day, Atila stooped like a beggar; and whereas Atila could wake the whole town of Holguín, many miles away, with his sublime crow, Paco Fortunato, when he was in the mood (for the beautiful hunk of a cock was by nature a vagabond and would often not awake till two or three in the afternoon), could be heard hundreds of miles away, by the yanquis at the naval base in Guantánamo and by the Virgin herself at El Cobre. So what happened was fated to happen, for Atila had been king of the finca for too long and certainly someone named after the scourge of the gods would not be usurped so easily.

After Paco Fortunato came of age to perform sexually, the white-feathered ladies of the henhouse paid little attention to anybody else. And why should they be blamed for desiring Paco Fortunato only and utmost (even if his performance wasn't all that his looks promised)? Who has never been blinded by the glare of the beautiful? Dare anyone cast away the first glance? It was too much for Atila to bear. Or was he too lured by the ruffle of the seven-seas tail? Was he . . . dare we say it? Was the scourge of the gods a bugarrón? It had been over six weeks since the white-feathered ladies had even allowed Atila entrance into the henhouse, much longer since any of them had allowed him anything more than a cordial, *Buenas*. So named after a barbarian, Atila became one. One evening after having dined at Elena Mulé's table and having sat through a recording of his favorite Verdi opera, which Elena Mulé played in her brand-new Edison cylinder, Atila, goatish beyond reason and inspired by the monstrous music he had just heard (an overwrought early Verdi work based on—you guessed it!), hid in the hole of the spearback rat not far from the henhouse and waited for Paco Fortunato to exit, as usual haggard from pleasing so many. When he did, Atila opened wide his once-bluest wings and darted from the spearback rat's hole and leaped on Paco Fortunato's back, doing to him what he had not done to any of the white-feathered ladies in over a year. Not surprisingly, Paco Fortunato did not put up much of a fight. He almost seemed to enjoy the whole business, now and then fanning his seven-seas tail as if asking for more. As he went into him a fourth time, Atila knew why Paco Fortunato's performances with the white-feathered ladies were never top-notch. *This* was his forte. Paco Fortunato, señores y señoras, was a marica!

The following morning, nevertheless, on the exact spot where he had been violated, Paco Fortunato died of shame, his seven-seas tail covering his corpse like a shroud. Elena Mulé left the body untouched, thinking that as it decomposed and if the sun hit it just right, it would turn into a beautiful tropical flower that she would name *siete afortunadas azulitas.* But to Atila and his madre-mistress's dismay, Paco Fortunato's beauty never decomposed. Atila passed by the corpse every day and lifted the seven-seas tail, hoping that maggots had begun to burrow into the flesh, but every day he was confronted with his cousin's offending beauty that would not fade, and thus Atila shook his head and his coral comb flopped from his left to his right and to his left again, and he muttered to himself in the language of cocks: "Coño, hijo de la gran puta, qué belleza." The white-feathered ladies made pilgrimages from the henhouse—risking their lives, leaving themselves open to attacks from the spearback rat— just to lift the seven-seas shroud and see their murdered lover and sigh as if all the joy and glory of life had been stolen from them too soon. Atila, in vain, tried to show them Paco Fortunato's true nature by bending over and fanning open his own tail and shaking it as Paco Fortunato had done his last night. But even though some haughty Cubans might argue this fact, the five shades of blue of the waters at Varadero Beach are no match against the seven blues of the seven seas, and every white-feathered lady, untutored as they were, knew that.

One evening, while Elena Mulé was playing her recording of various arias sung by Marioneta Alonso, then Cuba's greatest soprano, famous not only for her voice but for two other peculiarities (she was as bald as Queen Elizabeth and blind as Faith), Atila was touched by her rendition of "Habanera" from Bizet's *Carmen.* And he sang along. The music confronted and softened his spirit and he began to forgive Paco Fortunato for being more beautiful than he. He sang over the seven-seas corpse—alone, for it was dark and the spearback rat ruled the night—words in a language that he did not know but that sounded so appropriate. His voice came out of him in quadruple puffs of steam that turned to mist and fell on Paco Fortunato and woke him from his shame-ridden slumber.

Though Atila later abandoned him in an unforgivable act of cowardice, Paco Fortunato was Atila's first and favorite resurrected, perhaps because he was also much more than that. From that first day of his second life Paco Fortunato was as faithful and loyal to Atila as any bride of Christ is to her vows, and he shook his gorgeous seven-seas tail for him and only for him, forsaking forever the distraught white-feathered ladies. Atila did not take well to this at first. Too suffocating, he thought, too smothering. But who can resist for long the talent of a seven-seas tail? How often can one turn his face from such ultimate and vulgar beauty? And, really, why? Atila too eventually forgot about the white-feathered ladies, till one day the spearback rat broke into the henhouse and did away with them forever, leaving Elena Mulé as the only lady left to tickle and please, which (when he could pull himself away from the seven-seas tail)

Atila did, with his voice that topped the voice of any human, even the great, bald blind soprano Marioneta Alonso.

So now, six years later, what are you asking?

"Can you quicken the dead, Atila? Is your song that good?"

What? Are you blind, mi madre-mistress? Do you not see this hunk of a cock, who once was dead and now is living, this seven-seas-tail beauty fawning over me, his life devoted to me when he can have any feathered or non-feathered beast in the animal kingdom, male or female? And you, you mi madre-mistress, whom I am as devoted to as this one is to me, whom I have marched to peaks of ecstasy with my feathery tenor one night, with my tumescent baritone the other, like no manflesh ever will. Coño, le ronca, do you have to ask?

Show me, show me the way and I'll show you what my song will dare.

Elena Mulé, with her blue rooster in a cane reed cage, traveled overnight from the town of Holguín to the town of Bayamo, where a week before her sister Yolanda had given birth to a twelve-pound baby who could not breathe because of the hangman's umbilical cord wrapped around his neck. (Stillbirth is the kind, poetic term for this banal tragedy that should be better known as deadbirth.) Yolanda refused to bury her deadborn, for she was old and she knew she would not bear another child. A neighbor telegrammed Elena Mulé, and Elena Mulé went to console her sister and to help her bury the child in the proper manner.

Then why did she bring the rooster in that ridiculous cage, as if he were some type of rare parrot?—which, due to his vibrant plumage, a few folks on the train thought he was and they stuck their ignorant noses into the cage and yelped through the cane reeds: "Coco loco, caca mala," as if Atila were such an idiot that he would repeat such nonsense, even if he were a parrot. Why the questions about quickening the dead? Did Elena Mulé know the awesome powers of the very first blue rooster she raised *not* to be a fighter? Or was she simply trying to embarrass him?

They arrived near past dawn. Yolanda and her husband and their dead-born lived in a two-room tenement in the seedier district of town. He was a field worker. She knitted baby wear and used the money she made to make sure there would always be a bottle of rum in the cabinet when her husband got home. His back always ached and his feet were always swollen. The rum helped put him to sleep. When Elena Mulé knocked that morning he was already gone for the fields, one more time screaming at his wife that if that baby wasn't underground when he got back, he was going to cut it open and stuff it with stones and toss it in the river. Yolanda made promises she knew she was not going to keep; she knew that when her husband returned from the fields he would be too tired to be so angry. When there was no answer at the door Elena Mulé pushed it open and found her sister and two neighbors saying a rosary over a covered bassinet in the back room. She left Atila's cage in the front room. She hugged her sister and they cried together, and she joined them in the rosary, though Elena Mulé, unlike her sister, had never embraced the Christian god, nor His mother. When she asked to see the baby, her sister would not let her lift the knitted cover, which was folded over and tied at the base of the bassinet.

"When he breathes for the first time we will know," Yolanda said. "Llorará, like all babies, he will cry." Before Elena Mulé could say anything (*Me cago, how is he going to breathe when that thing is sealed like a coffin!*), her sister broke into the susurration of another rosary, for there were many Virgins to pray to before her baby could live. No one had opened the bassinet since the second afternoon after the deadbirth. They prayed to a hundred Virgins till their mouths were all dry and the fire of their five thousand Hail Marys was all ashes. At dusk the two neighbors left and Yolanda's husband arrived, stooped over and limping. He drank almost a whole bottle of rum and passed out hanging halfway out the window of the front room, mumbling to nightwalkers on the street below about babies who swallow stones and drown in the river. Elena Mulé took what little rum was left in the bottle and forced her sister to drink it, mixed with a little guava juice, for it looked like she had not slept in ages. She had two glasses. Elena Mulé lay down with her as they had when they were children in Santiago, cradled belly to back like spoons. She asked her what she had named the child. "Julio César," her sister said.

Elena Mulé said nothing. But she did not think it was a good idea to burden an innocent child with the name of a great warrior. When Yolanda fell asleep Elena Mulé got up, congratulated herself on the clever proportions of rum to guava juice, went to the front room, hiked up her skirt, crouched over the cane reed cage, and wet her rooster. Atila awoke. He did not move, keeping as dignified a pose as possible under such demeaning conditions, because he knew that his madre-mistress's water would bring him luck in his endeavor that night; and even more luck if he tasted it a bit, which he did, throwing his head back for a second. Elena Mulé did not dry herself. Before she returned to bed she undid the latch of the cane reed cage.

"Vaya, let's see what you dare do," she said. "Hasta mañana, enano."

Atila shook his tail briskly to dry off his Varadero-blue feathers. He walked across the front room, opened wide his wings, and hopped up on the small of Yolanda's husband's back. The weary drunk grunted a bit but he stayed in place. Atila watched through the window till the moon had sunk, then he went into the back room, where the two sisters slept. Stretching his neck upward, with his beak he undid the knot at the bottom of the bassinet. As soon as the cloth dropped to the sides, it was nose-noticeable that unlike Paco Fortunato, Julio César had begun to rot. Atila pulled the cloth down off the bassinet. The smell had permeated the knitted fibers of the cover and Atila tossed it aside with a flip of his neck. He opened his wings wide and leaped up to the edge of the bassinet. A child who cannot breathe in the womb, he knew, is born blue, not the blue of the waters at Varadero or the blue of the seven seas but the blue of varicose veins. The baby Julio César had progressed beyond that stage. His skin was now a pale shade of gray and an ashy pubescence covered his legs and his torso. His hair was wispy and fallen-leaf brown. One eye was open, doe-colored and creamy and far away. (Was this wink a dare? a mock? a prayer?) Atila perched himself on the deadborn's inflated belly, careful with the nails in his talons, arching them upward, wary that he might pierce the skin and all the fumes and critters of death come bursting out. He enveloped his wings around the child's head and lifted it, pressing it to his breast. He began to sing a dolorous aria from Puccini's *Gianni Schicchi,* softly in soprano. He sang all night and the gray child did not even attempt to breathe. At five in the morning Yolanda's husband appeared in the bedroom swinging a sugar sack full of rocks. He caught Atila on the side of the head and the blue rooster collapsed on top of the gray winking baby.

When Atila came to, the child was gone and Yolanda was waving a kitchen knife and screaming at her sister that the wicked rooster had swallowed her baby and that she was going to cut him open. They left Yolanda's tenement in such a hurry that they forgot the cane reed cage, so Atila had to ride on the train back to Holguín curled up into a ball and tucked under the lap of Elena Mulé's skirt, between her widespread legs, for there were no animals allowed on the coach unless they were caged. To console himself, to do something that would get his mind off his migraine, Atila sang and Elena Mulé's lips parted and she sighed the whole trip long. When she disembarked, many of the passengers congratulated her on her beautiful voice and they presumed the rosy flush on her face to be either typical campesina humility or the modesty of the crippled, for she walked funny.

A week later, in the middle of the afternoon, as Atila was riding the seven-seas tail right in front of the spearback rat's hole, challenging the monster to come after them, because such a brush with danger proved what an hombre he still was—even as he rode the seven-seas tail, and even if Paco Fortunato was terrified of such stunts and could derive no pleasure from them—Yolanda Mulé rode up in a cart-and-mule taxi from the train station in Holguín, holding tight to a bundle of knitted cloth and with a beatific smile on her face. This was enough to scare Atila more than a hundred packs of spearback rats. His hombre-ness melted from him like fat in a bubbling stew; and, still hinged to the seven-seas tail, he darted from there, dragging Paco Fortunato, who thought the monster had made its move and began to cackle like a hysteric hen (a habit he had acquired after his resurrection), backwardly along. They hid underneath a pile of bloodied white feathers in the haunted henhouse, where it was said the ghosts of the murdered white-feathered ladies still yearned and wailed for the body and tail of Paco Fortunato. Atila heard them and was immediately struck with another migraine, a condition he would suffer from for the rest of his life, and pulled back out of the seven-seas tail.

All day Elena Mulé called for her two remaining living roosters. "¡Atila! ¡Paco! ¡Vengan! Good news! Great news! ¿Dónde se han métío?" They did not believe her and remained hidden in the haunted henhouse for two days, till they heard a child cry and Paco Fortunato could not convince Atila that it was a trick of the spearback rat. This is what Atila learned when he dared venture out of the henhouse, that the baby Julio César had been reborn, that the evening after he and Elena Mulé had fled Yolanda's tenement, a basket with a baby in it appeared at her doorstep (just as her husband arrived from the fields), that the child was wet and bloodied as if it had just been born, though Yolanda was told that it wasn't from the womb that he was wet and bloodied but from the belly of the blue rooster who had swallowed him to give him new life, that once the news began to spread in Bayamo of this miracle, the people had begun to build a temple of stone in the center of town and called it San Atila el Milagroso. When Atila saw the baby, rosy-skinned, with Havana-brown hair and eyes lined in violet and drawn in with carbon, he knew right away that this wasn't the child that he tried to save a week back.

But how often does a cock get a temple dedicated in his honor? Who would protest if put in Atila's place? Who but a true saint?

"This is Julio César," the mother said. "Your resurrected."

How often does a mother get her deadborn's sentence rescinded? What fairy stories won't she invent? And . . . near the fields where Yolanda's husband worked, who heard the desperate cry of the guajira mother that her newborn, her liveborn had been stolen from right under her crotch?

Atila crowed a tinsel alto and the baby giggled and kicked his feet as if to dance . . . and winked. For the first time, and as always from then on, when Julio César was happy, Atila's migraine disappeared.

For more than a year, while they were building his stone temple at Bayamo, Atila and his madre-mistress visited every month and watched over construction—all done with volunteer hands. Atila, closer to a deity than anyone in that part of the world then (with the possible exception of José Martí—though he was a dead deity), was still forced to ride the train in his ludicrous cane reed cage, which Yolanda had her husband rebuild, since she had shattered it to bits the morning Atila had swallowed her deadborn child, though she would have nothing to do with the builders of the temple and was conspicuously absent on the afternoon of its destruction. The temple walls were made of limestone, and the stained-glass windows, designed by Elena Mulé and executed by a craftsman from Trinidad, depicted the great cockfights of many of Atila's greatest ancestors, the roof was red tile and atop the steeple was placed, of course, a blue weather vane. And who paid for all this? The people, claro, the same who volunteered their hands and their backs to build, who got to the cane fields a bit earlier, just as the still submerged sun began to hint at the shadows of things, so they could leave a few hours before quitting time and put in labor at the temple. Out of the back walls of brick ovens, the lining of workboots, and from behind the rims of Sunday straw hats, taped to the underside of cabinets and even out of the hem of abuelita's yellowed moth-chewed wedding dress, boxed up and forgotten so long ago in a miasma of dust under her bed, came paper money, not pesos, for those were not really ever worth saving, but green yanqui dollars, all into the coffers to build a temple for the resurrector. When it was finished, Elena Mulé had a separate cane reed cage made for Paco Fortunato and moved into the chapel with her last two living roosters.

At the first ceremony in the temple of San Atila el Milagroso, the honored rooster, perched on the pulpit, sang all the roles of Puccini's three-part *Il Trittico* (it was said that Marioneta Alonso, who had been impressed with tales of the singing cock, might make an appearance, but the bald, blind soprano never showed—perhaps if she had, things might not have turned out for the worst), a performance that lasted five hours and wearied all the congregation, most of whom had come with their recent dead, and had left them piled outside in the noonday sun. (No one in Bayamo had been buried in over a year, for everyone knew that once the temple was finished, and the resurrector within it, the resurrector would do what resurrectors are wont to do—bring back the dead. Thus, to avoid a pestilence, the mayor issued an ordinance that prohibited anyone from keeping their dead at home; instead the city bought a giant freezer, a block long and six stories high, from a yanqui company that manufactured snow for ski resorts—and was investigating the possibility of establishing tropical ski resorts in the highest peaks of the Sierra Maestra—and fashioned it with over a thousand coffin-sized compartments. There, for over a year, for a certain monthly fee, it stored all its dead, along with those of nearby towns for a higher fee. On the morning of the first ceremony there was a mad rush to get the dead out and bring them to the temple. Dear grandmothers and cancer-stricken uncles and the father who died of a coronary while lifting a limestone for the temple's eastern wall and the boy who fell into the wild hog trap and was mauled by the beast who had fallen in the previous day and his mother who died of sorrow—in those days, as doctora Sara Zimmerman would assert much later, it was still possible to die of such things—and the six teenagers of the suicide pact who hopped a wired fence and took turns inhaling nitrous oxide hooked to a tractor of the United Fruit Company and many many others, including pets too beloved to ever be thought of as beasts, starved kittens and ancient flatulent hounds and defeated roosters, all were taken out of the giant refrigerator and hauled to the temple of San Atila el Milagroso, in wheelbarrows and buggy carts and pine coffins affixed with baby carriages under each end. When they arrived a rubicund-faced man said in a hissy Spaniard accent that he was a papal nuncio and told them that they could not bring the bodies inside the wicked temple, for these were baptized souls and if they were to be raised from the dead, it was to be done in the living light of God, that he would watch them meanwhile.) So while the congregation restlessly listened to Atila's rendition of Puccini, its dear dead began to thaw and warm and rot. When they stepped out of the temple, half expecting to see their beloved up and around (wasn't it with his voice that the wondrous blue rooster woke the dead?), it was midnight dark though it was only four in the afternoon, and the papal nuncio had his robe tied around his head like an Arab virgin, covering everything but his steely eyes, and was waving away a horde of flies and mosquitoes and cicadas, that not content with feasting on the excremental dead had taken a liking to his sacramental odor.

There are differing versions of what happened after the people saw their dead mamás and papás, their abuelos and abuelitas, their mijitos and mijitas covered with suits of cicadas and helmets of black flies and veils of mosquitoes. Some blame the destruction of the first and only temple of San Atila el Milagroso on the papal nuncio who, without even consulting the monsignor of the local parish, had taken it upon himself to expose Atila as a fake and a charlatan, as he had recited prayers in Greek (written by Pope Pius XII, as inspired by the songs of Moses) to summon the seventeen-year locust a few years early, and thus it is said that the plague of locusts that descended from the heavens that afternoon was so monumental that it covered the town of Bayamo and made it night and it was not until four mornings later that the north wind blew the plague into the Caribbean Sea and anyone saw the sun again. All the dead were missing and the trees had no fruit or leaves and the palms were all bald so that they seemed like giant ridged gray phalluses shooting out of the earth.

Others, in a more rational attempt to explain the destruction of the temple, say that the locusts were right on time, that it was a larger swarm than usual—though not so large as to snuff out the sun! although, sure, it was overcast for a few days—and that, yes, some fruit was lost and a few palm fronds eaten, but this had nothing to do with what happened at the temple. Outside, the people found their dear dead and shooed away the humming insects and paid no attention to the nuncio and his twisted prayer chants, waiting for Atila to come out and do his thing, bring back the dead. But the blue rooster did not show. *That was the problem!* After his Puccini performance, he was taken down from the pulpit and locked into his cane reed cage in the chapel. Elena Mulé bolted the entrance to the temple and would not let Atila out to meet the congregation, nor it inside to meet him. Discomfited by the growing carrion smell of their beloved, irritated by the persistent drone of the settling-in locusts and their being locked out of the temple, which they had sacrificed a year of their lives and a lifetime of savings to build, the people grew restless. Someone threw a rock through one of the stained-glass windows. There were cheers. And more rocks were thrown till all of Atila's glass-painted ancestors were shattered. Elena Mulé, in an attempt to appease the mob, hoping that the locust-darkness would confuse it, sent out to them Paco Fortunato. The poor luckless handsome rooster wet and stained his limp seven-seas tail and forgot his greater voice and cackled shamelessly on the temple's front steps. Immediately, he was recognized as an impostor. Someone grabbed him by the neck and twirled his body till something snapped and Paco Fortunato cackled no more, then they plucked his seven-seas feathers and bashed him and crushed his body over the limestone walls and with his blood and with the luridness of his insides they smeared obscene words on the temple's iron doors. The nuncio stopped chanting and raised both his open palms as if in thanksgiving and proclaimed another victory against the pagans. "Down with the pagan temple," he yelled. "For the Lord our Jesus is great and He will reign forever!"

So the people went home and brought back picks and broadaxes and garden shovels, and with the same hands, with the same backs, with the same conviction that they had built the temple of San Atila el Milagroso, they began to destroy it, pulverizing it stone by stone; except that in fear of hurricanes from the Atlantic, they had built the eastern wall far too sturdy, and they could not take it down (though they brought in teams of Holstein oxen and tied heavy ropes to the base of the wall and the Holsteins pulled and pulled, digging into the earth with their wide hooves till they were almost buried alive); the following morning, the eastern wall still stood among the rubble-ruins of the house of San Atila el Milagroso. And the reason the dead were missing after the locusts were swept to the sea was not because the locusts ate them—locusts eat plants, not flesh!—but because afterward, the people of Bayamo, pledging never again to devote their lives to false resurrectors, reopened the town cemetery and laid their dead to rest. The papal nuncio said a brief prayer over every single grave and then led them in a procession to a funeral Mass at the town's Roman Catholic cathedral, proclaiming in the homily that the miracle of resurrection had been patented long ago by Our Lord and Savior Jesus Christ.

In all the commotion, all the high talk about the true Savior, Yolanda and her drunk baby-thieving husband and their child, who had been born dead but was now living, were entirely forgotten.

While they were busy murdering his lover, scribbling obscenities with his blood and the stuff of his lower intestines on the temple walls, Atila and his madre-mistress fled from a side door of the chapel, and once again rolled up into a ball and stuffed between her legs so that she limped and sang like a prima donna—and looked like one, since she was in her Sunday best, in a rose-colored loose-fitting silk dress with a blue-thread smocking at the collar and simple pearl necklace—they escaped from Bayamo, not back home to the finca near Holguín, but to hide in the Sierra Maestra, the rugged and prodigious massif in the southwestern hem of their tail-end province. From that day on, and for the next eleven years, Atila was convinced that one or another member of that first congregation of San Atila el Milagroso was stalking him down to murder him in the same fashion Paco Fortunato had been murdered.

They disembarked from the train at Santiago de Cuba and headed west along the Caribbean coastline by foot, Atila leading and stopping the campesinos in their buggy carts with his voice, hitching rides and eating whatever was offered to them for his song. They did not stop moving till they came to a village called Agua Fina, after a nearby creek whose waters were so transparent, so silky, that the villagers swore it was the tears of the gods and to drink from the creek day in and day out would promise immortality. And indeed many of the villagers seemed to have lived past a century already. But Atila and Elena Mulé were so distraught with any notion of resurrection or immortality, that though they were thirsty and had drunk little water in six days, subsisting mostly on coconut juice and the syrup of cane stalks, they refused to drink from the stream, but accepted from a Catalán storeowner named Miguel, who at eighty-six was one of the youngsters of the village, a meal of chorizo and crackers.

The Sierra Maestra is a wet, junglelike region that then, as now, was sparsely inhabited by farmers and campesinos who grew sugarcane and coffee and were for the most part isolated from the rest of the Island, iconoclasts who, from the early days of the Spanish colonization until Castro's Revolución many years later, have considered themselves at odds with the political goings-on of the capital on the other side of the Island. Thus, Elena Mulé wisely told the anciano villagers of Agua Fina, located on the foothills of the Sierra Maestra, that she and her rooster were fleeing from the reach of the despot then in power in Havana, one Gerardo Machado y Morales. Immediately the villagers took in Elena Mulé and her rooster as one of their own. They spent a week in the village feasting on suckling pigs and cask-aged rum. They danced and Atila sang his favorite arias from *Carmen* and all was joyful till Atila and his madre-mistress began—well, how else to say this without causing offense—to stink, for not only would they not drink the water from the tears-of-the-gods stream, but they would not bathe in it as the villagers bathed in it three times a day, and after a week they could not tolerate the scent of their persecuted visitors, so they sent them out with a young guide into the mountains, packing for them canteens full of rum, instead of stream water, and more chorizo and crackers.

The guide's name was Tati Hijuelos. He was ninety-seven years old. His hair was white and sparse and the muscles hung on his bones limp as a furled sail, but when it came to hiking and hurdling over the sharp jagged rocks the natives named after the fangs of wolves he was an expert. Not even Atila, who was seventy-five years his junior, spreading his blue wings and flying at times, could keep up with him. On occasion Tati Hijuelos would forget about them and move so fast up the side of the mountain that they would lose sight of him and he would have to trace his way back down and get behind Elena Mulé, and with his bony shoulder give her a shove on her graveolent rump and Atila a kick in his Varadero-blues tail, which sunk deeper the needles of his migraine. After three days, deep into the jungle, they came to the purlieus of a village called Sinsol. Tati Hijuelos said good-bye and pointed the way with his crooked finger.

"Tell them who you are and who you are fleeing from," he said, holding a hanky over his nose, "and they will be as hospitable to you as we were."

He hopped down the mountainside agile as a wildcat and in a matter of minutes had disappeared. Elena Mulé, the skin on the palm of her hands and on the knobs of her knees torn and bloodied, cracked open a fallen coconut with a sharp stone and washed herself with the juice and gave some to Atila to gargle and rubbed some of the oil from the meat on his comb and above his eyes to ease his migraine. They slept under a clutter of royal palms, covering themselves with dried fronds. The following morning they proceeded to Sinsol.

At the entrance to the village there was a gateway made of long flat boulders set one atop the other in a brave equilibrium. As they passed inside, the roof of the jungle grew so thick that the morning light vanished and the dirt road they were on was navigable only by feeling their way from tree trunk to tree trunk on the shoulder. Eventually the flickering lights from the village blinked from behind the dense mass of foliage and the winding-downhill road led them to a compound of bohíos built by the shores of an underground river. Elena Mulé saw a dwarfish man carrying a bucket of malangas and a torch. She told him who they were and the name of the tyrant they were fleeing from. The man answered that tyrants need no name, that they were all one and the same, and as Tati Hijuelos had said, he welcomed them and told them to follow him to his home where his wife would be glad to feed them breakfast. The man was about a foot shorter than Elena Mulé (who herself was not much taller than she was wide) and wore only a pair of work pants rolled up to the knees. His skin was so translucent that she could see the crossways of his veins and arteries running to and from the shadows in his chest. He had no hair at all, not even eyebrows or eyelashes (so that his expression was one of perennial bewilderment), and his pupils were from some angles salmon-pink, from some angles orange. The nails on both his fingers and his toes were long and curved and sharp as talons. His wife was dressed just like him and they looked so alike that the only way to tell them apart was by the pointy sand-colored nipples on her flat chest. She caressed Atila's tail and marvelled at his feathers as if he were a creature from another world. They ate boiled malangas and thin strips of meat that looked and tasted like shrimp. When their host told them it was poached albino grasshoppers, Elena Mulé became ill and she could not finish her breakfast. Atila was fine and asked for seconds.

After breakfast the hairless dwarf and his hairless wife took off their workpants so that they were completely naked, and around their sexes was as barren as the rest of their bodies. They told Elena Mulé and Atila that they were lucky to have arrived on a Saturday, for they would soon meet most of the other villagers. Saturday was the day of the celebration of the red stones. Unabashed, naked as they were, they led Elena Mulé and her rooster out of their bohío and further down the dirt road and soon they came to a stone amphitheater, the walls slippery with white moss, the roof a network of thick, hairy overlapping roots. They left the torch outside. A pyramid of flat stones, like the ones used to build the gateway into the village, glowing red, was set on center stage of the amphitheater, and one villager was tending to the stones, knocking the ashes off the ends and corners so they would not smoke, while others were carting in new stones in wheelbarrows, which were balanced, with the aid of large iron tongs, at the vertex of the pyramid. All the other villagers, whose looks were not so different from their hosts, hairless, with see-through skin and ruby eyes, were seated on the six levels of stone rows, naked and packed in, their legs pressed to their torsos, so that with the only light coming from the burning stones, their eyes flashed and their bony kneecaps shone. Atila thought he felt a feather plucked but he made no protest and when he sat down in the fourth row center he tucked his tail underneath him.

The roots-roof over the amphitheater was domed and thick and low, so that within it felt like being in a giant wigwam. The villagers chanted in unison. And as they breathed in, the glow of the stone pyramid dimmed, and as they let their voices out, it deepened. Soon, both Atila and Elena Mulé, so engrossed with the beatless rhythm of the chant, stopped measuring time, and without a grasp of then and now forgot about each other.

They later learned that the glowing stones were the ancestors of the villagers, some who had ventured away for lives in other villages, other lands, other times, and some like them who had never left their sunless spot and never deepened the pigment of their ghost-skin. As these fathers and mothers of time grabbed her by the hand and took her away from herself, Elena Mulé welcomed the villagers' monotone chant as she had always welcomed Atila's song, and permeating through the shimmering blue halo of air at the base of the pyramid, she spoke with all of Atila's ancestors. They told her how they had once been a peaceful tribe and how the father of their fathers, a black-feathered prince of the Nile, had raped Elena Mulé's mother when she was only nine, and how the child-mother had not survived the birth, split in two, and how Elena Mulé's grandmother, a witch who lived under the bed of the Nile, had cursed all of the black-feathered prince's offspring with a will to fight and to perish fighting and sent him, along with his illegitimate daughter, in a basket that floated into the sea, and the sea so washed them on their journey across the ocean that the black prince's feather turned blue. When Elena Mulé's spirit returned to the amphitheater, the place was half-empty and the body that was once again hers was naked and sweaty and parched. Atila had disappeared. She stood, knocking her head on the knotted-root roof. She looked at the villager who was her host and then at his wife, but they were both still in a trance, their salmon eyes rolled up and inward.

"Atila! Atila!" she screamed. "Where are you? Where are you, descarado? You are my brother, my cousin, my son. We are *all* related!" There was no answer, and Elena Mulé had lost so much water from her blood that she passed out. She came to again inside the bohío they had first visited, submerged in an underground ice-mud bath. The husband and the wife stood above watching her, Atila by their side. They had each plucked a different shaded feather from her rooster's tail and pierced their bodies with them, one through each ear, one through the navel, and two each through the fabric of their genitalia, he through the sac and through the underside of the glans, and she through the outer and inner lips. They suggested Elena Mulé do the same. They had heard in their trances at the celebration of stones that this was the secret to everlasting life.

Atila jerked his head at Elena Mulé; having submitted to a plucking of his tail out of courtesy's sake and looking as if he were suffering from some horrible molting disease, he wanted out of that crazy village.

The Man Who Played His Bones

Their hosts suggested the perfect place to hide was a village on the crest of the mountain range, near Pico Turquino, at 1,974 meters, the Island's highest point. The only drawback, they said, was that La Tiza, as the village was called, was famous for its high rate of suicides.

"You see," they explained, "unless a village was well hidden or out-of-the-way in these mountains, like ours and a few others, it became the property of the ravenous Spanish landowners; and the guajiros who worked the land had no love for it since it was not theirs, but rented, and the fruit of their harvest merely increased their oppressors' power. Some chose and still choose (for though we won the war of independence, most of the landowners never really left) to kill themselves to escape this vicious cycle. Gracias a Dios, our spot of land gets no sunlight and this frightened away the rich. Vaya, they are so easily frightened. In La Tiza, the landowners were frightened away by the ghosts of the suicides, who unearthed their own bones and crushed them to a chalky dust and spread it over the porches of the landowners' fancy cottage-mansions and in their drinking wells and rum casks. But even after the landowners left, leaving behind all their land, the peasant families that remained in the village were so eased by the habit of suicide that the ritual continued, even though there was no longer any need for it—the land was theirs and they had moved with their families into the landowners' cottages.

"There indeed you will be safe. The henchmen of the oppressors know better than to ever set foot in La Tiza again."

Because they could not find her rose-colored dress or her jewelry (the head priest at the amphitheater, the keeper of the holy stones, had confiscated them, and from then on, during the celebration of stones, he wore the dress as the holy garment and the pearls as the holy crown while he knocked away the ashes), Elena Mulé left the village of Sinsol with her blue cock Atila dressed simply, head to toe, in a thick coat of brick-red mud. They took the road uphill, again guiding themselves by feeling the knotty base of trees on the shoulder (for their hosts had not supplied them with a torch, for from a place where no light enters, the husband said very seriously, no light may be removed) and were thrilled when they saw the sunlight, in points and dashes like Chinese characters, breaking through the vegetation up ahead. They were out of the land saved by no sun. Just before she was able to see the shape of her rooster, soft-stepping ahead of her, humming a tune, Elena Mulé thought she heard him speak his mind (in the language of cocks, claro): "Y no seas boba, chica. We are not related. You are a woman. And I am cock. Those were dreams in there. God knows what drugs they were burning in that stony tent. . . . For if indeed you are the granddaughter of a witch who lives under the Nile and I am the descendant of a horny black-feathered prince who goes around putting his thing in nine-year-old girls, who the hell is that damn sister of yours who got us into all this mess?"

The first night they weathered heavy rains that washed the mud off Elena Mulé, and the following morning they had a breakfast of fresh coffee-bread and goat's milk at a peasant's bohío. The paltry wife ripped two of her dresses and sewed them together with her foot-pedal machine and gave Elena Mulé the new-fashioned dress. They continued up the mountain range towards the spine. Wherever Elena Mulé stopped at a bohío and asked the way to La Tiza the guajiros silently pointed up and westward, their faces ashen, but revealing nothing more of the history of this self-slaughtering village. On the fourth day after they had left Sinsol a blind peasant woman informed them that there was only one clan left in the village of La Tiza, the family of Mongo Pérez, and that they soon were destined to perish, and the village would be forgotten in the rumbas that tell the stories of the mountains. They hurried upward, as if racing against the final suicide. On the sixth day, crossing a high saddle near the Turquino peak, their breath so short that Atila could no longer sing to console his madre-mistress, it began to snow and the ground and the pines were so covered with snow that it reminded Elena Mulé of the photographs in books about los Estados Unidos that she saw when she visited the bookstores in Santiago de Cuba. The snow (though it was a thin and warm snow) fell so hard that it began to accumulate on her head and shoulders and Atila had to shake his comb and wag his shorn Varadero-blues tail to get it off him. It fell and blunted the sharp rocks sprouting from the mountainside that were the teeth of the jackal spirits buried there. It fell as if by the will, the rhythm of holy bata drums, coming from just above, just beyond, and when the beating stopped, the snow stopped, and when it could be heard again, it snowed again.

They followed the sound of the snow, Elena Mulé picking up her bird and setting him on her shoulder, because there was so much accumulation now and it was so soft that he sank in it, till they came to a promontory overlooking a canyon, above a wide river, on which was perched a tile-roof two-tier wooden cottage, its eaves heavy with snow. Nearby, on a jutting rock, a man in a heavy cassock that reached down to his bare knees stood against the sky that was a thin stretched-balloon blue, as if it could be pricked by a needle, and beat together two white log-thick sticks in a rhythm endearing to the gods. From him, or rather from the white logs that he beat against each other over his head, or down in front of him, or crouched beneath him, however the gods would ask him, spouted, like water from a spring, the wind ruffling it and then easing to give it back its flawless flowery symmetry, the snow that was falling over and softening the edges of the highest point on the Island. Approaching the snow-maker, Elena Mulé saw that the logs that he was beating against each other were really large bones, and she knew instinctively, though they appeared too big to be human bones (more like the thighbone of some fairy-tale giant), that these were the bones of his self-slaughtered ancestors.

When the man noticed that he was being watched, he stopped playing. He was so covered in bone-chalk that when he moved it fell off him in chunks as if he were a statue coming from inside a stone and when he blinked it dropped from his eyelids in sprinkles. He did not tell them his name, for he could not speak—his only language was the rhythm of his bones—but Elena Mulé assumed that this was Mongo Pérez, the patriarch of the last surviving clan. He moved past them into the wooden cottage, leaving powdery footprints on the porch like the trail of a clumsy ghost. Elena Mulé and her bird were hungry, so they followed him in. They found Mongo Pérez in the pantry, seated on a stool with his head bowed, playing two needle-thin bones that could have belonged to no creature larger than a pigeon. The snow cloud spouting from these bones, as chunks of the old snow kept on flaking off him, from the ridges of his eyebrows and the curlicues of his ears, was almost invisible as it dewdropped on his bare feet. Mongo Pérez fed them sausages and rice with pig's milk. But the meal was so covered with chalk that they spit it back out. When Elena Mulé spoke to him, he answered by playing his pigeon bones, but she could not understand. By the end of their first week there they got used to tasting chalk in everything they ate, and they strained it from their rum and drinking water and pig's milk with lace hair nets that must have once belonged to the Spanish landowners' wives and daughters. They daily awoke to the beating of the larger bones and to a heavy snowfall as Mongo Pérez greeted the day on his jagged rock above the canyon. Every month, Mongo Pérez climbed down a gorge from the mountain peak using a sharp digging shovel to keep his balance, and two days afterward, from below, he brought back fresh bones to play stuffed into a sack strapped across one shoulder and a hog flank strapped across the other shoulder, and in three covered wooden buckets he brought pig's milk and rice and rum. His skin was washed and rosy as if the top layer had been peeled away. Without the snow dust his nose and chin were sharper and he looked much younger, for his hair and beard were black. Elena Mulé told him that she too wanted to bathe, since both she and her rooster were white with the ubiquitous chalk. Mongo Pérez took out some fresh pigeon bones from a leather pouch tied around his waist and he played them. Elena Mulé was learning his bone-language and she understood that they were welcome to follow him the next time he descended the canyon. Atila crooned approval, with the thin mountain air and all the snow-powder, he was beginning to lose his voice, and he could tell that Elena Mulé was getting fidgety. When he mounted her belly and sang to her at night, she would not sigh. Even Puccini failed him.

They followed Mongo Pérez down to the river the next time and they bathed, washing away the chalk that tried to seep into their bodies, underneath their nails and in through their nostrils and every other available orifice. Atila gargled the chilly water. When Mongo Pérez undid his peasant's cassock and stripped, Atila heard Elena Mulé sigh as he had not heard her sigh in a long while, since before the building of the limestone temple. He could see why, for though a bit envious, even he was impressed with the sight, and he thought longingly of his murdered lover. From all

his bone-playing, Mongo Pérez had the shoulders and arms of an olym-
pian, but Atila was sure that this was not what Elena Mulé was whimpering about like a virgin. Out of Mongo Pérez's navel grew a phallus as thick
and long as the bones he played each morning, and when he got into the
river and washed it, the blood coursed through it as if it were borrowing
the force of the rivercurrent and the many veins that twirled around it
bulged with vigor and turned the shades of Atila's feathers against the
erubescent skin and the thing majestically stood. After he had washed
himself of the snow dust he rolled himself on the riverbank and turned
bottoms up and went at the fresh fire-colored mud as if it were a living
thing; then, draggled and naked, he took his digging shovel, his sack, and
his waist pouch and vanished from their sight, returning with the bones,
the hog flank, rice, rum, and milk, and he washed himself anew and put
back on his cassock.

The next time they went down to the river, Elena Mulé followed him
after he had spent himself on the rivermud. Having already adapted to the
mountain terrain, she was able to keep close behind. He crossed a dense
cane forest and descended further down the mountain through a coffee
field, till he came to wide cirque in a valley of plantain trees. His monumental misplaced phallus again became aroused and he made love to the
deep black mountain-mud. The walls of the hollow heard and they too
cried. He then took his shovel and dug out from the very spot a pile of
bones of various sizes, which he washed in a nearby pool. The larger bones
he put into the sack, the smaller ones in the leather waist pouch. At a bohío on the way up he bartered with a peasant woman, giving her some of
the bones in exchange for food and buckets of milk and rum. She was haggard, bent over, and blind, so she felt the bones with her hand for their
quality and nodded her head in approval; then she felt his navel-organ and
marveled at its shape and location as if she had never felt it before. Mongo
Pérez let her, but he did not become aroused. Irritated at this, the peasant
woman pushed him away and called him a marica. Mongo Pérez laughed
and waved his good-byes. The peasant woman happily played her newly
acquired bones on his departure—but when she played, it did not snow.

In half a year's time Elena Mulé learned the language of the smaller
bones (which Mongo Pérez explained to her were not pigeon bones, but
phalanges of the unborn from the bone-hollows of certain female suicides)
well enough that she could communicate with Mongo Pérez on a basic
level. In this way, every afternoon, seated out in the porch of the cottage,
after he had finished making snow for the gods, he recounted to her the
story of his family, the last clan in the village of La Tiza. Mongo Pérez was
not the patriarch. He was the eldest born and named after his father. By
the time of his birth, the Spanish landowners had long ago been frightened away and most of the villagers, except for a few ancient ones, had
done themselves in, so that the only reproductive couple left in La Tiza

was his parents. Even so, when his mother saw the location of his organ, growing from his navel like a misplaced hog's tail, she wanted to bury him, for she was sure it was a sign of evil things to come. His father, however, would not allow his firstborn to be murdered so. "No me importa de donde carajo le crece la pinga. All the better, he won't even have to pull down his pants this way!" They bore three more children, a boy first, with his organ growing from the proper place, because the mother had murmured so many rosaries to the Virgin of Cobre, who saw to it that there would be no confusions this time, and then two girls. During the last birth in the history of La Tiza, his mother died. She was buried with all of the other villagers in the distant valley of plantains, for during the time of the Spanish landowners the peasants were not allowed to bury their own on the land they tilled. The Spaniards thought it would poison the land. Since then, the burial ground had remained the same.

So that their clan would not perish, Mongo Pérez's father forced him to wed his younger sister and his brother his other sister, but the brothers could not bring themselves to lie with their own—Mongo Pérez because he was embarrassed by his deformity and his brother because he had never wanted to lie with *any* woman—so they went down the gorge to the river and taught each other how to rid themselves of their desires in the red mud. Proclaiming in front of the elders that he was just doing it to prevent the death of their village, the father drank a pint of cane rum and slept with his two daughters and showed his sons the bloody sheets to let them know that there was nothing to fear; but still the brothers disobeyed and they would not take their sisters as wives, preferring their own company and the moist warmth of the red earth.

In La Tiza, the generations of villagers, back to the times of the Spanish colonialists, have left their most significant mark on this world by the way they decide to leave it. There are the traditional ways (the ways of the world below La Tiza)—hanging, slit wrists in a tepid tub, heavy boulders fastened around the ankles and into the rivercurrent, the dive into the gorge, and, claro, the rusty musket with the butt-end pressed tightly by the knees and the other end brushing the palate—but Tizonians considered these methods vulgar and demeaning. There were, they knew, if not better, more inventive ways to go. The finale is after all what they, the living, most remember. Suicide is often a noble act, even when done wrong; but when done right, it is graceful and courageous, and it was, for the villagers of La Tiza, the purest art.

A campesino, before the turn of the century, decided to undo himself by swallowing mango pits till he burst open. He began with tiny round lollipop mangoes and progressed to the oval king mangoes. It took him six weeks and he swallowed one hundred and forty-two mango pits before his digestive canal popped open like an overstuffed sausage spilling all its poisons into his middle cavity. Out of his grave, from his fertilizing tripes, there grew sixteen different varieties of mango trees, whose fruit was served as a delicacy to the Spanish landowners of the following generation.

A woman, who was a divorcée and had moved to La Tiza after her second marriage, thought that by eating the brains of rats, surely a venomous thing, she would put herself to everlasting rest. Pero al contrario, the more she caught the rats in her giant traps and carefully peeled back the skin and chiseled open the breadcrust skulls and ate their brains, the less she slept and the more enthused she became with the adventure of life (and the less she cared about the shame of having been known by more than one man), scurrying up on the thatch of her bohío and building there a nest. One midnight, she was attacked and gnawed to death by a horde of rodents who did not want their brains eaten. It is said that in the end, the woman saw the logic of her death plan and rejoiced at being chewed to death by her brethren. Before she was buried, the Spanish landowners had all her teeth removed, which were not human, but iron-hard like a rat's, and many men wore them on gold chains as amulets so that their wives would never leave them.

A cane cutter, at about the time the landowners were starting to flee La Tiza because of the bone-dust on their porches, shaved all of the hair off his body with the sharp blade of his machete, and went naked into the cane fields, exposed to the torrid sun and to the dagger leaves of the cane stalks that pricked at him like fresh regrets and drew blood. He crossed six different fields before he ran out of blood and fell dead, one of his eyes poked out, the left side of his sac cleanly sliced open so that his testicle hung out like a rosy quail's egg on a string, and his torso lanced and pierced like a dummy after bayonet practice. Others, who later mimicked this suicide virtuoso, never made it past the second cane field.

The peasant workers were not the only ones to pursue, and at times perfect, the art of suicide; many in the landowning families, especially the women, were also quite talented.

The Duchess Josefina, the matriarch of the last landowning family to flee La Tiza, had grown so in love with a campesino boy that she could not bear the thought of leaving La Tiza back to the cold and arid mountains of Asturias. One evening, she wrapped herself in the six cashmere Bihar carpets that her husband had given her as a gift from his trips to the East and ordered the boy to beat the bundle with a churn paddle till it stopped moving. The boy was glad to oblige, since she had ordered him to do so many things that he enjoyed far less. The duchess thus died keeping true to the laws that royal blood must not be spilt to commingle with the unclean earth.

Her four daughters, whom the campesino boy fantasized about when the duchess made him crouch and ordered him to tickle there with his tongue, are the most famous suicide case in the rumbas that recount the stories of this village. They were referred to later as the bidet suicides, for their deaths were inspired by that French porcelain gift to the art of cleanliness that the user straddles like a midget pony to bathe her genitalia and her rump. Nearby the duchess's cottage there was a hot spring that was tapped as a water source for the bidet in her bathroom. The water had to sit and cool in a reservoir under the house for its natural temperature would surely scald the softer parts. The day each of her daughters began to bleed in the manner of women the duchess took each into her bathroom and showed her how to use the bidet and told her in a harsh tone that for the time she bled she must use the bidet three times a day, in the morning, after the siesta, and before bedtime, this way she would remain clean, and the smell of the serpent devils (for this is what the blood was, a reminder of and punishment for the sin of the first woman) would be kept at bay.

What terror followed by what joy each child must have felt!—for when the mother turned on the bidet, the warm jet of water that shot out of the brass upside-down faucet at the base of the basin was the temperature of what the child had always imagined a man's flesh to be (un poquito warmer than theirs), and as it cleaned out her insides and her mother handed her the rose-perfumed soap to wash down there, just like this three times a day, the child felt such giddy joy that it did seem probable that what her mother said was true, that she was washing away all the sins of all the women of this world back to the very first. The oldest girl washed five and six times a day, running by her mother and saying that she had to wash again because she was so afraid of the serpent, and the duchess who had straddled that bidet thousands of times and never once felt a tickle, smiled approvingly because the lesson had been well learned.

As each came of age, the second and third child also learned the ritual of the bidet, and soon also proclaimed a great fear of the serpent. The three older sisters so giggled and whispered around their youngest innocent sister, who would not feel these pleasures for three or four years, that she needled them to know what was so funny, and they answered, que nada, just that we're becoming women now, only that. And so much they loved to wash on the bidet, that they began to slaughter newborn piglets behind their father's back and use the blood to stain their panties to prove to their mother that, yes, they were bleeding again, even though it was only two weeks since the last time. The youngest sister soon caught on and she too stained her panties and experienced the pleasure of the bidet a whole year before she bled for real. It became so hectic in her bathroom that the duchess had her husband buy from the European manufacturer four more bidets for her house, one for each of her daughters.

On the day the duchess was buried, Bihar carpets and all, the daughters decided that she had died because they had lied to her, and the older one convinced them they should now do their rosaries and beg forgiveness of her and of all the women that had ever died for their sins. . . . And join them. They traced the source of the warm man-hot bidet water to a natural spring not far from their father's cottage. Intermittently, steam and misty water shot out from the geysers twenty and thirty feet in the air. They chose a group of four geysers where the water shot out the farthest. They rid themselves of their heavy mourning garments and while the geysers slept, they crouched over them as they did over their bidets, and said a prayer for the soul of their mamacita. When the steam and hot water shot out, from all four geysers at once, as if a river of fire water were rushing by right beneath them, the girls did not think of the duchess, nor of their sins, nor of the temperature of a man's flesh, nor of each other, nor of their homeland, which not even the oldest remembered. When the hissing gush of water the temperature of the devil's flesh hit their exposed parts, and they felt for a second a terrible pleasure that made them all at once one with the first woman, they all thought of how helpless a piglet feels before you slice its throat and collect its blood, and that's what they did, they shrilled like slaughtered piglets. A doctor who performed the autopsies in a hospital in Santiago de Cuba wrote down in his report that when he sliced open their torsos there was nothing more he could do, for their insides all were melted, and he could not tell for sure which organ was the stomach, which the pancreas, which the kidneys, which the lungs, which the liver, which the heart.

Mongo Pérez's sisters dreamed up their deaths inspired by the man who crossed the cane fields. They would go sweeter than the duchess's daughters. They hunted the cane forest for the thickest and pulpiest stalk. They cut it down and sharpened each end like a spear. One morning, while their father and brothers were out in the fields, they went to his bed and sat spread-eagled on diagonally opposite ends and placed the cane-spear, which they had soaked in coconut oil, between them. They opened their legs wider and scooted nearer to each other till the soft soles of their feet were touching and each end of the cane-spear began to enter them where their father had entered them. They pushed closer together till they could reach out and clutch hands and the force of the spear entering them passed beyond pleasure and they grimaced. They swayed, their soft backs bending like young palms in a whirlwind. And then, as if they had decided beforehand the exact time they would do it, the number to to's to the number of fro's they simultaneously pushed themselves into each other, so that their bellies slapped and their lips locked and the spear had split them each in two and once again their blood was on their father's sheets.

Mongo Pérez's father, always the Philistine, got drunk one night and slit his wrists. His brother drowned in the river. (But that was not a suicide, Mongo Pérez was sure; rather, he thought, that a current possessed by the duchess's four lustful daughters took a liking to the round mound of his ass plunging against the muddy bank and snared him away.)

After she had heard his story Elena Mulé began to care for Mongo Pérez with an almost maternal affection. She awoke before him and brewed cafecito and strained it with the lace hair net, and when it was too chilly, she made him wear a wool poncho over his cassock before he went out to play his large bones and converse with the gods. She did not watch him anymore when he took off his cassock to wash in the river, and when he grunted and howled atop the red mud, Elena Mulé swam faraway upstream so she did not have to hear. Atila was enlivened by all this, and one afternoon, awash with nostalgia, as if back in Holguín listening to a recording of Marioneta Alonso, he went to Elena Mulé while she was enjoying a siesta, the windows of the cottage bedroom wide open, the soft mountain breezes caressing her naked folds. Atila climbed on the mound of her belly; he tried to sing, but the lining of chalk in his throat and the thin mountain air in his lungs foiled him. In her sleep, Elena Mulé tossed her arm over him and pressed his head to her belly. Atila tried to nudge his way out but his madre-mistress's arm was heavy. Then he felt something that stopped him from trying to free himself. There were gentle eruptions coming from inside Elena Mulé's belly, not the chaotic rumblings of gas, flatulence in its journey, but a rhythmic toom-a-tum, toom-a-tum. Her heart! Her heart had fallen to her belly. Atila craned his neck upward to underneath her large left tit, grown even larger these days somehow, which was falling to the side of her like a pendulous papaya too heavy for its stem. Another heart! This one beating with a more confident thump-a-pom, thump-a-pom.

Could it be? She who had begun acting as if this deaf and mute man was her retarded son? What mother would take such advantage of her dumb child? Atila waited for the following morning, for if anything was happening, that's when it happened, under the cover of the snowfall.

He spent the night under the roof of a protruding boulder on a cliffside across the way from where Mongo Pérez daily played his bones. Atila was raging, crowing clouds of snow-dust, that ascended and disappeared in the crisp night air—he imagined these his prayers, prayers that Elena Mulé would prove him wrong, prayers he knew that like the little clouds of his song would never reach heaven. At dawn, Mongo Pérez showed up exactly as the morning's shiny red helmet peaked up from under the horizon. He played his bones, and as a cloud of snow descended on the earth, a shadow, barely discernible in the blizzard, crawled under Mongo Pérez's open legs and limbered up under the cassock until she was sitting directly over his navel, her legs and arms wrapped around him, her head poking out in front of him out of the cassock's collar and thrown back—all the monumental weight of his madre-mistress suspended on the navel-thing! Mongo Pérez continued to play and they rocked to the beat of his drum-bones and the snow fell harder and harder till, as if they were suing for pri-vacy, they became invisible.

That afternoon, Atila left the village of La Tiza, not bothering with farewells. When he would return, many years later, with the bearded lib-erators, both the village of La Tiza and Elena Mulé would be completely unrecognizable.

The Wall & the Prayer-Feathers

Had it not been for the voices, he would have lived his life out in the Sierra Maestra, would have known nothing of the bearded men who called them-selves liberators and may have lived to be a hundred, much longer than any of his ancestors. But as soon as he left La Tiza, Atila began to hear them, first as a susurration, as if someone were whispering too far inside his head, then night after night, clearer, as if he were approaching them. So he retreated. Though to no avail, because at last he heard them so painfully in another bout of migraines that it seemed each word was cut, crafted, and polished into the horns of a wild goat and then rammed into his head. The voices had the honesty and despair of supplicants; and Atila was in no mood to listen, things had been going just fine without them.

The second day after he began his descent from Piquo Turquino, he came upon the finca owned by the blind peasant woman who bartered with Mongo Pérez for his food and milk and rum. He approached her bo-hío and was pleased to see, sunning at the far end of a field, another rooster. He was a fanciful creature with an inner coat of feathers, orange and red and gold, covered by an outer coat of rougher feathers, brown and black-brown (as if the inner coat were the fire of his spirit and the outer coat the armor nature had supplied—not for his benefit, but for the bene-fit of anyone who might cross his path, so that he might not be burned to cinders). When Atila came closer he could tell by the way the talons were shaped and by the ridges on the toes that this was a young rooster and a fighting rooster. When he saw Atila he stood and opened his wings to re-veal all the flames inside him—so bright, Atila was blinded momentar-ily—and crowed obscenely. He then darted at Atila and with his beak pierced Atila's side, and backed away, his fire-wings opened even wider, and a bit confused now surely! When the fire-rooster darted again, he moved so quickly that he was able to dig a claw on the side before Atila pushed him off. Atila felt the blood on the underside of his right wing, and when he spread it open again to assume the fighting stance, he felt a stab that was almost a joy, for it brought him closer in touch with his long

ancestry of fighting cocks. After twenty-one years of docility, he was finally fighting, and not against a pansy like Paco Fortunato (for though
Atila loved him then and now, he could not consider such an effeminate
beauty a fighter), but against an experienced fighting cock the color of
embers covered by mud. Atila crowed an unheard-before note and he
knew that his grandfathers and great-grandfathers were at that minute
taking possession of his body. The fire-rooster began to circle slowly, his
eyes fixed on Atila's eyes, though Atila knew that this was a trick, that in
the fire-feathers there were thousands of other eyes more sensitive than the
ones fixed in his head, that could spot any weakness, pick out any vulnerability, any opening for attack. How did Atila, raised as an aesthete, on
Italian opera and Austrian violin concertos and the womanly verses of José
Martí, purposefully against this gets-you-nowhere violence, know this?
How did he too start seeing with his blue feathers, the battle-eyes of his
long and doomed ancestry sprouting on his spread wings?

It was in his blood. How else?

The fire-rooster circled some more, a bit baffled now, for his opponent,
who had seemed helpless at first, an easy half-round match, was now protecting himself like an expert, guessing all attack plans before he had any
time at all to pursue them, staring back at his thousand eyes with a thousand and one. This cornflower-colored powderpuff who was half his size, if
that, was going to ruin his siesta. He circled and circled and could find no
way to attack the blue dwarf. The siesta was definitely postponed.

Atila guessed that in being still, gyrating on his left talon to the beat
of his opponent's circle-dance, he had the advantage. His stillness revealed
very little. While the more the fire-rooster moved in circles around him,
the more Atila knew about him: the shape of the four balancing toes in his
talons, the sharpest nail in the long middle toe, the one in the right talon
sharper, which threw the kilter of his motion off for just a millisecond
when he stepped on it, raising by an all but imperceptible tad his center
of gravity; the fifth nail, the spur, sticking out, thornlike up the ridged
leg, again the one in the right talon sharper, shaped more like a gutting
knife than a thorn; the yellow down that covered the rest of his leg, thick
as fur, erect, making his bony legs look as bulky as his muscular thighs;
the left wing that drooped just a bit lower than the right one, perhaps because it had more mud-feathers than fire-feathers; the pouchy wattle that
dangled to one side or the other of his neck when he stepped; and of course
the beak, sharp as a fishing hook but crooked slightly to the right, for
which the fire-rooster compensated by continuously tilting his head to the
same side, straightening the beak, a motion that he was so accustomed to
doing that it had become involuntary, like a twitch. All these things com-
bined let Atila's thousand and one battle eyes know exactly when he had
to make his move—just as the longest-nailed toe of the right talon was
planted down, as the fire-rooster's center rose and most of his balance was

on his spindly legs and not his huge thighs, as he depended more on his weaker left wing for support (his right wing too busy coordinating balance on the right side), as the combination of his fleshy wattle bouncing around to his right side and the twitch of his head exposed the left side of his neck like a babe left out for the wolves.

Too easy, Atila thought, and the thousand and one eyes of his ancestors agreed. But he let the fire-rooster circle some more, tire out a bit, lunging at him every now and then but not too threateningly, so that his circles would get smaller and smaller, and his motions, as he grew in assurance, sloppier and sloppier, till it seemed to Atila that the poor thing was drowning in a bucket of syrup, and as the right talon went down and the wattle dangled and the head twitched, Atila lunged, pinning his twice-as-big opponent with his beak sunk into the left side of his throat, so that the fire-rooster crowed less obscenely now, begging for a quick and merciful death. But it had been a long time since Atila had his feathers tangled with anyone else's. It had been a long time since he had heard a heart beating so fast. So long, that Atila grew fond of the fire-rooster, and keeping his beak dug into the flesh of his neck, pressing against the windpipe so that the fire-rooster knew that any sudden movement would mean his air would be cut off, Atila began to explore with his left talon under the fire-rooster's tail, which wasn't as stunning as Paco Fortunato's tail, but handsome nonetheless. The fire-rooster was shocked. *Death! Death now! ¡La muerte ahora mismito!* he seemed to crow. *¿Qué es esto? What are you doing? You pervert! You gran bugarrón!* Atila adjusted his position and continued to explore till the fire-rooster was too weak with shame to further protest and Atila lifted his beak and held the fire-rooster's neck with his right talon and mounted him. So is the Greek fabulist correct when he asserts that it is not only fine feathers that make a fine bird? Or, what does mud and fire on the outside feel like from the inside? Or, aren't we getting just un poquito too personal?

Suffice it to say, that though Atila never found another lover with as fine command of his tail as Paco Fortunato, after the encounter with the fire-rooster, Atila took to loving many others in his eleven-year descent down the mountainside. Unlike with Paco Fortunato, Atila felt no guilt. And as he did the first time, when he covered the fire-rooster's corpse with his mud-wing so that it seemed a fresh dirtmound of a grave, so he did with all the other defeated roosters, at such a voracious rate, three or four a day sometimes, that the guajiro chicken farmers banded together and raided the old Spanish cemeteries, disinterred the bodies of the colonialists, plied out the gold from their skulls, melted it all together till they had molded a ball of gold three feet high, and offered it as a reward for the head of the wolfish dwarf cock with the Varadero-blues tail who was raping and murdering their finest stud roosters.

Atila escaped by heading westward on the mountain range, to a rockier and less inhabited region. For many days he did not eat, and when his hunger towered over him, he let go of his desire for other roosters and the thousand and one eyes of his ancestors grew blind again and the voices of his omnipresent migraine became the leathery lash tongues of two groups whipping each other like an irascible Greek chorus turned against itself. Finally, one of the arguing sides caught his attention and he was lifted from his place on the mountain to a point higher than the village of La Tiza, though he well knew that the village of La Tiza was the highest point on the Island. He saw a human mouth toothless and with many many tongues. He placed the voices. The ghosts of all the suicides. And through them Atila saw the Island as it was—as if he were flying over it— a one-eyed crocodile wearing a dress, and he saw the horny skin of the crocodile studded with rubies and black sapphires and diamonds, as if some brave soul had dared to seduce the crocodile and lulled her to sleep and while she slept, sewn with a sickle-shaped needle these jewels into her tough skin, into her dress made of mountain rock and even into her gargantuan see-all eye. The jewels, the voices said, are the great cities of the Island as they will be when you rule over them, and all the waters that wash her will be as beautiful and as varicolored as your tail. We will be your army of sirens, the voices went on, we will help you seduce her first, and later protect her by luring any invaders to her rockiest and most perilous shores. Atila had not said no, had not thought no, but simply doubted that he could ever reign over this great beast when the voices showed him a drastic alternative vision. The crocodile was on her back being devoured by a battalion of scavenger beetles—steel beetles that puffed steam flew in from the north and made a sound like quishy-washy when they chewed, and oak-colored beetles that swam in from the east and used their ashen wings as sails. The waters around the crocodile were brown, yellow, and crimson from her spilling insides. Atila fell back to the earth and the siren-suicides never tempted him again.

There would be others of better use to them.

Instead, the voices of the other side of the dueling chorus captured his attention. These were lonely, selfish, and less ambitious voices and they did not pray for him to save the Island from the treachery of history, but for far simpler things: one, an eighty-nine-year-old voice, prayed that the unbearable solitude of her old age be eased, either by death or by bearing now the children she had never borne, for there was time, she came from a sturdy line of centenarians so she could at least see her children into early manhood; another voice, just as old, prayed that her too-teeming womb would dry (wasn't it time already), there were always too many mouths to feed, and she could not stand it when her ancient but randy husband told the elder son at the time of a new birth, no matter how old the boy was, fifteen or eleven or even nine once, that he could not afford to feed him anymore, that he would have to go into the world and make do on his own, then a little pat on the ass and a *vaya-con-Dios* and she would never see her son again, for boys like trouble as much as trouble likes them. A guajiro prayed for mild weather with a little more rain so that the sugarcane and garbanzo bean harvest be plentiful, even though the land was not his; the finquero who owned that land was traveling to the capital for perhaps his last time, because he had grown so obese that it took four of his strongest servants to wheel him around in an ornately carved dolly-cart from place to place, and he prayed for a famine of such proportions that there would be no food left on the Island, and the livestock would starve and all temptations vanish so he would dwindle down to normal size. One mother prayed for the death of her son, who had fallen into evil ways with hogs and goats and other men, she prayed that his insides be stricken down with some black plague, that his outside be scattered with welts and lesions, so painful and humiliating that on his deathbed he may repent and not perish everlasting; another mother prayed that her son, who had already been reborn once, be reborn again—for a thief-surgeon from the capital had kidnapped him and drugged him and cut into him and stolen one of his lungs—even if she was to forget who he was. This last prayer Atila heard after spending more than a decade in the rocky wilderness. He had survived by drinking from hidden fountains that trickled like pinpricks from the surface of the rough-skinned land, by eating baby rattlers, attacking the nest when the mother had wandered to forage for her newborns, and eating also the tenderized rat meat that the mother brought back and coughed up and left behind in her desolation; sometimes the mother attacked him and Atila opened his wings and summoned again the thousand and one eyes of his ancestors, and as he had defeated the many stud roosters before, he defeated the mother rattler, though he did not even bother to mount her before he sliced off her head with his right spur. So it was amidst all these dead mothers and their devoured offspring that he heard this last prayer of a twice-grieving mother; it was the only prayer he had heard in all his time in the wild that deemed a response. He moved away from the wilderness northward, to the site of his fallen temple.

When he reached the purlieus of the town of Bayamo, he saw a radiant rainbow dust cloud rising from the earth. The nimbus changed colors as it ascended into the brighter light and loomed in shades of gold, vermillion, and avocado, lined with a metallic blue, and then unwove itself until it was unseen. Atila followed it until he stood atop a hill overlooking the eastern wall of the fallen temple. There were kiosks set up in the dirt ground all around the wall, on the inner side and the outer side, so that it looked like a bazaar. A horde of townspeople circled and circled the wall as if they were modeling for a painting of one of Dante's infernal levels, and once in a while a Condemned One would be motivated to stop at a kiosk and haggle with the kiosk owner, and if a transaction was agreed upon, the Condemned One would pull out gold coins or green yanqui dollars (it was the only two types of money the kiosk owners seemed to accept), and he would be handed a heavy parchment sheet and a blue feather, its point dipped in red ink. The Condemned One would then pass through the kiosk, in the front and out the back, and kneel in front of the eastern wall. Using his lap as a countertop, the Condemned One would scribble a prayer on the parchment and roll it up around the feather and insert it into a cranny of the wall. To exit he would have to pay another fee to the kiosk owner. Every hour or two, when his allotted portion of the wall was too stuffed with rolled parchment, so that there was no little crevice left to insert even the briefest of prayers, the kiosk owner would pull out all the rolls and neatly pile them and set them on fire. From these bonfires rose the kaleidoscopic cloud Atila saw.

He would later learn that after the destruction of the temple the city government had taken possession of the property on which the wall stood, and after its own attempts at dismantling it proved futile—at one point hiring a team of yanqui engineers, that with their delicate gauges (a theodolite so modern that it could measure the angle of a cricket's fiddle to the exact degree from over a mile away) and with their most sensitive measuring machines came to know the wall better than they knew the contours of their own wives, but still could not knock it down, not even with a modern form of silent explosives at that time being perfected by exiled German scientists in American universities—the city settled on a more inventive way to deal with the ineradicable reminder of its people's madness. It convinced the monsignor of the local parish to preach in front of it and proclaim that like the Jews have theirs now we have ours, our own wailing wall, just that it is an eastern wall and not a western one, but that due to the hurricanes this is more proper for a people of the tropics and that the Lord works in proper ways. Folks from every city and town of the eastern province made pilgrimages to relieve themselves of their greatest fears and sorrows; even the tyrant then in power in the capital made a pilgrimage to the site, hand in hand, like a newlywed couple, with the cardinal of Havana, who was arthritic and could not kneel by the wall so he laid himself face down in front of it and stayed there for so long that the tyrant joked that His Excellency's soul had just been granted a promotion.

The city government had spent a lot of money trying to tear the wall down—just on hiring the yanqui engineers and their frizzy-haired German scientists it had squandered two years of its budget—so now it needed to make some of it back. It hired some of its favorite merchants and rented them pieces of the wall where they could set up their kiosks, so now when a pilgrim wished to make a prayer he had to pay a fee, and of course his own paper and ink were no good anymore, for the acid from these, he was told, ate away at the sacred wall. Instead, the kiosk owners sold the pilgrims a specially treated parchment and the blue feather as a pen (which was in honor of the miraculous rooster the temple had been built for) and the red ink in honor of the blood spilled during the riot that destroyed the temple. The monsignor of the local parish vehemently endorsed this plan, saying that the prayer-fee was no different than the traditional tithe. For his part, he got a kickback for the new tower being added to the Catholic cathedral. For their part, the merchants got to keep up to twenty percent of the fees they collected.

Atila learned all of this and more later, that the color of the iridescent cloud he had followed to his spot atop the hill came from the burning feathers inside the prayer parchments, for the city could not find the appropriate blue feathers for their staged ritual on any fowl, so they bought a paint factory in a nearby town and dyed thousands of hen and rooster feathers, and when these burned they revealed themselves and sent up clouds of their true colors, lined with their false coat of blue. All this Atila learned later. As was true of him throughout his life, there atop the hill he did not think much before he acted, but let whatever song was surging in him guide him. And there atop the hill, Atila sang with his old voice for the first time since he had performed Puccini in the only ceremony in the brief history of the limestone temple. This time it was nothing as exalting as *Suor Angelica* that he sang. This time his song welled from another source altogether. It was a basso cantante aria, and it rumbled from within him, blasting away at the layers of chalkstone lining his throat so that the first few notes were spit out with a cloud of white dust. He did not recognize it at first, this not a work he knew well, not one of Elena Mulé's favorite operas, too dark for her tastes. It was from Arrigo Boito's *Mefistofele.*

There atop the hill was the saint returned as demon. When the pilgrims heard his voice they cowered and put their hands over their heads as if the three thrones of the Almighty were collapsing. The kiosk owners began to take down their tents and collect their wares. But the rumblings they heard were not from paradise, and Atila's voice was not meant to frighten them at all. It bypassed them, ignoring their fearful poses (now perfect for that painting they seemed to be modeling for) and as if blown by a vengeful hurricane wind headed for the eastern wall. In every crevice where there had once been stuffed a supplication the voice dug in, through every cranny a pleading pilgrim's breath had passed the voice squeezed by, and in every groove a lamenter's tears had sculpted the voice puddled. With his satanic verses Atila surrounded and strung up the wall and he did with it what six teams of Holstein oxen would not, what eight hurricanes did not, what thirty yanqui engineers and twelve German scientists could not, what a million's million prayers cared not, and what the cardinal of Havana dared not, he groaned a note six scales too low for the leftwardest piano key and then shrieked another six scales too high for the rightwardest so that they headed in a barrel dance for their target, and the eastern wall came tumbling down.

Father Jacinto's Great War of the Americas

There was a great carnival, a street fiesta, after the crumbling of the eastern wall. The same merchants who had been appointed the sacred gatekeepers of the prayer ritual set up the same kiosks that had served as portable temples around the mound of limestone rubble that had once been the same sacred eastern wall, and instead of selling parchment and blue feathers and red ink, they sold rum and pork rinds and corn frituritas and two or three of them put their kiosks together and draped heavy canvases over them and set up a funhouse, into which no children were permitted, for the fun was provided by a ring of belly dancers driven in from gypsy-town every evening. The fiesta lasted six days. More prayers were answered in those six days than in the twelve plus years the eastern wall had stood.

In the moonlight of the last night, late, after the line at the entrance to the funhouse had dwindled to three old drunks who frantically searched their every pocket, pulling out coins wrapped in lint, to see if together, all three of them could gather enough money to buy one of the dancers for a minute each, and most of the other kiosks had been dismantled, Atila, who had been pacing up and down the mound of limestone rubble, because the pieces of stone, still vibrating with the force of their fall a week before, were warm, and the heat eased his arthritic talon-joints, saw a naked boy, his whole body caked in fresh mud, peeking into the funhouse through a tear in the canvas and clumsily stroking himself, unable to manage the burgeoning heft of his thing. Atila crowed softly and the boy jumped, the fright deflating him a little, giving him more control of the task at hand. When he saw Atila, he seemed relieved that it was only a rooster and pulled himself away from the peepshow, and he snapped his fingers calling after the bird and began to stroke again. His fingernails were sharp and as long as Atila's talons and he was careful not to scrape himself, using only the palm of his hand, cupped around his penis as if it were a flightless bird. The mud on his hair and on his face was beginning to dry and crack and the boy seemed barely able to open his eyes and his mouth, through which he breathed, for his nostrils were clogged with earth. Atila crowed a bit louder, directing it at the boy, and the dried mud on the boy's face fell away in chunks. As if aroused by this, his burden eased, the boy seemed to be lifted by a little wind and was relieved. "Ay, gallito, gallito, mío," he said. "Are you the one who awoke me last week with your monstrous song? What a voice, gallito. It must have penetrated

the very core of the earth." He laid face up on the ground, frothing the
fluid on his belly, and stared at the moon and the stars, which after a while
seemed to frighten him, for he turned on his belly and, with his face dug
in the dirt, he fell asleep.

The following morning the boy awoke and shielded his eyes and raged
at the sunlight. He began to dig at the earth with his long nails, and in
less than a few minutes he had dug a hole big enough to bury himself.
Atila dug him out, but the boy swung at him. Atila had never fought an
opponent this large, who although still a youth, was five or six times the
size of the largest rattlesnake. He swung at Atila again, obviously furious
that he had been unearthed, and this time dug into him with his nails,
immediately drawing blood. Atila opened his wings and the wild boy
backed off, as if the light of a thousand and one more suns were upon him,
then he came at Atila blindly, with his head bent low like a bull, so that
Atila was easily able to scoot out of the way and take a swipe at his rump
as he passed. The wild boy yelped and fell to his knees and began to dig
himself another hole. Atila jumped on his back and with his right talon
on the boy's neck and his left talon clutching at his curls forced his head
back so that the boy's face was hit directly by the sunlight and when his
eyes widened, as if in surrender, Atila saw that they were so carbon-black
that he could not find the pupil and that they were lined with a thread-
thin strip of violet. Atila knew this boy who suddenly lost all his wildness
as his limbs went flaccid. Atila laid him in the first hole he had dug until
nightfall and then he dragged him to a nearby tributary of the River
Cauto and washed the wound on his buttcheek and all the earth off him,
and then with the boy's long brown curls entwined three times around his
beak, Atila dragged him to a nearby grotto and waited for the boy to
awake.

A one-eyed Jesuit named Jacinto de la Serna walked three miles from the
seminary every day to wash in the crisp waters of the tributary, looked all
around twice, gyrating his head to and fro, so as to gauge for any possible
intrusion, before he shed his robes and his sandals and his undershirt and
underpants and jumped in, wearing just the black patch over his left eye,
a golden medallion of the Virgin of Guadeloupe and a chunk of coconut-
flesh soap tied by a horsehair rope around his neck. Father Jacinto was a
professor of archeology and social science at the Belén College in the capital and was ending a two-year sabbatical with a visit to his mother in
Manzanillo. During his sabbatical he had visited as a guest and a scholar
at the Vatican, had been to la Scala, had gone to Paris, and had spent time
with the republican rebels in northern Spain, where he had lost his left eye
when their squad was ambushed one morning by Francoist troops. That
week he had been invited to spend time with an exiled republican

colonel—the war now all but lost—who dwelled in a finca near Bayamo, and as he washed in the river he was already planning a return to the capital. He was joyful for the first time since he had left Spain weeks before, and he sang hymns to the almighty Lord in thanksgiving for sparing his life. He was so enraptured with his own voice, that at first he did not hear the child's scream echoing from a cavern not too far away, and when he did—because he had been washing just above the waterline, just below his potbelly, rubbing vigorously and religiously there with the coconut flesh—he thought the child's scream was directed at him, that he was signaling him out to his friends for ridicule, so Father Jacinto headed out of the water and grabbed his bundle of clothes and threw them on, his body still soapy and the coconut soap forgotten and swallowed by the rivercurrent. Father Jacinto was so discomfited that it wasn't till he was more than a hundred meters from the river that he realized that the child's screams were not at all concerned with him. He turned back, astonished by the endurance of the child's lungs—he had not paused for breath since he had begun to scream. Father Jacinto tracked the cry to a cavern upstream. He ran, not giving much thought to what was making the child scream so. He saw a naked boy on his knees and digging furiously at the gravelly dirt within the cavern. Just as Father Jacinto was to go to him, he felt something dig into his lower leg and his first thought was that he had stepped on a bear trap, then he felt it on his other leg, and glanced down and saw the blue ruffle underneath his robe. There was a wild rabid rooster on the loose. He kicked the rooster away and picked up a heavy stone and threw it, missing the rooster by quite a margin. He stepped back out of the cavern to tend his wounds and the boy's screams became less piercing— perhaps because he knew help had arrived. Then his screams stopped altogether and were replaced by a voice more beautiful than any Father Jacinto had heard at la Scala, a melancholy melody that reminded him of Mozart's darkest late pieces. Not daring to enter the cavern by the same entrance, he climbed along one of the side walls, his leather sandals so useless for traction on the slippery rocks that he had to discard them, till he reached a nook above with a hole that opened into the main cove.

He saw that it was the rooster that sang, standing over a mound where the boy had been digging. Had he killed him and was now paying homage? this the boy's requiem from a chivalrous murderous rooster? ¿un gallo devoto también? Father Jacinto maneuvered his way back down the cave side with some trouble (it had been much easier on the way up and he thought this a peculiar symbolism). The soles of his feet were cut and the cuts on his shins were still bleeding, so he limped back to the river and waded in knee-deep till the cool waters, though they stung at first, had washed away most of the pain. He went back to the front entrance of the cave. The rooster was still singing and the timbre of his voice became more and more precise as the rapture of the chords darkened. Father

Jacinto was far too curious. He walked back into the cave, crouching a bit, his fingers curled, ready to do battle with the rooster if necessary. The rooster paid no attention to him this time and continued with his mourning. The boy, who had indeed been buried under the mound, had pushed his head back out of the earth and he listened, enthralled by his own death song, no longer terrorized. The rooster continued his memorial service for over two hours, improvising the whole thing, for at times he paused and stared away at the empty air as a composer might in the middle of knitting together a symphony.

Father Jacinto sat near the mound and crossed his legs, wishing someone as talented as this blue cock would compose a hymn for all of the dead at the hand of Franco's fascists. When it was over, Father Jacinto stood and clapped and clapped and yelled bravo and bravo as if he were at la Scala still, and the boy, bringing his hands out of his grave with some trouble, also clapped and spoke for the first time, mimicking Father Jacinto with bravo and bravo, and encore and encore. Atila did not bow, did not blow kisses to them, did not take seventeen curtain calls, did not clasp any bouquets. He had not performed—or so it seemed from his demeanor, as he stepped down from the mound and began picking at bugs from his wing-pits—for anyone but himself.

Father Jacinto spoke to the boy: "¿De dónde eres? ¿Y este pájaro es tuyo?"

"I come from under the earth. And no the bird is not mine. I found him . . . o mejor dicho, he found *me;* a week ago he awoke me from my earth dream with his demon song, and last night he caught me while I was fucking three viejas!"

Father Jacinto crossed himself. Atila continued to pick bugs off himself and chewed and swallowed them, and the one-eyed Jesuit imagined for a second that he was still in the rebel hospital in Granada, and that this was another morphine-induced hallucination. Still, even in visions, he had his duties. "You lie and you are sinful with women. Do you want to confess?"

"Yes," the boy said. He dug himself further out of his grave. "How do you play?"

"¿Cómo te llamas?"

"Julio César. ¿Tú?"

"Do you know who Julio César is?"

"This is a stupid game: *confess!* I just told you. *I* am Julio César. Now who are you?"

"I am Father Jacinto de la Serna."

"Whose father are you?"

The rooster stopped cleaning himself and he walked over to Father Jacinto. The one-eyed Jesuit stood up and backed away. The rooster folded his legs under him and sat by the priest peacefully as if he were sitting on the nest of a wayward hen. Father Jacinto crouched down like a catcher instead of sitting again.

"Do you want to play this stupid game of confess or not?" the boy said. "Whose father are you?" He dug himself completely out of the earth and Father Jacinto was embarrassed by the boy's nakedness and he could not help to stare at his genitalia, the dark droopy fruit fallen on a pair of large, round bagged riverstones. He offered the boy his robe.

"No, it will itch too much. But whose father are you?"

"Do you ever go to church? I am a father of the church. I teach at a school in the capital. Maybe you would like to come with me."

"You're not playing right."

The sun moved over the side of the cave and a beam of light, fluid as a tentacle, seeped through a crack in the roof and licked Julio César's bare feet. The boy jumped back and his breath quickened and he began to dig himself back in. Father Jacinto went to the boy and grabbed him by the shoulder. His body was feverish. As he struggled with him, all the time darting his one eye back to the rooster, who remained as before, still and meditative, Father Jacinto noticed a long fresh scar on the boy's left side that ran from the side of his belly, under the rib cage and up the sternum and the near his throat dipped downward again towards his nipple so that it looked like a palm twisted and cut in half by a thunderbolt had been etched on his chest. Father Jacinto hugged the boy close and traced the scar with his finger and asked the boy what had happened in a soothing voice that he used only when talking to younger children at the Belén school.

The boy pressed his face to Father Jacinto's chest. "That's how the surgeon from the capital stole my lung," he said. "That's how he killed me. He sells organs to rich yanquis. My mamacita told me stories about him. . . . I thought they were just stories."

Because he knew the boy was still playing confess, because he so much despised yanquis, rich or poor, Father Jacinto believed him. But the love growing in his heart forbade him from listening any further.

"I don't want to go to the capital," the boy said, "that's where the surgeon was from."

A Jesuit in love with a resurrected boy? Not so unbelievable. A doctor who steals from his own people to sell to rich foreigners? Not so unlikely. But organs? stolen organs packed in ice and covered with straw? for what? This is the late 1930s, the only transplant that has been attempted from one human to another is of the cornea. (And it is the Jesuit, not the boy, who has lost an eye!) Christiaan Barnard is a pubescent lad in West Beaufort, South Africa, decades away from conceiving his life's work, obsessed now with only one organ, which he hopes will never be transplanted from his body, though it is now growing heavy on its bough, and the lad has nightmares that it will one day ripen and fall off.

Human organs? from breathing unwilling donors? what fairy tales does a mother invent?

Through our simplest stories are woven the invisible threads of our unmentionable fears. Under the forests of our most fantastic narratives runs, like a serpent under the brush, the most realistic record of our history—just ask Jakob and Wilhelm. A mother who has once lost a child whispers till her dying day, to anyone who will listen, fragmented tales of lost children.

. . . Once there was a blue cock who was said to raise the dead with his wondrous voice.

. . . Once there was an old mother who gave birth to a hanged winking child, and the mother wanted to keep him but the father wanted to fill him with stones and throw him in the river, so the blue cock came and swallowed the winking child, and rescinded the sentence of the umbilical cord, and the child appeared as if fresh from a womb.

. . . Once there was a people so hungry for a savior that they believed all this and were deaf to the cries of a guajiro mother who had had her live-born stolen from right under her crotch, and sacrificed a year of their lives and a lifetime of savings to build a limestone temple for this blue cock, and they called him saint, and their dead went unburied to wait for the savior's return, and thus fashioned out of one fairy tale a fairy tale of their own.

. . . Once there was a blue cock who was said to raise the dead with his wondrous voice, and he had a hunk-of-a-lover and a rotund mistress, and they came with him to reside in his limestone temple, and the blue cock did have a wondrous voice, but like most wonders in our world it did not impress the dead at all, and this limitation, this failure in translation (for certainly the dead speak and hear with other noises, other notes), cost him the life of his hunk-of-a-lover.

. . . Once there was a limestone temple that in one brief locust-dark afternoon was, but for one hardy wall, destroyed.

. . . Once there was a saint returned as demon, and he finished the job.

. . . Once there was a winking child who lived in a second life.

. . . Once there was the case of disappeared children that police captains put at the bottom of their work files, children from the tin-shack towns west of the capital and from small pueblos throughout the length of the Island, even as far east as Oriente, children who would sometimes reappear, as if awakened from a dream, with delicate palms sketched into their chests, their bellies, the small of the back, the left side of their sacs.

. . . Once there was a thief-surgeon from the capital who was ahead of his time, he stole organs for a living, and sold them to rich ailing yanquis, whose own organs they had poisoned with their dissolute lives, and they also believed too much in fairy tales, as if the tropical heat had melted their cold logical minds, and were told that for their poisoned organs to heal they must eat the fresh healthy organs of others, and so they unpacked their pine boxes of straw and unmelted ice, and quickly sauteed kidneys with garlic and peppercorn and port wine, broiled liver with Spanish seasoning, stuffed hearts with minced onion and marjoram leaves, and wrapped tiny huevitos, no bigger than olives, in strips of bacon, and swallowed slices of lung raw, letting the little globules of air expand in their mouth and pop, each according to his malady, and all as shamelessly as if they were feasting on the innards of beast or fowl, and though they never knew the thief-surgeon's name, while their unhealing organs let them live, they considered him their savior.

. . . Once there was a winking boy who would need a third life, whose lung would be an appetizer to some decrepit yanqui in the capital (though the thief-surgeon consoled himself in that he had not killed him but stitched him up and left him to live after the drugs wore off; it was only when he needed a heart or a liver that he was forced to kill, when no delicate half-palm need be carved, just a blow to the head and a slit from the base of the neck to the pit of the groin).

. . . Once there was a thief-surgeon who drew half-palms with the genius of a court calligrapher, and on the chest, the bellies, the backs, the sacs, of the Island's children would forever grow these half-trees, the mark of their fortune, for they had *re*appeared, they had lived.

Once begun a fairy tale must needs continue. Just ask Wilhelm and Jakob. Just ask any in the ghostly drunken march of the capital's toppled tyrants. Or better yet, as Father Jacinto would have it, just ask the yanquis.

Father Jacinto lost the boy Julio César twice on the train trip from his mother's house in Manzanillo to the Alturas de Belén hillside where the college was located in the capital. The first time, at a stop in a town called Las Tunas, he thought the boy had run back home. Father Jacinto had stepped off the train to buy him a cola and a piece of candy at a market down the street from the station. When he came back the boy was gone. Father Jacinto had picked up a new habit since he met Julio César and his blue rooster, he would lift up the black patch on his left eye to make sure he wasn't dreaming, for in his dreams he could still see with both eyes. He did this now and looked around the coach, and the few passengers that paid any attention at all to Father Jacinto when he shook them and asked them where the boy had gone looked away from the stitch scars in his left eye socket and said the boy had walked out almost right behind him. He undid the pierced sackcloth tied over the tin bucket under his seat. The blue rooster was asleep. He took the tin bucket outside and turned it over and the rooster came tumbling out, rudely awakened.

"I've lost Julio César," Father Jacinto said to the rooster. The people who had not boarded yet, and those who were still waiting in line at the ticket counter and were too riddled with impatience to notice anything (cubanos back then had not yet mastered the art of waiting in la cola), turned and watched this scene, forgetting about their hurries.

"I've lost Julio César," the Jesuit repeated. This time the rooster seemed to comprehend, because it opened wide its wings and began to lead the priest out of the station in marching steps.

"Please wait for us, negro," Father Jacinto screamed to the conductor, trying not to lose sight of the rooster. "We won't be long. I need to find the boy."

"¿Sí, sí, cómo no?" the conductor said. "Not te preocupes, padrecito, we'll wait for you." He was going to call the local police, but he thought better of it, and told the engineer to ease the engines a bit. They were going to wait, and he crossed himself three times as if to prove it to Father Jacinto, who waved his mil gracias.

They were gone for two and half days. They followed a dirt highway that crossed through cane fields and headed northeasterly towards the ocean. They passed the finca of a certain don Piño who chased them with his hounds for twelve hours, and intermittently fired his shotgun into the air and announced his hatred of all comepinga sodomite priests. They came to a swamp region near Puerto Carupano, where the mangroves grew so prolifically that the entwining roots knit a landmass of their own; the blue rooster stopped and began to circle and look for the boy Julio César. They found him buried in the soft mud near the firm land of a nearby village; a cloud of mosquitoes had begun to devour him. The rooster sang its requiem again and the boy awoke, slapping his face and his arms to kill the bloodsuckers. Father Jacinto picked him up (he had shed his clothes again) and washed him in a lagoon near Puerto Carupano and tore off the lower part of his robe and fashioned for the boy a dress. On the way back they stopped at a young peasant couple's bohío and were fed boiled yucca and bread and the peasant's wife told them of a different road back to Las Tunas so that they would not have to cross don Piño's finca, and she told them she could not say why he hated priests so much for it would not be proper, but she did say that don Piño had been raised in a Franciscan orphanage and perhaps they had mistreated him. She gave the boy Julio César a pair of torn work pants that belonged to her husband and a blouse that belonged to her. Father Jacinto thanked them and blessed their thatch-roofed hut.

When they got back to the train station in Las Tunas it was packed with people screaming and yelling at the negro conductor, who had promised he would wait, who, not persuaded by their rage, would not move his train from its spot on the tracks, who had set the entire Island's train schedule back some sixty hours. At first, they were going to simply arrest the conductor; but a Siboney indian lawyer who was traveling to the capital, and was a man inspired by idealistic causes, protested that his arrest was illegal and racially motivated, to which the barefoot police captain guffawed, for he was a very dark mulatto and all his men were darker than him. Still, the Siboney lawyer insisted—somewhat pleased by the hopelessness of his argument—that as long as the conductor was in charge of the train, only his employer in the capital had jurisprudence over him, not the local police. The mayor of Las Tunas reluctantly agreed and the owner of the train company, a cubanized yanqui (an American-Cuban) named Theotis Q. ———— (someone, somewhere, somehow, long ago, had stolen his surname so now anyone whose station forbid them from calling him by his Christian name was forced to address him as Mr. Blank, or Mr. Dash), was wired.

He arrived in Las Tunas the following day down the opposite track, in his private two-car train, pulled by the most powerful locomotive of his fleet. Even though he was losing much money with this delay, and though he was known to be driven into fits of frenzy if any of his trains were a few seconds behind schedule, Mr. Blank, or Mr. Dash, did not fire the negro conductor. As it was, Mr. Blank, or Mr. Dash, also had a reputation as a progressive yanqui businessman, who as a young man had belonged to the American Communist Party. (It was there and then, it was said, that his surname had been stolen—or that he had simply lent it to a persecuted comrade who had forgotten to give it back.) He would not act so brashly. Instead, he invited the sixteen photographers and reporters that he had brought with him from the capital into the railway station and as he stroked his obscene raccoon-tail mustache, citing both Karl Marx and Adam Smith, debated with the Siboney lawyer the rights of his employee. It was in the middle of this debate, as Mr. Blank, or Mr. Dash, was scaling to Ciceronian heights, that Father Jacinto returned with the boy Julio César in his arms and the blue rooster perched on his right shoulder.

"All aboard!" the negro conductor screamed. "Se va el tren, chico. ¡Se va por fin!"

The following day, just as he had planned, Mr. Blank, or Mr. Dash, was depicted in all the front page stories in the capital as a kind and gentle employer, who cared for the rights of individual workers as much as he cared for profits; and one editor went as far as to claim that Cuba needed more yanqui bosses like Mr. Blank, or Mr. Dash, to show us how to run a company in a proper and Christian fashion.

At the railway station, after introducing himself and taking the boy

Julio César from his arms, turning just slightly to give the photographers his better side, Mr. Blank, or Mr. Dash, chatted with Father Jacinto, learned that the boy was a runaway and that the priest had taken him under his custody and was planning on giving him a proper education at the Belén College in the capital. Mr. Blank, or Mr. Dash, offered Father Jacinto a ride to the capital in his private two-car train. (He would cast out some of the minor reporters.)

"It would be much faster," he explained, "safer for the boy, now that the papers will make him famous."

Father Jacinto, so devout in his hatred of yanquis, no matter what political persuasion, no matter what social station, a sin he relished even more than his hatred of the Franco nationalists, lifted his eyepatch— though the yanqui, being a man of the world, did not blink at the skin-sealed pocket of the Jesuit's left eye—and answered curtly: "Gracias, pero no, you Mister This . . . you Mister That." And then he added after taking the boy back and walking past him: "Mucho gusto."

"Igualmente," Mr. Blank, or Mr. Dash, said in unaccented Spanish, not letting his disappointment show. "And please, oh please, call me Theotis . . . Theotis Q."

Father Jacinto fastened a leather sash to Julio César's wrist with a Mary-Magdalene knot that he had learned to tie in the mountains of Spain with the republican rebels (so named because once it was tied it was undoable and secure as the Magdalene's chastity belt after the Resurrection), and tied the other end to his wrist with a lesser gordian knot. They passed through Camagüey and Ciego de Ávila, and through the tobacco fields near Cienfuegos, where they stopped and Father Jacinto napped. When he awoke, the boy was again missing. He had chewed through the leather lash and taken the Mary-Magdalene knot with him. He also took the blue rooster in the tin bucket. Father Jacinto jumped out of the train, and though he said nothing to the negro conductor, when he stopped back in the railway station, after having searched for Julio César around the town and down the port, the train was delayed again at the station. The Siboney indian lawyer, with his arm wrapped around the negro conductor, was ready to do battle with Mr. Blank, or Mr. Dash, again, for the yanqui had already been summoned from the capital.

"Se te fue otra vez, eh chico," the conductor said. "Oye padre, me parece que el mocoso ese no te quiere." Father Jacinto smiled patiently. "Yes, he left me again. Se me fue." He threw up his hand with half the leather sash still tied around it. "But please don't cause any hassle on my account. I'll catch another train."

"We'll find him!" a gruffy voice said in English. Mr. Blank, or Mr.

Dash, had arrived. He had brought with him a team of yanqui investigators, with their dark glasses and telescopic binoculars and bulges, like tumors, within their dark suits.

"Lo encontraremos sin duda." Mr. Blank, or Mr. Dash, spoke again in his perfect Spanish. They searched for seven days, Mr. Blank, or Mr. Dash, insisting the train on which Father Jacinto was riding remain in the station till the boy was found, this time throwing off the Island's train schedule by over one hundred and fifty hours. The national guard was called in, but Mr. Blank, or Mr. Dash, had offered his men a hefty bonus and a lofty promotion as reward for anyone who found the boy and he knew they would not be outdone by the ragtag third-rate peasant soldiers.

On the eighth day, in an illegal raid of a fishing trawler from the state of Louisiana, they found Julio César buried in a tepid shrimp stew, in a giant tin pot, in the boiler room. The local police were called in because the cook of the fishing trawler had chased one of Mr. Blank, or Mr. Dash's, men with a cleaver, threatening to chop off all his appendages, starting with that little wee-pinky excuse for a dick, not because they had raided the boat but because apparently one of the investigators had made a crack about his shrimp stew, of how it smelled worse than a whore's twat at sunrise. The captain of the trawler, a Cajun named Richard Hadley, gathered all his men on deck and refused to let anyone take the boy, who stood by him, sopping with the foul-smelling stew. Richard Hadley had a heavy gait and a pronounced limp and the boat wobbled as he marched and questioned his men and questioned the boy. Mr. Blank, or Mr. Dash, had arrived, with Father Jacinto and an army sergeant right behind him. He congratulated his man who had almost been chopped to pieces.

"Sailor," Mr. Blank, or Mr. Dash, screamed at Richard Hadley, "you are in danger of causing a serious scandal with your kidnapping of this native boy. As one American to another, I demand that you release him, and I assure you that no charges will be filed."

Richard Hadley turned away from his men. He hobbled to the bow and looked up at Mr. Blank, or Mr. Dash, who was standing on the pier. "Sir," he said, "first of all, I am a fisherman not a sailor, so please get that right. Second, I have broken no laws. This boy came on my ship of his own free will and may leave it just so. It is his choice. But if he wants to stay and join my crew I will not let you touch him. And third, please don't address me as one American to another. I was born in Louisiana and have been a fisherman all my life and have never wandered farther north than Richmond, Virginia. You, from the looks of you (no matter how tropical you try to look in your linen suit and your pale moccasins and your expensive Panama) were born in some great colonial estate in Connecticut and have never dug your rosy little hands into the earth, much less dipped them in the wonders of the sea. No offense, sir, but we are not brothers!"

"Let the boy speak!" Mr. Blank, or Mr. Dash, said, clearly offended, and astounded that the hick sailor had guessed the state of his birth; his raccoon-tail mustache drooped.

Julio César was eating bits of stew off his own body, which made Richard Hadley's men squirm, and he said nothing.

"Young man," Father Jacinto spoke in broken English, stepping in front of Mr. Blank, or Mr. Dash. Richard Hadley, who was limping back towards his men, turned and beamed a smile: "Oh golly, I haven't been called that in a long time."

"That boy is a runaway," Father Jacinto continued, pausing as he translated his thoughts. "He needs help. He might even be, well . . . como se dice . . . un poquito retarded. He has not had much education. I plan to give him that. I teach at a very reputable school in the capital, and—"

"Enough of this nonsense," Mr. Blank, or Mr. Dash, said to the army sergeant. "Arrest that man! He is breaking international law!" As Mr. Blank, or Mr. Dash, shoved him towards the trawler, the army sergeant was clearly debating with himself whether his authority extended beyond the pier. Richard Hadley ignored them both. "Arrest him!" Mr. Blank, or Mr. Dash, said to his own men, who (though each held a nervous hand at the tumor on his side) were held at bay by the mad cook who still kept his rusty cleaver cocked in front of him.

"I suspect that this boy is a lot brighter than you think, Father," Richard Hadley said. "We have talked. We have talked a lot."

He took off his T-shirt and revealed his marvelously tattooed torso, with muscles so thick and layered that you could distinguish each single one slithering on another, so that his whole upper body seemed like a sack of serpents. He dunked the T-shirt in a water bucket and hobbled over to Julio César and wiped the boy's face, then he whispered something to him and patted him on the back. The boy spoke. He said that after he had fled from the train station two men had stolen his rooster from him and had chased him to the port, for they said they were hungry and the rooster wasn't a meal big enough. The rooster had tried to fight, opening wide his wings and darting at them, struggling for over an hour before they wrapped a sugar sack around him. Meanwhile, Julio César, afraid they were after his other lung, ran and hid in this boat. When the crazy cook found him in a storage bin in the cellar, cuddling with the rats, he took him to Captain Richard Hadley. The captain was kind, and when Julio César could not sleep, Richard Hadley told him a story of his life (*for our lives are many stories—not just one—often at much odds with each other*), how as a boy he had dreamt he wanted to be a fish, but his muscles were always so big and dense, even as a child, that he could not swim, and he could not be a fish, and his elders told him that the sea was not for him. When he was twelve, he stowed away in a trawler just like the one he owned now, and a lovelorn, whisky-sweating captain taught him how to fish, and later how to swim. He was joyful, for though his muscles kept on growing denser, and at first when he jumped in the water he sank, as if he were wearing the heaviest of diving belts, soon he learned how to fill his lungs with great breaths, till they were like balloons that counterbalanced the weight of his muscles, and he became an expert swimmer, and could now be with the fish in their world, as they lived and as they died. Richard Hadley told the boy that he was fortunate, for he knew the method of his own death: his serpent muscles had grown so ravenous, that no matter how many chunks of tuna he ate, they (the serpent-muscles) remained hungry for more, so much so that they began to eat at his bones after they got a whiff of the marrow. Eventually all his bones would be eaten, and his body would collapse (so in fact, the muscles were unwittingly plotting their own ends, a suicidal rebellion, a doomed feast). "I am like a house undoing itself beam by beam," Richard Hadley said. There was only one good note to all this: because there are so few muscles in the head, his skull would be spared from the bone-feast, and his brain would be un-damaged. "And that's where I store all my stories," Richard Hadley said, "under lock and key." He turned an invisible key at his temple and made a clicking sound and winked. Julio César begged to hear some of the sto-ries, and as he napped in the captain's cabin, he dreamt of a boy who be-gan as a boy and ended as a fish, boiled in a stew.

"I don't want to leave," Julio César said, his breath short after having spoken so long. He got on his knees and hugged Richard Hadley around the hips, his arms not quite reaching all the way around, and pressed his ear to Richard Hadley's backside to see if he could hear the ass muscles munching on the bone, and he rubbed his cheeks against Richard Hadley because he felt so warm, as if the serpent-muscles burned with energy even when they were still.

Father Jacinto was silent, unable to comprehend the inscrutable joy in Julio César's dark eyes, a joy that he had tried and failed to draw out ever since he met the boy; and now this yanqui trawler captain, this painted white man, un chusma, had succeeded even without trying.

"No quiero irme," the boy repeated.

Captain Richard Hadley made a chewing sound with the side of his mouth and fooled the boy into believing it was his serpents gnawing at his bones, so that the boy jumped back away from him, frightened. Richard Hadley laughed and went to the boy and spoke to him in whispers and Julio César shook his head vigorously and the captain consoled him by placing both his hands on the boy's shoulders and wiping his face again with the wet T-shirt.

Finally, even though Julio César was still shaking his head vigorously, Richard Hadley spoke: "Father, he'll go with you tomorrow. Tonight he will spend with us; we are going to prepare a great farewell feast for him."

The crazy cook with the rusty cleaver grunted.

Father Jacinto, who could now taste his disdain for the whole tribe of thieving yanquis, as if he were swirling sour milk and the yolks of rotted eggs around in his mouth, with a nidorous breath, spoke only three words: "Bien, regreso mañana."

And he brushed past Theotis Q. ——— punching shoulders with him and almost knocking the surnameless railroad tycoon into the ashen waters of the port of Cienfuegos.

The following morning, hand in hand, standing on the rotting pier, Father Jacinto and Julio César watched Richard Hadley's fishing trawler chug off into the Caribbean. It would be over twenty years, in a whole different world, when Julio César would lay eyes on Richard Hadley again. Father Jacinto could tell that the boy was holding back tears but he said nothing to console him, nothing to reprimand him. He simply led him away from there, and this time accepted Mr. Blank's, or Mr. Dash's, offer to ride in his private two-car train to the capital.

"He said that I wasn't made for the sea," Julio César said. "He said that I was too in love with earth. He said that I needed it more than it needed me, that what I could not get from the air now, because of my missing lung, I would get from the earth, that I would always be a landcrawler, and to be proud of it, for the earth has as many beauties and mysteries as the sea. He said he would think of me any time he came to a port and got drunk on aguardiente and rolled in the mud. He said he would think of me."

Father Jacinto did not answer the boy. From that moment on the child was his pupil and he would treat him as such, ignoring any conversation that did not deal directly with his intellectual development. That fall he enrolled Julio César in the second grade at the Colegio Belén, and even though most students were five or six years his junior, he still lagged behind them in grades and achievement. Father Jacinto tutored him privately at night, and because the boy had a habit of escaping from his dormitory room and digging fresh holes in the school's main lawn to sleep there—Father Jacinto could never force the boy to trim his fingernails close enough to incapacitate his digging—Father Jacinto had his antique, falcon-legged bathtub, which his grandfather had bequeathed him, filled weekly with fresh soil from the pineapple fields in Pinar del Río, and he let the boy sleep there at night.

Slowly, Julio César made progress in his classes, and in less than two years, caught up with students of his own age. He made a habit of reading *Don Quijote* while half buried in soil in Father Jacinto's bathtub. When he graduated from Belén, six years after Father Jacinto had enrolled him in the second grade, he had read Cervantes' novel eight times. At the graduation ceremony, only one student got more medals from the faculty and a bigger ovation from his peers. He was a bully, a tall boy who excelled in sports and more than once had arranged practical jokes involving the burial of Julio César, one time in a hillock of cow dung, another in a pile of discarded fish heads at a nearby canning factory.

The bully's name was Fidel Castro.

Father Jacinto liked Fidel Castro and he would often invite him to his room at night and lecture both him and Julio César on the evils of yanqui imperialism. Father Jacinto had visions. He said they were as powerful as the visions of St. John. Though as far as theologians can guess, St. John was not in the habit of smoking from a long curvy porcelain opium pipe as Father Jacinto was (after the tall boy had left, after Julio César had buried himself in his falcon-legged bathtub, which Father Jacinto had moved from the bathroom and placed next to his own bed, like a child's bassinet). He had visions of a war against the many-headed yanqui dogs, the pale wolves that for over a century had been stealing into our lands and feasting on the innards of our innocent people, a gory banquet to which no other tribe was invited thanks to the famous *doctrine*. Yes, yes, Father Jacinto believed the fairy tale of the thief-surgeon. He saw the angels of all the countries of Latin America uniting to slay the pack of yanqui Cerberuses. It would be the Great War of the Americas, greater and costlier than the Old World wars, for there it was brother fighting against brother (a family squabble really), here it would be the angels with the pure wine-dark blood of the Aztecs, the Incas, the Negroes and all other sunburned tribes against the rosy-blooded pale-hide northern hounds.

At this point in the vision, as Father Jacinto recounted it the following evening, or sometimes in the middle of a lecture in his class, Fidel Castro always became a little befuddled, for he noticed that both he and Father Jacinto—and, in fact, nearly a hundred percent of the student body at Belén—were as pale-hided and rosy-blooded as any yanqui dog, and he wondered aloud if they would be fighting alongside the White Wolves of the North in the Great War of the Americas.

"No, no, no seas, bobo," Father Jacinto assured him. "We will be with the dark tribes. We will be with the victors."

Fidel nodded unconvincingly and Father Jacinto lifted his eyepatch to get a better look at this doubter and Julio César was impressed because Fidel stared back at the one-eyed Jesuit and did not bat an eye.

Demon or Saint?

At that time, at about the end of the Second Great War in Europe, the University of Havana had seven schools, including law, medicine, and architecture. Although Father Jacinto had pushed Julio César to study archeology, since he had shown such an undisguised interest in, and need for, earth, Julio César decided instead to enroll in the school of philosophy, for no reason at all, except that when wandering the basement offices of that school's main building in the secluded side of the campus, where bearded students sat on stone benches under the shade of the eucalyptus trees discussing the New French School, he had been struck by a placard on one of the office doors that read:

PROFESOR JUAN SALTOS Y BRINCOS
DOCTOR DE DEMONOLOGÍA Y HAGIOGRAFÍA

There and then Julio César decided that while at the university he could make no better use of his time than to study the lives of devils and demons alongside the lives of angels and saints.

When he told this to Father Jacinto one evening, Fidel Castro, who had become a hesitant friend to Julio César, due to the many evenings spent together listening to the one-eyed Jesuit and to their common and abiding interest in Cervantes' knight-errant, said it was a good idea, for their Island was full of both demons and saints, and often you could not tell one from the other.

Fidel Castro himself, after abandoning his dream of traveling to the United States to try out for the professional béisbol leagues, enrolled in the law school; and his tenuous, not yet famous, friendship with Julio César continued.

While still at Belén, Julio César, against Father Jacinto's protestations, had taken a job as a cleaning boy at the house of doña Álvara Clarón, also known as la Gallega, although she was not from Galicia but from the outskirts of Madrid. Doña Álvara was in her forties but she looked much older. She had wide, relentless hips so filled in (and filled out) that even though she wrapped herself in countless red and black and yellow mantles, when she walked you could see the voluminous flesh shifting from side to side. She always wore sandals and her feet were flat and puffy and the toenails were untrimmed. Red paint was chipping off them like off the side of an old barn. On the back of her upper arms there hung a mass of fatty tissue that stretched and dimpled the skin and it dangled like a sackful when she pointed at something. Her hair was almost always at once parchment yellow and ratty black and a bruisy red so that it almost matched her mantles. Her face was grandfatherly ugly and grandmotherly kind, her nose bulbous and pocked from persistent acne lesions, her lower teeth stained from her habit of chewing tobacco, and her eyes a warm and soothing sienna from her yearning to accost and speak to perfect strangers.

She met Julio César at the fruit market. His torso was bare and doña Álvara saw the half-palm frond of his scar. She stood behind him in line and tapped him on the shoulder.

"Muchachito," she said. "I have a blue-feathered rooster that once sang about a boy with a half-palm etched on his chest. Do you want to come hear him?"

Julio César had not forgotten about his blue rooster, for on many nights he had dreams about his other life, before the thief-surgeon from the capital had taken out his lung and left him to die, before he had learned to need the breath of the earth, and he dreamed of his mother and she told him stories about lost children that turned into other dreams about a blue saint of a rooster named Atila. "Is his name Atila?" Julio César said.

"Mira chico, yo no soy loca, how should I know his name? And who goes around naming their fowl anyway? I didn't say my rooster speaks. I said he sang. In Italian, but I understand un poquito. Ven conmigo. I'll show you."

She paid for his fruit and introduced herself with an intimate hug and led Julio César across town to a brick building redundantly painted orange. They passed through an unlit hallway into a garden courtyard full of azaleas and cannonball flowers and African violets and begonias and many other flowers that Julio César could not name. In doña Álvara's room, which they entered through a door on the east side of the garden, the blue-feathered rooster ignored the young man; as they watched him expectantly, and doña Álvara coaxed him with *vamos, vamos gallito, canta tan bonito,* he shit three gray and green soft lumps and then opened his wings and scuttled across the room and hopped on the kitchen counter and shit again on doña Álvara's sack of guavas and bananas and zapotes.

"¡Maldito!" she screamed and threw one of her sandals at him.

As the rooster continued to leave his markings on the room and Julio César made a gesture for the door, more to get some fresh air than to go from there, doña Álvara mentioned that she needed someone to watch her garden, a man to protect her women. Since the young man was eager to get away from his one-eyed Jesuit guardian, who these days talked of nothing more than that devil Franco (who had wisely stayed out of the Second Great War) and of the evil yanquis, who now would think that since they had saved the world from the fascists they therefore owned it, he eagerly accepted the job. By the time he began classes at the University of Havana—the first to register for Professor Saltos y Brincos's comparative course on two of history's great dissidents, Milton's Satan and Santa Teresa de Avila—Julio César was living with doña Álvara. He had moved from Father Jacinto's living quarters after his graduation from Belén. The Jesuit had reluctantly agreed that it would be improper if he stayed, though he continued to give him the thirty pesos a month allowance, which Julio César spent buying exotic lingerie from a French store in the old city for the ladies who worked in doña Álvara's orange house.

Father Jacinto also bequeathed to Julio César the antique falcon-legged bathtub, which the young student set up in doña Álvara's court-yard and filled with garden soil and at nights, just when the house was beginning to bustle with activity, American and European tourists, in light-colored linen suits splotched with wine, coming in and out of the seven doors of the seven rooms that encircled the courtyard (yes, for even in doña Álvara's fetid room there was activity), Julio César would dig himself in and forget about everyone.

"Some protector you are," doña Álvara chided him in the mornings. "What am I paying you for. Just to sit around here and look pretty?" And indeed, it was exactly what she was paying him for, to remind her women that masculine beauty existed in the world, though they may never guess at it from the besotted tourists they pleased every night.

His friend Fidel showed up once in a while—Julio César had con-vinced doña Álvara to offer a discount for the students at the university, assuring her it would make her women much happier to have some young blood *inside* their rooms—and before Fidel left he would crouch by the an-tique falcon-legged tub and start speaking in amorous whispers till Julio César poked his head out of the soil. He played a game with his old friend, quizzing him to see how much he had learned about demons and saints. He would ask of prominent historical characters:

"Demon or saint?"

He started with easy ones. "José Martí?"

"Fácil. Saint."

"Adolf Hitler?"

"Más fácil. Demon."

Then he would progress to more difficult ones. "Roosevelt?"

"Which one?"

"Franklin Delano."

Pause. "Saint."

"Theodore."

Longer pause. "Demon . . . no?"

Then to almost unguessable ones. "Harry Truman?"

"No sé."

"Murderer," Fidel said. "Atomic demon."

"Juan Perón?"

"Tampoco sé."

"Yanqui-hater," Fidel answered himself again, "reformer and a saint!"

Then, not breaking stride, speaking in the same amorous whisper, he would end the game as always. "Julio César?"

"Which one, the emperor or the gatekeeper of the orange whore-house?"

Silence from the questioner.

"Actually it makes no difference, they are both poor devils."

"Why?"

"Porque sí, because they are betrayed."

"Fidel Castro?"

"De dos cabezonas," Julio César answered assuredly, "demon one day, saint the other."

Julio César could tell that Fidel liked this answer, that he was a man already comfortable with the multitudinous contradictions in his personality, that he had achieved as a youth that perfect clarity in ambiguity that evades most men all of their lives. He was prudish and fun-loving, he would lecture Julio César for drinking too much rum one day and the next would show up at three in the morning with a bottle of rum in one hand and a bottle of whisky in the other, singing salsa ballads, waking Julio César and dragging him to a nearby cemetery to watch the milky moon.

"La luna is like us," Fidel said, "like our sad little Island, living on borrowed means, its every step dictated by the light of the tyrannous sun, even though you would never guess it. It looks brilliant and beautiful all on its own." Then he would sing to his friend and sing to the moon.

He was good-willed and malicious, at times he cared for Julio César like a brother, and visited him every week, and eased the jolts of his loneliness, but just as easy, he would make a cutting remark or pull some prank to remind him who was still the jock and the bully and who was still the queer abused kid. One dawn, while Julio César was still buried in his falcon-legged bathtub, he heard Fidel's voice as he came out of the fourth door in the garden. He was drunk. He was mad because the alcohol had not let him perform. He kicked the falcon-legged tub and called Julio César a priest-lover and a marica. Then he stood over the tub and urinated on the packed soil, laughing all the while, and promised that when he ruled the Island he would hang all the curitas and all the mariconcitos by their cojonecitos.

"Ese los curas le metieron complejo de rey," doña Álvara often said.

The liquid felt warm and soothing as it seeped through the soil and spread over Julio César's arched back and buttocks. He was not insulted or outraged as Fidel had expected him to be. During his next visit Fidel apologized, but Julio César pretended he had no idea of what he was talking about and convinced Fidel that in his drunken haze he must have dreamt whatever he was apologizing for. They laughed and then played the saint or demon game. It ended as always.

". . . demon one day, saint the other."

Julio César could not imagine that the crude and vulgar fowl that belonged to doña Álvara was the same mythic blue-feathered cock—

descendant of a long line of fighting roosters back to the era of the great Turkish empire—that his mother told him about in the stories of his soil dreams. (Julio César could sleep anywhere. In fact, more than once, while playing canastas and chatting and drinking straight rum in doña Álvara's room, he had fallen asleep in her narrow bed—which she insisted on sleeping in, under the illusion that her mountain of flesh fit comfortably in—and she, on the pretext that she did not want to awake him, slid him over and most precisely balanced her behemoth rump on the edge of the bed, so that he would awake buried under her, gasping with his one lung for air, for soil is much more porous and oxygen-rich than grease. Sleep anywhere—but Julio César could dream only while buried in the earth.) The rooster of his dreams could sing Puccini and Verdi, the rooster of his dreams woke him from his one-lung death with the same magnificent high-low note that crumbled the eastern wall, and summoned, with another kind of song, a caring one-eyed Jesuit, and made possible for him this life he now enjoyed, *that* rooster was fried and eaten long ago, by the thugs who chased him into Richard Hadley's trawler. *This* rooster's highest achieved melody was the jammed-propeller prelude of his farts, followed by the visceral cantata of his diarrhea. Doña Álvara, nevertheless, started calling her rooster Atila, as Julio César said the rooster of his mother's dream stories was called.

During his visits, Fidel Castro mostly ignored Atila, recognizing his existence only when he stepped on one of his piles of green and gray mierda. Then he would search him out and give him a good kick on the side, which would send the rooster cackling away like a hen. "Marica!" Fidel would call after him, as if the fact that Atila was suffering from terrible intestinal diseases somehow cast a shadow of doubt on his masculinity.

When he had had too much rum, though, and the woman of the fourth door had already pleased him, Fidel would take to liking the blue-feathered rooster and, inspired by the stories that he had once sung Puccini arias, Fidel would try to teach him the national hymn, becoming very serious as he sang it, his back straightening, and his eyebrows, which were too hairy for such a youth, bending inward, as if the weight of his thoughts were too much of a load:

> *Al combate corred, bayameses,*
> *que la patria os contempla orgullosa . . .*

Atila tilted his head like a curious dog and his heavy coral comb dangled over his left eye as Fidel became even more stiff.

> *. . . no teméis una muerte gloriosa,*
> *que morir por la patria es vivir.*

It was impossible to believe that Atila could understand these words, so perhaps it was from the tone of Fidel's voice, which grew more and more impassioned as he worked his way into the song, accenting each phrase not by the rhythm of the language nor the meter in the music, but by their patriotic poundage, that Atila took his cue, for just as Fidel hit the part of how dying for the fatherland was to live, Atila, his head still cocked and motionless, betraying nothing, as if he had no idea that a putrid air was passing through him and was about to find a point of exit, let out a glorious fart, like the cymbals that clash in all great anthems, a rumbling that resonated within the cavity from whence it came so that a minor quake seemed to shake the bird and his wattle trembled like a furled sail on the point of waking to a cold northern gust. At these moments, bent with laughter, Julio César had no doubt that this incontinent diarrhetic unpatriotic mute rooster was the fabulous blue-feathered cock of his dream-mother's stories.

If he could resurrect others, why not himself?

In an attempt to revive his (Atila's) lost talent, Julio César snuck him into a performance of *La Bohème* at the Havana City Opera. As Marioneta Alonso—who was now an ancient diva of eighty-three (though, since she had been bald since her youth, and had always refused to don a wig, she looked not that much older than she had forty years prior)—insisted, as always, on performing on a bare stage, for obvious reasons, though she pretended all of them to be aesthetic, expressing fear that her delicate voice, its timbre almost unchanged for half a century (as if the Maker had decided that taking the woman's sight and her hair was enough punishment for a lifetime and could not persuade Himself to take her voice), would be swallowed by the hollows of the scenery, and removed any lingering doubt that she could pass as a bohemian virgin by her tingling rendition of *"Sì, mi chiamano Mimì,"* Atila was wholly uninspired. By the middle of the second act, Julio César had to get up and leave. He had hidden Atila in a bundle under the oversized dark wool suit that Fidel had lent him, and the bird had so lost control of his excretory faculties that Julio César smelled just like that famous vagrant in Havana's Central Park (who daily stripped down to his undergarments and sat on a stone bench under the tamarind trees and took a pose and did not twitch a muscle, till the pigeons thought that he was a statue and perched on him and relieved themselves; at this, the man would become aroused and the pigeons then perched and relieved themselves on this most convenient roost).

Julio César buried himself in his falcon-legged tub for an entire week to rid himself of the smell. Fidel then got back at him for laughing during the most solemn moments of the national hymn. He taught Atila how to caca on the topsoil of the tub, feeding him rotted corn soaked in spicy rum so his condition would worsen. When Julio César emerged from underneath on the seventh day there was a white crust an inch thick, cold as an ice cap, over his topsoil.

"I just missed you, mi socio," Fidel said. "I figured the fertilizer would make you sprout sooner. Y de todos modos, you owe me for a suit, so maybe you can go to your one-eyed Jesuit and let him caress you in exchange for some cash from his coffers."

Julio César wiped the feces crust out of his brown curls, which he had let grow too long for Fidel's taste, and out of his whiskers, which grew in patches, like a child in a school play who has glued not enough tufts of wool on his cheeks. Fidel, holding Atila and petting him as if they were now the finest of friends, threw the rooster up in the air when it began to relieve itself on him.

"Qué gracioso estás, mi vida," Julio César said, and naked as he was, covered with earth and frosty shit went inside the third door. The woman in there would care for him and wash him with a warm damp cloth.

The demon-saint would be alone, for it was Monday and all the other of doña Álvara's women were off.

SIX

Seven Against Him

The only time I left our house during that first week back was to find the flat malletlike stone I used to crush the coffee beans. El Rubio's vandals had raided the house after the storm and stolen the coffee grinder. I was careful with each morning's batch, crushed just enough beans and pressed them tight into the end of the stained cloth filter so that the brew was dark but not inky. Afterwards, using a torn paper bag as underliner, I spread the grounds out on the windowsill to dry, then saved them in the goods closet. (When I run out of beans I will use the used grounds, then I will dry them again and use them again and again till I have wrung from them all the flavor and all the darkness.) At first, the pigeons picked at the grounds, but I found a sack of rice and I spread the grains on another windowsill. They came in great numbers and when their wings grazed my hand I could not feel them. They were hungry and they pecked at the rice and at each other but they left the grounds alone. Myself, I was not hungry. Coffee was all I craved.

I returned four days after I had left, four days after I had kissed Alicia lightly on the lips and promised her that I would see her again soon, maybe in Madrid, maybe in Miami. These were the only words of love I could offer her then: "Te veré pronto . . . donde sea." Aside from the two who came with me, and Mingo the finquero who helped us, she was the only one who knew. Perhaps it was too hurried, too soon after the trial in which Fidel personally advised the tribunal that sentenced me to death, al paredón, only so he could show me his Savior-face later by forgiving me, completely, not even a prison term. (*Granma* called the total amnesty he granted the *traitorous comandantecito* an act that shows Fidel at his finest, *towering over his enemies with the grace and nobility of a god.*) I was sent back home stripped of all honor and rank, no longer a comandante, not even a compañero, but a mere ciudadano, the lowest rung in revolutionary society, but *alive, alive, mi vida,* as Alicia always reminded me, grabbing me by the shoulders and shaking me as if to wake me from my proud stupor. Less than two months later I left. October 3rd, a Wednesday. (That same day, the revolutionary government made law its draconian Second Agrarian Reform Act. Now all the land, all of Cuba, truly *belonged* to Fidel as he had always dreamed.) We filled the falcon-legged bathtub with fresh water. We tied the window shutters close with wire. The storm was on its way. Four days later, I returned. October 7th, a Sunday. Alicia had left our home. Another consoled her. The storm had passed. And though the eye swept through towns and villages further up north in the province, Guantánamo got it pretty good, the winds and rains of the outer circle lashing into us like a wheel of giant back-handed slaps, stirring the sea, who is our touchy mistress, to do us wrong. The bay rose and its waters made canals of our narrow streets, and a torrential river out of La Avenida, our only boulevard. Later, on the front steps of the National Revolutionary Police Commissar, as if our sea-mistress was out to show us that even at her vengeful worst she did not abandon the art of laughter (eso es muy cubano, *la risa hasta la tumba*), there on the front steps of the commissar laid out like a gift from the enemy were found a set of plastic machine guns and pistols stolen from the naked rosy yanqui boys on the beach at the naval base. Camilo Suarez, the police chief, the one with hair so golden, on his head and on his cheeks and on his arms and on his chest, and some maricas who gossiped about him said everywhere else as well, held the guns at arm's length till all the water drained out, and he put them up to the resurrected sun and inspected them and pulled on the plastic triggers and buffed with his sleeve the plastic barrels and from one of the toys he read out loud and then laughed: "*Ma the een da Oo Ese Aaa.* ¡Qué gran mierda!"

So how do I know this? I heard him. I was on the second floor of the hospital across the street. A window shattered during the storm so that the bedsheets and my bandages were soaked. Even though he was told I would not be able to speak, el Rubio questioned me three times, once before the storm hit, twice after. The last time I saw him, I heard him tell the surgeon in charge of me, after he (the surgeon) had said I might require surgery again, not to sacrifice too much of his time on me, for other, truer ciudadanos de la Revolución were now in greater need. "If he dies, he dies. ¿Así es, no, compadre? El Líder graced him with mercy enough and he dared not embrace it."

It seems natural. There was too much to worry about, too many injured by the storm to allocate any overdue importance to a traitorous comandantecito caught trying to escape, nabbed right in front of la Cerca de Peerless (the short fence put up by the revolutionary government), that was both barricade and gateway to the yanqui's land, the paradise of the tin roofs.

Alicia had no news of me for two days. She had gone to her mother's. When Marta finally brought her to see me in the hospital, a guard stopped them in the lobby and put a rifle to Alicia's cheek and told them they could not see me. Marta grabbed her sister by the wrist and led her to the stairway to the second floor. "Vamos," she said, loud enough to embarrass the guard. "He won't shoot. No me parece que es tan hombre."

At my side, Marta told me the story, proud of herself. I could tell by the way she spoke, as if to a toddler, that she thought I couldn't understand her. My head was light with morphine. It was as if already I had lost sense of my flesh. Marta demanded that my bandages be changed and that I be switched to a different room. The nurses did not listen to her and when she tried to do it herself they restrained her. Alicia did not dare approach my bed. She stood on the other side of the room, her hands gripping each other, palms together and pressed to her lips as if she were stifling a scream. Her eyes were dry and opened wide.

This is what we had figured: with the storm on its way, there would be too many other concerns and security at the border would be lax. The original plan had been to attempt the escape on New Year's Eve 1963, when soldiers would be drunk and careless. But this was better, a storm like an Old Testament scourge, a storm beautifully named Flora whose windy mantles we would use as cover and flee from our ruined patria.

There were three of us—myself , a young architecture student named Humberto who had already been caught the year before trying to swim across the bay to the beaches of the base (sentenced, because of his youth, because he had had his leg mangled by a crocodile crossing a river on his escape route, but most pertinent, because his aunt Pucha was an influential member of the local CDR, to only five days in jail), and another sort of veteran, a yanqui trawler captain whom I had first met when I was a child, and who had smuggled arms to us during the War from New Orleans, Louisiana, and who, after the triumph, after Fidel's alliance with the Soviet Union, was one of the few yanquis who traveled freely in and out of Cuba, usually through the naval base. His name was Richard Hadley. When he heard of my trial, of my sentence, he came to Guantánamo, said he would do anything to help.

"Even if it means helping me leave."

"Especially if it means helping you leave."

Our first idea was to stow away in Richard Hadley's trawler, drown myself in the pot of shrimp stew as I had done when I was a child, and simply sail into the base on one of his many trips. But Richard Hadley said this was dangerous, and he did not want to put his crew in peril.

"So, we will flee on land."

"We?" I said. Richard Hadley had a degenerative bone disease, and his limp had grown more pronounced since I had last seen him. (And about the only thing he did well, he said, was swim, every other activity felt as if there were a fire inside his bones . . . *even the mermaids know how useless I am, they flee from me when I approach them.*) Yet he decided to aid us in our escape *by land.* He would come with us, he had weapons, he knew the terrain, knew where the mines were planted, and he added boastfully, the border guards would not dare shoot a yanqui.

"How will they know you are a yanqui?" Humberto said.

"Porque I have a tattoo of the stars and stripes on my ass, and I plan to make it all too visible to them!"

And there was Mingo who did not want to leave because he said he loved the blackness of the Island's soil too much, but had vowed to help us. It was his finca we used as training ground, his '40s Ford pickup truck we drove (el Cacharro later riddled with bullets like in some yanqui gangster film), his stashed black market dollars that bought us most of our ammunition. He was against hurrying things, against changing the original New Year's Eve plan. The truck needed work, parts to be replaced. "Están jodío if el Cacharro doesn't run like the wind . . . bien jodío. Wait. Wait for the year to end."

I couldn't wait. Richard Hadley sided with me and Mingo understood. We had less than forty-eight hours to fix up el Cacharro. We tracked the storm and prayed for a direct hit. A friend of Richard Hadley who worked inside the base had snuck out some maps (from an article printed in a yanqui magazine some months before) of the naval base and its environs. We went over them like students cramming for an exam. We guessed at which fields would be most heavily mined. Richard Hadley seemed to *know,* and as he marked each mine on our map, he toyed with the idea of changing plans completely, of avoiding the mines and using his trawler to cross into yanqui territory by water, but finally decided that his ragtag crew would not be up to it, and given the rage of Hurricane Flora the bay would be unnavigable as well as unpatroled. We went back to the original plan, we would try our escape by land.

"I told you once when you were a young boy," Richard Hadley said to me, "you are a landcrawler and have always lived as one, and if you are to die, you should die as one."

My body was never returned to my family, never anointed for the journey afterwards. This was one of the most infamous revolutionary edicts. Like Creon, Fidel believed that those who died struggling against the native gods (that is, against him and Raúl and Camilo and the rest of the revolutionary court), did not deserve the honor of a grave or the satisfaction of a family's mourning, but deserved rather to be chewed up by birds and violated by stray dogs. So at the edge of Campo Santo, on the side of a rocky hill, after Marta had identified the body and signed some papers, after el Rubio had slipped off my wedding ring, eighteen karats to be used for better things, he said, to replace one of his many cracked molars, my face was shaved and my corpse was left exposed to the elements. My family and my wife were given a grave number, an empty plot whose same number was given to *many other* families of us the desecrated.

A wild long-haired goat, as if it had been sent by an affronted God to replace my loved ones, passed by and licked my ears and my seven wounds. Soon, it was as if that long grainy tickling tongue was healing me, the saliva undoing the botched stitches and reopening the wounds, waking me to my death. I heard the horns from the funeral march of the *Eroica Symphony.* I found the strength to stand. I wandered here, to my old home. At first, I could not tell for sure whether the shattered windows, the fallen teardrop chandeliers, my ruined record collection or the death of Atila, my old-as-the-century blue-feathered cock (who like Mingo was too in love with the soil of this land to accompany me) floating in the fountain by the terrace, his neck cracked, his coral crest limp with the heavy waters, was the handiworks of zealot looters or the signature of the indifferent winds of Hurricane Flora. Two deeds, however, revealed their authors pellucidly. Scribbled with coalish ink on my rebel portrait, like a hangman's noose around my neck, a poem:

> *Gusano, gusanito,*
> *muere aplastadito.*
> *Au revoir, traidor.*

And floating in the water we had reserved in the bronze falcon-legged bathtub was a long, smooth yellowish piece of waste elegantly curlicuing at both ends, by its elegant shape clear that it had passed through the sphincter of a skilled officer and not through the asshole of a common soldier, and by its gold speckling clearer that on its way out the piece of waste had brushed ever so slightly and been tinged by the aureate asshairs of none other than el Rubio. ¡Maldito! It wasn't enough that he had me murdered (for the final surgery was never performed), but he had brought his muchachos, his ñángaras, into my home and desecrated it. I had lost so much blood. I was thirsty. I drank from the water in the tub. Now, I use the shit-water every morning for my coffee. Like any true gusano, I subsist on decay.

I have subsisted on little before. I could have been a finquero, could have chosen to be addressed as don Julio, and in the country-that-was-then a well-off landowner, well-off till just about a week ago when the revolutionary government took almost every piece of land from every landowner. But that's beside the point, because I chose to give my lands up long ago, before any Agrarian Reform Acts, chose to give my lands back to the campesinos by choice, lands I had inherited from a teacher of mine, a Jesuit named Father Jacinto, who had inherited them from his Spaniard ancestors, rich black lands in the mountains north of here, lands mother of coffee and sugar and giant plantains and dozens of other crops. But I chose not to become don Julio. I chose to follow Fidel. Father Jacinto died shortly after I had graduated from the University of Havana with a degree in theology. My specialization was demonology and hagiography. I learned how indistinguishable devils are from angels. I was going to teach and perhaps someday go into the priesthood. I was learning to know God, who obviously was not willing to linger in the background of my life, who, like certain sections of Beethoven's greatest symphonies, demanded *all* attention.

The Church virulently fought Father Jacinto's will in the courts. In public, they claimed that he died an insane man, thus his will should be null and void and his property fall into the hands of the Holy Catholic Apostolic Church. In private, they whispered that he had been sinfully in love with me and had abused me as a child. Y claro, one can never know for sure the secrets of another's heart, but if Father Jacinto was in love with me all those years he cared for me, he never used his love in any harmful way. He treated me as a father treats his son, nothing more or less. The Church knew that!—and all its calumnies after Father Jacinto's death forever soured me against bishops and priests and all their blind fanciers. The courts miraculously declared against the Church. The land was mine. The last time I saw Fidel in La Habana, in those days after the contested will, he patted me on the shoulder and assured me that he would see me again, that I would not be a landowner for long. "No te pega, mi gran socio."

"I have not forgotten God *or* the Holy Mother," I answered him.

"God is tyrant on *their* side . . . the words of the tyrant's Son, however, will judge and condemn the Father and this time the story will be reversed and it is He the Father who will perish on the cross. Four years in those airless classrooms of the philosophy department and you never learned the ancient difference between theology and morals?"

Estaba loco desde entonces, mad enough to believe himself.

Flora was merciful. She knew our shame and suffering. She was headed straight for us. Hidden in Mingo's finca cottage, we listened to the Voice of America on Richard Hadley's ham radio. The yanquis were always better at tracking these storms than we were. The voice spoke to us from the main yanqui hurricane-tracking center in a town called Coral Gables, a suburb of Miami. Humberto said that in Miami the women were giant blondes with tits the size of melons and that they dreamed of Latin men as they lay on the white-sand beaches. Mingo added that this was true, but that the milk from their giant tits was sour because their pale skins let in too much of the tropical heat, so all their offspring perished from hunger. Richard Hadley told them in Spanish to stop *comiendo mierda,* and told the boy to stop dreaming, that the yanqui dollar-utopia was not much better than any utopia.

"La vida es una mierda, sea donde sea. Nothing ever makes man happy. Don't you go supposing that us fat yanquis are any better off than you or him."

"Then why are you helping us?"

"Because you'll never make it out without me . . . and Julio's honor has been shit on enough."

He had Humberto close his eyes again and assemble one of the M-14s we would be taking with us. He timed him with a wristwatch and looked at me and shook his head when too much time had passed. Then he slapped Humberto on the side of the head.

"They'll kill you. Muerto y medio. You won't be able to peek through the blackness of the storm." He slapped Humberto again and again, till the boy, in desperation, finished assembling the rifle and clicked on the magazine. He opened his eyes and handed Richard Hadley the rifle and looked at him with an unforgiving rage.

"Good," Richard Hadley said examining the rifle, "the winds will slap you a lot harder."

"Good, good, Humberto," I said. "My turn."

I knelt in front of Richard Hadley as he dismantled the weapon. I closed my eyes and took the pieces and put them back together faster than the boy, though Richard Hadley slapped me harder and more often. I know the blows were causing his bones as much pain as they were afflicting. It's just the wind, just the wind and I clicked on the magazine and without opening my eyes stuck the point of the rifle under my beloved trawler captain's chin. Humberto clapped.

"Some things you don't forget, my little man," Richard Hadley said and slowly eased the rifle point from under his chin. He took the rifle and disassembled it and closed his eyes and told me to slap him. I did, but not with much vigor, certainly not with the vigor that the winds of Flora would slap him. Richard Hadley stopped. He dismantled the rifle again. He grunted.

"Let the boy do it. You are far too kind, my little comandante."

Humberto smiled and knelt by him and began to slap Richard Hadley with a force still colored by his anger. Richard Hadley yelled: "Golly, yes, yes, that's it!" and though his disease sometimes made his hands tremble, put the weapon back together in a quarter of the time that I had done it.

"It's easy for you, viejo," Humberto said, gasping for breath from his effort. "You are a yanqui. Your country is full of guns."

Richard Hadley's face was rosy from the slaps and his cheeks trembled.

"Nothing is easy," he said to the boy. "You'll learn that the hard way tomorrow."

The first time I saw the wounds, I thought of the boy. I wondered if his were just as bad. I wondered if his body too had been thrown out on a hillside for the birds to pick and stray dogs to violate. There was talk that any time a young boy was killed trying to escape into the base, el Rubio paid a visit to the coroner's office and demanded some time alone with the body and that he would lay the corpse on the floor and unfold the shroud and pull his pants down and masturbate over the dead boy while cursing all who succumb to the vicious lust for yanqui things.

I thought about Richard Hadley. All the bullets had missed him as he had prophesied . . . as if the border guards, with their infrared lights, could see the yanqui flag tattooed on his ass. Less than a hundred yards from Cerca Peerless, after the winds of Flora had begun to whip, after we had abandoned el Cacharro (which they later peppered with bullets just to make it seem they had seen us from the start), after he had guided us through the mine fields (hobbling so fast he seemed like a wounded rhinoceros), after the boy had fallen, after I had lost my rifle (without getting off even one bullet) and I too had fallen, he wrapped his large body around me so that no other bullet would touch me. He whispered in my ear that he would now be a better landcrawler than I had ever been, and tried little by little to drag me nearer the fence. The yanquis had come. Their helicopters hovered over the other side of the border. Their jeeps sat on a hill. But they did nothing. They watched . . . and that is perhaps why the border patrol did not shoot Richard Hadley dead. They put a rifle to his temple, and when he spoke to them, in his broken Spanish, they knew who he was, they looked at the yanqui helicopters struggling against the oncoming winds, coming nearer and nearer to the border, at the jeeps atop the hill, their canvas tops lashing like angry tongues, and they forced

Richard Hadley to walk against the wind a mile to the bayshore, forced him to strip so that they may better see the legendary yanqui flag tattooed on his ass, forced him to enter the shark-infested, embroiled waters and swim toward the beaches of the naval base. I never knew if he made it. He was a great swimmer, but it was a great storm.

I was obsessed with the wounds. Every hour or so I stood in front of the cracked mahogany mirror in the parlor and examined them, tried to remember the order in which they came against me. There were seven. I touched the first one, just beneath the collarbone. Painless. I was now living only with the memory of my flesh, like an amputee lives with only the memory of his limb. The second one blew open the navel, which mawkishly gaped back at me like an eyeless socket. I dared not touch it. The other four that came against me in the belly made smaller more beautiful wounds, like small peonies whose countless twisted-out petals were wafer-thin layers of flesh thickened and opaqued with brushstrokes of a coruscant red-brown.

And the last wound taught me what I no longer was. In the sac where I still felt the dangling twinness of my desires, I saw nothing but the crusty cavern of my present frailty. This was the seventh one that came against me, at close range (from a pistol and not a rifle), while I was already sprawled on the ground, after Richard Hadley had been forced to walk to the bayshore and do the only thing he did well, swim, swim away. When he saw me, el Rubio professed that it was proper that I should die a woman and then he pulled out his pistol and aimed it at the dead boy, but thought better and did not shoot and cocked his wrist and made a shot-noise through his lips like another boy at play.

"This one is not dead, capitán," one of his men, crouched over me, said.

"He will be," el Rubio prophesied, sliding his pistol back into its holster. And then he argued with one of the army comandantes about who was in charge and about the yanqui trawler captain who had been let go and about bullets that may have crossed into yanqui territory and finally, as if an afterthought, gave orders to take me to the city hospital.

There are many privations in this world after the seven came against me. I cannot feel sunlight, or rather I cringe from it, like one whose skin is badly burned. It is an old feeling. On the second morning here, I was spreading out the used coffee grounds on the windowsill and the rays of the sun brushed my hand and it was as if it were being licked by those far-away flames. The skin was liver-spotted and the fingers crooked. Maybe I have been in this world after the seven came against me longer than I think. I pulled my hand back and ever since that day I try to brew my coffee before dawn and I collect the dry grounds after dusk. I let my beard grow (it comes in faster than before); they cannot shave me now, I will be a barbudo again. I stay within the inside-air shadows and I stay out of the courtyard, except during the afternoon thundershowers when I go out, naked as I roam, and wash my wounds. The rain does its work well. It will be difficult when the wet season ends. But the sun too does its work well. The grounds on the windowsill look and feel fresh. I drink a lot of coffee but I can't taste it or smell it. It keeps me awake. I'm afraid to fall asleep. I wait for the dawn to brew my coffee. I wait for the afternoon to wash my wounds. I wait for the dusk to collect and save the grounds on the windowsill. The rest of the day is filled with thoughts of what I no longer am; and I can do nothing to ease the torment, for my greatest privation is the music that I cannot hear. I was fooled when I heard a shadow of the *Eroica* as I awoke into this new world, tricked into willfully entering this realm of petrified silence from where the rageful Beethoven and the lovely Mozart are banished.

Two Trials

When the shit-water runs out for the coffee I must leave and go I know not where. Maybe to see him, mi gran socio. To the Marist house. There's clean water there. The naked statue of la Virgencita in the garden provides it. It flows into her from an underground spring and seeps out of her like droplets of sweat. The brothers at first thought it was a miracle. The statue has been revered ever since her mantle disappeared many years ago, stolen it was said by the ghost of a halfwit, una tal Delfina Gutiérrez, sent to the gallows convicted of stealing as many as twenty-eight wedding gowns from brides in the capital at the turn of the century. Crowds came from all over the Island to witness the sweating Virgin, till the scientists examined the holy sweat and the Church had to admit that it was no miracle. Just an underground spring. Just geology. Still, I'll go there and catch the Virgin's sweat in a tin pot, use it for my cafecito, to the place where he kept me before he pardoned me, before he sent me home, alive but branded.

It was the old house of the Little Brothers of Mary, on a hilltop in the country west of the capital where the royal palm proliferates and celebrates nothing but itself. The house was surrounded by brick walls with mortared broken-off cola bottles at the top. After the brothers were kicked out and sent to a government-run school in the capital, the bottles were chipped off and barbed wire was coiled along the top of the walls. It was to be the new holding quarters of anyone accused of crimes classified under *la dolce vita,* a catchword that was meant to associate our alleged crimes with the decadence of the European bourgeoisie. (Pues Fidel is a great fan of Fellini.) Many of my counterrevolutionary crimes as they were recounted to me (as if written by a skilled, if style-free, novelist) took place during my visit to Berlin, although all I remember doing there is meeting with a lot of stodgy Eastern military officials and sneaking to the West side one evening to listen to the Lithuanian violinist play Beethoven. Still, the tribunal assured me that they had proof, pictures and fragments of correspondences, that while there I met with la CIA and was plotting the assassination of el Líder. I wish I had been clever *and* brave enough for such things. True, I thought Fidel had served his proper time as head of the revolutionary government and that he should step down and allow for open and free elections at every level. I made this clear and plain to him (as early as his first visit to the United Nations) in almost every letter I wrote to him. We had fought for liberty. We had won not to replace one tyrant with another.

The night of my arrest, naked, dragged from my marriage bed, I was put in the backseat of a four-door Soviet jeep and driven, over three days and nights, to the former Marist house. The building, a Spanish-style two-level tile-roofed structure overlooking the adjoining countryside, was converted to its new purposes effortlessly. The comandante who questioned me during my stay, a lank-faced habanero with bad teeth, had been under my command in the Sierra. He was very proud that it had been his idea to use the Marist house. He had spent some time there as a child, when for a brief while the brothers cared for and taught orphans and runaways. He described it to Fidel as an ideal maze of tiny cells, endless corridors and cramped stairways that more often than not led nowhere. Till the very last night I was there, I knew only one room of the entire building. Before they moved me into the house and led me down a stairway I was blindfolded. I was told to take off the oversized clothes they had lent me and then shut in a nine-by-twelve windowless room. The only other things in the room were a sheetless narrow mattress and a tin bucket in the corner for my necessities. When they shut the door, I was in complete darkness. It was my first night. I had asked for a pillow and sheets. They said no, that I would use the sheets to hang myself.

Three times a day, before meals, the comandante was let into the room and a chair was brought in for him by a guard and a floor lamp with a long extension cord set behind him. They both saluted me and then the guard stepped out. The comandante spread his legs over the seat, the chair's back pressed to his chest, his arms folded around it. When the stink from the corner was too unbearable, even for the brief period he was going to be in there, he ordered a guard to change the bucket. He had no weapon. I sat on the mattress cross-legged, squinting at the sudden brightness that cast a full-body halo behind him. Three times a day his shadow pulled out two iron-folded sheets of paper from the inside pocket of his military jacket. He unfolded them. He separated them and held one in each hand. First he read from the paper on his right side, in an even undramatic voice, the oath of loyalty he had taken with me in the mountains. Then he read from the paper on his left, the list of crimes the revolutionary tribunal was considering against me. His voice rose with the seriousness of each offense, culminating with *conspiracy to assassinate el Comandante-en-Jefe*. Three times a day he asked me if I was ready to sign my confession. Three times a day I said no.

Though I could not make out the features on his face, the comandante seemed neither hurt nor pleased at my answer. He nodded his head and re-folded the papers and stood and examined my nakedness and picked up the chair and left the room. A few minutes later two other guards came into the room, both also unarmed, one carried a tin plate with my meal, the other a tin cup with my water. They too saluted me. I was forced to eat without silverware as they watched. When I was finished, they took the plate and the cup and removed the lamp and I was again in darkness.

One morning, about a month after my arrival, the comandante who questioned me brought in, folded over his right arm, my guerrilla uniform, which they had taken from Alicia. I was told to dress. The uniform had been stored in the same trunk as Alicia's wedding dress and it smelled of her. I was weak from malnourishment. My old warrior clothes hung baggy on me. The comandante helped me lace my boots and tugged at my beret to give it the proper tilt. Another guard brought a panful of water and a razor and a soap brush. The comandante fitted the pan under my chin and shaved me and he patted me on the shoulders and smiled at me with his bad teeth. "No mereces ser barbudo."

I was driven to the capital. My trial took place in a hall of the Palace of the Revolution. My lawyer smelled of rum when he introduced himself to me. After a few rounds of questioning in which I again confessed to nothing and the State presented its irrefutable evidence to itself, my lawyer pleaded in a high womanish voice for the tribunal not to sentence me to death. He opened a Bible and read from the Sermon of the Mount and from the Book of Daniel and as he was leafing through the thin pages, looking for yet another passage, the head of the tribunal told him they had heard enough that this wasn't a church but a courtroom of la Revolución. My lawyer apologized and added that he meant no offense to la Revolución and added furthermore that he found the Holy Book very much in keeping with many of the teachings of la Revolución, that nowhere in the bylaws of the revolutionary government was there a law that abolished God, that such law (if it did exist) was an impossibility, an absurdity. The head of the tribunal told him to sit down and to shut up. My lawyer obeyed, but he kept on leafing through his Bible and when he found the next passage he had intended to read he pointed it out to me. His dirty fingernail was pressed down under a brief verse:

Then the Lord spoke to the fish
And the fish spewed out Jonah upon the dry land.

He nodded his head vigorously as if I could not fail to see the great significance of this. I gave him a puzzled look. Then, as if inspired by my ignorance, he read the verse out loud, his voice deepening an octave or two. The head of the tribunal slammed down his hand and called my lawyer an imbecile and a cretin, unpracticed in the manners of the courtroom. Later, during my journey back to Guantánamo, I found out that my rum-swigging lawyer is kept on the revolutionary payroll simply to defend the undefenseable and that his piety is sincere, if ill-suited as an armor against the fell vengeance of la Revolución.

The tribunal convened in another room for less than half an hour. It was said that Fidel sat amongst them for a few minutes. I was sentenced to die. My lawyer could choose one of two methods, by hanging or by execution. "Al paredón," my lawyer said and then he turned to me and explained it was the more humane of the two. On my way down the steps someone from a small mob that had gathered there threw a rotten mango at me, it hit me on my right cheek and exploded. There was a great cheer. Blood commingled with the soft smelly pulp and dripped on my clean guerrilla uniform. The guards rushed me into the Soviet jeep and hurried me back to the Marist house. The mob ran after the jeep as far as it could follow it throwing more rotten mangoes. The guard in the passenger seat stuck his rifle out of the window and fired twice into the air. The mob halted its pursuit and they stood still and their anger seemed to be blown out of them as if they had collectively been struck by one of the bullets.

For a week, no one came to my cell except for the two guards who brought me my food. I had sheets and a pillow (apparently it was now permissible to hang myself). They no longer saluted me. My bucket went unchanged. I pressed in the bruise in my face to make it hurt, to feel *something*. One evening, as I slept curled up against the wall, I heard a commotion outside and then I heard the door open. The wall became crowded with shadows as they brought the lamp into my cell. Then the shadows disappeared and only one remained.

"Pendejo, you have betrayed us and anyone *but you* would pay with his life as the tribunal mandated." I knew his voice and I did not turn to look at him.

"*You* are the traitor," I said, "and sooner or later the whole world will know it."

"You are poisoned with hubris, mi amigo del alma."

"Blame what you will. It doesn't matter. My part is done with."

"I came thinking of your wife, of your family—"

"You came thinking of yourself, cabrón!"

"¿Así que así?" he said. "I have disturbed the revolutionary process for your sake and from shame you can't even turn and face me one last time. It ends up with me speaking to your hairy nalgas."

"Go, go do what you have to do."

The shadow grew on the wall and I felt a knee pressed into my back and a pistol barrel grazed my cheek with a delicate and sensual attention and then was pushed into my temple and I smelled the scotch on his breath that gave him the courage to come to me.

"I can finish you right here and no one will lift one cry against me."

I closed my eyes. There was a silence that I supposed naturally precedes the firing of a bullet into your temple.

"Did you conspire against me?" he whispered.

"No."

"Liar!" He lifted himself off me and left the room.

The guard who removed the floor lamp assured me I had sealed my fate.

Another week passed. The bucket in the corner overbrimmed with my waste and wet my feet and splashed back at me when I crouched over it. I asked the guards who brought me my food and water if they could please change it. They ignored me. One evening, after I finished my supper and I reached back to them the tin plate and the tin cup, they blindfolded me and grabbed me under the armpits (it must have been quite simple for them—I must have lost some fifty pounds during my stay) and led me up some stairs and down a long hallway. Then, to my surprise I felt fresh dirt under my feet and when I breathed, it was the pure mountain air. I was outside. They walked me a bit more and then threw me on the ground. I was out of breath. (I had tried to keep in shape by pacing to and fro in my cell, but there's only so much pacing you can do in a nine-by-twelve room, and so much energy you can draw from three meals of mush beans and plantains.) I was told to remove my blindfold. It was nighttime but the moon was bright. My sight, instead of weakening during my dark incarceration, had become adept at making out the nuances of shadows and I could discern four figures standing over me, three in front and one, much taller and more solid and more still, behind them.

"He already smells like the dead, comandante." I recognized the voice of my interrogator with the bad teeth. I sat on my knees, and soon I saw that two of the figures were wearing uniforms, another one a dress or a robe and the fourth figure, the tall and solid and still one, had its arms spread at its side, palms facing outward and it seemed to be wearing nothing at all. The middle figure, the tallest but for the one behind them, lit a match and put it to a cigar in his mouth and I immediately recognized the whiskers of my old friend. He had deemed it appropriate to visit me again, as if the memory of speaking to my hairy nalgas had left him un-

settled. He sucked on the cigar and when he let out the smoke it trapped
the moonlight so that his whiskers and his face up to his eyes were hidden
by a soft gauzy veil.

"He'll smell better once he gets out in the open air," Fidel said.
"Brother Joaquín will make sure he bathes before he leaves." He put his
arm on the robed figure to his right. "I have decided you should not
die . . . o mejor dicho, we have *all* decided, Brother Joaquín, here, and
myself and this comandante and many other defenders of la Revolución,
all of us have decided."

I sat still and pretended neither gratitude nor joy.

"Does this not make you happy, mi amigo, if not for yourself, then for
your wife who will not be a widow?"

I said nothing. Fidel gave Brother Joaquín a gentle shove in the back.
The brother walked unsteadily towards me, his hands palms upward in
front of him carrying a bundle as if it were an offering. He placed the bundle on my lap.

"Póntelo, mi hijo." In his sour breath I could smell his many years. He
walked back and rejoined the other three figures. I stood up and unfolded
the bundle. It was a robe like the one the old brother was wearing. I
stepped into it and remained standing.

"Bien," Fidel said, "we are now face to face." The two guards came up
from behind me and pushed down on my shoulders so I would sit again.
"No, no, por favor," Fidel said, extending his cigar hand towards us. "Let
him stand. I did not come here to shame anyone. Al contrario, I came here
to do honor to an oath of loyalty that I once took to defend this prisoner's
life, in any and all occasions, and which he took to defend mine. Here, under the statue of his devoted Virgencita, which the brothers claim is
miraculous and sweats compassion, I have come to honor my oath." He
put his hand on the legs of the figure behind them, which now as he
moved out of the way I saw clearly sat on a pedestal and was the famous
statue of the naked Virgencita. He wiped his hand on the seat of his pants.
"The tribunal's sentence has been overturned, Julio César Cruz will not
die! Tomorrow he will begin his ride back to Guantánamo in the company
of Brother Joaquín. My oath will not be broken."

"Bless the heart of el Comandante-en-Jefe," Brother Joaquín murmured. "I will accompany him well and deliver him to his wife."

"Will the free man now speak the truth of his crimes?"

"I am tired of speaking and respeaking the truth. I am guilty of none
of the crimes I was charged with and I have never broken that oath we
took to defend liberty in this Island above all."

Fidel waved his other hand in front of his face. "No speeches, por favor. It was a question that I did not mean for you to answer. Fear not, I
will not change my mind. *You will not die,* punto y final . . . it would make
a liar of me, a traitor."

"No, no, compadre, lie as much as you can bear it. Your own historians will absolve you."

"Comandante, por el amor de Dios," Brother Joaquín blurted, "take care not to offend he who brings with him mercy."

"It's all right, Joaquín . . . I will not be moved from my position no matter what the freed man says. And take care not to address him as *comandante* ever again. He is now a *citizen* of la Revolución, a role that of course brings with it its own, no less important, duties." He walked towards me. I had done all I could to anger him, to embarrass him. But so far he had withstood my taunts with the grace of a proper king and now he wanted to add the final touch. "Que Dios te cuide, compadre," he said, standing less than a foot away from me, and saluted me theatrically for the last time. I spit at him and though I could not see it I felt the spit run down his cheeks into the fabric of his whiskers. Brother Joaquín gasped and the guards came running towards me, but Fidel held them by calmly raising his cigar. He said nothing and did not wipe my spit off his face and went into the house and I was left out in the courtyard with the naked Virgin and with the shocked Brother Joaquín.

The following morning I was allowed to bathe and shave and given back the same robe to put on, which I saw now was a monk's brown cassock without the sash so that it hung on me like an oversized peasant's dress. They also put on my feet a pair of worn leather sandals that smelled as if they had been worn by a whole generation of hermits. I was then led back to my cell. It had been scrubbed clean and smelled of ammonia. The straw mattress had a clean sheet and the tin bucket had been removed. I waited. Even my desperate yearning for Alicia (to have her now so I could rest my head on her lap and she could pass her hands through my hair as we listened in felicity to Bach's saddest oboe concerto), did not diminish my hope that with my final insult Fidel *had* changed his mind and that this was to be the wait before my execution. When Brother Joaquín came in and told me to follow him, I asked him if he was not going to hear my confession.

"I have no power to absolve you, hijo mío, but there is *always* time to speak of our weaknesses." He knelt beside me and crossed himself and lowered his head. I spoke arrogantly of all my recent weaknesses and when I had finished and I had not spoken about the one who had brought me mercy, Brother Joaquín seemed pleased and he took out a small flask from under his robe and uncorked it and pressed his thumb to the mouth and tilted the flask. He made a cross on my forehead with his wet thumb. I wiped the cross away with my fingers and smelled the ointment. It was musty like old rain hidden in wet leaves. Brother Joaquín grabbed me by the elbow and said it was time for us to go.

I was not blinded. The guards outside the door, the ones who brought me my food, had abandoned their unkindness and they held me up when

I faltered ascending the steep concrete stairways. We moved through a narrow hallway into the main parlor of the house. All four of us then sat on a wooden bench and waited. Heavy drapes were drawn over the arched windows and the only light came from the votive candles in front of a porcelain statue of la Virgencita. It was a smaller version of the one out in the courtyard and no one had stolen its robe so she maintained her majesty as queen of our nation, but her face did not express the well-earned sadness that the naked one is said to possess, a sadness as if her Son had just died.

I heard horses outside and the two guards stood up. The two main doors were pushed open and I saw by the rushing sheets of light that it was already close to high day.

"Vamos," the guards said. They led me outside and the skin on my face tightened. I had not felt the unabashed warmth of daylight since my trial. We passed through the iron gates and through the underbrush in front of the house. I was squinting because the sunlight was falling directly on us, so at first I thought I was having a vision, as it is often reported the accused do as they are led to the execution site. There, in front of the house, led by two black stallions was a marvellous carriage of many colors, dusk orange and lemonade yellow and the deepest shameless scarlet. The guards pushed me on and I saw that the carriage was like a canopy on a horse-carreta and that it was made of individual feathers stolen from tropical angels and woven in and out of dead tree branches.

"Vamos," Brother Joaquín said this time, grabbing me under my armpit and parting some of the feathers and helping me get inside my vision. The floor was matted with straw. I sat cross-legged and the carriage was the perfect size, the top just brushing against my pate. The light changed. It passed through the tropical-angel feathers and became emanations of them and tattooed their shapes and their varicolors on my robe and on my palms, which I turned upward so that there these colored shadows were most crisp and my palms were like crystal pools. Then Brother Joaquín said, ¡Arrea! and I heard the swish of leather against hide and my carriage moved and all the colors ran one into the other. Once I got used to the rocking movement, I pulled one of the feathers and as I examined it I fell out of my trance. It was a leaf not a feather. My marvellous carriage was made out of croton branches folded together like thatch over a precarious skeleton of brittle stalks. I knelt and tried to stick my head out towards the front where I heard the horse's clatter. My face met Brother Joaquín's bony behind.

"Stay in there," he said. "I'll tell you when you can come up here and sit with me."

I pushed my head to the side and stuck my head out a bit. The two horses were so gaunt they seemed mere ribcages draped in hide. "Where are we going?"

"Home. ¡Dale gracias a la Virgen! You're going home. You are a free man. I could let you off right here if you want, but I don't really recommend it."

He said nothing more and pushed the feeble black horses on. Near dusk it drizzled and when the wind blew my carriage began to shed its leaves so that slowly, as patches of the gray landscape became visible and as I looked up and saw a half-moon half hidden by a yellow mist, my carriage began to look more and more like a birdcage. I faced my palms upward as I had done earlier but the sorry moon did not cast enough light for any reflection. Well after it darkened, Brother Joaquín began to speak to me, as if the two-ply mantle of the rain and the darkness would disguise his voice. He said he had disobeyed a command to ride me through the capital past the Palace of the Revolution, so that the gods of la Revolución could examine with dismay one of their fallen ones, paraded by them, as a last embarrassment, in a birdcage made of colorful leaves. Brother Joaquín had veered from the ordered path and taken a rocky and mostly untraveled road south of the city, we might now be considered fugitives and the mercy that had been granted me might well be rescinded.

"A mercy *you* begged for more than I did."

"O a lo mejor no," he said. "When they catch up with us, I'll just tell them I got lost."

Nobody ever did catch up to us. That first night we ate most of the meager helpings they had supplied us with for the entire trip and slept by the side of the road under an almond tree. In the morning, one of the two horses had dropped dead. We abandoned the birdcage carriage and Brother Joaquín unhitched the other horse and fed it the remaining food and hitched a pair of sackcloth bags over its hump and took the flask from his robe and wet his thumb and pressed a long cross in between the horse's eyes. He then mounted him and I walked alongside.

"What is in that bottle?"

"The Virgin's urine."

"The Virgin's urine?"

"The Virgin's urine."

"*The* Virgin?"

"Exacto."

"That's what you rubbed on my forehead this morning?"

"And what I just rubbed into this animal's forehead."

He patted the animal on the neck and stroked its balding mane.

"Why?"

"On you, to sanctify. On the horse, so that he does not lose his way and in turn lose us."

"The horse is dying."

"I know. So am I and so are you."

He spoke with the assurance of a madman. As we moved along the side of the road I was able to examine him fully for the first time. He was strait-backed with wide shoulders and so devoid of flesh that I could make out the angles of his skeleton through his robe. He had unlaced the front of his robe halfway down his chest and patches of creamy white hair poked out of his chest cage. His face was desperate, the features sharpened by a certain hunger that seemed to have fed even on the pulp of his lips so that they now hung one over the other like dried petals. His skin was almost colorless and single white hairs grew few and wide apart (like grass on stony ground) on his cheeks and on his chin. Only his dark cinnamon eyes were serene, floating in the cave of his skull. Their stubborn buoyancy lifted his chin and like two precisely calibrated weights balanced his unsteady frame on the skeletal horse and gave him the overall demeanor that enabled him to proclaim with absolute and blessed authority that he was carrying around a bottle full of the Holy Virgin's urine.

"May I see?"

He handed me the bottle. It was a fine crystal container with a round glass top corked at the end. The liquid inside was the consistency and color of sooty riverwater. I shook it.

"It doesn't look like urine." I uncapped it and smelled it. The fecundity of old rain. "It doesn't smell like urine."

Brother Joaquín extended his hand and wiggled his bony fingers in unison at me. I returned the bottle. He tightened the cap and returned it to the inner folds of his robe.

"Many years ago, near the end of the last century, there was a young girl named Delfina from a very aristocratic family in the capital who went by the surname of Gutiérrez. Delfina Gutiérrez was engaged to a young man named Israel. Israel was also of aristocratic lineage, but there was more color in his skin and from certain angles it was evident he was of mixed bloods. This concerned her parents more than it concerned Delfina Gutiérrez for she was a devotee of la Virgencita (like I am, like I have heard that you are) and had it not been that she was an only daughter and that her father was desperate for a *son,* she would not have married at all. She promised the Virgin that when her husband took her on the wedding night she would feel no joy. There was a grand celebration and Delfina Gutiérrez found that she could drink champagne and rum head-to-head with the most notorious of her parents' highbrow, world-traveling friends and after the ceremony that night, when Israel took Delfina Gutiérrez, she was so levitated with champagne bubbles and so overwhelmed with his liquor smell and with his sweaty belly-warmth and with the vein (thick as the stem of a sunflower) that ran up his forearm and through his biceps into the hairy thickness of his chest that she forgot completely about her promise and imagined the vein coursing through his innards down to where it reappeared, thick as before, in the skin of his thick organ and she gave in to the many joys of her man. The following morning she was so burdened with guilt that she told Israel that she was leaving him and that she would have the marriage annulled. To which Israel answered that considering the many times they had done it that night they had no more claim to have their marriage annulled than his grandparents who had brought sixteen children into this world. Delfina slapped him and condemned him for having made her feel so wickedly good on her most sacred night and left him. Heart-torn and unable to forget his new wife's unimaginable talents for passion, Israel went to live in his parents' house, where he would die in a most horrible fashion, still sick with love."

"Does this have anything to do with the holy urine?"

"I didn't say it was *holy*."

"You said you used it to sanctify."

"Mira, are you going to argue or are you going to listen? Shall I remain quiet as before?"

"Perdóname . . . go on."

Brother Joaquín threw his cinnamon eyes upward as if at once reading the script of his tale in the sky and troubling the deaf heavens as to why he was assigned this burden of guiding this traitor home. Then he lowered his eyes and everything was as before.

"Así fue, from that morning on, Delfina Gutiérrez's life began to disintegrate. Her parents, embarrassed by her situation and angered by her stubborn insistence to have the marriage annulled, told her she had to go and make a life of her own. And she did, taking odd jobs as a maid and in the tobacco factory and living in a one-room tenement in the old city in a neighborhood facetiously named by its poverty-stricken residents Las Palmas Blancas, for the cheap white paint peeled off the buildings' outer walls in great sheets that for a while hung from the walls like albinal palm fronds. Above her lived a strongman who trained with heavy weights all day and dropped them so that Delfina Gutiérrez's ceiling rumbled and plaster dust rained down on her. Three months after her wedding night, Delfina Gutiérrez, long unbathed and so covered in plaster dust that she had to lift the strap of her bra to see the real tint of her skin, peeled seven of these poisonous lead-laden fronds from her building, and stuffed her insides to kill the new life growing there. The fetus came out wrapped head to toe in fronds, like a fish ready to roast. After this, her mind began to deteriorate and she placed all the blame for her misfortune not on the sacred Virgin but on the maldito sacrament of marriage and she set out to rid the world of matrimony. She tried various tactics. She searched the societal pages in the paper for the weddings that her parents were likely to attend and during the service she stood up on one of the back pews and screamed that she was a ghost from the shameful past (which many believed due to the coat of white dust that covered every inch of her), that the groom had been her lover for many years, or when her anger was more pure, that the *bride* had shared her bed! Eventually barred from all wedding ceremonies, she set out following the mailman and stealing invitations from people's mailboxes, leaving white footprints so obvious that it was a minor miracle that this tactic was so successful (a miracle she attributed to the Virgin) that on one or two occasions couples of well-known families were married with only a handful present. Her most successful ruse, however, occurred to her the morning she received a package from her mother accompanied with a note:

> *May this beautiful piece of fabric and art remind you of all that you have left behind and help you restore your sanity.*
>
> *Te quiero, tu madre*

It was her silk embroidered wedding dress, which she put on before she knelt in front of her makeshift altar to the Virgin and whispered prayers of repentance and then took off the dress and set it afire in the alleyway, a fire that burned with such rage that it seared many of the white palm fronds of her building. What better way, she thought, to undo weddings than to undress the bride? For isn't the white bridal gown the central piece, the one unique and ornate symbol that proclaims and holds aloft for all the world the luxury of virginity?

"Delfina Gutiérrez stole bridal gowns. She bribed servants, snuck into gardens and cautiously climbed up trellises, dug into cellars and hid behind stacks of aged rum casks and even once seduced the gardener and drank with him shot for shot of black rum (a skill she was learning to master late nights in her tenement room after her novenas) till he passed out, and wobbly as she was, lifted his heavy jangly key ring, anything at all on the eve of a much heralded wedding to sneak into the bride's dressing chamber and make off with the bridal gown stuffed into a fifty-pound burlap sugar sack. She stole twenty-eight bridal gowns in all and twenty-seven weddings were postponed the following morning. Only one bride decided, against the advice of her parents, that she would get married anyway, that she would walk the aisle naked if she had to, but that she could wait no longer to ride on the seat of her beloved and have him slay the ugly dragon of her virginity. The parents, not knowing their child was such a poet, politely assented, and let her wear her mother's most modest white silk dress.

"Delfina Gutiérrez stole bridal gowns and stored them, burlap sack beside bundled burlap sack, under the untuned steel frame of her narrow bed. One by one, their whiteness began to blanch her dreams and after the first ten were stored under her bed, it was as if a London-style fog, like the one that opens that great Dickens novel, had settled in her dreamworld and the poor souls that peopled her dreams, her mother and her father, her beloved betrayer and even the figure of the Holy Virgin, were only themselves after they disturbed the fog, existing, that is, a few paces behind themselves. When she stored ten more gowns under her bed, the only dream she could dream was of a white child floating on a bark of white palm fronds in a white sea under a white sky. This is the dream that drove her to murder."

"Murder? I thought you said she was hanged for theft."

"I never said she was hanged."

"Bueno, the way the story is heard, how she was hanged for stealing bridal gowns and then after death pulled her greatest trick by stealing the Virgin's gown. ¿Así fue no? Isn't that why the Virgin is naked?"

Brother Joaquín said nothing for a while, and we kept a steady pace eastward on the rocky untraveled road. When I tired and began to complain about it, he invited me to jump up on the horse with him.

"¿Estás loco?—His poor legs will fold if I jump up there with you."

"Bien, then we'll stop soon, and then maybe I'll finish my tale."

We moved on. We filled his canteen at a brook that flowed near the road. The horse drank from the stream. When I complained that I was hungry, Brother Joaquín answered me that the horse must also be hungry. It was well after dusk when our rocky path wandered into the streets of a small town. Brother Joaquín rode up the main street and turned and circled the block (the side streets were unpaved and uneven and the black horse stumbled) and then he went farther up and circled again and kept on doing this every other block, past the solid square buildings of the main street, a bank still flying the national flag although the sun no longer graced it and a post office still flying a more tattered version of the flag and a bodega with its own flag hiding its colors like a coy virgin, limp on a hook over the empty outside stalls, and past a small brick church, its heavy wooden doors padlocked, its flag entangled on the iron cross above its humble steeple. When we came to the end of town, Brother Joaquín mumbled something that sounded like a curse and he pulled on the reins and turned the tired black horse around and we went through the town again in a reverse fashion, passing through some of the side streets on the opposite part of town, stopping at the town's movie theater to squint, in the darkness, at the shiny stills of an American movie starring Joan Crawford. Most of the tenement windows were darkened and those that weren't flickered with solitary candles. This was less common then than it would eventually become, just one of the endless *sacrificios* Fidel asked his people to suffer for the good of the twin sacred cows, Socialismo and la Revolución. To save on the precious imported fuel, entire sections of the Island would be blacked out on an assigned day of the week, sometimes for a few hours, sometimes from dusk to dawn. I often imagined the Soviet cosmonauts watching from their orbits in space as an entire province went black and I imagined the cosmonauts laughing at our crocodile-Island, which seemed to have been split in two or had its head chopped off or its wide tail hacked and this is how they conquered their astral boredom: wagering shots of vodka on how our homeland would be mangled.

"Ni un maldito drunk to be seen wandering the streets," Brother Joaquín said. "What's wrong with this town! Where's the cantina? Where is the whorehouse?" He looked down at me and smiled, a common man proud of his put-on worldliness. I hunched my shoulders. He turned his horse again and we headed back west past the bank and the post office and the bodega and the church and out of the light-deprived town. About a mile out, near a cane field, we saw a bonfire in the distance and as we approached we saw the shadow of a tilted structure that must have once served as a barn or as a storage house; gas lamp flames danced within the glassless windows and the beat of tambourines and maracas and drums swelled as we approached. A cadre of shirtless men, some young some older, some thin, some paunchy, were dancing around the bonfire. They stopped when they saw us near. The music rushed out of the barn and it no longer plunged into their bodies and passed by them and scattered.

"Buenas," Brother Joaquín said when we were close enough.

"Buenas," one of the men said, raising his hand and saluting in a friendly fashion. He was young, still more a boy than a man, and in the undulating shadows he was so full of bones he seemed a crustacean. His hair was long and black and hung thick over his ears and his brow, and his beltless pants, which fell below his sharp hips and exposed a patch of his pubic hairs, seemed to be held up by nothing but an urgent modesty.

"Venimos de allá," Brother Joaquín said pointing back towards the town.

"Es nuestro pueblo."

"What's your pueblo called?"

"It used to be called Ascención, now it is called Los Baños."

"I like Ascención better. Don't you? What's the whole town doing way out here?"

"It's la Vieja's ninety-fourth birthday and we knew it was our turn for no light. She likes to celebrate her birthday on the exact day. It just happens that today is our turn for no light."

"¿Quién es la Vieja?"

The young man pulled his pants up by the belt straps and grabbed a torch that had been spiked into the ground and signaled for us to follow him. The others gathered around us. They helped Brother Joaquín dismount and they looked for a place to tie the horse but there was neither fence nor rail so they kept on looking till Brother Joaquín assured them that the horse would not go anywhere, that it did not have the strength nor the will to flee. They dropped the reins and we left the black horse alone by the shadows of the bonfire and followed. Above the double door entrance to the barn there was a crooked painted national flag (in the torchlight the blue was greenish and the red maroonish) and to the right, in white bold letters, *C. D. R.* Brother Joaquín noticed this too and he grabbed me and whispered to me to let him speak. As they moved inside the barn, the men and their women and children began to absorb the music again and their bodies resumed their forsaken rhythms. The old woman was balanced on a sturdy mahogany rocking chair at the far corner of the room. She was twisted precariously forward. As we approached, her face became a mask of pale serpent hide, the pattern of wrinkles and cross-wrinkles tattooed in almost perfect symmetry. Her eyes were pale as weak tea and her mouth, due to the many absent teeth and the force with which she sucked on a cigarette stub on one side, was misshapened. She wore a rough canvas field dress and sandals. She was just barely summoning enough power to clap her crooked hands together and tap the ball of her left foot to the beat of the dance. She stopped when she saw us. She searched in the pockets of her dress till she found her glass case. She peered at us through her lenses as if looking through a peephole.

"¿Qué son estos? ¿Ingratos?" she asked the young man with the torch.

"No, they are travelers."

She put out her cigarette on the arm of the rocking chair, which was charred solid black with burn marks. She reached beside her on the floor and brought up a blond-wood case and set it on her lap. From one of her dress pockets she pulled out a bag of fresh tobacco, from another a worn leather wallet where she kept her rolling paper of dark tobacco leaves, folded like bills. She opened a tiny drawer on one side of the wooden case and stuffed it with the cut tobacco, then she took out a single leaf of the rolling paper and ironed it out on the chair arm with the ends of her fingers and inserted it into a slit on the opposite side of the box. Her cuticles were blackened all the way around forming tiny horseshoes around her fingernails. She turned a crank. The leaf rolled in. She slid a compartment door open on top of the box and pulled out a fat tight brown cigarette and wet the seam lightly with her tongue. She blew on it as if to cool it. "Bien. I don't want any ingratos at my fiesta. And take that torch outside, you're stinking up the whole place!"

Brother Joaquín approached her and introduced himself. He introduced me as one of his seminarians, which, thanks to the garment they had lent me back at the Marist house, la Vieja seemed to believe.

"I don't have much use for priests in Los Baños."

She took off her glasses and put the cigar-rolling machine back on the floor beside her.

"We are not priests. We are brothers. Devotees of the Virgin Mary. We are teachers."

"Well I don't have much use for the Virgin Mary either, but I do need teachers. The old church is now a schoolhouse. I am Delia María Delgado. I run the local Comité. They call me la Vieja, es de cariño. Perdónenme, I confused you with ingratos, those who live in our town, reap all the

benefits, but have refused to put their faith in the difficult workings of la
Revolución. Al diablo con esos. I did not invite them to my fiesta."

"With all respect, señora, we are traveling. We do not mean to stay."

La Vieja tried not to look offended. She signaled with her cigarette at
me: "¿Y éste? ¿Está mudo?"

"He is still a student," Brother Joaquín said. "He listens. He learns."
La Vieja nodded and sucked on her sparse teeth. "Bueno, la fiesta es de todos. Join in. I am ninety-four today."

"A los cien!" the crustacean boy shouted from outside. "Llegas a los
cien."

"Join in," she repeated to us, raising her arms as far as her bones would
allow her.

We were served rum from an oak cask and pasteles de carne, greasy and
still warm. The dancing continued outside by the bonfire and Brother
Joaquín stared and did not clap along, and when someone tried to hand
him a pair of maracas he wandered away from the dancing, inside again
towards la Vieja, who clapped along, though they left her mostly to herself, rolling her cigarettes and smoking them. She had again removed her
glasses so she did not see us approaching. I followed Brother Joaquín. We
sat on the ground by her.

"We will need to rest for a day or maybe two. Our horse is weak."

"Sí," la Vieja said, pretending to be listening only to the music.

"If there is anything we can do in return, for the school or—"

"You are teachers, no? Teach then the difficulty of faith wherever you
go, of faith in our land, in our people, and in our Líder. It's too easy to
throw your hands up in despair, too easy to abandon what we struggled so
long for. That's what the yanquis want, to infect our people with their easy
ways. El Líder will not have it and his people will not have it. Pero la pena
es que some of our people, coño, *are* infected. Discontents, doubters, de-
fachatados! They were not *ever* fit to be with us or of us. Those that cheered
him as he passed through here on the way to La Habana, those that kissed
his hands and caressed his beard and offered him and all his guerrilleros
their own baths and their own soap bars so that they may look decent
when they arrived at the capital, now those same ingratos huddle behind
their shut doors and speak of him as one speaks of a rabid dog! And their
own sons and daughters, their own brothers and sisters know better and
come and let me and el Comité know all about it. Imagínate, their own
kindred sees their wickedness! There are boys in this town, grandsons of
mine, no older than twelve, thirteen, or fourteen, that were rushed to the
coast and fought against the hijo de putas yanqui-loving invaders. I had
two grandsons die in the mountains. One in the Sierra, one in the Escambray."

I did all I could to remain silent. Brother Joaquín placed his hand on
my knee and pressed it, as if beseeching me to *remain* quiet. I now knew

where I was. After he had reached the capital, and ensconced himself as head of the provisional revolutionary government, Fidel had written to me about an odd occurrence in a village in the province of Matanzas where the rebel army had stopped two nights before they reached the capital en route from Oriente. The villagers, led by an old woman who seemed to be the ruling matriarch, had received them warmly and slaughtered pigs and brought out their rum casks and the whole town gathered in the central plaza to celebrate Cuba libre. But after the long festivities, way past midnight, the old woman went up to one of the guerrilleros, a young one of seventeen or eighteen, and started unbuttoning his shirt and when she had taken off his shirt, bent as she was, she crouched and started unlacing his boots and when his boots were off she pushed herself up and started undoing his belt buckle and his pants. The young guerrillero along with everybody else was frozen and he stepped out of his pants like an obedient child. The old woman gathered the uniform over her arm and it was only then that she noticed that the fiesta had suddenly turned quiet and that she noticed all the astonished stares of her townspeople.

Ay no jodan, she said to them, *I have changed too many diapers in this town and have seen too many pinguitas and too many chochitas for it to be of any interest to me! ¿Qué esperan? Muévensen. Get to your homes and boil water. These soldiers need baths and their uniforms need washing. They can't ride into the capital looking like this. Vamos, vamos. La fiesta se acabó. These brave soldiers have liberated you, the least you can do is offer them a warm bath.*

And the villagers, each woman and child and man, began to strip the guerrilleros in the same devoted fashion the old woman had done till the entire rebel army except for its leader was standing in the plaza in only their soiled undergarments. No one dared approach Fidel, who was a bit woozy with rum and laughed heartily at these strange antics. The old woman walked up to him and took his cigar from him and was going to put it in her mouth but thought better of it and handed it to one of the many children who horded around her, children who called her abuela, though it was told that she herself only had one son who had been murdered young and childless, and that she had never known a husband or a lover. *¿Y usted, qué? ¿Piensas que te vas a quedar sucio?* She untucked his shirt and unlaced his boot.

"Vaya at that time," la Vieja would recount to me less than a month later, on what she thought was her deathbed, "everyone was assured that this young idealist was the Second Coming of el Cristo. And when I went to undo his pants everyone gasped, you could hear them all in one, as if I was going to be struck by lightning just because he too like all his men needed a bath!"

She undid his pants and Fidel too was, like everyone in his army, in his underpants.

"Vaya, it didn't look like he suffered too much hunger in the Sierra,

porque he had quite a belly on him. Bueno, como ya bien se sabe, los guajiros de Oriente son los santos de verdad. They took care of the rebels.
They offered them everything, their homes, their food, vaya si no llevamos
por los chismosos, even their daughters. La verdad plena es que, *they,* and
not the rebels, and at the risk of committing treason, not Fidel, won the
war."

The villagers then took the guerrilleros—two to a home—and man,
woman, and child bathed them with sponges and lent them their beds.
The following day on their way out, Fidel kissed the old woman on the
forehead and renamed the village, against the protest of the village monsignor, Los Baños, the City of Baths.

I knew now where I was but I said nothing.

"Now *both* of you are mute," la Vieja said. "Teacher and student, qué
bien!" She took out her glass case and put on her glasses and turned to
look at us. "We will feed you and feed your horse, all three of you look as
if you've taken your fasting much too seriously." She laughed for the first
time and revealed her few yellow and brown remaining teeth and repeated
her vow that she would feed us and added that there were some clothes
that the parish priests had left behind that she would give to us. A naked
brown boy of about six brought her a glass of rum and she asked for two
more, which the boy handed to us. La Vieja lifted her glass, grumbled a
toast and threw the rum back in her throat with a quick deft motion and
then asked the boy for three more shots. The boy collected the empty
glasses.

"I make it here," she said while she waited. This time after the boy
handed us the refilled glasses he sat on la Vieja's lap and she let him wet
his lips with the rum. He asked the old woman to tell him a story. La Vieja
said that she was out of stories but that maybe the priests knew some.
Brother Joaquín did not correct her this time, did not insist that we were
not priests but Brothers of Mary, instead he pulled out the flask from one
of his pockets and held it up to the dim light. He casually mentioned its
contents and began his story of Delfina Gutiérrez again, from the top; but
before he had gotten past the wedding night with Israel, la Vieja stopped
him.

"Ya basta. That is no story for mi nietico's ears. ¡Qué cosas! I told you
I have no use for the Virgin Mary, and much less use for her urine."

So we sat silent the rest of the night and drank shots of rum and the
boy was ungratified and he blew horn sounds on an empty cola bottle and
heard no story.

Two mornings later, freshly bathed, fully fed, and with new garments on
our back, celebrant garb that the parish monsignor had left behind, which
Brother Joaquín put on more out of courtesy than anything, so that now

we did look like priests and not Brothers of Mary, and a couple of bottles of moonshine rum and chorizo and fresh bread in our makeshift sackcloth saddlebags, we set out eastward from Los Baños. La Vieja pointed us in the direction of the farthest town we could reach by nightfall and gave us the name of the woman who ran el Comité there. "She is like a sister to me. The sound of my name casts a spell on her, just say Delia Delgado and you'll be well looked after."

Brother Joaquín thanked her. We rode. Brother Joaquín was silent. I told him about Fidel's letter, about the night of the many baths. He said he had suspected as much, that la Vieja surely knew who we were, that she had probably bewitched and bedded Fidel that very night.

"Why all the hospitality then?"

"It is her duty. To make sure you reach Guantánamo safe, shamed and branded and safe."

"Why would they not supply a military escort then? Or send me on the train with guard?"

"No, no, mijito. You are not worthy of such *obvious* attention anymore. You get a piddling houseless unfed Marist instead . . . *and* the help and protection of a few CDR's and the matronly witches who run them along the way. You, comandante Julio César Cruz, the great guerrillero, the leader of the famous Fourth Column, once one of the native gods, now a native dog, must rely for protection on a frail monk and a band of abuelitas! ¿No ves? Nothing is left to chance. Shame has become a commodity and it is rationed out by the Party like all other commodities." He nodded his head, pleased with his insight. "I have just broken the law. I addressed you as comandante." He was pleased some more by this transgression. "He was merciful. He could have sentenced you to the lower Circles, as is the fate of all traitors. But he was merciful. He merely took from you your title, your right to *gravitas.* You, hijo, are in Limbo."

We rode on. The black horse (although it did not look it) was rejuvenated with its rest and kept a healthy pace so I didn't have to drag him forward by the reins. Early in the afternoon, we stopped in an open field and Brother Joaquín sliced the chorizo with his rusty blade and made sandwiches. He said he had not been able to sleep a wink in la Vieja's house the night previous. "I don't know how you slept through all the noise. She snores like a fat general." After he ate, he pulled out the flask of the Virgin's urine and crossed my forehead with his wet thumb, then crossed his own. The grooves in his brow softened and he laid back, shut his eyes, and fell asleep. The tall thick blades bowed over his face and shielded it from the sunlight and bowed over his body as if bent on interring him. I ate some more and kept my eyes on the road.

She seemed at first to be a child like the children that were leading her gray mule up the road. She rode on a saddle too small for the mule's wide back holding on with both hands to the horn. Her head was hooded with a white bedsheet and her body so crouched and tiny that it disappeared underneath the black shawl and behind the animal's thick neck. The mule stumbled and at times stepped off the road and down the pebbly embankment and the two boys that were leading it had to pull on the reins and grab it by the straps of the headstall and scream at it and wrestle with it from the sides. The miniature rider wobbled on its hump but her limbs remained still and she seemed unperturbed with her precarious mount. The grass was tall and the black horse had wondered away from us to a nearby stream, so they would have passed by us on the road without noticing us, for her hood blinded her periphery and the boys were too concerned with keeping the mule on a straight path. They passed by us in a cloud of dust. The mule stepped hard forward and back and forward and back on its progress as if to reassert her unwillingness to make this journey. I slapped Brother Joaquín on the side to wake him.

"¡La Vieja! La Vieja and her grandsons."

"¿Dónde?" Brother Joaquín stood and screamed with the rattly voice of the just wakened: "¡Oye! ¡Oigan! ¿Adónde van?" The gray mule stopped and its thick legs and thick torso and thick neck hardened. The boys let it be and dropped the reins. It was the young boy who had brought us the rum and another boy, taller and a few years older. They wore rough-cloth smocks that dropped halfway down their thighs, and their legs were exposed and their feet bare. The taller one reached up and grabbed the mule by the bit of the bridle. He wore nothing underneath and his genitals were exposed. He pulled down on the smock to cover them. The mule passed its tongue in between the boy's fingers. Brother Joaquín hurried towards them. "¿Adónde van?"

La Vieja lowered her hood. "She's blind. Ya está ciega mi maldita yegua. La pobre Marenga, she's older than I am." The gray mule's mongoloid eyes were covered with a yellowy film that hardened crusty white along the inner folds.

"¿Adónde van?"

"We're going with you."

"We're going to Oriente, all the way to Guantánamo. It's a long way to Guantánamo."

"I know," la Vieja said. "¿Qué crees? Don't you think *I* know that!" She flipped on her hood and signaled to her grandchildren to get Marenga going again. "Go fetch your horse, you'll easily catch up with us. We have just enough time to make it to Magdalena before nightfall."

Brother Joaquín went looking for our black horse.

Marenga would not budge. The boys tugged at it, their bare feet undermining their leverage on the pebbly trail. The smaller boy punched the mule on the neck and the mule groaned and curled its whiskery drenched leather lips.

"Basta, basta," la Vieja screamed. "We'll wait for the priest. ¡Basta coño! ¡Búsquenme la caja!" The older boy took a wooden cigar box from one of the saddlebags and handed it to la Vieja. It was fitted with a tiny lock. La Vieja opened it and pulled out her tobacco bag and the wallet of rolling papers and handed it to the boys. They did not need the machine to roll the cigarettes. The younger one held out his palms and the other one used them as a surface to lay out the paper and sprinkle the tobacco fillings. They had rolled six cigarettes by the time Brother Joaquín returned. They gave five to la Vieja and kept one for themselves. She gave them back the locked cigar box, which they returned to the saddlebag and sat on the trail and smoked their one cigarette, sharing two puffs at a time. The younger one licked the tobacco crumbs from his palms. "La yegua no anda," the older one said to Brother Joaquín said.

"What do you mean the mule doesn't work?"

"It won't move," la Vieja said. She stroked Marenga's neck. The mule nodded its head.

"It doesn't want to go," the younger one added. "It wants to go back home."

"No te pongas soquete, niño," la Vieja demanded. "It doesn't want to go back home. It just needs to be comforted, to be assured that we're not leading her to the edge of a cliff. This mule was raised in another world, in the world before la Revolución where the old have no purpose and are properly disposed. It is frightened. It does not know of our new world."

Brother Joaquín dismounted from the black horse and took out his flask of the Virgin's urine and crossed the mule with his wet thumb, on the brow and over the crusted eyes. The mule threw its head back and bared its teeth and was all in all shaken from its rebellious stillness, so the boys were easily able to lead it forward. "Vamos," Brother Joaquín said.

"It worked," the younger boy said. "That was the Virgin's piss. The Virgin, the mother of God. Her piss!"

"Better that way," la Vieja said. "De una yegua a la otra."

Brother Joaquín ignored this insult to our Virgencita and we moved on, the mule and the boys now setting the pace and the black horse struggling to keep up.

Magdalena was a farm town, north-northwest of the famous resort in Guamá, on the shores of Laguna del Tesoro, a sublime serene lake surrounded by swampland where many of the Party elite were known to vacation. It was there that Fidel had decided to spend a week of relaxation after his victory at Playa Girón some miles south. Thus the Committee for the Defense of the Revolution in Magdalena was one of the most well informed and influential in the entire Island. Or so la Vieja recounted to us as we approached the town near dusk.

"Aquí en Magdalena están más en la honda que en la misma Habana."

It was her way, I imagined, of further telling us that she very well knew, and everyone in this town would very well know, who we were, and that their mission was the same nevertheless, to assure our safe passage into Guantánamo. We stayed in Magdalena for two nights at the home of Rosa Domínguez, a woman not much younger than la Vieja who was the head of the CDR there. We traded in the black horse and the blind mule for a carreta led by a pair of fresh young mules. La Vieja and Brother Joaquín rode up front on the driver's seat, her cigar box on her lap now, the boys and I rode in the back. Rosa Domínguez and three of her great-grandchildren followed us in their own carreta. We made headway, past the port of Cienfuegos, keeping close to the southern coast till we reached the foothills of the Escambray Mountains. Our stops were mostly in small villages, though often we just hitched up canvas sheets over the carreta and slept outdoors; but wherever we went we were welcomed there by people who knew Rosa Domínguez or la Vieja either by name or by reputation, and always we stayed at the home of the head of the local CDR, most often a female, usually in her later years. *No ven, es tan claro como el amanecer, the old now have purpose!* All this changed when our party began to grow, for from almost every village the head of the local CDR, or if she was too occupied, her sister or her assistant, or if not her first-cousin or her assistant's assistant, set off with us in another carreta and brought with her two or three grandchildren or great-grandchildren for company and cheer. La Vieja neither encouraged nor discouraged anyone from following us. Except once, with the newspaper man.

To avoid a treacherous crossing through the Escambray mountain range we headed north. We left behind tobacco fields, acres and acres covered in cheesecloth to protect the leaves from the midsummer sun. After we passed through the city of Sancti Spiritus, we travelled on a dirt road parallel with the Central Highway, about a mile or so south. It was pasture land and the cows came right up to the edge of the road to graze. This, la Vieja joked as she pushed the two young mules on, was a path taken by denizens and thieves and revolutionaries and blessed ones so as not to call too much attention from the spiteful gods. She said she missed Marenga. She said it to no one in particular, as if she were addressing those same spiteful gods whose gaze we were trying to avoid. Past the city of Ciego de Ávila, our group, consisting mostly of old women and young children in a convoy of rickety carts, had grown to over fifty. A reporter from the *Granma* office at Ciego de Ávila began following us. La Vieja assured him, in a condescending tone, that neither she or anybody else in the group would answer any of his questions.

"¿Por qué no? I too am a servant of la Revolución! Why are you protecting a convicted traitor?" He rode alongside us on a healthy wine-colored thoroughbred. He wore a leather sombrero and veal-hide boots and a Safari jacket and all in all (even to his carefully textured beard) tried to emulate the look of Hemingway or of a modern Rough Rider. "Do you know who that man is, crouched in the back there, dressed as a holy man and playing balinas with your grandchildren? Certainly a woman with your reputation for insight cannot be so easily deceived!" He galloped closer to our carreta and offered la Vieja a black-market cigarette from a red pack. His fingers were rosy and long like Fidel's.

"Mira, joven," la Vieja answered, perched on the driver's box of our carreta, "en primer lugar, I don't smoke cheap yanqui cigarettes. Y en segundo, you, like every other minion-editor or puppet-journalist, know very little about what is really going on in this country. Your cities cannot begin to tell the stories of the soul of our Island, which is in the soil, en el campo. So go and hide in your square buildings and write your stories as they are dictated to you by the bureaucrats from the capital and leave the workings of la Revolución to us, to those Fidel intended to run it in the first place, us, el pueblo." I did not look up again and continued to play with Guillermo and Felipe, drawing a circle in the mound of dirt we had shoveled into the carreta, pretending our flat dull pebbles were round shiny marbles.

"Señora, to so defame *Granma,* the official Word of the Party, can easily be construed as a counterrevolutionary act!"

"Print it in your paper then! Print it that Delia Delgado is a contrarevoluciónaria, and then count the hours and days and weeks you will be laughed at and stripped of your measly position."

"Señora, por favor, I just came to get some answers."

La Vieja lit one of her own cigarettes. "No. You already have your answers and you just want to hear me recite them. Al carajo contigo. Clerks like you are the death of la Revolución! Poor Fidel, poor Che, if they will forever surround themselves with you city-hounds."

"Señora, por favor." His horse seemed to slow down of its own volition and he faded back behind us, though he stayed with the group for a few days, avoiding la Vieja, talking to other CDR officers who were more willing to pass on rumors, which the faux-Hemingway reporter later printed in *Granma:* that a volunteer band of CDR leaders, brave and noble women from the countryside led by the feisty and true-to-the-bone Fidelista Delia Delgado, were escorting the traitorous comandante Julio César Cruz to his home in Guantánamo, where they would turn him over to the chief of police of that city, un tal, el Rubio, who would then take him into the custody and that the tenuous stay of execution granted by the all-merciful Líder might yet be lifted and the traitorous comandantecito may yet be called to pay for his betrayal with his life.

La Vieja rounded up the group when she had read the story, and holding the crumpled smudge-gray paper in one hand, shaking it in front of her as if to rid it, letter by letter, of its lies, she insisted she did not want to know who spoke such basura to that mock-revolutionary, that sorry-ass excuse for a patriot, but that whoever did best not continue with us, best stay behind and return to their village and resign their position on the local Comité and return to the fields and dig their hands deep into the black soil and keep them there for a few weeks, a few months, a few years, till the worms start crocheting through their fingers, so that they may better come to know what la Revolución is truly about. The following day two parties of women and children did not continue with us; and la Vieja instead of being pleased that they had listened to her, was angry that indeed it had been one of them (one of *us*) who had spoken to *that sinvergüenza who dresses like a yanqui marica and is better suited to be dallying in the streets of Miami with all the other traitors (los cobardes que dicen que tanto aman a su patria pero al primer chance huyeron) than riding the trails of our Island.* "Damn *Granma!* Damn all the leeches in the capital, may the cockroaches eat them all! May the rats infect them with a thousand plagues and their bones all wash up on the shores of Miami Beach! Hacen miga a la Revolución." She folded the newspaper around the borders of the article and tore at the creases and folded the torn-out story and saved it in her cigar box.

A few days later, early in the afternoon, halfway between two villages, we were struck by the first tropical storm of the season, just a prelude to Flora, the storm we would use as a mantle for our escape attempt some two months later, but still of enough force to merit a name. We saw it approaching from the southern coast, the sky suddenly turned fluid, rolling in great gray waves towards us, as if the world had been turned on its head and the restless Caribbean spilled into the heavens. We tried to put up the canvas sheets over the carts for covering, but it was done so hastily that as soon as the first winds came our shelter went with it. We pushed the mules on, off the trail towards a grove of tangerine trees that provided some protection till the winds picked up and their delicate branches began to fly off like wisp and their trunks to bend low and lower, as if in forced repentance. The mules were now getting harder to drive; I had replaced la Vieja on the driver's seat. She was in the back, her two grandsons crouched over her, holding tight over their head our last piece of canvas. The mules buckled back. Brother Joaquín sat next to me, dexterously handling one set of reins and shouting directions at me on how to handle the other. It was the only time I heard him openly curse. During a lull in the winds, I heard la Vieja tell her grandchildren that Marenga would not have been afraid of the storm. The older one retorted that Marenga was afraid of her own shadow till she could not see it anymore. Brother Joaquín signaled to the rest of the party and we headed towards an embankment that separated one field from another and was the only protection in that flat and loamy country. There, we waited out the storm, and as far inland as we were, we tasted the sea salt as it pelted our faces.

Afterwards, la Vieja along with Brother Joaquín decided it would be safer if we traveled on the shoulder of the Central Highway, that way in

case another storm should threaten we could seek out shelter in one of the
many farmhouses. Army jeeps and trucks carrying soldiers and macheteros passed by us and ignored us, as if already we were ghosts, entirely
invisible. The days that followed the storm were warm and stunningly
beautiful, the sky taking on the deep-toned blue, as if painted on a dome
of pure sapphire that made it seem stone-solid, a blue that travelers world-
wide say the sky only takes over our Island.

La Vieja took ill. She had taken over the reins again, somewhat shamed
that she had listened to me and abandoned the driver's seat during the
storm. She bundled up in her shawl, still damp even though she had laid
it out to dry after the storm. She covered up the first sneezes and when
Brother Joaquín inquired if she was all right she answered that she had
never been ill one day in her long life. Brother Joaquín took out his flask
and wet his thumb and reached over to her forehead but she snapped his
hand away.

"Por favor, yo no soy Católica, ni Apostólica. Save your witchcraft for
the mules." She sneezed again and asked if her other mantle was dry. I
took it from the side of the carreta and gave it to her and she threw it on
as a hood. That night, we pulled off the shoulder of the road and unhitched the mules and slept under the stars. La Vieja huddled in one corner of our carreta and called her grandchildren to her and held them tight
and they asked her why she was burning so. Brother Joaquín sat vigil by
her. He tore at his garment and folded the pieces and wet them and applied compresses to her forehead throughout the night. He explained to
her grandchildren that God sometimes makes his favorite children suffer
the most. He told them of the many vicissitudes visited upon the legion
of saints. By dawn, la Vieja had no strength to resist him or his stories.

The following morning, we flagged down one of the military trucks.
Brother Joaquín explained to the driver and the comandante in the passenger seat who the ill woman was. He asked me to fetch the *Granma* article for him from la Vieja's cigar box. Guillermo and Felipe stared hard at
me when I ripped off the tiny lock; along with her tobacco bag and bill-
fold of rolling papers and a packet of typescript letters and the *Granma* article, there was a rust-spotted pistol inside the box. I quickly reshut the
box and handed the article to Brother Joaquín. The comandante perused
the story, then eyed me, then perused the story some more. His beard was
bushy but kempt and he wore an olive cap low on his brow. He stuck his
head out the window and barked an order. The canvas flaps flew open in
the back of the truck and two unarmed soldiers emerged. They picked la
Vieja up from the carreta, bundled up as she was and took her inside the
truck.

"Bien," the comandante said to Brother Joaquín. "We'll take her to
Camagüey." He eyed me again. Then he cast his eyes away from me and
away from Brother Joaquín and spoke to the other old women, the CDR

officers, and to their grandchildren. "Ustedes sigan. You'll find her there at the Revolutionary Hospital. She'll be fine. It's just a fever. Sigan. You'll be there by dusk. On my orders, the journey is now yours."

Brother Joaquín rehitched the mules and set on ahead, our carreta in the lead as always, even though la Vieja was no longer at its helm. No one passed us, no one questioned where we were leading them. We were silent, already mourning her it seemed. We pushed our caravan on towards Camagüey. Other army trucks passed by us, but we had shifted once again into the realm of the unseen. They brushed us with their speed and frightened our animals.

Our stay in Camagüey was the longest of the entire journey and we might have stayed there indeterminately had la Vieja not pulled the tubes out of her nose and her arms one morning and proclaimed that she was well again, that she was sick now not from pneumonia but from lack of oxygen from all the doctors and the nurses and the "little clerks" from the Camagüey Party Headquarters who daily crowded into her room and stole all her air. Her skin had acquired a rosy tone that we had never seen on her and the dirt had been scrubbed from her fingernails and from her toes and a nurse had put lipstick on her while she slept. She latched arms with Brother Joaquín and wiped off her lipstick with the sleeve of her robe and asked him to lead her out of that misnamed hospital. "The only thing revolutionary about this place is its name!"

On her worst night, a few days after we had arrived, when her fever climbed above 104 degrees, the night the young doctors assured us she would die, she asked to be left alone with Brother Joaquín and me. The doctors at first were reluctant. They whispered something in her ear, which she rejected by summoning all her strength and lifting her right arm and shooing them away.

"They think you would murder me on the eve my death! ¡Imbéciles!" Brother Joaquín and I tried to laugh with her. "How are my grandchildren?"

"Bien, bien. They have been very industrious for the Comité here in Camagüey."

"How is Marenga? How is my old mule?"

"We left her. We left her in Magdalena. ¿No se acuerda?"

"Sí. Sí me acuerdo. We left her." She signaled for us to come closer. She reached out and grabbed Brother Joaquín's hand and held it tight. "Complace a una vieja ya casi muerta, now that the children aren't here. Start again the story of Delfina Gutiérrez, the young woman who stole bridal gowns. I think there's something in that story. Tell me. Empieza el cuento otra vez."

Brother Joaquín was reluctant at first, but la Vieja pleaded and pleaded and Brother Joaquín relented and began again the story of Delfina Gutiérrez. This time la Vieja let him go, past the marriage to the mulatto aristocrat Israel, past the wedding night, past her escape and her move into the ghetto of Las Palmas Blancas, where the plaster peeled off the buildings in giant palmlike fronds and where the strongman above her caused storms of plaster dust, past her self-induced abortion and her nights with the drunk gardener, and past her dream of a white child floating on a bark of white palm fronds in a white sea under a white sky, the dream that drove her to murder.

"Murder?"

"Pues, everything in her life, now even her dreams, reminded her of the night that should not have been, of her broken promise to la Virgencita. She went to see her gardener again and drank with him and deceived him with hopes that one day she would become his wife. So together they plotted the death of her husband Israel, who, as I mentioned before, still torn with love, lived secluded in an out-of-the-way bedroom of his parents' home."

"The death of Israel?" la Vieja grumbled. "Qué bien, I like the allegory . . . the shameless aristocrats that under the guise of religion murder the heartland of spirituality. ¡Qué bien!"

"The evening of the murder she prayed at the altar she had erected in the corner of her tenement room. Plaster dust covered the statuette of the Virgin of Cobre, coating her dark face with a pale mask, little piles of plaster dust around the wicks snuffed the candle flames as soon as Delfina Gutiérrez had lit them, her ceiling rumbled and more plaster dust rained and Delfina Gutiérrez was sure that this was the Virgin's way of telling her she was listening to her prayers of vengeance. She peeled fourteen of the largest palm fronds off the buildings in her neighborhood and set forth to see her gardener. He would wait outside till she gave him signal."

La Vieja coughed: "Ay, qué horrible. Pero sigue, sigue."

"Israel was found by his mother three days later, wrapped in a white sheet so tight that the outline of his limbs and his fingers and toes, the features of his face and even his genitals were detailed like carved stone. His poisonous white palm-frond cocoon had dried and stuck to his skin and the coroners with all their chemicals could not free him from it and so he was buried in it. Six days later, after a brief trial in which no state lawyer dared defend them, Delfina Gutiérrez and her gardener were hanged side by side in a public execution.

"The gardener joined the silent throng of the dead and, as with most of them, was never heard from again, but Delfina Gutiérrez was not finished. A few hours after her body had lost its futile epileptic struggle against the rope, water began seeping down her legs and off the ends of her swollen toes, so that when the time came to take it down a small puddle had formed on the ground beneath the gallows' trapdoor. 'Oiga miren estos, caballeros,' the executioner called to his colleagues, 'se meó la muerta, pissed all over herself!' Her body was cleansed and dried and wrapped in a shroud and presented to her parents. The following morning, as the parents were trying to convince a reluctant priest to go ahead with a private church funeral, the shroud was soaked in urine. The parents immediately blamed the Spanish coroner for desecrating their child's corpse, blamed agents of the weakened almost doomed colonialist government, blamed the reluctant priest, blamed the murdered Israel and the hanged gardener, even blamed the cadre of nationalist rebels who were the only ones to speak up in her defense during the trial, blamed everyone except the child herself, who was still seeping warm urine from her four-day cold body. They returned the body to the government and asked them to 'fix it.' There was an autopsy conducted. The body was opened, the bladder removed, and still when left alone overnight it continued to wet itself! All the other inner organs were removed so that her corpse was now a cave and still Delfina Gutiérrez continued to urinate on herself. The government finally worked out a deal with her parents: they would command a priest to conduct a church funeral if they allowed their daughter's hollow flesh to be cremated. The parents met with the government priest and consented. 'La pobre,' Delfina Gutiérrez's mother admitted as she watched her daughter burn in a pyre of dried palm fronds, 'she was afraid to enter the kingdom of the dead.'

"Delfina Gutiérrez's ashes were scattered within the caves of the Virgin's sanctuary in El Cobre, but her crusade against the sacrament of marriage did not close. Her ghost was said to haunt chapels on the eve of weddings and break into the silver-door sanctuary behind the altar and into the monstrance to contaminate the Communion wafers with droplets of urine, so that the following day, during the service, a green mildew tainted the Eucharist and too many marriages could not be sanctified with the body of our Lord, and perhaps worse, she was said to visit this or that unfortunate home after the couple had returned from the honeymoon and leave traces of herself, in the black soil of the potted palms and the woody mulch of the orchid bed, in a mysterious tiny wetmark on the Persian carpet or a larger drenched wetmark on the bedsheets, in the moist washcloths used in the bath and in the sponges used in the kitchen sink, in the discarded coffee grounds or ripening fruits, left so much trace of her old self behind that the bride and groom felt tears well up in their eyes from *la peste* and both got on their hands and knees and sniffed behind furniture and in the corners of closets, blaming the house cats and the neighborhood stray dogs, blaming the rainy season moistness, blaming the grocer for selling them rotten produce, blaming the musty pages of their family albums and finally blaming each other for the insufferable dank stinkness that had settled on their home. And soon both their bloods were so drained that no matter what feats of arousal they invented, his organ remained limp and soft and useless as an empty wine sack and his tongue grew cold and his lips pallid and the only thing dry in the entire house was her vessel. So Delfina Gutiérrez continued her terror against the sacrament of marriage, so that hundreds of new husbands in the capital could only perform with strange women in sweet-perfumed houses, or with unsuspecting goats and dogs and mules (or the liver or pancreas of such beasts), or with young boys and with grown men who are third sex (los perdidos, los maricas), or even with certain species of mushy-trunk plants and certain makes of goose-down pillows, with anyone and anything, that is, except with their chosen wives, who felt as if they were being tongued by rum-drowned lizards when their husbands returned in the early morning hours and begged for forgiveness as they kissed them on the earlobes. And so it was, near the end of the last century, not long before our Island was finally liberated from the dominion of the Spaniards, that almost every new marriage in the capital was doomed to infelicity."

La Vieja had asked me to prop some pillows behind her and she was sitting up now, listening intently, as if she had stubbornly decided to ward off death until this story was done. "Qué diabla," she said. "Pero sigue, sigue." Brother Joaquín glanced at me and in his cinnamon eyes, in the tiny upward curl of his flaccid lips, I saw his strategy painted as evident as the mask of a comic actor. Like a serial novelist, with the promise of continued-next-time, he would help la Vieja ward off death.

"Sigue, coño. Sigue." She pushed herself farther up on her mound of pillows and adjusted her robe to cover her bony chest.

"Mañana. Sleep for now. Tomorrow I will finish the story."

"Sleep? How can anyone sleep after hearing such things. ¿Estás loco? I will not sleep again till you have finished this horrible tale."

"Mañana," Brother Joaquín repeated and held his hand to her forehead to make sure the fever had not returned and left the room.

"Está loco. ¡Ese cura está loco!"

La Vieja remained alive to hear the end of Brother Joaquín's story. And the story, I think, had served its purpose; for as I watched him relate it to her (watched him and watched her more than listened to the tale) I saw, in his untimely pauses, preceded by almost inaudibles, *pues, deja ver . . .* and followed by all but unhearables, *ay sí, entonces,* that Brother Joaquín was inventing this tale and with the same ease that a priest transforms wine to blood he had converted dirty riverwater in his fancy flask into the holy Virgin's urine, one of the many props he would use to keep *me* alive on our journey homeward. I chided him the morning we left Camagüey, before la Vieja had mounted our carreta: "You don't know the end of the story; that's why you couldn't finish it. You're making it all up as you go along."

"What're you talking about, viejo? This story has been around for years. You, yourself, saw the naked statue. ¿Dónde está la Vieja?"

"She is still saying good-bye to all the doctors and the Party cronies."

"She is right. They *are* parasites."

When she came out a side door of the hospital, they were still following her, young doctors who wished she would stay just a few days more to make sure there would be no regression, journalists who needed a few quotes with which to pepper their article to give it the flavorful sting of verity, Party bureaucrats and CDR foot soldiers who forced little notes into her fists, lists of names and offenses, reporting every one from grandparents to teachers to garbagemen for counterrevolutionary activities, and other notes, careful, if politically hazardous, recordings of hardships not yet eased by Fidel. On our way out of Camagüey, la Vieja sat in the back of our carreta, one cigarette in mouth and one in hand, for they had not let her smoke at the hospital. She rubbed her cheeks with her palms and the healthy rosiness vanished and a gray pallor emerged from underneath. She explained that she had rubbed some of the lipstick on her face to convince the foolish young doctors that she was well enough to leave.

We continued travelling on the shoulder of the Central Highway, making the triangle from Las Tunas to Holguín to Bayamo, which we reached on the 25th of July, the eve of the tenth anniversary celebration of the rebels' failed attack on the government armory there, the spark that would light the many future fires of la Revolución. There was a carnival atmosphere in the narrow streets that not even our ghastly caravan, nor its pale thin riders, could diminish. Naked-torsoed sweaty mambistas played their drums and barefoot children sang their songs of plenty, sang a comer judías todos los días.

Guillermo and Felipe jumped out of our carreta and joined these children and learned their words. La Vieja directed us to go on, assured us that they would be safe, to go on through though she saw how difficult it was to maneuver the mules up the congested streets, where roasting pits were set up on the intersections of every third block, and the sweet smell of slow-roasting pig-fat intoxicated Brother Joaquín and all the others driving their carts behind us.

We asked where the local CDR headquarters was and without inhibiting the movements of their dance, the women pointed us in one direction and the drunken boys in another and both offered us jarfuls of rum. I grabbed one and offered la Vieja a sip and then Brother Joaquín, though he declined (too concerned with steering the nervous mules through the street fiesta) and took a sip myself. La Vieja took another sip and then squeezed in the front of the carreta between us and told Brother Joaquín that she hadn't forgotten his promise to finish the story of Delfina Gutiérrez and then demanded that he forget about the taste of pig flesh and steer the mules off the main street.

One block to the south and about six blocks down a narrower, less congested road, we saw a shabby two-floor building marked with the white letters, *C.D.R.* Their own roasting pit was set up right outside, a small child in charge of rotating the impaled pig over the fire. We stopped and looked back to direct the others and saw that the throng of revelers had swallowed about two thirds of our caravan. Inside, there were a few old men playing dominoes and drinking rum from one wide-mouthed pickling jar which they passed clockwise around the table. We celebrated that night in Bayamo, we celebrated the first of Fidel's many defeats. We celebrated, drinking rum from jars and dancing to the *tantarantán* of the mambo drums and *¡azúcar negra!* of the salsa singer and chewing on crispy greasy burned pig-skin and savoring *tajadas* of pork loin. We celebrated the first of Fidel's many defeats, in honor of his subsequent and ultimate victory.

The festivities were still going on, more pigs being slaughtered, more casks of rum being hoisted up from cellars, and the drums and the dancing unabated, when we left town two mornings later, la Vieja forcefully gathering up all her colleagues and their children and proclaiming that we had eaten and drunk enough to last us all the way into Guantánamo. None of the Bayameses, even those that covertly referred to the story in *Granma,* were able to get any answers from her on what her plans were when we reached my hometown.

"I'll hear the end of that story," she said to Brother Joaquín on the road eastward from Bayamo. "That's what my plans are. I'll dine with Julio's lovely wife and hear the end of that story."

At the cavernous sanctuary for la Virgencita in El Cobre, Brother Joaquín showed us the quiet spot where the remains of Delfina Gutiérrez had been spread. La Vieja knelt in front of the likeness of our Holy Mother and recited a rosary of thanksgiving with Brother Joaquín and me, and forced her grandchildren to join us. The other CDR leaders and their grandchildren refrained, not daring, however, to voice their fears that the fevers had pushed her into senility.

In exchange for this courtesy (which is all I thought it was, for though she knew the words to the prayers, la Vieja never had been and, I was sure then, never would be a woman of organized faith), Brother Joaquín was persuaded to continue his story.

"And so it was, that near the end of the last century, the whole kingdom of matrimony was infected with the vengeful pestilent ghost of Delfina Gutiérrez. Couples thought it best not to marry, and lived together and risked their everlasting souls instead of risking the demise of their love. By the time the yanqui flags were lowered and our national flag raised in 1902, unblessed unsacramented love was rampant in the capital. The problem was so drastic that the newly established president don Tomás Estrada Palma secretly rode out to the outskirts of the capital with a small entourage and visited the Little Brothers of Mary at their cloister in the countryside (the house where we lived till 1960, where you were kept, viejo). The brothers were still mostly Spaniards then, or native

Cubans with a long lineage of Spanish blood, and they received the new president coldly. But don Tomás too had some pure blood running in him and he won them over with a woeful recounting of his three daughters' ruined marriages and they agreed to pray with him. They knelt under the Virgin's stone statue in their jasmine-sweet garden. The president refused the offer of a mat and knelt on the black dirt so that his white linen trousers were soiled. They said a novena and pleaded with the Virgin to call back her wayward devotee, to save the sacrament of marriage in the newly established nation. One of the brothers confided to the president that this was all the fault of our acceptance of the infidel yanquis, that now that they had gone, the Virgin was sure to take action.

"It took some time, but eventually the Virgin did lure the ghost of Delfina Gutiérrez into her garden. And the ghost, resentful at first, vented her rage on the soil of the jasmine vines and on the bed of wild orchids, but the more she wet the ground, the sweeter the jasmine perfumed and the more outlandish and colorful the orchids bloomed. When Delfina Gutiérrez complained that it was cold, the Virgin lent her the damask robe. But such pity did not weaken her and she continued to soak the soil, till it was said the jasmine aroma wafted all the way from that garden, through the thick foliage of the countryside, all the way into the open windows of the over-furnished quarters of don Tomás, and at his desk, just awaking from a siesta, he called in his three miserable daughters and offered them the happy news. 'Can't you smell it! ¿Están bobas, chicas? Smell it! Smell it! The Virgin has triumphed. Your husbands are yours again.' And house by house, the stink lifted from the capital and was replaced by the fragrant breezes from the Virgin's garden. Así fue; indeed, to this day it is the only triumph historians are able to attribute to the brief and troubled term of President Tomás Estrada Palma."

"Estrada Palma was a yanqui puppet," la Vieja said, nodding her head.

Brother Joaquín too began to nod his head but then shook it instead, as if both pleased and annoyed by the interruption. He stood and put out a hand to help la Vieja up, but she said she wanted to stay a while, and remained behind, in private prayer.

Arrival

La Vieja talked little throughout the remainder of our journey, only once did she become talkative, to tell me how well she knew the lawyer who had defended me, a poor man driven to drunkenness because he could not reconcile his Marxism with his deep-felt Catholicism. Then she added that she had received word from the Palace of the Revolution that we would be passing through her town. When Brother Joaquín asked her to elaborate, she told him that the story of Delfina Gutiérrez could not have possibly had a more sappy ending. We bypassed Santiago de Cuba through the coffee fields to the north and arrived in Guantánamo in the late afternoon of July 28, some two days after leaving el Cobre. The air was muggy and we were thirsty and we stopped on the shores of the Río Bano and filled our canteens and the children took off all their dusty garments and jumped in the river and bathed. We entered the city through a byroad near the railroad tracks and then turned west towards the town park. El Rubio and his army of uniformed thugs had been waiting for us on the western end near el Campo Santo, the cemetery, and by the time he heard the news of our arrival, most of our party had already made it to Parque Martí, on the northwest corner of town, a few blocks from my home. A small crowd of worshippers were already gathering outside of St. Catalina de Ricis Church. El Rubio met us there, setting his men and his bullmastiff Tomás de Aquino alongside his newly painted powder-blue Studebaker in a wall to stop our progress. Some of the children from our caravan, some of the younger ones still naked or wearing only wet briefs, dismounted from the carts and ran into one of the patchy yards. El Rubio was wearing a military uniform and not the black and khaki mismatched garments that his men wore. He was the tallest man in town, handsome, some said, though he had lived all his life tormented by his bad teeth and his narrow shoulders and child-bearing hips. His beard was yellow and golden as ever but his thick hair was greased back so that it looked not blond but a light sunset honey. His eyes were like melted drops of our Cuban sky in brilliance and his lips were thick and wet and pink and set in a childish pout. La Vieja and I were in the driver's box of the lead carreta. El Rubio held on by a leash to his bullmastiff, who try as he might could not hide his languid nature, could not put on a fierce expression. El Rubio shouted at his men to grab hold of the mules. He saluted la Vieja. Father Gonzalo and the rectory servant had made their way out of the parish living quarters. He was wearing crisp and white celebrant garb. He looked at me and Brother Joaquín in our own tattered and soiled celebrant garb and did not know what to say. He greeted me with a simple nod of his head. El Rubio approached the side of our carreta and saluted la Vieja again and said he had heard of her honorable mission. He unwrapped a chocolate bar and took a bite and offered la Vieja a piece. He said he had come to meet her to take her prisoner. Brother Joaquín was about to protest but la Vieja cut him off by raising her hand. She stared at el Rubio. "¿Y quién eres tú?"

"I am capitán Camilo Suarez of the Revolutionary Police, veteran of la Revolución." He put out a chocolate-smeared hand to help la Vieja down from out of the carreta but she did not take it.

"Mucho gusto, capitán. I am Delia María Delgado, chief officer of el Comité in Los Baños, in Matanzas, and an in absentia and honorary member of the Central Revolutionary Committee, and one of the founding

members of the National Association of Small Peasants, and a voting
member of the Federation of Cuban Women, and a tireless organizer and
agitator for the National Confederation of Cuban Workers and a close
friend and comrade of el Comandante-en-Jefe, and I know not, no tengo
la menor idea, mi capitán bellísimo (has anyone ever told you you look
like a yanqui movie star? un poquito como Mae West y un poquito como
Marilyn Monroe), what *prisoner* you are referring to."

El Rubio took a step back from the carreta and put his hand to his holster. Some of his men giggled at la Vieja's chide at his northern womanish
beauty. The worshippers had come forward and were standing behind Father Gonzalo, though he was telling them to go inside because services
were about to commence. I looked for Alicia, I looked for doña Adela, but
they were not there. El Rubio held his ground and did not step farther
back and tried, with his men, to giggle at himself. He said, almost casually, that his mother had been of pure Spanish blood (like el Líder's), hence
his yanqui-seeming looks. Then he changed his tone and said that in his
blood there was not a drop of yanqui-ness. He added that he was glad to
come face-to-face with such a respected and titled and old comrade in *la
lucha* and that she would find in the people of our city the truest of revolutionaries, in spite of the fact that the Devil illegally made his home in
our bay.

La Vieja looked at the wall of men blockading our way and at the two
men holding on to her mules by the bits, so still that horseflies rested on
their serious faces, and at the poor Tomás de Aquino, who had abandoned
his attack pose and was lounging on his belly. She lit a cigarette and
sucked on it a few times and then held it at the side of her mouth and
closed her eyes and massaged her sinuses with her fingers. "It is hot out
here. Mira, I am a sick old woman, capitán. I would like to die in my own
bed. I don't have time for this. What need have you to harass us?"

"Señora Delgado, by no means do I intend to harass you. Rather I came
to do my duty. To receive the prisoner you have so nobly, and under great
risk to your person, delivered."

"Capitán, dime si estoy equivocada, are you so out of touch in this flat
pueblecito so far from the capital, that you let hearsay dictate official revolutionary matters?"

"¿Señora?"

"I have no prisoner! I have rather orders, personal orders from el Comandante-en-Jefe, in a letter which I will show you if you so need, to
guide this *citizen* of ours safely home, to his wife, and from what I see, que
Dios lo proteja, to his townspeople."

"Señora Delgado, your tone is unnecessary."

"Capitán Suarez, your great ignorance is unnecessary. Como carajo you
rose to your esteemed position will forever be a mystery to me. I wonder
if Fidel knows about you. Lo dudo. Is this why my grandchildren risked

their lives in the Sierra? Is this why I have dedicated almost a whole century to the struggle for liberty, so that thugs like you, nalgones como tú, would inherit the power? Now get your men out of the way, and get your mutt's wide ass and your own wide ass out of the way, before I pull out my pistol and get you out of the way myself, one by one! I am a sick woman. I do not have time for you or your mariconerías."

El Rubio stood still, stunned, wordless; sweat droplets sprouted on his shiny tanned brow and stuck there. Father Gonzalo forcefully gathered his growing congregation and moved them closer to the church entrance. I finally saw doña Adela; I saw her try to make her way towards us and I saw Father Gonzalo physically restrain her with the help of other worshippers. Unnoticed, the group of children had snuck behind the wall of policemen. A small rock came flying from there and struck el Rubio square on the cheek and he let go of Tomás de Aquino and covered his head with one hand and pulled out his pistol with the other and shot it in the air.

After the ensuing melee, sixteen children, three of the other old-women CDR officers in our caravan, Brother Joaquín, and I were all arrested. Father Gonzalo was taken in and questioned and released with a warning that if his parish was in any way involved in any further disturbances, all further religious services would be considered counterrevolutionary in spirit and therefore prohibited. Two children were wounded by bullets and taken to the city hospital. One was struck with a bullet in the abdomen. He died two days later.

El Rubio confiscated all the mules and all the carts and la Vieja's cigar box but said he would not charge her with any crimes for there were no bullets in her rust-impaired pistol. La Vieja visited me in my cell and told me he did not dare charge her with any crimes because he must have perused some of the letters that were inside the box. She promised me that she would have the entire Central Committee descend upon Guantánamo and that soon we would see el Rubio dangling from a rope for his murder of one of her grandchildren. I protested that Felipe and Guillermo were unharmed, that I had seen them inside one of the cells in the Department of State Security. She answered that all children were her grandchildren and that one of them had been murdered and that the blond marica with the woman's ass would pay for it.

Alicia visited me in my cell a few days later. She tried to act strong, but I could see that she could barely summon enough strength to stand. Her cousin Héctor came with her and held her up by the arm. They both kissed me softly on the lips, for which the guards taunted Héctor and taunted me and told Alicia that maybe she ought to leave us alone. They visited me every other day, taking turns with la Vieja, for I was only allowed one visit per day.

I had one other visitor though. One of el Rubio's men came in with a pan of water and fit it under my chin and shaved me every day. A beard, el

Rubio proclaimed to me, was a badge of honor I did not deserve to wear. I said I could shave myself. He answered that it was more proper to let someone else strip me of my honor. I convinced him then to let Alicia shave me (which fit his twisted system of derogation just fine, more proper that I should be stripped of my dignity by a loved one), but Alicia did not have the strength, her hand shook and she cut me, so from then on, her cousin Héctor did it, his hand steady, his voice soothing, as if I were on my deathbed and had no strength to do the task myself.

Because, after two weeks, sixteen children still had not been released, and la Vieja still had not been able to assert her legendary influence on anyone in the capital, though she secretly wrote letters every day (which she sent out through factions of the local CDR who had turned against el Rubio after the child's death), Father Gonzalo went on a hunger strike. One morning, after the sparse-attended Mass, when Anita had set for him his cup of cafecito negro and his eggs lightly scrambled and his buttered and sugared toast, he pushed them back and said he would not eat till the sixteen children and the Marist brother and comandante Julio César Cruz were freed. And so he stood and walked to the Department of State Security and informed el Rubio that except for the taking of holy Communion, he was fasting in protest of the illegal imprisonment. El Rubio put out his cigar with a pronounced grimace and pulled out a chocolate bar from one of the drawers and took a bite and offered Father Gonzalo a piece and said that it was fine, that if he wanted to be *un santico y un mártir* on behalf of traitors that was his business, that he could not eat all he wanted, but to remember, *mi padrecito, that it is against the revolutionary laws to refer to that traitor by his former title.*

Eight days passed and Father Gonzalo's hunger strike was abided only by Anita, who did not stop cooking his meals and placing them in front of him, after morning Mass and after his early afternoon confessions and before rosary time, meals that Father Gonzalo regularly pushed away, wiping his brow as he complained about the August mugginess and asked Anita for a glass of water with a squeeze of lime juice, just a simple *vacito de agua con jugo de lima, por favor, mi vida,* and then asked her to please stop wasting food, that it was a sin, a charge Anita ignored till the eighth day, before Saturday Mass, when she replied that he was the one in sin, that hunger should not be so mocked, that it was one of God's most serious scourges and that He would not have one of His servants toying with it, just like no wise father would let his child play with his loaded pistol, that there are millions of starving children all over the world (and many even here in our socialist *culicagao* paradise of an Island, *pues perdóname, padre, pero es que estoy bravísima con usted,* who have no choice *when* they can stop hungering), *mírate, mírate ya el tipo de atrofiado que tienes, con pellejos de vieja y cara de muerto,* that he should not forget that he had once been a very ill man and that God had saved him not so that he now go and murder himself, which is the greatest wrong, which would be a sweet victory for el Rubio and the rest of the *malditos comuñangas* who tyrannized our people. "And what are we to do then? What? What are we to do with you under the ground? Who are the people going to turn to, to open their hearts to the grace of our Virgin and of our Lord? No puedo verte más así. Y voy y te repito, con mucho perdón, padre, it is you who are sinning." Father Gonzalo pushed aside the guava juice and the cup of dark black coffee she had prepared for him and protested: "If I am selfish, if I am sinning as you say, I am doing it with a sound heart and, more important, with sound mind. I have thought this out. They will not dare—"

"¡La mente es la loca de la casa!"

Father Gonzalo stopped; it was a phrase he had taught her and was wont as a young preacher to repeat, a phrase attributed to one of the mothers of the Church, Santa Teresa de Ávila, in a sermon where she railed against the Mind as the madwoman in the attic. Against his own teachings, Father Gonzalo further protested: "Es que no entiendes, mi vida, I am doing this for the guiltless children in that jail. I am doing this for Julio and for Alicia and for mi querida doña Adela. Please don't make it any harder than it already is." He reached out and touched her.

"¡Siempre has tenido complejo de mártir! Pero si así es. But you will not do this alone. Every proper Christian then should hunger with you. Tell them, tell them all tonight to join you."

"I have no right, Anita, I have no right to *demand* such sacrifices."

Anita put down her own coffee and pushed aside her own plate. "Yes you do, Father. I will begin. I will not eat with you. Tell them tonight and they too will begin, those that still believe, those whose faith has not been tarnished."

"I have no right, mi vida. Now go on, no seas boba, eat, eat, someone has to maintain this house, someone has to keep strength."

Anita raised an eyebrow and, as she had for eight days previous, asked Father Gonzalo to say grace over their meal (which he did as he had for eight days previous with a reluctant and absurd prayer of thanksgiving for the food he was not going to eat and the cafecito he was not going to drink), then she cleared both their plates, and battling her conscience, scooped the blessed contents, of rice and black beans and ropa vieja and tostones, into the garbage. Then, suffering another pang of guilt, she poured the juices and the remaining coffee down the sink.

"I will begin now. Mejor, así no tengo que cocinar. Tell them tonight and they too will begin; tell them and if they are the truly golden souls you always proclaim them to be, they too will begin." Anita began planning the great communal hunger strike with the same enthusiasm she reserved for her famous nochebuena meals for the hungry. "Imagine, imagínate bien, first your people fasting alongside you and then others who either are moved with pity or are fueled with a new rage against these malnacidos Fidelistas. Soon the yanquis in the base will take notice, and you know how they love spectacles!"

Father Gonzalo was going to tell her that naiveté was in its own ways a peccadillo, but he refrained. He reached for his water glass and moistened his lips.

That evening, prefacing his sermon with a long apology and proclaiming that what he was going to ask he was going to ask against his judgment and that perhaps his hunger was beginning to drive him into dementia (at this point he laughed, throwing his head back, as if to act out his onsetting madness), and clearing his throat many times and even stopping once to beg of some water from one of the acolytes, Father Gonzalo recounted this entire conversation with his friend and servant and quietly asked all his parishioners to join him in his hunger strike, for the sake of the children and for the sake of comandante Julio César Cruz and his wife and his own dear friend doña Adela. At the end of the service that evening, in the gallery of the half-empty church, Anita played the shoddy organ as if it were a battle drum. She played and the congregation and Father Gonzalo sang "Tu reinarás, Reina y Madre" loudly enough, as they did always, to disguise the horribly untuned chords.

El Rubio attended the first service the following morning. He put out his cigar before he entered the church and respectfully removed his military beret. He sat in the third pew from the front in an aisle seat and nodded to Father Gonzalo as he and his celebrants walked up the aisle to the altar. He stood and sat and knelt accordingly during the service, following the lead of the worshippers in front of him. During the homily, Father Gonzalo again prefaced his request with an apology and joked, though less jokingly, about his onsetting dementia and asked the parishioners to join him in his hunger strike. His voice had by now lost most of its well-known stoutness and failed at times to rise to the boldness of his conviction and often only the first few syllables at the beginning or the end of a phrase were audible. So, from all accounts of those present there, it was unclear whether he outrightly referred (as he had in the night previous) to the children, or to me by my stripped and illegal title, or to my wife, or to his friend doña Adela, who was there, two rows behind the captain of the revolutionary police force. Father Gonzalo forcibly raised his quavery voice when he added that he would not ask such sacrifices if he did not think the cause was most just and proper and action urgent. Before the homily had ended, el Rubio had put on his beret and left. Careful eyes in still heads recorded his disrespectful failure to kneel at the aisle and keen-tuned ears heard him snap open the leather strap of his holster, and both eyes and ears traced his every step out.

Father Gonzalo later admitted to me that he was ready to join us in our imprisonment that day. He expected el Rubio to be waiting for him in the front churchyard, ready to charge him with the usual list of invented crimes against la Revolución. He said he was afraid, not of el Rubio or of jail or of his growing hunger and nausea, but of handcuffs, because as a child he had once been tied to a bedpost by a senile aunt and lost all feeling in his hands. But there was no one waiting to handcuff him. He walked out of the church and at the low end of the front steps turned to greet the worshipers, most of whom, as most had the night before, held tight to his outstretched hand and whispered to him words of endurance and assured him that he was first in their prayers and that it was a good idea to have others join him—*esa Anita es una brava, siempre lo ha sido*—and that they deeply regretted that presently they could not include themselves in his noble efforts, pues, because of age or failing health or family duties or job duties or, two or three women even had the heart to admit on behalf of their sons and husbands, simple lack of courage, it was impossible for now, *aunque claro, our hearts and souls are still with you.*

"Sí, sí, ya entiendo," Father Gonzalo said to each and every one of his parishioners who turned down his call to hunger, "es mejor así, someone has to keep the strength." And then he added with a constrained smile, making sure Anita, standing a few steps from him, did not hear: "No apologies necessary. It is perhaps too much to ask." Only one other hunger striker was recruited from their dangerous efforts that morning. She was the last one to exit the church, using a borrowed cane now, half her weight supported there and the other half on an acolyte's tensed arm.

"Estoy contigo," she said, stopping two steps above him so that she could look into his eyes. "Nunca me ha caido bien la Iglesia ni los curas (not that I consider the question of God an outdated one, al contrario, I consider it one not broached often enough, and I hate to say the priests I've known have tended to make more ado about the cloth than about the soul), but I see that you are different. You have the true revolutionary zeal, not like this blond one, no como ese soquete con melena de yanqui, embarrado con el poder. I'm with you. They are my children and your friends. I have never fasted on purpose in my life, and I may be too old to learn new things, but al carajo, I'll try. I'm with you."

La Vieja recounted to me that evening when she visited my cell the whole of the service and, with a jittery joy, the look on Father Gonzalo's face when she told him she was going to join him in his hunger strike. "Mira chico, he measured me up and down and side to side as if guessing if there was any flesh to sacrifice to the gods of hunger and he tried hard to ignore my persistent wheeze and tried harder, el pobre, to ignore the shame swelling in his chest, that I was the only one, a stranger among all his beloved followers, a comuñanga, as I heard his servant call me, that took to heart his command to join him in his hunger strike.

"'No, no señora,' he says, putting his hand on my shoulder, 'no está usted en condición—'

"I push up from my cane and throw my chin back. '¿Cómo dice?' He starts again but as if weary in his effort of commencing to explain to me how I would surely die in a hunger strike of any length, he seems to re-arrange his thoughts and like the general of a humble army who is wont to draft the feeblest conscript rather than no conscript at all, takes me into his ranks. 'We are three now,' I say to him, and I tap my cane on the stone steps, 'but soon we will be in the millions.' Pero el pobre, fasting has him distracted, he misses the allusion."

When la Vieja told me of Father Gonzalo's hunger strike (it was the first I heard of it), I convinced her to pass on the word to Brother Joaquín and to the jailed children so that we too may join them. On the second day of our attempt to refuse the food that was offered us, to leave the black bean and meat-scrap mush on the tin plate untouched, el Rubio had us rounded up and manacled and brought to a large holding cell in one of the higher floors of the Department of State Security building. It was a large spare windowless room flooded with artificial white light. There was a gallows-like wooden contraption set up in the center of the room. There was a child hanging from one of the beams by his strapped wrists and strapped ankles. His fingers and his toes wiggled fretfully like the legs of an upturned roach. He must have been one of the children in our party but I did not recognize him. His head was stretched back and down by a makeshift rope harness knotted to a lower parallel beam. His nostrils were pinched shut by a wooden clothespin. He was alternating between sobbing and heavy breathing through his mouth. We were made to line up on opposite walls. Some of the younger imprisoned children also wept and kept their chins glued to their chests and would not look. El Rubio entered and climbed the platform of the wooden contraption. He was wearing a white T-shirt and no weapon. His boots made no sound as he walked. He carried a tin plate in his left hand, a fork in the other. He commanded everyone to raise their heads. He repeated his command once and again till everyone obeyed. He stroked the child's head. He asked him to stop crying and as-sured him and us that no one would be hurt and forkful by forkful he stuffed all of the contents of the tin plate into the child's mouth till the child had to stop breathing and stop sobbing and chew and swallow.

When el Rubio was finished, scraping the plate of the last bit of mush and putting it in his own mouth, and spitting it back out on the fork and forcing it down the child's throat, he smiled and turned in a full circle so that all of us would see his lip-locked smile. "Pues ven, no one is hurt and

this child now will not die of hunger, and none of you, while you are imprisoned under my command, will die of hunger. I will have no deaths on
my conscience. Fácil, if I have to I will feed each and every one of you,
from the oldest to the youngest, in this same manner." He stepped down
from the platform and said that now he was hungry himself and commanded one of the guards to take the child down and stroked the child's
hair again and left the cell with the empty tin plate and the fork still in
hand. All further visits from outsiders were suspended. Our own hunger
strike had lasted a day and a half and we were shut out from our supporters. What I know now in this place where memory is breath, is what Father Gonzalo and doña Adela recounted to me the day after Che Guevara
concluded his brief visit to our town.

La Vieja insisted that their hunger strike be made more an event, that
the art of a protest, of rebellion, is to do it in the eye of the public, that
without witnesses rebellion is an act of egoism, an endeavor in self-
aggrandizement, that in this sense, she went on in more familiar terms,
protest is the exact opposite of prayer, whose grace lies in its solitariness
and its doom in publicness. She convinced the present head of the Guantánamo CDR to build a small platform outside the Department of State
Security jail where we were held. The three of them, la Vieja, Father Gonzalo, and Anita awoke at four every morning and went to sit on the platform, waiting for the government employees and the warden and el Rubio
to arrive. La Vieja convinced Father Gonzalo to undo his shirt so that they
may see the shape of his ribcage, already too evident, as his orange-brown
skin, like dull leaf foil, made a cast of his hidden architecture. She also
nailed a placard to a post near the platform and in red paint (which was
also supplied by the CDR) marked the days Father Gonzalo had gone
hungry and in a smaller red number the days she and Anita had gone hungry. Few spectators were attracted at first, some devout who came and recited a rosary for the Seven Sorrows of Mary with Father Gonzalo and
Anita. (La Vieja sat between them, silent and solemn, so that it could be
supposed from first looking at them that the rosaries were addressed to
her, that she was a vision of a visiting deity, the final and proper answer to
so many thousand lamentable susurrations.) And children also came intent on enjoying the last days of their summer, and a handful of field
workers also came who had nothing better to do till the sugarcane harvest,
sipping rum from old Coca-Cola bottles and offering it to the children
and to the devout and even to the hunger strikers. Only the children
drank with them and only then did la Vieja abandon her trance. She called
each child that had been drinking to her, and took from them the cola bottle and turned the bottle on its head to spill its contents, then she set the
bottle beside her and returned to the mold of her solemnity.

When el Rubio found out that the CDR had helped in constructing the platform for *la vieja enana y el curita mártir y su criada tortillera,* he had the old woman who was the leader fired and replaced with his own pariente, Ana Josefa Risientes, known to everyone in Guantánamo as Pucha, a younger revolutionary who he said had fought alongside him in la Sierra (though I don't remember her from there) and was sure not to turn on him. La Vieja was appalled and demanded that such actions were illegal and traitorous, that the CDR was an organ of the people and that only the people had a right to replace one leader with another. Helped down from the unsteady platform by two of the drunk field workers, who only after emptying a few bottles had the nerve to approach her, la Vieja stumbled to el Rubio's powder-blue Studebaker one morning and lifted her cane and began striking the hood and the windshield with all her force and called him an assassin and a child molester and a degenerate. El Rubio smiled, mindful as ever not to show his teeth, and had his men restrain her. As he wet his fingers in his mouth and passed them over the scratches on the new paint job, he casually commanded the arrest of the two field workers. It was la Vieja's last show of outward strength.

Through the newly established leadership in the CDR, el Rubio repossessed the supply of red paint and the brushes, so that after a few days no one was sure just how long the strikers had gone hungry, and he began to spread rumors that the hunger strikers were cheating, that they returned to the parish every evening not to rest as they said but to feast on Communion wafers and milk and pork provided by a certain counter-revolutionary finquero and that they rationalized such fraud on the traditional misericord allowed to monks when fasting became too unbearable. These are not true protesters in the revolutionary sense, el chisme went (so widespread that it even made it to us in our solitary cells), but run-of-the-mill, hocus-pocus papists. La Vieja, it was said, as invention mounted upon invention and bred the most ludicrous tale, was the worst, was actually the Mother Superior of a Matanzas nunnery of such wile and stealth, such a bruja, that she had once even fooled el Comandante-en-Jefe during his victorious ride into the capital. To counter this, la Vieja insisted that they would not abandon their platform at all. She had the floor of the platform spread with hay, and on it the three hunger strikers made their beds. She had a makeshift outhouse constructed of palm fronds and cane sheaths and a rusty metal bucket set behind the platform. She convinced Father Gonzalo and Anita to stop taking Communion, for this weakened their stance and the wafers, consecrated or not, were bread and bread was food. And she challenged el Rubio to set a watch on them, a challenge that, claro, el Rubio turned down but that others soon took up.

Pucha herself, as the seed of the rumors she had planted began to blossom into a bush that seemed to burn with the flowers of truth, began to believe her inventions, and had an emergency subcommittee set up within the CDR to watch the hunger strikers and keep vigil over them. Nine members, seven women of sundry ages and two teenage boys, took turns, in groups of three every third night, watching the hunger strikers. They set up a long table directly across from the wooden platform and set on it three gas-lamp lights and their coffee thermoses and sat behind the table and at first watched the hunger strikers as if they were judging a competition. But as early as the third round of watch they grew weary and took to bringing magazines to read and cards to play with and when this failed to relieve their boredom, they took to setting giant *jutía* rats loose under the platform and to bringing baskets stuffed with fresh pastries (guava and cheese pastelitos and chicken empanadillas) to taunt the protesters. "Pues que rico están los pastelitos hoy," they voiced to each other from behind the glare of their gas-lamp lights and they set basketfuls underneath the platform so that the rats would not wander far from there and what the rats ate they accused the three hunger strikers of eating, and so they reported in their biweekly subcommittee reports to Pucha, that the three protesters were cheats, mock-rebels, frauds, stooges of the yanqui imperialists.

By the second week, Father Gonzalo's third week, the hunger strikers had strength only for stillness, so free of motion that their life could only be judged by the moistness of their eyeballs and the slow-motion blinking of their eyelids and the ceremonious fashion (on la Vieja's voiced command every half an hour) in which they simultaneously reached for the water bottles at their sides that the church ladies took turns replenishing. They wet their lips and took only a sip, un buchito nada más, for they had no energy to visit the outhouse more than once a day.

When Doctor Isidoro Antonio Mestre, a young pediatrician famous with the town children for the dulcet softness of his voice even as he pinched them with vaccines, was moved to visit them at the beckoning of his devout mother and with his stethoscope check their heart rates and the pattern of their breathing, he was arrested on the spot and the recent permission that he had been granted to leave the Island with his family for Madrid revoked. "Te jodiste, viejo," one of the guards said as he placed handcuffs on him, and tapped hard on the cone of his antiquated stethoscope till the drum cracked. "Too bad, they say Franco feeds his loyal subjects the sweetest ham in the world!" Within three days, the young Isidoro Antonio Mestre was charged and convicted of sixteen counterrevolutionary crimes; among the lesser ones (these which fell under the notorious category of *la dolce vita*) were his unaccented fluidity in the English language, his effeminate passion for the opera, and his arrogant and gross display of his medical degree from the yanqui University of Chicago and of cardboard cutouts of yanqui cartoon characters, such as el ratón Mickey and el pato Donald, on the walls of his office. *Our children deserve better,* the state concluded in its brief and foolproof argument and recommended as punishment, along with the revocation of his permission to leave, the divestiture of his license. And so the tribunal sentenced and so it was quickly done, an English-language thesaurus, ticket stubs from the Chicago Lyric Opera and rare recordings of *Tosca* and *Turandot*, the medical diploma, el ratón Mickey and el pato Donald and the deaf stethoscope all confiscated and burned.

From then on, except for the church ladies and a handful of the grandmothers of the imprisoned children, the hunger strikers were alone. The field workers were beginning their preparations for the sugarcane harvest and the children were starting their classes.

On Friday September 6, the thirtieth day of Father Gonzalo's hunger strike, la Vieja was not the first to rise as usual from her bed of hay and use the metal bucket. And when doña Adela and the church ladies came near dawn with their rosaries in hand to awaken the other two, she still had not risen and they found this strange and went to her first and touched her for the first time and put the water bottle to her lips, but her body was losing all its warmth and she thirsted or hungered no more. They awoke Father Gonzalo and Anita and gave them water and before they removed la Vieja's body from between them, they prayed as usual, and Anita said she had heard la Vieja in her dreams at the moment she left and she said that the words she uttered were the words of our Lady and Mother speaking through one of her devoted ones and she repeated them as a prayer for the dead.

El Rubio wanted la Vieja's body. He came flanked by Plácido the coroner and a hospital physician and pointed to the giant rats that nested under the platform and recited, in rote, prophecies of plagues and pestilences and epidemics if the dead were not disposed of properly. And Plácido the coroner nodded reluctantly and added in a pleasant voice that he would care for the body with utmost respect. Father Gonzalo answered them that there was not enough blood or flesh left in that poor old body for any microbe to prosper and he too pointed at the rats and picked up a baby *jutía* that was scurrying about in the hay by the tail and held it over the body to prove that nothing living or hungry could care for the carcass of la Vieja's spirit. He threw the beast on the corpse and the beast poked its pointy whiskered snout into the corpse's open mouth and lifted its head and looked about and showed no further interest as Father Gonzalo had predicted and fled to join its brethren.

"Take the body," el Rubio commanded despite the proof. The coroner and the physician moved towards the platform so that Father Gonzalo had no option but to defend his proof in another, less familiar, manner. Pobre

Gonzalo, whose dementia was probably now more real than when he had joked about it some weeks before, pobre Gonzalo, whose own father had been an army colonel and whose grandfather had fought alongside the great warrior Antonio Maceo, whose two saddest memories were the time as a young boy, during the tyranny of Gerardo Machado, he had been forced to march in a military parade with a pike on his shoulder, and the time he had to break the news to his father and grandfather, cara a cara, that he was entering the novitiate, news that both men reacted to with disgust and indignation, shaking their heads and smacking their mouths as if trying to overcome a sour taste, assuring him in mocking tones that the clergy was haven for men who could not, or worse, wanted not to (*¿entiendes, no, muchacho bobo?*), find women, pobre Gonzalo, who had fled from the soldier's life because the very thought of violence made him stomach-ill, picked up another baby *jutía* and whirled it over his head and slung it at el Rubio, aiming it at his head but hitting him instead on the shoulder so that it clung for a moment there, petrified, till el Rubio grabbed the babe rat by the neck and squeezed all breath out of it and threw it back on the platform so that it lay beside the human corpse. His men had jumped out of the powder-blue Studebaker and were standing behind him with pistols drawn and cocked and aimed at the frail form of Father Gonzalo.

"No vale la pena," el Rubio said. "Put your guns away. Let them stuff the dead rat inside the old witch and let us wait and see what they do with her, for they will not break soil in our town to bury her without our permission." He turned on his heels and his men and the physician followed him. Plácido lifted his hands as if to beg pardon, then he too turned and followed.

The Minister's Visit

Somehow, perhaps through the usurped leadership of the CDR, news of la Vieja's death made it to the capital, for after they had washed her body and dressed her in a white cotton robe formerly used by a seven-year-old acolyte and fitted her into a tiny pine box fashioned for an untimely death, after an eight-day vigil, which had seen la Vieja's gray flesh sink into the pockets of her skull and her breathless suspiration contaminate the chapel with a sweet rotten smell, that not incense, nor myrrh-scented candles, nor a crateful of apples pricked with cloves and wrapped in cheesecloth and hung on nails at the sides of the coffin could combat, as the mourners planned to lead an illegal funeral march from St. Catalina de Ricis to Campo Santo, police barricades went up all over town and many streets were blocked off and el Rubio announced a mandatory rally at the yard across from the railroad station. Kiosks were set up and new bulbs screwed into every street lamp and six pigs were slaughtered and set on a roasting pit. A dance was announced and the hunger strikers' platform was cleared of hay and transferred to the yard to serve as stage for a salsa band. This was a good night, el Rubio announced as he opened the feast, the Minister of Industry was paying a visit to Guantánamo. He was due in town early in the morning.

Near dawn, after many hours of eating and drinking, el Rubio, his mop of hair dark with sweat and fallen over his brow, called for a halt to the music and took the stage and unveiled a new painting of the minister slouched like a giant over a tiny chessboard, his eyes intense and black and true as always, his left hand stroking his famous goatee, his right hand half open like the beginning of a question, his white king safe in one corner, shielded directly in front by a pawn and a couple of squares on the side by a rook, contemplating a move. It was to be presented to compañero Che as a gift the moment he stepped off the train. And furthermore, el Rubio added, as an act of revolutionary mercy in tribute to the minister, he had released the Marist brother and six of the delinquent youths from prison and he beckoned them all, along with the resentful hunger strikers, to join them now in this feast of pardon, this celebration of liberty.

When Che Guevara arrived at the train station in Guantánamo, not on the ten o'clock of Sunday morning as had been expected, but on the six o'clock train from Santiago, the Death Express, many did not recognize him (*¿Cuál es? ¿Cuál es? ¿Ése, ése?*), could not reconcile the thin lank-faced patchy-bearded pale man in the baggy olive uniform with the giant in the portrait (*No chica, ése no. El otro, el flaco, el flaquito*), could not tell exactly who he was till he put on his black beret and approached el Rubio and put his arm around him and whispered something in his ear and shook his head and whispered something else to his bodyguard and then was whisked away in the powder-blue Studebaker standing by.

Che Guevara visited me in my cell and asked to be left alone and we reminisced about our days in la Sierra and he told me of his visits to South America and to Mexico and of his ever progressing plan for a united southern continent. Then, in a quiet voice, he added that there were many stubborn weeds, pretty and yellow as dandelions, yet to be plucked from the soil of la Revolución, but that no serious planter abandons his land because of a few deep-rooted weeds and he begged me to have patience, *how poor are they who have it not,* and he sucked on his asthma spray, kissed me on the cheek, chided me for my thinness and promised me that I would be home with my wife before he left town.

Che Guevara visited St. Catalina de Ricis Church and marched at the tail of la Vieja's funeral procession, alone, his black beret in hand clutched to his chest. The powder-blue Studebaker, on the guise of providing protection against snipers, idled patiently behind him. At la Vieja's grave site, a plot donated by the city government, as if speaking only to her and not to the minister, nor to the hunger strikers, nor to all the other mourners gathered, Brother Joaquín knelt and began again the tale of Delfina Gutiérrez, *to more properly finish it, mi querida, como te prometí.* "Pues ya sabes," he began, "of her marriage to the mulato aristocrat Israel, of the dreadful bliss of her wedding night, of her escape into the ghettos of Las Palmas Blancas, of her abortion induced by the poisonous white palm fronds, of her drunken nights with the gardener, of her theft of twenty-eight bridal gowns, of her dream of a white child floating in a bark of white palm fronds in an abominable white sea under a perverse white sky that drove her to the white murder of her husband, of her hanging beside her second lover, of her stink attacks on the sacrament of marriage that at the birth of our republic threatened all newlyweds in the capital, of the first president's visit to the Marist house in the hills of the country, and of the jasmine-sweet victory, that so failed to convince you and that the president proclaimed as his own political triumph. Ya sabes todo eso. But the president's mortal victory is not the Virgin's, whose most human grace is that she is more interested in our character than in our happiness, and her most precious promise is that she would console us in our sorrows and make them hers and assist us in our deaths and make her everlasting life ours. So she did with Delfina Gutiérrez. When the mountain winds blew and the ghost-child became too cold, the Virgin gave her her robe and when Delfina Gutiérrez wet the robe and was overcome with a violent attack of escalofrío, the Virgin beckoned the ghost-child to come into her, to make her sorrows one with her who has known the greatest of all sorrow and the ghost-child at first was hesitant to share her solitude, but in time obeyed and entered the still naked form of the Virgin and that is why to this day that sacred statue seeps, through all its pores, a substance that is hers and not hers, a liquid that is as many parts vengeance as it is forgiveness." Brother Joaquín reached into his robe and removed the crystal bottle and uncapped it and poured its blood-brown contents on the fresh mound of la Vieja's grave. The softened dirt drank it as soon as it received it.

That evening, before Che boarded the train on its way back to La Habana, el Rubio granted me and the twelve remaining children our unconditional freedom. After forty days, Father Gonzalo broke his fast with bread and guava juice and that midnight he and Anita took Communion for the first time in four weeks. I never saw Che again, but I know that he did not take his portrait gift, for it still hangs to this day on the wall of el Rubio's office at the Department of State Security, and he tells anyone who dares admire it that it was a gift *from* the minister *to him* on the occasion of his prodigious visit to our town.

Alicia received me in our home, but I could no longer be a husband to her, the man she had married no longer existed, the *guerrillero* who had broken into the tiny mountain schoolhouse to retrieve hidden arms had been erased from the blackboard of history like yesterday's lesson. I left her to the care and caresses of her cousin and when Richard Hadley appeared, I searched for others just as discontented as I was and began to plan my escape into the paradise of the tin roofs.

When I returned here to this house in which we made our marriage, much less a *guerrillero,* much much less a man, with these seven wounds against me, naked as the sacred statue of la Virgencita, my skin liver-spotted and my fingers crooked, my ears deaf to the orchestrated clamor of the virtuous symphonies, my wedding ring a molar in the mouth of my enemy, my old-as-the-century blue-feathered cock floating in the fountain by the terrace, his neck cracked, his coral crest limp with the heavy waters, my falcon-legged bathtub desecrated with a golden *mojón,* my wife a lover to her own, in her an unborn daughter who will, bear my name though not be my own, my only strength my memory, my only solace my prayers to our Lady and Mother, my only pleasure the pale cafecito from the reused grounds and the brief and sudden afternoon showers that wash my wounds, I suspected too well my one unlisted crime, for which no tribunal had the wisdom to condemn me, the where-and-how with which I forgot the patience that Che so urged, that allowed him and all the living to live on.

BOOK THREE

Exile and the Kingdom
of Forgetfulness:
A Tale in Tongues

SEVEN

Wordeaters

As doña Adela kneaded the dough, she realized it was too wet, as careful as she had been, she had added too much water and now nothing could be done. She had no more flour. She could get no more at la bodega till the following month for both her ration card and her daughter's card were mobbed with "X's." And there was not even close to enough money in the yellowy, over-handled envelope she kept under the porcelain statuette of Santa Bárbara to buy flour through la bolsa. Hasta el pan de Dios nos lo quitan. As she pressed the dough trying to squeeze out the extra moisture, she had an idea. She went to her bath closet.

It was filled with labeled vials and jars full of flower pollens and seed extracts and eastern spices that her daughter Alicia used to perfume and animate her morning bathwater. She opened a few vials and smelled them and with some she tilted the bottle and wet her index finger with her tongue and pressed it against the powder and tasted it, either nodding her head in approval and setting the container on one side or puckering her lips and shaking her head in a tremble, putting the container back on the shelf. She selected five vials and one small jar to take with her. In the vials were granules of crystalized honey and dried shavings of coconut meat and essence of orange and papaya blossoms and dust of eggshells, and in the jar, red tiny diamond-shaped bits, bittersweet as they melted in doña Adela's mouth, that Alicia had labeled as *sangre de rosas* but doña Adela had once heard Marta say that it was the blood of doves turned to glass under the sacred fire. She added a sprinkle of each to the soft dough, kneading it in one at a time till she felt the dough become substantial to the touch and then she added half a sprinkle more of crystal honey, a pinch of eggshell dust and after a moment's hesitation one more sprinkle of the glass blood. The dough turned pinkish. And she waited till it rose.

She lit the oven and set the flame just right and shut the trapdoor and then molded the dough and set it on the lightly greased cast-iron pan.

While she waited for the oven to heat, she put the five vials and the jar back in the bath closet, exactly in the place they had been. When the bread was done and the kitchen full with its aroma, doña Adela set it on the windowsill to cool. The red crystals had melted and the crust was colored brown with purplish streaks. She boiled six boniatos and peeled them and pureed them; along with the bread and a tortilla flavored with scraps of ham fat—it would have to do as that day's almuerzo. She placed on one end of the long kitchen table four settings and took the bread from the windowsill and set it there too and alongside it the eighth of a stick of butter that was left for the month. She covered the puree and waited, restless and tempted to brew some coffee, though she had set the limit of coffee to only once a day so that it would last past the second week of the ration month.

Half an hour later, towards the front of the house, she heard shouts. She heard the cries of her granddaughter coming from outside on the veranda. "¿Ay Virgencita, qué ahora?" Doña Adela hurried to the front door. When she opened it, Marta ran inside with the girl in her arms.

"Adela! Adela!"

"Where is Alicia?"

Marta put the girl down and Teresita screamed, her little hands tightened into fists and shaking in front of her. "Take her into the kitchen," doña Adela said, her voice calm and steeped in a mother's authority. "Go now, Marta, ahora, no seas histérica. Take Teresita into the kitchen." Marta obeyed. Doña Adela then shifted her housedress and buttoned the two buttons she had undone in the kitchen while cooking and wished she had not forgotten to jump into her slippers when she hurried to the front door. She stepped out into the veranda and grabbed the rusty chain of the porchswing when she felt her mind begin to swim. She focused her stare on the faces of the mob gathered below on Maceo Street, packing the street from the near curb all the way across. She was surprised that she recognized so many of the faces, some from Mass, others from the market, others yet who had once considered her a friend and during the early days of la Revolución had ingratiated themselves to her, knowing she was the mother-in-law of an influential comandante, and others still who she could not believe would ever harm her family, whom she had watched grow up and babysat for, and even one, the daughter of a still dear friend, a handsome mulatta who cast her handsome round eyes downward, whose birth she had assisted.

"¿Qué quieren?" doña Adela said, pretending she had never known any of those faces.

No one in the mob answered and its center began to spread open person by person and its wings spilled into the sidewalks and revealed what was buried within. Doña Adela put her hand over her mouth as if to keep herself from making any noise. Her daughter was paraded out to the head of the mob, her right arm held by a young man who was rumored to have replaced Pucha as the chief of the local Comité. He was lank and pale and shabbily garbed in an oversized campesino costume. Whatever fear Alicia felt her face did not betray it. She stared directly at her mother, the afternoon shadows concealing the rage in her eyes. Her hair was let out and doña Adela was surprised it had grown so long past her shoulders and there was even a glint of gray here and there that doña Adela had not noticed before. Over the past months she had lost emotional touch with her daughter, had let her sink back into the quicksand of grief without lending a hand, let her disappear just as the government had wanted her to disappear. Alicia wore the white sashless caftan she had brought back from her five-month sojourn in the mountains, as if she had been waiting for these people, as if she had known the sacrificial role she would play and dressed for it.

"¿Qué quieren?" doña Adela repeated, this time her voice cracking.

"¡Evidencia!" someone from the mob's heart shouted.

"¡Evidencia! ¡Evidencia!" many repeated, from its guts and from its wings.

"The people want evidence," the young man holding Alicia's arm said. "Evidence we know is in that house, evidence that will show her forever a traitor to la Revolución."

Doña Adela looked at her daughter.

"Give them nothing, mamá," Alicia said, not trying to raise her voice above the shouts of the mob. The mob roared its disapproval and gathered closer around her. A girl no older than ten or eleven, dressed in a pionera's uniform, with the flag-colored pañuelo around her neck, stepped up to Alicia and spit in her face. When Alicia did not wipe it off, she spit again and again till the young man chief of el Comité shoved her away. The mob's center doubled over with laughter. The young man raised his free arm and waved them to stop and he pulled a white handkerchief from his pocket and wiped Alicia's face. Alicia recoiled from his touch and was no longer able to hide her tears.

"Mira como llora la sinvergüenzona!" the pionera said. The mob laughed some more.

"¡Silencio!" the young man screamed. He looked at doña Adela. "¿Bueno?"

Alicia was now sobbing, her head bent low.

"Whatever you want," doña Adela said and went inside to look for what she knew they wanted. She passed the kitchen on her way to her bedroom and was surprised to see el Rubio, sitting at her kitchen table feeding her granddaughter a buttered slice of bread, surprised to see a whole block of butter in the butter dispenser. Teresita had stopped crying.

"Where is Marta?"

"Buenas." El Rubio smiled. "I brought some mantequilla. Pues, I figured you would be short. I came in through the patio. Marta is out there. Llorando la pobre. . . . Wonderful bread, never tasted any quite so good." He buttered the boniato puree and ate some with the same fork he fed Teresita.

"Will they let her go if I give them what they want?"

"Señora Adela, perdóname, but I am not here to protect Alicia; I am here to protect you, your other daughter (or I should say, discúlpame, your husband's other daughter), and your beautiful granddaughter, esta muñequita. Alicia is in their hands. Should the business of the people of el Comité be any business of mine, or of anyone on the municipal police force? Don't these people police themselves? . . . but I do suggest you give them whatever they ask for."

Doña Adela ran to her room and lifted the statuette of Santa Bárbara on her console and took the envelope of money and the two folded manuscripts that were hidden there, one, the copy of Alicia's Sermon of the Seven Kisses, and the other, her handwritten transcript of Beba's translation of the English children's story. She went to el Rubio and shoved it all in front of him. El Rubio looked inside the envelope and handed it back to doña Adela and said that he saw no need for petty bribes, besides, she well knew, no matter how few, that yanqui dollars were highly illegal (not to mention terribly unimaginative and dull in their color scheme). He opened the manuscripts and examined them, ahemming this and ahumming that and refolded the manuscripts and gave them back to doña Adela. "Your daughter's handwriting? That's good. Pero mejor that you give it to them. The gesture will seem . . . vaya, como digo . . . more sincere. Mejor que no me meta yo. What good will it be for anybody if I get involved? And be wise, don't show them the yanqui dollars, it'll just get your daughter in more trouble!"

Doña Adela told him that he was a coward and called out to Marta to come back into the kitchen and chastised her for leaving her granddaughter alone con este gran defachatado. El Rubio said that there was no need to insult the only compañero in the whole town who dared come to her aid and to the aid of their loved ones. He pointed at her granddaughter with his fork. He ate the puree and asked if there was more. He said he had heard of her famous recipe for mutton kidneys and that one day she would have to copy it down for him. When Marta had come into the kitchen, doña Adela stuffed the envelope down her breast and went out to meet the mob again. She held both manuscripts aloft in her right hand, shaking it so the papers ruffled. Alicia had been engulfed by the mob again, its wings folded in on her.

"¡La evidencia! ¡La evidencia!" the mob cheered and it pushed closer to the veranda where doña Adela was standing.

"Give me my daughter and it is yours."

The young man chief of el Comité walked up the steps of the veranda and stood in front of doña Adela with his hands out. "Por favor," he said. "No quiero lío."

"I want my daughter in the house first."

"Withholding evidence is a crime as serious as any your daughter has committed."

Doña Adela cast a quick glance at the mob. Still, she could not see Alicia. Two women and the young pionera walked up to the veranda. One woman put her hand on doña Adela's shoulder and forced her to fall back on the blue porchswing. As she tried to regain her balance, the pionera grabbed the manuscripts from her hand. She leafed through them but the young man chief of el Comité told her there was nothing in the papers that would be of good to her as a pionera of la Revolución. She gave him the manuscripts. He walked down the veranda steps and held the manuscripts aloft as doña Adela had. The mob burst into cries of joy. A woman screamed at the young man chief of el Comité to read from the manuscripts, to prove here now and forever señora Alicia's treachery. "Read for yourself," he said. He flicked the manuscripts in the air. The sheets flew apart and floated downward like giant confetti. Doña Adela tried to get up from the porchswing but she was pushed back down by one of the women up on the veranda.

"¿Mijita, dónde estás?" she muttered.

The mob raised all its arms in unison and reached for the sheets. In silence, the people read the criminal's manuscripts. Those that didn't manage to grab a sheet looked over the shoulders of those that did. The pionera brought a sheet back to the young man chief of el Comité. He thanked her and looked at the sheet and told the mob that there was no use reading in silence, to read out loud so that all the people may know of Alicia's false heart. They read out loud. "Louder!" he commanded. "Loud enough so that even the yanquis at the base hear you."

He showed them how and the people did as he did, some reading from Alicia's sermon, some from the translation of the Lewis Carroll story. The words spewed shouted and incomprehensible from the sides of their mouths and sentence by sentence they wove the text into a crown of thorns. When they were finished, the young man chief of el Comité tore his sheet in half and then in half again and gave a piece each to the women up on the veranda and a piece to the pionera and kept a piece for himself and he commanded the mob to do the same. He put the paper in his mouth and began to chew on it like a goat and the mob cheered and did like he did, masticating in unison, loud and vulgar with open mouths, and then someone screamed that *she* should be the one eating her own words and they dragged Alicia to the front again. Doña Adela screamed for her daughter but the two women held her down. The pionera tossed her wad of chewed paper at Alicia and it stuck to her neck and they threw Alicia to the ground and forced the wad in her mouth and moved her jaw with their hands so she too would chew on it. Doña Adela began to throw punches at the women who were holding her down but they laughed at her and called her abuelita. One by one they regurgitated their cuds of paper and made Alicia chew on them. When they were done her caftan had been torn open and her breasts were scratched and exposed. The young man chief of el Comité walked up to her and spit his cud, not at her but at her side, and the mob cheered this gesture of mercy and all followed him away from there.

By the time doña Adela reached her daughter and wrapped her in the shawl that had been draped on the porchswing, Alicia was trying to heave back up parts of the paper she had been forced to swallow, but nothing came out, except for a noise that reminded doña Adela of pigs at the slaughter.

After doña Adela had thrown el Rubio out of her house, threatening him with a kitchen knife, Marta put her arms around her sister and promised vengeance. Doña Adela reprimanded her and picked up her granddaughter and said that what they had done to Julio César not long ago and what they did to them now they would do to the girl as well soon, that it was foolish to fight these thugs for they would surely emerge victorious and to think on her defenseless niece when any thoughts of vengeance possessed her. Marta said that they may as well pack their bags and leave for Miami if they were going to take this abuse and torture like a chorus of ruined saints.

"Maybe that is what it has finally come to," doña Adela said. "Maybe it is time for us to put in for permission to leave. No, mi vida, you are absolutely right, we are no saints. Why fight anymore, when this will always be the outcome?" She scrubbed the silver el Rubio had used, and let it sit in hot water, as if he suffered from some highly contagious disease, and told Alicia to try and eat; but she would not, and held on to her sister, the promise of vengeance more a consolation to her than food.

The first complaints in the late days of 1970 came from people indirectly involved with the business of el Comité, informants and ad hoc members who, for sundry reasons of security and secrecy, did not attend the weekly meetings; and they were filed jointly with the local postmaster and at el Rubio's office. Pieces of mail from el Comité's office, announcements of members' weddings and of new births and recent deaths, and other more delicate documents such as detailed minutes of a previous meeting or affidavits necessary for corroboration of counterrevolutionary offenses, were not arriving at their destination; or if they did arrive, they came torn and smudged and soiled and illegible as if some barn animal had grown fond of the taste of the ink and tried to lick it off.

The postmaster, an eighty-seven-year-old spinster named Paca Córtez, convinced el Rubio to let her conduct a private investigation first. She dug out the rusty bicycle she had not dared use since the days when la Revolución was young, oiled the chains and attached training wheels and, with her gnarly mahogany cane tucked under one arm, took turns secretly following each of her carriers, and aside from the infractions that (all but one) she already knew about or suspected: that one carrier was a borrachón and carried in his bag two flasks of rum, which he sipped on diligently and emptied just as he emptied the last pieces of mail from his bag; that another carrier, her forty-year-old grandnephew Miguel, a man so cursed with dark long-haired beauty he seemed trapped in the jewelcase of his looks, entered one of the buildings on his route, a Renaissance-style stone house with colonnaded galleries, built under the shade of a giant ceiba, that was the home of the town's alderman, an older bachelor as well known for his revolutionary zeal and talent in cultivating exotic orchids as for his tastes in love, that daily her grandnephew bypassed the stone post-box that was the open-mouthed face of a Roman god and entered through the front door without knocking and was inside for over an hour, much longer than needed to deliver any mail, but doing what, Paca Córtez cared not to ponder further, for whatever his weaknesses Miguel was her most efficient and best-liked carrier and women her own age sighed with joy at the mere sight of him, mouthing that if they were only twenty years younger . . . ; that her only woman carrier was a consummate whore, and that she too like the grandnephew took time off from her afternoon route to visit her queridos, though, unlike her grandnephew's, hers were various and of the more vulgar vein, factory workers and drooling retirees in their stained undershirts, and her appearance, of tired eyes, pockmarked face, blunt features, and pork-fat limbs, did not begin to offset the shamelessness of her profligacy—these and many other sins Paca Córtez discovered (even the one of which, as she reported, she had had no inkling, one carrier, whom she was forced to dismiss and charge under the counterrevolutionary crime code, who took so much interest in his work that he became an expert at distinguishing, by the care and slant with which the addresses were scripted, which pieces of the daily mail were missives from tormented lovers, which from wronged friends, which from wistful faraway relatives in the yanqui diaspora, and some of these he stuffed inside his pockets and took home and at night steamed open and read, and some he kept as mementos under his single mattress, and some he delivered only weeks later), but none that explained the complaint at hand, that some devil was busy eating the words off certain pieces of mail addressed from the offices of the local Comité. All this and more she jotted down (omitting all of her grandnephew's sins) in a thirty-page handwritten report delivered in person to el Rubio's office.

Paca Córtez put her bicycle away. She suggested to el Rubio, in a postscript of her report, another tactic. She had the young man chief of el Comité keep close track in a journal of correspondence mailed to her house. She stopped going to the post office and instructed her carrier, her grandnephew Miguel, to take all her mail to her address. She waited on the rocking chair in her porch and took her bundle from him by hand. She sifted through it and daily found nothing from el Comité. She called the young man chief of el Comité and he assured her that at least four pieces were being sent to her every day. Some time later, many of the pieces began to appear in her mailbox, wet and smudged and illegible and weeks late. Miguel assured her that he had not put them there; so she took him off his route and put him in charge of personally picking up the outgoing mail from the offices of el Comité and hand-delivering it, piece by piece. He complained that he did not want to be taken off his route, that he had been on it too long and that his customers had grown accustomed to his presence in the early afternoons and that they bid him into their homes for cafecito and expected his personal services. Paca Córtez answered him that she well knew just how *personal* his services were and how much he was bid into *certain* homes and she promised to reinstate him on his route when this crisis was solved, with a lighter load so he could spend as much time as he needed admiring the orchids at his friend the alderman's stone house. For a while this worked, announcements of quotidian milestones and the other more delicate documents from the offices of el Comité arrived at their intended addresses crisp and legible and punctual. Paca Córtez reported to el Rubio that she was content that the problem had been solved and all was well till the morning Miguel and the mailbag of outgoing mail from el Comité disappeared.

Paca Córtez did not call el Rubio. She dug out her bicycle again and rode to the stone house. She parked her bicycle under the giant ceiba. She knocked on the door with her cane, as forceful as if she were a landlord coming to collect rent. The alderman opened the door. His reading glasses were perched on his beaky nose. He showed no surprise. He was tall and bald and brown as a creole egg and wore a light blue guayabera and neatly pressed trousers.

"Buenas," Paca Córtez said, her cane still aloft.

"Buenas."

"¿Dónde está Miguel?"

The alderman removed his glasses and took a step back, as if afraid she might swing the cane, and motioned with his hand for his guest to enter. Paca Córtez stood her ground and asked again the whereabouts of her grandnephew. "Mejor si entras," the alderman said. Paca Córtez lowered her cane and stepped past him. She said that she had often heard of the famous beauty of his gardens and of his home in general, but that sadly she had never before been invited to visit. The alderman answered that he was a very private man, a recluse really, and that he had only become a public figure in service of la Revolución.

"Hmmm," Paca Córtez said. She was led past the dark foyer through a loggia that was lined with potted palms and crotons and hanging ferns and faced one of the sunlit patios. There were open passageways to every room of the house fitted with low wrought-iron grills. Paca Córtez leaned up against the loggia railing and stared out into the patio. There was a young poinciana tree in the center and under it a bench and the three brick walkways that led from the bench were hidden with low-creeping vines. "That's my favorite spot to read," the alderman said, "late in the afternoons when the light falls less harsh."

"¿Dónde están las famosas orquídeas?"

The alderman motioned for her to follow like a guide leading a tour. He pushed aside the grill in one of the passageways and led her into a room where the floor was of an exquisite veined marble, its base the color of his guayabera. In the center was a mahogany dining table with eight chairs. On one wall hung a Bruegel-style painting of a peasant feast and on another a giant portrait of a black Madonna. The room opened onto another larger courtyard. Some areas of this courtyard were well lit, others were shaded by small tangerine trees and parts of the open air roof above were sheathed by a giant muslin sheet that puffed like a canopy with the breeze. Paca Córtez adjusted her glasses. "Mi Edén," the alderman said as he parted the low iron grill and led her through the doorway.

Paca Córtez leaned close to the railing. At the center of the garden, in a bricked-off circle of woody mulch, between the light and the shadow, was a profusion of flower spikes each with six or more startlingly white flowers with yellow upturned lips. They hung on the slender spikes as if ready to flutter off. The alderman told Paca Córtez the scientific name of the flowers, which sounded too heavy and vulgar for their airy beauty. He said that every year he managed to fool a few of his orchids, by keeping them in pots in the coolest rooms of his mansion and fanning them with artificial breezes, into believing it was a long spring, and when they bloomed, transplanted them into the center of his garden.

"It is the only one of my orchids on which I play such an obvious trick. ¿Vale la pena, no? Does not their presence excuse such a transgression? Not that such a trick is not without its dangers. The plant sometimes becomes confused and angered and in an act of rebellion against its removal from the natural course of seasons, the foliage becomes diseased and spotted, a rash act of self-destruction in a final effort to save itself from the eternal spring! Thus, most of my plants I let bloom as their nature mandates. It is just this one, this one that I can't resist tampering with."

Paca Córtez followed the alderman into the garden and towards the center bricked-off circle of woody mulch. He knelt by the plants and passed his fingers over the green leaves. One or two of the plants, though flowering as if healthy, were indeed struck with a rash of tiny yellow spots. "Qué pena," Paca Córtez said. And the alderman agreed that it was a shame, but he assured her that the plants would recover their health once he returned them to their natural course. He showed her other varieties in his garden, some that grew on pots, some on carefully balanced mounts of stones and rocks, some on the slender trunks and branches of the tangerine trees and others that sunk their tangle of roots into the brick walls or around the wooden rails of the upper balustrades and their flower spikes seemed to grow on air. The alderman showed Paca Córtez one variety that he said was his own hybridization from three Philippine varieties. The flower had a swollen crimson lip and blood-brown petals that fell off on each side, long and floppy with tiny hairs, like a hound dog's ears, and its crown was triangular and twisted and pure white splashed with dots of bright red, like a murdered princess's tiara.

"Mi pobre *guajira guantanamera,* that's what I have named it. It has taken me over half a century to bring into existence. I plan to have it officially recognized at the next international orchid show in Rome. . . . That is, if I get permission from the government to attend. ¿Qué crees?" He took a pot and presented it as a gift to Paca Córtez. She took it and thanked him; and half-forgot as to the purpose of her visit, she added that he would surely get permission to travel to Rome, she could not see what suspicions the government would have about such a devoted servant of the cause, and she commended him on his beautiful home and on his stunning garden and begged a thousand pardons before she asked him why a man who lived so shamelessly as *un puro aristócrata* was so interested in the success of la Revolución. The alderman grew serious. He took out a handkerchief from one of his pants pockets and wiped his bald pate. He picked up another pot and took the one he had given her and led her out of the garden. "You have come looking for your nephew, no es así, señora? I will show you where he is." In a room with large airy windows curtained in lace, Miguel was asleep in a wide bed. His body was tucked under white linen and his head supported upward by a mound of pillows. His brow was bandaged and there was a small round bruise on his right cheek. Paca Córtez heard the alderman sigh at the sight of her dormant grandnephew. He put the plants he had brought up on a bedside table and shook Miguel on the shoulders till he woke. "Tienes visita."

Miguel opened his eyes and pushed himself up on the bed, keeping his body covered with the sheets.

"Hombre," Paca Córtez said. She pointed at the alderman with her cane. "¿Este diablo te ha hecho daño?"

Miguel looked at the alderman and he said that on the contrary, that his good friend had saved him from harm, that he had offered him shelter and care, and had been reading to him before he fell asleep.

"What happened to you then?"

The alderman excused himself and said that he would brew some coffee.

Miguel waited till the alderman had stepped out of the room before he began to relate the occurrences of that morning. He had gone to pick up the mail from the offices of el Comité the night before, and had taken the bag to the postal office to sort it out and mark it as usual and was out the doors on his delivery route before sunrise. He had not yet reached his first stop on La Avenida, when he was set upon by a band of women dressed in white sheets and sandals. Their hair was loose and wild and fell over their faces so that in the predawn shadows he could not tell who they were. They demanded he hand them the mailbag. He asked them who they were and the one that was their chief, a slight woman with long brown hair, said that they were the wordeaters and that they were hungry since they had not eaten in over a week. Miguel then laughed, sure that this was some sort of prank, or perhaps a test that *you, ti-íta, had set on my loyalty,* and asked them what it was they ate and they answered that they liked best words spiced with mendacity and envy, words stewed in the sauce of shameless plots and kindred betrayals. They demanded the mailbag again, for they said it was full of such words. Miguel laughed again and protested that they were mistaken, that these letters he carried contained announcements of births and marriages and divorces and deaths, the common business of life, and he threw the mailbag over his shoulder and was about to proceed on his route when they set upon him and dropped him to the ground and pressed his forehead to the gravel and, so he could not follow them, stripped him of his uniform.

"I wrapped myself in old newspapers and came here. It was nearby. It was the home of somebody I could trust. I lost the mailbag. I'm sorry."

The alderman returned carrying a silver tray with two tiny porcelain cups of steaming cafecito and one larger one with tepid tea. He put the tray down and pulled out a chair and motioned for Paca Córtez to sit. He handed her one of the smaller cups and handed Miguel the other one and took the larger cup for himself, confessing he drank tea for coffee disagreed with him. They sipped in silence.

When Paca Córtez was finished, she put her cup down on her lap; she adjusted the bun on the back of her head. She looked at the alderman and waited till he cast his eyes away from her.

"You are someone we can trust, are you not, señor?"

"Claro."

"Claro," Paca Córtez echoed him. She looked at her grandnephew. "It is good they did not hurt you. They promised me they would not."

"You know these women?"

"Claro. You know them well also . . . and so does your trusted friend here."

"Ti-íta," Miguel said, "what is going on?"

Paca Córtez looked at the alderman again and this time he did not cast his gaze from her.

"Señora Córtez, I think *I* know what is going on," he said. "And what is going to prevent me from going with all this information to the Department of State Security?"

Paca Córtez remained serene, more concerned with a small coffee stain on her dress than with what the alderman had just threatened. She put out her coffee cup so the alderman would take it from her. She grabbed her cane and leaned on it and stood.

"Mi querido concejal, what kind of a world do you suppose you live in? Do you think it mirrors at all the false peace of your gardens and your airy rooms? No, no, no. Bien sabes que no. This world we live in rather mirrors the condition of your badly ulcerated stomach, bleeding from within and without, diseased from its own excesses."

The alderman wondered out loud how she knew of his illness, which he admitted to no one, not even his dearest friends. He pointed with an open hand towards the man in the bed.

"There is one person to whom you confess all your weaknesses," Paca Cortez said, "and she is more a beloved to your heart than all the beloveds that have ever lain with you in that bed put together."

The alderman was silent.

"Do you not write to your sister in the capital on the first Friday of every month?"

The alderman nodded.

"How many people do you think read those letters before your sister does?"

The alderman shook his head. He blushed from the eyebrows up to the apex of his bald crown.

"Voy y te repito, what kind of a world do you think you live in, mi querido concejal? Do you think you are the only one with the wiliness to lead a perfect double life?"

The alderman sat on the bed. He put his hand on Miguel's leg. "You work for el Rubio?"

"He thinks I do, and I unveil just enough of the precious secrets of our town, so that he believes I'm perfectly loyal, vaya, just enough for him to believe that he needs me. People are silly, things they will not dare say face to face or whisper into a telephone, they casually write in a letter that they will hand to a stranger who will hand it to another stranger and another one and so on, till it arrives at its trusted destination. There are not many sinners in this town, from the most petty adulterer to the most dangerous and devoted counterrevolutionary, that have evaded my scrutiny. Of course, I cannot do it all myself, I have many that work for me, readers to sort through most of the nonsense that people write to each other. That poor man I had so publicly fired last week was one of my finest and fastest readers, but there had been too many complaints of unreceived mail and we needed a scapegoat. El Rubio promised him if he confessed to all our invented crimes, if he let us paint him as a tormented and perverted soul without attempting a defense, we would buy him a nice home in the suburbs of Miami, in a little residential area called . . . como era, ah sí, muy bonito el nombre, the Grove of Coconuts, o algo así, and set up for him and his family an envious life in the land of plenty, a promise that, of course, el Rubio could not keep. This poor servant of la Revolución is now in prison, and if he is not murdered there, he will serve out his full fifteen-year sentence, and by that time even his wife and his children and grandchildren will have no choice but to believe that he is the devil-traitor the tribunal condemned. *That* is the world you live in, mi querido concejal, no matter how well you hide from it, within your lovely rooms, among your ever blooming orchids or behind the puppet-mask of your political post." Paca Córtez walked over to the bed and caressed Miguel. "This beautiful soul, my sister's grandchild, I saved from all this *sucieza*. Lucky for you, no crees, that I let him be nothing more than a humble carrier. Saved him till the end when I had no choice but to get him involved, and with him you, mi querido concejal, for it is only with your aid that we will be able to succeed in our battle against el Rubio and his cronies in el Comité."

The alderman made a gesture of protest with his mouth and Paca Córtez comforted him and assured him it was safe, that his most heretical letters to his sister, the ones full of counterrevolutionary diatribes and jeremiads over lost worlds and unkept promises, were in her possession and that el Rubio had never lain eyes on them.

"I did not send them off to her, to your sister, for your own safety, because I knew other, less forgiving eyes, would dwell on them."

"Who is with us?" Miguel said.

"Many, many are with us, my dear." She recited a long list of names from memory, mostly women, including Pucha, the former chief of el Comité and cousin to el Rubio, and Alicia Lucientes, the widow of comandante Julio César Cruz, and her feisty sister, who was the one that led the band that ambushed Miguel early that morning. She asked the alderman if he could be trusted to join them.

"What choice do I have?" the alderman said.

From that morning on, the wordeaters made the alderman's stone house their headquarters and from there unleashed their word-ravage on all forms of revolutionary literature. They progressed from the mail to propaganda posters where Fidel's entire speech from the previous Sunday was printed in miniscule type, to finally sabotaging the *Granma* office and making off with whole packets of the daily government paper, which would later turn up on certain citizens' doorsteps and on el Rubio's desk at the Department of State Security as a mushy ball of gray pulp, like the innards of some strange fruit from an old black and white yanqui movie world.

Paca Córtez fooled el Rubio as long as possible into believing that she was conducting her own investigations on the plague of wordeaters, till el Rubio could tolerate no more of her delays and called a rally in Parque Martí to publicly denounce the wordeaters, whom he referred to as locusts attacking the life tree of la Revolución. He spoke as all public speakers had learned to speak by that time, his head dancing to the furious rhythm of his rhetoric, his index finger often pointed in accusatory fashion at the heavens, his whole body leaning forward on the podium, in these and in every other gesture shamelessly mimicking el Comandante-en-Jefe. He ruffled the sheets that contained the text of his speech in the air and challenged the wordeaters, if there were any mingled in the crowd, to come eat these words if they dared. When no one approached the platform, he called the wordeaters cowards and devils and he pointed to the steeple of St. Catalina de Ricis Church and he said that today these monsters eat the sacred words of man and tomorrow they will eat the holy words of God and he compared their cheap form of terrorism to the fascist book burnings. The alderman and Paca Córtez and many other appointed politicos and civic leaders sat on the platform and listened and applauded at his every cue, seemingly unsuspectful of the fate that awaited them. El Rubio ended his speech (as the great ball of the sun lowered itself into the steeple of the church and spilled its light down one side like a pierced yolk) by mosquitoing and sucking the blood-truth from the Gospel of St. John, and he assured la Revolución's faithful that just as in the beginning was the Word and the Word was with la Revolución and the Word was la Revolución so in the end the Word and la Revolución would outlast a thousand plagues.

That very evening, before they had a chance to disperse, all but one of the fourteen appointed politicos that sat on the platform, as el Rubio spoke to the gathered crowd in Parque Martí, had been replaced. The mayor, the alderman, the school chancellor, the fire marshall, the councillor for field workers, the chief of the factory workers, the city manager, the province commisary of the Communist Party, the foreman at *Granma*'s local printing press, the city's minister of culture, and the postmaster Paca Córtez were all removed from their posts and arrested and charged with neglecting to defend the words of la Revolución. Only the young man chief of el Comité survived the purge. The former chief of el Comité, cousin to el Rubio, was wanted and missing, purportedly having fled into the mountains with the band of women that were the core of the word-eaters.

On that Saturday morning, some moments before el Rubio delivered his six-hour speech, Alicia and Marta and Pucha and the other women conferred with Paca Córtez under the poinciana tree of the alderman's first garden. They tried to convince her not to attend the speech, for it was already rumored around town that el Rubio's speech was a ruse to gather in one place all the politicos that had been plotting against him. Paca Córtez said that then perhaps it was proper that they, who were most at fault for digging the city and the whole Island into this shithole, should pay. She told the band of women to flee into the foothills of the sierras that very afternoon, and there hide for a few months and recover strength, just as the rebels had done a decade before. She waved her cane in the air and said that she had no strength to climb mountains.

"And no more talk of this . . . el viejo, mi querido concejal, poor man, he is afraid, he wants to go with you; but el Rubio will grow suspicious if all fourteen of us are not sitting right there on the platform, like chickens rounded up to have their necks twisted and their feathers plucked. So no more talk of this . . . take Miguel with you, he is all the man you will need."

Paca Córtez had the band of wordeaters abandon their trademark loose-fitting ceremonial white caftans and had them disguise themselves in worn field workers attire, with large straw hats and heavy boots. They lit candles under the poinciana tree and chanted prayers to San Lázaro and Santa Bárbara. They asked Paca Córtez to join them but she said she had forgotten the habit of prayer a long time ago and that she knew the gods only through a colorless and fragmented memory, and that she thought of them almost as one thinks of the vanished loves of childhood, only in rare idle moments. She let them pray and went to get the alderman who was saying good-bye to his orchids and promised him that even if he did not make it to Rome, his hybrid orchid with the ears of a hound and the ruby-spotted crown of a murdered princess would live and thrive in the gardens of men for ages to come, and she consoled him further: it was proper that his improbable looking flower had been named *guajira guantanamera,* for when gardeners of future ages, of yet undrawn countries, raised it, they would admire its tragic beauty and consider the honor and glory of the Cuban peasant, of that Island that by then (many centuries onward), from its most fertile sugar grasses to its highest sierra, may have well been swallowed by the encroaching sea.

Just as Paca Córtez left the stone house, one hand on her cane, the other on the alderman's arm, her grandnephew Miguel drove up in a flatbed truck and the women mounted it and pulled the canopy shut in the back. The alderman kissed Miguel on the forehead and asked him to be careful. As they drove west, they saw the people lumbering to the rally. They passed el Campo Santo and near the shores of the Jaibo River they were stopped by the military police and questioned briefly as to why they were not attending the rally. Miguel dismounted from the truck and undid the canopy in the back; he signaled to the women dressed as workers and said that there were early harvesting preparations to do in some cane fields to the north and that just because the previous year's sugar harvest had failed to reach its famous goal of ten million tons was no cause to lose hope for the upcoming year. "El trabajo siempre primero, ¿no compadre?"

The officer agreed with this oft-repeated maxim and commended him on his sense of duty. He prophesied in a whisper to Miguel that though it was mostly men who had fought to give it first life, it was women who would save la Revolución, and he let the truck pass. They headed towards the township of Soledad. They stopped and were fed by a Jewish bodeguero who asked no questions and as they ate inside the truck Pucha convinced Miguel to forsake the journey westward to the foothills of la Sierra Maestra, that it was better to keep within striking distance of Guantánamo, where guerrilla-style, coming and going, they could continue their assault on the words that were the links to the chain of la Revolución. "What good can we do hiding in the mountains, imitating the actions of our enemies? The new revolution will not come from the mountains; al contrario, when the people are sick enough of toda esta mierda, it will rise from the hearts of the cities, it will bubble up like lava from the sewer tunnels. We have started something and made my maldito cousin nervous. What good can we do hiding? Paca offered herself as sacrifice to save us, I say that now it is up to us to offer ourselves, to save our sons and daughters and their children and the children of their children, and in the process we may even save *ourselves*. If we hide we are no better than those that fled. If we hide we might as well build ourselves a raft and float to Miami."

They took a vote, and nine against seven they chose to stay in Soledad and continue their gorge on the word-crusted monster of la Revolución. They rented rooms in the house of a retired wrestler who had once performed for the banned gypsy circus (and hated la Revolución simply and unapologetically because it had destroyed his career) and began to plan their second wave of assaults on revolutionary offices in Guantánamo.

From the first days of their fugitive stay in Soledad, Alicia yearned for her daughter; and since they were forced to cleanse themselves in an outdoor shower in which an intricate gadget, similar to an old-fashioned pull-toilet tank, dumped water over a wicker screen ceiling (the wrestler's old house was not equipped with running water or any other modern convenience save for a rudimentary electrical system), she yearned for her falcon-legged bathtub. She did not yet miss her mother, but she accounted for this by the fact that she was still angry at her. They had fought much after the incident with the mob and doña Adela had threatened that if she (Alicia) abandoned now her home and, more important, abandoned her daughter, for the sake of some futile cause, she (doña Adela) would apply for immediate permission to leave with Teresita on the freedom flights to Miami, and that she herself would denounce both Alicia and Marta and the whole band of women to el Comité, *so they can do what they want with you this time!*

"Adela, no hables barbaridades," Marta said. It was the morning before the day they sought refuge in the alderman's stone house, the morning before the day of el Rubio's speech. They were sitting at one end of the kitchen table having breakfast, watery coffee and revoltillo boosted with water and black-market cream. Teresita was still asleep.

"Barbaridades no, I am thinking about my granddaughter. You are both grown women, you can do as you please. I am an old woman ready for my death, así que por mí no, but that child is helpless; and I will do what I have to to protect her."

"Pero coño, Adela, can't you see that that is exactly what they want, to turn mother against daughter and daughter against mother. This is how they succeed. Can't you see that you're playing right into their net."

Doña Adela looked at Alicia and ignored Marta. "Any sentence you bring upon your head you bring upon her. Piensen eso bien before you continue playing your dangerous games." The two sisters were silent. Doña Adela continued. She told them further that they were embarrassing her by persisting in the celebration of their santería rituals. "How am I supposed to explain such things to Father Gonzalo or anyone else at the church?"

"Father Gonzalo doesn't care about such things," Marta said. "He is a man of faith, and faith is faith, no matter what guise."

"Marta, por favor," Alicia intervened.

Doña Adela paused just long enough to give Marta a chance to remain silent, then she told them some of the abhorrent things the children said to Teresita at school. She reminded them that this woman Pucha, whom they now considered such a trusted ally, had more than once, up to no less than six months before, tried to destroy them, had sent el pobre Héctor to his death, and that because she had lost her prominence within the Party she was *una frustrada, una resentida* and still a dangerous woman.

"We all have sins to be forgiven."

"Mira Marta, I'm not talking to you. I'm talking to my daughter. I'm talking about my daughter's daughter. Maybe someday if you change your habits, you too will have daughters and feel differently."

Marta pushed her plate aside and stood up from the table and left the kitchen.

Alicia looked at her mother. "That's how you expect to get through to her, by insulting her." She stood and said that she was going to go wake her daughter. That evening when she put Teresita to bed after dinner she told her that she was going on a brief journey, she asked the child to take care of her grandmother. "And don't ask too much about me or tía Marta, it'll just upset her. We'll return soon. There's just some things we must do."

"Are you going to go see papi and Héctor in Heaven?"

"No, bella. There are no trips to Heaven. Fidel does not allow them."

"Abuelita says we can get permission from Fidel. She says we can all go soon. All we have to do is get permission. It just takes time because so many people are asking to go."

"Sí, mi vida, it takes time."

The child kissed her mother and put the covers over her head. "Don't be gone long, mamá, so that you'll be here when the permission comes."

Alicia kissed her daughter through the covers. "What do the kids tell you at school about your mother and about your aunt?"

Teresita pulled the cover down to her chin. "They say nothing." She pinched her eyes shut and yawned. "They say lies. They make fun of me because you won't let me be a pionera. They call me gusanita."

"You can't be a pionera. We are not communists."

"I know. That's what I tell them. I tell them we are Catholics not communists. But they still make fun of me and the teacher lets them."

"You're going to have to be strong. I can't keep you out of school, mi vida. I've told you that. It's against the law."

"It's a communist law, mami. The teacher told us about the policemen with Russian watches who know exactly at what hour we go into school and at what hour we leave. She says that because of la Revolución even guajiro children in the mountains now have to go to school and learn how to read. It's a communist law, mami, and we are not communists."

Alicia did not say anything else. She watched her daughter till her eyelids trembled and slowly drooped downward like heavy plantain fronds and she had fallen asleep. Alicia went to meet Marta who was waiting for her at her house on B. Street. She did not say anything to doña Adela and now, as the time stretched at the wrestler's house in the outskirts of Soledad, she wished she had and she wondered how much pressure el Rubio was putting on her to publicly denounce them, under the guise that it would be best for the child.

The wordeaters continued their attack on revolutionary targets in Guantánamo. They snuck into the city in Miguel's truck in groups of eight, disguised as workers. Miguel taught them how to pry open the bottom of mailboxes, and they avoided the mail carriers who were now each accompanied by as many as three of el Rubio's foot soldiers; and Miguel tutored them on the exact times each citizen was wont to go retrieve his mail or his copy of *Granma,* and thus many revolutionary documents and many copies of the Party paper continued to disappear and reappear as ruminated cuds devoid of words, and all this they performed, to the chagrin of el Rubio (who was sure the whole of the citizenry was on his side and would in no way assist the locust-women in their endeavor to eat away at the life tree of la Revolución), in the clear light of day, and they were back in the wrestler's house in Soledad before nightfall.

On each trip into the city, the wordeaters brought their host back a clean and uneaten copy of *Granma.* He proclaimed that the best way to defend one against the enemy was to keep track of all his lies. As they prepared the evening supper, the wrestler sat in his favorite rattan rocking chair, under the only functioning lightbulb in the house, wearing nothing but a pair of his black elastic performance trunks and a pair of golden spectacles, unawares completely of the fubsiness to which slothy retirement had reduced his body, rolling the ends of his dirt-colored mustachio, and he read to them the lies that had been printed in that day's edition, often ad-libbing cynical insertions and ornery addenda, especially to the text of Fidel's Sunday speeches, and sometimes inventing a whole separate parallel text on taboo subjects such as the betrayal of Che or Fidel's one and only testicle in such an authentic mimicry of the dry *Granma* style that Miguel wondered out loud one evening if their host might not indeed be an agent of the regime.

One evening, the wrestler stopped reading long enough to peruse a story in the local section, and he informed them in his monotone reading voice that this he was not making up, that the whole gang of wordeaters, *this new species of counterrevolutionary terrorist, these adders likely hatched in the incubus of la CIA,* had been charged with the murder that had taken place late the previous spring, the death of a comrade finquero who had provided them with shelter and for his favors was repaid with a merciless middle-of-the-night assault in which he was beaten senseless and dragged to the river and drowned. And as footnote to that story it was added that two of the previous leaders of the wordeater gang, the former city alderman and the former postmaster, had been sentenced each with a fifteen-year sentence, but that the former postmaster on learning that she would not be free again till her hundredth year had promptly suffered a coronary and passed away.

". . . *promptly* suffered a coronary," the wrestler repeated. "That's exactly what it says."

"Pobre Paca," Alicia said. No one looked at the wrestler or questioned the verity of this story.

"So you are now hiding and abetting accused murderers," Pucha said finally.

The wrestler let the paper rest on his round hairless belly. He took off his spectacles. He leaned forward on his rattan rocking chair. "Let's not kid ourselves, vieja. You worked for these sinvergüenzas. Accused is as good as convicted en los tiempos en que vivimos."

"We will pray with all our hearts tonight," Pucha said.

"Pray all you want," the wrestler said, "pray to all the gods in the pantheon, but that's not going to change the way things are now run on this Island. Las cosas se jodieron."

Alicia did not sleep that night and before dawn she snuck out of the wrestler's house. She wore only the white ceremonial caftan and a set of keys on a leather necklace. She would be a plain target when she entered the city of Guantánamo. She hitched a ride in a real worker's truck and mounted in the back. None of the workers questioned her or asked her name and they pretended not to know her and to be too tired for anything but silence, but the driver knew exactly where to drop her off without being told. By the time they reached the city limits of Guantánamo the night had turned gray and by the time she arrived at the doorsteps of her mother's house and dismounted the truck the gray had turned to light entire. No one said good-bye to her. She used the keys on the leather necklace and entered her mother's house without knocking. She passed though the hallway by the kitchen and saw her mother sitting there sipping on her morning cafecito. She did not greet her. Doña Adela stood and asked out loud for a blessing from the Mother of God. She followed Alicia to the doorway of the bedroom where Teresita slept. She heard her daughter tell her waking granddaughter not to believe anything she heard from that moment on, to always remember this moment as the truth for, from now on, her ears would be filled with lies and counter-lies and the truth would only live on in this brief moment in this small room as they held each other, like a rare jewel buried under the floor of a deep sea. By the time she had finished talking to her daughter, el Rubio's men had already made their way into doña Adela's house. El Rubio trailed behind them, his mane of blond hair ungreased and disheveled, his eyes puffy, his shirt unbuttoned revealing his sunken chest and grotesque belly, the old scar on his left cheek rosy as if from a recent injury. He pushed his men aside and approached doña Adela. He asked her for some coffee and doña Adela told him there was none left. He moved towards the doorway and saw Alicia kneeling by her daughter's bed. "How long have you been housing this criminal, señora Adela?"

"Toda mi vida. ¿Es usted tonto, capitán? She is my daughter and I have housed her all my life."

"I wish there was no need to do this." El Rubio had apparently decided not to be rude no matter how crassly he was treated by the old woman. "I wish each and every ciudadano had faith in the process of la Revolución so that I could retire to a house in Varadero. Wouldn't that be a perfect world?" He signaled to two of his men and they moved into the room and lifted Alicia away from her daughter. Teresita called to her mother and asked her if this was a dream.

"The first time I did this I hoped I would not have to do it again." El Rubio was still speaking to doña Adela but she was no longer listening.

The Isle of Pains

Alicia walked out into the rickety, rotted dock with eyes downcast and with a look that some who watched the spectacle mistook as shame. She had not been allowed to wear her ceremonial white caftan, so she chose instead to wear a simple light blue dress and leather sandals and a scarf of a somewhat darker blue than her dress, tied over her head. Two soldiers led her out to wait for the ferry at the end of the dock. They held lightly to the backs of her arms, their rifles strapped on opposite shoulders. An army comandante wearing dark-tinted glasses followed behind them. He carried Alicia's small brown suitcase; his belly was sucked in and his chin high and he had all round him the air of a silent snotty servant. Another soldier was left behind by the road, sitting in the jeep. The townspeople who had followed the Soviet jeep from the train station to the harbor were not allowed on the dock and gathered behind a military barricade, but Alicia could still hear some of their insults. The comandante had already commanded them once to shut up and now he turned and did so again, so that for a moment, except for the surface restlessness of the sea and the caw of some low-flying gulls, all was silent. The comandante stepped up in front of Alicia all the way to the very end of the dock and looked out into the horizon, then peered at his watch. "Idiota," he muttered.

Alicia looked at her own watch. It was past noon. They waited. The call of the townspeople swelled again and gradually drowned out the motion of the sea and the cries of the hungry birds. The comandante grabbed the rifle from one of the soldiers and followed the path of one of the birds and shot. The hit gull dropped headlong into the sea as if diving for food. The comandante laughed and then he turned and screamed at the crowd that one of them would be next if they didn't shut up once and for all. The mob began to disperse. Mothers led their children away first and then the young people left and others, till finally there was only two old women left there, in black shawls and veils, holding on to each other, and one of them screamed that she was not afraid to die for speaking the truth and she waved and shouted that she wished the ferry with the murderess on it would drown. The comandante ignored her. He handed the rifle back to the soldier, crossed his arms and faced the ripply waters.

After more than an hour of waiting, a fishing boat appeared from the southeast and they heard the awful noise of its engine almost as soon as they saw it. As it came closer they noticed that it moved low in the water and rocked back and forth wildly as if trying to taunt the sea into a quarrel and its noisy engines did not leave behind much of a wake. At its helm was a bare-chested old man with grizzled cheeks and a bare sun-spotted crown with long white hair on the sides and back. He was screaming but could not be heard over the engines. He circled in front of them once, then idled the boat into the dock. The soldiers grabbed the ropes and secured the boat.

"Separate yourself, woman," the old man continued to scream as he stepped unto the dock, "separate yourself from these sons of la Revolución who have ruined my day. Separate yourself for you are no longer a citizen of the Island, but an exile in the Island's island. . . . How is a man supposed to feed himself and his family if he is not allowed to fish?"

"Cállese, Charo," the comandante said. "You've already been told that the government would reimburse you for your day lost. Bien sabes that we have always taken good care of you."

"Sí, sí verdad. I forget myself. I forget the goodness of el Líder." He walked up to Alicia and sat there staring at her till she looked back at him. "So this is you? ¡La traidora Alicia Lucientes, tan bella y tan mala! You have been willed by the ones that will to come live with us, as if our island were a sanatorium for the wicked-hearted. They think that if they can put half a sea between you and them they will be rid of you. If I had been the judge, I would have been wiser, I would have sentenced you to the firing squad. Así mismo, bella, al paredón. But Fidel is too old-fashioned, muy caballero, he does not like to have the mothers of our children shot."

Alicia did not respond but continued to look at him. His skin was white at its core but stained full with amoeba-shaped orange and brown spots that melted into each other. His eyes were black and they sparkled like unused coals.

"Charo, déjela, you are not here to play judge. You are here to take us where we are going. Do you know how long we've been waiting?"

The boatmaster turned from Alicia. "Perdóname jefe, it is my piece-of-shit boat that is slow not I, and it hates to toil in the sea as much as I love it. Bueno vamos, although I see no sense in this, what has been willed has been willed, vamos, Alicia Lucientes, separate yourself from your old thoughts, you are going to your prison without walls and there are no kings to betray now. Your only ruler will be your solitude and the only one to rebel against will be yourself. I have come to bring you into the heart of the Isle of Pains. But beware. This puke-green sea quells forever the fire of memory. He who crosses it, will find on reaching the other shore that he has not yet lived. Bueno, ahí está, forewarned is forearmed, though you will not remember what I have said. Qué pena, coño. We always forget what we should most remember."

"Estás muy filosófico hoy, ¿no, Charo?" the comandante said.

Charo nodded and said that his wife belittled his ramblings with the same phrase and with the same disdain—but what did women know about the harshness of the world? They climbed into the boat. The lower deck was a few inches deep in water. Charo proclaimed that this was a mere inconvenience and no danger. The comandante seemed unconvinced, but he ordered his soldiers to let loose the ropes and yelled at the soldier waiting by the jeep to pick him up in four days. The two old women still behind the barricades waved, still offering the same devilspeed wishes they had wished before. Charo screamed back at them that the sea was too finicky and refined a creature to care for the taste of his godawful leaky trawler.

The journey across el Golfo de Batabanó, from the southern coast of Cuba to the town of Nueva Gerona on the northern tip of the Isle of Pines, was some fifty-odd miles. Charo's boat took over five hours to traverse it, the boatmaster at the helm simultaneously yelling obscenities at the frothy sea and at his growling boat throughout, as if both were beasts in need of taming.

They landed on a rocky and barren beach late in the afternoon. Charo anchored the boat on the shallow clear waters. They waded onto shore. The comandante carried Alicia's suitcase aloft over his shoulders. A group of army soldiers was waiting for them on the beach. Charo bid good-bye and said to Alicia that they would surely meet again, and took her aside and whispered to her that this smaller island overrun with pines was a truer paradise than the other Island because here no face was a stranger to any other, and all were bound in the kinship of *las penas de la vida,* a utopia less heavenly but truer than the ones cooked up on the bigger Island. They separated Alicia from the boatmaster and climbed a peak and walked on foot to the road and mounted horses southward to the town of La Fé. Alicia rode double with the comandante. He held the reins wide at her side, his chest pressed to her back. She spent the night in a cell of the Department of State Security. The morning after, they took her wristwatch from her. She would have no use for it here in this backward place, she was told, as if the mechanical keeping of time were a notion recently conceived. They moved on, to the forest lands in the southern half of the island. They turned east.

The horses climbed. They saw the flora give way to masses of rock hundreds of feet high that rose like ill-formed fortress walls from the nearby plains. From the summit Alicia could see beyond the fortress walls, beyond the valley they encircled, to the Caribbean. They moved toward the giant rock masses and began to descend. They abandoned the horses and left them in guard of two of the soldiers and continued to descend till all vegetation vanished and the ash-green limestone surrounded them from the sides and from above, and the sunlight was shattered into pieces, peeking in through cracks and clefts in the stone, and soon was absorbed into a dense mist and disappeared altogether. As they traipsed through a tunnel, directly into the heart of one of the rock masses, they left soldiers behind one by one like crumbs of bread, as if to facilitate their return from the netherworld they were journeying into, till their group consisted only of the comandante and Alicia and four other soldiers, and almost without knowing how they got there, they came out on the other side to a world as large and as surfeit with sunlight and vegetation as the world they had left behind, though Alicia noticed that for some reason, perhaps the exuberant birdsong, everything here (even herself and the comandante and the four soldiers) seemed differently alive. They led her through this new land to the front yard of a small bohío with shuttered wooden windows and before she knew it, the comandante and the soldiers had disappeared and Alicia was alone with her small suitcase at her feet. She did not search for them, instead she examined the small hut. She concluded it was a sort of temple, for planted on the thatch roof was a tall iron structure, three times the height of the hut, in the form of a twisted cross. It was secured to the ground with pikes and steel cable. She picked up the suitcase and walked towards the door. There were voices inside in a language that was not Spanish. She knocked. There was no answer and she knocked harder.

"Sí, ya, ya voy." It was a woman's voice, less crisp than the other voices. The door was pulled half-ajar and Alicia was welcomed into the flickering darkness.

"Vamos, entra," the woman said, "el niño is watching his muñequitos. The light darkens the glass and the birds are too loud."

Alicia entered three steps into the room. Before her eyes became adjusted, her suitcase was taken from her. She was told that she may sit and watch the end of the program if she liked. She looked for the source of the flickering lights with her eyes and found it perched on a wooden cabinet in one corner of the front room to her right. It was a small television set, also the source of the foreign voices. Black and white yanqui cartoon characters, a pair of loud-mouthed magpies, were fighting each other, taking turns squashing each other's head into their bodies with tennis rackets as if they were made of pliable clay and not bone and flesh and feathers. The squawky voices seemed to Alicia perfectly suitable for the language they spoke.

A child was crouched on the dirt floor directly opposite the television set. His hair was long and dark and tucked behind his ears and he was naked except for a pair of torn shorts and had his arms wrapped around his legs. His face below his eyes was veiled in shadows. He giggled at the antics of the muñequitos whose every move was reflected in his eyes.

"Ése es Joshua, mi hijo," the woman spoke from the other side of the room, on Alicia's left. "This is my home." She was seated at a small wooden dining table, clear but for a wooden cigar box, and wore only a housedress, and like her son was barefoot. She offered Alicia some coffee and again said that she may sit and watch the end of the program if she liked. She tapped the seat of the empty wooden chair next to hers. "We have been waiting for you, Joshua and I. Joshua salude." The child waved his hand without looking at Alicia.

"Who are you?" Alicia said, remaining still by the entrance to the hut.

The child made a hushing noise and an irritated gesture with his hand. The mother made a cross with her index finger to her lips and whispered to Alicia that she should not be so impatient, that sometimes the gods behaved as if they were creatures without any rhyme or reason, but that she should not be fooled for this was just theatrics, a dance that concealed more than it revealed, for there was purpose inherent in every action and commandments of the gods, even when such purpose cannot be known by us. Alicia asked her if by the gods she meant the criminals who ran the government. The woman answered that she too had once thought exactly in those terms, *bueno hasta diría peor,* but that now she was the chief of the 333rd Committee for the Defense of the Revolution in the Valley of the Nightingales, and was renowned the whole length of the Island, from Pinar del Río to Baracoa, as the most talented rehabilitator of those who have lost sight and sound of the hidden glories of la Revolución.

Alicia picked up her suitcase. "Mire, I am leaving." She started for the door.

"And where will you go, Alicia Lucientes? Do you think that door opens out, just because it opened in? How long will you and yours test the endless mercy of el Líder?" She reached for the wooden box and opened it. She pulled out a silver lighter and a medium-length cigar and peeled the ring off and bit a small piece off the closed end and lit it.

"Come and sit, Alicia Lucientes, come and watch the end of the program with us. We get wonderful reception, no? The signal comes all the way from Kingston. Come and watch with us, la televisión is a wonderful invention, it soothes his nerves. After the muñequitos my son and I will take you to your new home. He does not care for anything else, just los muñequitos . . . and, claro, the Sunday speech. We will introduce you to some of the other residents of our valley, all who like myself had at one time or another staked their lives and the lives of their loved ones for the sake of toppling la Revolución, and who have come to see the error of their ways." She sucked on the cigar and let out a few puffs. "We have seen hundreds like you, Alicia Lucientes; do not think that your thoughts and deeds, no matter how horrible, are the first to be wicked"—she tapped her breast with her free hand—"for wickedness has lived here long before us and will live here long after we are past."

Joshua made the hushing sound again and his mother scolded him this time, begging him to show a little kindness and hospitality towards the new villager and to put on his poncho, for it was disrespectful to appear so naked in front of a stranger, especially a woman who was not his mother; besides, he knew it was a rule that during the sun hours he may not remove any of his clothes. Joshua spoke for the first time. His voice was deep and throaty and did not belong to a child. He told his mother to stop nagging him, that he was her son not her husband, that he would show kindness and hospitality to the stranger, in time. She knew he always helped her with the new ones. He looked at Alicia for the first time and mumbled a greeting. He told her that she should sit, for it would be another fifteen minutes before he was through watching. He corrected his mother and told her that actually the rule was that he may not remove his poncho while he was *outside* for the sun would color his skin. He was inside now and there was no sun to color him. He pulled down the waist of his shorts at one side to reveal no visible tan line and proclaimed that from his groin up, he was as white as his father had made him.

Alicia sat in the empty chair next to Joshua's mother. Between cigar puffs, she leaned over and whispered to Alicia questions about her journey, to which Alicia made no answers. She then whispered that her name was Maruja and apologized for not having introduced herself sooner. Alicia remained silent, shifting her eyes back and forth from the attentive young man on the floor to the black and white images of belligerent cartoons from Kingston.

That afternoon Joshua and his mother led Alicia to her own bohío. After the yanqui cartoon program transmitted from Jamaica had finished, Joshua's mother had stood and opened all the shutters. Light and birdsong flooded the inside of the bohío. The entire house was one room, with two narrow twin beds at right angles in one corner near the television stand, a kitchen table with two chairs, and a small iron stove and an oversized freezer box. A doorway in the back led to what Alicia presumed was a bathroom. A single portrait of Fidel, while he was still a rebel in the mountains, framed in dark wood, unperturbedly adorned the bare walls.

Joshua stood and shut off the television. He was thin and tall, and broad-shouldered as a man, and his limbs were sinewy and long and his shorts hung low on his small hips. He had a strong face with a Roman nose. A scant fuzz barely darkened his jawline and his chin and the fold above his thick lips. His face and his torso were indeed as white as a yanqui virgin, but his legs below the hem of his shorts and his feet were sunned to a coffee-brown, and looked as if he had borrowed them from a member of another race. His mother told him again to put on some clothes and Joshua grabbed a dirty oversized cotton poncho that was crumbled on top of his bed and threw it on. It fell down to the hem of his shorts and covered his arms to the wrists. He smoothed his long black hair back behind his ears and tied it in a ponytail. He said he was ready.

Maruja put out her cigar and put on a pair of workboots. She was younger than the impression she had given in the darkened room. She wore only a light coat of lipstick as makeup, her eyes and her hair were as black as her son's, her movements as agile, her skin smooth and only a tinge darker, and everything about her, except for the chipped nails on her hands, was of a woman not of the country, a woman still vain enough to care for her looks, but youthful enough not to mournfully dote on them. She picked up Alicia's suitcase and a campesino hat and followed her son out of the bohío. She made her son wear the hat.

They kept up behind the quick-paced barefoot Joshua through a narrow dirt road, across a shallow ford, till they came to another meadow with another bohío on it almost identical to the home of Maruja and her son, except for the absence of the twisted steel antenna.

"This is where you will live," Maruja said.

Alicia asked them what was going to stop her from fleeing in the middle of the night. Joshua's mother answered that nothing or no one was going to stop her either from leaving or others from visiting.

"The thoughts of your consummate redemption will be your only guards."

Joshua laughed at this and said there were army soldiers who had made their homes in nests in the pine trees throughout the valley so long that they had sprouted black and gray feathers and that some of them could even fly with their rifles slung over their wings, and that they went mostly unseen because they traveled from pine to pine only after the moon had fallen, and that neither he nor his mother were allowed to leave or receive visitors without their permission.

"These giant black birds, though you cannot see them, will be your guards, señora, for they will always be watching you. They are all over. They even speak to each other like birds and sometimes the songs you hear are the real songs of the nightingales and sometimes they are not. Don't let my mother confuse you too much with her fancy talk."

Maruja scolded her son, this time more harshly than before, and told him to keep his wild children's fantasies to himself. "La señora Alicia va a pensar que estás loco."

Joshua paid no mind and continued: "We are all prisoners of the invisible birds." He pushed away from his mother and touched Alicia on the shoulder, he whispered that he would tell her other things later, that there was no need to upset his mother on this her first day in the valley. He opened the door of the bohío and swept his hand towards the inside in a dramatic gesture of welcome. They left Alicia alone and Maruja said that her son would bring her food and cooking ware later that evening, and that if she wanted to write to her family in Oriente, she would also be provided with ink and paper.

Her new home was furnished more sparsely than the other bohío. There was only one chair by the dining table and only one bed and no television set and no icebox and no portrait of Fidel. Alicia decided she would hang her icon of Santa Bárbara, which she had had her mother hide in the fold of her suitcase along with a wad of pesos. She sat on the bed and listened to the birdsong that might or might not be real. It was the first time she had been alone since the morning she had left the wrestler's house in Soledad. She lay down on the bed, which was improbably comfortable and remained still, in a half-slumber with her eyes open, till it had darkened and she heard a restless scratching at the base outside her door. She heard Joshua's voice calling her to open the door. Then she heard him screaming obscenities and the scratching at the base of the door ceased. She did not stand from the bed. She called back that the door was open. Joshua walked into the bohío with a makeshift torch in hand, a splintered broomstick with a piece of oiled cloth wrapped around one end. Small pieces of flame flew from the cloth like fallen stars and withered on the dirt floor. His breath was short. With fire from the torch, he lit a gaslamp that was hanging above the stove. He placed a cloth sack on top of the dining table and signaled for her to come to him. He waited till his breath settled before he spoke: "Ven, quiero que veas a mis amiguitos."

Alicia stood from the bed and walked to him. He pointed his torch towards the door. There, a few steps back from the doorway, sitting on their hind legs like obedient pets, were a pair of long-haired brown rats, so big and hirsute that they looked like exotic hounds. The tops of their skulls were shaved in a circle in the manner of monks. They squinted at the light pointed towards them, and lowered their heads and covered their snouts with their front paws, but did not move. Their bald heads shone like twin moons. Alicia stepped back, away from the door.

"Don't be afraid, señora. They're friends. Jeremiah and Ezekiel. Named after prophets. Mamá made me memorize all of the books of the Bible in order and so I have named all my friends, from Genesis on. This time I skipped one. I should have named these two Jeremiah and Lamentations, but I skipped one. It's a bad name for a rat, so I skipped one. Mamá was much more serious about the Bible back when I was child. She still leafs through it now, every so often . . . ay, pero I shouldn't have told you, her friends at el Comité don't know, so don't tell them when you meet them. I shouldn't have told you. . . . Jeremiah and Ezekiel—they are brave like prophets. They protect me from the invisible birds." He stepped outside and sunk the torch into the ground next to them and told the beasts to watch the fire and not to let it go out. When he came back into the bohío, he shut the door and told Alicia again not to be afraid.

He wore the same dirty poncho and ragged shorts and was shoeless. He opened the sack and put out a set of tarnished silverware and a tin of rice and beans, still steaming, and a tin of meat strips and green peppers and a jug of water. He said that his mother had cooked for her today, but not to expect her to do it every night. He said that she would not want to be eating his mother's cooking for too long anyway, for sometimes when she could not get enough real meat from outside the valley, she slaughtered his friends, the rats, and with their sinews and insides made a godawful stew, which she served at the meetings of el Comité, and her poor friends there, not wanting to offend their chief, forced it down gulp by gulp. "She has murdered twenty-one of my friends in the last three years, from Genesis on down. Only two were spared, the one named after me, Joshua Dos (because she thought it would bring her ill favors from the gods to slaughter a beast named as her son) and Song of Solomon, who clawed his way out from under her knife and fled, never to be seen again. Perhaps Song of Solomon roams these valleys still. Twenty-one of my friends she has murdered for the sake of her friends who hate her stew anyway and eat it only because they are afraid of her, but she is afraid of *you*. Vaya, not because she believed you murdered anyone, but because she thinks my father sent you here to embarrass her."

"Your father? Who is your father?"

"My father is the one who owns this valley, this whole island; that is why ours is the only bohío with electricity, the only one with a television. I thought they might have told you about my father when they brought you here; they tell others, pero se hacen los bobos. I'll tell you the whole story one day, my father does not want to embarrass *me*. I am almost eighteen; soon he will need me to run his lands. That's what he says in the letters mamá hides in the thatching of our bohío. Soon the invisible black birds will work for me."

"I was told nothing of your father, or for that matter of your mother or of you."

"Bueno, it doesn't matter anyway. Come and eat, you must be hungry."

Alicia had moved back to her bed. "I want to be alone."

"Señora, no one is alone on this island, especially in this valley, *that* my mother and all her friends will surely teach you, that this wish to be left alone is the first vice of the counterrevolutionary criminal, that this wish, even without being acted on, is already a sin against the community of la Revolución."

"You speak very eloquently for a boy."

Joshua knitted his brow. He passed his hand through his hair and tightened his ponytail. With the same hand, he puffed up the meager patches of his beard. "I am almost eighteen, y además, I can't help but talk the way I do sometimes. Mamá and her friends never shut up!"

"Then you do not really believe what you say, you're just parroting your mother."

"No, I do believe, most of the times. I believe in mamá and her friends (most of them anyway). You will like them, I think; vaya, a veces me jo-den mucho, but they mean only good. And mamá believes in me, she trusts me, and so will my father soon. Pero mira, come and eat, your food is getting cold. I'll leave you alone as you wish, I'm just telling you what mamá thinks about such wishes from newcomers. . . . Do you know when I like to be alone? When I run. Some days I do it right before the sun comes up, some days right before it falls, some days both, depending on when mamá needs me. The black birds are too busy then, settling into their nests for the day or preparing for their night travels, to care about a solitary runner." He moved towards the door. "So I know what it feels like to want to be alone. I'll go now. But eat before your food gets cold. It's real meat. She can't murder my friends for now. I stole her blade and she hasn't been able to find a new one. Eat. You'll need strength for when you meet my mother's friends tomorrow." He stepped outside and shut the door slowly. Through a crack in the wooden window shutter, Alicia watched his torchlight bounce softly away.

She felt tired and she lay on the bed again and slept. She dreamt of a young man dressed like Joshua in ragged shorts and a dirty poncho, and his face was that of Joshua and of many other young men, and at times Alicia thought she was near her husband as he had been when he was fighting in the mountains, and at times she thought she spoke to her cousin through the chain-link fence of a labor camp, and at times she was in the presence of unbathed young men with shaved heads that she had never known, who spoke with the sureness of the blessed and moved with the abandon of the possessed. When she awoke the oil in the lamp had been all but fully consumed and the flame gave out only a meager halo of light. It made Alicia think of saints not yet canonized. Almost without giving notice to the hollow ache in her belly, she stood from the bed, sat at the table, and ate the cold food as a hungry animal might have, with-out pause to drink from the water jug or ponder on the flavors. When she was finished she pushed the empty tins away from her. She went to the bed and tried to sleep again but she could not. She remembered that after her first night on the island they had taken her watch and never returned it, but in the darkness she made the motion of looking at her wrist anyway, a gesture that pleased her for it made evident that though they could take from her her husband and her cousin and her mother and her daughter and all her earthly loves and all her earthly possessions, they could not steal from her her habits and her thoughts and therefore could not steal from her her last and truest life. She let her hand rest on the bed, for all her complacency still ignorant of how long she must wait till morning.

More than an hour must have passed, though it was difficult to tell. The darkness inside the bohío had only changed because now the flame in the lamp had completely died. She felt thirsty. She began to taste the sourness of the cold food she had eaten. And now she did what she had not done during her meal, she paused to ponder on its texture and on its flavors. The rice was old and salty and many of the grains hard like sun-dried larva. The beans were lumpy and mushy and tasteless except for a certain cheesy sharpness. The meat was stringy, its natural sweetness hidden too well by gobs of gelatinized grease, and the peppers soppy and overripe.

Alicia tried to remain in bed, but she felt her heart crawl down to her belly and beat down there, demanding she do something. She went to the table and fumbled for the jug of water. She drank from it twice, but could not wash away the surging memory of her meal. She drank again but the water seemed to slosh inside her and she became as if seasick and fell, losing consciousness for what seemed no more than a few minutes. When she was able to stand again, she stumbled to the back door of the bohío. Her right arm had broken the fall and her wrist was numb. She passed through a narrow wooden unroofed passageway to the outhouse. She knelt over the makeshift tin toilet and vomited till the muscles in her belly could squeeze out only inclement gasps of air. She moved away from the toilet and crouched in the opposite corner of the outhouse, her back to a tin tub no bigger than a newborn's basin, and stayed there till she saw the sky gray and then brighten through the holes in the threadbare thatch roof. She did not move when she heard someone knock on the front door and did not move when she heard Joshua call out for her. He seemed more embarrassed for himself than for her when he found her, still crouched where she was. He apologized and said he was afraid something might have happened to her, said that he would bring her fresh water from a nearby brook so she could wash up. Alicia nodded. He returned some moments later with a pair of washcloths and two buckets of water and a crude piece of soap. With one bucket and cloth he cleaned the remnants of vomit from the toilet. Alicia made no protest. As he scrubbed, he laughed and told her that he too had little tolerance for his mother's food. He set the other bucket and cloth and the soap by her. He told her she should clean up a little bit for she was going to be meeting his mother's friends later on that morning. Alicia thanked him and asked him to bring her toiletry bag from her suitcase. She did not mention the soreness of her wrist. He brought her back the whole suitcase instead and set it by her.

"I dreamt of your friends," Alicia said before he stepped out again. "They were young and guapo like you. I hope your mother never gets to them."

Joshua lowered his eyes. "She will," he said. "But I'll find others to tame and shave. There are many books in the Bible. One day I'll show you how I trap them and tame them." He left Alicia alone again.

He was waiting for her inside the bohío seated at the table. He stood and poured some coffee from a thermos into a small ceramic cup. He complimented her on her choice of clothing, a plain off-white summer dress. She had tied her hair back in a ponytail like his. He said she looked like a new woman. He handed her the coffee. "This will make you feel better. Besides you're going to need plenty of it to stay awake during the meeting. They tend to run awfully long, especially when they first meet a new resident. Sometimes I have to force my mother to throw everybody out because it's already time to watch my muñequitos. It's even worse on Sundays. But you'll see."

After Alicia drank her coffee, he took the chair that she had been sitting on and threw it over his shoulder. "Everyone brings their own," he explained. "There's not enough room in mamá's house to keep all those chairs. Don't let mamá know I carried it for you."

"Why? She would not like that her son is a gentleman? ¿Cómo que no?"

"You don't know mamá yet. Vamos. I'll hand it to you just as we approach. Vamos. There's breakfast there if you're hungry. . . . Don't worry, mamá doesn't cook too often for el Comité. They beg her not to trouble herself. One of the other ladies usually makes breakfast for the meetings. Her cooking will sit much better in your stomach. Vamos. They are eagerly awaiting the new resident of the valley. No one was late this morning."

An Odd Request

Near the end of the long meeting around Maruja's kitchen table, the eight other members and Maruja seated in their own chairs, Joshua seated crossed-legged on the floor beside his mother, Maruja informed Alicia that it was a tradition that a new resident could make any request at all and if it was in any way under the power of el Comité to fulfill it, no matter how outlandish (as long as it fell under the code of rehabilitation), it would.

Alicia asked that her daughter be brought to live with her.

"Impossible, mi vida," Maruja said immediately. "It is you who were convicted of crimes against la Revolución, why place that burden on your daughter as well. Besides, no seas loca, such a request is not within our powers to fulfill."

Alicia was silent.

"Something else, chica. Vaya, something more simple."

"My husband's bathtub."

"¿Cómo? A bathtub?"

"My husband's bathtub."

The other members of el Comité, seven in all, six elderly women and a youthful-looking middle-aged man, began to confer in whispers, leaning their heads one to the other. Maruja looked hard at Alicia, as she reminded her comembers that it was not only impolite to conduct any of the business of the meeting in whispers, but that it was strictly against conduct regulations, that they must shed, once and for all, this habit of their former lives.

"Pues, what do we think of this request from our new resident?"

"Where is your daughter?" Joshua said. "How old is she?"

"Niño, por favor," his mother tapped him on the head. "We've moved on from that subject. Is la jefa's son going to ignore regulations as well? The bathtub. The husband's bathtub. What do we think? Is it within our powers? Is it proper?"

"Esto, I did not find it proper to say this when I introduced myself to you, señora, but I knew your husband." The middle-aged man spoke. He was seated next to Maruja. His name was Marcos and he was fair-skinned, though his arms and face were burned by the valley sun. He had light-brown hair with streaks of gray on the sides and in some curls that fell on his brow. His looks were enhanced by a long thin scar that ran along the right side of his jawline and by his womanly lips and his thick eyebrows a few tinges darker than his hair. His voice was low and soft and somewhat ungrounded to his appearance. "I fought in the mountains, and although I did not serve under your husband's command, I knew him, knew him well. We became disillusioned with the progress of la Revolución at about the same time, about the summer of '62, just before his trip to Berlin; by then I was serving in the Ministry of the Interior in La Habana and had lost touch with him. Vaya, as you must know, your husband was not a politician, claramente, or he would not have turned down all the offers for high-ranking offices in the capital. He was not much of a diplomat either, though he attempted that briefly after the War. I imagine that he did not return to his finca near Bayamo partly because he fell in love with you, but I imagine that mostly he did not return because he saw it as an absurd thing for one of the heroes of the War against the landowners to remain a landowner himself. His lands he donated to the State a long time before the Agrarian Reform Acts. He became simply a retired warrior, living on a pension. And no being grows disillusioned more quickly than a warrior without a war. That's why most of them turn to politics. Y esto, without meaning to offend anyone, or breach any regulations, I think that's why Fidel has remained a politician for so long, why he has been unwilling . . . bueno, let's say, why the people have not let him, relinquish power."

"Marcos is one of our more recently titled neighborhood chiefs, Alicia," Maruja said, her voice easily overcoming his. "He has been in the valley for less than a year. Imagínate, and already a chief. He has made quite a comeback since his days at el Boniato prison, has caused quite a stir among our valley folk, oye, y no te vayas a pensar, not only because of his looks. His people chose him because they know he will represent them well, is not afraid to speak his mind, to stand up for them when he has to." She tapped Marcos playfully on the thigh. "The future of our country depends more on men like him than on any other, on our thousands and thousands of prodigal sons . . . and daughters, claro."

Marcos nodded his head in silent concurrence, but he did not look at Alicia.

"Pero chico, so much wonderful talk, and you did not address the issue at hand. Qué es esto, is no one going to follow protocol? What will our new resident think of us? The tub. The tub, carajo. Can we get it? Should we fulfill this odd request? But first, tell us more Alicia, tell us what this bathtub is like, tell us why you want such a simple thing."

"It is heavy and long and deep and its legs are the carved talons of a falcon; it belonged to my husband, and I have bathed in it since the night of our marriage, and after my husband was murdered, it was my only solace. When I was submerged in it, I saw him and I spoke to him."

"His ghost?" One of the elderly women spoke and leaned forward on her chair. She looked at Alicia with her wide milky eyes. They were so advanced with cataract that it looked as if the pupils were hidden within a glob of lard. Unlike the other old women, her gray hair was not tied back in a bun and fell loose over her shoulders; all this and her loose-fitting white frock gave her the appearance of a halfwit in an asylum. "Did he speak back to you?"

"Don't be silly, Josefa. You are too in love with witchery. It will be the fall of you."

Josefa leaned back on her chair. She muttered that one does not fall from the same cliff twice.

"His ghost," Alicia said. "Yes, his ghost, if you like. Although he did not speak back, he had not the will nor the strength."

"We have not yet had any ghosts, mute or not, visit anyone in the valley," Maruja said. "Yours would be the first."

Josefa grunted and Marcos, across the paper-littered table from her, smiled.

"But, if it is that important to you, and if we can ascertain that it does not violate any regulations, and ghost or not, your husband remains to this day unpardoned for his sins against la Revolución. We are sorry that you lost him, but we are more sorry that he saw it fit to turn his back on his honor . . . so that his death was more a suicide than a murder." Alicia began to protest in a loud voice and Maruja raised her hands in front of her, palms out, as if to shield herself from Alicia's barrage of words, and she spoke over her, begging her not to take offense, proclaiming that neither Alicia nor her husband had any enemies at that table, that she was merely presenting the facts of a personal history as had been presented to her, that on the contrary, as was evident from Marcos's tale, her husband still had more than a few admirers in the folds of la Revolución, ". . . but we should not dwell on that, for the poor wandering soul of your husband has nothing to do with this. It is *your* bathtub now, and you need it for your peace of mind; for we all well know that ghosts are nothing but the emanations of troubles in our own mind."

Josefa grunted again, though Maruja ignored her and continued speaking to Alicia: "And it is, after all, nothing less than your peace of mind that all of us here at el Comité are interested in. Thank you for coming today and introducing yourself to us. I am sure, that though you may feel a bit awkward amongst us now, as the days pass and as your routine becomes more regimented by your duties, you will feel as welcome here in our valley as if it had been your home for years. And, indeed, with that purpose in mind, we will do all we can to find your bathtub with the legs like the talons of a falcon and bring it to you. Now, if you'll excuse us, we have other business to attend to."

"I have one other small request," Alicia said as she stood, "(aside from the bathtub), that my husband and his heroic deeds never be conjured up again in my presence."

"You are quite right," Maruja said in a conciliatory tone, sifting through some of the papers on the table, not looking at Alicia. "Perhaps it would be best if none of us mention your husband again. I too know how it hurts to lose the father of one's child."

She tapped her son on the shoulder and Joshua stood and helped Alicia with her chair and led her out of his mother's bohío. Marcos and Josefa and two of the other neighborhood chiefs mumbled their farewells. The others were silent.

A Repeated Tale

"Who was your father?" Alicia asked Joshua at the door of her bohío. "If he was a rebel, he must have known my husband, or at least known of him."

"My mother said to me, last night after I brought you your food, not to speak to you of my father again."

"You told her we talked."

"She gets things out of me; she knows how, she's been getting things out of people for so many years. Una experta. Some even say she got me out of my father against his will. Don't laugh. She got the story of the bathtub out of you."

"Do you think she has any intention of honoring my request?"

"I never know her intentions, and it is dangerous to guess at them." Joshua put the chair down. "I have to go back to watch my muñequitos and then see to my friends. But don't worry, the story of my mother and my father is the favorite one of the people in the valley, it is so often told that even the nightingales know it by memory, and if you listen closely to their song you'll hear them telling it. Y claro, the invisible night birds know it as well as anybody else, but you won't hear it in their song—they are too well trained, they know better."

"Who was your father?" Alicia repeated, but Joshua turned and disappeared into the brush. The blackened sole of his right foot was the last Alicia saw of him for over eight weeks.

She entered her bohío. She pushed open the wooden window shutters whose hinges were so rust-eaten that they creaked and trembled like palsied limbs. The noon light streamed into the bohío like water down a cataract. She sat at the dining table and poured herself some coffee from the thermos Joshua had left behind. She watched the clouds of dust celebrate the light and decided to put the buckets and rag Joshua had brought her to good use. She followed the song of a finch to the stream, which was no more than thirty paces behind her bohío, and drank from it with her cupped hands and knelt in it, soaking the lower half of her dress, and relished in the coolness and the sweetness the stream borrowed from the earth. She sunk her right hand deep into the water till the soreness washed away. She loaded up the buckets with fresh water, making two trips for she could not carry both. She thought of the first inhabitants of this island that is the eye of the other crocodile-Island and conjectured that they probably lived not much different than how she was living now, in the first days of her enforced exile, following the song of birds and setting their simple houses near running water. As she scrubbed the floors and the walls and in the crevices of the two windowsills and the doorway using her left hand, she tried to follow the tribunal's logic in sentencing her to this valley penal colony, this return to the beginning, to an innocence both she and her husband before her had long abandoned. But how can one remain innocent while trapped inside the guts of a rotting crocodile? And how can one pretend to so easily wash off the bile that has crusted into every available nook of the body, trapped under any fold of skin and buried into every cuticle? Only a serpent can so easily slough off its weathered self, only a serpent is so well found for the journey backward into innocence.

The finch whose song she had followed perched on the windowsill and interrupted her thoughts. It chirped insistently and flapped its wings as if demanding recompense for its assistance. Alicia gathered some of the grains of rice leftover from the previous night's meal and cupped them in her palm and tossed them out the window. Other birds, robins and thrushes, came to join the grateful finch and soon muscled it out of its prize. Alicia said out loud to her defeated bird not to be disheartened for the rice was old and over-salted and that she would pay it its due with much better rice in days to come. The finch flew away, ostensibly unconvinced with this promise. It too, apparently had lived through many of the unkept promises of la Revolución and its Líder. As she watched the other birds fighting for the last of Maruja's poison rice, she saw her husband's comrade appear from out of the same brush Joshua had disappeared into. He was wearing the rough-canvas pants and faded blue guayabera that he had worn at the meeting, but now he also donned a wide-brimmed campesino straw hat, which he laced down under his chin with a piece of thin rope. He carried with him a paper bag. He waved when he noticed Alicia had seen him and continued approaching.

"Maruja sent me with some more of your necessaries," he said, coming to the window where Alicia was and not the door. "Fruit and vegetables and stuff . . . no meat: Joshua told us that it did not agree with you." He smiled now and Alicia felt a blush and moved away from the window to open the door for him. "Believe me, her food doesn't agree with any of us."

"Does Joshua tell his mother *everything*."

"Joshua is a boy, señora, a boy with body of a man. . . ."

"Please, call me Alicia."

He set the bag down on the table and began to remove its contents, yuccas and boniatos and plantains and cloth coffee filters and a jar of ground coffee beans, ". . . A boy who dreams he is the son of an emperor."

Alicia sat on the bed, which she had fitted with the one set of sheets she had brought, discarding the old ones and bundling them aside. "Who was his father?"

"No one knows. All we know here in the valley are the stories his mother invents and has others at her beck and call repeat and repeat."

"What is the story?"

"Ay señora . . . digo, Alicia, I, for one, I'm not in the habit of repeating her lies."

Alicia was silent for a moment and then she said that she was only interested in the lies of the mother in how they affected her son, and that to him these stories certainly weren't lies.

Marcos threw his hat back so that it hung by the thin rope around his neck, neatly wedged under the Adam's apple, like a garrote. He shook his head and chuckled, as if in pity of an ignorant. "Do not grow too fond of Joshua, querida Alicia. That is exactly what his mother wants. He is her best source of information."

"What is the story?"

"It is a simple one really: Maruja tells Joshua, and tells others so that they may tell others more, that her one and only son is the rightful heir to the throne in La Habana, that one afternoon back in the days while she was still a staggering girl of the country, el Líder, while in the outskirts of La Habana, after having been defeated in his first election, seduced her and raped her and her son is the fruit of that night"—Marcos could not hold back a hacking spastic laugh, dislodged from his innards like a tickling hairball—"pero perdóname, I do not have much of a knack for storytelling. Others do the lie much better service, adding their own fantasies, and sometimes our deified emperor takes the shape of a massive bull, sometimes a strutting rooster, sometimes a horny he-goat, sometimes even a delicate swan, although, I, for one, have never seen a swan on the Island, except at the zoo, which is where I think Fidel belongs, with the monkeys not the lions."

Alicia did not join in with Marcos's second fit of laughter, now set to chords of loosened phlegm. He passed his tongue over his upper lip and the back of his hand over his mouth. He swallowed and collected himself before he spoke again. "It's all right, no need to fear my talk. Maruja and her cronies are too inefficient to be feared. Her reputation as the finest doctrine rehabilitator on the Island is a sham . . . bah, Joshua, the heir to the throne."

Alicia thought that his mocking counterrevolutionary talk masked much more fear than he was aware of and that Maruja seemed much more competent than he thought, but she did not give voice to her thoughts, instead she steered the conversation in a more absurd direction: "But just as a matter of logistics, Fidelito is older, and a legitimate son. Would he not indeed be the heir if there were any heir at all?"

"Bueno sí, but in this version of history Fidelito does not exist, he is a traitor by the simple fact that his bitch-mother and all her family were traitors. . . . He has *unfit* blood, is the way the text of the story goes."

"And does everyone here believe all of this?"

"The boy believes it. The rest of us pretend to believe it and give the story its due reverence by repeating it as often as we can."

"I thought you said that you, for one, did not repeat her lies."

"I did say that. And then I went ahead and told you the story. I have lived in the world of la Revolución too long. I have become a master in compromising what I say with what I do."

"And you have come here to suggest I do the same."

"I came here to bring you some fresh vegetables and home-grown coffee from our side of the valley. Our land is the most productive in the valley, y claro, we share the wealth as we ought. As I said, Joshua told us of how you were ill last night." Marcos finished removing the contents from the bag and sat on the chair and rubbed his lower lip with his index finger. "You will act as you see fit to act; you are famous for that, no? My campesinos here tell stories of how you bewitched a poor old farmer and drowned him, vengeance for having turned against you. They say you and your people are strong and true to each other, and like locusts, who, though without a king, all swarm as one."

"I am a mother and a daughter and a sister, and was once a wife and am now a widow, nothing more." Alicia rubbed her wrist again. "I fell last night. It's bruising."

Marcos stood and came and knelt by her and took her hand to examine her wrist. He said he only meant to relay what others were saying, that surely there was no foundation for any of it, that the campesinos were only to be heard for the spirit of their speech and not for its content. He said that perhaps they were hungry for a new savior, some Joan of Arc this time instead of a fabled Christ-like figure descending from the mountainous wilderness.

"The campesinos are much better off now than they have ever been," Alicia said. "If anyone has benefited from la Revolución, it is they. They need no Juana de Arc, especially one so old and devoid of innocence as la que está sentada aquí."

Marcos looked up, not trying to hide his surprise.

"What? Reformed already, and have been here only a day and a half?"

"I have never said otherwise, and neither did my husband, and neither do *my people*. At heart, I am more a socialist and a patriot than all the overfed murderous swine who roam the Palace of the Revolution. Our quarrel has been and always will be against the Fidelistas' consolidation of power, through the military and through its thousand and one ministries and councils and directorate, in the capital, in the provinces, in the cities, down to each individual maldito CDR (even here in this valley prison) and to each poor child who is forced to wear his red hanky around his neck, and chant their propaganda like nursery rhymes."

"Sí, sí, tienes razón, in all but in calling this valley a prison, when it is instead an exile. Fidel is a great admirer of the Roman emperors, and he learned from them that those that pose the greatest threat to you, you do not send into prisons, plots are too easily hatched in the incubation of cells (how did he hatch his own plot but in a prison not so far away from here?), instead you send them into exile where they lose touch, where they grow soft and lose their will to struggle."

"Peor, this valley exile, then we are no better than the cowards who fled to Miami, with their diamonds and gold nuggets as suppositories."

"Exacto, that is the aim," Marcos said and pressed his grip on Alicia's wrist, so that she instinctively yanked it away.

"Cuidado," she said and handed him back her wrist. He examined it some more and touched lightly with his index finger as if he were examining the texture of precious coral. He decided it should be bandaged.

"Bandaged with what?"

Marcos went to the old discarded bedsheets lumped in one corner and cut into them with his teeth and ripped off a long strip. He bandaged her wrist tightly, so that she could feel the circulation falter, and tied the ends in a knot.

"I do not see how we are to grow soft lacking so many necessities."

"I'll go get some ice from Maruja and come back." He laughed again. "See, this *lack of necessities* is just one of the many ways with which she keeps control over the people in the valley. She is the only one with ice! The Icewoman!—vaya, she deserves that title as much in a metaphorical sense as in a literal one. We are living as if this were still the nineteenth century. It is part of our penance. Pero no te equivoques, do not think all of us are as loyal to her as we pretend; for she is afraid of even her closest allies in the valley. Josefa for her witchery (as Maruja calls the santeros); and María, esa vieja that was so quiet and still at the meeting, nodding at everything Maruja said, you should see how she talks behind her back. Mira coño, *she,* ella misma, is not as loyal to herself as she pretends, even afraid of her own self. No, Alicia, we are not that much different from you. All of us here in the valley, except for the native guajiros, but even Maruja, at one point or another fought against the injustices of la Revolución, and are now trying to work our way back into it, wiser, but no less dissatisfied. And do not think that half the country is not quietly like us, less insolent and more inveigling, but no less dissatisfied."

"What was Maruja's crime?"

"You need ice for your hand." Marcos made a gesture, as if to go search for the ice.

"My hand is fine coño, it's too late for the ice anyway."

Marcos made a puckering gesture with his lips, as if he had just tasted an unripe fruit, and sat on the floor next to the bed. "Esto, as far as I can tell, and perhaps the reason she is still here with us, her greatest crime is one that she is still gloriously unrepentant for—her fantasy that her son is the heir to the throne in La Habana. Vaya, this story is repeated as often as other stories about her, so I will try to tell it sifting, as best as I can, the fine facts from the coarse fiction. Pero bueno, al fin y al cabo —who knows truths from lies?

"Because of her knowledge of biblical texts, she was given a good position in the National Library after the triumph of la Revolución, although who knows why, since too much reliance on religious faith, in those first austere days when a new creed was being written in stone, made you *ipso facto* a counterrevolutionary. But I think one of the assistant directors (a staunch gruff woman with muscled arms) took a liking to her and to her extensive knowledge of the Bible and hired her. Not much later, when one of the many ideological purges of the National Library brought down both Maruja and this assistant director, it was alleged that they had been caught in one of the stalls of the ladies' bathroom of the Library, half-naked and in the heat of a perverse affair of love. No lo creo; for there was a more substantial reason why Maruja and many of her colleagues and supporters were fired and arrested. She lived with her son in a small apartment in La Habana Vieja, on Cardenas Street. To the many who saw her daily at her desk in the Library and paseando, hand in hand with her young son, whom she dressed impeccably in linen boy-suits and knee-high socks and leather moccasins, on the cobble-stoned cathedral plaza, she led a quiet untroubled life. There was no sign of the passion that was consuming her.

"Every afternoon at her lunch hour, Maruja donned a pair of dark round sunglasses and a colorful yellow silk scarf over her head and disappeared for an hour; none of her colleagues knew where and none grew suspicious that she never accepted their invitation to eat lunch at the ice-cream parlor down the street from the Library. She was a woman after all with a young son who was rumored to be mildly retarded. Only her supervisor at the Library knew the details of her son's true condition, the trances he would lapse into in the middle of some invented war with columns of tin soldiers, or during a reading lesson late at night, when his face would go blank, all the familiar gestures whited out, his only movement a smacking of the lips, the illness the doctors at the clinic diagnosed simply as the petit mal, which had to be closely monitored lest it devolve, *que Dios lo proteja,* into the grand mal, or full-blown epilepsy. Maruja, though, did not go as suspected to check on her son, to monitor him. Joshua was alone in the apartment on Cardenas Street during her lunch hour, his feet dangling over the second floor iron-grill balcony, the seat of his linen suit stained with rust, sometimes falling into his trances for hours on end, so that his mother had to shake him out of it when she arrived at dusk, before she diligently proceeded with his nightly school lessons.

"As her supervisor told her to take as much time as needed with her son, Maruja exited the Library and walked two blocks east and then two blocks north, so that no one would see her mount the bus headed for the Vedado district, to a small park across "L" street from the Hotel Habana Libre, where she would sit on a bench under an almond tree and eat an egg-salad sandwich, and wait for the two Russian jeeps that daily approached the front entrance of the hotel around one-thirty. When the jeeps arrived and the four olive-drabbed men with their tilted berets all entered the hotel, Maruja wiped her mouth and walked across the street to the entrance of the hotel and greeted the doorman, an older mulatto man with an inch-thick sheet of snow-white hair, and asked him how el Líder was that day. *Bien, bien como siempre,* the doorman always answered and smiled *¿Y usted, cómo está? Yo bien, bien como siempre,* Maruja always answered as well, and smiled as well too, but said no more and took the bus back to the Library."

"She was stalking Fidel," Alicia said, "and this stupid doorman could not tell?"

"Don't forget this was eight years ago, and Maruja still held on to that sort of girlish beauty that vanishes so quickly. The lovelorn doorman thought Maruja was interested in him, and the daily arrival of Fidel and his cronies just an excuse to approach him."

"¿Y qué hacía Fidel?—going every afternoon to the hotel. Una puta, me imagino."

"No chica, Fidel doesn't flaunt that sort of thing. His erotic affairs he pursues alone, like a wolf. (Ahí está, a wolf! If Fidel were going to metamorphose into anything when he raped a country girl, it would be no bull or cock or goat, but a wolf!—a fat wolf!) But it was no prostitute he was visiting. La cosa es mucho más simple. Why do you think Fidel is the only one who came down from the Sierra with a full belly, trailed by an army of live skeletons? Why didn't any of the thousand foreign journalists covering the victorious ride to La Habana ask themselves *that* question? I'll give you the simple answer: he is addicted to milkshakes, loves them more than he loves his three daily shots of whiskey, more than he loves his cigar."

Marcos went on. He told Alicia how in the mountains many of Fidel's bravest guerrilleros were sent on missions in search of bohíos with ice boxes (since most dwellings in the mountains were without electricity) who would gladly donate a hunk of their precious ice, and let them get whatever drops of milk they could out of their shriveled-titted goats, when they were told it was for Fidel's daily milkshake. Back in the rebel camp, the guerrilleros wrapped the chunk of ice in a pañuelo and crushed it with their boots and stirred the watery milk into it and arm-wrestled for the honor to bring it to Fidel's bungalow. So it was that Fidel made his daily visit to the Hotel Habana Libre, not to bed any whore, as many on the outside might have improperly guessed, but to sit on the round mahogany bar and drink his daily milkshake, prepared expertly, just as he liked it, by Luisito Cuzco, the small indian bartender, with the ice crushed into small pieces as it had been done in the mountains, with no blender, but with the heel of his workboot.

All this Maruja learned from the snow-capped mulatto doorman as she daily engaged him, bit by bit, in more flirtatious conversation, on one day taking off her dark glasses so that he may gaze into her eyes, on another lowering her yellow scarf so that he may wonder at her thick black hair, and finally coaxing him into showing her the lobby of the hotel and the sealed entrance to the bar where Fidel was enjoying his merienda with three of his chosen comandantes and no bodyguard and a few other clientele of the hotel, usually Europeans, who were carefully selected by the secret police and given clearance, to make it seem as if Fidel was casually dropping by to visit them. For even though it is often noted by the mythmakers that Fidel has never used a bodyguard, he has, and security was much tighter around him in those days than it is now; vaya, con razón, *la CIA* had already begun its strange and lame campaign to have him assassinated. But Maruja, of course, did not know this, and she made up her

mind that she would one afternoon sit next to him and have her son legitimized, right then and there, at the round mahogany bar of the Hotel Habana Libre. She grabbed the mulatto doorman's long bony hand and
caressed it and hinted to him how much she would be honored to meet el
Líder, to for one moment of her lonely life grace in the presence of a mangod, how she might be willing to pledge her life to such a man who was
brave enough to lead her to him.

"Ay, no señorita," the doorman answered, his pupils dilated, his body
rigid as a youth, already falling under the spell of her caresses, "I would if
I could, but I have strict orders that he cannot be bothered, that the brief
half hour that he is in there is his only time of peace in his long day.
Porque coño, they say that even in his sleep he is consumed by his passion
for the destiny of our people, and has horrible nightmares of the pale monsters invading from the north. For he is sure that it is at night that the
next yanqui invasion will take place, one in which they will use a hundred
times the men of Playa Girón. El pobre, even in his bed he cannot rest; so
he stays up all night, and often visits, unannounced, the fancy homes of
the heads of the Central Committee, or of his most trusted comandantes,
and keeps everyone awake, wife and children and grandmother and all,
talking away the nightlong, one ear to the conversation at hand, the other
to the much-augured buzz of yanqui warplanes. . . . Ay señorita, believe
me, for you I would do almost anything, but this, this is beyond my powers. If you want to grace in the presence of a mangod, you might have to
wait for el Señor Jesucristo when He comes again."

"Bien," Maruja said, moving away from him, putting on her dark
glasses again and refastening her yellow scarf over her head, "pensaba que
eras más hombre que todo eso." From behind her sunglasses she noticed,
as soon as she moved away from him, how all his years rushed back into
him, like pigeons flocking all at once for a meager spread of crumbs, and
his chest caved in and his spine bent with their burden, and she knew he
would find a way to help her.

Two weeks passed and Maruja sat under the almond tree and ate her
egg sandwich and did not approach the entrance of the hotel, though the
doorman waved with both hands at her and signaled excitedly for her to
come to him. Maruja held her place and after the two jeeps arrived and the
four men dismounted and entered the hotel, she walked to the bus stop
and waited for her ride back to the Library. On the second morning of the
third week of her estrangement from him, the doorman, as soon as he saw
her arrive, abandoned his post and walked across "L" Street to the bench
where she sat. "You can see him mañana," he said. "I have spoken to him,
I have arranged it. You can go into the bar and see him while he is having
his milkshake. You can even have a milkshake yourself, he said . . . if you
like."

Maruja, who had never seen the doorman do anything in the presence

of the four olive-drabbed men but nod his head in a pathetic fit of servitude and hold the door open for them, was skeptical. "We'll see if you are
a man of your word, mi querido viejito." She stood and did not wait for the
jeeps to arrive that afternoon and took the next bus back to the Library.

She arrived the next afternoon at the park across "L" Street wearing the
same silk yellow scarf over her head and the same impenetrable sunglasses,
but wearing instead of the flag-blue skirt and blouse that was the uniform
of the Library personnel a tight-fitting summer dress printed with sunflowers with straps over her shoulders and the hem a few inches above her
knees, and a pair of black leather moccasins. She carried no purse. She had
taken the day off from the Library, telling her supervisor that her son was
too ill to be left alone.

As the two jeeps arrived and the four men dismounted, all at once
turned their heads and looked towards the park, and then, as if they had
seen nothing, cast their looks away from her and entered the hotel as
usual. The doorman waited fifteen minutes, glancing at his watch continuously, and finally waved for Maruja to come to him. As she stood and
reached the curb on the opposite side of "L" Street, she felt, in the watery
weakness at her bare knees, the first misgivings about the entire enter-
prise. What if he had her arrested on the spot? What would happen to
Joshua? Doubly a bastard and now orphaned for her impertinence. She
struggled against these thoughts and pictured her son in a hand-colored
photograph, his eyes closed, his cheeks rosy, his arms spread open, his
light birdlike body lifted aloft by his smiling father, the palm-haired
crown of a green mountain and the blue-on-blue sky as background, as in
the so many other photographs she had seen of his father with so many
other strange children. This image strengthened her as she continued
across "L" Street, not looking one way or the other for oncoming cars,
abandoning her baser sense.

"Cuidado, muchacha, por el amor de Dios," the doorman said as she
approached him. "Do you want to get killed on such a glorious day as
this? Vamos, vamos, I have timed it perfectly. He is a busy man. Es hora o
nunca." He held her by the arm and led her to the sealed entrance of the
bar. The door opened and one of the bearded comandantes came out and
said he had to search her and he was about to put his hands on her when
the door opened again and there he was standing in front of her, the man
she had last seen in person as a bull, or a cock, or a goat, o lo que sea. He
wore horn-rimmed glasses and his manner, though somewhat agitated,
was so refined that it seemed improbable he could transform himself into
any beast.

"No te atrevas, comandante." He wagged his long index finger. "Don't
you dare put your hands on my visitor." He turned then to Maruja.
"Perdóname, señorita, but my men are more paranoid for my life than I
myself am. ¿Pero justamente, no? I have been at the head of our govern-

ment less than five years and I am already on the verge of setting an Olympic record for survived assassination attempts. The pharisees in Washington, those bunglers who long ago abandoned the ideals of their Founding Fathers, want me hanging from a cross, but they are not good enough carpenters to build one that will hold my weight." He caressed his paunch and smiled. "But still, if it were solely up to me I would sit with my bare feet dangling off the malecón wall every evening at sunset, shirtless, letting the mist of the crashing waves baptize me as it nightly baptizes our land. ¡Pero no me dejan los muy cabrones!—protecting me as if I were a child. Is a man to be forbidden such simple pleasures for fear of death?"

Maruja stood silent and still before him. She did not remove her scarf or her sunglasses, so there was no way he could yet tell who his visitor was.

"Pero está muda mi bella visitante. You say nothing, but of course you say nothing. What can you say to such absurd ravings? Of course, a man is not to be forbidden such simple pleasures, else he is no longer a man. Who are we to guess at the calamities that will befall us, and befall us they will, so it is vanity to try to circumvent them—hence my creed for the good and honorable life is derived from the only worthwhile book in the whole damn Bible, to seek pleasure in toil (as well as seek pleasure in pleasure). All my speeches, my endless endeavors to please our people with pleasing words, ever have been, and ever will be, anchored by that theme. Coño, perhaps I *will* go to the malecón this very night! If I can have such a one as you accompany me. I will be safe, for the wicked are frightened of such tremendous beauty."

Maruja removed her sunglasses and lowered her scarf, but it had not the intended effect on the speaker. Instead of retreating from her in fearful recognition, he moved closer to her with his sorrowful hazel eyes and his lips parted in both fascination and a mounting curiosity. She returned his look and countered his snappy amiability with a witless enmity. He then performed a gesture she had often seen him perform during his speeches, in the long pauses, when he cast his eyes heavenward and shaped his lips in a puckish pout and brought his arched hands together so that they touched only fingertip to fingertip, forming like the skeleton of a dome, and ruffled through the text in his head (for rarely was it scripted on paper), skipping over paragraphs that for the moment had no relevance. He did this now, making it clear to her that all his previous (seemingly unstudied) rambling had also been (like all his speeches) a very carefully wrought text of which he now saw fit (perhaps because of the look she had returned) to skip a few paragraphs.

He returned his eyes to her and examined her whole person less dissimulatively, scanning up and down. He then shifted his eyes to his comandante: "Y dónde carajo was she going to hide a weapon wearing a dress like that?" He put his hand on the comandante's shoulder and laughed out loud. "No te digo, que Dios me proteja. It is quite clear that those souls whom I hold dearest to me, pressed up against my chest, as if by sheer will I could push them into the chambers of my heart, are the greatest of fools, and will sooner or later infect me with their folly."

He turned and went back into the bar without signaling for Maruja to follow.

"A veces se levanta así," the comandante said to Maruja. "And he keeps that level of energy going all day, till he falls down exhausted wherever he has ended up, for he refuses to establish a permanent residence. Tiene su toque de gitano."

When Maruja and the comandante entered the room, Fidel was already seated at the round mahogany bar, leaning forward on his seat and chatting in whispers with the impish indian bartender. A veil of smoke from his long Cohiba blurred their features. The room was full of people, Europeans, over-dressed in cotton sweaters and woollen scarfs for a laggard late summer afternoon (but perhaps properly bundled-up for the air-conditioned chilliness typical of all Cuban hotel bars, for even after the triumph of la Revolución, hotel managers did not relinquish their fears that the pale foreigners would be offended by the muggy tropical airs), seated at tables set near the walls covered with ceramic murals of Amazonish women in improbable coy sexual stances and war-painted indian warriors in frozen snarly belligerence, but Fidel and the other two comandantes were the only ones at the bar. The Europeans and the waiters that were serving them, except for momentary glances in their direction, seemed to ignore Fidel and his retinue too well, as if they had been practiced.

The bartender glanced in the direction of the newcomers and leaned closer to Fidel to whisper something. "Otro, otro batido, entonces," Fidel said so that everyone in the room could hear him, "my visitor is here." Now, everyone in the room, without exception, stopped their business and looked towards the bar. The bartender scooped some ice in a towel and wrapped the ends together and handed the makeshift icebag to Fidel, who set it on the bar and held it in place by holding down the tied-up ends, his Cohiba in the corner of his mouth, its ashes sprinkling down on the coat of his olive uniform. The bartender then hopped up on the bar and raised his arms and began a flamenco-style dance, clapping his hands over his head and stomping alternately on the cloth icebag with one foot, then the other. As he danced he sang, in a voice that was half his and half-borrowed from the spirit of his extinct ancestors:

> ¡Qué viva Cuba!
> ¡Qué viva Fidel!
> ¡Qué bajo de su torre
> con su mente lista,

Y mando al Batista
Pa la porra!

"Así, así, Luisito," Fidel encouraged him and let go of the icebag lest his fingers be crushed and clapped along.

When Luisito was finished the patrons all broke into an orchestrated applause. Fidel opened the icebag and examined the texture of the crushed ice and declared it perfect as always. "Luisito, make me another one, for I will need two today. I have a visitor."

When her milkshake was ready, Maruja was led to the bar by her accompanying comandante. The patrons could not help but to sneak a few extra glances towards the bar.

"Qué maleducado soy," Fidel said, looking at her for the first time since he had examined her body so brazenly at the entrance of the bar, "but I have not asked you your name."

"No," Maruja said. She did look at him and kept her gaze fixed on the sunlight rushing in through one of the high windows behind the bar as if there were no glass there at all. "But I am sure you know anyway." She pushed aside her milkshake. "For though you might have forgotten it from the night when you first saw me, your men must have refreshed your memory."

"Sí, they told me that you work in the National Library, but that is all I know."

". . . it was the Saturday night after Batista's *golpe de estado,* and you cried some because your first attempt at getting elected to a national office was not to be, you cried like a child who is not let out to play, you cried like a child in my arms before you set out to prove yourself el machón, to reestablish your lost glory by having your way with a defenseless girl." Maruja noticed that the chattering of the European patrons had all but ceased and that her voice bounced from wall to wall, doubling and redoubling, so that it seemed that the painted figures of the murals had been blessed with speech.

Fidel stood from his bar stool. The comandantes aped him. Luisito took a step back and his mien was instantly transformed from that of a cheerful performer to that of a person who is witnessing some horrible natural disaster and is frozen in helplessness. One of the comandantes put his hand on the Walther pistol in his holster and spoke: "What are you saying, señorita?" Fidel raised his hand, lit cigar nudged in place between index and middle finger, to signal he would take care of this on his own, then he brought it down hard on the mahogany bar, which prompted a blizzard of ashes on the backside of his hand and the sleeve of his uniform and an audible synchronized gasp from the Europeans and a cringe from Luisito. He spoke loud enough so that even the painted figures on the ceramic murals could hear. "I have shown you all the kindness I can afford to show a stranger. Pero es una gran pena, when the most beautiful women of our Island are hired to the enemy's work." He now turned and faced the Europeans, who looked at him not in apparent fear but in that unique type of delighted and unconcerned awe typical of a theatre audience at a first-rate performance. He pointed at her with his cigar hand as if she were a specimen at a lecture. "Aquí está el perfecto caso, señoras y señores: this is why the yanqui dog will never succeed in his attempts to obliterate me—his agents are not fanatics willing to perish for a cause, but our own natives, paid with dollars, like whores." He turned back to Maruja. "You will leave my sight now, for this, as your *friend* must have told you, is my time of peace; but I will see you again, bella, and you will repeat your traitorous calumnies."

"¿Pero estaba loca esa mujer?" Alicia said. "Así mismito, in a room full of strangers and armed comandantes, she accused him of rape?"

"Así mismito," Marcos went on. "And as she went out, she told him that she was no whore and that no yanqui dog had paid her any dollars, but that she did what she did for the sake of his son, who was healthy, but in dire need of a father to play with. Fidel spoke at her trial, not as a defendant (for remember she had been accused of moral perversion for the invented incident in the bathroom of the Library) but as judge over the judges of the tribunal, to whom he told that if the court failed to find the defendant guilty, history and the native gods of the Island's black soil would unleash a thousand plagues upon them. Maruja was sentenced to fifteen years at el Morro prison (a harsher underworld than el Boniato where I served my time, pues vaya, a prison and worse). Joshua was put in an orphanage where his *little illness* worsened and he began to suffer full-blown epileptic fits. He once described them to me as a demon in the shape of a scorpion that grows within him, till neither his body nor his soul belong to him. The revolutionary doctors, convinced that the seizures were a symptom of a greater illness, the plague of idleness, prescribed the rigor of daily discipline as a cure. Joshua was forced to join the Communist Youth League. He never wore his linen suits again. In time, the seizures were spread out over longer and longer intervals and became less and less severe, till they disappeared altogether. The scorpion had been squashed by the miracle of la Revolución. And Joshua became that truest and most foolhardy kind of convert, one whose faith has cured him.

"As for the poor old doorman, he never held Maruja in his arms as he had dreamed, and when he learned of what had happened inside the bar, he resigned his post without prompting. It wasn't until she was released from prison some five years later that Maruja was reunited with her son and finally revealed to him the prodigious identity of his father."

"¿Pero y eso?" Alicia said. "It isn't like Fidel to forget those who have offended him."

"Bueno, let's just say she came to some sort of agreement with Fidel. It is said by those who fabricate and refabricate these tales, that Fidel went to visit her at el Morro on the first Sunday of every month, disguised as a blind and old campesino, barefoot and in a frayed-brim straw hat and dark spectacles, his beard so caked with talcum-powder that little puff-clouds rose from it with his every move and his head seemed to be suspended in a low fog. He was accompanied by a just as ridiculously costumed Celia Sánchez. Thus they became Maruja's estranged father and sister from the fishing village of Cojímar. They talked for an hour during each of these visits and after five years they came to the agreement that if the alleged rape was never again mentioned by Maruja, she would be released and sent with her son to live in this secluded valley (famous before us because in the eighteenth century escaped Negro slaves made their first homes as free men behind the huge limestone walls) and help establish a colony for the purpose of rehabilating couterrevolutionaries like you and me. In return for her pains, the State would make sure that once Joshua turned eighteen he would be sent back to the capital to meet his father and from thereon be treated just as if he had indeed issued from the loins of el Líder.

"As you can see from what I've told you, Maruja keeps her first promise only halfway, from her own tongue there is never a mention of the incident, but she has a thousand other tongues at her service, keeping the sordid tale alive. As for her second promise, she has been more true. She is now, in her own demented manner, a devoted servant of la Revolución and its leader, and has in this village almost single-handedly rehabilitated thousands, *from the most base pervert* (that's me) *to the blackest witch* (that's Josefa), as she puts it, and helped reintroduce them into the society of la Revolución. And colorín colorado, *that* finally, señora Alicia, is what you and I are here for, so that some day we too may be as efficient servants as she is.

"But now, Joshua is almost eighteen, and whether Fidel keeps his end of the promise or not, will change our village forever. But that is still half a year away.

"As for you, you should enjoy your time of idleness till Sunday, for that is when, after most of the village gathers at Maruja's house to hear Fidel speak from her television set, you will meet all of them and become an official resident of our village, and be assigned the appropriate duties, as a worker and as an apprentice servant of la Revolución and your time will no longer be yours but belong entirely to Maruja. I am somewhat embarrassed to say that it is she who sent me here, to talk to you, to tell you most of the stories I have told you, for she preaches that the true revolutionary finds a proper use for every resource, and even my corrosive brand of cynicism, as she calls it, can be put to work if tamed properly, very effective against the iron wills of so many of the counterrevolutionaries who have passed through this purgatory. And I am that now which I once was, that which I afterward despised, against my rebellious conscience, I have become again (though not blind to all its ills as I first was) a true servant of la Revolución, and therefore a true servant of the future generations. Now I will go look for ice."

Alicia laughed openly for the first time since she had left Guantánamo, in the same harsh manner with which she had laughed in el Rubio's face when she had been asked by one of his thugs to sign her confession of murder. (A laugh of initial resistance, though less than four hours later she had signed the confession to lessen the charges against her sister and the other women arrested at the wrestler's house. This memory soured the pleasure of her present laughter.)

"What are you, Marcos, old compadre of my husband? I thought better of you when you dared to question Maruja during the meeting. Is this the up-to-date model of the New Man of la Revolución, is he like the poet who after volumes and volumes of song and lascivious lay, laments his reams of sins in a one-page retraction? If it is, then I am glad that my husband never lived this long, for although they broke him and turned him into a shadow even before they murdered him, a man no longer able to love his wife, his homeland, his own life, at least he never turned into this." She leaned towards him and placed her bandaged hand on his head, "A mock repentant, an apologizer more than an apologist, a castrato singing the inhuman notes of a lost paradise, no mejor digo, a paradise that never was. Me perdonas if I sound too insulting, y que me perdonen todos los santos, but my Julio is better dead than this."

Marcos stood. He shook his head. "You judge without full knowledge of the world where you have been sent. You judge now with a widow's mournful rage, with the ungracious grief of a mother estranged from her child; but in time, si Dios quiere, you will judge differently, you will judge with the unencumbered unadorned wisdom of an exile (a true exile, one banished from our land and not one who has fled to the enemy with riches in tow), and, a lo mejor, that will be your only salvation. . . . I will go get ice, once and for all." He left and returned soon after with a bag of ice, which he held tight against her bare bruised wrist and he stayed many hours, till after the moon had fallen, but she asked him no other questions and he said no other words to her except to warn her to ration her food carefully till Sunday.

Four days later he returned to lead her back to Maruja's bohío to listen to Fidel's Sunday afternoon speech.

The Devils in the Clock

Joshua was not there among the throng of villagers creeping in and out of Maruja's small bohío, in groups of seven or eight, like fire ants into the hull of a dead roach, just to get one peek at el Líder, atop the platform in the Revolutionary Plaza, sweat stains on the armpits of his olive uniform and on the brim of his olive cap, crowded by a sea of admirers, waving banners and placards and chanting responses to his sermon, which the villagers and Maruja also chanted.

"Cierren la puerta, coño," she screamed as one group entered and another exited; though all the windows were shuttered, the light from the opened door drowned the improbably small black and white image of el Líder on the screen. When it was Alicia's turn to enter she hesitated, but Marcos grabbed her lightly by the arm and led her in. Maruja did not look at her or greet her but kept her gaze fixed intently on the screen and talked back to it with phrases like *así mismo* and *la verdad, la verdad pura, coño*. Earlier that day, on the way from her bohío, Marcos had told Alicia that he had often objected to Maruja about this method of watching the Sunday speeches. He had explained to her that Fidel's speeches were purposefully so long, so that no one could muster the concentration to *sit* and listen to it from beginning to end, that is, he defeated his listeners, even as he tried to educate them, he out-patienced them just as he had out-patienced his professors at the University of La Habana and Batista and his Rural Guard and three yanqui presidents and would out-patience the Second Coming Himself, if need be, for the sake of our people. It was a virtue Fidel learned from the Jesuits, though all bustle and flurry on the outside, his avid gesturing, his mania for soliloquies (this, his heavy mask in the mad theatre of the imperial throne), on the inside an inner core of sanity and patience as consummate as the practiced stillness of a Tibetan monk, as solid as the limestone walls that surround this false valley. So, the proper way to listen to him was not to try to outdo him in an intricate game where he has made up all the ground rules and revealed them to no one. It is as silly as to have sat blindfolded across a chessboard from the great Capablanca.

"No—the more advantageous way to listen to his speeches (and clearly I am not the only one who believes this *or* practices it), the way perhaps he means for us to listen to him, is with one ear to his rhetorical trumpet and the other ear to the everyday trumpet of revolutionary life—the crickets on a freshly harvested field, the scrub of clothes against the washboard, the tedious murmurs of la cola at the start of the ration month, the cry of a child, the songs from an afternoon of rum, the groans from a sweaty evening of love—so that one may be properly integrated into the other,

just as the Jesuits use their concrete intellect to levee and dam the torrential river that is the word and will of God."

Maruja had looked at Marcos, unmoved to change her habit of sitting
for six or seven hours straight *looking* at Fidel and not just listening to
him. "Mira muchacho, por favor, it is that kind of sophisticated university
babble that got you in trouble in the first place, maybe if you had never
known how to build such airy castles with your fancy language, you
wouldn't have written all that counterrevolutionary trash. . . . Coño, para
mí es obvio, a man speaks, you listen to him, he speaks wisely you look at
him, you listen harder. It is rude to go about and do other things while
you *pretend* to listen."

After their allotted fifteen minutes were up inside the darkened bohío
with the flickering black and white screen, during one of Fidel's long
pauses, which the crowd at the plaza filled with shouts of *¡Venceremos!*
¡Venceremos! or antiquated doggerels aimed at the enemy:

> *¡Arriba! ¡Abajo!*
> *¡Los yanquis pal carajo!*

Maruja flicked her hand and signaled for one group to exit and the other
one to be let in. On the way out, Alicia said to Marcos, still within hearing range of their host, that both he and Maruja were mistaken, that the
best way to listen to Fidel's speeches was with no ears at all.

"He carps like a disgruntled housewife!"

Marcos hushed Alicia and led her out and took the trouble to introduce her to many of the villagers from his side of the valley. Most of them
addressed him as *jefe*.

The throng of villagers enjoyed their Sunday afternoons much more
outside of Maruja's bohío than within. They went in and came out with
somber faces and murmurs of approval at all the work that had been done
and greater work that lay ahead for the continued progress of la Revolución. Yet when they had been out for a few minutes, or before they had
been selected to go in, it was as if not a thought could be wasted on anything but idle pursuits. Barefoot boys, encouraged by their fathers, raced
up the twisted-crucifix antenna, apparently unbeknownst to Maruja, who
redundantly cursed the thousandfold accursed phantom of el-indio-de-
mierda Batista (who had recently abandoned his rotted brown body in
Madrid) for her bad reception every week, precisely during the course of
the Speech. Men played music in improvised drums made of rotted palm
stumps and maracas made of hollowed-out coconut shells, and at times
with their gitano voices and their primitive instruments seemed to drown
out the ubiquitous birdsong of their valley. And the words they chanted,
unlike the crowd at the Revolutionary Plaza, were heated with the fire
wheel of love won and love lost and not with the bonfires of politics and

revolution. Farther away, in a clearing hidden by a grove of shrub pines, women lined up to have their fates told by Josefa's cowrie shells. The woman Maruja had chastised for witchery at the CDR meeting was still very much a practicing madrina and had baptized many of the guajiro villagers into the realms guarded by the *orishas.*

"Maruja, la pobre, is out of touch with our world here in the valley," Marcos admitted.

"Very much like the one she is in love with," Alicia said.

She went to line up to see the madrina Josefa, who sat crouched on a cloth of satin with her long frock covering all of her body below her neck, on which hung two collars of polished beads, one crimson, the other white. She smoked hand-rolled cigarettes and flicked the ashes into the air. Wild grass grew thick in the meadow all around her, but in a circle around where she sat the ground was bald with wear. Alicia prostrated herself before the madrina and informed her that she was an initiate of Elegua and the madrina seemed to take offense, and said that she knew, that it was clear from the moment she saw her enter Maruja's bohío, that despite the outward appearance of her eyes she could see better than most, that it was obvious from the history of Alicia's cunning dissent against the government and from the scars on her cheek that she did not yet have, who her protector was, that she needed to be offered no such information for, *unlike the sinvergüenzas who run this Island,* she was no charlatan.

Alicia passed her hands over both cheeks. *What scars?* Josefa apologized. She meant no offense. Josefa picked up the sixteen small cowrie shells spread on the satin to the left of her. She passed her hand softly over the sawdust held in a tray to the right of her to make sure the previous divination had been completely erased. She shook the shells in her left hand like a gambler. She asked Alicia why she had come to consult the madrina.

Alicia said that she had no fee to offer the messenger spirit.

Josefa stopped shaking the shells and laughed. She said most of the people had grown so poor, not only in this valley, but in the whole of the Island, that many of the messenger spirits had joined the Party and their fee was now paid by the State, that even Alicia's own powerful protector, the wiliest god Elegua, was forced to switch from his favorite meal of rooster and opossum with rum, to the tendons of mice with black-market watery yanqui beer. She quickly added that she was joking and stopped laughing. "But seriously, hija, pretend you have a coin in your hand and whisper your concern into the air. I trapped un pajarito last night and offered it as sacrifice this morning. The gods know we do what we can. Besides, Elegua is the messenger of all the orishas, and his paths to this world are many, paved or not."

Alicia held both her hands pinched in the air, more as if she were holding a consecrated host than a large invisible coin. "Where is Joshua?"

The madrina, as was her duty, betrayed no astonishment to the question. She shuffled the cowrie shells from her left to her right hand, at each take transferring fewer and fewer pieces from one closed hand to the other and drawing with the pinky of her right hand either a circle or a slash on the sawdust. When she was finished she examined the pattern on the tray and let the cowrie shells fall from her hands like shattered crystal and closed her eyes and recited, in a borrowed high voice that belonged to the spirit of a young boy, from the memory of Ifa, the oracle that reveals the destiny of all beings, humans and deities:

Ifa is the master of today, Ifa is the master of tomorrow, Ifa is the master of the day after tomorrow. To Ifa belong all the days of the week. Ifa's oracle was performed for Bird. Bird was the son of the Fire and the Air and was to live in his inherited domain all the days of his life. But Bird grew fond of the fishes of the Sea and the critters of the Earth, and soon found he could not do without them and spent many days away from his home of Fire and Air. Afraid that other winged creatures would usurp his titled domain of Fire and Air, Bird built great aviaries on the plains of the Earth and on giant cane-stalk barges floating in the Sea, and there imprisoned all fowl and all winged things that were blessed with thin blood by Almighty God. Feeling his abandoned domain was safe, Bird grew smug, and he spent all his days inspecting his prisons in the Earth and on the Sea; and his own blood grew thick and heavy as gravy, and his wings withered, till he was no longer a creature deserving of his inheritance. And Almighty God stripped Bird of his title and of the power of flight, and with a thunderous tempest, stirred by Oya, tore asunder all the aviaries so that all the other fowl and winged things might be known together as birds. And Almighty God consoled the usurped monarch of the Fire and the Air by lending him the energy of Ogún, so that he plunged the mysteries of his exile, and invented tools, guns and powder and steel-wings and engines, that helped him regain a tiny part of the kingdom he had abandoned. Thus, he shall never forget the folly that led to such great loss. This is Ifa. This and no more. Asona.

The silence that followed the recitation of the oracle was interrupted by Marcos, who rushed ahead of the women who were waiting in line and informed Josefa that it was her turn to go listen to the Speech.

"Me cago en ella," Josefa muttered in her old voice. "Se acabó la fiesta." She gathered the cowrie shells and put them away in some inner pocket of her frock and stood. The sawdust on which she had drawn the diagram of the oracle she gathered on both hands and blew into the air murmuring a prayer in the old tongue of the Africans. The afternoon breezes challenged her and blew back some of the holy dust into her face so that it stuck there like caked-on make-up and forced her to bat her eyelids like a coquette.

The carved tray that held the sawdust, the sacred *opón,* she hid under a mound of polished riverstones behind her, amidst the wild grass.

"Come on, come on, she is waiting," Marcos said.

"Let her wait, coño," Josefa said. "My group will not go in without me."

On the way to Maruja's bohío, past the line of women whose concerns would not be addressed that afternoon, Marcos warned Josefa to take off her beads, and she did and put them in the same inner pocket where had put the cowrie shells.

Later, after the Speech was finished, Maruja joined the people outside and the drummers stopped drumming and the dancers stopped dancing and the children voluntarily interrupted their games and all the revelry in general came to a halt as the people gathered around her to receive their instructions for the following week. Maruja assigned Alicia to Marcos's neighborhood, and gave her directions to his bohío where she would report the following morning for her work detail. She ended as she did every Sunday, insisting to the people of the valley that only through the drudgery of work and toil would they be able to build the patience and integrity necessary to distill any joy from this harsh world. The people, led by their jefes, cheered, as they always did.

In the following weeks, Alicia worked in the coffee fields and alfalfa plains in the higher lands of the valley where Marcos was in charge. After she was given her work uniform (a pair of workboots, a long-sleeve khaki workshirt, a heavy blue canvas jumper-dress and a wide-brimmed straw hat that smelled of the labor of those who had worn it before her) and instructed on what to do, she avoided the other workers, and set out on her own and did not join in their field songs. When she returned to her bohío near dusk, she shed her clothes and washed them in the cool stream and then waded in till the waters reached her waist and lowered herself in and remained there till the moon had crossed from one end of the sky to the other. She then hung the clothes on nails sticking out from the beams of the outhouse and returned to her bohío and ate as much as she could stand. After her first week of work, when Marcos provided her with paper and ink, she wrote three letters nightly by the dim halo of the oil lamp, one to her daughter, one to her mother, and one to her sister. These she handed to Marcos on the following day and he promised that he would personally seal them in an envelope and mail them without letting anyone in the valley break the seal. Some nights she wrote a fourth and fifth letter, but these she did not mail, but folded into a square and hid in the lining of her suitcase. They were addressed to ghosts.

The workers were paid twice a week, on Tuesdays and Fridays, in bags of food and soap and other necessaries and oil for their lamps and wood for their stoves and (if so requested, on Fridays only) half a bottle of rum or outdated newspapers and faded-color magazines from the main Island. At the end of each week, each worker's production was carefully noted in a black leather journal kept by the jefe, the neighborhood chief. Saturday was politics and re-education day. And the workers would gather at the home of the jefe, and the work journal was carefully examined by all. The less productive of the group were made to explain their slackness, and invariably they offered salvos, some commonplace, such as advanced arthritis or sunstroke, some more daring and sublime, such as yanqui sloth syndrome, a condition, cousin to greed, where the mind refused to be ennobled by work and toil unless it was properly recompensed with wealth. Those suffering from yanqui sloth syndrome were tended to and pitied by the other workers as if they were indeed in the grasp of horrible illness.

Every week Alicia was among the top producers, this due not to any feat of endurance or devotion to her task, but mostly to the fact that on Wednesday afternoons when the jefe was away for the weekly Comité meeting in Maruja's bohío, the other workers, men and women and children alike, would cease their laboring and abandon the fields and climb to the cataracts of the main river and shed their work clothes and naked wash away their exhaustion under the crystalline falls, rejuvenated for Thursdays, which for no logical reason had been designated the longest workday of the week, when they would arrive in the fields before dawn and not leave till after the stars began to pierce the sky. On Wednesday afternoons Alicia remained in the fields. This stubborn penchant for separateness, this affronting aloofness, did not help ingratiate her with her fellow laborers.

Sunday, of course, was Speech day.

And how casually did the weeks tumble one upon the other, how cleverly were the long seven days disbanded one from the other (so that many in the valley grew to forget the old Roman names and knew the seven days by their more useful, though much clunkier, names—so that Monday was First-Work day, and Tuesday First-Pay day, and Wednesday Meeting day, and Thursday Long day, and Friday Rum day, and Saturday Journal day, and Sunday, of course, was Speech day; and how easy then to shuffle all the weeks together, as if in an imaginative card trick, not unlike the ones practiced by Josefa to divine the future and retell the past, so that the necessary ligaments that we use to hinge together dense pockets of time and thus make it bearable, the swing from night to day, from spring to summer, from child to man, from work to play, from truth to fantasy, seemed more like the twined tether of memory and regret that holds the beast from its baiters. Thus, it was the law of the valley, only through the drudgery of continuous labor, through the dull devotion of Sisyphus, could the illusion of time be shattered and the wanton gods avenged. "Y que no me digan nada," Maruja was wont to repeat, "my revolution here in the valley is more cosmic than Fidel's Revolución; he freed you from the imperialists, I will free you from the devils in the clock." And indeed, throughout her long stay in the valley of the nightingales, Alicia never saw the exacting face of a clock or a wristwatch.

"¿No ves?" Marcos explained to Alicia when she brought up the issue one Sunday night on their way back from the Speech. "Where there are no clocks there are no calendars, where there are no clocks and no calendars there is no history, where there is a continuous present, no history, no progress, no memory, and without any of these, there is no loss. She has gone much further than Dali who set fire under his clocks; in this little valley, she has set fire to the whole course of human history and is out to restart it, with her son as emperor!"

Alicia thought of the melting clocks of the Catalan painter who was a frequent visitor to the capital before la Revolución. She wondered what he would think of this valley without clocks, where time was forced to assert itself through other beings, through the remolded countenance of clouds, the shifting silt-lines of the river and its tributaries, or the shrill virtuous notes of a lewd little bird. (Thus, Alicia's alarum to rise near dawn was no bell from a clock but the abrupt hollow created by the silence of the nightingales.) More cunning than the swine-loving demons in the Book of Luke, the legion of devils cast from the clocks by Maruja's inquisition possessed (without belittling themselves by seeking permission) any other available thing in the valley, living or nonliving.

"For even a devil needs a place to call home," Marcos added to Alicia's ruminations with a half-smile.

Not Like a Prodigal

Much later, after Joshua had disappeared for the second time, Alicia thought how easily she might have gotten lost in the shuffled weeks of Maruja's ambush on history, had not Joshua returned on a muggy wind-less night, after a near two-month absence, bearing an unexpected gift and news of an imminent visit. It was a Friday and she was in the stream wash-ing her work clothes. When she heard his voice calling her from the front of her bohío, a bucketful of blood plunged from the cave of her chest to the pit of her belly. She attributed this not to a rush of joy (for though she had often thought of Joshua during his absence, she had never really missed him, not, claro, the way she missed her daughter and her husband and her cousin, but not even in the same manner she missed the flat streets of her hometown, or the most common acquaintance there) but from an embarrassed fear, for she was wont to walk back the thirty-six paces from the stream to the back of her bohío in the nude, her washed uniform draped over her arm. She tried to hurry out of the waters to reach her wet

uniform on the shore but saw the blaze of yellow and orange light from
Joshua's torch making its way around the house and proceeding in a
roundabout fashion towards the stream. She waded back deep into the
stream and hid her nakedness in the dark waters.

He called out to her again and after the third or fourth time, Alicia
abandoned her plan to try and reach the wet uniform and responded:
"¡Aquí estoy!" She saw the light change course one last time and head directly towards her. Joshua approached the shoreline with his torch held
aloft over his head. His hair was loose and stringy with sweat. He wore
only a pair of olive drab pants, like her husband had worn in the Sierra
during the war; they were too wide for him and fell low on his hips and
the shadows that fell from his heaving chest danced on the pale skin of his
belly. He lifted his arms above his shoulders, presenting himself. He was
thinner than before and the shadows falling from his ribcage made it seem
like a pair of twin narrowing circular staircases. There were rosy welt-
marks around both his shoulders and around his waist. A small flame flew
off the torch and was heading for his face but it died before it reached its
target, as if snuffed by the wet fingers of his guardian orisha. Joshua lowered his arms and crouched and caught his breath and lowered the torch
farther to just above the surface of the waters so that it washed out the
stream's blackness and made it transparent. Alicia covered her breasts
with her arms and took a few steps backward on the slippery riverstones
and lowered herself farther in the water, so that her chin was submerged.

Joshua lifted the torch. "Oh, señora Alicia, you are so quiet, so unwel-
coming, I just wanted to make sure it was you." He planted the torch on
the shore and walked into the stream up to his ankles. He smoothed his
hair back behind his ears. The light that gleamed from behind him now
made him into nothing more than a shadow. He lifted his arms again. "I
have returned! Pues, aren't you glad to see me? I have returned, and not
like a prodigal."

Alicia said nothing. She thought of the many things she could tell this
impertinent young man, but she had been struck mute. Joshua leaned forward and let himself fall into the waters. He remained in the shallow and
knelt and drank from the stream with cupped hands and splashed his face
and smoothed his hair. "It's too hot," he said. "You are smart to spend your
time in the river." He walked back to the shoreline and saw the wet
clothes. He laughed. "Are you completely naked, señora? Shall I go into
the house and get you something?"

Alicia nodded.

Joshua disappeared with the torch and returned bearing one of her
white summer dresses and hung it on the branch of a willow that grew
aslant over the stream. The dress hung still there, no breeze toyed with it.
In the playful deceptive shadows of the torchlight it seemed as if a young
girl had hanged herself there, and stoically waited in the air for a more

proper rest. Joshua disappeared again and said he would wait for her by the front of the bohío with a surprise for her.

Alicia waited till Joshua's torch was well away and let the breath of night return gradually. She trusted it less now than before. She hurried out of the stream, using her arms to push her out of the deep water. The dress was still visible and she reached for it and quickly put it on. It stuck to her skin. She lifted her arms over her head as if beckoning any adventurous breeze to traverse the humid night, but she remained as wet as she had been in the stream. She put her arms over her breasts again and walked to the front of her bohío. Joshua was seated by the front door, his arms on his knees, the torch sunk into the ground beside him, his bald friends, Jeremiah and Ezekiel, and two new ones, presumably Daniel and Hosea (although they might not yet have been named for their heads weren't shaved), all across from him, strapped on like teams of horses by two twin harnesses around their torsos to a long closed cart, Joshua's chariot. When he saw Alicia, Joshua smiled and with open hand signaled to the chariot. "Ahí tienes."

Alicia looked at the long chariot, then back at Joshua, then back at the exhausted giant rats strapped to the chariot, their bodies sprawled on the ground like a napping pride of lions, their long front legs stretched before them, then back at Joshua.

"Have you gone mad, muchacho?" Alicia said. "¿Qué es esto? Where have you been?"

Joshua continued to smile, and signaled again to the chariot. "¿Estás ciega? Has my mother plucked out your eyes?"

"I have asked for you, para que sepas. Your mother said you were away conducting official revolutionary business for the Comité. But others rumored that you had fled from her and gone to the capital to await your eighteenth birthday within striking distance of your father. They said if he did not recognize you as promised that you were going to murder him."

"I told you you would hear that story. The people of this valley have tongues longer than salamanders and imaginations more twisted than the fallen angels. So . . . you have asked for me? Aquí estoy, returned from my journey to your land, to your home, with your request to el Comité fulfilled. My mother, on rare occasions, can be very, very kind." His caramel eyes opened wide and he signaled again to his chariot. "¿Pero coño, sigues ciega, mujer?"

Alicia looked back to the chariot, she noticed its familiar giant egg shape, she looked at its wheels that were not wheels but talons dug into the mud, like those of a falcon burrowing into the home of its prey. She gave a short scream and ran to her prize, forgetting about the resting giant rats, who scrambled out of her way as far as their rope and harnesses would let them. Alicia passed her hands over the rim of her bathtub and walked a full circle around it, looking for familiar rust marks on its sides. "Pero, niño," she said. "How? How?" She did not notice her bare feet becoming increasingly tangled in the harness ropes, nor did she hear the helpless squeals of Jeremiah and Ezekiel (and Daniel and Hosea) who were dragging behind her, ass backwards, their claws unable to sink into the muddy earth.

Joshua stood and went to Alicia: "Cuidado, the ropes, you'll fall." He knelt beside her and freed her foot from the rope. He felt her hand on his head.

"Ay, mi vida, niño precioso, you have been to Guantánamo, you have seen my daughter."

Joshua stood and Alicia put her hand on his cheek. She trembled.

"How is she? How is my daughter? How is Marta? How is my mother?"

"I saw them all. I met many people from your town. I will tell you. But first tell me where you want your tub, so I can set it up for you."

"Inside. Inside the bohío, by the stove. So I can heat water. Ay, verás, there is nothing like a warm bath to purge the body . . . ya verás, even in this weather, to soothe the body and calm the mind." While she was talking, Joshua crouched over the bathtub and measured its width with his arms and then walked arms still apart to the front door of the bohío. His hands could not pass through. He repeated the same process, the second time measuring the height of the bathtub, not taking the legs into account, and walking to the front door. Again, he could not pass through because of the spread of his arms. "No hay manera, the back door is even narrower; it won't fit. You'll have to continue to bathe under the stars. No te preocupes, the invisible birds watching us are not concerned with nakedness. It bores them."

Joshua ordered the rats to rise. He spoke to them gently, with the benevolence of a master who knew well-treated servants work better than resentful ones. He lined up Jeremiah and Ezekiel on his left and Daniel and Hosea on his right. He picked up the largest harness and strapped it around his shoulders and around his waist. He asked Alicia to reach him the torch, and sunk his feet into the earth and heaved and pulled with the aid of his friends and the falcon-grip loosened from the earth and Joshua dragged the bathtub around one end of the bohío to the back, halfway between the outhouse and the back door. Its trail cut deep into the earth and Alicia remembered it had taken three men and her husband, one on each leg, to move the bathtub from the moving truck into their house in Guantánamo. Joshua removed his harness and sunk the torch into the ground and patted his animals and took some pellets of food from the pocket of his pants and fed them. They ate and rubbed their snouts against his ankle and circled once around him and rested. Joshua's breath was again heavy with the brief but tasking exertion and sweat glistened on his brow and above his lips. He said he wanted to jump in the river. He asked her to accompany him. They left the torch behind and the moon had already sunk so she did not see much of his nakedness when he took off his pants and casually handed them to her. They were heavy with sweat and mud. He jumped into the stream and splashed around like a child and teased her to come in and join him, that no harm would come to her for her mother had taught him the proper respect that la Revolución demands from all compañeros for the sacredness of a woman's body. When he came out he chided her for her cowardice and Alicia again could find no words with which to chastise his boyish effrontery. She reached the pants to him with her arm fully extended. He thanked her and said he would help her heat water for her first bath under the stars; and while they waited, he reasoned to her chorus of protests, he could tell her how he managed to fulfill her request to el Comité, by journeying all the way to her hometown on the eastern end of the Island and stealing the bathtub from the *cabrón rubio* who had made it his.

The Tale of the Tub (Prologue)

He boasted that when her daughter Teresita had first seen him, she had instantly fallen in love. After that, she could not bare to look at him, wrapping her arms around her grandmother's waist and sinking her face into her belly.

At first, he had gone to Alicia's old house. There was no answer at the front door and no answer when he rattled the iron-grill door of the courtyard on the east side of the house. He went around back and saw a small indian woman dressed in a black frock, her hair shorn down to a thin layer of fuzz the color of cigar ash, coming out of the henhouse, six limp white dead hens held by the scruff of the neck in one hand. When he made known the purpose of his visit she told him in a sibilant voice that la señora Alicia Lucientes no longer lived there, to which Joshua answered that he knew, and he tried to pull out the letter his mother had provided for him, but the indian woman continued in her harsh wheezy voice, asserting that this was now the home of comandante Camilo Suarez, and that if he had any business with said comandante he could go see him at his office in the Department of State Security and that if he tarried any longer in her presence she would have him arrested for trespassing, she was busy preparing the evening meal and she had no time for vagrant children.

"Are there many guests expected tonight?" Joshua asked.

"Guests? ¿De qué hablas, muchacho? Everyone in this town knows that el Rubio always dines alone, exactly at six in the evening."

Joshua raised his eyebrows and signaled to the six dead hens.

"Ay mijo," the indian said, her shoulders slumping, her voice softening, "you *are* a stranger amongst us." She laughed and raised the hens
above her head, "Three and thirty and three hundred of these he would eat
if I let him. Ves, he doesn't really eat the flesh, despises both the white and
dark meat, what his mouth waters for is the innards of these fowl, he will
eat a sauteed liver in one swallow, and close his eyes and moan when he
crunches on the grainy gizzard, and gob down scoopfuls of giblet with coconut stuffing, leaving the impure flesh, as he calls it, for me and his precious hound Tomás de Aquino, but he best likes a *pastel de corazoncitos,* pot
pie made only with the core of red onions and slices of chewy poached
heart, *this,* y no se lo diga a nadie, he can be bribed with. Ay sal de aquí,
mijo; abandon your quest. You do not want to meet my rotund master, for
I am afraid that he will take a liking to you, that dangerous liking which
surpasses even his obsession for slippery innards of beast and fowl."

Joshua pulled out his mother's letter and held it open in front of her.
The indian hunched her shoulders and said she could not read, but not to
shed any tears for her (as was the wont of many revolutionaries) for she was
proud to be illiterate, because the dumber you are in this world the less
you are likely to fall into the gutter of men's thoughts. "I am sixty-four
and still a virgin, in mind *and* body." She rubbed her velvety gray skull
with her free hand, as if to signal that this was as far as she would let her
own hands, or anyone else's, caress her own body.

"Fine," Joshua said, opening the letter in front of him and following
its contents with his index finger. "I will tell you what it says; it will do
no harm to your chasteness. . . . I have express orders from Maruja
Irigoyen (my mother), the chief of the 333rd Committee for the Defense
of the Revolution, in the Valley of the Nightingales, in the Isle of Pines,
to retrieve from this house and bring back to our valley a certain falcon-
legged antique bathtub that is the property of one Alicia Lucientes, former resident of this house and now resident of our valley."

The indian woman shook her head and walked past him towards the
kitchen of the house. "Like I said, niño, go back to your mamacita before
el Rubio sets his fat claws and his fake teeth on your boyish flesh, for
that sort does not repulse him. . . . I have to work now. You have been
warned." She closed the kitchen door.

Joshua went to the second address his mother had written down for
him, doña Adela's house on Maceo Street. Alicia's mother cracked the door
open a few inches and asked what he wanted. He talked to the slit of her
face, explaining who he was, who his mother was, the whereabouts and
condition of her daughter, and finally, the purpose of his visit. The old
lady said she did not know who to believe anymore, but that she had no
choice but to force herself to believe him, and that she was glad to hear her
daughter was alive and in good health and not in a prison. (Once she
found out that Alicia had been coerced to confess to the murder of the fin-

quero Mingo and had been taken out of Guantánamo, she pressed el Rubio for information on the terms of the sentence, how long, where it would be served. El Rubio's reticence to her questions, the way he scratched his chin with the naked short barrel of the polished derringer, which had been a gift from a famous yanqui novelist after the Sierra War, and suggested to doña Adela that she write the Department of State Security in the capital, for he could not tell her anything—only that it was good that one daughter confessed and thus saved the other one—made her mother fear that Alicia had been sentenced to the firing squad.) So she was unsure of how to deal with Joshua (even as she revealed all this parenthetical history to him, and he to her his task at the beck of el Comité of obtaining the falcon-legged bathtub), unable to deduce to whom the boy pledged his allegiances (for surely no one who worked for *any* Comité, or spoke the same tired jargon of revolutionary glory and revolutionary progress, could sympathize with dissenters like her daughter). Nevertheless, she pulled the door back and asked him into her home.

She looked like a soul condemned to insomnia, her white hair frizzled, her eyes bleary and half-shut, her body bent low like a palm after a windstorm. (Later, after Joshua had accepted an offer to sleep that first night in Alicia's childhood room, unused by Teresita now, who since her mother disappeared could only fall asleep in her grandmother's bed, doña Adela told him that the bags under her eyes, heavy as ripe plums, functioned as a reservoir for all her poisonous tears, and that if she lived to see the day when her granddaughter had become a woman, she would puncture them, and collect the venom of all her grief in a cup, and drink to her death.) She introduced him to the child not yet grown into a woman who was holding tight to her faded housedress, as if afraid a wind might pick her up and take her. She offered him coffee and some guava pastelitos she had baked that morning, assuring him that only one type of guava was pulpier and sweeter than guava picked directly from the tree, that was guava picked from the sheet-covered cartons of the black-market trucks; but told him he must wash first, for he looked and smelled as if he had spent a week in a pigpen. Joshua spread open his arms to display his dirtiness. Doña Adela said that the cloth of his poncho that hung from his bones looked like sooty gray wings of a city pigeon. Joshua said that his journey from the Isle of Pines had taken over two weeks, hitching rides along the Central Highway, and that many days he could not find any river or pond to wash in, although many times he refused offers to shack up at homes from solitary men and women, and even from whole families, who picked him up in their shiny Russian jeeps or rust-eaten Oldsmobiles or carts-and-buggy. His mother had warned him not to become entangled with any strangers along the way, for their kindness was sure to be a lamb's cloth that hid more perverse notions.

"Así mismo, but you are no stranger, you are Alicia's mother." He sniffed under his armpits. "And you are right, I smell like a rotting carcass."

The girl walked alongside her grandmother towards the bathroom door and only lifted her head a touch from her grandmother's belly, just enough to peek with one eye, when she heard her mother's name. Doña Adela left her outside as she went inside to run a bath for the visitor. When Joshua crouched and tried to talk to the girl and asked her age, she turned and faced the wall and covered her face with her hands. Joshua smiled and passed his hand through her long brown curls and said that there was nothing to be afraid of, that he was a friend of her mother. Teresita mumbled that she was not afraid, and that if he was truly a friend of her mother he would bring her back, so that the same thing would not happen to her that happened to her father before she was born. Joshua promised that the same thing would not happen to her mother. Teresita said she was almost seven, and old enough not to believe any promise from a comunista.

"I want my mother back, that's all. Can you do that? Can you tell her to come back?"

She turned and looked at Joshua for the first time and Joshua forced himself not to lower his eyes from hers though he had no good answer to her plea.

Doña Adela came out of the bathroom and handed Joshua a clean towel and fresh bar of soap. She let Joshua into the bathroom and told him to reach out his poncho and shorts to her when he had taken them off.

"Why, señora?"

"To burn them, muchacho."

Joshua laughed. He reached out his clothes to her. "Señora, if you can just wash them, por favor. They are the only clothes I own."

Doña Adela muttered that all the waters of the Caribbean could not wash the filth from such rags, nor all the perfumes from France make them smell clean again. She went into her closet and rummaged into it, through housedresses and church dresses, all the way back into one corner, where was stored, folded over the bar of a wooden hanger, the only article of men's clothing she possessed, an olive drab guerrilla suit, her dead son-in-law's fatigues. She set them out on the bed. The old cloth gave off a whiff of smoked tobacco and man's toil. The girl asked why it was so wrinkled and why it smelled so bad. Doña Adela said she did not know for she had washed it thrice and pressed it before she stored it away. She imagined a suit of war had no need to be cleaned and ironed and when left to its own devices, like a skilled drunk, reverted to its truer nature. She took off the silver star pins from each collar of the shirt-jacket and put them on the dresser and from the pockets of the fatigues and the suit she gathered a handful of cedar chips. In a box below, in the same corner of the closet, were a pair of black military boots. She put these out at the end of the bed. The leather was dull and cracking, but it would have to do.

Joshua was watching them through the half-cracked door of the adjoining bathroom. He made a noise and stepped into the room with the towel wrapped around his waist. His hair was loose and fell over his ears and on his shoulders. Doña Adela told her granddaughter to leave the room. Teresita asked doña Adela why she was giving away her father's uniform. She said her mother would not approve.

"Sal niña, I am not giving it away. I am letting him borrow it. I'm letting him take it to your mother on his back. Sal niña, go to the kitchen, can't you see that this boy is almost naked."

"I have not looked at him, abuela," Teresita said and turned her chin up and left the room.

Joshua glared at the fatigues with unabashed fascination. "I cannot wear that, señora. It should have been buried with him."

"Well, it wasn't. In fact, from stories we hear, we're pretty sure he wasn't buried at all, left out for the vultures to peck at his bullet holes. All we know is that they gave us a number that marked a grave, and that that same number they have given to many other grieving widows . . . y por favor, don't repeat any of this to Alicia, she is still under the fantasy that that empty piece of earth, number 687 at el Campo Santo, holds the dear bones of her Julio . . . and stop staring at these old pieces of war-cloth as if it were Santa Teresa's hand!"

"Have respect, señora. If you yourself didn't consider it a relic you wouldn't have stored it away so carefully."

"I stored it away so carefully because I suspected some day we might have use for it. Y da el caso que ese día ha llegado. For all your comuñanga talk, I see in your eyes that you care about my daughter, and she would be glad these old rags were put to use on your person. If you're going to do battle against el Rubio, you might as well be dressed like a warrior, a noble warrior who loved liberty enough to die for it."

Joshua put up his hands, closed his eyes, and turned his head to one side and shook it. "Con mucho respeto to the memory of your daughter's beloved, but I am not planning to do battle here against anyone, much less a comandante of the revolutionary police force. I will show him my mother's letter, and he will give me what I came for."

"Ay, qué inocente eres muchacho, this Island is a conglomeration of little tyrannies, and no little tyrant pays attention to any other one. Sometimes, when they are inebriated enough by their little swig of authority, they don't even pay attention to the Papa Tyrant." She picked up the olive drab shirt-jacket and cargo pants, and held one above the other in front of her. Joshua walked towards the crooked old woman and towards the flaccid ghost in the uniform. His towel dropped from his waist, but he did not notice.

"¡Muchacho!" doña Adela threw the fatigues towards him. Joshua caught them and covered his nakedness with them. When doña Adela walked out of the room, he stepped into the pants and buttoned on the shirt. Except for the expanse of the waist and the length of the sleeves, the fatigues fit him fine. He remembered his mother once describing coman-dante Julio César Cruz as a thin man, and she said that Fidel should have known from Caesar how dangerous it was to surround oneself with thin men, and Joshua now wondered how much weight he had lost during his journey if a thin man's pants were baggy on him. He rolled the sleeves and put the boots on without socks. They were near the right size, but he could not tell for sure for he was, by now, unused to footwear. He squinted into the small vanity mirror above the dresser. It was stained with so many tiny white spots that it hardly served its purpose. Joshua saluted himself in the military fashion and looked away. He turned his head and smelled at his shoulder, and bounced inside his boots and shifted inside the shirt-jacket, all as he tried to feel for the other presence inside the guerrilla suit, but felt only the weight of the clothes. He looked back into the damaged mirror, coming closer to lessen the disorienting effects of the stains and scratches, and could not decide whether to tie his hair back or let it loose. He remembered pictures he had seen of Che and of his father, after their descent from the mountains. He wondered if there was a cap or a black beret stored somewhere inside the old lady's closet. He thought of the last time he had worn clothes similar to these, the olive drab short-sleeve shirts and knee-length shorts of the Communist Youth League. He re-membered the care with which he washed and starched and ironed his three uniforms on Sunday afternoons, the eagerness with which he dressed the following morning, pretending the stiff cloth was a suit of armor. He was still a boy then. When they arrived to their exile in the Valley of the Nightingales, his mother forbid him from wearing *los trajecitos de los comu-nistas*. He adopted the garments of the native campesinos, the straw hat and poncho and canvas pants to protect against the sun in the fields. Even-tually, because of the intolerable heat, he had ripped his pants into shorts, and because he could run faster without them, he had no use for the heavy boots. His mother cried at nights as she massaged whitening cream into his legs, which were turning, despite her great efforts, the color of *un ne-gro cualquiera.*

Joshua leaned closer and peered into a clear corner of the ruined mir-ror. He ruffled the meager patches of hair on his chin and on his jaw. He did not look like a rebel. He took the long black hair from both sides of his head and spread it over his cheeks and above his lips and under them in the shape of a beard. He grimaced. He groaned in dismay, for he looked like a child in a costume; or perhaps worse, like a woman disguised as a man. Doña Adela knocked and he let his false beard fall. He straightened himself and gave her permission to enter. She clapped once and put her prayer-folded hands to her lips. "Ahí estás, you look as valiant as Julio ever did!"

"I look like an imbecile, an impostor."

"No, no, muchacho, believe me, I know, I have known plenty of men who have worn this costume over the past fifteen years, and you look as good, as valiant, como te dije, as any of them, even Julio. It is a sad fact of our country, that too many of our people like to dress in uniform."

"Valiant? I don't need to look valiant—"

"You will, muchacho, you will if you're going to lock horns with el Rubio. Ves, when my daughter was arrested, he took possession of her house, her furniture, even most of her wardrobe. (I don't want to think what he does with her dresses, for his servant certainly doesn't wear them.) And yes, even Alicia's prized bathtub, which was bequeathed to her by her husband and had been bequeathed to him by a man of God, so that now a devil washes where once a minister of the Lord did. Así son las cosas de la vida."

Doña Adela sat on the bed. She pressed the butt of her palms into her eyes and said she was glad that he had come for she had been crying for two months straight, but she would not cry now for she could not cry in front of strangers. She was glad that he had come, and that the news that he bore of Alicia's safety was like news from a messenger of God, and that she had never been sure what the angel Gabriel had looked like to Mary. Now she knew. He was not blond and he did not have pearl white wings and he did not wear velvet robes. The master painters had been wrong, equivocado completamente. Now, after all these years of hearing the story, she knew exactly what Gabriel had looked like to Mary, a lissom man not yet a man, with long black hair, wearing the garments of a fieldworker, a beggar, and wings, wings like a grimy Havana pigeon. Sí verdad, equivocado, though in some details, she had to admit, the master painters had been right: the bare feet of the angel, the way the Virgin holds her hand aloft, protecting herself, arresting his advances. She pressed the bones of her hands farther into her eyes and could not help but weep in front of this stranger. As he moved to console her, she got up and made her way with unsure shuffling steps out of the room. She warned him through her tears not to waste any pity on her, for she was beyond implacable, and that not even the pillars of her faith were of any use against the weight of her desolation. It was late. She must busy and prepare dinner for her granddaughter and her guest. "There is not much meat on you. I am afraid you need a much better meal than I can give you."

Joshua remained in doña Adela's house till the following morning. After dinner, a pale arroz con pollo, made only with wing bones and stale pitipuá, they drank coffee and sat on the two chairs in the living room. Teresita sat on her grandmother's lap and tasted the coffee by sticking her tongue into her grandmother's cup. She grimaced at its bitterness and wiped her tongue with the palm of her hand and sank her head back into her grandmother's breast. Doña Adela told Joshua much more of her life than she imagined she could tell anyone except Father Gonzalo. She said she had just taken her white pills and they made her chattery before making her sleepy. She spoke to this son of a Comité jefa, this likely informant, as if he were indeed a heavenly messenger, a confessor come to unburden her. She told him of the shameful manner in which her late husband, que en paz descanse, had left this world. She made a damnatory gesture towards the heavens. She told him how she had first been against her daughter marrying a guerrilla, for she had never been taken in by the sham that was and always would be this mock-revolution. Many, though, had been enthusiastic at first, even the parish priest, her close friend Father Gonzalo. But even before her son-in-law's murder, Father Gonzalo had seen the lies for what they were and turned bitterly against the revolution. Now, to save his church, he makes certain compromises, and attends Comité meetings, and knows more about the secret goings-on in this town than all the informants put together. Though in his heart of hearts she knew he had surrendered: in private, he said that even prayers were fair game for the regime, the words of the faithful flew up but were trapped in the thousand revolutionary snares set up all over the Cuban sky. The only hope now, he admitted, was exile, which was a fate more noble than one incommunicado to God. He helped many fill their permission-to-leave forms, and had contact with the yanquis in the base and helped others in ways that put his person, and the very future of the parish, in danger. "Of course, I should not be telling you any of this, God knows if you're not a demon disguised as an angel and have already destroyed my daughter and now come to destroy the rest of us."

But, convinced that such a demon would rouse to defend himself against such accusations and Joshua did not, she continued. She told him of her daughter's first arrest and unfortunately of her experimentation with santería, that primitive religion practiced by the uneducated. She told him of Mingo's death. A drunk farmer who drowned in a river during one of his binges. She told him of Alicia's return from the mountain, a changed woman, distant and disrespectful, not only with the authorities but with her own mother and daughter. She told him of the mob that had gathered outside her house one afternoon and forced her daughter to eat the regurgitated cuds that were once the copy of her sermon and the English children's story. She told him of her daughter's sister and the women who had banded together in vengeance with Alicia, and of their assault, in turn, on the words of la Revolución, and of the death of Paca Córtez, and placed her hand over her granddaughter's ear and, in an undervoice, told him of the recent murder, in the lower circles of the tower prison in Santiago de Cuba, of the town's former alderman, as he slept, stripped and knifed a hundred times in the back by men he had helped send there, cursed as a marica and a fiend with two faces, his delicate white skin cut open and peeled back so that it mimicked the petals of his most garish ruby orchids. She told him of the fate of Marta, who, poor girl, so traumatized, so young when her father had died, so crazy a mother, had never matured emotionally, had never desired a husband and children and a family. She had been sentenced to a rehabilitation camp near the yanqui naval base, the same camp where Alicia had once, long ago, spent some days. She told him of what he knew, of the confession of murder Alicia had been forced to sign to avoid a mass accusation of her sister and all the other women involved. And finally she told him about el Rubio, the massive effeminate gold-maned black-minded police captain.

After Alicia had disappeared, her fate a secret, he had moved into her house. He had tried before to move into the alderman's stone mansion, but learned the lesson many petty tyrants sooner or later learn, that their power is not as absolute, nor their domain as far and wide, as they imagine. The 83rd Neighborhood Committee for the Defense of the Revolution wanted the mansion for itself, and even though el Rubio had hand-picked its current chief and many of its leading members, el Comité took him to civil court and won their claim, on the punitive damage charge that it was they who had suffered the most harm from the alderman's treachery and from the ravage of the wordeaters and thus should be compensated in fashion. El Rubio retorted that it was he who had rid the town of the plague of wordeaters, he who should be rewarded. The judge, who perhaps had lost some previous power struggle with el Rubio, and apparently unthankful at having survived the latest purge, agreed with el Comité. El Rubio moved out of the alderman's stone house and reestablished a specious peace with the young man chief of el Comité, for they needed each other as bread needs butter. He moved into Alicia's house. And from there since the day of the trial, he has tried to undermine the young man chief of el Comité, who had proved, by his manly drooly hunger for a chunk of the power pork, that he was no marionette, that his appetite was as real as el Rubio's taste for the innards of beasts and fowl.

There were many in el Comité still loyal to el Rubio, still willing to do his bidding, generating rumors and turning brother against brother and son against father in the name not of la Revolución, but of the blond hog who is the police captain.

"So if you want to dupe him, go to him not as one ready to die for la Revolución, go to him as one willing to die for el Rubio . . . a Rubioista."

Joshua returned to Alicia's house on B. Street early the following morning, still wearing the fatigues and the black military boots, his hair tied back in a ponytail. He went around the back where he had seen the indian servant the previous day. The henhouse was locked and no one was around.

He went to the wrought-iron door that was the entrance to the courtyard. It was locked. He rattled it once and called for the servant. A dog barked lazily inside, apparently not so interested in the identity of the intruder to come to the gate. Joshua had not learned the servant's name and called for her simply ¡India! ¡India vieja! A man came to the gate and stood on the other side. He was wearing a long white terry-cloth bathrobe that fell almost down to his ankles. He was barefoot. His toenails were spongy, eaten with fungus. His hands were in the pockets of the robe and seemed to be supporting his basketball belly. His hair was wet and slicked back and his beard trimmed short and, though there were streaks of gold in both, Joshua could not tell for sure how blond they were. His eyes were an iridescent blue, like the wet feathers of certain rare birds. He was chewing on something, though it was hardly noticeable for his jaw was locked shut, pulsing at the hinge. His neck was long and womanly. He examined Joshua, casting his gaze upwards and downwards more than once, and then let it rest on Joshua's face. He smiled without showing his teeth and swallowed. "¿Qué quieres, joven?"

"I want to see the comandante who lives in this house."

"¿Eres militar, joven?" The man's voice was soft and pleasant.

Joshua remembered doña Adela's advice that the best way to deal with el Rubio was one, not to get lulled by his ingratiating, almost affectionate, manner, that despite his obnoxious breath, was capable of seducing many a soul, and two, never to answer any of his endless questions with something as simple as the plain truth. "Yes, I am in the military. I am visiting from La Habana."

"And what do you want with the comandante who lives in this house?"

"I have a message for him from my father."

"And who is your father?"

"An important man in the capital, but I am not allowed to say who . . . not yet."

"There are many of those, aren't there? There are many important men scattered throughout this Island."

"Not many as important as my father."

"Do you have papers, joven? Or am I to stand here, fresh from my morning bath, out of uniform, and believe every little lie that issues from your pretty mouth?" Joshua was moved to silence both by the ugly accusatory tone that the man had suddenly taken and by the unfitting compliment to his appearance. The man passed his hand through his hair and it had dried somewhat and Joshua could see how blond it truly was, some strands as pale as white gold.

"Don't be afraid, joven, contrary to the vicious rumors that slither like snails from the mouths to the ears of los envidiosos, I am no marica, nor am I the son of yanquis!"

"I had not heard either of those rumors, comandante."

"There you have it: here in front of you is the comandante who lives in this house. And now you've heard from his own mouth the worst that has been said about him, not that he is a corrupt police chief or a scheming politico, not even that he is so fat that he can't afford to sleep on his belly for his head won't reach the pillow and his ass falls from behind him like twin sacks of lard, but that he is a marica and a yanqui. In 1971, the two worst things one can be on this Island." He stepped closer to the locked gate. "And do me one favor, won't you?" He waited for a response. "Won't you? ¿Sí o no?"

Joshua hesitated. "Sí."

"Tell la señora Adela, when you next see her, to have a little more respect for her sacred dead, and not give away his old war uniform to any vagrant boy, filled with lies, who knocks at her door." He produced a key out of his robe pocket and unlocked the gate door and opened it. He came close enough to Joshua so that Joshua smelled his rotted breath. "Now, we'll start again. See if you can let your girlish pink mouth utter something close to the truth this time. What is it that you want, niñito, with the comandante who lives in this house?"

Joshua felt a fountain of tears welling up in his chest. He wrinkled his nose and tightened his cheeks and pressed down against the surge at the back of his throat. He knew this feeling well, knew how to fight it, knew it from when another woman had dressed him, in a fine linen boy-suit with knee-high socks and leather moccasins and left him alone in a dark apartment on Cardenas Street. But he was almost eighteen now, almost, at last, the son of his father, ten times the man of this petty *policitica,* and though he felt his lips tremble and imagined el Rubio tasting them and tasting his cheeks and tasting his brow with the invasive tongue of his breath, he would not cry. He reached in the pocket of his fatigues and produced the letter his mother had written. He handed it to el Rubio. El Rubio handed it back to him without perusing it.

"Al fin, joven, you come out with *some* truth. . . . I do not need to read your mother's letter. The woman has already told me of its contents, of your odd quest. You forget, you read her the letter yesterday. Liars should not be so forgetful; and neither should you have let la vieja Adela fill you with so much fear. The answer is simple, I cannot let you have your golden fleece, the falcon-legged bathtub. It does not belong to Alicia anymore, it does not belong to me, it belongs to the State. The State has seen fit to let one of its *loyal* servants live here, eso es todo; usufruct: the right to use and enjoy the property of another—it is an ancient Roman legal term that the modern capitalists, the vile yanquis, do not comprehend, they wrongly believe that to use and enjoy something one must own it first, que pena. Pero la cosa es, pertaining to the object of your quest, that I as a mere *user* cannot give away property that is not mine. Pero, I have looked through my old clippings of *Granma,* I once wanted to be a lawyer, so I save all the trial stories. Your mother is one of the redeemed ones! She has risen above her past self, according to these sources, and is now an expert at what she does. I understand she would not ask for things not deemed necessary for the purpose of the revolutionary rehabilitation of said prisoner, Alicia Lucientes. And your father; yes, that story I have heard too—"

"We do not consider our valley a prison," Joshua spoke with a renewed boldness, even as he tried to shut his nostrils and callous his whole being against the miasmic aura of the police captain, "nor our residents prisoners."

"What I was going to say was—" el Rubio put his hand on Joshua's shoulder and gave it a light tug towards him—"that I would be willing to help your mother, be willing to give you the due respect as the son of your father, if you in turn were willing to lend me a hand, for as I am sure la vieja Adela has told you (for all her righteousness and saintliness, her tongue is as long as anyone's in this town) I have some problems of my own, with some ingrates trying to reach for power beyond themselves, beyond me, even beyond the scope of la Revolución."

Joshua nodded his head, and el Rubio took it not to signify that yes Joshua had heard from doña Adela, but as a silent approval of alliance against the young man chief of el Comité. He pressed his hand into Joshua's shoulder till it began to give downward. "Bien coño, your mother has raised a proper revolucionario. Your *father* will be proud to have sired such a son." And before Joshua could protest, el Rubio was giving him a tour of Alicia's old house. The long brick-paved center courtyard opened out from a semicircle of four rooms, the atrium, the main parlor, the dining room and the airy kitchen, in which a fat bullmastiff slept, all sparsely furnished, el Rubio explained, because of a disgraceful bonfire the mad widow had set to a pile of fine Cuban mahogany pieces one New Year's Eve after her husband's suicide.

"Suicide? Sí, that's what my mother tells us at el Comité. But wasn't he shot down by border patrol while trying to flee into the American base?"

"Like I said, suicide. Your mother is correct. A man may kill himself in many ways. Suicide." He led Joshua through the two bedrooms. One furnished only with a sewing machine and a wooden chair, the other only with an unmade bed. El Rubio explained he did not let the woman into his bedroom. Finally they came to a blue-tiled bathroom, more spacious than either of the bedrooms, with a toilet, a bidet and a small sink in a far corner and a narrow shower stall in a near corner, and at whose exact center was placed Joshua's prize, the falcon-legged bathtub. El Rubio said it was not bolted down and could easily be moved out of the house if he saw fit, though outward theft from the State did not sit right in his heart.

"Perhaps," he suggested, "we can find some sort of loophole in this law of usufruct."

Out of the bathroom, a sliding door in the hallway led to another smaller courtyard, darker than the main one, the walls and floor and trellis-ceiling carpeted with creeping vine, and bordered by a bed of yellow rose bushes and white poppies, several in full and regal bloom. El Rubio explained that the secret to such beautiful flowers was to line the bed before planting the bushes with a carpet of human hair. This he learned from the man who had once been the town's alderman, something to do with nitrogen. He reached his hand to the side of Joshua's face and caressed a lock of his hair that had come loose from the pony tail and he said that such princely hair would surely lend beauty to the most homely flower. Joshua jerked his head away. El Rubio took no notice of this sudden brash gesture and led Joshua back to the rear entrance of the kitchen. He left Joshua outside, excusing himself to get dressed. He told Joshua that he knew the way out, and asked him to return that evening, for dinner at six, if he liked.

"Your servant, mejor digo, what do you call her, your woman. She said it was well known in this town that you always dine alone."

"*The* woman, not *my* woman. I am not an owner of land and much less not an owner of other living beings. The woman is clever. Alone? Yes, she is clever. Come then and I won't be alone. Come dine with me and afterwards, I will know your true self."

El Rubio said that after dinner there would be a test of Joshua's loyalty to la Revolución, and therefore his loyalty to its only proper defender in this far-eastern town, himself. When Joshua asked what kind of test it would be, and expressed mild disapproval at his innuendos, el Rubio laughed openly, for the first time revealing his teeth, some rotted black and brown, some capped in very pale gold, alternating like the keys of a tiny piano box that emitted not sound but an outrageous and irreplicable cadenza of stink so dungy, so like the thing it wasn't, that it seemed to mask the promise of some future sweetness. "Nothing immoral, joven, don't get so nervous," el Rubio explained, unsuccessful this time at dissimulatively breaching the distance between himself and Joshua to put any hand on him, "a simple feat that I have recently begun to use to test all my recruits, easy pickings for someone as well schooled in revolutionary mores as you."

"I *may* return," Joshua said, heading towards the front of the house.

"Yes, you may," el Rubio shouted at him, his hand extended, unshaken. "You must."

Joshua did not go to doña Adela's house, though he was tempted. When doña Adela interrupted their conversation the night previous and put Teresita to sleep, she turned on the television tube, hidden in a scratched and stained console. She said she could not miss a single episode of the nightly serial *novela* for she would lose the string of the story, and it was the only thing, aside from the rosary and the white pills, that made her nights tolerable. Joshua revealed to her that the only two things he was allowed to watch on his own television in the Valley of the Nightingales was Fidel's Sunday speech and the afternoon cartoons. Doña Adela said, keeping her droopy hypnotic gaze fixed on the fuzzy black and white screen, that Fidel's speeches were blacked out in her house, but that her granddaughter was also an avid watcher of cartoons, and that her favorite was el conejito Bugs, who never gets caught by the fat-nosed yanqui hunter Elmer Fudd and dresses up in costumes that fool everyone. Joshua was tempted to return to doña Adela and Teresita. He missed the afternoon cartoons and missed his mother, and even missed Marcos and some of the senile old women of el Comité. He wanted to please them; he wanted to please Alicia. He had decided that if he could not have the falcon-legged bathtub, he would steal it. Perhaps he could convince el Rubio to relinquish it, but if not, he would steal it. He would dupe el Rubio and steal it. For obviously el Rubio was not a man easily affrighted, which had been Joshua's original ploy when he went to see him that morning. He looked behind him to see if he was being followed. He was on one of the main streets and it was improbably deserted, the only human presence certain town women sitting in the shades of their veranda, stretching their blouses at the neck and fanning themselves with fan-shaped pieces of discarded cardboard boxes. The naked sun was directly overhead and Joshua had trouble finding even his own shadow. He could not risk returning to doña Adela's house, for el Rubio would certainly find out. He seemed to know far too much for a nobody police captain in a provincial town so far away from the capital. It made Joshua uneasy to think how flagrantly el Rubio had expressed his affections.

He went to the park and read the front page of *Granma,* which was plastered on the public kiosk. He read the date carefully and used his knuckles to figure out which months were long and which were short and calculated the days till his birthday. He wandered the square city blocks and marvelled at the impossible flatness of this town where no house was higher than any other, and the only thing that looked down on any roof was the yellow steeple of the church. He thought that only the lowest regions of the netherworld could be this flat, that paradise was certainly a progression of mountains and valleys like the island where he lived. He returned to the park and watched the old men playing chess on the benches. They wore ragged clothes and their hands were unwashed and their beards unshaven. They drank from rum flasks hidden within their coats, and their only evident dignity lay in their eyes, and in their furrowed brows and in the silence with which they examined the board and planned three or four moves ahead. In between games, Joshua spoke to them, and asked them which way led to the famous yanqui naval base, but they either laughed uproariously at him, as if he were joking, and told him the yanquis don't look kindly on jóvenes in Fidel's uniform, or they nervously reset their pieces and restarted their games.

He asked them where he might find a man named Father Gonzalo, and at this they grew serious and queried him on what he wanted with a harmless man like Father Gonzalo.

Joshua made no answer and moved away from them.

In the early afternoon, a wash of cinerous clouds spread over the sun and thickened over it, and all at once there began a downpour of rain that continued so for over an hour, not once catching its breath. At first, the heavy drops shattered like fine glass on the pavement of the park's paths, scattering pieces in all directions, and then when ponds and rivulets began to form, the heavy drops splashed into the gathering water with the carelessness of children at play, forming tiny circles of waves that ceaselessly clashed one into the other and merged the ponds and the rivulets so that soon the entire park was a tiny sea. Joshua sought refuge in the antechamber of the yellow church and some of the old men who had been playing chess joined him there, counting their black and white pieces to make sure they had not lost any in their flight from the deluge. A priest came out of the church and joined them. He was a short balding man, with indian skin and a kind smile. He wore a starched white guayabera and black trousers. He chided the old men that the only time he saw them inside the house of the Lord was when it rained and that in Genesis God had not seen it fit to save the unfaithful from the Great Flood. One of the rattiest-looking old men, drunker than the others, retorted that could his reverend grace not see by their barbaric appearance that they were not men but beasts, that this degeneration from man to beast was the ineluctable fate of any man unlucky enough not to have fled from this Island. At this, he put his arms around one of the other old men and wrapped one leg around him and began humping, and begged his reverend grace not to worry for the flood would soon subside and knights would mount upon bishops, and pawns creep like ivy upon rooks, and queens bestride over kings and all would be fruitful and multiply and be as abundant as flies on a donkey carcass. The priest, in an embarrassed effort to ignore him, walked up to Joshua and extended his hand. "I am Father Gonzalo, monsignor of this parish. I do not think I have met you, young man. Are you stationed nearby?"

"Beware of the Rubioistas!" the same drunk old man said and raised his arms and wiggled his fingers as if a goblin casting a spell. "He has been looking for you. He has been asking about the road to the paradise of tin roofs. Beware, beware of the demon come to hide in the house of God!" Some of the other men held him back and reprimanded him to show a little decency, not to mention common sense. They begged pardon of Father Gonzalo and of Joshua and explained with their thumbs tilted towards their mouths that he'd had a little bit too much.

Joshua took Father Gonzalo's hand and introduced himself. His hand was small and soft like a woman with servants, but his grip was strong. Joshua said he was in town doing some business for the revolutionary government; more specifically, for a former resident of the town. Father Gonzalo held on to Joshua's hand and put his other hand on Joshua's shoulder. He walked him past the old chess players, whom he nodded gravely at in an apparent gesture of forgiveness, and into the nave of the church. Once inside, he let go of Joshua, who stood in amazement within the temple, his eyes wide, his breath uneven, examining the stained-glass windows one by one, unable to make out the figures of angels and saints and apostles and Virgins and Christs (as Father Gonzalo pointed and named them) that had all been made indistinguishable by the darkness outside of the church, their beings pulled apart and transformed into a jagged puzzle. "I have never—" Joshua said and did not complete the phrase, opening his eyes wide and staring, providing his own light, as Father Gonzalo directed, and renewing his effort to solve the riddles of cut and colored glass. "I have never been inside a church," he said when he dropped his eyes and his shoulders and relented. "This is the first."

"It is one of our traditions that the first time inside a new church, you make three silent prayers, and out of these one would certainly be answered."

"Three wishes? Like when you find a genie?"

Father Gonzalo laughed and said yes, like when you find a genie. Joshua sat on one of the pews and said he would wait to make his three wishes, for he did not want to hurry and forget something. He looked again at the stained glass. He pouted.

"I would not want to live in this town," he said, as if involuntarily he had blurted out his first wish. "One cannot make out friends from enemies. That old woman Adela says she is your truest friend, but she said to me some things she should have not."

"Sí, doña Adela, she came to confession this morning. We talked all morning. Her sins are brief but her grief is long." Joshua smiled and thought that most likely el Rubio was right about the length of the old woman's tongue. "She is very relieved that her daughter is alive and well, that someone is caring for her."

"Why wouldn't she be alive and well?"

"Many terrible things have happened to her family, to all of us in this town, since the triumph of la Revolución."

"All great change is terrible in some way. Terrible things have happened to my mother as well, but this is not the fault of la Revolución, it is the fault of the nature of things. The old woman is almost delirious, she said I was an angel of God, or a demon disguised as an angel, she wasn't sure, after the dinner she spoke to me as if in a trance, she told me many things, perhaps some that she should have kept to herself—"

Father Gonzalo explained that doña Adela was on medication. She had fallen apart after Alicia had disappeared. Sometimes *los calmantes* did this to her, she spoke fantasies.

"Sí, the white pills, but she is not mad, she is not making up stuff, and I'm afraid that she is more a danger to her friends than to her very real enemies; pues, that is why I came to you, I cannot see her again, so tell her not to worry; her daughter is alive and well and will remain alive and well, away from this town, which is the worst place for her. Perhaps some time in the future, if we can convince my mother, Alicia can come back for a visit, to see her daughter. The police captain does not care for her, or for the memory of her dead husband. Did the old woman tell you I was going to see comandante Suarez?"

"Be careful with el Rubio."

"Yo no soy bobo, padre. I know what I'm dealing with. I know corruption when I see it. That man can be charged with crimes ten times as serious as the murder of a drunk finquero. But my business is not to convene tribunals. I need to get what I came here to get." He pulled out his mother's letter from a pocket of his fatigues. "It is by order of my mother's Comité. But this comandantecito, aside from being a pervert, has no respect for the process of la Revolución. He is no model revolutionary; but I suppose, for the time being, you are stuck with him."

"Is it true what that old man said? Were you looking for me? Were you asking for the way to the yanqui base? Many young men pass through this town, in many disguises, with stories more absurd than yours, but with only one purpose in mind."

Joshua stood, straightened his shirt-jacket with both hands and scooted past Father Gonzalo into the main aisle of the church. He looked at one of the bigger stained-glass windows behind the altar in one last effort to envision the shapes hidden there. He spoke to Father Gonzalo without looking at him. "Be careful, padre, I know you mean well, but be careful who you choose to proposition with your doubtful mode of salvation . . . *and* be thankful I am no *chivato.* Save your charity. I am not one of your runaway children. Those young men that pass through here looking for a better life, tell them that it is not in the land of the rich yanquis, tell them it is here"—he poked the left side of his breast—"in their Cuban hearts, in devotion to a cause that too many have foolishly abandoned. You are a priest, are you not? A good one, I imagine, from how much even the street bums admire you"—he pointed to the antechamber where the drunks were gathered—"so you must know the value of sacrifice, and the wickedness of the wealth that is the yanquis' only claim to holiness. La verdad es, I was looking for you to give this message to the old woman, that one day she will see her daughter alive and well, a productive citizen of la Revolución. My mother is good, she will help Alicia succeed where before she had failed. *And,* I was looking for the way to the yanqui base because I wanted to see what was so alluring, what indeed had bewitched Alicia's husband into the suicide mission that ruined the life of his family, what glory he saw, and others still see, in this barbed-wire encircled city where yanqui warships dock and the Cuban sun shines off the roofs of foreign houses."

"Muchacho, I have put myself and my parish at risk too often to be afraid any longer. El Rubio knows everything about us there is to know . . . even the many things that can land me in jail for life and ruin this parish, those same things *that doña Adela should not have told you.* But he does not move against me for some reason, he turns his gorgeous mane the other way, perhaps because he knows the people need some form of consolation, or perhaps, as you say, because he is so steeped in corruption that he has lost his footing and has no way of distinguishing the shore from the horizon. Or, perhaps, a combination of both. So, muchacho, I am not afraid of you as *chivato,* for I have already made myself and all my others as vulnerable as possible. My duty is to the well-being of all the people in this town—even those who are just passing through."

"How long will *you* stay and continue to perform this duty, padre? How long before you decide that the well-being of the generations that have not yet been born on this Island, who in the silence of their unmade wombs have never heard the rumors of a yanqui paradise, is not worth the sacrifice of the meager years left in you?"

Father Gonzalo was astonished at the loftiness that had in a moment transformed the boy into a man. It no longer sounded as if he was merely parroting the speeches he had heard. Father Gonzalo was too weak to match it. "I don't know how long. Estoy viejo y muy cansado."

"El Rubio does not move against you because once la Revolución starts to work in this town, his power vanishes. Without counterrevolutionary agitation, without young men being sent to their deaths for the promise of a false paradise, he is out of a job."

Joshua turned and walked down the aisle towards the exit.

"Muchacho," Father Gonzalo called. Joshua paused. "I will give doña Adela your message." Joshua nodded and continued on his way out. Father Gonzalo called again. "The way to the base is through the road southward that leads to the town of Caimanera, or go across town and follow the railroad tracks, that too will get you there. There is a hill beyond the alfalfa fields, from its zenith you can look down at the airport on one side of the bay and the tin roofs of the main yanqui town on the other . . . be careful, there are murderers perched in towers on our side . . . oh, and if you see small wooden half-buried boxes, do not step on them, they are mines."

Joshua thanked him and left the church. The old men were spread on the cracked gray marble floor of the antechamber and had restarted their games. Joshua slipped past them unnoticed into the rain.

Dinner for the New Man

His clothes were still wet when he arrived for dinner at el Rubio's borrowed house on B. Street. During the storm he had roamed the empty streets of the city, crossing eastward till he found the railroad tracks and following them south. By the time the storm had passed he had crossed the Guantánamo city limits. He noticed it was later than he thought. The dusk light was spread thick with abandon over the whole western half of the gray dome sky (in soppy strokes of violets and globs of red and countless washes of orange) as if trying to redeem itself for the lost day. He turned back. The wrought-iron door at el Rubio's was ajar. Over the puddles of the brick-paved courtyard there stood a long table covered in crisp white cloth. Many white porcelain bowls of food were set out on the table. Their contents were all similar, mounds of mush, earth and wine colored; and Joshua thought that along with the insides of animals, the police captain also ate blood-soaked Cuban dirt. El Rubio sat at one end. The indian servant in a black gown was mopping the steps under the tile-roof awning that led into the open kitchen. She grumbled in low tones directed at the head of her mop. Joshua greeted her but she did not turn or raise her head to salute him. A lone chair and silver was set at the other end of the table.

"Bueno, Joshua," el Rubio said, signaling to the blood-brown feast on the table "as you can see the woman has a very Gothic imagination. I asked her to prepare a simple dinner for two! For three, I meant, for she usually joins me at six, but as you can see she has not set a place for herself. She has grown peevish. She says there's too much cleaning up to do. The storm blew right into the front rooms. Blew out the flames under her pots and pans three times. Bad timing too, the woman had just waxed the floors. But look at this, she came through anyway, come, come, sit down, taste this—" He had already begun to eat and washed down his mouthfuls with a goblet of red wine and wiped his mouth with one or the other end of the tablecloth, leaving it streaked like soiled underpants. His dog sat by him, its tongue lolling out, its breath desperate. "Mmm, pork brains au beurre noir, the woman speaks no *francés,* but she can certainly cook it; mmmm, braised to perfection, see the trick is to poach them first (isn't that right, woman?), without peeling off the outer membrane, and then, before braising them in a cast-iron pan, mind you, not dropping them in till the butter is so hot it has begun to turn brown and black, to cover them lightly with spiced bread crumbs, for brainmeat on its own offers little in flavor; it is its texture that it is prized for—no other organ of the beast's body melts with such grace and delicacy in the human mouth. It is like tasting the fat of phantoms! Oh, and one other important secret, the brains must still be warm from the beast." He turned his head and lifted his fork to the indian. "Was it yesterday or the day before that this pig was slaughtered?" The indian was bent over a bucket, wringing the mop with violent twists, her small hands all stretched and twisted fingers, and she did not answer him. He fed his dog with his own fork. "You see the brain is a very perishable thing, it has to be eaten on the very day the beast is slaughtered, or at the most the day after. With veal and lamb you can preserve it for a bit longer, but the swine's brain starts to poison itself almost immediately after death. This is why the Jews don't touch it"—he tapped his temple with the handle of his fork—"they are clever, esos judíos. A dead pig is as dangerous as a hungry tiger. Only the skin is safe, burned to a crisp. Ay, el chicharrón, that greatest of Cuban delicacies. But how can we, as the top of the food chain, belittle ourselves to eat the hide of such a base creature (it is our national bird, no?—the yanquis have the majestic eagle as their emblem, we have the mud-rolling pig!), with the little black hairs that haven't been singed off, erect on it, as if the beast were in the throes of lust? Urgh!" He tightened his lips and cringed. He patted the dog's great head. "But you, you love chicharrón. Don't you? Don't you, baby?" He let the beast lick his hand and then turned again to his servant. He raised his voice, as if to indicate she must not have heard him the first time. "Woman, *I said,* was it yesterday or today that this beast was slaughtered!" The india grumbled something that could as well have been yesterday or today or ten weeks ago.

Joshua stood unmoved by the entrance to the courtyard, shifting on the mud and slush that had penetrated the cracked leather of his borrowed boots. He remembered he had loosened his hair as he walked in the storm and now he searched in vain in his pockets for the band to retie it. He took the thick strands from each side and wrapped them around each other in the back and tucked the tail in to hold it in place. El Rubio watched him and ate another mouthful and banged the table with his fisted hand. His goblet of wine teetered and regained its balance. "Me cago en mi misma madre," he said. "Did she conceive such a monster that no human will eat with me?—not the woman, not the beautiful compañero, only this beast!" He stood and walked towards Joshua, sauntering, fork still in hand. He did not look as obese in his wide-fitting uniform, the wide black belt of his jacket pressing his monumental belly in.

"You came because you were hungry, no?" He took Joshua by the hand and led him towards the long table. Halfway there, Joshua snapped his hand away and said he could make it to the table on his own.

"Está bien, está bien, mi cielo," el Rubio said, returning to the table and bending forward, sticking his nose over the other dishes, "no need to get upset. I was just going to point out some of the other marvellous things the woman made."

"Don't call me that. Don't call me *mi cielo*. It sounds stupid. You are a comandante."

El Rubio straightened and came back to Joshua, his movements now angled and military. He poked Joshua in the chest with his fork. "That's right, a comandante, I fought in the Sierra, and fought in the Escambray and continue my fight, daily in this town, against countless counterrevolutionaries." He poked Joshua again and held the fork in his chest, as if he were about to press it in. "And when you, mi compañerito, have fought in one-tenth of the battles that I have fought in, then perhaps you can tell me how a comandante is *supposed to behave*." He pulled the fork away and threw up his hands in a womanly fashion. "¿Pero qué hago? Carajo, I don't want to quarrel. I want to eat, before everything gets cold. I want *you* to eat! Ay mira, mira, this is a masterpiece, veal hearts stuffed with coconut shavings. The woman is a genius! ¡Un monstruo! We'll open a restaurant in Varadero when I retire, she as chef, me as host. Wouldn't I make a congenial maitre d'." He caressed his paunch. "Vaya, I'd have to lose a little of this." The woman grumbled from the steps in response. El Rubio sank his fork into the praised dish and brought a tasting for Joshua. He dangled it under Joshua's nose but Joshua kept his lips pressed tight. El Rubio waited. The indian servant dropped her mop and came from the steps. She stood beside them. She folded her arms and glared up at Joshua. The dog came over and sat by them.

"Whoever does not eat my cooking is a traitor to la Revolución!"

El Rubio giggled and shook his head vigorously and said that *claro, claro, a traitor and a half, even his dog knew better,* the woman was more than correct. He began to rock the loaded fork and said that this was the heart of yanqui veal stolen from the base, a blond veal with blue eyes, and that any true compañero would not pass up the chance to chew on the heart of a yanqui anything. The india abandoned all her previous crabbiness and giggled along.

Joshua stepped in between them and sat by his setting on one end of the table. He reached for the veal heart dish and ate forkful by forkful directly from it. The meat was packed with flavors, like a very rich liver, augmented by the familiar and frightening tang of one's own blood on the lower lip. The coconut stuffing complemented it just right, changing its slippery texture and making it swallowable. He finished the entire dish, letting the bloody gravy slide down his chin, before he looked back at his hosts, who were staring back at him, their hands clasped in front of them, their heads nodding in approval, like proud parents. The india slapped el Rubio on the shoulder. "Te lo dije," she said, before returning to her mopping chores. "Certainly the boy is no traitor. We are safe. Aunque sea el hijo del mismo diablo, he is no traitor."

Joshua, an old hunger now stirring inside him (he had refused breakfast from doña Adela that morning and eaten nothing all day), reached for other dishes. El Rubio, back at his place at the opposite end of the table, described them as the young man ate in silence, and the bullmastiff came and sat pleadingly by him.

"Ay, sí, sí, that one is exquisite, cow's tongue stuffed with goose liver; imagine, close your eyes and imagine as you chew it all the tongues that have ever lengthened in slander against you—¡ay, qué placer! Give me, give me, coño, don't eat it all." He stood and reached across the table for the dish. "No ves, in its form, in its texture it is exactly like a human tongue. You have eaten the tip, which is the tastiest part, because it is the most versatile, it knows both the salty and the sweet, and it is where thoughts often get stuck and cannot be made into the words. You have eaten all the sugary and briny unsaid words." He fit the pieces of the sliced tongue together and traced, with his knife, the cleft that divided it in two. "And this line here a chinaman once told me is the central line of our energies, it runs down the body and comes out our assholes into our holiest organs. ¿Ves?—from one versatile tip to the other! And that is why the tastiest parts of the beast are the organs deep within, for they are the keepers and transmitters of the energy, from one opening to the other. The flesh, the common flesh enjoyed by so many, is repulsive to my tastes. It is a suit of armor strapped and plaited over the skeleton to protect the tastier organs. It is as absurd to eat this armor-flesh as it is to eat the bones that hold it in place. Only animals relish the flesh, though my poor Tomás de Aquino will eat *anything*. The outside is common and bland (and remember this not only as a rule for developing a more sophisticated cuisine, but as a dictum for life in general), you have to dig, strip the armature away and dive into those cavities full of blood and urine and shit pools, to find the tastiest pieces of the beast."

El Rubio stood again and passed two dishes to Joshua, one, the brains au beurre noir, the other as of yet unidentified. He kicked his animal away. "Vamos, vamos try the first, but don't chew, don't chew, remember what I said about brainmeat. Let it melt in your mouth like a Communion wafer. Don't chew, you'll ruin the experience! Here, have a little burgundy, it'll go well with that other dish. Go ahead, taste it, see if you can tell me what it is."

Joshua was working hard on not chewing the chunks of pork brains, letting the pieces turn to jelly in his mouth before he swallowed. For all he had eaten, his hunger had not much dissipated. Perhaps, he thought, el Rubio had such a belly on him, Tomás de Aquino had such a belly on *him,* because this sort of food did not perform the natural role of food, to sate hunger. He washed down the last bit of brains, before it had fully melted, with a mouthful of burgundy. He sunk his fork into the other dish, some honeycomb-shaped organ cut into small pieces and floating in a mushroom sauce, and sprinkled liberally with kernels of white corn, sparkling like unburied jewels. Its aroma was stronger than the other dishes, and as he bit into the first forkful, Joshua realized what el Rubio meant, for in both the burgundy and this dish (which along with a honey sweetness that was consistent with its shape) there lingered a smack of some substance that made Joshua's cheeks blush at tasting it.

El Rubio's demeanor brightened. "¡Ahá! ¡Qué bravo! Already you have guessed, already, by the expression on your face, I see that you have guessed. Sí, sí, joven, you are enjoying the most delectable delicacy of them all. That is why I saved it for last. Magnificent and glorious goat tripe!—the beehive mouth of Hades, the sinkhole to the shit-canals! You have passed my test with flying colors joven! It is only the transformed soul, the true New Man of la Revolución, who is ballsy enough to chew on the spongy mouth of Hell with such relish, who has enough guts, yes guts (there is no other word), to venture into this most inner sanctum. Here, here, don't eat it all. It is too much for one person."

Joshua's impulses forsook him. He would have liked to throw the remaining contents of the dish on el Rubio, and on his shorn-headed servant, turned again from her mopping chore and clapping inaudible little claps with her tiny hands, prayerlike in front of her face, and on Tomás de Aquino, his tongue hanging out like a trembling limb; but he continued to eat the goat tripe with mushrooms and corn, each forkful becoming more and more gratifying, and the next more and more craved, as if he were eating backwards in time, and the more he chewed and swallowed the honeycomb tissue, the more he wanted more, till el Rubio stopped complaining that there wasn't going to be any left for him and sat back on his chair and clasped his hands behind his head and watched with a bemused and satisfied smile, moving only to refill Joshua's wineglass each time he emptied it.

As he was running in the darkness, barefoot and shirtless, away from el Rubio's house, Joshua tried to piece together the events following dinner that forced him to flee, without his borrowed boots and shirt-jacket. He ran parallel to the railroad tracks towards the hills north of the alfalfa fields in Caimanera, searching not for the paradise of tin roofs, but for the familiar (though long absent) fiend that had for a moment possessed him. The old woman Josefa had often told him that demons were wont to haunt the purlieus of paradise.

After he had finished the goat tripe, Joshua leaned back on his chair, extended his legs and let his arms drop to his sides. El Rubio continued to refill his wineglass, trickle by trickle from the burgundy bottle, till it spattered on the tablecloth and threatened to overflow, for Joshua made no move to have any more. He (el Rubio) said something of a dessert, a soufflé made from bitter cocoa and creole eggs from a hermaphrodite rooster. Joshua let his head fall back. He was going to pat his stomach and say he could not eat another thing for days, but he could not lift his arms and his tongue felt numb and leaden, as if some fat soft creature had invaded his mouth and died there. El Rubio had moved behind him and he put his hands on Joshua's shoulder. "I told you," he whispered. "It was too much for one person. You should learn to listen to me. It is not good to overindulge in tripe. It can prove downright toxic. But look at you, you are all wet. You'll catch pneumonia if I let you sit here like this in the evening chill."

With the heel of his palm, he wiped beads of sweat from Joshua's brow and pushed Joshua's flaccid body forward and removed his shirt-jacket. He threw it towards the india and commanded her to wash it. He circled in front of him, squatted, and removed Joshua's boots and wiped the mud from his feet and in between the toes with the tail of the tablecloth.

"What you need is a warm bath to shake you from this stupor. Woman, a bath, run a bath for el joven. He has proven quite a hero! Let him feel the pleasures of the falcon-legged bathtub and so that he may know why it is so difficult to part with it, why the murderess wants it back!"

El Rubio slid one arm under Joshua's legs and the other under Joshua's back and lifted him from the chair. He stumbled backwards and came down on one knee.

"Coño, you are heavier than you look. . . . Or is it the wine?" He tried to get up but could not muster the strength. He shouted to the indian woman, directing at her the rage for his evident weakness. "A bath, woman, a bath I say, why are you standing there like an idiot!"

He rocked Joshua's body up and down and Joshua burped and tasted the fluids of his stomach inside his mouth and felt a ticklish string of drool seep out.

"Good, good, it will pass," el Rubio said in a lullaby voice. He adjusted the bulk of the limp body so that Joshua's back rested across the thighbone of his raised leg. Joshua's head fell back and hung from his neck with the urgent pendulousness of a ripened papaya. His hair came loose and grazed the brick-paved floor. El Rubio wiped Joshua's mouth with his shirtsleeve and passed the edge of his thumb over Joshua's lips, then he cupped his palm on the back of the head and lifted it. "Let it pass, mi cielo. You have proved a Hercules in your appetite for the tastier tissues. Pero acuérdate, it is true that many, gods and mortals alike, have ventured into the underworld; but he who while in that land tastes the fruit, belongs there."

Joshua could not make any sense of the words that were spoken so softly to him. He figured, by their tone, that they were meant in kindness and condolence. He burped again and gurgled out bits of the honeycomb tissue coated with burgundy-flavored phlegm. He closed his eyes (the only voluntary motion of which he was presently capable) and felt the nausea ebb for a moment, but in a snap it returned and his left eyelid began to quiver, as if some tiny insect were trapped in its folds.

"Woman," el Rubio screamed, as he readjusted his hold on Joshua. Thrusting his belly forward and leaning Joshua's body back on it and locking his arms to form a bottomless cradle, he heaved himself up with a great grunting effort. "Woman, I say, why don't I hear water running? The situation is getting ugly here, coño. Woman!"

At this, perhaps disturbed by el Rubio's voice, the trapped insect in Joshua's left eyelid began to grow. First, it extended a loosened leg past the bridge of the nose into the other eye, so that it quivered even more violently than the left one, then it burrowed with its mandibles downward into the centerpoint of the head, so that Joshua felt a buried throb as if someone were stabbing him from the inside out, then the growing critter began to unfold and whip its pointy tail, stinging first the cheeks, and down to the lips and the jaw and into the throat, snapping the vocal chords, so that Joshua's head began to rattle from inside like a live maraca, and his whole body fell into the rhythm of the infernal noise.

"Woman!" El Rubio grew nervous. Joshua's possessed hand boxed him in the ear. His heels buckled into his thighs. El Rubio extended the spastic body away from him and cautiously set it down as if it were a live wire. Tomás de Aquino whimpered and hobbled into the kitchen. "Woman, I say!" The india ran towards Joshua and gently pressed one knee into Joshua's chest. She forced open his mouth and pressed four tiny fingers down on Joshua's tongue. "Don't bite me," she admonished Joshua, holding his jaw open with her other hand as if he were a crocodile. "I know you can hear me. Por favor, don't bite my little fingers off."

At the sound of her wheezy voice, as if in choreographed moves, Joshua's body slowed its floor dance, and his limbs lost all spring again and his hips all rhythm and his jaw loosened and he rested, the eyelids still, as if in a deep slumber. The trapped insect had escaped. The india slowly pulled her hands out of Joshua's mouth and wiped them on the folds of her black dress. Joshua was at peace, and in his trance, his absence, as if with eyes and ears that did not belong to him, he saw and heard the woman and her master arguing.

The india shouted at the man she worked for.

"¿Idiota me dices? You could have killed this poor boy. ¡Idiota eres tú!"

El Rubio sighed. He rubbed a spot on his thigh where Joshua had kicked him. He shrugged. "It is your cooking woman, not mine." He shrugged again. "Is the bath ready?"

"You are not touching *this* boy! Are you blind to such an obvious omen?"

"Woman, el joven had a bad reaction to your food. If it is any omen at all, it is that the gods don't give a shit for your food. But who cares?

Fortunately for you, *I* love your food. Now do as you're told. A bath will help purge him."

The india picked up Joshua's head and put it to her breast. "I said that you are not touching *this* boy. It is enough with what you, what we, have already put him through. He rebels against our spell. The gods are with him."

"Woman, you know I don't believe in your magic."

"No you don't, though you are the benefactor of it, though you have seen my spells and implorations work a thousand times, witnessed how they cursed the blood that runs through the veins of your enemies and brought unhappiness to their homes. What else but my *magic* would have brought down such a mighty hero like Julio César Cruz? What else but my *magic* would have delivered so many shorn-headed mujercitas and so many more innocent muchachitos to a disgusting beast such as you?"

"Woman, please, the neighbors like to listen. You too have had your pleasure in this."

"Let them listen. Yes, I have had my pleasure. Let them listen. What do you care? You don't believe. I'll tell them all. I'll tell this very boy here what we did, see if he doesn't wring both our necks." She pushed Joshua's head back away from her chest and held it in both hands and spoke to it abjectly, sotto voce, with a rueful seriousness, as if she were addressing the skull of a long-lost loved one, or the shadow of a confessor through a screen. "Last night, after I had told him about you, this ogre here swallowed 104 kernels of white corn. One hundred and a-four that's eight times thirteen, the numbers of the two wiliest orishas. One hundred and a-four—we have tried other numbers, other combinations, but only this one works—"

"Woman! ¡Cállese!"

"One hundred and a-four, swallowed the kernels whole without chewing. (He knows how to do it by now.) Without chewing, like pills, for we must pick them out of his shit the following morning. All one hundred and a-four, for if one is missing the spell is ruined—"

"¿Pero estás loca? What if the boy is hearing this? Woman!"

"Where do you think I was this morning when you dropped by for a visit?" She leaned closer and whispered into his ear, ". . . under a gaslamp in the henhouse, picking white kernels out of his morning shit! Found only eighty-two, so I made him drink two cupfuls of seawater. Eighteen more came out as he crouched down and the watery shit splattered over the terrified hens. The last four I had to go in there with my little fingers and find myself."

El Rubio flexed back his leg and extended it, landing the point of his boot square on the india's sternum, separating her from Joshua. Tomás de Aquino howled in the kitchen. "¡Loca, te has vuelto loca pal carajo!" Joshua's head dropped and bounced on the brick-paved floor. He stirred. He brought one knee up. El Rubio crouched and wrapped his hand around Joshua's waist and lifted him onto one shoulder, holding him tight, one arm wrapped around his thighs, one hand pressed on his buttocks.

"That's right," the india tried to scream but her pierced lungs would not let her. She clutched her chest where el Rubio had kicked her. She spoke in a gurgly low voice, as if a flood, summoned by her master, were rising to drown her voice. "You are all his, the spell is simple but powerful. The gods cannot save you. You ate the kernels, in that last dish, that touched all his insides. He is in you and dwelling in your softest parts and you are his forever." She coughed and her mouth filled with blood. Her body was twisted with convulsions and the veins in her neck thickened and she struggled in vain for one more breath. And then, like a spent swimmer, she gave one last jolt upward and let go, as if something had been ripped from her insides.

Joshua came to his senses. A lightness tickled the insides of his head, as in the dreams where the invisible black birds captured him, their claws sunk into his back, or when he drank the rum Marcos made in the tin tub of his outhouse. He struggled and el Rubio tightened his hold. He closed his fists and slammed them into the small of el Rubio's back where he imagined the kidneys hid, buried under all the fat. El Rubio laughed, as if a woman were attacking him with her small clumsy fists. Joshua grabbed the back of el Rubio's jacket belt and pulled himself downward. He tumbled off el Rubio's shoulder. El Rubio toppled backwards with him and held on to the hem of Joshua's pants. "No, no, mi cielo, qué haces? Don't listen to that witch. Stay, stay and I will bathe you." His blue eyes had gone gray, and for a moment Joshua imagined the spell of the white corn was working, for he felt no scorn, no loathing for this fat marica with his hand on his leg. "Stay, mi cielo."

Joshua jerked his foot away and hurdled over the folded lifeless body of the india. Her head rested on its side, with one cheek in a pool of blood. Her eyes remained open. Josefa had once told Joshua that those who die with their eyes open die wisely, for the spirit has no use for eyes. It is better to leave them here on this earth, where others may find use for them. He remembered this as he ran out of the courtyard without looking back, without further lending an ear to el Rubio's shameless supplications, or the bullmastiff's piercing howls.

High in the Banyan

Joshua ran past the town of desolate small streets of Caimanera till he saw the skeletal shadows of the towers near the frontier. He turned west towards the river and crawled on all fours through the bushes and the high grass. The mines were easy to avoid, hidden in little pine boxes, clunky and evident even in the thickening darkness, like a scattering of disinterred child-sized coffins. He circled around them. When he came upon the fiend, the companion of his childhood who had so often inhabited his body, who was a scorpion egg that hatched in his left eye and grew to inhabit all of him, he was amazed and a bit frightened to see that he was as black as the invisible birds that lived in the pinetops of the valley. But he wore no uniform and carried no weapon and lived in the water and not the trees. He was naked, knee-deep in the river near the yanqui base. The blinking lights of the yanqui airport were within sight, they beckoned and teased with all the promise of a giant Christmas tree. The top of the fiend's bald skull, the bones of his wide shoulders, the ripples on his chest and in his belly caught the moonlight, caught the flickering yanqui lights. He let himself be visible. He was turning in circles urinating, and the steamy stream was his whirling tail. The river was infested with crocodiles and they surrounded him and snapped their jaws as the tail of the fiend slapped off their snouts. They too seemed to fall into a trance, paralyzed by the same little illness. And for all their sinister crackling, they knew better than to come any closer.

"Hey!" Joshua screamed, struggling against the mesmerizing effects of the fiend's circling tail. "Hey! ¿Qué haces aquí? Are you too abandoning us? Fleeing into the stolen yanqui land?"

The black fiend was startled at the sound of a voice. His sparkly tail disappeared and the crocodiles snapped out of their trance and came at him.

"Coño, coño, me cago en tí," the black fiend screamed, as he high-stepped over the snapping jaws onto the shore. He came at Joshua and tackled him. And then suddenly they were surrounded by flashes of green light that seemed to emit from the bushes and the grass, as if the very earth and its progeny were burning from inside and alerting the guards in the towers that there were traitors amidst. No, Joshua thought, I have not come to cross the frontier. The earth is wrong. I am no traitor.

The crackle of the hungry alligators was joined by the crackle of machine-gun fire. The bullets pierced the air and slashed into the riverwater. Sirens wailed. The black fiend grabbed Joshua by the hand and they ran, hurdling over the wooden-box mines, deep into the wilderness and away from the spray of machine guns, away from the ghostly green flames, and away from the blinking stars of the yanqui airport. They climbed a banyan and settled on one of the higher branches, one that shot no roots earthward. They heard the barking of dogs beneath them and they heard more machine-gun fire and when they grew tired of hanging on to the branch, the black fiend threaded a thick vine through his legs and arms and he lay stretched like a hammock. He told Joshua to lie on top of him, for if the guards shone their lights up into the tree, they would surely pick out his pale white-ass torso and shower it with bullets. Joshua obeyed only after the frontier guards began to randomly spray nearby treetops with bullets, only after the fiend had told him his name. He lay belly up on the human hammock whose name was Triste and the hammock threw up his legs and wrapped close his arms and shut in around him like a cocoon. Triste assured him they were safe, that not even with the eery green light that for some reason Triste called *inferior* red could they be seen. He would not let them be seen. His skin would grow cold and dark and colder and darker till it absorbed *all* light, even the green light that makes heat visible, and the giant banyan itself would be consumed in the utter blackness and disappear with them. Joshua wanted to believe him. Wrapped in the hammock of flesh, he felt untouchable. They were as invisible as the black birds of the valley.

High in the banyan, invisible from the ground as they were, the white one inside the black one, the warm one inside the cold one, hanging pouchlike from a thick vine like the leathery roost of some winged branch-hopping lizard, they talked in whispers.

Tell me.

Tell you what? I am hot. I can barely breathe. I don't like this.

That's too bad; I don't like it either. I am cold. I can catch pneumonia. But if we switch positions, they'll marry us with their bullets.

Marry us? Óyeme, you're not a marica are you? Is this whole mierdero town full of maricas?

This whole Island is. Ya casi no quedan hombres en Cuba. What's the point? . . . Marry us—I meant the bullet that kills one of us, kills the other, we are one when the bullet comes, married.

You are *a marica. ¡Oye!*

Tranquilo, muchacho, don't toss around like that, the vine will rip. Tranquilo, I don't go for boys with bleached hides. You are much too white.

I am white. I am proud to be white. Sin pena ninguna. My mother is of Castillian blood. My father is the whitest man on the Island. But I am no marica, keep that in mind if you get any urges. Respeten a los machos, coño. That is where all your troubles stem from, maricas don't respect men when they are true men. You think all men are, at heart, maricas and pájaros and bugarrones.

Al contrario, we go far beyond respect, we treat the true macho with the sort of adoration that only the Virgin Mother deserves. . . . Who is your father?

El comandante Fidel Castro.

¿No me diga? Bueno verdad, the whitest man on the Island. Why were you fleeing from your father's house then?

I wasn't fleeing. I was looking for you.

For me?

I thought you had left for Miami a long time ago. That's what the doctors at the Communist Youth League said when the seizures disappeared, that my faith in la Revolución had driven the fiend, the possessor away, sent him packing with the gusanos to Miami.

The possessor? ¿Estás loco, muchacho?

*But they lied. You were here. You had not left. You were hiding in Guantá-
namo the whole time and you possessed others. You drove the heroic comandante to
suicide, you drove the widow Alicia to murder, you drove the old woman to madness. My mother knew it. That's why she sent me on this mission, to face you one
last time. But you won. You grew in me again, you won the last battle and you
were crossing the frontier at last, a victor, against me, against el Rubio, against the
india who summoned you with her implorations, even against the poor crocodiles in
the river.*

*Save your breath, muchacho, we may be up here a long time. I wish you were
making sense so that I could defend myself, but you are talking like one who has
just awoken and is not sure whether he is still trapped in the worlds of his dreams.*

Joshua did not heed the warning to ration his breath. He went on talking
for the entire two days and nights they spent atop the banyan, his ramble
interrupted only by short naps or when Triste, annoyed with the endless
tale, closed in the cocoon so tightly, sealing the cracks where flesh joined
flesh, so that there was no air to support speech. But even then, once the
cracks reopened a little bit, Joshua did not heed the warning to shut up
and ration his breath. He told Triste of the apartment on Cardenas Street
where he spent his days alone as a child. He told him of sitting on the
rusty iron-grill balcony and letting the little illness descend on him, a relief from the sweltering heat and the babble of the vendors and passersby
on the street below. It was like being asleep and being awake at the same
time, the only discomfort a blunt pain in the hollow of the nape. He did
not notice the day turn to dusk, turn to evening and came to only when
his mother shook him and told him it was time for his lessons, his geom-
etry problems, his Bible reading and his daily memorization of a Milton
couplet, not in translation, but in the original. English would serve him
well, his mother said (when his time came). Joshua shivered, his eyelids
trembled, the pain had moved up into deep inside his head, but he had
not noticed. The day had passed unnoticingly and his mother was back. It
was time for his lessons. He had mastered the nature of spheres and cylin-
ders, he could feel them orbiting in his mind. He had reached the section
in the Bible where the Lord commanded his namesake to cross the Jordan.
He could recite the fall of the rebellious angels in the wishy-washy language of the enemy. It was time for his lessons and the little illness ebbed.

Then one day they had to leave the apartment on Cardenas Street. One
day, his mother revealed to him the identity of his father. His mother
called him the whitest man on the Island. When they took his mother
from him and transferred him to the State hospital, the little illness worsened. The tic in his left eyelid spread its tangle of roots deep inside his
head and used the pulp of his brain as nutrients. The fiend grew like a

weed in rich soil. It took his body. It took his mind. It snatched for his soul. He told the doctors it felt as if a scorpion were growing inside him. The doctors told him the scorpion was a yanqui scorpion. They told him his illness, they called it a *grand* illness now, was a symptom of his bourgeois degeneracy. *El trabajo te curará,* they said. *Work will cure you. It will make you a man.* He was put into the Communist Youth League and sent to the cane fields for six months. In the fields, where the cane harvesters joked that the sun shone as if it suffered from an incurable fever, his seizures vanished as the doctors had predicted. How could he not then believe in la Revolución? What ingrate does not believe in the miracle that has saved him?

He did not see his mother for five years. By the time they informed him that he must accompany her in her exile, he had forgotten her. He had no family. He had risen in the ranks of the Communist Youth League, was a *vigilante,* an informant to several CDR's. La Revolución was his family, his compañeros, the brothers he had never had. *No,* the leaders of the Communist Youth League said, *no te equivoques, la Revolución has not gone as far as to forget the need of mothers. You will accompany her. You will watch her to make sure she does not stray from the path again.* During the trip to the Valley of the Nightingales, in Charo's leaky boat, still wearing his crisp Communist Youth League uniform, he did not speak to her. When she tried to force conversation, he dug in her bag for her black leather Bible and leafed frantically through it. His mother laughed; she said it was obvious no one had bothered to continue his daily lessons. She stumbled over to him and looked over his shoulder and helped him find the passage he was looking for. She pointed at it with her dirty fingernail. "Read it. Read it to me."

Joshua refused. He shut the book.

"Read it, goddamn it," Charo shouted, turning from the wheel.

His mother reopened the book and found the passage again. Charo repeated his command and said it was a capital crime against la Revolución to disobey a captain in his boat. Joshua read, shouting against the wind and the roar of Charo's boat engine with the words from Matthew:

> For I have come to set a man against his father, and a daughter against her mother, and one's foes will be members of one's own household. Whoever loves father or mother more than me is not worthy of me; and whoever loves son or daughter more than me is not worthy of me.

"Coño, está jodío el chico comunista," Charo said, "what a thing for a young man to read to his mamacita. Toss that vile book into the sea!"

Charo's scorn was just a prologue for the scorn with which all the native islanders treated the new villagers. These were the ancestors of the runaway slaves that had established the first homes in the valley. They had seen the white soldiers, the Fidelistas, the legions that served the whitest man on the Island, in their olive drab come and go. But now they had sent one to live among them. *Envidia,* his mother pronounced, after all, they were the first in the valley with a generator, which ran the refrigerator, the television, the air conditioner (part of the deal his mother had made with his father—*if I'm going to move with mi querido hijo to a village stuck en el año de la cometa, give me at least the modern conveniences*). In 1968, the tide of progress, the glory of la Revolución, had not yet washed over this remote valley surrounded by limestone walls hundreds of feet high. Joshua told Triste how his mother tried to win the natives over with the wonder of electricity, cooling their water with crushed ice (which turned to hooks of anguish within their rotted mouths) and inviting them to her bohío to watch Fidel's speeches on the black and white console (which seemed to them like a gray demon's rattle compared to the ubiquitous coloratura of their bird-infested land and the chill air like the unfathomable breath of a long-interred corpse). Ultimately, she could only win them over by becoming one of them, by toiling in the fields just as hard, by forcing her son to stop wearing his young communist uniform, by sharing the fruit of her labors just as generously; and by reading to them from her favorite book of the Bible, which rendered the simplicity of labor as the only human gesture devoid of vanity. It was clear, these men and women and children, descendant of runaway slaves, who had not intermarried, who had obstinately kept their blood dark and thick with the bile of suffering, had built an ideal revolutionary community long before the gaunt bearded white gods had descended from la Sierra. La Revolución had not come here because its doctrines and tenets, fresh and vulnerable as newborn babes to the overprotective regime, were deemed here old and stalwart as the tallest pine. Or as the native islanders put it more bluntly: *esos dichos del Che y de Cara de Coco son más viejo que cagar sentao.* Here was their home, the mother told her son, here he would become a paragon for all future revolutionaries, here he would learn from the truest and oldest revolutionaries on the Island, these sons and daughters of slaves, to outshine his father for when the time comes to dethrone him from his seat in the capital. "But cover your head and your body from the sun. Inherit the blood in their hearts, not the pigment of their skins."

But it was they (the natives) who risked inheriting the pigment of *his* skin, they who were not as stubborn in keeping their dark lineage pure as his mother believed, their young women who taught him the rules and strategies of love and who over three years bore six children each colored like coffee with *un chorrito* of milk, future heirs to the throne in La Habana who were kept hidden in the bohíos and not allowed out in the fields or near the river to play with the other children, future heirs to the throne in La Habana who would never know of the white face of their grandmother or the whiter bearded face of their fabled grandfather, whose flesh color resignedly revealed the heritage of both the sinners and the sinned-against.

The second morning dawned, and high in the banyan, invisible from the ground as they were, the white one inside the black one, the warm one inside the cold one, hanging forebodingly from an overexerted vine like a giant black pod of misery over the earth, they heard the nearby barking of dogs and they whispered.

I am thirsty.

Sorry, that line has already been used by a very famous persecuted one. Think of something a little bit more original.

I wasn't trying to be original. I'm just thirsty. What is wrong with you? With all of you?

They have made us crazy. We have let them make us crazy.

I'm going to go crazy if I don't get some water. Let me go. I'll sneak to the river and get us some. What is wrong with you—aren't you human? aren't you thirsty?

I haven't been talking quite as much as you have. . . . If I let go of you, those dogs down there will make your pretty white flesh look like shredded coconut pulp.

Oye, oye, I told you, no funny stuff. Don't call me pretty, I am not a girl. Vaya, la Revolución gives liberty, to all, even maricas. Pero respeta, keep it amongst yourselves. I told you, dejen a los machos tranquilo.

If we were to leave los machos alone, it would be no fun being a marica.

Oye, te dije, respeta. ¡Ay! Wait till my mother hears of this, wait till she learns that I spent a whole night inside the flesh of another man, a man blacker, and more pure a descendant of slaves, than any native of the valley.

I am not a man. You said so yourself. I am the fiend that possesses you. I am the scorpion of your childhood dreams. Forget about your thirst, go on with your story. Another day and the dogs will have their tongues hanging down to their paws. They'll tire of looking for us and climb back up in their towers, and we'll climb down and sneak to Guantánamo.

Ay sí, Guantánamo, I have not told you why I came.

Joshua told Triste of the tub that had belonged to the Spaniard Jesuit and then belonged to comandante Julio César Cruz and then belonged to his widow Alicia and now belonged to the fat fairy they call el Rubio.

Alicia? You know Alicia Lucientes?

Yes. I will tell you.

Yes, tell me, for though I have never met her face to face, she has a place in my heart.

Joshua continued to speak to forget his thirst. He told Triste of the others who were sent to the valley, to recover from their lapses of faith under her mother's care. With the aid of the natives, and through her sermons on the beneficence of simple labor, she had become a sort of priestess; she had established a reputation. *The finest revolutionary therapist on the Island, Granma* reported in a back-page story. The weak, the renegade, the infidel were sent to the valley like the ill to a sanatorium.

Alicia arrived not long ago, a convicted murderer, an eater of revolutionary words, her own reputation also solid: *the most famous dissident on the Island.* The invisible black birds, like the unseen storks who transfer unborn souls into our world, dropped her off at the entrance to her mother's bohío. As early as the third afternoon of her stay, his mother proclaimed that this most famous dissident ever sent to the valley, this wordeater, this murderess, would be her most renowned convert. Thus Alicia's odd request to have her falcon-legged bathtub brought to the valley must be fulfilled. She said she could converse with the ghost of her husband when she bathed in it. Joshua's mother said that all phantoms must be exorcised, that she would convert the ghost of the dead comandante, if necessary. She sent her son to look for the falcon-legged bathtub.

Joshua told Triste of his journey to Guantánamo, of his visit to Alicia's mother and daughter, of el Rubio and his indian woman. He told him of Father Gonzalo's system of aiding and abetting runaways to flee into the yanqui base. He told him of el Rubio again, and of his foul breath, and of the india, and of her black frock and shorn scalp, of Alicia's old house and of the simple majesty of the falcon-legged bathtub, its fullness and flexures as alluring and beckoning as a cubanita's hips. He told him of the feast of innards, described to him the vaporous qualities of brainmeat, of the current of blood still coursing in the flavor of heartmeat, and he told him of the spell of the white corn, the imploration of the fiend of his childhood . . . and finally, he told him how el Rubio had punished the india for revealing their secret, how he had planted a boot on her chest and murdered her. *And I ran from there like a coward, without my prize, without my falcon-legged bathtub. I did not dare fight this blond devil.*

Triste spoke at length for the first time:

There's a story of the Sierra that the one that I once loved told me. I do not know how much of it is true. It is about a guerrillero with a blond mane and a blonder beard. Fidel—your father—had ordered his execution for some perverse crime involving a guajiro's young son. (It was the first law of the rebel band that no harm shall be done to the villagers of the mountain, that their crops shall not be stolen, that their animals shall not be slaughtered, that their bohíos shall not be pillaged, and that their mothers and daughters shall not be raped. They forgot to mention their sons.) Early on the morning of his pronounced death, before it had brightened, the blond man visited the rebel chief at his cottage in La Plata. He asked to be left alone with him. The guards laughed at this. What, they said, are you planning to take el Líder with you? But your father, being your father, never one to turn his back on a dangerous situation, shooed the guards away. He was left alone with the condemned blond man. The blond man took off his boots and his uniform, took off his undershorts and handed them to your father. The brittle sun-toasted hairs shone on his concave chest and on his engorged belly and on his spindly legs and on his woman's arms like bristles of gold. He asked your father for a knife.

Your Father, knowing that the man was a virtuoso with a blade, but knowing

*also that no creature in so meek a state would dare raise its hand against him,
searched for his stiletto and handed it to him. He turned his back on the condemned
man to fix himself some cafecito. The condemned man waited, the steel held aloft in
his right hand, till your father turned back to look at him. He reached down and
grabbed his testicles with his left hand and stretched the skin of the sac and put the
knife to it. He mumbled that this and much more he would do to save his honor and
to be allowed to devote his life to la Revolución. Your father stared at the man. He
waited. And as the blond man started to slice into the skin of his sac, your father
grabbed the blade. Thin streams of blood spread over each side of the sac. Your father
grabbed the condemned man's cojones. He told him that once, when he was a student
in La Habana, he had held in his hands the eyes of a man that had been blown
out of his head by a terrorist bomb. He said that it had felt not much different than
these little huevos. He said it was not surprising that these two organs that were not
quite inside and not quite outside the body should have the same texture.*

*He stood. He let go and wiped his hand on the seat of his pants. He told the
condemned man that this vile act was a further proof of his cowardice and that he
was not impressed. He called in the guards. He repeated what he had said when he
first proclaimed the death sentence. He said he hated to lose such a skilled soldier.*

*As word got around the rebel camp of the blond guerrillero's attempted self-
mutilation, others were more impressed than your father. They debated in hushed
conversations whether any of them would have the courage to commit such an act,
even to save their lives. Che himself was heard to say that the ability to repent is
one of the most sacred of human attributions. That it is not on the weakness with
which a man commits a crime but on the sincerity and strength with which he re-
pents that he should be judged.*

*Pressure was put on your father to revoke the sentence; and though it was never
officially revoked, your father must have listened, for the execution was postponed
and postponed and postponed till the events of the war, the lack of skilled guerrilleros, erased it from memory and the blond guerrillero was given back his rifle
and bayonet and joined the column with Alicia's husband, commanded by the boisterous comandante Barba Roja, and proved his bravery in skirmishes against
Batista's Rural Guard, charging into enemy strongholds, with the abandon of a
man already dead, and advancing his fame with each blow of his bayonet into a
rural guardsman's chest. Because Alicia's husband wanted nothing to do with the
post-war government, this blond guerrillero, whose death sentence had never been
lifted, was given command by Barba Roja over the revolutionary police force in
charge of the city of Guantánamo. This is the man you feasted with, this is the man
living in Alicia's house. Apparently, he has not forgotten his talent for raping
young boys, has not repented for his sins as well as Che imagined. We will go to
this little dictator (doña Adela was right in calling him that); we will take from
him the falcon-legged bathtub. And if necessary we will fulfill the sentence that has
never been lifted, we will carry through the forgotten command of your father.*

Joshua, throughout this, heard the voice of the black man whose flesh
surrounded him, as he imagined his namesake must have heard the voice

of the Lord as He instructed him to cross the Jordan, from nowhere and from everywhere at the same time, so that he not only heard it, but he smelled it as unnerving as the sweat of the black natives of the valley and tasted it as pungent as cut tobacco leaves and felt it as the electric tingle of untouched flesh and saw it as pinpricks in the mantle of darkness, and the man who was blacker than any he had ever seen promised him the same promise beyond the power of mortals: *Let me and I will not fail you, I will not forsake you.*

Joshua responded, he squirmed inside the black hanging egg like a chick ready to crack open its shell, and he forgave himself for letting the black man love him, for the black man was no man at all, but the fiend that had been in him so many times before.

High in the banyan, invisible from the ground as they were, the white one inside the black one, the warm one inside the cold one, before the dawning of a third light, the dogs had ceased their barking, the frontier guards had relented and returned to their skeletal watchtowers, and the cocoon opened and the weakened vine threaded backward through his arms and his legs, and Triste fell to the earth and like a mountain cat landed on all fours. He quickly rose to his feet and caught Joshua in his arms. They ran from there. Triste unearthed his campesino costume from a hole near the river and they waved good-bye to the crocodiles and sneaked to the bus terminal and took the first packed worker's bus back to Guantánamo.

An Annunciation

Alicia stopped him. She did not want to hear the end of the story, not now. It was already ugly enough as it was. Her home town was one of the provinces of Hell. Visitors returned with calamitous tales like gods from the netherworld.

They had boiled water potful by potful on the iron stove. Twice Joshua had to interrupt his story and go fetch more wood. They filled the tub halfway up and by the time they had poured in the last potful, the growing night breezes had cooled the sitting water. Alicia brought out her suitcase. It clinked like a loaded milkcrate. She had collected in discarded rum bottles certain oils and extracts from the native herbs and fruits of the fields. She had done it just to fill her evenings, when tired as she was, sleep would not come. She did not dare imagine she would ever again sit in her falcon-legged bathtub. She did not think that Maruja and the women of el Comité could fulfill her second request any more than they could fulfill her first request for the company of her daughter. She sat on the edge of the bathtub and asked Joshua to sit by her.

"It was you, after all, and not them, who fulfilled my request."

Joshua sat just far enough from her so that their legs would not touch. Alicia said she had not noticed before, but that indeed he had the same type of body as her husband, and that is why he fit so well into his guerrilla pants.

The bottles were unmarked, so she sniffed at the lip of each to make out its contents. She reached each bottle out to Joshua and let him sniff. Some she recorked and put back into the suitcase, some she used, adding a few drops into the bathwater and stirring it with her hand. She did not ask Joshua for his opinion, though once or twice he gestured as if to offer it. She said that though it might not seem it, there was a precise art to this admixture of aromas and alleviants.

"Even water, our purest element, can be made purer." She said she was an expert at it, that if she lived another life, she would become an inventor of perfumes and medicines, a healer of the stinking and the unsound. She would not marry or ever have a lover.

Joshua said that beautiful women, no matter how independent or successful, always had husbands and lovers. It could not be helped.

Alicia said she would choose then not to be beautiful.

Joshua said that one does not choose such things, that a woman has no power over her beauty, or for that matter, over her ugliness, whereas a man has no use for his beauty and can overcome his ugliness with feats of strength and courage.

"If you would have known my cousin," Alicia said, "you would have seen how you are mistaken, you would have seen how effortlessly beauty can stir in the shape of a man, without paint, without jewels, without gowns, artless and benign as the west wind." She added crystalized pollen dust from one of the bottles into the bathwater and stirred it in with her hand. She looked up at Joshua and smiled at the thought of this young man, shaped like her husband but with the head of a girl, who so desperately wanted to grow into a man, a guerrillero, a true son of his father. Would he have fought in the Sierra had he been born a decade earlier? And would he now be one of the overfed swine roaming the Palace of the Revolution? His innocence crushed by the weight of military titles and appointments to councils and committees and ministries?

"In fact," Alicia said, frightened by the thoughts she knew she should not word, "although it is clear your mother has as much distaste for mirrors as she does for clocks, if you want to see how much *use* beauty has in a man, you should go to the river tomorrow morning and stare at your reflection."

"I am not of that kind, señora. And I did not say that beauty has no use for a man, I said a man has no use for beauty, the more he wallows in it, the more his manhood vanishes."

"Is this what they are now teaching young compañeros? And what of the beauty of women?"

"Oh that, claro—¿cómo no?—that a man must appreciate, but even then not so much as to go weak for it."

"No seas bobo, what great man has not fallen into the epilepsy of love a hundred times, at least once irremediably. Didn't Mark Antony forsake Rome for Cleopatra, David murder for Bathsheba, and that pale English king renounce the throne for a yanqui divorcée?"

"It has not happened to my father."

"No, así son las cosas de la vida, unfortunately it has not happened to your father."

"He has kept true to his pledge to keep the welfare of the Cuban people foremost on his mind. His bride has always been this Island."

Alicia thought that one look at Celia Sánchez, Fidel's most famous paramour, with her narrow hips and fleshless form, her mule's gait and guerrillero's wardrobe, would at once explain why his father had never knelt at the altar of feminine beauty. But these thoughts she did not word, lest Joshua might take it as an implicit offense of his mother, a less famous though much more beautiful rumored paramour. Instead, she stirred the water one last time and thanked Joshua for bringing her the bathtub, and told him that he best go, for she wanted to step into the water before it cooled too much.

"Pero señora Alicia, I have not finished my story. I have not made the announcement that I came here to make. I'll wait. I'll go into the bohío and shut the windows and the doors. I will not peek. You must trust me."

Alicia began to protest. Joshua stood and raised his voice: "On my honor as a compañero, you must trust me." His voice grew deeper and he pounded the edge of the bathtub with the side of his hand. "I have not finished my visitation." He stood and went from her and entered the bohío through the back door.

She did not see the shadow of his arms pull in all the wooden shutters, so her valley home seemed as if it were closing its eyes on its own volition. *He has not finished his visitation,* Alicia grumbled to herself as she turned her back to the blind bohío and stepped out of her dress, covering her breasts with her arms till she had lowered herself into the bathwater—*his visitation!—el pobre, he has believed my mother, ha cogido complejo de ángel.* She put her head back against the edge of the tub and stretched her legs out and let the purified warm bathwater do its job, remove her from her senses, so that she lost track of time and forgot the weight of her limbs and her organs and the more cumbrous heft of her thoughts. Later, when she had dressed without drying, she walked to the back door of the bohío, arms again crossed over her breasts, and knocked lightly. Joshua opened it. The gaslamp was lit. He looked bemused. He told her that throughout the length of her bath (almost three quarters of an hour) he had heard her speaking to her husband and to her cousin and to her daughter. Alicia said he had misheard, that she would not be speaking to her daughter for her daughter was not yet a ghost.

Joshua assured her that this was so, that her daughter was not yet a ghost. He asked if the water was still warm, and if she may permit him to bathe in her tub.

Alicia told him it was not good practice to bathe in someone else's water unless that someone else was your lover. She looked for a reaction in his eyes, in the curve of his lips, in the shade of his cheeks, but saw only a child waiting expectantly for permission. She told him that he was welcome to do as he pleased.

"Bien," Joshua said. He stepped lightly around her and went outside. Alicia shut the door. She set her chair by one of the shuttered windows. She turned off the gas lamp and sat on the chair. Gingerly, with the point of her index finger, she pushed the near shutter out till she had sight of her bathtub and of him. He was already out of his pants, his arms raised upward, as if he were praying to the moon. His dark thick-muscled hairy legs and lean pale smooth torso made it seem as if he were the fruit of some unholy coupling, a creature of the lower orders, half-man, half-something else. When he was done stretching, he turned to the bohío and called that he did not know any ghosts, then he corrected himself and said that yes, in fact, he did know two ghosts, but only one that he wished to speak to. Alicia did not move, did not blink. He stepped into the tub and settled in facing her, his head resting on the opposite side of where Alicia's head had rested. He called out that the water was still warm. He splashed it on his face and on his hair. He submerged his entire body and stayed under for more than two minutes. When he came up, he hung his arms out of the tub and breathed in gulps, the cage of his ribs pushing out on his skin. He spoke not raising his voice, as if he well knew that she was watching him and would not miss a word he said. On their journey back, Triste had tried to show him how to breathe underwater, though it was clear he had not learned so well. Before that, high in the banyan, Triste had shown him how to make love, that he had not learned so well either, though he would get better at it, it was just that he was not one like Triste, like her cousin, like el Rubio. But la Revolución makes room for everyone, el Rubio should have known that, should not have had to resort to his devilish schemes. La Revolución is tolerant and wise, it encompasses all humanity, all acts, all sexes, even the third one. It was just that he, the son of his father, was not one like them.

"He's coming, you know, your beautiful-like-a-woman cousin's giant black lover. He's coming to recount to you the tale of your cousin's death. He's coming to beg forgiveness in the name of those that could not save him. He's coming to our valley. He too now is a dissident. He will be blamed for both murders, though he only committed one. Vaya, with my help."

Joshua stretched his legs one at a time, raising them and holding his ankles with his hands and pressing his forehead to his knee. He then submerged his entire body again and remained under far longer than the time it would have taken to drown any air-breathing beast or brute.

EIGHT

Monologue of Triste the Contortionist:
The Thirty-Mile Swim

¿Qué cómo? How else? I swam.

No me crees. I see it in your eyes. You don't believe me. How else does a fugitive like me, un negrón tan jandango, get to see the most famous dissident in the Island. I took off from Playa Girón, walked into the waters, desnudito, así salí, y así llegué y te asusté.

Gracias. Gracias. The blanket is good. I was getting cold.

How else? I swam. The longest stretch was over thirty miles. No me crees. . . . I see it. You don't believe me. But one day (when we're both free), I'll show you. It *is* thirty miles from Playa Girón to the most northern point of Cayo Largo. Me llamo Pedro Ovarín. But no one has called me that in a long time. I've been known as Triste all my life. Ever since I was a kid, ever since I first put my left foot behind my right ear (like this), ever since I could graze parts of me with the tip of my tongue, in my abuelita's bed under the mosquitero, that other children dared not even touch with their hands (*that* I won't show you . . . I'm sorry. Perdóname if I am vulgar). I am a contortionist, a famous one who once loved one that you once loved. My abuelita said that I was a happy child till I started twisting myself into odd shapes. No me acuerdo. I have no memories of happiness.

¿Cómo? I swam. How else?

You are beginning to believe me. Your eyes are beginning to know who it is that I am. I promised him that I once loved that you once loved I would see you. So now you see me.

And it *is* thirty miles, though you don't believe me.

Gracias. Gracias. The soup is good. I was getting cold. I love garbanzo stew. What a great sense of humor Fidel has, no crees?—imprisoning you near a town called La Fé, where the gods shit colored stone, in a hole full of nightingales, surrounded by forests where they mine for nickel and tungsten.

Do you know what tungsten is? It's a metal that most fires can't melt. You can't bend it like this or like this (don't be so amazed, that's only my fingers, you should see what I do with the rest of my body); tungsten is not a contortionist, it won't bend, even in the fires that flow in the hidden underground rivers of the earth. It would make the best prisoner—tungsten is immune to torture.

He too was imprisoned on this island that is the eye of the Island. So he was once you. He that murdered the ones you love was as you are now, inside the eye, trapped in a hole from where you can't see ni puta mierda. Perdóname, my tongue is dirty. He was a good swimmer too—Fidel. ¿No me crees? But he never tried to escape from this island prison. I swam *in*. You believe me now. Yes, I'm tired.

Gracias. Gracias. The cafecito is good, better than the blanket, better than the stew.

I told you and you believed me. I promised him—not Fidel, but the one that I once loved that you once loved, and *he* believed me. I could see it in his eyes. So I had to swim in; and I'll swim out when the time comes, because I am a better swimmer than Fidel. He never dared swim out. He was pardoned, as a child is pardoned.

The one that I once loved that you once loved that his men murdered, do you remember his name? Is that why I have no memories of happiness?

Don't tell me! I swam. Water gets in my ears. It drowns all my memories.

¡Ay! Gracias. Gracias. The rum is good. Me encanta el ron, more than the blanket, more than the stew, more than the cafecito. I'll remember now. And then I can tell you why I came here. How I swam.

Give me a hint. What was his hair like? The one that I once loved that you once loved.

Don't tell me. I swam. I'll remember.

It was like wool, like tufts of black wool before it is woven into yarn. Ves, I remembered. My abuelita is wrong. I do remember happiness, even if sometimes it is twisted out of shape, like the ringlets of his hair (once, he let it grow long—he did not shear it until they made him—and just like his hair was then, wild and dark brown and twisted and twirled into all shapes, such was my happiness). That's what I had chosen. Do you remember happiness? Do you remember brushing your cheeks against his hair till they were scratched with joy?

You are beginning to believe me. What was his name? Do you know?

Don't tell me! I swam. The water gets in my eyes. But if I can just have a bit more, maybe things will clear up.

Gracias. Gracias. Yes, that's good. It is no longer cold. I love rum. It heats me up inside, better than the blankets, better than the stew, better than the cafecito, mucho mejor. I swam. The longest stretch was over thirty miles.

You are beginning to see him, the one that I once loved that you once loved. His eyes? What color were they? Give me a hint. Don't . . . don't tell me! I remember. My abuelita was wrong when she nicknamed me Triste.

His eyes were sometimes the color of a long-aged cognac or sometimes the color of boiling honey. And I did not like it when I loved him and I did not see them, for when I loved him, the one that I once loved that you once loved's eyes closed, and just from under the lids, light-droplets the color that was the color of his eyes seeped out and clung desperately to his curled thick eyelashes like water on a dolphin's back and then were blown out into the air and dispersed and disintegrated as stars that have lost their course. This was the wilderness in him, that clung to his eyelashes in ochre dewdrops, that was my happiness, that my abuelita will never know. She called me Triste. And now they all do, and it is who I am.

You are beginning to remember happiness. I believe you. What did your abuelita call *you*? Do you remember his name?

Don't tell me! I swam. Why else wouldn't I remember. I swallowed too much seawater. It changes me on the inside. It blanches my memories. His mouth? His lips?

His lips, they were full, as if three or four extra layers of flesh had been stretched there and softened and colored over time by his breath, like the flow of the warm undersea shapes a coral reef. I remember. Sometimes too they were salty and when I tasted them I thought of the seawater. But we were far from the sea. We could not swim. Yet his lips were salty.

Gracias, pero no. Gracias, no. No more rum. Not yet. Not now. Not while I'm remembering what his breath tasted like.

Don't tell me! I'll remember. I was not Triste, though everyone called me that.

Like a late spring breeze peppered with pollen, yes, flowing with invisible nectars, not too warm, though warm enough; breath I could taste and swirl in my mouth and feel its heat in my chest when I let it in me, and much much more intoxicating than this rum. I'd be drunk for weeks and I'm still hungover to this day, even though I swam, and the sea with all its galvanic stings should have cured me.

You believe me. You know. That's good. Now I'll take some more. Gracias. Gracias. The rum is good. But it is a poor man's moonshine compared to his breath.

And when I loved him, the one that I once loved that you once loved's breath stuck to me and I did not bathe till I knew I could touch him again, and my skin, all of it, smelled of him, because his breath had sunk into my pores and spread throughout so that I was him, and when the guards would separate us, for weeks sometimes, sometimes longer, and I loved myself, it was him I loved and I called his name from my tiny cell where my head would bump if I stood up and where I defecated and urinated in one corner and crouched in the opposite corner, my head turned to avoid the stench, and *then* my abuelita was right.

What was it that I screamed when I loved myself as I was loving him. Give me a hint. Do you even know? What did your abuelita name you?

Don't tell me! I'll remember. I swam. The longest stretch was over thirty miles. I walked into the waters at Playa Girón and the three girls that were the girlfriends of the soldiers were alone on the beach and as I walked into the waters afterwards, their girlfriends stared, porque estaba desnudito, así como llegué y te asusté. They stood and shielded their eyes from the sun with their hands as if saluting me (like their soldiers had taught them, seguro), and they followed me, they waded in as if they smelled their soldiers' sweat and their soldiers' spit on me. But the seawater is harsh and it washes quick, ridding the skin of its memories, so the girls waded back to wait for their soldiers who were still with each other. I swam long (thirty miles was the longest stretch, from Playa Girón to the most northern point of Cayo Largo) and my encounter with the soldiers left me empty, so on the white-sand beaches of Cayo Largo I loved myself and he was not there, the one that I once loved that you once loved. His breath was not in me. And what's the use of loving yourself if you're only loving yourself, if there's no one's breath seeping through your pores, if there is not a trace of what it was like to once have your arms around him so that his smell was yours, not yours to keep, but yours as your own body is yours and will not be yours at the day of reckoning.

His body. I remember. My abuelita was wrong. Por favor, don't tell me. I remember.

Holding him was like handling a caged bird. In every muscle, even the tiny ones that wiggled his monkey toes, there twitched the hollow-boned urge to fly, so that it felt as if I would let go, he would take off from me (like the magic balloons abuelita bought me at the circus the first time we went) and soar into the boundless blue sky and become a speck and then vanish, as if he had found a portal to another world. How could I let him go then, even after I had loved him, hidden by the tall gray-green stalks in some unshaven lot of the cane field, even though the dagger leaves stabbed at us, and we knew that the guards knew we were missing, and even though he could not really fly away, for he would have done it a long time ago and abandoned all his tormentors, those heartless bestias who also professed to love him, but in the end murdered him.

Don't stir. It is not something you don't already know and have not known for a long time. You would not be here in this island that is the eye of the Island, trapped in a hole from where you cannot see ni puta mierda.

I'll have some more rum. You should have some yourself. Gracias. Gracias. This at least numbs the brain, dulls what I remember. It is almost as strong as the seawater.

Though when I wake, I always remember. My abuelita was wrong.

We were lovers almost from the start, and though he was very young, fifteen then, he was not innocent. He had been a lover before. This I knew from the first night, when after a performance, he came to my sleeping cart with a bottle of bourbon. I could not stand the bitter taste of it. *He* drank it without grimacing. He said his maestro had taught him.

What was his name? The maestro? The one that taught the one that I once loved that you once loved how to drink bourbon and how to fly?

He talked at length about him. There was not much room inside my cart, so he sat on my bed and swigged the bourbon straight from the bottle, and he pushed closer to me, letting his hand wander up my thigh, saying how great I looked all twisted and bent on the St. Peter cross. *(Chévere, your arms and your legs looked like black serpents choking a young tree! And your long white nails were the twenty fangs with which the devil ate the baby Jesus.)* He'd had too much. I took the bottle from him and he fell back and passed out in my arms. I leaned my face close to his and his breath smelled like fresh cut pine wood. I kissed him on the cheeks, tucked him in my bed, and left my sleeping cart. I finished what was left in the bottle, growing more and more accustomed to the tongue-pricking taste of the liquid that was the color of his eyes in the gaslamp light. I remember. My abuelita was wrong. Although I was not sure if the great pity I felt was for him or for me. In the morning when I returned to my cart he was gone. Four nights later he came back and he did not pass out and I did not leave.

What did your abuelita nickname you? What was his name?

Don't tell me! I'm swimming in rum and I'll remember.

Much later, after the liberators came down from the mountains, bearded and thin, but not thin like the one that I once loved that you once loved was thin, not lithe like him, but thin like starved, so you could count their ribs, even the little tiny one that's no longer than the thumb at either side of the belly, after they had decided who would share in their liberty, and after they had excluded us and hunted us down and forced us to learn the process of love again, taught us like children what was right and what was wrong, o mejor dicho, forced us to unlearn what was wrong, to forget everything back to the first time when that uncle who is only three years older takes me to a barren field on the edge of his father's finca, and forces me to pull down my work pants—they are stained and sticky with the sweet syrup of the cane stalks, so a lo mejor he just wants to wash them in the river—and I am tired and do as my uncle says, and even though my skin is black-black-brown, darker than the darkest cup of cafecito, de negro puro, as my abuelita says, I can see a patch on my lower legs, from where my work pants were rolled up to where my boots cover the ankle, where my skin is impossibly darker from the mud-sputter of the felled stalks; my uncle likes this, and when my ankles are resting on his shoulders in that barren field at the edge of his father's finca, he passes his tongue over that darker part of my legs, and I concentrate on his rosy tongue as it too blackens from the mud of the cane fields. I'll never let my uncle know how much it hurts because he sees it in my eyes watching his tongue, sees that beneath the riptide of pain passing over my body there runs a more powerful undertow of pleasure, a lightning current of joy, which I won't forget, long after my uncle who is only three years older has disappeared and a brigade of other men has taken his place. I remember; no matter what the liberators who came down from the mountain and decided who will share in their liberty did, no matter what my abuelita named me.

Gracias. Gracias. The rum is good. It frees my tongue. Sí, sí, ¿cómo no?—have some yourself.

When they had rounded us up and put us in their work camps they pretended to make us soldiers. They called the camps Military Units for Aid to Production. We were sent to the same camp, the one that I once loved that you once loved and I. I thanked Changó and all the saints for that, but cursed them in the next breath because they had let me become a slave again. Monday through Friday we were out in the fields. Fidel had promised the world the world's weight in sugar. And though every year he falls far short of the goal, he promises even more for the following year and sends his henchmen out to gather more slaves. Saturday was conscript relaxation day, which meant that families that worked all week at the factories or at the mills were forced to volunteer time in the fields while we got to play fútbol games with the warden's team. Changó forbid we were to win, though we did once or twice, no matter how tired we were from our labor in the fields, and paid for it on Sunday.

Sunday was conscript education day.

Aside from a few intellectuals and artists, mostly poets, whom Fidel had begun to gather up early on, almost as soon as he took power (though Fidel's real attacks on the intelligentsia hadn't begun, that would come later, when *they* who were supposed to be the forefront thinkers of our land finally dared to question the sacredness of la Revolución), most of us were maricas, as we were always reminded, for every sentence the guards uttered to us either began or ended with gran cacho de maricón, even to the poets, many who weren't really maricas, but who had always sympathized with us. As a reward, they were lumped in with us, addressed with the same insults.

I remember. Sunday was conscript education day.

There was the room with the magazines and the green projector and the machine with the four levers, each one with a different colored plastic cap, one red, one yellow, one black, one green, a four-note pianito with an infinite number of chords. I was the only one, it seemed, who could concentrate hard enough, keep my mind enough away from the pain, to discover which lever corresponded to which wire. I told the one that I once loved that you once loved in the fields the following Monday. He said he did not care, that he did not want to know, as did most of our other campmates. Why did I imagine that they *would* want to know? That if the bearded pianito player on the other side of the long wobbly table spread with open magazines and black and white glossies pushed the green lever all the way down, then the electric current would not flow through the wire attached to the folds of your anus (that was the black lever), nor through the one attached to your right testicle (that was the red one), nor through the one attached to your left testicle (that was the yellow one); the current would flow through the one attached to the underside of your penis, to the fleshy triangle where the head meets the shaft, which Sunday after Sunday had become scabbed and scarred, and from whose apex emanated the numbness that lasted for weeks and spread to the other points of their unholy sign of the cross. The green lever was the pianito player's favorite. The others did not want to know. But I remembered.

Sunday was conscript education day.

After breakfast we would wait and see who was selected. A doctor checked us, made sure the burns from any previous sessions were properly healed. On Saturday nights some picked at the scabs and scrubbed them raw to make them seem worse, but no one ever went more than three weeks without visiting the pianito player. After they had selected us we sat on the floor in a room next to the pianito room. We heard the shouts of who was weak and who had not learned the last lesson.

Sunday is conscript education day.

When they call me in I strip down in front of the others, but I know that they will not look. If they do, then it is noted, and it is a sin paid for not much later. I walk into the room with the four-note pianito. There are three men in there, all in uniform, their crotches bulging and trembling as if some tiny field mouse has been stuffed in there and is struggling to get out. Every time I visit, it is three different men. From the look on their faces this assignment is obviously a reward. There is a long wooden table on which lie closed magazines wrapped in brown paper. The four-note pianito, a simple metal box that someone buffs and shines every Saturday night, is set at the far left hand end of the table. In its corners I can see my broken reflection. Long wires, all the same color, a ghastly gray, sprout from under it like roots. At the end, three of the wires are shaved and welded to a thin metal plate, square and thinner than a coin; one wire is thicker and is shaved longer than all the others and the silver filaments at the end are opened and spread out like a spider with many legs. I know why. There are three finger-long pieces of medical tape dangling on my side of the long table. There is another longer piece of tape, which dangles just short of the floor. There is an empty chair on each side of the table. The one on my side is fitted with three leather straps on each arm and on each leg and another thicker strap around the seat. It is bolted to the concrete floor. Behind my chair is another smaller table on which is mounted a green crank-by-hand movie projector. A film is reeled in and set to go.

"No me mires la cara, negrón, maricón," one of the men says. I obey him. I lower my eyes. But I remember his face. Its skin is the color of wet sand. I remember his eyes. They are yellow, sprinkled with coffee dust. "Have you forgotten your place, negrón, maricón?"

I have not. I remember. I know exactly what to do. I have been in here too many Sundays. I give my back to the three men and bend down and rest my torso on the long wooden table. I feel four hands on my back, pressing down. I feel the field mouse bulge of one of the men brush against my right thigh. I try not to imagine who it belongs to. I hear him wet his finger in his mouth. He reaches into me and prods around with his wet finger, then he pushes his finger into me and leaves it in a moment and plucks it out. He grabs the thicker wire, the one I know is connected to the black lever on the four-note pianito. He wraps the shaved end of the thick wire around his finger and pushes into me again. When he pulls out I feel some of the silver filaments stay in and some spread out over the soft flesh around my anus. He rips a piece of the medical tape off the end of the long table and fixes the wire in place.

"Your asshole stinks, negrón, maricón." He spanks me softly, like a reluctant parent disciplining a child.

Sunday is conscript education day.

My eyes are still closed. The four hands on my back ease their pressure and they lift me and throw me back into the seat with the straps. Before I am strapped in, my bare feet are hoisted up and a shallow steel pan half-full of water is slid under them. My feet are lowered into it. The water is cold. The straps are buckled. The field mouse bulge of the man who stuck his finger in me is brushing against my right shoulder. Then it is not. I hear two more pieces of tape ripped off the end of the table and the man's fingers (they are still moist) lift my sac and affix two thin cold plates underneath it on each side, making an "X" with two pieces of the medical tape, plates connected to wires connected to the red lever and to the yellow lever. Then he lifts my penis and lifts the head and pulls the skin back and rubs the head between index finger and thumb and he lets my penis drop. I hear him smell his fingers, sniffing deeply as if having walked into a kitchen where his abuelita is preparing arroz con pollo.

"You are still not washing like we showed you, negrón, maricón."

He pulls the skin back again and affixes the last wire to the underside at the bottom of the head and wraps the longest piece of medical tape all the way around so that the skin remains pulled back. Then, with the loose ends of the tape, he affixes my penis up against my lower belly. He goes back to my right side and I feel the field mouse grazing me again. I try not to think about it. If my penis becomes aroused it will peel off my belly and want to stand on its own. I tell myself that I will not let this happen. But the pianito player is good, much better than the guards with the field mouse bulges. Aside from the magazines and the glossies and the films, he has at his command (depending on how far he presses down each lever and at what angle) the full range of chords of his instrument. He can please just as masterfully as he can hurt. He keeps a proper balance. He tickles. He stabs.

I hear the pianito player enter the room. I hear him sit down and slide his chair in. I hear him tap the thumb of his right hand on the table. I know the other four fingers are hovering over the four levers of the pianito, the index finger over the green, the middle finger over the red, the ring finger over the yellow, and the pinky over the black. He is waiting for me to open my eyes.

Sunday is conscript education day.

The pianito player is a simple-faced man with warm hazel eyes and a heavy peasant beard. He wears a sergeant's stripes, but his military jacket is three sizes too large on him and he is obviously not a military man. He wears also around his neck, dangling from a leather necklace, a cross whittled from the shell of a coconut. Because of this, because we have never known his name, because we only see him on certain Sundays and because he looks like a pastor, we call the pianito player Father. He approves of this.

"What is your name?" Father says when my eyes open. His voice is gentle. He remembers, but I must repeat it. We must have the same conversation every Sunday like a litany.

"Triste."

"Triste. What a beautiful name. Who named you that?"

"My abuelita."

"Triste, do you know the story of the angels of the Lord who came to stay at Lot's house?"

"Yes, I do."

"What did the men of Sodom want at Lot's door?"

"The men at Lot's door wanted to fuck the angels of the Lord."

"And what did Lot do?"

"He offered them his two virgin daughters instead."

"And what did the men say?"

"The men said no. They wanted to fuck the angels of the Lord."

"And what did the Lord do to the men of Sodom through the power of his beautiful angels?"

"The Lord struck the men of Sodom blind, struck them all blind, both great and small."

"Triste, since your last visit, in either thought or act, have you been at Lot's door?"

With his left hand, Father has begun leafing through the magazines with the brown covers. I do not lie to Father. It is no use. He plays the pianito too well. I can feel the current before his fingers even touch the levers. I can taste blood on my lips when there is none there.

I tell Father the name of the one that I once loved that you once loved, the name that I now cannot remember, then Father knows that I have confessed my sins and my education may begin again.

The Name of the One That He Once Loved That She Once Loved

"Héctor."

Monologue of Triste the Contortionist: At Lot's Door

Gracias. Gracias. The cafecito is good. Too much rum—you shouldn't have let me drink that much. I was tired. I dreamt of the white-sea tobacco fields after you told me his name. I dreamt before I was asleep, as I listened to the beautiful noise of the nightingales. You are fortunate after all. Fidel has banished you to a paradise. Thank you for telling me his name. Thank you for letting me dream of the white-sea tobacco fields again.

I dreamt of him as he had been that Christmas we were arrested, the day I dug into his chest with my long fingernails and pulled out the amethyst eye that had been his brother's eye, and in my dream other eyes danced out of his wound, varicolored like the set of marbles my abuelita had once given him when we stayed in her bohío on the edge of her brother's finca. My abuelita was always kind to him. Héctor was upset over his brother's disappearance. (We did not know then Juanito had been taken. We thought he had just upped and fled and Héctor took it hard, saying his brother had abandoned him, just as his maestro had.) Héctor swallowed all the marbles, twenty-six of them, one by one. That night I pressed my ear to his stomach and I could hear the marbles clinking against each other, as if children inside his belly were playing with them. It took ten days for him to pass them all. He hid at dusk out in my abuelita's brother's tobacco fields, under the cover of the cheesecloth that is like a giant mosquito netting that protects the leaves from hungry insects and from too much sun. The field is full of shadows when it is covered with the giant cheese cloth. It is a placid white sea. The phantoms of the blind men at Lot's door passed through the air and through the surface of the white sea. They danced around Héctor when he shit the marbles and Héctor's dark pinga stiffened and the skin lightened as it grew and he rubbed it against my bare back when he was finished, after he had wiped himself with the leaves lower down on the plant (because these were the driest). He rubbed against me under the cover of the white sea as I broke apart his warm lumps (that were sometimes soft and passed like mud through my hands and were sometimes hard and had to be pressed with both palms to crumble them) and I looked for the marbles that had passed, like a miner sifting for gems. It took him a week and half to pass all the marbles and every afternoon we would go out under the giant cheesecloth that is a white sea and strip and he would rub against me and ask me where I thought his brother had fled to and I would not answer and count the marbles that had passed and later I would wash them in the river. Like the phantoms of the blind men, we too could live under the surface of the white sea, but now and then we needed to come up for air.

Gracias. Gracias. I'm sorry I brought no clothes. But the swim was long. I feel like a ruined Roman emperor wearing all your blankets and bedsheets.

After I dug into his chest and pulled out the eye that was the amethyst eye and swallowed it so that the guards would not take it, Héctor fell into an unwakeable sleep, slept for two days in the military truck they kept us chained in, slept when they dragged him into the holding quarters in the abandoned hotel, and slept till they questioned us five days later. In the truck the wound bled till it entirely soaked his gray T-shirt but Héctor slept. His eyes were gyrating behind their closed lids and a light that was the color of his eyes was seeping out. I knew then he would make it. I knew what he was dreaming about. My chained hand was just able to reach him. (After I had dug out the amethyst eye a guard, who thought we had been fighting, came into the truck and beat us both in the ribs and in the stomach with the butt end of his rifle and tightened the chains around our chests and around our waists. I pleaded with him to get Héctor a doctor. *Que muera,* he grumbled, *los maricones merecen morir.* But Héctor did not die. Not yet.) His eyes were gyrating. I was just able to reach him. I undid his belt buckle and grabbed him and stroked him and tickled him underneath with my long fingernails like he liked till the light that was seeping out of his eyes flickered and my hand was wet with him. I tasted my hand and it was full of life. I thanked all the saints that my tongue had not been chained. The guard was wrong. Héctor did not die. Not yet.

Later, when they asked Héctor how he had been wounded, Héctor did not answer them. They presumed he had tried to commit suicide, that shame had finally brought him low. When they asked him if he still liked to put hard penises in his mouth he looked up at them, sleepy-eyed, with a tight-lipped smile, and told them he would much rather have them up his ass now. . . . I feel as if I know you well, señora Alicia, but still perdóname. Pardon my dirty tongue, pero la verdad es la verdad. I will not refrain from telling you everything just as it was, not even these parts. I will pretend I am not speaking to you but to the wild nightingales outside your windows, who in spite of their song know well of the savagery of this world.

The two guards who were with the questioner, the blond police captain of Guantánamo, el Rubio, beat him and opened his wound again. When he asked me the same question I lied. But they knew and they beat me also, till I told them the truth and they made me recite all the places in my body I loved to have hard penises, as el Rubio poked me with his finger in all the different spots of my body he wanted me to recite. That week we were given work clothes for the fields and sent to a labor camp in Camagüey. There were five months left in the sugarcane harvest.

In the bus on the way to the work camp our hands were manacled to the bars of the seats in front of us, one long chain running through all the manacles from the front to the back of the bus. The windows were shut. It was a hot January morning and inside we could barely breathe. Héctor sat behind me. He was unconscious again. In those days after the arrest, it was as if he had been struck with the sleeping sickness. He would awake only when we were moved from place to place and then fall right out again. His wound had become infected and there was no color seeping out from under his eyelids. There was enough give on the long chain so that I could twist my torso and reach back and touch his face. The man seated next to him, an old gypsy with a long cigarette-yellowed beard, who had been a laborer at the circus, had his hand on Héctor's thigh. I slapped it off. "Tranquilo viejito sucio." The old man snickered. Three of his front teeth were missing.

"Is it true that this pollito is yours?" he said.

I ignored him and he put his hand back on Héctor's thigh. I slapped it off again. Héctor's pulse was distant. Little by little, I stole enough give on the long chain that bound us all together—the men up front yelling back at me every time I managed to gain a link or two—so that I could reach back and pull up Héctor's work shirt. The old gypsy stared and put his hand on Héctor's belly and rubbed it in circles. I slapped it off a third time. With a needle I had fashioned from the shaved-down tooth of a metal comb they had neglected to take from me, I pierced the infection under Héctor's left nipple. Pus streamed out and ran down his belly and collected at his navel in a pool. The old gypsy dipped his finger into the pool and put it in his mouth.

"Está rica la leche del pollito."

I ripped off my own work shirt and cleaned Héctor's wound as best as I could. I undid the hem of my work pants and with that thread and the metal needle I temporarily sewed up Héctor's wound with five clumsy stitches. As I was trying to lower Héctor's work shirt back on him I noticed that the old gypsy had snuck his right hand behind Héctor and inside his pants and was fingering Héctor's ass and masturbating with his other hand. The old man came and a small wet spot spread on the bulge of his work pants. I threw a punch at him but the chain didn't reach and my arm snapped back. The men up front took this opportunity to steal back the give on the chain and my body was yanked away from Héctor and away from the old gypsy who still had his hand in him. "Your pollito is dead," he said. "His asshole is cold as an ice cube."

The men up front had stolen all the give in the chain and my body was pressed forward, my wrists pressed against the bar of the seat in front of me and I could not move. I turned my head and saw that now the old man had his head buried in Héctor's lap.

"Cold," he mumbled, his toothless mouth full. "Cold all over."

When we got to Camagüey and the guards mounted the bus and they found him, with his head still buried in Héctor's lap, they beat him on the head with their rifle butts till his head was thrown back with one blow and smashed against the window. I heard his skull crack at the end of their rifle butts. He emitted a tiny moan, not much unlike the snicker I had heard previous. Then the guards began to pound their rifle butts into Héctor's chest. I started screaming that he was unconscious, that he had nothing to do with the old gypsy, that he had been raped. The guards pushed me forward. They saw my shirt was ripped off. They laughed and asked me if the old gypsy had tried to rape a big negrón like me too. They hit me in the back with the rifle butts. I fell off the seat and they pushed me forward with their boots. I was still manacled and as I lunged past the seat in front of me it felt as if both my arms up to the elbow had just been dipped into a pool of fire. The sensation spread up my arms and into my chest. Héctor never felt the beating, never woke up as they pounded their rifle butts into him. They broke eight of his ribs and one jagged end punctured his left lung. They took him to a hospital in the city. I got away with just a bad wrist sprain, though I couldn't hold a fork in my right hand for a month, and in the fields I had to swing the machete left-handed. All my hours I thought about Héctor, and regretted that I had listened to him and dug out with my sharp fingernails the amethyst eye that was his brother's eye from underneath his left nipple. He would not have caught the sleeping sickness. I would not have lost him.

Gracias. Gracias. Estoy muerto de hambre. Me encanta la tortilla. Yes, yes, more cafecito also.

That is why they did not let you see him for over three years, because it took that long for him to recover. It took that long for him to regain the rhythm of his breath and the cognac color of his eyes, that long before I could show him again that hard amethyst ball that was his brother's eye and roll it over the rosy ridge underneath his left nipple, the old socket sealed shut till four days after his death, a massage Héctor liked because he said that as I gently pressed down with the stone on the scar, the nerves danced underneath and they tickled his heart.

But I'm getting too far ahead of myself, I'm skipping over too many parts in my eagerness to let you in on la verdad of those last days. I must go back, back to the white sea, for under it swim the reasons why I dug out the stone that was his brother's eye from under Héctor's left nipple and swallowed it, why he succumbed to the sleeping sickness that permitted the yellow-bearded gypsy to rape him and the guards to break his ribs and rupture his lungs. I must return to the white sea, if for a few moments, señora Alicia.

We had so much fun under the cheesecloth of the tobacco fields for the ten days that he passed the marbles that he challenged me to swallow them now. We had washed them in the river and were keeping them in a pouch made of tobacco leaves, the ones high up on the plant, which are the strongest. He said that if I could hold the twenty-six marbles longer than ten days, then he would let me do anything to him under the surface of the white-sea tobacco fields, let me follow my lust for him to *any* measure. Claro, I agreed. If I couldn't, if I passed the marbles in less than ten days, then *he* would be the master and I the slave. Again, I agreed. Just the same. To heighten the thrill, we would keep our hands off each other till the bet was over. To this I was not so quick to agree. "It's just a game," Héctor said. "It'll be fun." So I gave in.

The sheriff had told my abuelita that morning that he was sure Héctor's brother had run away, had gotten sick of the circus and fled, maybe back to Santiago de Cuba to find his mother. Two weeks before, my abuelita and I had ridden in her mule and buggy through three towns westward and then three towns southward. Not one villager had seen the boy with the amethyst eye. It was past midnight by the time we returned. Héctor was waiting for us, sitting at the kitchen table, drinking bourbon. My abuelita snatched the bottle away from him. Héctor cried. I asked him if he wanted to go visit his mother at the asylum to see if his brother had gone to her. He said no, his brother had not gone to her, his brother had been taken. I asked him how he knew. He told me he just did. My abuelita said she did not understand. The following morning my abuelita and I went out again in her mule and buggy and she brought him back the gift of the varicolored marbles.

"Vamos, Triste," he said. "Swallow them. It'll be fun."

My abuelita was right. He was still a child. So I agreed to play his game. I swallowed the twenty-six marbles as he drummed with joy on an overturned tin milk bucket.

In those days I was studying ancient Assyrian texts and learning to master the inner movements of my body as well as I had mastered the movements of my limbs. On certain weeks I fasted, I fed only on coconut juice and drank water with lemon juice. I drank seawater to cleanse my insides. By the fourth day of my fast I could feel my stomach inside me as tactile as I felt the fingers at the end of my hand. I moved my stomach from wall to wall of my belly-cavern. I could undo my small intestines and tie half-knots in them. I could drop my heartbeat to ten or eleven beats a minute and without moving any part of my body, without exerting myself, I could raise it to over two hundred beats a minute and break into a sopping sweat simply by bending backwards, by doing what yogis call the bow. Other weeks I gorged, I filled my insides to see how far I could stuff myself before I lost control of my functions, cagándome donde sea. I ate everything my abuelita fed us and then I left Héctor and ran to her old brother's finca cottage on the other side of the mountain and ate there, sat at the same table with my uncle who is only three years older while he felt me harden underneath the table. He stroked me and stroked me, so vigorously that the table began to rumble, and his old blind father lifted his head from his plate of congrí, and moved his muddy eyes from side to side. I saw sweat droplets being born on my uncle's upper lip, but I did not wet his hand like my uncle wanted me to. I had learned to control *that* also. Irritated, my uncle banged his hand on the table (the one that had been stroking—it was rosy with exertion and the veins pushed up out of the fair thin skin). He screamed at his father never to serve this ingrato food again. His father lifted his head again and when he laughed rice flew like pellets out of his mouth and he told his son to stop talking nonsense, that I was only a child.

Héctor and I went to the fields under the white sea late in the afternoon of the day after I swallowed the twenty-six marbles. I had already eaten seven meals. I was ready to explode. I left a pile at least a foot high. Héctor sifted through it with his long fingers. Not one marble. He accused me of cheating. The following day he kept a close watch; again I held myself and out in the fields under the white sea late that afternoon, I crouched and left a bigger pile than the day before. Again Héctor searched through it in vain, soiling his arms up to the elbow. Again no marbles. Again he accused me of cheating. He said I had tricked him, that I had not really swallowed the marbles. I told him I would prove his accusations false the next day. He told me he was not ever going to let me touch him again. He left me. I saw him later, masturbating furiously under the folded yellow and gray leaves of a dead plantain tree. His work pants were down to his ankles and his underwear just below his knees. His torso was much darker than his lower body, as if he had been dipped feet first in some kind of cleansing solution. I could tell when he came, his ass squeezed tight and dimples formed on each side. He wiped his hands on the dry leaves and ran into the kitchen of my abuelita's bohío to try to find where she had hidden the bourbon. I knew, but I did not tell him and I did not want to play this game anymore.

The next day Héctor dug twenty-six marbles from the pile I had left behind. He smiled wickedly.

"Yo soy el dueño y tú el esclavo," he said. I knew my abuelita would not like us playing this game for her mother had been a *real* slave, but that afternoon under the folds of the white sea, I was glad to be a slave, I was glad to follow my master's every command. By evening, as we emerged out of the white sea, Héctor shoved me and set me free and he said I should not have felt sorry for him and let him win.

The following week, while we were readying to join the gypsy circus for its winter tour, someone left a package on my abuelita's doorstep. It was a shoe-sized box wrapped in butcher paper. Inside was a tiny leather pouch with Héctor's brother's glass eye, clean and polished. That night, I told Héctor where abuelita had hidden the bourbon.

Drunk, Héctor sliced his chest open with one of abuelita's kitchen knives, right underneath his left nipple, and buried his brother's eye there. He had me stitch it shut on each side with my abuelita's sewing kit, so that the glass eye, with the amethyst facing out, would not pop out. It took twenty-three stitches, thirteen on the inside, ten on the outside.

Why?

(I know you're too gracious to ask so I'll do it for you.) Why should I do such a foolish thing, assist him so in his madness? I have no answer, señora Alicia, only that his grief touched me so that I was again his slave, as I had been under the white sea, and I would have done anything he asked.

But you know all this, you know how Héctor became the acrobat with three eyes. But what you might not know is what he became like after he recovered from the fevers, the attack his body put up against that foreign object in his chest. That part he hid well from his family and from other performers at the circus and even from my abuelita who (after the photographer who had become his guardian abandoned him) assumed the role of his protector and housed him whenever he was not touring with the gypsy circus.

Three things happened after the fevers, after the amethyst eye in his chest became like an eye that sees, that scar-lining around it rosy like lids, the hair above from Héctor's nipple like eyelashes. One, he could not sleep. Later he became proud of his talent for insomnia, but at first it frightened him and he kept me up at night, pressing wet tobacco leaves against the eye on his chest because it would not shut and kept him from sleeping. When he gave this up he would get up and wander the fields and then return to my room in my abuelita's bohío and sneak under the covers of my bed, waking me by nestling in with his back to me and pressing the cold muddy soles of his long feet up against my thighs. Two, he could not get drunk; which doesn't mean that he did not drink—al contrario. He never stopped drinking his bourbon now. He drank two or three bottles a day (switching to rum when he could not find a yanqui to sell him bourbon) and was always sober as a surgeon, alert as an owl. And three, he was never satisfied sexually.

That winter it started, bad enough so that sometimes I would not see him for five or six nights straight; and when other performers—acrobats and strongmen and even clowns—would give me the smug look, I knew Héctor had come to their cart the night before. But Héctor cared for none of them and eventually he would come back to my cart, knock timidly on the door to wake me, bottle of bourbon in hand, and sneak under the covers and press his soiled bare feet up against my thighs. The longest he spent with anyone was the three long weeks he went to the luxurious sleeping quarters of Georgina the Manwoman. Georgina was a prima donna and a yanqui—from New Orleans, though I think she might have been born in the Middle East and was once a confidant of Héctor's maestro, señor Sariel. She was a big draw and demanded the finest accommodations. (Georgina, as she proved during her no-children-admitted show was both man *and* woman, but he preferred to be addressed as *she*.) Her sleeping quarters were like a powerful sheik's traveling tent, with wooden platforms covered with serapi carpets that established four different levels—her bedroom of course on the highest, the bed the size of a small pond, covered in white linen and surrounded by a silk mosquitero. It took ten hours and sixteen men to put up and dismantle her tent as we moved from town to town. The yellow-bearded gypsy who raped Héctor with his finger was on Georgina's crew, and I can imagine how happy he was during those three weeks, cutting an eyehole in her tent so that he could return at night and watch Héctor's ass bouncing in the candle shadows of Georgina's fourth platform, or his long feet fluttering in the air and getting tangled in the silk mosquitero like a giant pigeon trapped in a thick cloud-sheet. *That* vision—the yellow-bearded gypsy watching from outside and loving Héctor from there—hurts me more than Héctor being there in that bed, with that freak of nature who had the face of a wounded angel and the organs of a man covering the organs of a woman. Y que Dios me perdone otra vez, I was glad when the guards cracked the old gypsy's skull.

After Georgina, none of the other circus performers could satisfy Héctor. He was hurt, for this time he had not left. She had thrown him out one night and told him it was time she find herself un hombre de verdad.

"Ya estoy cansada de maricas," she said to him on the last night, and handed him his bundle of clothes and led him out of her tent, naked as he was. "I need a *man*. Adios entonces, mi bellísimo, mi mariconcito." She kissed him on the cheek and patted him on the ass and drew shut the tent folds. Héctor cried as he cuddled in next to me that night, but I did not have the strength to console him or to make love with him, even though he was aroused all night and kept pushing his ass into me. I just held him.

By then it was the late summer of 1957. When we got back to my abuelita's bohío near Baracoa to rest for the upcoming winter tour, Héctor escaped to the mountains, where the bearded liberators were hiding. Héctor scribbled a note and left it on my grandmother's kitchen table under an empty bottle of bourbon, saying he was going to become a "revolucionario." Without him, attendance was cut in half at the gypsy circus and the few who attended spent most of their time at Georgina's show, or heckled Jorge the Ringmaster when he announced the substitute for the acrobat with three eyes, a dwarfish Chinese–Puerto Rican tightrope walker named Cundas with a round kind face and feet *bigger* than Héctor's. Which is how Jorge answered the hecklers.

"Miren coño, how can you not be impressed! Look at those magnificent feet!"

Cundas would then balance himself on one foot and lift his other foot from the rope and wiggle the six-jointed toes, and the strip-muscles on the balls of his foot vibrated like the strings of a piano during a violent symphony. Still, the people were not impressed and they renewed their shouts for the three-eyed acrobat.

When Héctor returned to my abuelita's late in the spring of the following year and snuck into my room, and under the covers of my bed cuddled beside me and pressed his feet to my thighs, I thought for a second it might have been someone else. His feet had grown a few inches—as if in envy of Cundas—and were crocodile callused and when I went to rub his cheeks I found whiskers.

"How is the revolution, mi barbudito?" I whispered into the nest of the back of his head.

"Llena de mariconerías," he answered and began to push his ass into me. This time I did find the strength to forgive him and to please him.

Gracias. Gracias. I will have a bath if you have drawn one. It will be an honor. This tub is almost holy. Un rélico de tipo. The bath is good. Warm. It heals the wounds of last night's rum, yesterday's swim.

He had served under your husband's brigade. This your husband may have never told you, how he first came to know your cousin Héctor. But it wasn't at the circus. Your husband became a big supporter of the circus *after* la Revolución triumphed. He knew Héctor in the mountains. Héctor penetrated the jungles of the Sierra in less than a week and made it to the rebel headquarters, high at La Plata. No offense to the memory of your fine husband, señora Alicia, but Héctor told me that once he had made it into their midst and they saw how beautiful and harmless he was, all the guerrilleros took to him, even Fidel. And your husband filled up this very same tub that I'm in, that we stole, that one was murdered in (sí, sí, that tale will come), and after he had filled it and made the water warm as you have done for me, your husband bathed Héctor, washed his limbs with coconut soap, for Héctor had not eaten much since he fled from my abuelita's bohío and he was too weak to wash himself. They fed him banana bread and goat's milk and dressed him in a campesino's smock and let him rest for two days, even if he could not sleep. When they roused him, they gave him cups and cups of cafecito and more bread and goat's milk. Héctor became so joyous and wired that he danced for the rebels and did somersaults in the air. They gave him a guerrillero's uniform and boots and a rifle (by then the rebels had raided many of the government's armories); but he gave them back the rifle and the boots and the uniform—keeping only the faded-olive wool beret.

"The jagged rocks will make picadillo of your feet, muchachón," your husband said to him.

"No, comandante," Héctor said, affixing his beret and saluting your husband. "I can walk on the edge of una navajita without getting cut. It is my art. I am a ballerino with wings!" He did another somersault and your husband's men applauded and your husband's mute blue-feathered rooster tried to crow but his vocal chords were as untuned and useless as those of a sea-buried piano. The men demanded that both Héctor and the rooster come with them when they moved east on the mountain range. But your husband feared more for the lives of this monkey-boy and his rooster than he did for his own.

"This is a war, not a circus," he grumbled to his men.

"War *is* a circus!" one of the men answered. He was an aging, weak-kneed guerrillero who grew gray whiskers no thicker than Héctor's and had once been a well-off tenured history professor at the LaSalle boys preparatory school in the Oriente province. Your husband did not feel like debating the merits of war with him and he reluctantly agreed to bring Héctor and his rooster along.

Because he could move so much faster than the other guerrilleros along the rugged terrain, Héctor soon began to lead. It was humid and warm. Winter only visited them at night when the long rains were chilly and misty and slow-falling, like shavings from a frozen heaven. Héctor tore his guerrillero's smock at the collar and pulled it down below the shoulders and tied the sleeves around his waist so that it hung on him like a long wide skirt. The guerrilleros behind him whistled and your husband reprimanded them as if they were schoolboys. Héctor moved on. He wrapped his feet tightly around the jagged rocks—perhaps this is why they grew so much in eight months—he willfully stretched them on those rocks to better handle the sierra-terrain. And that is why he so easily fled from them when he decided it was time, why your husband knew better than to chase him.

But at first he was fine, a vowed revolucionario. It was the third and last indulgence Fidel allowed your husband. The first was the mute blue-feathered rooster, which your husband carried with him everywhere perched on his shoulder. Then it was *this,* the falcon-legged tub. It took four men to carry the thing with them. Fidel had a fit when, a few weeks after they had landed on their victorious and promised return from Mexico on a leaky boat named *Granma,* your husband disappeared with six men and went to Bayamo, to the finca where he had lived after his university days to claim his bathtub and his rooster. Your husband was clever though. The first night he met up with Fidel he had water boiled in a rusty cast-iron pot and let Fidel be the first one to bathe, the other comandantes, even Che, washing him and then drying him off as if he were already the emperor and they his slaves.

"It's still a danger," Fidel said after an hour-long bath. "But we'll keep it. It'll lift our spirits."

Fidel's brother Raúl berated him. "¿Somos guerrilleros o niñitas de baño?"

Fidel took the towel from your husband and wrapped his index finger with it and stuck it in his ears to dry it off, then he scrubbed dry his beard. He felt drowsy and he knew how to end the argument right away. He wrinkled his nose.

"Bueno hermanito, from the smell of you, if there's anyone who needs a bath around here it's *you!*" He motioned for his cigar and lit it. "Fill the bath for Raúl."

"¡Nunca!" Raúl said. Fidel shrugged his shoulders and sent Che after him. "We'll keep the bathtub, compadre," he said to your husband. "But Raúl is right, it might prove dangerous to carry it along with us. So we'll hide it somewhere till we have established a permanent camp; then we'll come and get it. ¿De acuerdo?"

"¿Cómo no, comandante? De acuerdo."

Fidel winked at him and suggested he take a bath if Raúl was not willing. He combed his hair with his hands and stroked his beard, which had grown to cover his Adam's apple, and put back on his dirty military garb.

Eight weeks later they established camp at the high point of La Plata. The falcon-legged bathtub was retrieved and installed there. They built a wall of palm fronds around it and called the room a chapel. Fidel himself made ration cards out of palm bark for his men, entitling each of them to four baths a month. Fidel carved the cards with his own bowie knife, marked them with a star as each man bathed.

"I am now teaching you the way so that you may later teach others," he spoke from the other side of the palm-frond wall as he fashioned a crooked star on the palm-bark card, while his guerrillero, submerged in the falcon-legged tub, reached down under the water and scrubbed his groin, then lifted his ass and washed down there too, "that luxuries are not to be hoarded, that riches are to be shared equally. It's as simple as the seventh chapter of Matthew. I don't know why los curitas can't plainly see that, why they are not screaming their support for us from the pulpits at *every* morning Mass."

Your husband disagreed with all this ration business but he said nothing. Vaya no era bobo. His only protest was to demand that he too be issued a bath card, even though he knew that Fidel himself bathed in the tub every day (and that *that* was the real reason he did not want your husband taking it with him in his campaign eastward), with the excuse that soaking his joints in the hot waters eased his toothache and Celia had not yet sent a maldito dentista. Your husband knew otherwise, that at times—and this you won't read in any of the government's history books—in the middle of leading the rebellion against Batista's regime, Fidel was engaged in re-reading all of the works of Dostoevski, and the chapel was the only place where no one dared to bother him. But your husband did take the tub. It was his.

Your husband recounted all this to Héctor after they had set camp on a woody ridge east of La Plata, the first night of the campaign that would eventually capture Santiago de Cuba and establish it as temporary capital of the Island. They set up the tub and built a fire under a wigwam fashioned with moist palm and banana fronds—to protect the fire from the misty rain and so as not to give away their position—and heated water and Héctor bathed first and then most of the forty-nine guerrilleros and then your husband, all in the same water, heated after every three or four men with a fresh boiling pot. Héctor asked your husband who Dostoevski was, if he was some famous general like Napoleon, and if that was why Fidel was so interested in him and your husband pulled out from one of his bags a beat-up copy of *Crime and Punishment* with a cracking fake-leather cover and on whose title page Fidel had scribbled: *Fidel Castro '53*. That is, it was dated from the time that he too was a prisoner on this island that's the eye of the Island. He gave it to Héctor. Héctor brought it back with him to my abuelita's bohío and I helped him to read it sentence by sentence, one or two a day—ves, his formal schooling had mostly stopped after his mother had fled the first time when he was thirteen, so he read at an elementary level. Over five years later, when we were arrested and taken from the circus, he was still reading *Crime and Punishment* and had made it near the end, to the beginning of the sixth part. Later, while hidden in the cane fields near the labor camp in Camagüey, I asked him if he remembered the last sentence he had read.

"Claro, cómo no, mi amorcito," he said solemnly. "'*A strange time awaited Raskolnikov.*'"

Héctor liked to be dramatic this way. "'A strange time awaited Raskolnikov'?. How much stranger could things get for him?"

Pero coño, señora Alicia, you are letting me wander ahead of my story again. Vaya, stop me if you have to! Ah! This bath is so wonderful. I was wrong. Your exile is not such a bad thing. Estás mejor que los corbades que huyeron como ratas para Miami. Yesterday, on my way in I saw again the young man who brings you your food and coffee and rum. No, not such a bad thing at all. Guapísimo que es. I talked to him for a while: he was glad I had come to see you as I had promised him. Joshua. Bello. Joshua, a king's name. Maybe Fidel is doing you a favor by keeping you here, on this paradise full of nightingales and ruled by a beautiful young king. In the mainland things are worse by the day. ¡No dura mucho el reino del hijo de puta ese!

Ever since he got captured inside a hut after the raids on the barracks at Mocanda, Fidel forbade any of his troops from sleeping *inside* during any guerrilla mission away from La Plata. So after they had bathed, your husband and his men put out the fire, they spread their canvas sleeping bags over the jutting and falling roots of the banyan trees (and in the orange moonlight the bullish trees looked as if they wore dresses), and the guerrilleros crouched under the dresses and slept. It rained and there were many leaks in the dresses and Héctor became very cold and your husband wrapped him in one of his blankets till he stopped shivering. While they were huddled together, your husband finally got up the nerve to ask Héctor about the eye stitched under his left nipple, and Héctor told him all and many overheard and did not sleep that first night of the campaign. Your husband promised Héctor that when la Revolución triumphed no such things would happen to anyone, and perhaps in a moment of rapture brought on by sleeplessness he promised Héctor that he would find his lost brother. When Héctor assured him that his brother was dead, your husband then promised him that he would find the body, so that it could be given a decent burial, even if he had to drag all the rivers of the Island. Then he whispered into Héctor's ear a poem Martí had written about the glorious dead. Héctor recited it to me word for word, teary-eyed, when he returned to my abuelita's bohío.

He was in your husband's brigade for a month and half (before your husband joined with Barba Roja), the guerrilleros barely keeping up with his lead as he invented shortcuts over the insurmountable steeps, and (from what Héctor told me much later, after I had dug out the amethyst eye from underneath his left nipple and he could again become drunk and loose-tongued with his bourbon) they could barely keep up with the acrobatics that he introduced them to at night. Vaya, esto con todo respeto, to Héctor's great disappointment your husband never participated in the orgies under the dresses of the banyan trees, though certainly he knew about them. Pero creo, y vaya it's only a guess, that that is why Héctor fled from them, because he had fallen in love with your husband and your husband could not reciprocate that love. So he came back to my bed in my abuelita's bohío where he supposed I would be desperate for his return. He was not wrong.

Your husband never sent anyone after Héctor. He knew that there was no danger of Batista's Rural Guard capturing him and therefore no danger of him turning traitor. Your husband knew very well why Héctor had fled. When Fidel asked about Héctor later, when all the columns came together to descend upon Santiago de Cuba and upon Guantánamo, your husband told him that Héctor had fallen off the side of a cliff and his head had burst open like a rotten mango. Some years later when Fidel saw Héctor perform the Lazarus Rumba at the gypsy circus near La Habana, he stood and clapped for five minutes, and of course, the rest of the crowd did the same, and because of this great ovation initiated by el Líder we thought we had our benediction. That night, however, Fidel wrote a six-page letter to your husband. It dealt mostly with official matters, but it ended like this:

> . . . I was at the circus and saw the child with the amethyst eye on his chest, the one that impressed us so in the mountains long ago, and that now you have made yours. He seems to have gotten most of his rotten-mango brains stuffed back into his head; he is still as talented as he once was. Too bad he did not remain with us to join us into our ride into the capital, porque además de ser tan talentoso, es un muchacho guapo. I know how much you love the circus and love this boy who deserted our rebel forces and went unpunished, and who will indeed remain unpunished, pues now he is part of your own family; and as far as I am concerned, he is the only reason why I fight Raúl and the CDRs on their aims to shut down the gypsy circus. Talent like your cousin's should not be repressed! But as for the rest of the performers—they are a band of deviants and misfits and a detriment to la Revolución. The CDRs are absolutely right about that! Pero bueno, ya basta con el refunfuño.
>
> Cariño, Fidel

Your husband read Héctor the last part of the letter and asked him how he should answer.

"Cariño a Fidel también," Héctor said.

Héctor later stole the letter from your husband (though he said your husband had given it to him) and I have it now, hidden in an old suitcase under my dead abuelita's bed. Your husband never seemed to have answered Fidel's letter. Pero vaya, este cuento triste ya se sabe, a year later your husband was arrested on trumped-up charges and later was murdered in the eye of a hurricane and three months after that the gypsy circus was shut down forever and we were arrested and taken to the labor camp, labeled unequivocally as deviants and misfits *and* counterrevolutionaries.

So it was simple: Héctor knew that if they labeled him a deserter they would single him out and punish him for the crime even Fidel had said would go unpunished. When it was evident we were going to be arrested, he asked me to pluck out the amethyst eye from under his left nipple. I did. I dug it out with my fingernails, and Héctor was no longer the child with the blue eye in his chest, he was just another common deviant, and like the hero of the novel that was Fidel's favorite, a strange time awaited Héctor.

He did not remember the bus ride, nor the yellow-bearded gypsy raping him with his finger, nor the guards beating him and rupturing his lungs. The first thing he remembered after I plucked out the eye from under his left nipple was the two steel Chinese balls that had other balls inside them and rung like faraway church bells. They were heated and pressed downward along the ridges of his lower back and around and around his tailbone. He was in a hospital bed that had no mattress. He was suspended on it face down. His upper torso up to his collarbone was in a cast that smelled of rotting wood. His chest was itchy, as if it just had been rubbed by rough wool. His arms were opened like the wings of a dead bird, resting within a long cagelike contraption and fastened with metal clamps at the wrists and at the elbows. His legs were held aloft by a similar contraption, also clamped at the knees and at the ankles. He could wiggle his fingers and his toes. His head was secured in place by an iron halo. He imagined he looked like some flightless creature, caged in a skeleton of shiny steel. He sucked in air and pushed it out with the muscles in his belly. Long needles buried in his chest punished him for breathing. He smelled mierda and old urine. He asked questions but the person who was massaging him did not answer, did not speak at all. Héctor shut his eyes tight and tried to sleep again. He had been dreaming of the white sea. He could not sleep, not till the man who was massaging him—now he could tell it was a man by the rough dry hands—reached under the bed and turned an unoiled crank that screeched like burning angels and Héctor's body rotated till he was face up. He still could not see the man's face. The man put two pills on Héctor's tongue and poured tepid water down his throat. The man's forearms and the back of his hands were carpeted with coily black hair. When he was sure Héctor had swallowed the pills— sticking his index fingers on the inside of his cheeks and spreading them, then prodding with his thumbs under the tongue (his hands smelled like something burned), he turned the crank again till Héctor was face down. On the way out he patted Héctor on the butt, and it was then that mi nenito realized that he was not wearing anything but the cast that smelled like rotting wood around his chest.

"Dormirás ahora, mariconcito," the man said. Before Héctor passed out from the pills he caught an attack of the shivers, un escalofrío violento.

From then on, with his skin, Héctor knew every callus on the man's hands, at the bases of the palms and between the fingerjoints and on the fingertips, till they felt not like flesh at all but like the shell of a sand animal, though the heated Chinese balls felt good, soothing as he passed them over his lower torso and his legs and the soles of his feet.

"It's to keep the circulation going," the man once said and patted him harder on the butt. "¿Te gusta, no, *mariconcito*?"

"Sí me gusta. Are you a doctor?" Héctor said, but the man did not answer him again.

The man fed Héctor a cold compote every morning and late every afternoon. He poured water down his throat three times a day. The first time Héctor had to relieve himself he asked the man what to do. There was no answer. Héctor held it for a while, but during feeding time when the man turned the crank and he was face up, he let it go. The man laughed at him and wiped Héctor with a hot cloth and left the pieces of waste there overnight. After he was finished wiping him, as if to punish him, he did not feed him, and turned the crank again and heated the Chinese balls more than usual and they burned his skin so that it stung for a few days. Still, every time Héctor asked permission to relieve himself, the man did not answer and the man laughed wildly when Héctor finally could not hold it in, and the man always left the pieces there overnight till a gray dry crust had formed around them like a cocoon.

One day, he heard an orderly, the one who cleared the aluminum waste pan under him, address the man as Dr. Gómez.

"So you *are* a doctor?" Héctor said, almost relieved. No answer again.

When his breathing became easier, when it seemed to emanate naturally from his chest, Héctor spoke and all he heard was an animal sound; then he realized he had not been speaking out loud before, but only inside his head.

One evening, Dr. Gómez visited him and told him that it was time for his physical, for soon he would be freed from the cast and the iron halo. Héctor was face down on the suspended bed. The clamps were released at his knees and at his elbows. The blood rushed through his limbs. His lower back and his ass and his legs and the soles of his feet were covered with coconut oil. The crank was turned and his belly and his groin and the front of his legs and feet were also covered. The crank was turned again so that he was face down on the bed without a mattress. Dr. Gómez began massaging him with his hands. All over. He even pushed his fingers up his lower back, under the cast, and pressed down with the fingertips on the emaciated muscles. That felt the best. The oil smoothed Dr. Gómez's hands and softened the sand-animal palms. The steel Chinese balls were just the right temperature when he put them to Héctor's skin, as if they had been heated in some feverish region of his own body and released now to comfort him. They glided over the coconut oil and became slippery—but even when Dr. Gómez dropped one, the perfect temperature did not change.

"Ahora sí que te vas a sentir bien, mi mariconcito."

The Chinese balls were now moving by themselves over his body, rolling near the edges of the steel exoskeleton. They passed over the mound of his ass, close to the ridge, but they did not touch each other, down his hamstrings, to the pocket behind his knees where they paused, down the calves and around the cape of his toes, back towards the front of his body, up his shins to the protrusion of the knees and hard in on his thighs. Héctor felt as if he were moving, as if he were using each muscle the hot Chinese balls passed over in perfect unison the right one to the left one. So that at first he was pulling in a heavy weight and then crouching and then jumping and then curling his feet. The Chinese balls touched and clinked as they settled on his belly and the faraway church bells rang. Héctor was face up now. The crank had been turned and he had not heard it. He was alone in the room with the Chinese balls. They began to move again and made the return journey to the small of his back and settled on the spoon-dips in the back of his upper hipbone. He was face down again. He felt Dr. Gómez's fingers again. They opened the cheeks of his ass and with the coconut oil his ring finger went in easily, then two, then three, the longest one tickling him from the inside till Héctor came into the waste pan below. Héctor was breathing so hard that the buried needles in his lungs (which he thought had been removed) pierced him again.

"¡Así, así, mariconcito!"

The Chinese balls moved again. They found Dr. Gómez's fingers and he pushed them in. The first forced the muscle open and it felt as if it were tearing. The second one went in easier, the muscle relaxed and not torn. It swallowed it. Dr. Gómez laughed like he laughed after Héctor relieved himself. He pushed the balls farther in, till again they began to move on their own and turn one on the other like planetary orbs and Héctor came again and this time Dr. Gómez, on his knees by the bed so that Héctor could see his bearded chin for the first time, with his trousers at his ankles and both his palms around his penis, came with him, together into the waste pan, and Dr. Gómez's come was yellowy and it colored Héctor's as it mingled with it and Dr. Gómez laughed louder and stumbled up and kissed him and stuck his nose and his tongue where the Chinese balls had gone in. Then he turned the crank and waited for Héctor to release the balls. Héctor was numb and he could not feel them come out but he heard them as they hit the aluminum pan. One, then the other. Dr. Gómez had not stopped laughing.

"You are almost well, mi mariconcito." He never returned.

A week later Héctor was released from the bed with no mattress. He weighed eighty-seven pounds. He caught pneumonia and spent a year recovering in a sanatorium near the capital before they returned him to the labor camp, still thin, at one hundred and twenty pounds. At the time of his death, almost a year after you saw him, two and a half years after he had come to the labor camp, he was almost a picture of health. He weighed one hundred and sixty-four pounds.

Imagínate, when he returned, thin as a street dog, I was at once both horrified to see him so, and thankful to all the saints that mi nenito had lived! At first, I could only see him when we were out in the fields. He was still ill enough to have to spend nights at the infirmary, but not ill enough to be excused from working the fields. *El sudor en la frente is the key to the good health,* the camp physician said. That was his second favorite saying. *El trabajo los hará hombres, ya verán,* that was his favorite. I was always the strongest and the most productive machetero, so the guards always gave me a bit of leeway out in the fields, let me stray out of the sight of their telescopic Belgian rifles, for this I repaid them with favors when they were away from their noviecitas for too long. I convinced them to be lenient with Héctor—and they soon figured out what he was to me. Héctor was so weak when he arrived that he could just barely lift the machete above his shoulder (though because of his fear of snakes, he always kept a grip on it, even while we sat on a shaved part of the field for the meager almuerzo), much less swing it with enough force, low and lower to the ground to cut the stalks properly. The guards let me go to him for two and three hours a day and cut side by side with him, so that his productivity would seem normal.

At nights I saved my meal portions for him—stale bread and strips of dry chicken—and wrapped them in a cloth coffee filter I had stolen from the kitchen, and hid them under my straw mattress. In the morning I would hide it down my crotch and take it to him out in the fields so he could have a second breakfast. Monday and Friday they fed us strips of pork. These too I saved for him. I myself subsisted on the watery black bean soup they gave us for lunch and sometimes at dinner. If I was really good to the guards, in the endless afternoons inside the cabs of the conscript transport trucks, two or three of them at a time, if I made the rolled-up windows steam with their long sighs, they patted me on the head and called me *negrito bocón* and rewarded me with yanqui chocolate bars. These too I saved for Héctor. Soon he was strong enough to be released from the infirmary and transferred to our barracks. He even enjoyed going out in the fields and breaking a sweat. And of course, it was still only in the fields where we were bold enough to touch each other as we wanted to, under the cover of the green-gray stalks or by an old abandoned Spanish church near one of the cane fields, on whose worn steps we knew each other like twisted angels.

Late in the afternoon I would escape and do my duties with the guards and Héctor would sulk and often ignore me for a few days and not eat the meal portions I had saved for him, or the yanqui chocolate bars I had worked so hard for. There was nothing I could do: the guards needed to be pleased—los santos bien saben, most of the times, especially after Héctor arrived, my skin ached when it came into contact with theirs—if not, they would never let us have our own time together.

In six months time Héctor was healthy *and* beautiful again, his musculature naturally rebuilt by the long hours in the fields and his skin bronzed into wholesomeness by the cloud-melting sun. The guards started asking me when it was that I was going to bring him along to join us in our late afternoon sessions. "Tiene el culito rico ese muchachito," they said.

I refused to let myself even imagine their hands on mi nenito.

"Qué va, Héctor no," I told them, as if I were not a prisoner and they not my guards. "No sabe nada. He won't know what to do. He's very inexperienced. Very meek."

"De toda forma, tiene el culito rico. We'll *show* him what to do."

"Qué va, Héctor no. No y no."

I worked harder to please them so that they would forget about Héctor. (And for a while they did.)

Héctor liked to take his shirt off when he worked in the fields. I forbade it. He liked to shower both in the morning *and* when we returned from the fields. This too I forbade and told him to cut back his showers to three a week, though in the harvest months they forced us to shower every day. The old guard in charge at the barracks let us shower as often as we liked because he got to watch; and often the guards from the fields would come and watch too, under the pretense that they were watching us so that we would not touch each other, and when someone would get aroused they would walk over to him and beat him under the falling water until he was no longer aroused. And when no one would get aroused, they beat someone for pissing into the drain or soaping himself too long in certain parts, for they said these were pervert codes we had established. Some of us they never beat—those that pleased them, and those that they hoped would one day learn to please them, so Héctor and I were immune to the shower beatings. Héctor loved long showers. He just closed his eyes and sat under the warm ducha and let it massage his head, and eventually his thick hair would soften and fall over his eyes like heavy drapes. Everyone loved to watch him—and a few other campmates were beat for doing so, as if the guards had now also taken to protecting Héctor because they knew that one day he would be theirs.

Monologue of Triste the Contortionist:
The Passion of Comandante Federico Sánchez

The guards rarely forced themselves violently on any of us. Pero oye, don't get me wrong, naturalmente, there were a few incidents here and there of rapes and forced acts, but most of them enjoyed the process of seducing us, luring us with promises just as they did with women. There was an officer in the camp named Federico Sánchez who had fallen unabashedly in love with Héctor; and all the other guards, bueno nada más que sabían bretear de eso, for Federico Sánchez was in his late thirties and had never been married and still lived with his mother in her villa outside of La Habana four months a year. Federico Sánchez was a lieutenant-colonel and had been in the mountains during the latter part of the Revolutionary War (after Héctor had fled) and later had commanded troops against the counter-revolutionaries in the Escambray Mountains not far from our labor camp, so he had rank over most of the other guards. Behind his back, the other guards called him *doña* Federica la Marica. Pues sabe, his mother was quite the aristocrat and contrarevolucionaria herself, bueno, still is—her villa has become a fort guarded by her six German shepherds—and she sends letters to *Granma,* calling Fidel a child robber and a soul kidnapper. The editors, as if to liven up the pallor-prose editorial page, sometimes publish her letters. Escribe bello; parece que tiene complejo de escritora. Every time *Granma* publishes one of her long letters, they say Fidel reads it and laughs heartily and then has the entire editorial staff fired. Federico Sánchez knew that behind his back the others called him doña Federica, but it just gave him that much more pleasure when to his face they addressed him as *mi* comandante Sánchez in tones both of love and fear.

Federico Sánchez was in love with Héctor and Federico Sánchez was second in command at the labor camp. He might have saved Héctor and Héctor might have let himself be saved, for aside from his one deformity, comandante Federico Sánchez was a handsome man. He was short though well proportioned, with broad muscle-cupped shoulders and tree-trunk arms. He too, like Héctor, was a mulatto, though his skin was even lighter than Héctor's and his hair, which he always trimmed short, much thinner. He had thin archless black eyebrows that almost touched each other and long eyelashes and hazel eyes specked with cyan. His nose was Roman (like his idol Fidel) and his beard was much darker than his hair and neatly trimmed. His lips were thin, like a yanqui's. He had a long lizard tongue, which he had the habit of stretching by placing its tip against the back of his lower teeth and pushing it out, so that tiny rosy bumps on its surface seemed to grow and harden like a thousand aroused nipples. And it seemed that from many years of doing this his lower jaw had been pushed forward so that he had a serious underbite. Pero al fin y al cabo, even with these oddities, even with his deformity, which he hid rather well with his dark-green leather glove (except claro, when his arm was at his side and a breeze blew and the three middle fingerless fingers and half the thumb bent in the breeze like young tobacco leaves), not a bad-looking man. Because of the accident—a rusty Belgian pistol that blew up in his hand—he never carried a firearm, his only weapon a long seven-inch bowie knife sheathed in black leather on his left hip. Yet, for whatever reason, maybe the scary size of his tongue, or maybe because he suspected what others called him behind his back and needed to make up for this weakness, he wielded more power than any comandante in the camp, even his one superior officer. Federico Sánchez might have saved Héctor.

At first he tried to pull Héctor from the Sunday education lessons, but the comandante in charge of the camp, an avid worshipper of the Virgin of Cobre, a man we called Cara de Jamón because his face was so fleshy, would not allow it. Then, Federico Sánchez had the gall to use his mother to free Héctor from the camp. He told Cara de Jamón that his mother was in need of a servant who could not quit, for all her other servants, hidden in their shack rooms behind the patio walls, tuned in to Fidel's Sunday speeches on their battery-operated radios, had become full of revolutionary zeal and quit, and the villa was falling apart and the prize German shepherds were beginning to look mangy. He wanted then to *borrow* Héctor during the four off-harvest months, and use him in his mother's villa near La Habana. Cara de Jamón, who had become somewhat disillusioned by la Revolución's recent tirades against religion, and especially in its insults to his Virgencita Santa, agreed to have one of his little soldiers—for that is what he called us: *mi soldaditos*—serve time as a criado to an unrepentant aristocrat, simply because Federico Sánchez's mother was also professed to be a great devotee of la Virgencita. They left on the first week of July, just the two of them.

Héctor returned two weeks later under heavy guard. He was wearing a soiled cream-colored linen suit, a torn untucked light-blue linen shirt, and on his left foot one ruined ox-blood leather Italian shoe, the sides all mud-crusted. His right foot was bare and bloodied in between the long toes. His face and his hands and his hair were covered with streaks of yellow paint, like a tribal warrior. He was marched by us; but he did not look at any of us, his eyes downcast, and I noticed then that even his eyebrows and eyelashes were stained with yellow paint. He was put in solitary confinement, in the hole where you can't stand up. We didn't see him again till the end of that summer, when he suddenly appeared one day, asleep in his old bed at the barracks, barefoot but still wearing the same linen suit, now stained with urine and mierda-splotches. We were returning from a nearby mill, which is where we put in most of our working hours during the off-harvest months, and were tired and ready for a meal and a bed, but two or three of us skipped dinner and stripped Héctor—he had lost some weight again—and dragged him to the showers, where the old guard ran a warm shower for him and, as we scrubbed the smell off him with our soaked and soaped workshirts, we noticed the tiny rectangular burn-scabs on the skin of his penis and on his ass and the inside of his upper thighs. He had spent some extra time with Father. The old guard turned his gaze away from the naked Héctor, either in shame at his complicity or in

repulsion at their marring of his beautiful organ. Later that night, after
the other men had come back from dinner, he handed me a jar of aloe balm
and he let me sneak into Héctor's bed with him.

"Sabe, I don't approve of this *they* do," he said without looking at me.
I thanked him for the balm. "Y cuidado," he added, "because I am lenient
doesn't mean that *they* will be!"

In a couple of weeks' time the burns had mostly healed and the old
guard made me sleep in my own bunk again. A couple of weeks more and
we were out in the fields again. When we were able to sneak away, which
was not as easy as before, for I was by then out of favor with the guards,
Héctor was finally able to open up about what had happened in the villa
of Federico Sánchez's mother.

"Pues vaya," he said, brushing the blade of his machete against his un-
derchin, not looking at me, his shirt off and tied around his waist, "right
away la vieja didn't like me. She knew, mi amorcito. She knew exactly
why the old pervert had brought me there—not to help her, but to fuck
me without having to bother about anyone finding out. A mother knows
these things. *My* mamita knew about me the moment she first saw me after it had happened with mi maestro, señor Sariel. This mother knew too.
Así que vaya, right away she didn't like me. She gave me that sideways
look and that little grunt in the back of the throat that you almost can't
hear.

"*Do you have any experience in domestic help?* that's the first thing she
asked me. And Federico Sánchez broke in right away, his face reddening,
waving the finger of his good hand at her: *Mamá, this is not an interview. I
have brought you help for this falling-apart excuse of a house and you should be
thankful and not so pedante!* Es verdad, la vieja era un poquito pedante, no
sólo en carácter, but in the way she looked and smelled. Even standing
across the room from her, her skin gave off a sharp smell, like garlic covered up by cheap lemony perfume. Her face was caked with white
makeup, y claro se había hecho la cirujía (it looked like her face had been
fixed many times), but you could still see the wrinkles lining up like toy
soldiers, around her lips and around her eyes. After her son had told her
off, her white makeup began to crack and she gave us *both* the grunt at the
back of the throat again, and then she left the room. At least the dogs
liked me. These were supposed to be the vicious animals that fought off
the Fidelistas when they tried to take over the villa, but they spent that
whole first day licking my hands and my crotch, and they wouldn't stop
no matter how loudly Federico Sánchez called them off me. Vaya, parece
que estaba celoso, ¿no ves, mi amorcito?—*he* wanted to be licking my fingers and my crotch. In the jeep, on the ride up, he almost said it outright.
¿Ya sabes cuanto te quiero, Héctor? he said that to me, not waiting for me to
answer, *How much I would do and risk for you? Ya sabes.* What could I say to
this?"

Federico Sánchez could have saved Héctor. Héctor knew this but he would not have it. He did very little domestic work around the house. In fact, without his mother's knowledge, Federico Sánchez had hired three other servants to make Héctor look superefficient; they came in to do the housework after midnight when his mother was well into her Valium-sleep. Federico Sánchez paid them with rum and with forged ration-booklets for meat and dairy products. Héctor did help Federico Sánchez paint the exterior of the main house. He paid Héctor with bourbon, which he bought from a yanqui who was *íntimo* with his mother.

"Did you take off your shirt while you were helping him paint the outside of the house?"

"It was very hot, mi amorcito. And you know how much I dislike clothes."

(Poor Federico Sánchez.) He did not know how much Héctor disliked clothes. He thought that Héctor was stripping for him, displaying himself as lovers do one for the other. Poor Federico Sánchez who bought Héctor the finest linen suits woven by the Italians in the old section of the capital city and silk briefs and socks woven by los chinitos in La Calle del Malecón, who bought Héctor all the bourbon he could drink, and when Héctor was too groggy to protest (when the bourbon had made all his limbs heavy and his heart fond for *any* affection), poor Federico Sánchez dressed him and undressed him like a doll, and right before dawn—when he suspected his mother would begin wandering the long hallways of the house, drinking the first of her two dozen cafecitos negros to offset the pills, and then kneeling in front of the porcelain statue of the Virgin of Cobre, murmuring rosaries till noon—he paid the night servants and let them out and then carried Héctor to his own bedroom and gave him water and three aspirins to drink and washed his forehead with a warm damp cloth and kissed him on the cheeks and on the bridge of his nose and then set under his ruffled-hair head three goose-down almohadas and drew the mosquitero and curled up on the pink-marble floor beneath his bed without pillow or blanket and slept there beside one of his mother's German shepherds, who nibbled on his fingerless fingers, and stared at the contours that Héctor's body cut on the soft mattress and dreamed of Héctor's breath that stirred the air with such sweet snores. Poor Federico Sánchez who thought Héctor would grow enamored of this life in his mother's ruined villa, rising late in the afternoon and costumed in linen and silk and drunk on bourbon.

"It was very hot, mi amorcito," Héctor repeated. "You don't think I was trying to get that fingerless pervert all horny for me do you? It was very hot. And I liked the paint when it rained from the brush and splashed all over me."

Doña Sánchez wanted her villa-house painted the same color as the Church of San Francisco down the hill from her. But it wasn't as if she had much choice, for the whole neighborhood was being painted egg-yolk yellow. It was the surplus paint on the black market. (Yellow paint, for some reason, is always surplus on the black market.) The priests at the Church of San Francisco got a good deal on it and Federico Sánchez, due to his military stature, got a better deal. Doña Sánchez wanted the wooden storm shutters on the windows and all the wooden doors and doorways on the main floor painted in old green. ("Sort of the color of that ridiculous glove you wear," she said to her son, and at the moment she had said it, one of her German shepherds, as if on command, on a mission to shame him, licked the three fingerless fingers of Federico Sánchez's right hand.) And the many wrought-iron balconies running along the second floor, as well as the pillars in the inner courtyard, she wanted painted snow-white. The parapet and the steel urns that lined the house on the front, she wanted painted clay-red.

"Yellow, mamá," Federico Sánchez said. "Yellow—that is all we have. Todo todito amarillito."

"¿Las puertas?"

"Yellow, mamá."

"¿Las ventanas?"

"Yellow, mamá."

"¿Hasta los balcones?"

"Yellow yellow yellow, mamá!"

"¡Ay qué horrible! Va a parecer la casa una tortilla."

"Mamá, we won't do it then! I'll go right back with Héctor to Camagüey." Federico Sánchez stretched his tongue.

"Yellow," doña Sánchez said relenting, "yellow then, todo en el color de la Virgencita, las puertas, las ventanas, los balcones, hasta el ojo de mi culo píntenmelo amarillo!"

Héctor laughed and all that day he imagined sneaking the longer bristles of his yellow-soaked paintbrush into the *eye* of doña Sánchez's wide ass. When Federico Sánchez asked him what he was giggling about he told him and Federico Sánchez laughed also. He laughed at his own mother with glee.

There were four and a half gallons of paint left over when they had finished painting all the outer walls and window shutters and doors and doorways and balconies and doña Sánchez's villa-house looked as if it had been pissed on by King Midas. Héctor suggested they ride around the capital and donate the leftover paint to the people whose house looked most in need of a paint job; and Federico Sánchez said that it was *una idea magnífica, noble. You are finally becoming a son of the revolution!* He dressed Héctor in a new sand-colored linen suit and the light-blue linen shirt buttoned all the way up to his neck, though Héctor complained that it was too hot to be all buttoned up, and the custom-made ox-blood Italian leather shoes that Federico Sánchez told Héctor had belonged to his father, and unfortunately Federico Sánchez's feet had never grown to his father's monumental size of fourteen and a half. His father had been a giant, measuring almost seven feet. Héctor, who was about six feet tall, had to look *down* to meet Federico Sánchez's gaze as Federico Sánchez spoke to him. And the truth hit Héctor with a stupefying clarity. Poor Federico Sánchez was a bastard. And even if he had been a giant like his father who was not his father, Héctor thought that he would never have worn any of his father's fine clothes anyway, because the only time he saw Federico Sánchez out of his military uniform was late at night, when he curled on the pink marble floor next to his mother's German shepherd. And even then he did not wear the fancy linen pajamas that the servants laid out for him, but a tight-fitting white T-shirt, which showed off his thick chest and his boa-arms, and long boxers and a pair of black socks and, of course, his olive-green leather glove, which he never removed and which during their stay had become spotted and streaked with bright yellow paint.

The shoes fit Héctor just fine, with plenty of room for his giant monkey-toes. It was the first and last pair of shoes he owned since he had run away from home when he was thirteen. He found shoes so uncomfortable that he never wore the work boots they gave us in the labor camp, not even out in the fields. I tried to convince him in the showers one night, playing on his fear of snakes, telling him that las culebras like to suck on naked toes, but Héctor just brandished an invisible machete at me. *¡En seis mil pedazos las corto!* The soles of his feet eventually grew so callused they were tough as hooves.

They loaded up the paint and got in Federico Sánchez's jeep and drove east; and though Héctor knew that the bad neighborhoods of the old city were due west, he said nothing. Federico Sánchez made no conversation either. They drove in silence till nightfall and near the beach town of Varadero got off the main highway and followed a sandy road to a small wooden cottage on a hill from where Héctor could hear the drumbeat of the waves. The sky trembled with torch-flame stars and the moon shone like polished silver.

"It's so bright we can paint tonight," Federico Sánchez said, unloading the food and the fresh water and the paint cans, and handing Héctor the case of Kentucky bourbon that he had gotten from his mother's friend, that former assistant to the former yanqui consul, who despite the embargo and the thousand other yanqui laws still vacationed on the Island every winter. By the front door of the cottage, Héctor tore the case open and broke the seal on the first bottle and drank straight from it.

"Pero ven acá chico, no tanto coño," Federico Sánchez said, grabbing the bottle from him. "We are going to paint tonight. I wasn't kidding." Héctor grabbed the bottle back from Federico Sánchez and took another swig.

"Fine, I'll paint by myself," Federico Sánchez said, then he forced a smile and put the three middle fingers of his ungloved hand softly under Héctor's chin. "Puñetero, tan bonito y tan malagradecido que eres!"

Federico Sánchez took off his military jacket and opened one of the paint cans and started painting the outside walls of the wooden cottage, while Héctor found the highest point on the hill, not far from the house, and sat with his back to Federico Sánchez and, with his bourbon bottle in hand, stared at the coruscant moon-foil sea. Every time Federico Sánchez got down from the ladder to retrieve his dropped paintbrush or to move the ladder along the wall he was painting, he went over to Héctor and grabbed the bottle of bourbon from him and took a long swig. He did not say anything to Héctor. After six trips to the bourbon bottle, when Federico Sánchez stumbled back up on the ladder, he pointed with his sopped palm-gripped brush at the different constellations and told stories about them, mostly plain stories his mother had once told him as they sat on the roof of their villa-house and bemoaned their fate as a wife and son abandoned by the giant man whose secret life with other men they had never imagined. Héctor seemed uninterested in the stories till Federico Sánchez began to tell of the Hyades and of the giant who hunts them.

See that little cluster there, high up, right in front of you, all bunched together like too many diamonds on a ring. Those are the Hyades, the daughters of Atlas, the giant who carries the world. There are six, but you can only see five, and I'll tell you why. Mira, así va el cuento: Zeus, the god of all gods, had a lover and her name was Semele, and his wife knew about this lover and had her burned alive with Zeus's own flames; but before she died, Zeus was able to snatch the child from her belly, and so that her wife would not find him, he gave the child to the daughters of Atlas to care for him, and they named him Dionysus and raised him into a man, and the man was beautiful, with long dark locks and a body so lovely he would never clothe it, and this son of Zeus became the god of wine and the god of orgasms, and he left the daughters of Atlas and wandered the world spreading his religion. But twice a year, during the rainy seasons, he returns to the sky to the women who raised him—Zeus rewarded the women for saving his son by making them stars—and he pleases them like only the god of orgasms can; that's why you can only see five out of the six, for one is always behind them, on the look-out for the coming of Dionysus, and when he comes, one is always with him, being pleased.

Now, there is a giant hunter, who is in love with Dionysus and wants to have him, and his name is Orion. That's him there, to your right, up, up, see his torso and his legs and his bow and arrow and see that long thing sprouting from his side, bent and twisted like a massive oak branch and lit at the end with the brightest star in the constellation, that thing that the many prudes say is Orion's sword, but we who know, who look at it right, can plainly tell that it can't be his sword, that it is too beautiful and, in its outrageous curves, too full of desire to be a sword!—

that it can be nothing but his raging hard-on for Dionysus, the god who pleases the Hyades but will not have him!

The yellow paint from the brush Federico Sánchez pointed tremulously at Orion's bent desire for the god of orgasms dripped down his gloved hand and down his arm, but he did not care; he had gotten mi nenito's attention and Héctor was listening to him and staring with lips-parted awe at Orion's wonderful pinga. Federico Sánchez dropped the brush but this time he did not climb down to retrieve it, instead he took off his green leather glove—it was saturated with yellow paint—and he hurled it to the ground from the ladder as if challenging someone to a duel. He stuck his finger-and-a-half hand into the moon. To Héctor, its shadow on the white-plate moon looked like the head of a baby elephant with a stump-horn, *no no, no un elefante, un bebito rinoceronte.* Héctor laughed and swigged more bourbon as he told Federico Sánchez this. Federico Sánchez dug his hand out of the moon. He told Héctor to forget about his hand and to concentrate on Orion and on his bent and unrequited love for the god who was too beautiful to wear clothes. He pressed his naked finger-and-a-half hand against the bulge on his crotch, and later Héctor would see the yellow stains there, like a mutant child's finger painting.

But Orion too is beautiful. Mira, mira, if you can cast your eyes away from his long lovely pinga. Look at the rest of him! Look how the muscles ripple in the ball of his shoulders as he pulls back his bow, his legs firmly planted and spread in the sky, his hair and beard the color of the night, trimmed short like a warrior, his face twisted in longing; pero carajo!—how can you avert your eyes from that oak-branch pinga that never rests, that is even in the way of his vision! And how can the Hyades not see it and try to make it theirs, these poor and sad women who are alone for most of the year, waiting for their lover who is almost their son. They lure the giant hunter, promise him what they cannot deliver, and get to sit on the oak branch that never rests to cure their dank stenchy sulphurous below-the-girdle solitude. Again and again they sit on the bent branch and ride the skies like witches, but Orion never rests beside them for it is another that he is bent for.

Federico Sánchez had made his way down from the ladder and his voice had lowered and he was speaking directly into Héctor's ears. He reached toward Héctor's neck with his ungloved hand and deftly, with his pinky and half his thumb, undid all the buttons of his shirt. Then Federico Sánchez, working with his hand as if it had not a finger and a half but six or seven fingers, undid the belt buckle and the buttons of Héctor's pants. Héctor took another shot of bourbon and laid back on the sandy ground and kept his eyes on Orion. His shoes came off and his pants and silk boxers slid off him. He felt Federico Sánchez disappear for a second. He was angry at himself for being so aroused. And just as he thought that he could easily put his pants back on, he felt a cool soppy grainy tongue lapping at his thigh, covering it with thick cold-blooded saliva, all the way down his leg, to the callused soles of his feet and in between the long toes and then up the other leg. Héctor looked away from Orion and lifted his head. Federico Sánchez, his eyes so open they were almost perfect circles, his long tongue stretched against his lower teeth, so that even in the moonlight, Héctor could see the countless erect rosy mininipples, was painting him yellow. He was holding the brush with his good hand, and just now he was getting to the part Héctor imagined he had wanted to start with, but had denied himself the pleasure of at first, like a child who saves the best part of a meal for last.

Héctor felt his testicles shrink when the brush, covered with sand dirt and saturated in bright yellow paint, came in contact with them. He wished the other part down there would shrink too. But it didn't. It jumped up and down on his lower belly as if beckoning the brush. Federico Sánchez complied. Then he wriggled Héctor out of his shirt and went on to paint half his torso up to his nipples.

"¡Mi niñito el color de la Virgen!" he said when he was finished, standing open-legged above Héctor. "The giant Orion has come. He has captured his boy!" Héctor laughed, for even in the position they were in, Federico Sánchez looked nothing like a giant. Federico Sánchez took another shot of bourbon. He took off his T-shirt; under the shag of black hair Héctor could make out the well-defined torso. Federico Sánchez stood on one foot and took off one boot, then the other. He let himself drop down on Héctor and began passing his iguana tongue over his belly, meticulously washing away and swallowing, lick by lick, the coat of paint the color of the Virgin. Around his aroused penis and his shrunk testicles Héctor felt as if Federico Sánchez was going over him with a moist thin strip of fine-grain sandpaper. He turned his gaze back to Orion and then Federico Sánchez grabbed him and stroked the shaft with the three nubs of his bad hand and rubbed the head in circle motions with his thumbstub and kept his tongue at work below the testicles and soon Héctor's eyes rolled back away from Orion and his eyelids fluttered and his tongue poked the inside of his right cheek and Federico Sánchez pulled in his own tongue and encircled his mouth around Héctor and swallowed him.

When Héctor looked up again Federico Sánchez had stripped and, standing, still spread-legged over Héctor's body, was pleasing himself as he had pleased Héctor, the three nubs and the thumb-stump working in the same manner (a mist of yellow paint flying off from the jerk and pull and shining like pollen-dust when it caught the moonlight). His legs too were hairy and muscle-cut and his organ very miniscule compared with his other limbs, the head flat and lined with thick streaks of purple, which reminded Héctor of some mushrooms he and his brother had once picked and eaten in Mingo's finca. Federico Sánchez's come bubbled out of him in three-quarters time, like a syrupy salsa, and mingled with the yellow paint and fell in string-gobs on Héctor and tickled him as it slid down the sides of his belly searching for the dry ground. He carried Héctor into the cottage, threw aside the mosquitero, and set Héctor down on a wide bed dressed in white linen. Héctor felt the wet grainy brush pass over his back and buttocks and in between his legs, and from the smell of the paint and all the bourbon he had drunk, he passed out.

"Así que de veras, I don't know if he fucked me or not, mi amorcito," he said to me, "pero vaya, his little mushroom was so tiny, that even if he did, I was so drunk that night, I don't think I would have felt it."

The next morning when Héctor awoke he felt a dull pain in his right foot. There was a gash three inches long across the sole, right under the ball. It had stopped bleeding but when he tried to walk it opened up again. Federico Sánchez was passed out next to him, his body smeared with yellow and red and brown stains, the tip of his tongue, which was hanging out of one side of his parted lips, resting against the lower one like an exhausted guerrillero, also covered in paint and in blood. Héctor wiped off his own blood from Federico Sánchez's seven-inch bowie knife and took it with him and he took the clothes Federico Sánchez had bought for him (he would need them as cover) and he took two bottles of bourbon (these too he would need to fight back the pain in his foot and the hunger as well, for he searched for money in Federico Sánchez's clothes and in the jeep but there was none to be found—a prestigious comandante of la Revolución, Federico Sánchez needed no money, he simply demanded goods and services, which worked everywhere except in the black market). Héctor left the cottage and washed as well as he could in the sea. The cut on his foot stung and he limped as he came out of the water. He would have taken the jeep, but of course he had never learned how to drive, so he escaped on foot. He told me his first plan was to go back to Guantánamo and seek your help, señora Alicia, but he made the mistake of hitching a ride from a campesino who was the head of a local Committee for the Defense of the Revolution, and in his mule and buggy, the man, while giving a well-acted speech on the evils of la Revolución, rode him directly to a local national guard station.

"His finger wagged like Fidel's as he spoke," Héctor told me later. "I should have known."

Federico Sánchez almost died of lead poisoning. He was ill for many months. That is why they kept Héctor in solitary confinement for so long; they were readying to charge him with murder and hang him. But Federico Sánchez recovered—and whatever story he concocted when he returned, it saved Héctor's life, for a while, long enough so that he could recount to me what had happened, long enough so that he died for the sins that he came to the labor camp to die for and not for a trumped up murder charge.

Federico Sánchez returned to the camp just as the sugarcane harvest began that year. A week later, Cara de Jamón was transferred and Federico Sánchez became the head comandante. He moved into the wooden cottage by the river. The wrinkled queen who worked as his servant (Federico Sánchez personally selected Cuco la Loca, the oldest and least attractive marica in the camp for this service) said that in the bedroom of the house he installed a large abstract painting streaked with dirt-brown and vivid reds, but mostly done in yellow, the shape of arms and legs and torsos bending into each other. This was the only acknowledgement Federico Sánchez would make of his past life. He treated Héctor as if he had never known him, addressing him with the same insults the guards used on us. Héctor took it all well; pues, was glad. He hoped that Federico Sánchez's face would soon blend unrecognizably with the others who watched us. Little did he know that Federico Sánchez had already begun planning his murder, which he wanted done not by some blind revolutionary tribunal, but under his command.

The guards shunned me that harvest season. I was no longer welcome into the cab of the conscript transport truck. I had been replaced, and thus I could demand no favors from them, no special time to sneak away with Héctor. They watched me swing my machete through the telescopes of their rifles.

"Ya estás viejo, negrón," they taunted me. "We're harder for younger meat now! Any idea where we can get any? How much time do you expect us to wait for the mulatico, el del culito rico, the boyfriend of doña Federica la Marica!"

Eventually they *did* lure Héctor into the cab of their truck. Héctor assured me he did it for my sake; but I needed no explanations, I knew him. Ever since his maestro first taught him the pleasures of it, Héctor could not do without the feel of another man's flesh, vaya, the simple smell of a man made him as joyous as drumbeats make the possessed, as pleased as bread makes the holy. And though Federico Sánchez must have suffered much, his heart emptied at hearing the telling and retelling of the way Héctor bit his lower lip and gasped when you first went into him and the way his eyelids fluttered, like poinciana clusters caught in a stiff breeze, and his tongue made a bump on his right cheek right before he came, this was all part of Federico Sánchez's plan. It was written. He knew that eventually Héctor would begin to ask for favors, for time to see me.

We met every Tuesday, supposedly because it was the day Federico Sánchez drove into the town of Las Ceras, about ten miles southwest of the camp to lecture at a military school there. But Federico Sánchez was going to town to spend his passions on other boys. Pues, this part of the story I got from Cuco la Loca, who waited on Federico Sánchez hand and foot, and even accompanied him into the boys' whorehouse run by a former comandante, a retired compadre of Fidel—all ages of boys, whose mothers were told they were being recruited for the service of la Revolución, in every shade of skin color from dark brown to yanqui-looking rubios with eyes like the mountain sky. *It's a good thing that I like HOMBRES!* Cuco la Loca told me, *¡Hombres peludos, con los cojones como los huevos de la avetruz! If not, I would have gone crazy in that house. All manners of little not-yet-men.* Cuco la Loca helped Federico Sánchez undress and sat by the bedside and handed the flask of bourbon back and forth to Federico Sánchez as he went through boys that resembled Héctor in everything but the long callused high-arched feet and the scar under the left nipple. And Cuco la Loca said that Federico Sánchez massaged the feet and pulled on the toes of the poor boys as if trying to stretch them. He also said that he was half in love with his employer till he saw his pitiable pinguita shaped and sized like a mushroom and streaked with purple. *Te juro, even some of the boys had to hold back from laughing at it.* When Federico Sánchez returned to the labor camp, stumbling from the bourbon, he called the guards who had watched Héctor and me in the fields through the telescope in their rifles and he asked them to describe exactly what they had seen; and when they weren't graphic enough, Federico Sánchez slammed his gloved hand on his long mahogany table and screamed: "¡Así no fue carajo! Díganme bien." And when the guards came to the part when Héctor's eyelids fluttered and his tongue poked into his right cheek, he would stop them by raising his good hand as if to proclaim an oath and dismiss them and then he would ask Cuco la Loca to shut off the lights and help him out of his clothes, and he would lie naked, faceup on his mahogany table and sob like a widow, his hairy muscular chest swelling and falling, softened with sorrow.

One Tuesday, when he had drunk more bourbon than usual, and played with the hired boy's feet so long and so hard, pressing and pressing the bones between the palms of his good and bad hands, that the boy forgot he was a worker in service of la Revolución and remembered that he was a child, and began to cry, Federico Sánchez demanded that he stop crying, that his real *boy* never cried, no matter what he did to him. When the boy would not stop crying Federico Sánchez pulled out his seven-inch bowie knife and pinned the boy down, and slit a gash under the boy's left nipple and told the boy as he began to scream that *now* he looked like his real boy and demanded again that he stop screaming. The retired comandante who owned the house and owned the boys asked Federico Sánchez as he left that day, *con mucho respeto, compadre, y sin crear lío,* never to return, handing him back the knife he had wrested from him when he burst into the room. That night, Federico Sánchez interrupted the guards when they were telling him about my meeting with Héctor.

"Next Tuesday, grab him in the middle of his sins and do what you have to do to reform him. Let him know the wrath of our Lord that, pronto o tarde, strikes down all sinners."

Cuco la Loca did not warn me. He was afraid for his own life.

On Tuesdays after almuerzo the guards called Héctor into the cab of the transport truck and then let him go see me. After he had met up with me, we would walk to a nearby river, un arroyo, and he would not let me kiss him till he had stripped down and crouched by the shore and grunted out all the semen and then washed. Although I did not mind the smell of another man's sex on him, he insisted. "Primero la aborción," he said as he crouched over the smooth stones and the juices, sepia-tinted by his innards, poured out of him with every grunt and slid into the river like pale baby moccasins. "Pues, I don't want to become pregnant, mi amorcito. Only by you. The others are all forgotten." He grunted one last time. Sometimes I would join him in the river and if the waters had risen enough we would both go under the surface and kiss for the first time there. It was a stolen private moment, but we knew we would not stay under for long, for if the guards were watching (we never knew for sure) they would become nervous and disturb us. So we came out of the river and everything else we did unabashed, under the afternoon sky, in the plain sight of Changó and all the saints, till the afternoon they took Héctor from me.

In the cab of the conscript transport truck, early that Tuesday afternoon, one of the men put his lips to Héctor's ear, as he bounced his hips on him, and whispered no obscenity, no special request, but only a few words of deepest fondness, *Don't go see Triste today, bellísimo. Por el amor de Dios, no vayas a ver a Triste hoy.* And he wept as he came inside Héctor.

"He cried—¿lo crees?" Héctor said crouching by the river a few hours later, for he paid no attention to the one warning he was given, and he came and saw me anyway. Héctor pressed the muscles of his belly and grunted a few times. He looked down and smiled.

"Mira, mira, mi amorcito," he said. "Look at all the tears he shed."

After he had washed we went far away from the river to the ruins of a brick church built by the Spaniards in the last century about a mile and a half south of the cane fields. We held hands as we walked through the fields, Héctor wearing only his work trousers and his wide-brimmed campesino hat and carrying his machete in his other hand, although today he was not looking out for snakes, carrying the weapon limply at his side as if he was unaware he had it. We heard our followers rustling behind us and sang love songs to each other for their benefit. When we got to the steep church steps, whose edges were worn smooth by the long-ago pious, I stripped. Héctor took out a silver flask that the guards from the transport truck gave him every week filled with bourbon and took a few gulps as he watched me and then took off his hat and his work pants and put down his machete. He offered me some bourbon. I refused. He seemed hurt at first, but an idea came to him and he immediately brightened.

"Let's have sex like the twisted angels, mi amorcito," he requested. "We haven't done it in a long time."

I stood on my hands on the lowest step and stretched my legs upward and back to the highest step so that my body was like a bridge into the holy temple. Héctor approached me and stood on his tiptoes over me, reaching up and grabbing my shins, so that he was a canopy over my bridge, and I felt the warmth of the sun off me and on him.

"More, more," I commanded him. "Your body will stretch more, mi nenito."

He stood higher on his tiptoes and grabbed lower on my shins and I felt his muscles stretch like when a drumskin first dries, wanting to tear away from his bones and I felt him hard against my belly.

"¡No, no, sin toquar!"

"I'm trying, coño."

"No. You are not clearing your mind." I felt my voice leave me through the top of my head and bounce off the stone step. "You are thinking of other things."

"I am thinking of that man's tears, mi amorcito." I felt Héctor's voice cut into my body through the muscles in the floor of my pelvis. "I am thinking of snakes. I am thinking, what if I never taste you again and have to spend the rest of my life tasting them inside that truck."

"Forget everything. You are here now. You are with me. You are a twisted angel. Close your eyes and forget everything."

"Sí, sí, mi amorcito. I will forget."

For this to work, our bodies (with the exception of where he was grabbing my shins) could not touch, so that his flesh and my flesh would know each other not by contact or penetration, which is the common way, the way of man and all the animals, but by nearness, which is the way of faith, the way man knows Changó and all the saints, and the way Héctor knew his brother and the many other dead when he performed his Lazarus Rumba.

"I don't remember the Lazarus Rumba, mi amorcito," he had told me a few days before. "I don't remember being famous and adored."

Sí, sí, mi amorcito. I will forget. Héctor's voice was all inside me now, like a breeze caught in a cavern. It rippled the pools of my blood. He let go of my shins.

I closed my eyes. I waited till I too had forgotten.

¡Ahora! ¡Ahora! ¡Mi nenito! My voice bounced again off the smooth stone and it caught under Héctor's heels and pushed him off the tips of his long toes. Héctor floated above me for a moment and I knew him as I will know him for the rest of my life. I knew him by the marvelous cosquillitas of his nearness. Then he fell on me and I tasted the sea-water sweat on his inner thighs and, twisted as we were, we made love on the smooth church steps.

"¡Maricones y brujos tambien! ¡No jodan!" Their rifle butts wedged us apart. "¿Cómo se atreven? This is sacred ground!" A blunt blow to the side of my head knocked me out.

When I came to I was sprawled on the church steps. I smelled and tasted bourbon on my face. They had woken me up so I could watch. Héctor was still naked, sitting on the ground, his arms resting on his knees, his pinga still half-hard. There was blood on his face and on his arms. A cowboy pistol was pointed at his face. Héctor, his eyes squinting because his face was to the dying afternoon sun, glared at the guard. "Go ahead, hijo de puta!" he taunted him. It was the first time I heard him raise his voice to any of the guards. "Do it if you dare. See what doña Federica la Marica does with you! Do it if you dare! Do it, hijo de la gran puta!"

Héctor lunged for his machete. The guard lowered his pistol and fired into Héctor's back, then he kicked him over and fired into Héctor's chest and into Héctor's belly. I don't remember how many shots. I don't remember screaming. I don't remember Héctor's body bouncing on the ground like an epileptic. I don't remember Héctor's blood splattering on his murderer's boots turning there into black oil-slick globules. I do remember after he was dead seeing his beautiful long toes quiver in unison, like the wings of a pigeon who will never fly again. My twisted angel had been taken from me. I had no strength to remain conscious.

Nunca gozaré otra vez.

Of what happened later, all that I know now I learned from that poor old queen Cuco la Loca.

"I know this boy tried to escape," Federico Sánchez told the guards on the front steps of his cottage, Héctor's body lying underneath them, still naked, its face uncovered, its eyes unshut. "I know that you had no choice but to use force. You will forget that this happened. This boy died of hepatitis. In order not to spread the disease, his body will be burned and the ashes sent to whatever relatives you can find. *If* you find any. Many of these degenerates, in shame, have abandoned and forgotten about their families."

The murderers moved to pick up Héctor's body.

"Un momento," Federico Sánchez said raising his left hand. He looked at Héctor's face for the first time. It had been spared.

"The eyes will not close, mi comandante," one of the murderers said as if apologizing for a mistake.

"Go wash up. All of you. Leave the body here. I will have my servants carry it in the house and have Dr. Domínguez from the infirmary conduct an autopsy."

"An autopsy, mi comandante?"

"¡Pero coño, están sordos! Leave the body!"

There was complete silence except for the sound of the river current, which Cuco la Loca often said always passed by that house with the whispery rumble of freshly pumped blood. Federico Sánchez stretched his tongue. The murderers, all of them, turned and walked away from the cottage by the river. Federico Sánchez waited for an hour, standing over Héctor's body, staring at his face. Watching from one of the upstairs windows, Cuco la Loca thought he heard him speak to the corpse. *Puñetero, tan bonito y tan malagradecido que eres.* Cuco la Loca was horrified at the thought of having to carry Héctor's body into the house. But he was upstairs waiting for the order. The order never came. Federico Sánchez knelt by the corpse and cradled it as the Virgin did with her Son and picked it up himself and washed it in the river by scrubbing a smooth round sun-bleached stone on the wounds and then he carried it into the house. The body was not burned till almost four days later. Federico Sánchez took one of his mother's linen bedsheets and used it as a shroud and laid the body on the mahogany table and kept a vigil over it, drinking bourbon and talking to it. And when the sheet became stained with the darkening blood he wrapped it in another one and another one, so that by the fourth day he had used almost all of the linen sheets his mother had given him to take with him. Cuco la Loca was in charge of bringing Federico Sánchez the fresh linen and the bourbon twice a day. He brought him pork sandwiches and tamales and black bean soup also, but Federico Sánchez did not eat. By the second evening Cuco la Loca had to hold his breath when he walked into the study. On the third evening he became ill and vomited right outside the door. Federico Sánchez went out to him and patted him on his hunched back and told him that *these were the wages for our abominable Sin.* On the fourth day Federico Sánchez opened the seven linen sheets, one by one, and with his bowie knife cut into Héctor's bloated body under the left nipple and dug in under the ribcage and pulled out Héctor's brittling heart, which but for a scrape, the bullets had spared. That night, a group of guards, led by the one who had warned Héctor on the afternoon of his death, broke into Federico Sánchez's cottage and in a quickly assembled tribunal in the parlor just beyond the study where Héctor's body lay, charged him and convicted him with treason to the principles of la Revolución. That same evening, in the backyard of the cottage by the river, Federico Sánchez was executed. The order, we heard later, had come directly from La Habana. It was still said that Héctor died the way Federico

Sánchez had said he died, and that his body was burned to avoid the
spread of hepatitis. Federico Sánchez's own body was transported to his
mother's yellow villa near the capital, where it was said his mother sicked
all her mangy German shepherds on the coroners, who fled, leaving the
starved dogs to tear with their untrimmed paws at the thin-paneled pine
coffin.

Monologue of Triste the Contortionist: The Tale of the Tub

Señora Alicia, this world is strange. It is said that certain survivors of the
Nazi death camps at times look back on those days with an eerie nostalgia, for not only was it a time of the most unimaginable horrors, but it was
also the time of their youth. And who does not find a glint of joy even in
the most wretched youth, and who does not, in the later years, yearn for
that glint of joy. That is what your cousin is for me. He is my lost joy, my
lost youth, my everything that I will not ever feel again. And I surprise
myself, at times I too feel this perverse nostalgia. Héctor is with me again
in the telling of all these horrors. It is Héctor's ghost I follow from place
to place as I pass through the rest of my life, from nothing to nothing
more.

When pressure from international humanitarian groups and European
intellectuals became too great, Fidel forced his brother to shut down the
homosexual labor camps. One day, the gates were opened and our uniforms and our work boots were taken from us and naked we remained inside the barracks. Father came and inspected us one last time. He no
longer seemed deserving of that nickname. He had grown bitter and cynical. The room with the pianito had been shut down in the time of Federico Sánchez's death. His beard had grown longer and grayer and he
played with it incessantly, twirling the pointy end around his forefinger.
He no longer wore the cross whittled from a coconut shell. His eyes had
darkened to a brownish yellow, the hue of bile. He inspected our groin areas and our backsides, making sure all the old wounds had healed, snick-
ering and shaking his head and muttering to himself that he had never
seen such healthy packages in all his life, that now all his work would be
for nought and things would surely go to ruins. Some of the men became
aroused during his examination and Father grew disgusted and spit at his
side and examined these men no further. He prophesied that due to the
shutting of the labor camps, los maricones would roam rampant on the Island, unpunished for their perversions, doing great damage not only to innocent others but to their ignorant selves. When he was finished with his
examination, he pulled out a wrinkled piece of paper from his coat pocket
and read out loud to us in an affected and sonorous voice (so unlike his for-

mer tones of kindness) a passage from Paul's first letter to the lust-struck Corinthians, a passage punctuated by the second shortest verse in the Bible: *Shun fornication!*

Afterwards, naked as we were, we were forced to sort through a pile of old rags and a separate pile of old shoes. This would be the costumes of our exodus, the discarded tatters of the meekest guajiros. I found only a pair of shorts and someone else found me a mismatched pair of worn leather moccasins that fit me. Then the gates were opened and we were evicted from our prison-home. The new comandante in charge of the camp, the one that had warned Héctor on the day of his death, watched from the porch of the cottage by the river, smoking a long Montecristo. He had joked in his farewell speech to us a few days before that now that the camp was closing he was going to have to become a proper man and find himself a fleshy-hipped cubanita for a wife. I waved at him as I passed the gate. I will always remember him not as the man who daily raped the one that I once loved that you once loved, but as the man who with a few coura- geous selfless words had tried to save him. The cottage was far away from us and I don't know if he saw me, but he did not wave back. I wonder what they all did after the last one of us had left the camp. I wonder if they stripped and made love to each other like we had shown them in the cab of the conscript transport truck. I wonder what happened to the old guard who was in charge of the showers. I wonder if he still lives. I wonder if he thinks about Héctor now as often as I do.

I joined a group of about ten of us that included Cuco la Loca and some others whose homes were in Oriente. Most of the freed conscripts, no mat- ter where they were from, headed west, for the capital; there, right under the tyrant's nose, they were sure their brand of love would be freer and eas- ier to find. (Many maricas still thought of Fidel as their protector, and blamed the persecutions and the labor camps on the evil influences of his brother!) Pero sea lo que sea, I wanted nothing to do with the capital. I wanted to see my abuelita before she passed into the other world. From the few letters I had received from her, it was clear—from the trembling of the script, the loss of reason in all matters except for the meticulous de- tailing of all her countless pains and discomforts and the exact herb that a padrino had prescribed for each one—that she was on the brink of death. Our group separated from the larger group and headed east.

We did just as Father had feared we would do. We were like a gang of tigers freed from a zoo. Through each small town or large city that we passed we roamed the night and seduced young men (the more recently married, the greater the catch) who were more than eager to escape their boxed existences and join us. They too had been imprisoned. They too had now been freed. We did just as Father had feared we would do. We ran rampant and infected the innocents with our newfound freedom. This, we proclaimed, was a new era for la Revolución. The '70s would be ours, *la década de los maricas.* Our group had grown to over thirty by the time we crossed into Oriente, headed for Santiago, there to establish the new capital of a freer Island. We were biased. We knew that the eastern side of the Island, specifically the easternmost province of Oriente, was the hotbed of everything that is worthy in our history. Our many rebellions and revolutions against colonialists and imperialists, the most sensual and native dances like el son, the most renowned padrinos of santería, the remains of José Martí, el Comandante-en-Jefe himself and even Our Blessed Mother, all called Oriente home. Oriente was the *real* Cuba, and Santiago therefore the *real* capital.

That's where they were headed and after one last night of *la gran bachata de los pájaros*, as Cuco la Loca referred to our romp through the towns in northern Oriente, I parted from them. The night before, I made love to everyone in the group who would let me, even the pellejosa Cuco la Loca, and then I left never to see one of them again.

I headed for my granduncle's finca, or rather the government's finca run by my granduncle, to say good-bye to abuelita. She had promised me, in a rare lucid moment in one of her letters, that the padrino had taught her certain ways to keep Death at bay. One was to fry seventeen scorpions in corn oil with slivers of boneset root, and leave it on the doorstep—this was Death's favorite meal and Death would eat the scorpions one by one and break into a great sweat of satisfaction and forget altogether his purpose in visiting that house. Another was to paint a live turtle blue and make it circle the house seven times then let it wander around the yard without getting lost. Death would get on all fours and follow the creature around like a fool, amazed that such a being existed, and tormented that it was unknown in Death's kingdom, Death again forgetting the purpose of his visitation. My abuelita wrote that she was in great pain but that she would use these and other stratagems and that she would not die until she saw me. I imagined Death might grow a bit wrathful when he found out how often he had been duped.

I hurried home. I knew I was near when I saw the patches of white sea. My granduncle had owned one of the few tobacco farms in the province of Oriente (most of the crop best suited to the other side of the Island, where the nights are longer and cooler). Now the government owned it; and blind as my granduncle was, he still ran it, unwilling to abandon the land that had been taken from him by the progressive agrarian reform acts.

When I reached my abuelita's cottage it was near dusk. A menagerie of blue turtles roamed all about the yard so that from far away the cottage seemed to be sitting in the center of a small pond. I squinted to see if I could make out Death on its haunches trying to sniff out the secret of these immortal creatures. I saw instead my abuelita come to the doorway. She wore no clothing and the rags of her white hair fell on her bony shoulders down to her shriveled tits. Her skin hung loose on her bones and her sex was completely bald and pushed inside out so that her folds swung like a pouch in between her legs. The only flesh in all her body was bunched up into a ball in her belly, so that she seemed like a skeleton on the fourth month of its pregnancy. She leaned on two white canes, which lent her the balance her fleshless bones could not. Her arms, her legs, the skin draped over her ribcage and even the bones of her feet were all stained with splotches of blue paint. There was a faraway dilated look in her crusty eyes that may have been caused by the fumes from the paint, but more likely a sign that my abuelita had lingered with the help of the blue turtles way beyond the point of her allotted time.

I tiptoed over the turtles, careful not to crush any, and approached her. She let go of the canes and made a gesture to hug me but instead fell in my arms. She was light as a bird.

"Coño, Triste, por fin," she wheezed into my chest, "I am sick of painting these monstrous long-necked critters. What do you call them?"

"Turtles, abuelita, turtles."

"Eso mismo. . . . Perdóname, mi amor, I would cry if I could, but there are no tears left in me, the worms in my belly have drunk them all."

Later, when I questioned my granduncle about abuelita, he assured me his sister had died nine months prior. His son confirmed this and made a move to put his arm around me, as if in condolence, but I ran from them. That night, after the workers had abandoned the fields, I buried abuelita under one of the patches of white sea, so that she may live forever in the breath of her beloved cigars.

I rushed to Santiago to find Cuco la Loca and the others from the camp. I had imagined it would be easy to find them, just listen for the raucous shrieks of all those mad queens, their shouts of *¡Libertad! ¡Libertad!* as their grizzled-chin married lovers topped them. But Santiago de Cuba was a changed town from the last time I had visited in the mid-60s during el carnaval. It was now a town beset by an unholy silence, a silence trapped in by the surrounding mountains like a fog, a silence that may have been confused by the tone-deaf for the warm silken stillness of the siesta hour, but that in its un-Cuban coldness bespoke of a failure from which there was no rebounding. Perhaps it was the lame conclusion of the much-heralded ten million ton sugar harvest the year before, perhaps the many other empty promises and calls to sacrifice coming from the capital, perhaps a realization that the gods they had welcomed into their city from the Sierra a decade before no longer deserved to be prayed or sung to.

I walked the city streets. The townsfolk who during that carnaval years before were all smiles and camaraderie, sharing rum and kisses with perfect strangers, now walked past me with their eyes averted. A schoolgirl with a red pionera handkerchief noosed tightly around her neck screamed at me that I should put some clothes on, that it was indecent to go around so naked. (I was still wearing the shorts and mismatched moccasins I had snatched up at the labor camp.) Her mother tried to hush her but she continued to scream, the veins in her neck rushing with indignation, her mouth twisted in revulsion, her dark eyes lit with righteousness. I heard others join her and I walked on, not looking back. I followed the streetcar tracks uphill on the main boulevard. The side streets became as shady and noiseless as a graveyard of heroes.

Then, as I neared the top of the hill, a great confusion of tongues erupted, like the wails of animals trapped in a burning barn. It grew louder and louder as I climbed. It was the only memorable sound I heard in that city on that day. It was a primitive inchoate song like none I had heard at even the wildest carnival, a chorus of fury entangled with a chorus of yearning, like two champion roosters in a pit. I turned into Padre Rico Street and followed the wild song up a series of steps to a three-story high peeling pink courtyard wall. Beyond the wall, atop the twin domes of the main structure, were visible a pair of lanterns with round arched windows. From there the voices emanated like steam surging from a hot spring.

It is Héctor's ghost that I follow from place to place as I pass through the rest of my life from nothing to nothing more; and here it had wandered, to the place he had dared come only once as a man, here to the asylum his mother had been committed to after her countless phantom pregnancies. Was she still alive? Still giving birth to invisible twins, year after year? I tried to discern her voice among the tormented many, tried to discern the cries of her brood of invisible twins, and even, sure that his ghost *had* ventured here, tried to discern the call of the one that I once loved that you once loved. All for nought. I heard instead the voice of my abuelita, I heard her lucid and wise as she had been before the blue turtles, I heard her say that a soul condemned becomes indiscernible from any other.

I waited till the last glint of light had vanished from the sharp points of the broken cola bottles and I fled Santiago de Cuba. I roamed the Island from end to end living on the natural generosity of our people, till I too decided, like your husband, that to save any shred of my dignity I must flee from this my land, must make like a worm and burrow out.

I decided to go through the yanqui naval base in Guantánamo.

Perhaps Héctor's ghost was leading me by the nose towards you, señora Alicia. But by the time I reached Guantánamo, you had already been taken away. I went to the monsignor of the parish to try to get in touch with your mother, but she was accepting no visitors. She had suffered a breakdown and her heart was weak, the monsignor said. He asked me if I needed help with anything else, if there was another reason why I had come to Guantánamo. I lied.

I stayed in a tenement of workers in the red light district on the east side of the railroad tracks, not far from your old home (inhabited by the blond police chief) on the other side of the tracks. I traded favors with the men in exchange for a worker's costume and leftovers of their meals of congrí and ropa vieja. I slept on the rickety wooden floors of whatever room I was let into and waited for Héctor to come to me in my dreams, like the angels of the Lord come to sleepers in the Bible, and lend me the courage to take the bus to Caimanera, the gateway town to the west end of the yanqui naval base. But the Lord held his angel back, Héctor never came into my sleep, though the workers did, stumbling with rum, kicking me and dropping their trousers (this no more than three feet from their slumbering wives and children) and pleading, *vaya, otro favorcito más, mi negronsón.*

When I tired of this, I left the tenement and went on my own to Caimanera, without Héctor's spiritual lead. Him too, it seemed, I would abandon in my foolhardy quest to retain my dignity. I waited in Caimanera for two more days, sleeping in another tenement, but now posing as a worker so that I owed favors to no one. Then I moved west, staying in the barns of two State ranches, moving towards the Caribbean, towards the Aeropuerto Tres Piedras in the yanqui base. I had been told by someone I had met in the shrine of El Cobre, a young thin poet from the capital, that this was the least protected section of the frontier, that the revolutionary militia suffered from a severe phobia of the roar of yanqui warplanes. The boy was right. The watchtowers on the Cuban side were scattered so far apart that anyone, if careful with the billows of concertina wire and the conspicuous boxed mines, could have crossed the border under the cover of darkness. A shallow river infested with crocodiles, running parallel to the Cerca Peerless, posed a much more serious threat than the guards in the watchtowers. I buried my campesino costume near the river and hypnotized the animals in the river with the stream of my urine as I had done with serpents in the time of the gypsy circus and was ready to abandon Cuba and abandon the spirit of the one that I once loved that you once loved, when I heard the voice of the messenger that *you* had sent.

Sí, señora Alicia, for I believe that without knowing it, the Lord, through you, had sent Joshua to me in place of your cousin to keep me here in this godforgotten land where I belong, and where the spirit of Héctor is condemned to its purgatorial penance.

A boy in a pair of guerrilla fatigues. At first, because of the fairness of his torso, I thought he was some wayward yanqui marine, but when he spoke I knew he was a soul of this Island. And he was as beautiful in his fairness as your cousin had been in his swarthiness. (I should have known, the Lord always sends angels unforeseen.) When the guards heard us and shone their infra-red lights on us and opened fire we ran and hid atop a giant banyan. Throughout the two days we spent there I heard Joshua's story and heard of you and heard of the horrible fair-haired man they called el Rubio who had stolen from you your home, your husband, your freedom and ruled Guantánamo like a petty tyrant.

When the border guards had tired of looking for us, we flew down from the banyan and went to meet with this tyrant. I had somewhat convinced Joshua while up on the banyan (although indeed he had done most of the talking and in a way convinced himself more than anything) that the only way to save Cuba, to save la Revolución, was to get rid of the tyrants one by one, beginning with the little ones. I dug up my campesino costume and washed it in the river. The crocodiles stared at us through their periscopic eyes like the guards had stared at us through the lenses of their rifles at the labor camp, half in hunger and longing, half in fear and revulsion. We waited for dusk of the third day, and in Caimanera hopped on a workers' bus to Guantánamo.

I wanted to try again and see your mother, to tell her who I was, to perhaps relate to her the story I have related to you, so somebody would know, so that it would not be so easily erased from the history, but Joshua insisted that there was no time and led me directly to the open courtyard gate of your old house on B. Street. There was a powder-blue Studebaker in near mint condition parked in front of the garage door. Its coat shone back the winking streetlamps and the dying moonlight as if ridiculing their meagerness. Joshua moved in, treading softly on his tiptoes. He signaled me to follow him. I heard the growling of a dog within the courtyard and froze. Joshua continued to move in. When I reached him he grabbed me by the arm and whispered to me that el Rubio's bullmastiff Tomás de Aquino was at least nine hundred years old, and could barely walk, not to mention that the poor beast was terminally ill with laziness. I held on to his arm and we moved in together. It stunk like a swamp and I heard the buzz of hungry insects, loud and menacing as live wires in a rainstorm. A light was on in the kitchen beyond the haze of the fly-infested courtyard. Tomás de Aquino was huddled in a corner of the kitchen and growled at us again but did not move, did not even have the will to lift the huge bulk of his gray head or to defend himself against the swarm of flies prodding into his ears and his enlarged nostrils.

The courtyard was still set with the remains of the feast of three nights before. A dark cloud of large flies with gossamer wings buzzed over the long table and coated the white porcelain bowls crusty with leftovers; they circled the lip of the empty bottle of burgundy and empty glass at one end of the table and many had drowned in the half-full glass at the other end. The denser swarm of flies converged on the far end of the courtyard and hovered, blacker than the very night, like a guilty soul unwilling to leave this world and meet its judgment, but just as unwilling to rot in its old house, over the little corpse, the shorn-headed indian servant.

Joshua loosened himself from my grip and waved his arms in front of him to open a pathway through the swarm of flies to the table, but no sooner had he walked through it than it enveloped him, dense as a single creature. But Joshua seemed unafraid, familiar with this phenomenon. I thought of Héctor. I thought of his maestro, the famed old moor señor Sariel, who knew the mind of flies and performed his own act during his days in the gypsy circus with a swarm of white-winged horseflies. Joshua too seemed a man who knew the mind of flies. He moved at ease among them. He lifted the porcelain bowls to his nose to make out their contents. He chose one and took it to the kitchen and put it under the head of Tomás de Aquino. The old bullmastiff let his long tongue fall from his jaw and lapped up the soupy contents, drowned flies and all. Joshua returned to me. He told me that Tomás de Aquino, like his master, loved chocolate.

"That I just gave him," Joshua whispered to me, "was bitter chocolate soufflé made with creole eggs from a hermaphrodite rooster. It was the only dish I did not get to taste the other night. It is nice that the old dog will have a sumptuous last meal. He deserves it. He has been a good beast to a bad master."

A pair of flies shuffled in circles on Joshua's brow like thoughts restless for flight and it was then I knew for sure the unnamed purpose of our visit to your old house, why there had been no time to go see your mother. Our deed must be swift as the furies, invisible as breath, silent as the falling sun. "Petty tyrants have no use in the process of la Revolución," Joshua had said to me atop the banyan. I thought of my uncle who is only three years older. I thought of Father. I thought of Federico Sánchez. And thus we were bonded in our purpose.

I went to move towards the corpse of la india and her indecisive soul, but Joshua held me. He said that there was nothing that could be done, except what we should do. He moved again through the swarm of flies, like his namesake parting the Jordan. This time I followed him. We moved through a hallway into the inner house. Joshua opened one door to a bedroom furnished only with a sewing machine and a wooden chair and a straw pallet; he opened another door to a room with an unmade empty bed covered with a mosquitero. We moved on down the hallway. Joshua put his ear to the last door and tried to open it but it was locked. He lunged at it with his shoulder till it flew open. Tomás de Aquino growled from the kitchen.

El Rubio was soaking in your falcon-legged bathtub in the center of the blue-tiled bathroom. He roused from his slumber and looked at us with blurry eyes and asked Joshua who was this negrón that he had brought into his dream. He fished unsuccessfully with one hand for a porcelain pipe and a lighter on one side of the tub. Joshua walked over and handed the pipe to him and lit it for him. El Rubio thanked him and reached out with his free hand and touched Joshua's leg and muttered that it was strange that after three days of dreaming of *you, mi niño bello, you have become almost real. I have been waiting for this.* Joshua nodded and said that he knew and lit the pipe again till all the opium extract had burned. He motioned me to come towards them. El Rubio became agitated. He took the curvy porcelain pipe from his mouth and sat up in the tub. He said the pipe had once belonged to a man of the cloth, the same man who originally owned the bathtub, that it was now State property, that he used it but did not own it. ". . . and who is this black demon you have brought with you, mi vida?"

Joshua knelt by the side of the tub and took the pipe from him and took el Rubio's hand and caressed it and put it to his bare chest so that el Rubio closed his eyes and sighed. Joshua motioned me to stand behind them. He kissed el Rubio's hand and then nodded at me.

Without being told I knew what was expected of me. I cupped both my hands over his thick crown of golden hair and pushed his head underwater. Joshua continued to caress and kiss el Rubio's hand and suck on the end of his fingers and not until the very last moment did el Rubio realize that he was an accomplice to his own murder. His hand withdrew from Joshua's lips as if from a rabid flame and curled into a palsy fist and just as suddenly drooped and splashed into the water. I kept both my hands on the crown of golden hair for many long minutes till Joshua laughed with a delirious joy. At almost the exact moment Tomás de Aquino drowned, unable to lift his snout, heavy with flies, from the sop of the bitter chocolate soufflé.

Before dawn we buried all three bodies under the bed of poppies and yellow roses in the inner courtyard, unmoored the falcon-legged bathtub from the tile floor and loaded it into the powder-blue Studebaker and abandoned Guantánamo forever. Joshua had plucked a white poppy and he wore it behind his ear, his legs hanging out of the passenger seat, innocent as a schoolgirl. Up the Central Highway, I sat him in between my legs and taught him how to drive, so that when he left me near Playa Girón, he managed, in jumps and starts, to control the Studebaker.

"That's all right," he assured me, "there's no way I can harm myself. This thing is like a tank . . . a boat—maybe I'll drive it right across the gulf of forgetfulness."

I promised him that I would come and see you in my own time. I swam. The longest stretch was over thirty miles. Me crees, señora Alicia. Ahora sí me crees.

NINE

Assassination as Birth

The second time Joshua sailed to the bigger Island from the rocky shores near Nueva Gerona, on the smaller island, he did not call on Charo the Crosser, the owner of the leaky trawler. And for all the stories that were later invented to support the myth of the Newer Man—of how he crossed the bay on a raft of 432 live shorn-headed *jutías* (more rats by far than all the books in the Bible to name them, so that many rats were christened by names with numerals as suffixes, such as Daniel 2, or, more oddly, Second Corinthians 3), a live raft 18 feet by 24 feet of giant rats strapped together by a hemp net woven by the Newer Man's mother, fashioned with 432 miniature harnesses, a live raft with 432 little hearts, 432 whip-propeller tails, and 1,728 skinny long-nailed unwebbed paws that kicked and kicked and took two and a half days to cross the Gulf of Batabanó, kicked and kicked till the 432 little hearts, one by one, burst, till the 432 whip-propellers, one by one, limped, and the raft (no longer a live raft) sunk some three miles off the coast of the bigger Island and forced our already wearied and dehydrated Newer Man to swim the rest of the way—no one knows for sure what the historical truth is. The facts are, as reported by *Granma* and kept in the file cabinets of the Party factkeepers, that the prisoner Joshua, a young man with no last name, the son of a mad old prostitute in exile in a remote nightingale-infested valley of the Isle of Youth (as the Isle of Pines has been renamed) arrived for the second time in the capital city on Tuesday, September 26th, 1972, three days after his nineteenth birthday.

A year before, he had come to the capital disguised in an outdated guerrilla uniform from the days of the Sierra and was captured trying to sneak into the Palace of the Revolution. El Líder was in the middle of a marathon interview with the renowned Italian journalist Gianni Denti, and during one of the breaks (requested by the journalist and not by el Líder, for el Líder can talk longer than most journalists can listen) he was told of the young man who had been captured and of his outlandish claim. El Líder cut short his interview and allowed for a private audience with the prisoner. Gianni Denti asked if he might watch, to get a feel for el Líder at work. At first, el Líder said it was out of the question.

Redondamente no. But Signor Denti persisted (with his polished wooden grin, his obeisant half-bows, as if he were in the court of some feared Ve-etian count), till el Líder agreed, on the condition that the encounter with the young man would be considered off the record. And so Gianni Denti, all teeth and spittle, stayed and was told to hide in an antechamber of el Líder's office, the door cracked open, so that he might listen if not watch. He waited, pen and pad in hand, for the young man to be brought in.

"I thought I said off the record," Fidel demanded.

"Sí, sí Signor Presidente, this is for my own use. No se preocupe."

The young man was brought in and forced to sit in one of the un-tanned leather chairs in front of the well-ordered mahogany desk. Fidel had his back to him, perusing the bookshelves on the other side of the room. Before he acknowledged the prisoner, he went to his desk and clicked Signor Denti's tape recorder on. He glanced towards the half-cracked door of the antechamber and caught the one wide peering eye of the obsequious Italian. He suppressed a smile. He dismissed the guards. He looked at the prisoner. They held on to each other's stare as he sat in his own chair and poured himself a whisky and crossed his hands behind his head.

Gianni Denti has kept the conversation that ensued, as promised, off the record . . . for the most part. Now and then, he has lent the rights (for a substantial fee) to this or that part of the transcript to certain respected *European* journalists and writers (never to a yanqui) working on articles about, stories on, el Líder and/or the state of the Island. It is known for in-stance, from an article in *Le Monde,* that Fidel spoke with the young pris-oner for over two hours (twice interrupting the discussion to fetch a blank tape from somewhere in the antechamber), at one point offering the youth a whisky to soothe his nerves, that he had asked the young man his name and that the young man had said Joshua. "Ah, like the prophet," Fidel had said and asked him his surname, and the young man had said he had none; and that indeed, when the records were checked, the young man's sur-name had been blotted from his birth certificate, and under the heading of Father the word *ninguno* was typed. It is further known, from a lengthy story in *El País,* that the young prisoner was of extraordinary beauty, with dark eyes and long black hair tied back in a tail and fine European features and a chin almost beardless, and that Fidel twice complimented him on it. Also known, from a mostly inflammatory article in the pages of the Ger-man weekly *Die Zeit,* was that the young man professed to be heir to Fidel Castro, a charge twice dismissed by el Líder, at first with: *Even if it were so, even if I had known your mother, even if I had the genes in me to father such a buen mozo (in all humility, less possible, unless all your looks come from your mother, and then I am sorry I did not know your mother better than you charge I knew her), but even so, if all the fruit of my loins should, by law, be considered my heirs, there*

*would be a thousand poppy-eyed princes holding poisonous spoonfuls at my table.
Could the Virgin charge the Lord with patrimony?* And secondly with: All *the
children of the Island are children of Fidel Castro! The laws of heredity are the
laws la Revolución overthrew forever. Can you call the Christ a bastard?* From
another article in *Le Monde*, this one confirmed by a footnote in a review of
a thick biography of el Líder in *The Times Literary Supplement*, it was known
that after the lengthy interview all charges against the young prisoner
were dropped (as Fidel is wont to do with most political charges, even
when it means great danger to his own person) and he was released to return to the Isle of Pines, back to his dejected mother and his dreams of
finding his lost father.

A year later he had returned, this time washing up on the shores of the
southern swamps of the Island, not in the ceremonial guerrilla costume,
but in a dirty poncho and ragged shorts and a pair of wooden-soled chancletas that clicked and clacked with a murderous beat, *un tremendo zapateo*,
as he made his way inland, through cane fields and forest to the town of
San Antonio de los Baños, then to Lourdes, towards the capital. Many
helped him, sons and daughters of la Revolución who fed him at their tables and let him, unbathed as he was, sleep between them in their beds.
He moved inland, till he had reached the Vedado district, and came onto
"L" Street, to a small park across "L" Street from the Hotel Habana Libre,
to a bench under the shade of an almond tree, where he slept round the
clock, knitting together siesta after siesta, for three straight days. In his
half-slumbers, when he raised his head and squinted his eyes and looked
around to make sure that the world around him had not disappeared or
that someone had not mistaken him for a corpse and buried him, he did
not see the two Russian jeeps that daily came and went to the front entrance of the Hotel Habana Libre, did not notice the three men in olive
garb dismount and hurry in, nor the shadow of a hunchbacked old doorman, his stature melted by servitude, struggle to open the door for them,
as they all did in the stories of his mother's days, when she sat on that same
bench, under the shade of that same almond tree, eating an egg-salad
sandwich.

And there, in his marathon of siestas under the shade of that almond
tree, we must, for now, leave this Newer Man, this hero with no surname,
for the rest of the story is told to us by *Granma* and by the yellowed files
in the cabinets of the Party factkeepers. Joshua disappears forever from the
pages of *Le Monde, El País, Die Zeit*, from the footnotes of *The Times Literary Supplement*. On page 586 of el Líder's biography by a libelous yanqui
journalist, he loses his first name as well as his last name, he is an innom-
inate boy from the country, one of the many luckless characters snared in
the web of Operation Mongoose, the failed yanqui mission to rid the
world of Fidel Castro. The story is told in one paragraph:

Many of the assassination attempts were badly bungled. Mostly, because the CIA was in the habit of hiring Cuban nationals to do the dirty work, paying them in bundles of up-front dollars and promising their safe passage to Miami, whether the attempt was successful or not. Only one attempt, on New Year's Eve in 1972, long after Operation Mongoose had been allegedly scrapped, nearly succeeded. Castro was in the habit, since his first days in Havana, of stopping every afternoon by the frigid air-conditioned bar-and-grill of the Hotel Habana Libre and drinking a milkshake. (Along with whisky and cigars, Fidel loves ice cream and milkshakes.) It was no secret, and many Europeans vacationing in the hotel purposefully waited till two o'clock to have their lunch so that they might get a glimpse of him. The CIA, of course, knew about it and suborned a new employee, a young untutored campesino recent to the capital, to try and slip a cyanide pill into Castro's milkshake. The next time Castro came in (jubilant, for New Year's Eve in revolutionary Cuba is not only the farewell to the old year, but the anniversary of the rebels' victory, the farewell to tyranny), he ordered a whisky instead of his usual milkshake and the boy with cyanide pill in hand fell into an epileptic fit and was arrested on the spot. The Fates had intervened again. (According to Granma, *the boy served less than a year in prison for his bungled attempt, but this is highly unreliable for* Granma *was forbidden from using the boy's name in its coverage of the story.)*

So here is the Newer Man in the service of the enemy. This is the best *Granma* and the Party factkeepers can do. This is the information they feed to the yanqui biographers (most of whom would be much better suited for writing coarse fiction), this is their finest insult. This cliché of working for *la CIA*, long after *la CIA* had realized that it was useless to try to murder a man so smeared with a tyrant's luck.

But should not this yanqui biographer have been better-versed in the march of history, the history of revolutions (since he was writing about one)? Should he not have known that threats from the outside are followed on the heels by threats from the inside, that rebels rise against revolutionaries, that once a New Man sheds his skin he can metamorphose into nothing else but a Newer Man? In revolutions, there is no retracing of steps. (Someone should grab all these incompetent yanqui historians by the ear and force them to read their Carlyle!)

So, perhaps this story can be better told.

By October of 1972, nearing the decade anniversary of the missile crisis, *la CIA* had most of its energies directed eastward, towards Laos and Saigon, and inward, burrowing, along with its notorious cousin the FBI, into every tavern, every meeting hall, every dormitory room of every yanqui college campus. Fidel Castro, though certainly not forgotten, was more certainly no longer the main obsession. So a young man with no surname, sleeping on a bench under the shade of an almond tree, would not have been approached by sunglassed men in dark suits and offered a sack-ful of dollars and one single cyanide capsule. We ought to be more imaginative than that. We ought not to accept such unoriginal stories from such official sources.

Perhaps this story can be better told in the tongue of the people, since the yanquis, incompetent as they are, are in control of the publishing empires, and respected journalists like Gianni Denti have taken to hiding in the antechambers of Silence.

A young man without a surname, sleeping on a bench under the shade of an almond tree, weary from a hazardous crossing over the Gulf of Batabanó on a raft of live rats, perhaps suffering from sunstroke . . . one late afternoon awakes. He is well rested. He has slept four-and-a-half scores of siestas. His vision is clear, no need for cafecito, no need to recall dreams. It is near dusk. The harvest sun behind him is reflected a hundred times on the windows of the hotel across the street. The windows are frosty with dew, with the Europeans' air-conditioned homesickness. The droplets glimmer like old gold. Except for a few passing cars on "L" street, it is desolate. The jeeps that he has never noticed are not parked in the front driveway of the hotel. He hears music, and he knows it is this music that has awakened him. He sits up and tries to guess where the music is coming from, tries to follow its rhythm with the wooden soles of his chancletas. The song backed by drums and *tres* guitars is a call to a party.

> *La fiesta va a comenzar,*
> *El que venga como quiera, no lo dejen entrar.*
> *Póngase un saquito para que puedas entrar.*

He looks at his dirty poncho, at his ragged shorts, at the soot under his toenails and he knows he will not be let in. Many come and are welcomed.

> *Yo voy a pasar. Pase, usté.*
> *Yo voy a pasar. Pase, usté.*
> *Yo voy a pasar.*

Suddenly the gatekeeper has a change of heart. He says he has new orders.

> *Un momento, caballero. Por favor, no pase, usté.*
> *Pues tengo una nueva orden, que aquí mismo cumpliré.*

The guest, dressed in a most elegant Italian suit, is annoyed.

> *Pero señor, si yo vengo con corbata, saco puesto y bien plantao,*
> *Por favor, señor, aquí no me deje parao.*

The gatekeeper, unafraid to insult the guest, unafraid to be blunt, explains himself.

> Usté no puede pasar, compai,
> La fiesta no es pa los feos.
> Ve y cámbiate la cara, compai.
> Tú mismo te tiene miedo.
> Feo, requetefeo, compai.
> No es na peor que ser feo.

Joshua laughs. He has stood and has captured the rhythm of the song with the soles of his chancletas. The current moves up his brown hairy legs into his hips. He has not danced since he was a child and listened to the street musicians from the iron-grill balcony of the apartment on Cardenas Street before he fell into his trances. He feels for the first time a part of his world. Dancing is the talent of the Islanders. There is only one Cuban who never dances. Joshua continues to dance and laughs again.

The poor guest in the fine-cut Italian suit has not been let in, for, as the gatekeeper has put it, the party is not for ugly people. Though the song is old, he knows why it is sung now.

El Líder had made a State visit to Paris. He was welcomed in the presidential palace, he toured the Louvre, he was photographed in front of the Mona Lisa. And all throughout his visit he forsook his usual military garb for a custom-made midnight-blue Italian suit. *Granma,* for a moment forgetting its respectability as the Party's Word, printed a short caption under one of the photographs: *¡Coño! ¡Qué guapo!* But the picture told a truer story that a hundred flattering captions would not alter. In his custom-cut Italian suit, el Líder looked like a petulant itchy child forced to dress up for his First Communion in hand-me-down ill-fitting clothes.

Did the three Italian tailors who were summoned from Milan to the Palace of the Revolution, these card-carrying members of the Italian Communist Party, do this on purpose? Did they intentionally cut the shoulders so high and bunch the cloth in the upper back so that el Líder looked hunchbacked? Did they infuse the lapels with a wish to fly so that they constantly flapped and waggled like the wings of a heavy pelican? Did they sew the hem of the pants just high enough so that in a full-length photo, with his large leather moccasins, el Líder looked like a clown, *un payasón,* as one of the underground mimeographed quarterlies put it? Did they snicker as they mistaught him how to tie a Windsor knot so that it was thick as a fist pressed up under his Adam's apple? Did not anyone have the heart to tell el Líder that these three Italian tailors were most certainly traitors to the Party, agents of *la CIA,* or worse, of the banished Sicilian mob that once ruled the capital, that they set out, from the first cut of cloth, to make him look like a barbarian at a ball, the Philistine among the Civilized, the Untutored among the Sophisticated, and the Ugly among the Beautified? Who could have guessed looking at him so misdressed, so uneasy, tugging at his collar, straightening his fat-fisted tie, holding down his lapels, that he too was an heir of Rousseau and Danton and Marat? How great the skill of three demonic Italian scissors, three traitorous Italian needles that made the exalted look so lowly.

And so the song that Joshua hears, whose rhythm he captures in the rattle of his chancletas, in the turbulence of his hips, was heard all over the capital in those days.

> *Feo, réquetefeo, compai.*
> *No es nada peor que ser feo, compai.*

And those that sing it embrace this young man with no surname. The bartender at the Hotel Habana Libre is named Luisito Cuzco. He is no taller than five feet and has brown smooth cheeks and large brown eyes punctuated by almost hairless triangular eyebrows. He is a Siboney indian. There are few of these left on the Island. The Spaniards, with the blessing of Rome, were of two minds: conversion or genocide. Luisito Cuzco is a survivor of an extinct race. So he lies. He invents a home. He claims he is from Ecuador. After reading Che Guevara's journal of his travels through South America, he borrows the name of a mythical city and makes it his own. People do not question him, so he invents a lineage. He is Inca royalty. His many friends hence call him *la princesa*. He plays the *tres* guitar and calls his band Los Rumberos Incas. He welcomes the young man with no surname. For one, this is the type that attracts him, for another he knows what it is like to be a man without a place, knows how to endure in the harshest climes, like the weeds that thrive in the sea. Joshua divulges his real name before he realizes that this may be a capital mistake. He tries often to lie to Luisito Cuzco but finds it difficult. In every conversation the indian is always a few steps ahead. *No jodas a un jodedor:* that is his favorite phrase. Luisito Cuzco gives Joshua a job, lets him sleep in a cot in his tenement, shows him how to play the güiro and lets him sit in with Los Rumberos Inca. He cannot guess, as no man can, what awaits him, how he will be repaid for these generosities, how soon he will join his murdered ancestors.

El Líder was back in his military garb. He seemed himself again, boisterous and chatty, tarde tras tarde, as he drank his milkshake. (He either had been shielded from the heavy ridicule over his Milanese wardrobe or purposefully ignored it.) He bragged that Paris was the second most

beautiful city in the world, more illustrious than Moscow, more provoca-
tive than New York.

"Pero vaya, somewhat . . . cómo te digo . . . illusory, like a beautiful
woman without a heart, a phantom princess, no match for the fiery living
soul of nuestra Habana."

Luisito Cuzco leaned into the bar. He took back the empty milkshake
glass and washed it in the sink underneath him. He placed it aside, for el
Jefe and el Jefe alone drank from this glass. "Eso va sin decirlo, comandante." He looked for Joshua to ask him to bring more glasses from the
kitchen; but Joshua, as usual when the Comandante-en-Jefe was present,
was not to be found.

"Why are you afraid of him," Luisito Cuzco asked Joshua after a session at a nightclub in the Vedado district. "He is just a man like you and
me."

"I am not afraid of anyone."

"Entonces, why do you always hide when he comes to the bar?"

"Mira, no te confundas. I am not a communist. I am an orphan. I have
told you the story. I came to the capital because someday I am going to go
to the university. Y que importa, whether I see him or not. Like he cares
about anybody but himself. Like he cares about us, the people. Why aren't
Cubans allowed in that club we played tonight? What's this tourists and
Russians only? Is that the triumph of our Revolución? Mierda, they don't
even know how to dance! Why do we even *play* there!"

"Sabes bien why we play there, they pay us in dollars."

"Yeah okay, just don't let *him* see your dollars while you are fawning
over him and crushing the ice for his milkshake."

"Coño, I have been good to you. I am not a communist either."

"No, claro que no, you are a princess. An Inca princess."

Luisito Cuzco laughed, he put his arm around Joshua's waist. He
had about him the uncomplicated ease of a commoner and was almost
a foot shorter than Joshua so that in no way could the latter interpret
this gesture as threatening. They walked in silence. And Joshua eventually put his arm around Luisito Cuzco's shoulder, so that they walked
entwined like a father and son walking home from a *béisbol* game. They
had walked less than a block when the streetlamps went out all at once.

"Otro apagón," Joshua said. "Can't we ever go a whole night without
one in this *maldita ciudad*? Can't you speak to *him* about it?"

In the incipient darkness, Luisito Cuzco tightened his grip around
Joshua's waist. "You played well tonight. La gente te quiere. Maybe you
can stay with us for a while."

Joshua loosened from his embrace and crossed the desolate street and
walked ahead.

"Oye," Luisito Cuzco shouted after him. "No te pongas bravo. Just a
thought. I know you came here to do other things." But he had lost

Joshua in the shadows of the unlit street. He quickened his pace lest for some reason the boy should decide to leave him. He cursed himself. He had let his feelings intrude. He had wandered from the script. He had said the wrong thing. It might prove costly. But when he reached his tenement building, Joshua was sitting on the steps out front, his head between his knees. Luisito pulled a flask of Havana Club out of his back pocket. This was another of the advantages. The manager nightly slipped him a flask of rum. Joshua, for the first time since Luisito Cuzco had known, accepted the offer of the flask and tilted his head back and took a long gulp.

"Maybe we ought to get you some new clothes, now that you have become so popular. A real dancer's outfit. Vaya, prestao, you can give it back to us when you leave."

The days go on. Good, Luisito Cuzco, thinks. Let the days go on. Joshua has not worked up the nerve. And the more the days pass, the more his resolve is likely to weaken. He is caught in more lies. Like an unskilled storyteller, Joshua cannot remember what came before and what should naturally follow thereafter. But Luisito Cuzco does not correct him. He lets him invent as many past lives as he cares. Joshua does, however, prove a skilled barback, and a more skilled musician and performer. The people really do love him. Fat-cheeked Russian women with smeared-on lipstick and platinum hair throw themselves at him in the nightclubs. Russian soldiers and European bankers on the dance floor mimic the furious zapateo of his wooden-soled chancletas, the churn within his ragged shorts. But they are not Cuban, and you cannot fake such things. There are no dancers on the dance floor. Near the end of each show, Joshua puts down his güiro and moves center stage, next to the microphone, next to Luisito Cuzco, who croons into it:

> Oye, mírenlo, y mírenlo bien, poque horita se va,
> El niñón, se va, y que se va, se va,
> Que te vacunen, que te vacunen hoy
> Pa que lo sepa y lo sepa bien,
> Así que aprovecha, coño, aprovecha bien,
> Que te vacunen, que te vacunen hoy
> Po que el niñón ya se fue, y que se fue, se fue.

Joshua takes off his poncho and waves it like a scarf over his head, and twists it around his torso, and rubs it on his hips and on the back of his legs. He closes his eyes, throws his head back. His knees buckle as if he is about to fall, though he does not fall, just at the last moment, he recovers and comes up and buckles again and recovers and comes up and again and again.

The women abandon their men, they crowd as close as they can near the lip of the stage, and reach out their hands and graze the inside of his thighs with their long fingernails. They are foreigners. They are ignorant of the art of this dance. They do not understand the words. They do not know that it is the man who is supposed to do the chasing. The woman who resists. If the woman gives in, there is no dance, no motive for the art. Joshua frowns and slaps their hands away with his poncho and tries to restore the proper order, thrusts his hips forward with the force of a kettle drumbeat. For a moment, as he watches him from the corner of his eye, as he wets the head of the microphone with his spittle, Luisito Cuzco thinks that the boy has lost himself in the dance, become a conduit for the holier spirits and thus exorcised of his baser purpose, and is (for a moment) truly beautiful, nothing more than un rumberito bello. He repeats the chorus again and again in succession, till the words come unglued from their meaning and are nothing but servants to the dance.

Joshua dances and dances till one of the foreign women leaps on to the stage and tackles him. She is wearing a dress two or three sizes too small. Her stomach is folded into three separate rolls. She straddles Joshua and bounces on him, wailing her own incomprehensible lyrics in her tongue, her fat arms in the air, the plentiful flesh slapping to and fro like a pelican's pouch.

After this night, Joshua dances no more with Los Rumberos Incas. He works with Luisito Cuzco at the hotel during the days, and stays in his tenement at nights, cross-legged on the twin cot. He remains in the small room each night as if he were already a prisoner, though Luisito Cuzco urges him to go to the malecón and spend time with others his own age, to dangle his legs over the seawall and let the Caribbean mist baptize him, the salty sea air blow loose the cobwebs in his mind. Joshua does not listen. Each night before the apagón comes, he has drunk all the Havana Club that was left over from the night before and he is passed out facing the wall. When Luisito Cuzco arrives he calls out to the boy to make sure that he is asleep, then he flicks on his silver lighter and goes through the sugar sack where Joshua keeps his meager belongings, the little treasures he has collected during his short stay in the capital, a Russian watch stuck at 2:30, a worn leather wallet carved with indian figurines that he found in a garbage bin at the hotel, his güiro (which Luisito wouldn't take back), a silver necklace with no medallion and two separate bundles of bills secured with rubber bands, one of the pesos he has made from the hotel, a thicker one of dollars, his cut from the band. Luisito Cuzco touches the pockets of the dirty shorts Joshua wears even in his sleep. He rattles the wooden-soled chancletas to assure himself they have not been carved with a hidden chamber. Night after night, he finds nothing—no pistol, no dagger, no small bomb—to confirm the dire prophesies of the men in the Russian jeeps, the uniformed barbudos who accompany el Jefe.

Why don't they just arrest him and charge him with all their prophesied crimes? It's not like they need proof or solid evidence. They have never needed such things before.

Why have they put *him* in such a spot? He is just a bartender, an amateur rumbero, a foreigner in this Island that once belonged to his ancestors.

Luisito Cuzco thinks of fleeing the capital, fleeing the country as many have done, but he does not, he is not of that class, he stays at the Hotel Habana Libre and he daily serves el Jefe his milkshake and he does not dare subtract or add a word to the prophesies of the bearded men.

On Sunday, December 31, 1972, thirteen weeks and five days after Joshua had arrived at the capital, the bar-and-grill at the Hotel Habana Libre was unusually crowded, there were no seats available at the bar, and it was two deep with early celebration. All the formica-top tables were full of diners. It was past two in the afternoon, and Luisito Cuzco was shuffling from one end of the half-parabola bar to the other. Joshua kept him supplied with a constant stock of clean glasses from the kitchen, and near past one was forced to jump behind the bar to help him serve drinks to the thirsty Europeans who had never known such a muggy and warm New Year's Eve. The Europeans paid with dollars and Luisito Cuzco did not let Joshua handle the money.

"Just serve the drinks," he said. He quickly showed him how to make a daiquiri, the most common order. "I'll take the money from them." Joshua grew distracted, ignored the patrons who shouted their drink orders at him. He watched the pale green bills change hands. There were none left in his sack at home.

He had lied to Luisito Cuzco one last time. He needed more dollars than were in his bundle. He had told him that whores do not deal in pesos. Luisito Cuzco had said what he always said when he caught Joshua in a lie.

"Óyeme, no jodas a un jodedor."

At first, he tried to get Joshua to rejoin the band, luring him with the promise of plenty of more dollars. But Joshua would not consider it. He said he did not want to get trampled by European elephants. He said he would find the dollars somewhere else. So Luisito Cuzco gave him the dollars anyway, enough to purchase the powdery content of the glass vial, which he had had for over a week and kept on him at all times, now hidden in his pocket and at nights, because he knew Luisito Cuzco went through his belongings, wetted with Havana Club (to disinfect it) and then with globs of saliva (to lubricate it), inserted into his rectum.

The apothecary was an old surgeon in one of the government hospitals, he was also a sometime photographer, a sometime gardener, and a sometime santero . . . and a long time ago, it was rumored, had stolen organs and sold them to rich ailing yanquis. He ran a pharmacy from his apartment where he sold relics to the faithful, and from where he sold his poisons to anyone who had the dollars to pay for them. The apothecary, like the whore, did not deal in pesos.

Joshua remembered his name, he remembered exactly where he lived, remembered exactly that you had to enter through a garden in the back, with creeping vines hiding the walls and the ground carpeted with marigolds and touch-me-nots and begonias. And after he came to in the hospital bed, when the bloated scar-cheeked comandante with the greasy mustache began his endless sessions of interrogations, it was the first thing he wanted to know: *Who sold you the vial? Where does the traitor live? What does he look like?* Joshua was disoriented, but he remembered exactly, feature by feature, the globular bald head, the gaunt gray cheeks unhidden by a base of ruddy makeup, the thin painted mustache like Clark Gable, the absent lips and bad teeth and yellow eyes, the pale green surgeon scrubs and yanqui cloth sneakers with no socks.

PÍO GORRAS
36 CALLE DE LOS POSEÍDOS, APARTAMENTO 16
(POR FAVOR DE PASAR POR EL JARDÍN ATRÁS.)

He remembered exactly, the sofa with a threadbare blue cover, the apothecary's great-granddaughter in a stained pajama skirt, her tangled hair and pink blotches on her forehead, sucking her fingers and watching the transaction from the doorway to the kitchen.

"For the rats, huh?" Pío Gorras said louder than necessary, as he siphoned the crystalline powder into the small vial. His fingers were long and thin and the nails faultlessly manicured. (His hands were his only decent feature.) "Sí, sí, coño, es la tristísima verdad, this city is infested with giant rats. This will do it. Make sure you use *all* of it. Some of these rats are very powerful."

Out of spite, or a growing sense of conviction in the properness of his bungled attempt, Joshua said nothing. He rubbed the back of his head. He played the amnesiac. There were many in this city who could do much good with poison, bought with dollars, from Dr. Pío Gorras.

"Okay, así va a ser, bien," the bloated interrogator said. His cheeks were mushy, pitted and carved with the characters of a severe boyhood acne. He scrubbed the palm of his hands on them as if to smooth them. "We have men who will help you remember what we already know too well, réquetebién."

Joshua closed his eyes and rested his head on the mound of pillows. He wondered if he had been drugged or if the haziness he felt was a hangover from the fit he had suffered.

Ask any fool on the street, he wanted to shout. *He will tell you where the apothecary lives. They will write it out for you on a little sheet of paper, with a note in parentheses warning that you must enter only through the garden in the back. They will tell you this entire story like a fairy tale their mothers once whispered to them. He is one of you, a loyal member of the Party, a renowned surgeon, perhaps on the payroll at this very hospital. Check your drug inventories! Count your poisons!*

But he said nothing. He rubbed the back of his head again.

"No me acuerdo. I don't remember anything."

Your name is Joshua. You are the son of a whore. You have no father. You were arrested more than a year ago trying to break into the Palace of the Revolution. El Líder consented to seeing you and graciously pardoned you and sent you back to your whore of a mother. And it could have stayed at that, a foolish guajirito, who makes a judgment in error, who has the fortune of meeting el Líder and chatting pleasantly with him. It could have stayed at that, something, someday you might have recounted to your grandchildren.

But now, you will never live so long. Did you think that we would not keep our eyes on you? Did you think we would so easily forget? ¿Eres bobo? El Líder is full of mercy and grace, especially for the young, but it is up to us, el pueblo, to protect him like he cares not to protect himself. He is our voice in the world, but here, we are his eyes, we are his ears, we are his shield, without us he is a lamb in the field.

From the moment you set foot in this province we had our eye on you. ¿Qué piensas, niño? La Revolución has ten thousand eyes! Every family that you stayed with on the road to the capital, every wife who kicked her husband out to let you rest in her bed, every abuelita who cooked you arroz con pollo and kissed the back of your head, every schoolchild who let you into their hopscotch games, all of them, one by one, reported your actions to their local vigilantes, who reported immediately to us.

Do you think us blind? Do you think us morons? Do you confuse the Christian grace of el Líder for stupidity?

Your name is Joshua. You are the son of a whore. Y ahora, it is rumored, the fucker of a traitor, the fucker of the widow of a greater traitor, herself a murderer and as much a whore as your mother. Una puta y media. You have no father. And we watched you fatherless as the devil come to do the devil's work. We fell asleep with you under the same almond tree, in the bench where your whore of a mother once sat and stalked our Líder. We awoke you with our song. Yes, our *song. For even when el Líder is ridiculed, the shameful words become ours as they must become ours so we can tear them to pieces till they no longer make sense. We entrusted you to one of ours. For the indian Luisito Cuzco, que en paz descanse, was a man true to his ancestors, true to his land, he was one of us, a devoted member of the Party, and he detested singing the song that lured you into his trap, but he sang it anyway, he sang the shameful words of ridicule for the greater good. And later, he let you* sing them *for the tourists at the nightclubs. The foreigners haven't changed. Wherever they come from, all they want is to use our land, to get drunk on our rum, and toasted on our beaches, to fuck our daughters and piss on our fields. So Luisito*

Cuzco had no heart to sing these words to them. So he let you sing. He let you dance. ¿Más propio, no? For you are a greater scoundrel than they, this is not their land and they should have no love for it.

He hoped you would forget. And we, we also hoped. Though we could have arrested you the minute we heard you had returned to the mainland as you had been forbidden to do, taken you and thrown you in el Morro for a thousand years, for the crimes that were already full-born in your heart. Yet, we hoped. El Líder hoped. He said you would not dare. He said, in the end, you would not want to. He said it knowing that you are the son of a great whore, spawned in disgust and birthed in bitterness and raised in iniquity. As if there are angels that dare do battle with such demons as you. ¡Como si hubiera remedio! Still, we hoped.

And for what? For you to attempt your wicked deed in our holy day of commemoration. ¡Le ronca! How could you not know how closely you were being watched? How could you not guess that Luisito Cuzco called you behind that bar on purpose. He is the capital's fastest bartender and could have easily handled twice the crowd that was there. He knew what was hidden in your pocket. He stuck his finger into your hairy ass every night and felt it. How does it feel? ¿Le ronca, no? You think full bottles of Havana Club were left behind by chance?

We have defeated many devils. We know exactly how careless the wicked are. And there you are, Joshua, son of a whore, night after night your culito fingered by a half-sized indian, fingered and fingered like a new whore's cunt. There you are, Joshua.

But still the act had to be attempted, it was written, and you were condemned long before you acted. For how was he to miss your face, though you turned it away as you reached into your pocket, as you fumbled with the vial, as you dug the tumbler glass into the ice and reached it out to Luisito Cuzco . . . and after he poured the whisky, after the foreigners cheered and toasted and gathered around el Líder, after he complained that he still had no drink to toast with, you had already started, you had emptied half the poison powder into the tumbler of whisky, you had tossed the vial aside and it was then that the avenging angels found enough courage to descend upon you, to twist you into all sorts of shapes, and pull the tongue out of your head and set your eyes a-twirling and toss the poisoned whisky on your cheeks and throw you back against the rack of bottles and deliver you unto us, unto the hands of him you wanted dead.

You had done it all in the eyes of Luisito Cuzco, and because the angels did not descend on him, our men did, three of them hopped the bar and jumped him, and whipped him with their pistols, and proved again that men know more about murder than angels. But the greater torture is yours, it would have been a blessing to die there behind that bar, Joshua, son of a whore.

Joshua opened his eyes. He had been listening and not listening, for he knew the fold of the story till the moment the bug of his old sickness began to twitch in his eyelid and kick its trapped legs. He looked at the interrogator. He knew he was as full of lies that sound like the truth as any of his father's people.

"If you know so much, carajo, why are you asking me where the apothecary lives?"

The interrogator stood. He walked to the side of the bed. In a calculated and even gesture he threw back his left arm and slapped Joshua with the back of his puffy hand. It was how Joshua came to know that his arms and his legs were secured to the bed with leather straps. He could not defend himself. The blow was of such force that it jolted Joshua to the opposite, the right, side of the bed. The IV needle on his left arm popped loose and dark blood squirted from his arm and stained the bedsheet. He tasted other blood and felt it stain his dignity.

"If I hit you so again a thousand times, it would not begin to counterbalance the violence you attempted to inflict this afternoon, on us, on your people, on your country, on our Revolución! Begin whispering prayers to the father of all demons, for you will soon meet him."

He screamed for the nurse, a small mulatta wearing only the upper half of her uniform and black slacks, who hurried in and knew exactly what had occurred but said nothing. Her eyes averted, she dutifully reattached the IV needle to Joshua's arm and pressed a gauze to the cut on his lip and took his pulse and touched his forehead and promptly exited the room.

"Prepárate, muchacho," the interrogator said. "This is only the beginning. We are going to round up the whole nest of traitors. And we will not be pushed. We will do it in our own way, in our own time. We have finally made a nation out of this Island, and we know that the world is watching, waiting for us to trip up. So we are careful. Prepárate bien, muchacho. You will live, but you are going to come out of this a new man."

This then, in that room, in that hospital where perhaps the ancient apothecary Pío Gorras, the renowned surgeon and member in good standing of the Party, the sometime photographer, sometime gardener, sometime santero, sometime organ thief, was or was not employed, paid for his services in pesos, claro, and not dollars; this then, in that room, the evening after the assassination attempt, the evening that was the thirteenth anniversary of the rebels' march down from the Sierra, that would have been the assassination day of that other leader, had he not made like a roach at a rumba and scrammed, this then was the birth pangs of the new man, or the Newer Man, as he must be known for the sake of the finicky genealogists.

For how does one attempt patricide and fail (fail miserably, cowardly, buckling under the weight of ancient demons) and not be metamorphosed? With what wherehow are we to pinpoint the who, to overcome the tunnel vision of the yanqui biographers, the laxness of stiff-lipped

Party factkeepers, the yeasty bitterness of scarred interrogators, and see assassination (even the attempt) as birth? And why should we?

(¿Por qué?)

Porque así son las cosas de la vida. Porque even a New Man, like a new Studebaker, gets old. Porque it's not the shell that crumbles with rust first, not the chrome that is dulled by the noonday first, not the whitewalls that are blackened with the mud-sputter of our cane fields first; no que va, the problems start on the inside, so that we can't remember when the air-conditioning compressor compressed or when the windshield wipers wiped, when the starter did not have to be coaxed on and prayed to and screamed at like a deaf and petulant deity or when the brake pedal responded to anything but a violent thump, as if to squash a jutía. Porque no matter how ingenuous we are at finding spare parts in the black market of our soul, long after the odometer of our heart has stopped reading the correct mileage (just add a hundred thousand miles, or is it two hundred, or three—coño, is our Island so big!), long after the speedometer of our breath knows how fast we are going, and the compass of our mind can barely guess in what direction, in the end we must improvise, we must invent. Porque así son las cosas de la vida. Porque we must make the newer of the new. Porque, coño es fácil, we do it by reverting to simpler times. Porque somos y seremos a very fecund-headed and adaptable people. Porque look at how long after la Revolución our Studebakers are running and there is not one single running Studebaker in all the boulevards of yanqui-dom. Porque we cannot only think in metaphors, we can drink them, we can eat them, we can light our rooms with them, we can fall madly in love with them . . . *and* we can drive in them. Porque it doesn't take much ingenuity to replace a carburator with a rumor-mongering vigilante, a cooling fan with grandmother's Sunday abanico, a crankcase with a Miami exile, a piston skirt with a rumbera's scarf, a muffler with a rolled-up copy of *Granma,* a steering column with the steely words of Fidel's speeches, a surefire starter with Martí's *Versos Sencillos,* a gas tank with a Soviet subsidy, a viscous coupling with . . . bueno, you get the idea. Porque that's why our Studebakers are still running and theirs are not. Porque we make the newer of the new.

With man as well as with Studebaker.

Within Alicia's Bohío, in the Colony of the Newer Man

"They should hire better writers than that!" Alicia slapped down the two-week-old copy of *Granma* on her kitchen table.

"Who?" Marcos said. His shirt and pants were drenched in sweat from the fields and he stood by the bed not wanting to sit on it and soil it.

"Who? Todos, the paper, the Party, whoever is inventing all this mierda . . . that boy my lover! This is how they shame Julio, even in his grave, this is how deep their vendetta plummets."

"Kind of boring, if you think about it," Triste said, snatching the paper and spreading it before him. He was sitting cross-legged on the floor, shirtless, mud-splashed from the fields. He ate a sandwich and smudged the bread with his hands. He drank straight from a rum bottle. Alicia admonished him again to go wash his hands. He protested that it was not dirt nor grime nor soil but the color of his skin melted off by the harsh sun. He put his rosy palms up as if to prove his theory. "Vaya, kind of boring (you're right, they *should* hire better writers than that). They could at least have had him doing something with *me*! Imagínense, vaya to put a more lurid twist on the whole scandal: *Nameless Assassin Secret Lover of Fugitive Negrón.*" He poked each word of the imaginary headline in the spread copy of *Granma.* After spending a few days in the valley, Triste had been convinced to stay. What better place, after all, Alicia had said, for a fugitive negrón to hide than in this colony first established by runaway slaves.

"No le veo la gracia, Triste. Joshua is likely dead . . . or worse. Besides, you are not a fugitive. You did them a favor by murdering el Rubio. He was too ambitious, ese hijo de puta. You did them a favor. They know it. That's why they have not touched you."

Triste took another gulp from the rum bottle. "Bueno, Alicia, perdóname, but I also have . . . vaya, como digo . . . my charm with the men they send from the capital. They have more than *touched* me. That's why I can joke a bit, I know that Joshua is not dead, some of the men have whispered it in my ear. There will be no public trial, as rumored. Fidel will once again display his ample patience and return the boy to his mother, as if nothing at all had happened. Mercy, these men say in my ear, is enthroned in the heart of all natural kings. Now where the hell do you suppose they got that from, for these gruff men are not poets at heart."

"Shakespeare," Marcos grumbled. "It's from somewhere in Shakespeare."

"Shakespeare? No, no, Virgil maybe."

Alicia twisted her mouth with disgust. "¿Pero qué le pasa a ustedes? Those men are full of lies. The revolution has no use for mercy and the truth, nor for Shakespeare and Virgil (wherever it's from). It never did. It is lies that are holy writ, that instill fear, that pit neighbor against neighbor."

"Miren, whatever they have done with Joshua, or plan to do with him," Marcos said, "it's ruined everything here in the valley. Every week they send a different squad of men with a new list of questions and accusations and pilfered quotations from the great poets. We till the fields and drink our rum and listen to the Sunday speeches at Maruja's and pretend our lives are still the same (even *she* does not mention her missing son, as if he never existed), but our lives are not the same. Our simple life in exile has come to an end."

"Sí, pero no seas tonto," Triste said. "They know they have to keep on changing the men they send here, because they know that the longer the soldiers stay here, the more they become part of us and less part of them. The bird songs in this valley dissolve all the rhetoric of their precious revolution. If we can convince enough to stay, as we have two or three already—¿no es así? (one which I will take credit for), pronto, prontísimo we'll have a standing army. Charo will be running a one-way ferry, trip by trip building the new rebel army."

Marcos went to the window and stuck his head out. He looked both ways as if he were to cross a street. He closed the wooden shutters and fastened the latch. "Triste, soldiers from the capital have always lived in this valley with us. They come and they stay and they don the garment of workers and work the fields and let their skin grow so dark that they become as one of us. But they are *not us,* believe me, I have had many work in my side of the valley, attend our meetings, break bread with us, drink rum with us. Then one morning they are gone and others have taken their place. Those that stay are the eyes and ears of those that leave. ¡Qué cosas! They do not stay to form a new rebel army. They stay because they are told to. Joshua used to refer to them as the invisible black birds. But they do not hide up in trees, they hide among us, at our work, at our meals, at our committee meetings. Now with all this, they are not even bothering to hide. They are building a set of new bohíos near Maruja's house (a Complex, they call it) . . . I suppose because it's near the river and because they can tap into her generator. They now keep their olive uniforms and stand in the fields with their rifles slung over their shoulders. They no longer get their hands dirty. They are suggesting a conspiracy now. They plan to arrest and charge Maruja and all three of us. They just need to extract a full confession from Joshua. . . . He is in el Morro, they say, and is ready to talk, to accuse us all."

"Lies upon lies upon lies . . . when they come in here, I do not talk to them. I do not answer any of their questions. They threaten to take me to the capital and have me charged and executed in place of the boy. They threaten to charge my old mother and my poor daughter. They threaten to charge my sister. I'm surprised they don't threaten to charge the ghost of my husband. I'm surprised they don't threaten to dig him up and murder him all over again. Sí quieren oír la verdad, Joshua is already dead and all of us are soon to follow. My only wish is that they let me see my daughter one last time before they do me in."

"No, no puede ser, señora Alicia, ya verás, the men have whispered it in my ear. . . . Yo conozco a los hombres and they do not lie in those brief moments. Ya verás, time will tell."

"Dicen that his horse is the color of Martí's."

"How the hell did they get a horse into this valley," Marcos said. "We've been trying for years to get mules in here, to drag our plows, and we finally figured that the only possible way to get any beast of burden into this fertile land was to put wings on it and let it fly in."

Josefa was sitting on the bed knitting. "They could have flown it in . . . by helicopter."

"No, negra, que va, we would have heard a helicopter, no matter what remote part of the valley they decided to set down in. Besides, I don't think that the Party has any more than three working helicopters."

Josefa grunted. She did not like to be addressed as *negra* (after all she had only an eighth of black blood). Triste, to her disgruntlement, always insisted on using this address, no matter how often she asked him not to. She had been tempted to put some curse on him, but there were too few on their side and she did not want to risk losing anyone, even someone as disrespectful as the giant negro. Besides, it was obvious that some greater power had cast a curse over all of them who met in Alicia's bohío every evening. "Mira negro, the way you chug on those rum bottles, a yanqui atomic bomb could be dropped in this valley in the middle of the night and you would not hear it."

Triste laughed. He stretched his long body over backwards like some creature that was both cat and serpent and reached out a rum bottle to Josefa. "Vaya negra, maybe it will do you some good, relax you a bit. Offer it to Elegua if you can't have it yourself. Coño, even orishas enjoy a good swig now and then, I don't see why you shouldn't."

"Okay, señores y señoras, basta, don't start," Marcos stepped between them. He grabbed the rum bottle and set it down on the wooden table. "I am worried. Alicia should have been back by now. It is almost dark."

Josefa was agitated. She knitted in furious sharp little gestures, as if her needles were pens, and she were scribbling, with both hands, backwards and forwards, in an alien script. "Maybe she is at the Complex, waiting for the arrival of the Newer Man, waiting to make those *Granma* stories come true."

"Coño, por favor, Josefa . . . y tú también, Triste, let's not turn one against the other."

"I say only what my shells tell me. Voy y repito, my shells say his horse is the color of Martí's and his heart the color of his father's."

"It must be black indeed," Triste said, ". . . the heart, not the horse."

Marcos went to the door and opened it and stood looking out. The nightingales had begun their chatter though there was still a thick glob of orange and violet bleeding over the sharp ridges of the western valley walls. It was Wednesday. Marcos had gone to the weekly meeting in Maruja's

bohío. She had announced in a blubbery speech the return of her son from
a prison in the capital. It was the first time she had said his name in over a
year. She had finished the announcement by reading a passage from one of
Hemingway's novels, a passage that reminded all present, in typical Hemingway fashion, of how this world breaks everyone, but that some become
stronger at the broken places, a passage that made it obvious why the author had so much loved this Island of broken souls. There had been no
mention of a horse, although rumors among the native guajiros and within
the chance of Josefa's shells were that it already roamed the valley, grazing
at night in the alfalfa fields and sleeping during the days in the cavern of
the limestone masses that surrounded the valley, that it was of long blond
mane, and sixteen hands tall and white as Fidel's ass, with a streak of brown
along its broad chest, that its wings were already shriveling and they would
never be able to lift him away from the valley, and that it was destined to
be ridden by only one man. Some of the guajiros had drawn the unseen
horse on their spread bedsheets and colored the figure with pigments derived from lime in the valley walls and colored the landscape with pigments from the very grasses and earth and trees that were represented.
Some gave the horse wings, as it was believed necessary of any animal of
such size that was to come into their valley. None, as of yet, painted a rider
on the horse. They flew their creations on beams outside their bohíos like
banners. The soldiers from the capital, in turn, sunk giant poles in front of
their bohíos at the Complex and flew the national emblem, but they did
nothing to discourage the natives from flying their own homemade colors.

None remembered how the phrase the *Newer Man* came into common
usage. Maybe it was a reaction to all the rhetoric of the soldiers from the
capital about the New Socialist Man, maybe, in fact, the phrase itself was
a part of the foreign rhetoric, repeated to the natives in hesitant susurrations and into cupped ears, to cast on it a shadow of insurgence, taint it
with the bold streak of revolt, to make the natives believe it was of their
own making. But in the whole year of Joshua's absence, there was no
doubt, neither among the natives nor the foreign invaders from the capital, who would most certainly be cast in the role, who, and only who, was
deemed to ride the unseen horse.

Alicia did not return till after the nightingales were well into the second movement of their symphony (the casual adagio of the middle
evening hours), after the moon had begun its fall, after Triste and Josefa
had declared a pact in their bickering, she almost run out of yarn, he almost run out of rum. And the way Alicia walked into her bohío, moving
with slow weighted gestures, as if she were the only creature awake during
the siesta hour, the careless manner in which she threw down her straw
bag (empty but for a pair of two overripe mangoes that instantly perfumed
the air with their sweet and sour effluvience) by the doorway and passed
both her hands through her too quickly graying hair, carelessly revealing

the fuzz under her armpits, the way the sweat clung to her upper lip and glimmered with the light of the gaslamp like beadlets of liquid silver, the way she casually grabbed the rum bottle from Triste and swallowed the last gulp (no one had ever seen Alicia drink rum), the way she lit an unremarkable fire within the iron stove, and set the big heating kettle atop it, and filled it with three bucketfuls from the stream in the back, making three separate trips, the way she refused Triste's offer for help to lower the kettle from the stove and take it out the back door by shooing him away with a flick of her hand, the way she heard none of the small questions that Marcos posed her and said nothing, not that she was tired and she was going to have a bath, not that there was a reason why she was three hours late for their nightly meeting, not that she was hungry and had they saved her a plate of food, not to leave her alone to get out, but nothing, not a grunt, not a sigh, gracefully nothing, they knew instantly that she had seen him, that the one who would ride the unseen horse had been mercifully returned to his mother, just like the foreigners from the capital had so many times whispered in Triste's ear, they knew it as surely as if she had walked into her bohío and proclaimed with open arms: "I have seen him!"

When he appeared to her again, two weeks later, Alicia still had not uttered a word, and for all anyone knew she had not heard a word, had been deaf to the thousand rumors flittering about every native's ear, infinite and restless as black flies before the rainy season, fashioning truths through the sheer force of their numbers. And it was these very flies that established for all that there was a studied purpose to Alicia's newfound dumbness, that the old Alicia, the traitor's widow, la contestona contrarevolucionaria, the convicted wordeater and murderess, la santera, la Católica Apostólica, the most famous dissident on the Island, would not do in this inchoate colony of the Newer Man, this valley-state to be ruled by a son pardoned for the greatest sin. This and more the multitude of flies buzzed for all to hear.

When he appeared to her again, it was a Wednesday. Joshua's mother and the other Comité chiefs were busy with their weekly meeting. The workers were bathing in the falls and Alicia remained alone in the fields as was her habit. Joshua rode his white horse to the bottom of a hill at the edge of the coffee field. He had named the horse Obadiah 5 and it would be the last name he would pilfer from the holy book, for he had stopped trapping jutías and baptizing them. These were games of his youth. Obadiah 5 did not have wings; but he did have two pale bowlike streaks on each flank, from his withers down to his thighs, where, the flies buzzed, his wings had once been before they withered. Joshua dismounted and wrapped the reins around the trunk of a young palm. He rubbed Obadiah 5 on the brown stain of his breast. The horse nodded and pressed his large head into Joshua's shoulder. A government soldier was watching from nearby, his rifle slung over his shoulder, his hands on his hips, his large straw hat the only discordance in his military garb. Joshua dismissed him with a wave of his hand and waded through the bushes into the field in Alicia's direction. He too wore a straw hat and a loose clay-colored work shirt, unbuttoned down to his belly, and heavy work pants.

Alicia did not look up from her tasks till Joshua had reached her and extended his hand down to help her pick some berries. She noticed that two-thirds of his pinky was missing and as he helped her pick the fruit, the stump, like the phantom of an epicure's pinky, stood erect and apart and motionless as if it had forgotten how to cooperate with the other fingers in the labor of the hand. He knelt by her and leaned into her till the brims of their hats touched. He spoke to her softly, certain that she could hear. "My father says that some of the most beautiful of the Greek and Roman statues have certain digits of their hands and feet missing." He laughed nervously and grabbed her arm with his mutilated hand. "I know you can hear me, Alicia."

She had to look up at him, but she did it as if she had never known who he was, with a thin smile spread like a see-through veil over her face. She took up his other hand and examined it, and counted out loud the joints of each finger.

"What I did," he said, "I did for all of us. I did for my mother, I did for you, I did for the negrón who saved me in Guantánamo."

"Uno, dos, tres. Uno, dos, tres . . . Sí, todos están. Your other hand is fine. But your father is right. He is after all a very cultured man. Take off those boots. Let me see your feet."

Joshua put his hand under her armpit and lifted her. She had grown light as a girl.

"Vamos, Alicia, vamos. You are overworked that is all. Our sun will do wicked things if you don't pay it its due respect."

She stared at his boots. "Vamos, muchacho, no tengas pena. Let me see your feet. I will count those two." Joshua led her down the hill to the horse and found a canteen in the saddlebag and held it to her lips as she drank. He pulled out a small cloth from one of his pockets and soaked it with the canteen water and washed the dirt and the tiny dead insects from her face.

He lifted her onto the saddle and climbed behind her. "No!" she screamed. "No! Take off those boots. Let me count your feet!"

He grabbed the reins with his right hand, cupped his left hand over her mouth, kicked Obadiah 5 on the flank with the back of his boots and they dashed away from the coffee fields towards Alicia's bohío. She yelled out a few more muffled cries and then, as Obadiah 5 sped to a full run across a wide meadow, her small body went slack and leaned back into his and she took the stump of his pinky and put it into her mouth.

"Así," he whispered in her ear, "calmadita. It's all right now. Those days are passed. I have made peace with him . . . as must we all. I have made peace with all my demons. I'll let you count my feet all you want."

The Ghost in the Yellow Scarf

She returned to Guantánamo for the first time, six years later. The place was no longer home to her. She returned to Guantánamo as visitor. She was accompanied by Joshua and Triste. This time, Joshua joked before their departure, they should take the train, though perhaps it was less reliable than hitting the road. One thing the main Island's revolution had surely accomplished is that trains would never run on time, as they do in fascist countries. When they reached Adela's house on the corner of Maceo and Narciso López Streets, a whole day behind schedule, Triste and Joshua waited on the steps below the porch. They were both dressed in the clay-colored field wear that was the new uniform of most all the residents of the Colony of the Newer Man. Alicia wore a loose-fitting white cotton dress and leather sandals. She knocked once and the door unbolted and opened on its own, a slow and cautious swing, as if an invisible servant had been standing on the other side waiting for her knock. She entered her mother's home alone. There were four suitcases by the door, one, her mother explained in a whisper, was the girl's, two were hers, and one was Father Gonzalo's. Though the monsignor didn't know. He was being stubborn. He had sworn to her, on his medallion of la Milagrosa, that he was not leaving, that he was the servant to the misery of his flock. *Así mismo dice, el pobre.* The suitcases had been by the door, stacked next to the chipped wooden console of the black and white television set, for almost four years. Adela passed her hand through her hair, which was greasy and knotty and receded halfway up her skull, like the tide of a dirty inlet. She had shrunk almost half a foot and walked with a wary shuffle, her feet never leaving the floor and leaning with one hand either on the spare furniture or the wall. She wore a loose-fitting faded blue housedress and pair of anklet stockings that bunched up at her swollen ankles. The skin on her face was spotted and pallid and gathered underneath her chin just like the ankle stockings. Her eyes were so bruised with grief and sleeplessness it seemed she wore a carnival mask behind her eyeglasses, which she did not use, but let rest low on her nose so that she could peer over them.

Alicia reached out both hands to her. "Mamá," she said. But the old woman treated her as if indeed she were nothing more than a casual visit.

"Así," she said, and did not grab Alicia's hand.

"We are waiting for permission," the girl explained. "Abuelita, why aren't you wearing your shoes?"

The old woman did not answer.

The girl pointed to the suitcases. She looked at her grandmother as she spoke to the visitor. She had come into the living room unheard, wandered in from one of the back rooms. Or maybe, Alicia thought, she had been lurking in some corner unnoticed. She wore a pair of faded American jeans cut off just above the knees and a simple white threadbare T-shirt that took no care in concealing the richness of her dark nipples. She had grown very tall, but the curves of womanhood had only begun to mold her and her gestures were still those of the child she had not seen in so long. Her hair was long and tied back, black curls tucked behind her ears and falling down her shoulders. She wore leather sandals and on her left foot a braided ankle bracelet made of black hair. Alicia found it strange that though she wore no make-up and no paint on her fingernails, her tiny toenails were coated with a thick coat of beet-colored gloss.

She pointed again to the stack of suitcases, as if directing the visitor's persistent attention away from her.

". . . though we had to empty mine, for tonight I have to change my clothes fifteen times. Abuelita says that's the tradition. And all in all, even counting the dresses that were packed away, I only have nine."

"No importa," Adela said. "We'll unpack my suitcase. I'll lend you six of mine."

Teresita giggled. "Ay abuela." She threw up her eyes and put her hand over her mouth, as if she were trying to imagine herself in the shapeless sheets that were her grandmother's housedresses.

"Ay mijita," Adela said. She shook her head and with a turn of her chin pushed the girl's eyes away from her and towards the visitor.

"Buenas," Teresita said. "Are you Benicia? Where is your camera? . . . *are* you this woman, la Reina de los Quince? We have your business card. Qué raro, I thought you looked different. I thought you were much younger."

Alicia turned to her mother. "You did not tell her I was coming?"

Adela shuffled over to one of the two colonial-style chairs that were the only furniture in the living room besides the television console. The cover of the chair was torn at the corners and the spongy stuffing poured out of the holes like dirty bathfoam. Adela leaned on her granddaughter and sat. She let out a long sigh. She shook her head.

"No, I could not. Por ahí dicen que me he vuelto loca, perhaps it's true, maybe in my delirium, I forgot to tell her. And what did I know? A cable from a government agency? How many times has the government lied to me, and how many times have I just passed the lies along to this innocent?"

"Ay abuelita, no seas drámatica, what cable? what government? You did tell me." She turned to the visitor, a gaunt woman with sad carbon eyes and a yellow scarf tied over her head, out of which poked strands of

gray hair like tendrils of old Spanish moss. She could not stare long at the
visitor's eyes. "But she didn't tell me you were coming, she said we were
going to your house. She says you have arranged your garden beautifully,
with flowers and creeping vines and potted palms and a swing and even a
stone well. Where is your house? Past the railroad tracks, by the river,
right? Qué raro, I thought I knew you. Do you live far away? I must have
met you. I think I have. Pero my abuelita hasn't finished the adjustments
on my dress yet. It's still too long. It was once my mother's. Her wedding.
No está en moda, sabe. Her wedding, that was a long time ago. It's still
too long, even though I am much taller than she was. Abuelita still has to
take off maybe another five inches. But why do you look at me with such
horror? I'm sorry, de veras, we did not know you were coming so early.
Abuelita said you would not be ready till later this afternoon." She turned
back to her grandmother. "Vamos chica, are you going to finish the dress?
I know your hands hurt"—she knelt by her grandmother and massaged
the old woman's hands—"un poquito más, and then no more favors till
the day I get married."

"Five years . . . five years, and not one word from you." The old woman
freed her hands from the girl and shook them at the visitor. "I made phone
calls. I wrote letters. And what was their answer . . . in cables just like the
one I received a week ago. *In the interest of national security . . .* that's it, you
can imagine all they invented *in the interest of national security.* There were
rumors that you were involved in the murder of the police captain and his
servant and even in the attempt on ese-hijo-de-la-gran-puta Fidel. Good,
good, I said, let her be involved. Let her be the assassin with her lone
hands. La gente dice que me he vuelto loca. I do not leave this house. I let
her, this poor saint, stand in the colas. Gonzalo has to come here to give
me Communion. The women at Mass whisper about me. ¡Hipócritas!
Gonzalo says that they are afraid to visit me because they cannot stand to
look at the grisly mask of my suffering." She waved her hand under her
face as if she were displaying a piece by a tormented and disturbing sculptor. "¡Hmmm, Cristianas no son!" She gave her hands back to the girl.

"Sí me duelen, mi santa. . . . Each day that passed I became more and
more sure that my only daughter, whom I carried for nine months, aquí en
este vientre, had been ripped from our lives without as much as one word
of condolence . . . in the interest of (maldito sean todos) national security."
She glared at the visitor, who saw in the ashen eyes of the old woman, the
whites like embers, that she had run out of tears long ago. "So why, Alicia, should I have believed the words on that yellow piece of paper that
came here a week ago, informing us that you were coming for a three-day
visit . . . a *visit,* mi única hija, after eight years, a *visit!* ¡Maldito sean! And
why should I let you into this house? Why should I let you ruin the
tenuous peace this child has found at last . . . as an orphan in the hands
of the glorious revolution, both her father *and* mother murdered by el

sinvergüenza Fidel. You are dead, Alicia, there are votive candles in my room lit for the benefit of your departed soul. Jesús, María y José, why should I not be mad!"

Teresita stood. She put her hands under her grandmother's arms and tried to lift her up. "Vamos, abuela, what are you saying? Did you forget to take your pills? No hables tonterías. And how many times have I told you to keep your shoes on. Vamos, you're going to scare poor Benicia. She looks old, doesn't she? Older than I thought. It's okay, you don't have to finish the dress today." She turned to the visitor. Her eyes saw exactly how changed her mother was, how unique her own mask was, made by a sculptor at least as tormented as the one that had molded her grandmother's face . . . but she continued to speak as if her hawking voice only suspected what her eyes knew. "We'll take the pictures some other day, señora Benicia . . . really, you can go now . . . some other day. It doesn't matter what day really. It's just that she is ill, la pobrecita . . . it was the death of my mamita that finished her. Where are your shoes, coño? Those stockings are slippery and you'll fall again. . . . There, there abuelita, you've frightened poor Benicia. She came to help us celebrate, but look, look how she weeps. Mírala, abuelita, mírala. Ay qué llanto, la pobre Benicia."

The visitor spoke for the first time to the girl: "Your grandfather, in the days prior to his death, would not keep his shoes on either. Many times your grandmother and I had to go fetch him to wherever he had fled, his shoes in a bag with us."

Teresita let go of Adela. The old woman had trouble gaining her balance and grabbed tightly to one of the arms of the rickety chair. She swung her other arm in the air.

"¡Ahí está!" she said to the girl. "Imagine that, she has come to bury *me*. I do not wear shoes so that surely means that I will soon die! You are unorphaned for three days, mi santica. Your misery begins afresh. ¡Ahí está carajo!" She negotiated a temporary truce with her balance and slipped back down into the chair.

"Ay, mamá," the visitor said. "Ay, mijita."

"No. No que va. Mamá is gone. She got permission. She got permission because she so missed papá. Dícelo, abuelita. Tell the poor photographer the truth. No!" She let out a little whimper that seemed a prelude to a long lament. She ran from the room and left the old woman shoeless and the visitor (the photographer, la reina de los quince, or the ghost, or whatever the carbon-eyed lady was) waiting with her mouth half-open as if some sham priest had held back from her the Host.

She had locked herself in the big room nearest the patio, the one down the hallway from the kitchen with the double French doors. Alicia pressed her face to the glass panes frosted with palm trees and creeping tropical vines, peering through the clearer sections where the palm fronds were etched. Teresita had drawn the curtains of the two large windows that faced the patio. Though she could make out only a shapeless obscurity, Alicia persisted. She knew her daughter would see the mass of her face pressed to the glass, a featureless rosy glob like an October moon, just as she had seen her own mother's face when she had imprisoned herself in that room in the days after her husband's death, in the days when the child had been conceived. She did not knock on the door or rattle the knob as her mother had done.

Adela explained that of the three bedrooms, it was the only one they used now, sleeping side by side on her marriage bed. "She abandoned her own room not long after you left. What was I to tell her? She slept (she still sleeps) with her arms wrapped around my waist. Ay, mi santica. It is her room now, more than it is mine. It is peopled with her dolls, crowded like a city with their little houses. She makes them herself with scrap wood that she finds near the bay, in the heap that was once the old Spanish fort. She checks the scraps for termites, for water rot, as diligent as if she were building a house for herself. Remember how good she was at building sand castles as a little girl. Remember, Alicia. Gonzalo says she was a master architect at the age of three! When we get there . . . because we are going, mija, we are going, the suitcases are packed . . . the great exodus has begun . . . when we get there, al gran Miami, she will go to the finest American university. There is no need for architects in Cuba."

They sat at one corner of the long kitchen table, as had always been their habit. Joshua was silent. He had graciously refused an offer for coffee. He had announced that he and Triste would be staying at the home of the new police chief, the stone house built under the ceiba tree. Adela told him not to expect much, that all the orchids except the black ones had long ago perished. Joshua nodded, as if he understood. His hands were spread open and even at the table, in a conscious effort not to hide his butchered finger, the mark of the new covenant with his father. Triste had gone to fetch Father Gonzalo. Adela warned him not to alarm him, to feed him the news of Alicia's arrival in small doses. "He's very frail these days, as we all are." She made an effort to smile but her wizened lips and her wan cheeks had lost touch with that art.

They let the noise of the barrio that seeped in through the ironwork of the open window above the sink—the busy after-school chatter of the pioneros (incomprehensible as the noise of compounding waves), the raunchy holler of the fruit cart salesman (a vulgar and brave black-market aria), the insistent yelp of stray hounds (as if any could offer respite from the hunger numbing their fangs)—serve as ersatz for the cordial conversation they dared not have, of the valley land the visitors had come from, of invented crimes and fantastical punishments, of the new course of the revolution, of the phantom who sat naked, bullet-ridden, still unaneled all the way at the opposite corner of the long table, unnoticed, as if he too had long been locked up in an unlit room, thirsting for the fresh coffee the visitor had refused (though from its pale hue, like second man's bathwater, and its ignoble lax aroma, like rained-on bundles of newspapers, it did not seem much different from the cafecito he had made many years before with used and reused grounds from the windowsill), he who had served as husband to one, as son to another, as hero to the last, and as missing father to the girl, the girl not there in that kitchen anymore than he was there.

Thus, with these unsayable words, these undirectable glances, at one corner of the long kitchen table, Adela's head lilting forward like a nocturnal flower at the first light and then suddenly jolting up as if struck by an electrical blow from the inside, fighting off any form of sleep as she had done now for so long, they waited for Father Gonzalo.

Alone in the hallway, patient, describing the feast that was to take place the following day in the holy celebration of a child becoming a woman, the monsignor was able to get Teresita to unbolt the lock, but when she opened the door he lowered his eyes, he pressed them shut with the conviction one tightens shutters before a storm, he pressed his chin to his sternum, he whispered to his God to give him strength to withstand the affront of the child's utter nakedness.

"¿Qué quieres, Gonzalo? Did you come to hear all my vile sins? Will I be pardoned for being a woman before my time?"

Father Gonzalo held shut his eyes. He continued to talk to his God, Who soon answered him. Fragments of verse skipped across his mind like the foamy gurgles of a windstruck sea, as if his God were reminding him of what he had once known well:

> He ido marcando con cruces de fuego
> el atlas blanco de tu cuerpo. . . .
> Historias que contarte a la orilla del crepúsculo,
> muñeca triste y dulce, para que no estuvieras triste.
> Entre los labios y la voz, algo se va muriendo.

He muttered to himself God's answer. He did not open his eyes till he had raised his chin and he knew that they would be cast upward, staring into the girl's own glittery burnt-sugar eyes. Eyes so improbably like those of the one who had been her true father. Things were known from the beginning. Even his old friend Adela, in her outrageous silence, even she knew.

"Niña, por el amor de Dios, never abandon your dignity. Put something on."

He made a move to reshut the door, never taking his eyes from hers, but the girl took one step forward and kept it ajar with her bare foot as stop, the foot with the anklet of braided black hair, the only thing she wore.

"Tomorrow I will be fifteen. I will be a woman. Does the body of a woman offend you Father? You have been standing out here for over an hour, talking to yourself como un loco, trying to get me to open the door and now you want to shut it? Look, look at my body so that you can better understand my sins. No tengas miedo. Look."

"Your mother wants to see you."

"The ghost in the yellow scarf? ¡Qué tonta! What a bad costume. She came disguised as Benicia. Do you know Benicia? Do you know her story? ¡Qué tonta! As if I would not have recognized her the moment I looked into her suffering eyes. Qué raro, you are afraid of naked women but you are not afraid of ghosts? Who has come with the ghost? Has the angel with the dirty wings come? Tomorrow I will be a woman. Did you let *him* know?"

Father Gonzalo again muttered to himself God's harsh answer:

He ido marcando con cruces de fuego. . . .

"Dios santo, mi hijita." Alicia had been standing in the hallway. She had removed her yellow scarf. She remained still, her arms heavy at her sides. She stared like one who has been gouged suddenly and irrevocably by the bitter arrowhead of obsessive love. Had she not known her own daughter before this? Had she willed herself to forget, in the vain hope of postponing the pain that now struck her at her side, above the loin, like a fisted cramp, there where the flange of the arrow had lodged, and from where a wine-dark grief suffused all her insides? Had she lacked the courage to foresee the woman her daughter would become?

She was halfway out of the room, her foot jammed against the door, naked, her chin held high, her torso erect as an Ionic column, her fully formed breasts thrust forward as if she wore an invisible corset, the nipples so dark they seemed smudged with black earth, her thin arms unabashedly at her sides, her hands loose, her long legs slightly parted, slightly open, unconcerned with the vulnerability at their apex, all of her, towering over the diminutive confounded monsignor. Her hair was still tucked behind her ears falling behind her. She turned her head to her mother and her eyes filled and overbrimmed and rivulets glistened down her cheeks, but her body remained rigid, her chest did not heave, her belly did not convulse, her torso did not collapse. Only her eyes betrayed her sorrow. Alicia did not rush towards her, for this was not the helpless child, *mijita,* that had once been her daughter. This was a woman, *ya una mujercita,* that but for a feeble-minded grandmother and a well-meaning wearied priest, had made her way alone in the world, *mi vida,* fatherless all her life, motherless half of it.

Alicia memorized the body of the woman so that never again would it be so sinfully absent from her reveries. In every detail she saw the beauty marks, the charcoal streaks of the darkness from whence she had come forth, in the thick black eyebrows that converged on the bridge of her nose and almost touched each other as the Creator almost touches Adam near the dawn of the sixth day, in the marbles of her glittering eyes, as if some mad chef had let sugar sit too long over a fire, in the claret cast of her un-painted lips, droplets of blood mixed in equal parts with droplets of mud, in her mountain soil nipples, in the wisp of black smoke that surrounded her navel and vanished halfway up her belly, in her pubic mound, hidden by a tangle of unearthed roots, in the dusky glow of all her skin, especially the cheeks and the brow, and in the countless dolors that Alicia imagined pierced like black nails into her daughter's sacrificial body. And to all this, Teresita had added her own touch (as if not to be outdone by the cruel cleverness of nature)—she had fashioned a braided shackle around her left foot, from hair that may have been her own (for it was just as black), or may have been one of her lovers', as her grandmother suspected.

"How can you blame the child?" Adela had said in the kitchen in the only brief spurt of conversation while they waited for Father Gonzalo. She addressed Joshua and not Alicia. "How can you blame her for wanting to be loved as she deserves to be loved? I would not blame her even if she turned whore!"

Alicia did not move towards her daughter till Father Gonzalo grabbed her by the wrist and led her there, to the open door of the room, and used the mother as a mantle to cover the daughter's nakedness. As soon as her mother had placed her arms around her, Teresita's rigid body collapsed with all the force it had used to remain still and naked and undaunted in the presence of her mother's unmasked ghost. After she regained her bal-ance, Alicia led her daughter into the room. Father Gonzalo closed the door behind them. In the darkness, they trampled houses and stepped on the citizen-dolls of Teresita's toy city, till they stumbled onto the bed and fell one on top of the other.

Alicia sat up and adjusted herself so that she held her daughter's head on her lap. She cuddled close. She passed her hands through her daughter's long hair. She massaged her temples. She spoke to her, the words muffled by the vasty deep of her indomitable grief.

"Mi vida. Mijita. Ya una mujercita."

She alternated the tone, cadence, and order of the phrases as she re-peated them, till it sounded as if she were softly crooning a rumbero's lul-laby.

Sweat slicked Teresita's brow and moistened her hair. She too found the courage to speak. She proclaimed that she was not afraid anymore, that she had become used to ghosts, that there were many in the barrio, that though she could not keep track of them, her abuelita could, peeking through the slats of the closed shutters of the front bedroom, out into Maceo Street.

"No está tan loca como dicen. She beckons them in and they pass through the narrow gaps between the open slats. They visit with her. Feeble as she is, she must stand, for the spirits always insist on sitting in her rocking chair. She lets them. She knows how peevish spirits can get. She leans on her canes as long as she can and listens to their updates of the gossip from the next world. She seldom interrupts, except when she is astonished by something, some sin that passed unheard through this world—'¡No digas!,' she says—or when she has already heard a story— 'Ay, ya ese cuento es más viejo que yo,' she says. She repays them by lighting votive candles for their quick passage through purgatory. The room is filled with candles. Gonzalo thinks it's a hazard, but abuelita pays him no mind. Many of the candles are for you, mamacita, even though you never visited with abuelita."

She asked how many of her houses were trampled, how many of her dolls had been squashed. "They too will become ghosts. ¿No es así, mamacita? Don't some dolls have souls? I know that I am too old to believe that, but I do."

She expressed doubt, for how could it be that a ghost had such ponderous steps, such rough hands, such a pulpy voice. "How could it be, mamacita? Have I wrongly summoned you back into your rotted body? I could not help it. In school there is una asentada (well, she was still a novice then, but she was desperate to be initiated, to feel the weight of her orisha in her), una mulatica with big green eyes like a crocodile. We call her La Cocodrila. She is the niece of a renowned madrina in Baracoa. It was her idea—after I told her your story one afternoon, after I told her how you had stopped sending letters, how abuelita had received a cable that informed her of your burial in the Isle of Pines. 'Aha,' she said to me. 'if she is buried then she can return. Only the unburied are doomed never to return to their loved ones.' She said she would tease the secret of some spell from her aunt, even though she herself was still a novice and had no skill yet to command such power. When she returned from a visit to Baracoa, she was very excited, her green pupils expanded till there was almost no white left in her eyes. This would be her first imploration of the orishas. She said all she needed from me was a lock of your hair and a lock of my own hair. I knew abuelita kept a lock of your hair, which she had saved from your first haircut, in a waxy envelope in her Bible, between the first and the second letter to the Romans. I stole it. One night, we went down, past the railroad tracks, to the river and trapped a bullfrog, which we would use as sacrifice. La Cocodrila slit the bullfrog's throat and caught the blood in a coconut shell. She made me put my finger in it and it was cool like the coolness of the river. She cut a sliver of coconut flesh. It had soaked up the bullfrog's blood like a swab of cotton. She broke the sliver in two as if it were a consecrated Host and ate her half and gave me the other half for me to eat. I handed her the locks of hair, yours and mine, and she dipped them in the shell and chanted to her gods, to the moon, to the stars, to the riverstones. Then she washed the locks in the riverwater and braided them tight, one to the other, and tied the braid to my ankle. She warned me never to take it off, never to wear high heels, never to raise my braided foot above my head, and never to cover the braid with a stocking, else the spell would be broken. 'The day your mother's hair turns all white in the grave, white like the unstained meat of half this coconut, her heart will bleed again and she will remember that once her hair was black as the midnight. And she will come to see you.' And she was right, mamacita, you waited. How sad it must have been for you, waiting in the mirror of your tomb, till *every* single strand turned white."

Alicia listened, even as her three-phrase song continued, even as it trilled and grew loud and plaintive, like the wail of an Arab widow. From here till the end of her life, there would be no stopping of that song she had invented in that dark room where she had spent her first days as a widow, where her daughter had been conceived and where she now held her as if only an instant had passed, naked, sweating, chattering of spells and implorations, of how the mother that now held her in her arms was a sad spirit condemned for a brief while, through the magic of a crocodile-girl, to go back into its shrunken white-haired corpse.

Alicia listened, even as her three-phrase song continued long into the night, a piercing ululation sustained by the breath of her calamity, so that soon it surpassed the wail of *twenty* Arab widows, and the many neighbors in the barrio who began to listen heard it. It drowned the love ballads on their tocadiscos, the mambos on their transistor radios, the cries of their own children. And the old remembered a night, many years ago, when Alicia's mother had suffered her first *grito del corazón,* in the patio of her sister's house, under the giant fig tree, when her nephew had lost his left eye. They remembered how the blood-soaked pillow could not muffle her cries, how they awoke from nightmares of tortures and stake burnings to find that the wail was as real as the sweat on their sheets, and thus they assured their young ones: "The old woman is readying for the grave. She has regained that great voice she lost so many years ago."

But the young ones heard something else. They recognized Alicia's sad song as *el llanto de los quince,* which they had not heard since the trinary deaths of the blond police captain, his shorn-headed indian servant, and the massive bullmastiff Tomás de Aquino.

The Bakery Administrator's Daughter

Once, in Guantánamo, there had been fifteen Studebakers like the powder-blue Studebaker that had belonged to the murdered police captain. Once, before the triumph of la Revolución, before el Rubio had sprouted filaments of old gold under his armpits and on his chin and around his navel, before he had worked for the yanquis inside the naval base, before Colonel MacDougal had expelled him under suspicion of spying for the Batista government, before he had ventured to the Sierra, hungry and barefoot, his services at first rejected by a guerrilla comandante because he did not own a gun, before el Rubio had ever dreamed of owning a car, any car, much less a yanqui car, much less a Studebaker, there had been fifteen of them in the small provinciality of Guantánamo. *Imagínense, quince Studebakers en este pueblecito de guajiros.* Actually over half of the Studebakers belonged to soldiers in the yanqui naval base, but in those days passage to and from the paradise of tin roofs was common—many Cubans, like el Rubio, worked inside the base and many soldiers visited the town when on leave—there was no Cerca Peerless, no mines, no river infested with crocodiles, no bay infested with sharks, no watchtowers.

The flaky upper-crust families, the type of families that put ads in the local newspapers looking for "white Spaniard maids," or those families less aristocratic, less bleached in their lineage, who had connections with the ruling regime, the type whose mothers and daughters, y hasta la anciana abuelita, dyed their hair the color of el Rubio's natural hue, resplendent and ochery as just-sifted riverbed gold, had made a ritual of leasing the fifteen Studebakers from their owners on the fifteenth anniversary of each daughter's birth, the day she was welcomed into womanhood. Fifteen couples would be invited to ride in the fifteen yanqui cars to the feast in the Centro Municipal near Parque Martí, where along with the father and her daughter they would dance to a mamboed version of a Strauss waltz.

After the triumph of la Revolución, some of the families that had not fled had tried to continue this ritual but were thwarted when they found that el Rubio would not lease his Studebaker (which had come into his possession when one of Batista's henchmen, a sergeant in the Rural Guard, had fled with his family on the eve of la Revolución, leaving behind any possessions that could not be stuffed into one of his fourteen suitcases, or hastily sewn into the lining of his evening jackets, worn dutifully as dresses by his four young daughters, or into the virgin crevices of his own body) for the purpose of this outdated bourgeois ritual. Thus the celebrations went on for a few years, marred, misnumbered, truncated, sometimes with seven Studebakers, sometimes with four and finally with as few as two, the fifteen couples crowded into the spacious cars like clowns in a circus. Finally, when el Rubio had amassed enough power and been appointed chief of the revolutionary police, he sabotaged the engines of the two remaining Studebakers and forbid, by decree, the celebration of *las fiestas de los quince*. Never having sired a child, never having known the luxurious joy of doting on a daughter, he had underestimated the will with which Cuban fathers want to please their daughters. The celebrations went on, more outrageous than before. The shells of the two remaining Studebakers were bought and fixed over twin mulecarts, and once more the fifteen privileged couples jammed in, their suits and dresses grown more and more shabby with the passing years, badly tailored, the lining of suits poking out of the hems like hounds' tongues, the seams of the dresses clustered and bulged like the flesh of creeping slugs; and too many of these dresses the señoritas proudly wore, their chins cocked, their faces painted, their hair stiffened like baked meringue, their gazes askant, as if they were attending a ball at Versailles, bore the vestigial traces, in their heaviness, their loud patterns, their patchwork, of drapes and furniture upholstery. It was murmured in the local CDR, after the minute book had been shut, that in less than five years of progress, la Revolución had left every window of Guantánamo naked and every chair or sofa bare as a skinned rabbit. Still, they celebrated. Against the decree, in badly tailored suits and hull-thick dresses they celebrated. Two lame mules hung with cowbells tugged the husks of two Studebakers, their rusty exteriors garlanded with hibiscus and branches of crape myrtle, their hollowed interiors jammed with fifteen couples armed with claves, castanets, and maracas, past the Department of State Security, past the office of the man who had decreed against them, and they aimed their great joyous noise at him, daring him to rejoice along for another *niña* had become *una mujer*.

Y las mujeres son la gran alegría de este mundo. La mujer was what the Creator created after He had created everything, after He had rested, and with this final masterpiece He topped even Himself, so went one of Father Gonzalo's sermons during one of the illegal celebrations. Yet illegal as they certainly were, el Rubio could not hector any of his men to take action against them. As soon as they heard the clickclack of the claves, the raptap of the castanets, the swishwhoosh of the maracas, they laid down their arms and grew deaf to any orders and threats that el Rubio barked at them. They too were fathers of Cuban daughters. Not even el Rubio's loafish bullmastiff Tomás de Aquino (no father himself, for his grotesque belly had made it impossible for him to mount any bitch) could be persuaded of the seriousness of the decree and at each pass of the mulecart Studebakers, he got off his monumental behind and followed the caravan, adding his baritone howl to the percussive harmony.

El Rubio was patient. He kept the decree on the books. But he stopped barking orders and threats to his men, he let them lay down their arms, let the two-cart Studebaker caravan pass, let Tomás de Aquino follow doltishly along. He listened with a tolerant ear to his bullmastiff's over-the-top, harsh-tuned, off-the-tracks, traitorous aria. He listened to the subtle threats in the suggestions of the ladies from the local CDR that the decree, if looked at in the wrong light by the wrong Party higher-up, could *itself* be deemed counterrevolutionary. All the while he said nothing and let the people, with the lashing of their tongues, set their own trap.

There was an administrator of a bakery who had a daughter just shy of fifteen. The administrator was rumored to be terminally ill. And it was said that as a farewell gift to his daughter, he was planning to throw the greatest *fiesta de quince* ever seen in Guantánamo, even more extravagant than those celebrated by the wicked aristocracy in the days before la Revolución. This was absurd of course, for the administrator, even though there were always long *colas* at the bakery and he was more accustomed to the orange fire within his brick ovens than to the yellow fire in the heavens, was paid a measly sum of pesos that was just enough for him and his family to get by. Still, on the evening before the appointed day, seven cases of Dom Pérignon were carried in by two mulatto men through the back door of his house on Calle José Martí near the shores of the Bano River. A few minutes later a massive slaughtered pig was carried in on a pole, through the same back door, by the same two mulatto men. (Cashier clerks at the bakery, el Rubio recognized them.) And then a second pig almost as large, and then three bunches of unplucked white gallinas, tied together by their legs and hung upside down like dead flowers. A barrel was rolled in, possibly rum, and bags of fruits and vegetables and rice followed, then branches thick with flowers, deep red and pinkish white. More black-market goodies than el Rubio had ever seen amassed at one time. He watched from the driver's seat of his powder-blue Studebaker, hidden at the edge of a blooming guava grove near the river. Every time the mulatto men disappeared into the house, waved in by the bony liver-spotted hand of the old administrator, el Rubio put down his binoculars and wiped the lenses with his shirt. He saw more than he could believe, for after all the food was smuggled in, another truck pulled up, and the two mulatto men started unloading hunks of shiny red metal and polished chrome and black-leather bucket seats and whitewall tires whose bands were pearly and unspotted as a bride's new dress. And then another truck from which was unloaded three sets of conga drums and enough brass trumpets and trombones and fugelhorns to supply a small symphony orchestra.

"Qué cojones," el Rubio muttered. He tried to wake up Tomás de Aquino sprawled on the passenger's seat next to him, just to make sure he was not the only one who witnessed this abominable spectacle, but the bullmastiff flicked his ears and exposed his yellowed fangs. Had Tomás de Aquino known that there was so much comestible booty gathered together in one place, had he listened to his master and raised his large

helmet of a skull, he might have charged the criminals with the proper
courage of the police dog that he certainly was not; but Tomás de Aquino
was wont not to pay any heed to his master, and he went on snoozing in
the passenger seat, content, as most of the Islanders, on dreaming of riches
that he knew would never be his.

El Rubio continued to watch till the day turned bright and the whiff
in the morning breeze of sizzling pig hide awoke Tomás de Aquino, who
struggled up and sat on his haunch and poked his cavernous wet nostrils
into the air, mawing each open, as if the smell of the thing alone could
ease his eternal hunger. Before Tomás de Aquino broke into a hunger
seizure, el Rubio rolled up both windows and mud-tailed out of the guava
grove. He decided he would let them have their last supper. He asked one
of the vigilantes of the local CDR to take note of everyone who attended
the fiesta. She returned to him that night with a list of over a hundred citizens who had attended as guests, the twelve citizens who had served as
musicians, and the five citizens who had been employed as servants. She
was tipsy, un poquito jumada. She said she had gotten too close (vaya, she
had needed to get close for champagne corks launched from the patio were
whizzing into the street endangering any passerby) and the administrator's wife (*una mulata buen moza, with fleshy hips and sumptuous breasts, she
won't be a widow long, eso es seguro*) had caught her peeking through a crack
in the red-brick patio wall; but instead of reprimanding her, she had invited her in.

"Vamos, entra, rejoice and party like a true cubana. You comuñangas,
all of you, have forgotten what fun it is to be Cuban! My husband has decided to remind you before he goes to his grave. Vamos, entra. Alleluia,
my daughter is a woman today!"

El Rubio nodded, he said that perhaps she should consider adding her
own name to the end of the list. The vigilante sobered up instantly, her
eyes widened, she insisted she had done it out of duty, to get a closer look,
a better count. Y vaya, once she was in she could not refuse their hospital-
ities, else they get suspicious. El Rubio said he would take her sense of
duty into account, but added her name to the list anyway. The morning
after, he went to the house on José Martí Street and arrested the bakery administrator.

At the trial, the names were made public. The administrator's name
was Roque San Martín. His daughter's name was Benicia. She was legendary among the long-tongued neighbors, for since the day of her birth
her father had not allowed scissors to touch her chocolate hair and it had
grown to graze her ankles. He himself, it was said, combed the knots out
of it every evening. Roque San Martín's coffee-colored, wondrously curved
and much younger wife was called Yéyé. Each of the guests that attended
the feast, beginning with the vigilante, was called by the revolutionary
tribunal to testify against their generous host and his family. Only a hand-

ful ignored the summons. Only a handful listened to the urgings of Father Gonzalo (who it was revealed later had been briefly at the feast to bless the debutante). In a sermon on the Sunday after the arrest, he proclaimed, mirroring the twisted logic of el Rubio's charges, that there had been no feast on St. Anthony's day, that he had not been there when he went there to bless the child-woman and that all those he saw there, at the greatest fiesta de quince he had ever attended, even during the era of the aristocrats, had certainly not been there either. This, he said, is the way el Rubio and the tribunal should be addressed. Any and all statements infected with nonsense. But only a handful listened to the urgings of Father Gonzalo. Of the 104 guests who had been at the feast, over ninety, including the vigilante, including the two mulattoes who worked for Roque San Martín and helped him purchase the black-market booty, gave concise, clear and descriptive statements of what had transpired on the evening of St. Anthony's day.

Sure enough, from what the tribunal heard, from what it saw (for there had been three photographers hired for the occasion, two who dutifully turned in their negatives to the tribunal), Roque San Martín had made true on his herculean boast—not even in the wicked prerevolutionary days had Guantánamo seen anything like the fiesta for Benicia's fifteenth birthday. As the guests arrived they were handed a single camellia, some white, some red, some bicolored. The guests were then escorted by Yéyé into the main patio where the roasting pit was set in one far corner, and in another corner the two mulatto bakers were assembling an automobile, an Italian convertible. Rum was scooped from the very cask with a wooden ladle, set in the third corner, and distributed liberally, so that it wasn't long before things got rolling, before the guests got anxious for the debutante and her father to appear, for someone to pick up the trumpets and trombones and fugelhorns gently laid on the stools atop the band platform in the fourth corner, for someone to jump behind the drums and pound them, like a tumble-rough lover, like a giant-handed masseuse, to their better life.

"Sí, sí, ya viene la música. . . . But first, antes que nada," Yéyé announced, silencing the expectant guests. "The bath."

A shutter on the second-floor window of the house flew open and the sickly Roque San Martín stepped out into the small semicircular balcony. He was clearly on his last days, his face so deflated that it hung on his skull like a hood, his chest sunken and his spine bent inward like the opening of a final question, the last three wisps of hair on his pate like weedgrass that had endured a long drought. Still, he had found the strength to don his most elegant linen guayabera and now that he was outside he found it proper to put on his most stylish Panama and was liberally sucking on a dark long Hoya, which his wife wouldn't let him smoke inside the house. He found the strength to lean forward on the wrought-iron railing and smile, a frightening gummy smile, and he signaled to the guests gathered on the patio below, with the back of his free hand, as if he were a nonagenarian pontiff on the balcony at St. Peter's square. The guests cheered his presence like wearied pilgrims and they raised their rum-filled glasses to him. They shouted that with God's help he would overcome his illness and see his grandchildren, that God owed it to them, for He had not worked a miracle in Guantánamo in a long, long time.

Roque San Martín grew serious at hearing this. He sucked on his Hoya and spoke with the abandon of the faithless. "Ay no me jodan señores y señoras. Cancer is a most terrible fate. My innards are a nest of scorpions . . . besides I am atheist!—and the only time I believe in God is when I look into Benicia's brown eyes, when I bury my nose in the fragrance of her hair. Her beauty has been all ours, her mother's and mine, for fifteen years, and under our stern aegis it has blossomed, ya verán, ya verán . . . for the time has come, the shield must be removed, from here on her beauty is the world's and her admirers will be as countless as the stalks in a cane field." But, as if unable to imagine his daughter wooed and pursued by so many, Roque San Martín fell into a fit of hacking and coughing, his frail frame doubling in on itself like a spent world, his lit Hoya slipping out of his fingers, bouncing off the wrought iron railing and spiraling down to the patio like a misguided missile. Yéyé moved towards the spot underneath him, as if to catch him in case he too came tumbling down. Roque San Martín pounded his chest and gargled in a gulp of air and waved her off. "No es nada," he wheezed.

"Do you need help with the tub?" Yéyé called.

"No coño, I said, no es nada. I am fine. Dying, but fine."

There was cautious laughter below. "Así estamos todos en esta maldita Isla."

"Bueno, basta, the time has come." Roque San Martín summoned all his powers and disappeared into the penumbral room behind him, from whence in a few moments emerged, as if moving on its own will, the great white bow of the magnificent bathtub in which the girl-woman Benicia lay, the back of her head resting on the edge, her long, long never-scissored hair falling over the front, her face hidden from the guests below, her nervous giggles audible. Feeble, dying, Roque San Martín pushed the monumental bathtub out onto the balcony till its stern touched the iron railing and his daughter's brown and thick and knotless locks fell halfway down the balcony, unswayable by the gentle spirits of the early summer breeze, smooth as a cataract of caramel.

"Aquí va, aquí va," Roque San Martín called from the shadows, popping open bottles of champagne with the vigor of a young barman, the corks shooting over the red brick wall into the street, and emptying them into the tub. "Aquí va, coño, put your masks on and witness the first bath of the woman, my daughter the woman! Put your masks on, carajo, respect her dignity."

Benicia's giggles erupted into outright shrieks as the chilled foamy baptismal French bathwater rose on her virgin body, till it lapped up against her bare nipples like a prophecy of the many eager suitors to come. And before the guests knew it, the band had snuck onto the platform on the fourth corner and began to play a mambo, and their attention shifted from the balcony, so that only a few recalled seeing (their carnival masks in place so that eyes that saw would not be seen seeing) Roque San Martín lift his shrieking shivering daughter from the bathtub (naked and newly a woman as she was, her melonous buttocks goose-pimply) and straddle her in his fleshless arms and carry her into the darkness of the room, and, again, before anyone knew it, they were down on the dance floor, she in a flowing white linen dress, her hair doubled and tripled into a bun, carrying her father through the dance as if he were a lifeless strawman.

From there the feast went on, there were photographs of Benicia in the driver's seat of the motorless Italian convertible, photographs of a rainstorm of camellias that flooded the bucket seats and frame by frame buried the driver up to her neck, photographs of balloon-cheeked trumpet players, à la Louis Armstrong, whose joyous notes seemed to tear through the black and white flatness, photographs of the guests possessed by the spirits of the drums, their eyes white, their mouths agape, their knees bent and their arms akimbo, a fuzzy photograph of the two-faced parish monsignor as he touched the forehead of the debutante with moistened fingers, and finally, photographs (these that irked the tribunal most) of the two monumental plump-haunched pigs hung over the roasting pit, their hide charred, their flesh visibly tasteable.

Certainly, the tribunal concluded in a caustic note after reviewing all the evidence, the bakery administrator could go to the grave pleased that he was a fouler aristocrat than all the foul aristocrats who had ever tarnished the history of the Island. ¡Pura degeneración! And before it passed its harsh sentence—fifteen years imprisonment for the administrator (one year for each of the eight counts of embezzling from the bakery, one year for each of the four counts of illegal sales and purchases, one and a half years for his irreverent tirade on the witness stand in which he hurled insults at el Rubio, among the kindest being that the poor police captain did not want girls to become available women because he wanted all the young hombrecitos for himself, and one and a half years for the incestuous overtones of the champagne bath—the tribunal expressed its fondest wishes that the convicted, terminally ill as he was rumored, would live to serve every minute of his sentence), three years imprisonment for his wife (for shamefully letting her daughter be used as a pawn in her husband's sick immoral and rebellious masque), and complete loss of custody of the child Benicia whose virgin hair was shorn, military-style above her ears, and whose upbringing would be resumed by the Communist Youth League of the province of Oriente (it was not, the tribunal expressed its fondest hope, too late to make her a loyal compañera)— it set in stone el Rubio's decree against quince celebrations; from here on, celebration of the feast was strictly prohibited, its venomous bourgeois roots unearthed by this incident, and anyone caught in any semblance of a celebration of a girl's fifteenth birthday would be prosecuted to the fullest extent of the revolutionary code.

Y a propósito, the tribunal's judgment went on, *to rid us of the temptation, perhaps it would be wise to abolish the fifteenth year of a young woman's life altogether, so that legally (if not chronologically), she leapfrogs from fourteen to sixteen, thus erasing any vestiges of this sham ceremony from the annals of our history. A cubana is a woman, una mujer propia y derecha, when she devotes her moral nature to the principles of la Revolución, not, magically, when she turns fifteen, and her father sees fit to pawn her off to other men. La Revolución has always sought to vanish the horrid discrepancies between the sexes inwrought in our culture. The way a girl becomes a woman should be no different from the way a boy becomes a man, through her deeds in service of her society. All this, of course, deserves further consideration and it is beyond the scope of our power to implement, though we will send a letter to the Central Committee and to the Minister of Culture in the capital with our recommendations.*

Young women, of course, still turned fifteen after fourteen. The Central Committee and the Minister of Culture in the capital never answered the tribunal's letter. How could they, with a sober face? Young women, still, when the time came, turned fifteen. No committee or minister on heaven and earth could change that. ¿Quién se atreve a usurpar la naturaleza?—¡ni el Señor mismo! But now there were no fiestas, no father with the rebellious heart of Roque San Martín, no daughter like Benicia who would ever feel the tickle-joy—under the armpit, in the shallow pit of the navel, on the rosy hills (esas colinas inexploradas, jamas pisadas) of her woman parts—of a million frisky bubbles of Dom Pérignon.

So on what man would fall the burden of commemoration? To what sad soul would the banished angels of womanhood reveal themselves, when girls after fourteen (and musn't they?) naturally turned into women of fifteen?

On no man, no man . . . for what man had the cojones with which to lavish a daughter with feastly love after the heavy sentence that fell on Roque San Martín, what bull had not withered into an ox? So on no man, no man at all . . . but on a short-haired gorbellied loose-sphinctered flat-muzzled misery of a beast. Angels, especially banished angels, have the strangest preferences for who should serve as their messengers in this world. And so they appeared, one afternoon not long after Roque San Martín's trial, to the bull-mastiff Tomás de Aquino. He, no visionary, was lounging on the sun-warmed bricks of his master's inner courtyard, thoughtless almost (as was his wont) except for the close attention he was paying to the expanding bubble of fetid gas that was vacillating in his belly, unsure of whether to escape out the back door or the front. And would not his namesake, the angelic doctor, have lectured el Rubio's bull-mastiff that it is exactly when we are paying the most dire attention to the basest matter that heavenly creatures see it best fit to visit us, that it is only in those moments of desperate scrutiny to our impure flesh, esta carne como ropa vieja, that we are vulnerable at all to God's better beauty, to the grace of the immaculate? It was so for the soot-footed Virgencita in her dusty dwelling, it was so for the old gray-haired Elizabeth in her long and barren marriage, and it is so for all beings. The wind, any guajiro knows, howls fiercest past shuttered windows.

But in our story, another wind, a reeking wind lengthened in swirls— like the vaporous tail of a plummeting fiend—in Tomás de Aquino's mid-section so that he had to shift the heft of his thick torso over to his left and cast his prodigious haunch heavenwards to facilitate release; all this, forcing his huge head askance, setting his jaundiced eyes directly into the sunlight that torrented through the iron-grill roof of his master's inner courtyard; and there from the pure nimbusy yellow of afternoon light to the sick yellow of excess bile passed the banished angels of womanhood and possessed this most brutish seed of a vile murderous race (for no man, no man at all, found them worthy for their avenging task).

On that afternoon, less than a week since the sentencing of Roque San Martín and his family, less than two weeks since the last quinceañera feast on St. Anthony's Day, so suddenly and heavenly struck, Tomás de Aquino let out a monstrous tympanic fart and he rolled back his leathery lips and exposed his vulpine fangs and assumed the mantle of his mission.

He sang.

No, no, no, chico, not sang. That is too casual and watery a word. Tomás de Aquino did not sing, not if a song is melody and harmony and rhythm, not if a song is the metered whispers and thunders of a river, not if a song is a deep-tissue massage to the noise-sore soul. No this was no song, no cantata, no madrigal, no aria, no hymn. Perhaps a fugue, yes a fugue maybe. Qué va, no, not even that. This was discord, jagged vengeance of the sort unmatched by all furies of pandemonium, unimagined by even the most modern composers; so Tomás de Aquino most certainly did not sing. Later, they were to name the sky-piercing wail that first burst from his lungs that afternoon like the cry of a thousand tortured demons *el llanto de los quince* (the wail of the fifteens), as if all women that had not become, our *would* not become, women, by decree, had lent their caged voices, their ululant tongues, all the anger of their thwarted womanhood, to this basest of beasts named after the most celestial of saints. Later, mothers and grandmothers, sisters and aunts, cousins and neighbors (indeed all women who had properly become women when it had been legal to do so) were to join Tomás de Aquino in el llanto de los quince, so that the unsevered silence that was once common during the height of the siesta, at the low night hours when roosters slumber and diarists scribble, in the brief moments just after prayer, all were swallowed by the thousand-voiced harsh protest against el Rubio's inhuman decree. Yet on that first afternoon, it was Tomás de Aquino alone, no man, no man at all, and no woman either, but he, humble flatulent he, whom the banished angels of womanhood visited.

And many years after Tomás de Aquino had drowned in a pool of his own vomit, his death synchronized to the second with that of his master who never had the luxury of knowing that his last anguished opium-laced breath would be his last, many years after the feasts of quinceañera had become common again, the decree against them still in the books but degenerated into the sort of law that it is wiser not to enforce, better left, like old parchment, unperused, it was Benicia San Martín, her hair grown past her shoulders again, her old beauty somewhat rough-hewn by her boxed blooming years spent sleeping in bunkers, wearing olive fatigues, and marching in combat boots, who architected the great feasts of quinceañeras, who, after graduating from the Communist Youth League, had been wise enough to set up her own business, a business that had nothing to do with her training as an electronics technician, a business that was, without mincing words, the family business, a business that fed and clothed her and her reunited family, her delirious mother Yéyé—the stunning mulata of the once-sensuous lips droopy now and slippery with dribble, of the irresistible curves forever shrouded now by the stale urine-stained sheets of the bed she would not abandon—and her decrepit father, who had been released from a Santiago jail and given back his house and welcomed back by his family, who against his better judgment obeyed the wishes of the tribunal to endure till he had served every minute of his sentence, though he had only served half of it, because at some point he had seen the light and signed a document that detailed his conversion to the creeds of la Revolución, that with its marvelous drugs and brilliant surgeons had excised all traces of cancer from his polluted body, and now, sound as a dollar but hollow as a peso, wandered the hallways of his house like a phantom, in a ripped soiled undershirt and low-hung underpants, raising chickens in the drape-drawn living room, condemning his daughter's *illegal affairs* and boldly proclaiming that he was only waiting, waiting till his daughter's hair again touched her ankles so that he may step in peace into his grave, *y maldito sea el día that she had ever become a woman y se me metió en el coco a mi celebrarlo, y maldito sea San Antonio and all his days*, a business with no government license, legitimized instead, yanqui-style, with a business card, a whorish red allegro script on a white background,

Benicia La Reina de Los Quince

which she handed surreptitiously to any inquirer, palm to palm, folded in two, as careful as if it were three crisp yanqui hundred dollar notes, which is what it was worth, sí, como no, as much as nine thousand pesos on a monthly basis, for so large was the urge to celebrate a new womanhood after the murder of el Rubio and the silencing suicide of Tomás de Aquino.

The banished angels of womanhood, suddenly unbanished, shifted their allegiance to Benicia, La Reina de los Quince, the fairy godmother of present and future quinceañera celebrations, who would do her all to make sure that a young woman would remember this day for the rest of her life, especially for the older ones, the ones in their late teens and twenties who had missed out on their celebrations during the ban period and now came to her with their own bundle of pesos or wrinkled black-market dollars, to reclaim their right. The business was run from the palace of la Reina, the same house where Roque San Martín had staged his infamous St. Anthony's Day feast and now raised chickens and tormented the clientele with his derelict appearance, with his gargly taunts that nothing his daughter would do could match what he had done, that the champagne bath at eight hundred pesos was a sham, soda water tinted with a little bit of coffee and sweetened with a few drops of cane juice, that the linen dress the quinceañera could rent, at 150 pesos, had been altered and re-altered so many times that it had more stitches than a baseball and more stains than the shroud of Turin and stunk worse than a whore's bedsheet, that the makeup the new women would wear for the photo session, personally applied by Benicia, for a mere thirty pesos, had been concocted from the waste and blood of his chickens, that the hibiscus and rose bushes and potted palms set up in the patio for these same photo sessions, at five hundred pesos (even though his daughter was no photographer by trade—*a television repairwoman, carajo, that's what they made her!*), were fakes, as plastic and devoid of fragrance as a capitalist's soul, that the waltzes she played for her measly parties were from records so scratched and from phonographs so antique that the marvelous Strauss "Tales from the Vienna Woods" sounded more like "Wails from the Corner Brothel."

And what could Benicia San Martín, as the quinceañera's mother placed her hand on her daughter's chin and turned her daughter's eyes away from the mad old man, say to the father who had brought her so much joy on that St. Anthony's Day so long ago? What but a most mild retort?

"Cállese, papacito. Cállese, por favor. This woman just wants to make her daughter happy, like you once made me happy." And at this, Roque San Martín would hunch his bony shoulders and snivel like a boy and wipe his hands, stained with the blood of slaughtered chickens, on the seat of his underpants, and shuffle back into the living room, and mutter to his daughter that her hair was far too short for anyone to believe that she was a fairy godmother of any kind.

Y quién sabe, perhaps Roque San Martín was right, for the more Benicia let her hair grow, down past her wing-bones stretching towards the foothills of her buttocks, not as dark now, not as thick, streaked with long strands of yellowy gray, like threadings of gold in a countess's gown, the more her business thrived, till she was able to afford real camellia and gardenia bushes and a faux-brick well, which she set up in the center of her patio for the quinceañeras to lean against during the photo sessions, and new Irish linen dresses in six different sizes and styles and boxes of makeup, which she purchased from the local theater company, and even, near the collapse of her business, a Rolleiflex camera, which was said to once have belonged to the town's most famous and notorious photographer, Armando Quiñón (somehow having been pilfered from the bonfire that destroyed all his things on the day of his suicide), that made it almost impossible to take a bad picture, and she even, once or twice, found enough real champagne on the black market for the quinceañera to take a puddle-bath and was able to hire a quartet from the town's symphony to play live waltzes at the fiestas.

So it was wallowing in so much relative success, to the surprise of her father, who now made it a point not to show his face when prospective clients came over, to even tidy up the living-room coop and box all the gallinas in the kitchen, her hair now past the lift in her buttocks, that Benicia San Martín headed to the house on the corner of Maceo and Narciso López Streets. Her client, a boyish girl, named Teresa Cruz, had failed to show up for her preliminary makeup and photo session. Perhaps, Benicia thought, her mad abuelita, the once respected and respectable doña Adela, widow of the libertine Teodoro, mother of the most famous dissident on the Island (though Benicia thought her father better deserved that honor), had not finished the dress, for she had insisted on not renting one of Benicia's newly purchased dresses for her granddaughter.

"I will make her my own from the moth-eaten shreds of her mother's wedding dress," she had said on her visit to Benicia's patio. "That at least I can do for the poor girl. It is said that madwomen make the finest dressmakers!" And she smiled wickedly and pressed a bundle of pesos, mingled with dollars (to give it heft), into Benicia's palm and shuffled off on her two canes.

Roque San Martín, who had been peeping through a lifted drape in the living room, prophesied to his daughter that soon, much too soon, the Island would be full of people like him and the mad old Adela, too weak to walk but too proud to die. This, he shouted to his daughter, was the glory and future of la Revolución, a nation of immortal invalids.

"Por favor, papacito," Benicia said, not looking at him, separating the dollars from the pesos, "if the vigilantes hear you saying such things they'll throw you right back in jail."

"No, no, mijita, we are the tamed, the cured, the undead. We are no good to them in their jails, better to have us raising gallinas and knitting shut holes in moth-eaten dresses. Let them cast their sad nets elsewhere. Hacia usted, mijita . . . hacia usted, and all your illegal affairs."

"¡Sshhh, sumuso, papacito, por favor! Los vigilantes have ears cupped to every wall!"

And such she feared was the reason the girl Teresita Cruz had not shown up for her appointment. Someone had found something out and whispered it to someone who whispered it to someone else who whispered it in a wrong ear. Such were the perils of running a private business not sanctioned by the government, and Benicia had coursed through them many times before (greasing the greasable palm, tickling the ticklish hand—a full quarter of her profits she reserved in her coffers for bribes), but she had never been challenged by the return of the piteous wail known as el llanto de los quince. She, like the many, had thought it had died forever with the death of el Rubio and his grotesque bullmastiff. But on the porchsteps of señora Adela's house, as she arrived to investigate why the girl Teresa had not shown up for her preliminary makeup and photo session, she heard it again. And she asked herself if hounds too have more than one life. And even as she pleaded with the angels of womanhood not to abandon her side, she resisted the temptation to cup her ears, for she knew others heard it too, and she knew that the girl inside that house would never turn fifteen, her life never rightfully and ceremonially steered into womanhood, and that this, this again would be the fate of all the not-yet-women of Guantánamo, for they too heard it, even the unborn, all infected by this song that was not quite a song, not quite anything but the high-pitched noise of mourning, like the squeals of a violin tuned to the echoes of Inferno's steepest canyons, they too heard it and mimicked it, and so Benicia knew, right then and there, on the front porchsteps of the house in the corner of Maceo and Narciso López Streets that she was ruined, ruined till the day they would bring home the lamenting mother (to whom the banished angels of womanhood had now turned), in a pine box, on the six o'clock from Santiago, for not till then would any girl in Guantánamo become a woman again.

So resigned, Benicia San Martín made some quick calculations in her head. She figured that for her ever-blooming camellia and gardenia bushes, for her faux-brick well, for her fifteen finely tailored Irish linen dresses, for her Rolleiflex, for her battered tocadisco and collection of Strauss waltzes, through la bolsa, she could procure enough yanqui dollars to sustain her ailing family for about a year. "After that, papacito's gallinas better start laying golden eggs!"

To make sure Roque San Martín would see that day, she went home, and with a kitchen knife, butchered off her gray-threaded brown locks. When he saw her, Roque San Martín shook his head and said only that it was very unfit for a young woman to live so long with the incontinent ghosts of her parents. Then, just as matter-of-factly, with a most dignified patience, he set out to teach his gallinas how to cackle *el llanto de los quince*.

"Who knows, it may one day serve as our national anthem," he said to them, "for what right-minded girl would want to reach the age when she would need to bear children on this god-forgotten futureless Island!"

TEN

Lamentations

How, mi niña? How have we arrived where we were not going? Whose star led us here? I have come here to this song-infested valley one last time, to this kingdom of forgetfulness to prepare myself. This time I mounted Charo's leaky trawler with an almost-joy. I took off my chancletas and danced around in the puddles of his deck as if drums were playing inside me. I danced till Joshua and Triste restrained me, afraid that I would punch holes in the rotted wood, or that I would fall overboard and drown, or even that I would throw off my shawl and throw off my dress.

"Coño, la vieja Alicia has finally gone mad," Charo said. He started the engine and it coughed and hacked and gargled like an old smoker waking at dawn. He warned us, as he always does, of the dangers of crossing the Gulf of Batabanó. "This puke-green sea quells forever the fire of memory. He who crosses it will find, on reaching the other shore, that he has not yet lived. Bueno, ahí está, forewarned is forearmed, though you will not remember what I have said. Qué pena, coño. We always forget what we should most remember."

How does Charo himself always remember if he's crossed this sea so many times? When asked this, he shouts over the old-man rumble of the engine that some impossible fires burn like forgotten gold in air pockets of the darkest canyons of the sea, that they persist by breathing in the very breath that they breathe out. And he is right, for it is with one of these impossible fires that I borrow from him, the Crosser, that I can see you now, here where I have come, followed by the Newer Man's black-garbed soldiers, who laugh at me through the telescopes of their rifles, followed by the Newer Man himself, his wingless horse patient, trotting, not even breaking a sweat, to the openings of the caverns in the valley's eastern walls, where, in their nests, the wild giant jutías nurse their young with more talent than I nursed you, my only daughter, their hairless fallow bodies wrestling for every available teat, the mother still, but for a brush of her hind leg to unglue one and make room for another that has been left out, and in her forepaws she holds one more that will go hungry, that she cannot make room for, and licks shut its unopened eyes—¿no ves? less than a mother-rat I was for you, and yet, not ever a woman, your only child's tongue sticks to the roof of your mouth, mi pobre niñita, mi santa, as your abuelita calls you. Where can I run to in this isle of pains where my shame does not usurp my shadow? In what hole can I bury these shriveled tits? For even in the narrow deadend tunnels of these walls, where breezes dare not travel, where the mother rats burrow to bury their hungry, where the world's acid light has never cut, there it is, in the shape of your eyes, in the sharpness of yellow needles. Here lives the perpetual fire that feeds on itself.

Mi santa, as your abuelita calls you, once you were the picture of beauty, an icon to make all angels envious, in your lacy dresses that she so diligently made for you (even as her sight failed and she was forced to count each stitch out loud lest she forget), and your flowing coffee-black locks (which she braided also counting out loud):

> *una dos tres,*
> *que bella mi niña es,*
> *cuatro cinco seis,*
> *quien no la queréis,*
> *siete ocho nueve,*
> *la tierra no se mueve,*
> *diez once doce,*
> *la loca es la que cose*

and your eyes whose marbled depths tempted even the men of God to whisper *if only*. Sí, mi vida, así mismo es, even the men of God. For who did your abuelita not tempt with her santa, her niñita? You were the daughter she never had, for papá stole me from her the second I was born, even though your abuelita knew he had another daughter out there somewhere, in his lives lived apart from her. She let him steal me, perhaps with the thought that with me, one day she could steal *him* back. Poor papá. There *was* another daughter, your tía Marta, who, thanks to your abuelita, you hardly knew. She is happy now. As happy as any Cuban can be in Miami. Papá loved her too. His happiest moments were spent offstage; and then one day, just like that, after we had retrieved him from the olive house, he dropped in front of the bathroom mirror, in the wings of our lives, his heart stopped before he even had a chance to finish shaving the left side of his face, to perfume his neck, to wipe himself. Wickedly . . . wi-cked-ly . . . your abuelita refused to perfume his corpse, for she said it would attract all his whores to the funeral house like flies to carcass. *Qué bueno, they will never see him again,* she said with an awful satisfaction, standing over him.

And before she called for Father Gonzalo, she made me shave the rest of his face, right there on the bathroom floor, as if she could not stand, at the end, the thought of touching him, even with the shaving blade. Imagínate, I was about your age, maybe a bit younger. Sí, hasta más jovencita. *I am only a girl,* I said pleading with my eyes. *Do not tell me you are only a girl,* was her answer, standing above, reaching me the blade, which she had simply picked up from the floor and not even rinsed. *Finish shaving your father, it will be an embarrassment if Gonzalo finds him like this.* (Gonzalo who knew intimately of our thousand little embarrassments, but who kept his well hidden from us.) *Defachatado vivió y defachatado murió.* I took the blade from mamá. I rinsed it with hot, hot water. I knelt on the cold floor. I steadied my one hand with my other hand, held it by the wrist. I shaved the foamy side of papá's contorted face. ¡Qué mala!

Y al final, she failed, for the flowers that bloom on your abuelito's grave in Campo Santo were not brought there by her. The chinese orchids, the naked-lady lilies, the begonias, the turkish roses, the bougainvillea that creeps over the tombstone like a lover's thousand fingers. What a marvel! Though you have never seen it (she would never permit me to take you there), papá's grave shames all others in Campo Santo. There are so many that remember him. Yet not one bush was planted by his wife. ¡Qué mala!

She saved all her compassion for you. The second you were born, no mejor digo, mucho antes, in the days after you were conceived, she consecrated you with all the bitter reserves of her unused love. She made you her santica. And you were hers. I too let another steal my only daughter. And who did she not dare tempt with you, with her prize? Me. The butcher and the baker (your abuelita, with you in hand, never made colas). The servants of God (how many times did Father Gonzalo's vision stray from the theme of his homily to dwell unchastely on your face?). Even papá's barefoot ghost, who would not be so easily tempted, who taunted your abuelita by wandering our house too cheerful for a ghost, by failing to fall in love with you as so many had fallen for you. Papá's barefoot ghost, who came and went from our house as rashly as when he had not been a ghost, whom your abuelita blamed for every single domestic disturbance from the very afternoon of his burial. When we returned from the cemetery, fruitflies had infested our kitchen, and their tiny darting almost invisible lives drove your abuelita into a frenzy. She chased after them, armed with the lace handkerchief she had not used, twisting her body and swinging her arms about as if she were possessed by an angry orisha. Not bothering to change, to remove her widow's veil, she single-handedly slid out both refrigerators and the stove to find the source of their numbers. But there was no spilt syrup, no rotting mango, so naturally your abuelita blamed papá. It was the stink of his cologne that was attracting the flies. Some whore must have snuck into the funeral parlor and doused him with it!

"Desgraciado, ya salió," she proclaimed. "I smell him. He cannot stay put! Even in his grave!"

In the weeks to come papá's ghost was to be blamed for the milk turning sour three days before its date, for the chicken pot pie burning to a crisp, even though it had been in the oven for less than half an hour, for lost pieces of mail, and for the dark stains on the brick floor of the patio, caused your abuelita said by the ghost's escupitajos, for not even in the hereafter had he learned his manners. Poor papá, though none of it was his fault at all. The fruitflies nested in the rotting apples pierced with cloves that your abuelita hung with cheesecloth in the kitchen, like shrunken heads, to ward off evil spirits. The milk turned sour early because it had not come directly from the farm (la Revolución's labyrinth agrarian bylaws assured that), the chicken pot pie burned because our stove was so ancient that the dial settings for the oven had been rubbed off by wear, our mail was lost because our mailman was a drunk, and the stains on the patio floor were from the rotting fruit that dropped from the plum tree because papá was the only one that ever cared to pick them.

But for his greatest sin perhaps papá's ghost was culpable, most of all your abuelita blamed papá's ghost for his infidelity, for coming and going with as little regard for others as when he had been a man. Not even in his grave, not even for his granddaughter, so many years later, would he stay put. In this your abuelita was not wrong. Many years after his death we were not sure on what day, what week, what season papá's ghost would drop by for a brief visit, on what morning we would notice your abuelita's rocking chair rocking, rocking all by itself for no reason at all. Poor papá. It is his charm, his restlessness that is yours.

Little is lost by any single death, mi vida. Little.

Remember the story I used to tell you when your abuelita would let me have you, the story I used to tell you before bedtime. ¿Te acuerdas, mijita? Your abuelita did not like the story. She said it was too morose for a young girl. My ti-íta Edith used to tell it to me and my cousins when we were children, and we had liked it. And you liked it. Remember. Remember the old willow who lived alone near a wood, the old willow whose branches were tears, misty and yellow, the old willow who had wept so much, so long, that all her eyes had gone blind. ¿Te acuerdas?

"And how many eyes did the blind willow have?" you asked, snuggled against me in that dark room with so many moons.

"As many eyes as she had branches, and branches of branches."

"And how many eyes is that?"

"Many many eyes . . . over a hundred, over a hundred hundreds, more eyes than a cloud of flies."

"And why did she weep?"

"She wept for many reasons. She wept because she was alone. She wept because she had once been one in a family that formed a majestic grove near a brook where poets came for shade and inspiration. But there had been a drought and all had perished but her. She wept because many came from faraway lands to the base of her trunk, maidens and madmen, emperors and fools, to recount the tale of their sad lives, came from faraway lands only because they knew she would weep for them as no one else would. She was a great weeper! But mostly, she wept because it was the thing she knew how to do best. She had no ears so she could not hear. She had no nose so she could not smell. She had no tongue so she could not speak. She had only eyes, eyes brimming with tears."

"And why did tears make her blind?"

"Because tears are like little fires surrounded by a bubble of seawater."

"Tears burn," you said. "I know."

"But on her death, she was rewarded by God. She was planted by a stream in the gardens of Heaven so that all who saw her may be reminded of the world they had left behind. So that they may never forget. There is no purpose in Heaven without memory of this earth. God needs this earth as much as we need his Heaven."

"And she wept even then? Even in Heaven she wept?"

"Even in Heaven, for God had asked her not to stop doing what she did best."

"Poor willow. Even in Heaven."

And then you snuggled tighter against me and kissed my neck and slept, your breath like a baby dragon.

Even in Heaven, at last, where she was going all along. *Mi vida. Mijita. Ya una mujercita.*

You first touched me in the basement of the schoolhouse. If I could now touch you back, my dear Julio, touch you as if my fingers were waking from a long bloodless sleep, as if your warrior's hull were the petals of a pale virgin's cheek. My hand dares not. It is as unsure, as petrified as the hand that did not reach for you as the schoolchildren watched.

"Vamos, señorita," you said, "por favor, por el amor de Dios, direct me. It will be safer for the children if I do not linger here too long. The Rural

Guard is everywhere. I cannot say for sure that they have not followed me here and are surrounding the schoolhouse right now. Vamos, señorita, por favor."

I saw, and the schoolchildren saw, the rusty pistol tucked into your pants, aimed down at your crotch. But even in the unlikely chance that such a weapon functioned, that it was loaded, I knew, and the schoolchildren knew, that you would never use it. Not on us. I was not afraid and the schoolchildren were not afraid. You were no warrior yet—though on your entrance into our room you had announced that you were a guerrillero, a revolucionario, an enemy to the tyrant. Had I not felt the blood plummet out of my heart, my limbs grow numb, my brow cold from something far more startling than fear, I would have felt pity, a lo mejor even revulsion, for you looked far too feeble, too desperate—barefoot, mud under your toenails, thin as a grave-dweller, the armature of your ribs poking at your oversized grimy campesino smock, your cheeks and your hands soiled, your beard and your shock of hair twisted into intricate knots, as if by some wicked design—to be a proper enemy to anyone, even the impotent indio tyrant.

No child cried out. They seemed in fact to welcome your intrusion into the drudgery of their multiplication lessons. They gladly put down their nubbed pencils and shut their notebooks and rested their faces on their hands and watched you, watched us as if we were playing out a scene in a yanqui movie. The skeletal lunatic prophet comes to the wistaria-covered country schoolhouse. I could have made you vanish. I could have turned back to the chalky dogged logic of the blackboard where 6 times 6 was 36 and 6 times 7 was 42, and click by click, with the end of my pointer, like a hypnotist, I would have taken back their attention, made you less interesting than a lump of melting ice. Strange as you were, armed as you were, they were still far more in awe and fear of me than they were of you. But your hand moved, and I knew, and the schoolchildren knew, it was not moving for the pistol. Your dirty hand moved and it reached for mine.

"Vamos, señorita, por favor. I was told by the Comandante-en-Jefe to ask for no one, to search for the most beautiful woman in the school-house . . . that she had the key to the trapdoor, that she would direct me to the basement."

Later you invented stories, you told me you had seen me through a grimy window as you scurried up to the schoolhouse like a sand critter, that you had caught a glimpse of the side of my face, of the slope of my bare milky shoulder, as I wrote out the multiplication tables. Later you invented stories to seduce me, as if you needed to, as if I would love you for the dangers you had passed, and you would love me that I did pity them, as if I indeed were one of those schoolchildren whose multiplication lesson you had so conveniently interrupted and not the woman who held back her hand from you, to the thrall of the schoolchildren, who seemed to know this drama better than we who were playing it.

I went to the bottom drawer of my desk and fetched my key ring and motioned with it, jingling you out of the room. You, as obedient as any of my schoolchildren, followed me to the trapdoor in the back, across the schoolyard. "I know he has come to see you." Your voice was whispery, sheepish. "I know you have done this, vamos, unwillingly. But you will not live to regret it. I know you have done this more for the safety of your children than for our cause, but it is one and the same. When they are men and women, they will be glad they had such a teacher as you. Many guajiros are joining our ranks . . . our army is growing, but ten thousand men without weapons are useless in the struggle against the tyrant."

As usual, you exaggerated, the rebel army then consisted of a few hundred men, if that.

I undid the lock and threw back open one of the trapdoors. The noise frightened you. You crouched down and hunched your back and looked around. But you did not imagine that I had done it on purpose. You helped me open the opposite door and you repeated in my ear that you were not sure you had not been followed. We laid the other heavy wooden door gently on the ground. The planks were spongy from the recent rains. The sharp sweet stink of gunpowder, like aged cheese, wafted up from the basement. This pleased you. You craned your neck and peered into the opening, your shoulder blades poking up like arrow heads under your smock. The cloud of fear and doubt had melted from your face. The gunpowder was very important, you said, it was needed to set booby traps for the Rural Guard.

"You are no warrior," I said. The strong smell was not a good sign. It meant that some of the ammunition had likely gotten wet.

"How?" you said, growing nervous again, backing off and wrinkling your eyes like a cat who has come across an unnerving odor, again darting looks into the woods that surrounded the schoolhouse.

"It has rained. There are leaks. I warned him. I warned your friend the lawyer. But like most lawyers, he seems to lack any talent for listening. Maybe lawyers and graduate students aren't the best bunch to be leading an army against Batista. Though, bien sabe todo el mundo, he is no warrior himself, no matter how many military titles he attaches before his name. Couldn't you find any professional colonels in Mexico?"

You smiled. You let me mock you. Mock your cause. You were not yet so enamored of la Revolución.

"It has rained?" You pushed your fingers into the moist earth. "Coño, I *know* it has rained, señorita! I have slept under the rains since we arrived from Mexico. Mírame, coño, am I not a creature of these rains? But the comandante said you had put the weapons in a dry place! That is why he brought them here."

"The earth leaks. I told your friend the lawyer."

"Sí, the earth leaks . . . El Comandante-en-Jefe would not know that."

And you put out your hand again and this time I took it and led you into the basement. The shadows emboldened you. (Were you a ghost even then, at the height of your life?) You pretended to forget why you had come. You grazed against me in a manner that had nothing to do with your duty, your mission. (In this, your friend the lawyer had been different—dry-worded threats, fixed gaze, two paces apart, all business.) You said that I was right, that you were no warrior and that you would not be a warrior again when the tyrant was overthrown. And, as if this promise had been asked of you, you touched me to prove your sincerity. Your hand ticklish as a rain breeze on my bare shoulder. You asked me for permission to return, to return when there were no weapons to gather. You asked me for permission like a schoolboy. I did not answer one way or the other. I could not. But making no answer was too clear an answer, so you touched me again, desperate, with the weightiness of a drowning creature, before you gathered up the sack of rifles and the casks of gunpowder and left me there in that dank hole under our schoolhouse, waiting for your return.

It was only when the schoolchildren asked me that I realized I did not know your name. So they helped me invent stories about you, calling you simply el Esqueleto. And now I know that it was these stories more than anything else that made me unable to forget, that taught me how to touch you back.

Ay, si pudiera . . . that I could bring them here to me now with their stories. My children, grown as they are now, proper servants of la Revolución. That they could teach me again not to know your name, your part, your destiny. That they may invent worlds where neither you nor any of the rebels ever existed: an isle where a ragtag band of men whose skeletons grew on the outside like sea-crawlers fought and defeated a large army of ponderous green bulls, and in the waste of the battlefield grabbed each of the slaughtered bulls by the fleshy pouch and sunk in their blades under the throat and slipped it down the belly and peeled off their rough hides and like the savage indians of yanqui lore wore the skin of their enemy as armor for future battles. The men whose skeletons grew on the outside would rule the mountain for many generations, the children said, for they were protected and guided by the skinless ghosts of a thousand enemies. My children, who had trouble with 8 times 9, but somehow knew their world as well as the fates did.

And so they taught me to know you, by peeling you skin by skin. How many visits did you make to our schoolhouse in Ermita? How many skins did you let me peel off in that dank basement, till I touched you, touched you like none of your enemies, none of your compañeros had ever touched

you. And as the ends of my fingers, the inside of my lips learned every part
of you, guessed at shapes I did not know, you remained still as a fleshless
bone, your only movement the breath that passed through you, humming
and sighing like a wind through a hollow stump. ¿Qué pasó? What happened to that revolutionary patience with which you let me love you?—
which I now mimic (this ferocious torpid mockery my only tribute to you,
my lost, lost husband), here, hidden in the walls of this valley, as dark and
as dank as that basement, no longer aware of what is night or what is day, the
nameless jutías *my* compañeras. Like me they will no longer serve, will no
longer sacrifice their children and so are condemned to spend their days here
in these holes where runaway slaves once hid, having neither life nor death.

To touch you now, to guess at the shape of the wounds that took you from
me a second time, in those moments after you had lived, before you had died.

A kiss, Héctor, a kiss to a square of your cheek pressed against the cold
chain-link fence. A kiss knowing I may not ever kiss you again. A kiss
with a woman's passion, even though you would not give me your lips.
You rarely gave me your lips after we were children. At some point, you
started to complain that my lips tickled yours, and each time we tried to
kiss, you pulled back and burst out in laughter and wrapped your arms
around yourself as if I were torturing you with feathers. Pero, when we
were children, te acuerdas, primito bello, when we were children. Te
acuerdas, hidden from your mother and your brother, and later hidden
from your teacher and from the photographer, sometimes under the nose
of your blind father, as he listened to the sordid affairs of his radio *novelas*
(berating the out-heroding narrator when unconvinced with the plot, as if
it were the poor actor's fault that the writer had failed), te acuerdas, esos
besitos, half-dry, half-moist, like a first nibble into a veiny plum we could
not eat.

You rarely gave me your lips afterwards, even in that room where you
consoled me with your hands, wakened me with the needles in your eyes,
where you led me beyond grief. Remember our childhood song, our kissing song:

> *Besitos besitos, en los labios labios,*
> *Besitos besitos, saben a mar a mar,*
> *Besitos besitos, somos diablos diablos,*
> *Besitos besitos, te voy a dar y dar.*

With it, we went where our kisses would not, we gave to each other what
our kisses could not.

"Sí, sí, all right" your father said when he heard us (he could not guess
that it was any more than a song of children), lowering the volume on his

radio, demanding we play out the tale better. And so we did. I played the beautiful dark scorned widow and you the mulatto son of my husband's mistress, or something like that. You seduced me with your humility, with your apologetic existence, with your love for your dead father, for blood, you said, is the greatest tie. And you moved to kiss me. And I let you. I let you touch my lips with yours. But at this, your father interrupted, again the action was becoming too unrealistic for his taste. How did he know we had let our lips touch if he was blind? What sounds did we make?

"No, niña boba, así no," he said, becoming narrator and writer and director all at once, "you turn your head. You let him approach you. Let him move to kiss you. Sí, sí, all right. He is as handsome, as desirable, as much a man, as your husband once was, perhaps even more so . . . the lure of the prohibited and so on. Yet, at the last second you turn your head, so that his kiss lands on your cheek. And with this you are revenged. With this little gesture you prove both your bitter love and your monumental contempt for the dead man that is his father and your lost husband. This is where life is, in these simple gestures, rubied with both tardy forgiveness and persistent rancor. This is life, coño. Sí, sí, all right."

Then your father turned the volume back up, only to find that inside his radio the husband's son had already bedded the dark-haired widow, and he clenched his fists and berated the poor actors some more, proclaiming that it was not so and could not be so in real life, that it was odious to the senses to believe such trashy fantasies. And there we left him, a most disconcerted realist judiciously grieving; and we escaped to where I would not turn my head, where we could taste the tiny drops of the Caribbean in each other's half-dry half-moist lips.

Rarely again after we were children, after you learned other arts and began forgetting our song, did you give me your lips. Yet, I knew how to love you through others that better suited your needs. I loved you even through Julio, through my own husband I loved you. Right next to him, from the fourth row, facing the center ring. I followed you to your death camp, just to kiss you once more on the tiny square of your cheek pressed against the cold fence. I welcomed into my heart the giant twisted man who was your best lover. What would your father say of this, our story? ¡Ay, nuestras ilusiones! O how he would berate the poor luckless narrator of our lives!

"¿Pero qué es esto? Vamos a ver, vamos a ver if I got this preposterous story right. There, the widow, sealed in her mother's room, wrapped in a musty old shawl that she found in a corner of the closet. Sí, sí, all right, her rage is real enough, I'll buy that. Against God, against nature, against all conventions of grief. Her husband was no longer hers, a soldier stripped of his rank, his honor, banished. Though this poor man's St. Helena was his own family, he was condemned to be a mere ciudadano, a mere husband. Sí, sí, all right, I'm with you, I can see *his* rage. Old soldiers are strange, and it is believable enough that one can be in a state of complete exile, even in the midst of one's own family. All great stories are full of that. So the widow is a widow before she is a widow. Sí, sí, all right.

"But let's go back to her, sealed in her mother's tomblike room, wrapped in a musty old shawl that she found in the corner of a closet. Bien, bien, the cloth of her ancestors, of the dead—her wish to join them maybe. A mock shroud. She plays with jigsaws in the dark, feeling the riddly curves of the pieces as she imagines she feels the holes that riddled her husband. She plays music. It smooths and deepens her grief. Her husband's favorite violin concerto. They danced to it, made love to it many a time. They even heard the famous Lithuanian violinist play it once during their honeymoon in Berlin some years after the War. What was his name? Details, coño, the soul is in the details, you clumsy lazy devil. Look it up. *Make it up,* if you have to . . . but give me a name! Heifetz. Ahí, ahí, all right, Jascha Heifetz. Sí, sí, all right, his name sounds like the tightening of a string. His fingers are worth a thousand heavens! His bow a thousand beauties! It is his recording that she plays (who? who? Paganini? No. No. Beethoven. Sí, sí, all right, the master's singular violin concerto, perfecto), but there is a scratch on the record and it skips and the widow does not move to slide the needle, she is too concerned with the shapes at the end of her fingers, she lets it skip and skip and skip till the strings magically become drums. Others move the needle. The mother who brings the food and the water that the widow hardly touches. She slides the needle. The priest who offers her the condolences her soul must reject, like a bruised muscle cringes at too pressing a touch. He slides the needle. Sí, sí, all right. The ghosts also, for it is true, they are most likely to appear after a recent death, as if to escort the unwilling soul away from the living. The ghosts too slide the needle.

"But this other visitor? No le da un carajo about the stuck needle. Why does she accept him? Why does she let him lounge on the bed behind her, like . . . like a what?—*a slumbering cat consoling her with his purrs.* Hmmm? Sí, sí, all right, but let's fix this a little. Let's turn down the volume, for here is where things start to go awry, bueno, como se dice, to overstep the modesty of nature. Vamos a ver. You, mi niña Alicia, you play the widow. Heed, heed: all joy has been wrung from her heart. Still, she must live; *and* unless we decide to kill her right off, at the top of the story, she must be played! Take any of your aunt's scarves, let that serve for the musty old shawl. Props: use them well, they are extensions of character. Things, things, treasure them, all earthly things are from God's toy box. You, mijito Héctor, you play this last visitor. Heed, heed: the monstrous act is not yet formed in his head. He too has come merely to console. He has heard of the murder of his dear cousin's husband and has left the touring circus, and come, as the mother comes, as the priest comes, as the ghosts come, merely to console. Vamos a ver, where does he break company from them. Sí, sí, claro, the record, the Beethoven . . ."

And this time, as I imagine it, your father changes not a thing, for once the radio narrator is not to be outdone, for once your father's play, with us as puppets, follows gesture by gesture what is not heard from inside his radio. The realist is converted. The unimaginable takes place again and again. You come into that dark room. You are the only one who has not bothered to knock. The record is skipping. It sounds like a rumba. The Lithuanian violinist is playing a rumba! (Your father would be wrong in insisting on the name. I never remembered it.) You do not move to slide the needle. You let it skip. I do not look up. I know by the weight of the steps moving towards me that it is not mamá, that it is not Gonzalo, that it is not papá's barefoot spirit (although it is his light steps that yours most resemble, like those of a pigeon). I know it is you. You pass by me and go directly to the bed behind me. You lounge, sí, when you are not in the air, you always lounge. When you are not a pigeon, you are a cat. I feel your hand reaching out for me as you pass but you do not touch me. Then, when you have passed, I hear your voice. Delicate, soft, as if afraid that if you speak too loud I may break. But your voice has always been a balm to my heart.

"Mi primita, mi pobre primita bella."

I answer you, the first time I have spoken since Marta and I returned from the hospital, since el Rubio himself, beret in hand, brought news of Julio's death. There would be no funeral, no burial. He asked forgiveness, it was not his doing. It was the law of the land. The State took the responsibility of burying its traitors. Vaya, merely to prevent the making of false martyrs. He handed mamá an envelope. In it was a document of burial, with a grave number. El Rubio's joy burst through his mock-mourning like the day's first light through a fine linen mosquitero.

I have not spoken till I answer you in kind.

"Primito, thank you for coming. I know they must be very disappointed that you abandoned them so early in the autumn tour. Mi pobre primito bello, how *is* the circus?"

"The circus is nothing without me. But for you, for you, I would abandon the world."

"Sí, eso lo sé, mi pobre primito bello. Julio always said the same thing . . . that the circus was nothing without you."

"I will rejoin them when they pass through here, it is only a few weeks."

"Good. You will rejoin them. I thought for a second that you too were a ghost, the way you did not touch me when you just passed by."

I do not feel you leave, do not feel you come in all those other times, do not feel you shift behind me, yet soon (on what day? after how many visits?) your hand is on my shoulder, soft as lips, peeling off the musty old shawl.

"You have lost weight, primita. Your bones are poking at you from the inside. You should eat. Does la vieja not cook for you?"

"Mamá doesn't like it when you call her that. She thinks it is disrespectful."

Your fingers tremble like grounded feathers, they make soft circles at the base of my neck. You say mamá has gone to the bodega. You say she will be a long time waiting in the cola. You say the priest is hearing confessions. You lift me from the floor with ease. When we are side by side on the bed, I unbutton your shirt. I poke your belly, I tell you where they have shot him. You are ticklish still.

It is your cooing laughter I hear now, here in the echoes of this limestone cave. The soldiers in their black garbs are sharp-shooting outside. They hunt for the crow and the raven, for any bird that dares to be as invisibly black as them. They hunt, while they wait for me to come out. They have followed me here through the telescopes in their rifles. I am the blackest bird of all, I have taunted the eagle and ridiculed the hawk, and the raven and the crow speak to me as if I were one of them, a compañera. They break God's commandment as they are wont (they are clever and rebellious creatures). They inform me of the hour of my death. It is not far away. But they are wicked, they tell me not the manner nor the method. Instead, they teach me the harsh language of ghosts.

Vamos a ver, I'll take this sheet of muslin they furnished me with. *Sí, sí, all right,* I hear your father: *things, God's things, use them, reuse them.* One of Joshua's black-garbed soldiers, pretending kindness, caught up with me on my flight from the Valley of the Nightingales, or as it has been renamed the Colony of the Newer Man. He held his rifle at his side. He looked at me with his naked yellow eyes and lied right through them. He said it might get cold inside the caves. He handed me this sheet of muslin. It was wrapped neatly in a triangle like a flag, or a newly woven shroud. I took it. I knew I would find use for it. But not as they expected me to find use for it. ¡Bobos! Do they really expect that I will do for them what they must do themselves, that I will wind tight this muslin and knit one end through a curtain of stalactites and the other around my neck?

No. No. ¡Réquete no! What they must do, they must do themselves.

This sheet of muslin already soiled with six nights of slumber, with the musk of the jutías who huddle by me, taking and giving warmth, with the invisible inside-rain that falls like dew from the cave ceilings, will be the musty old shawl. Sí, sí, all right, I will sit and wrap it around my shoulders. The ridges on this floor, so marvelously sculpted by the persistent unfelt inside-rain, will be the curves of my jigsaw pieces. The wind whistling in through the hairline cracks of the limestone walls will be the fugacious sadness of the Lithuanian violinist.

So you must come, for I am in greater need of you now than I was then. You must abandon whatever phantom circus you are performing with and come to this fortress wall where I now dwell. Come, as your giant twisted lover came.

Everything is set. Ahí, ahí, do you hear it, the wind is stuck . . . it is playing a rumba, but it is more like the lashing of a whip than the heartbeat of a drum. The wind is different than the Lithuanian violinist. Don't you hear it. Now, come, come as you once came, come without knocking, come and also be different. Let me swallow the seawater of your lips and, drop by drop, drown.

You have forgotten our kissing song, our song of children. We are not that anymore. We have gone way past being children. Come, inhabit the stuck wind. They shot you like they shot him, shot you in those soft places in the belly where I touched you, the spots where you were most ticklish. Aquí y aquí y aquí. But do not despair. Bullets cannot kill the wind. The Lithuanian violinist is stuck on a rumba. I will let the muslin sheet drop. Your hands are like kisses. Your eyes like a pincushion pierced with gilded needles. Your lips burn like coral. Let your lips sear shapes in me, aquí y aquí y aquí, primito bello. I too must know your ends. But let us first conceive a hundred daughters of ghosts, let us repeat our sin again and again till it is as much ours as salt is to the sea, till we know it as well, as naturally as we once knew our childhood song.

Mamá . . . Gonzalo, I hear you both, not in your prayers, not in your hymns, not in your whispery conversations (your hands kneaded together, your brows aching towards each other across the corner of the kitchen table), I hear you in the thump-pa-clump, tatatap, thump-pa-clump of your dance. Is it the dry wind? Is it hurling cannonball-sized rocks against the limestone walls? Are the more ferocious brothers of nature rebelling against this republic of the Newer Man? No, it is too hesitant, too timid a noise to be that sort of wind. Sí, it is your dance, a miraculous sort of performance, for both of you can hardly walk now, one with toes weighted with poison, the other with four legs and no arms, a thing perhaps more pathetic to hear than to watch, thump-pa-clump, tatatap, thump-pa-clump. This freak dance is all you have had since the music of your friendship faded so long ago, since that day when papá fell half-shaven in front of the bathroom mirror. Gonzalo arrived minutes after you put the phone down, you thought he would take longer, you thought I would be finished with my task, but I was just getting the last scruff off papá's neck, and as soon as he saw me there knelt on the bathroom floor with a blade against papá's tranquil Adam's apple, trying to get at a clump of longer hairs that he must have missed morning after morning when he shaved (what did all those young mistresses feel when they put their lips to this token of his slovenliness?), he screamed: "Alicia! Alicia! ¿Qué haces?" and he moved to grab me, but you threw yourself on him. You wept. Now . . . you wept,

wept with desperate little breaths as if your lungs could not match the urgency of your sorrow. And as he held your body up, his eyes still on me, his balance in peril, you danced your freak dance. And I, knelt there on the cold floor by my clean-shaven father, was no longer only a girl.

After the triumph of la Revolución, after Julio was murdered, after I turned my face away from our God, there over the corner of the kitchen table, over the wrinkled envelope that held the lies about my husband's corpse, you and Gonzalo made a pact. (Mamá did you really think I did not know the truth? No soy como tú. I would have surrounded that unnamed numbered grave with a wall of rose bushes, would have built castles of mud over it higher than any tombstone in Campo Santo, it would have outmarvelled even the flowery monument made by papá's whores . . . but Julio was never buried, there or anywhere, and I knew it, even if you never told me.) In an effort to crush my devilish rebellion you made Gonzalo one of ours, to him one day you would bestow your treasured granddaughter, and he in all his loneliness would welcome her and love her far too much.

And although he says that he will (that he must) die in this land, one day he too will add his suitcase to the stack by the door of your house, next to the television console. To Calle Ocho in Miami you will take your last dance, thump-pa-clump, tatatap, thump-pa-clump, la vieja y el cura making all that noise, what will the exiles say (those pale souls who are not quite so sure anymore when they call themselves Cubans)? They have been yanqui-ized, they are not used to such spectacles.

Bang your two canes, mamá (it will be more purging than any grief), wiggle your poisoned toes, Gonzalo (it will be more soothing than a hundred sermons): thump-pa-clump, tatatap, thump-pa-clump. Remind the exiles in Miami how we dance with our sorrows, remind them before they throw you in the homes where they put their old mothers and their decrepit priests.

There is a fire. I smell it. It is your soldiers, I know, they are still waiting. They are roasting a pig. It must be night again. Maybe a bit chilly. Is it winter already? Have I been back that long? How many winters have I missed? How many soldiers have waited outside that narrow hole from whence I traipsed like a rat into my last home? (How old is my daughter?) I know the one hour, but I have forgotten all the other hours that led to it. Why not just come here and get me? Why not just do what must be done? Have you forbidden them? Will *you* do the deed, escort me to my hour? You, the truncated Newer Man. I smell it, the aroma of fat flesh sizzling over the bonfire, the sweet odor seeps in through the invisible cracks in the wall, seeps in here where no fire can exist, except Charo's fire, the fire that burns with its own breath, here to where the earth is undoing itself with the aid of the starved newborn jutías for whom there was not enough milk. A mother chooses. Some she lets live, some she gives back to the earth.

A mother did not make this world. It is the messy handiwork of fathers who so easily forget their deeds and misdeeds, who are not forced to choose before there are any choosings. Though you will say that your father chose, that forgetfulness is the direst choice of all. You too, like my Teresita, an only fatherless child. Only she, she suffered the sin of the father twice. I too was forgetful.

Ves, Joshua, I have watched you watching me the way a young man should not look at a woman so old beyond her age. I have watched you watching me with that disjointed unaimed novice look. Even now, even as I have stepped into the costume of a woman twice my age, this frizzled coronet of gray, this mask folded with sorrow, these shriveled tits, these bones that huddle close to the earth, for the hour they know is not far away. I, a woman only forty-two, who could pass as anybody's abuelita. I have watched you watching me. I have seen it darken. There is only a shadow's difference between the eye of the lovelorn and the eye of the murderer. (The poet knows.) I have watched you. It does nothing. You are a tyro. You are not your father's son.

I have cut off my hair and used it to bed the nests. I have been diligent, I have woven the cloth into the hairs, made it sturdy, for soon they will not have me, crawling in on their front paws as they come, dragging their bellies, they will have to build their own nests. I have cut off my hair. All my lovers have forgotten me. Why then do I smell you crawling into this hole? Vaya, mi negro, your beauty is preceded by your musk! You still smell of *him*! After all these years. Have you not washed your soul in so long? . . . since that hour when you saw pigeons dying in his feet? . . . or have you been sleeping with ghosts? You were right, there is no use in loving yourself if you're only loving yourself, if there's no one's breath seeping through your pores, if there is not a trace of what it was like to once have your lips on his, on his so that his breath was yours, not yours to keep, but yours as your own breath is yours and will not be yours in the coming hour. We have borrowed so much joy from him, mi negro, borrowed it as carelessly and as frequently as if we were moons, but the misery has been all our own, deep as the craters where the caresses of the borrowed light never reach, before we had lost him, before we even knew the flavor of his breath.

Is that why I smell you coming, negro? Do you still follow from nothing to nothing more the one that I once loved that you once loved, the one father of my child, here, where he is lodged like a prayer in my lungs, like a pin in my heart, like a worm in my offals, like a fever in my mind?

What happened to your uniform, mi negro, again you arrive

desnudito, con los huevitos escogeditos, your black skin glistening, and now it is you who bring the comforts; the blanket, the thermoses of cafecito and garbanzo stew, the rum, all in a bundle that you dragged behind you through the narrow holes in this cave. You look much better naked. Vaya, I have never told you that, tenía pena, but its the truth. I see what my Héctor saw. Don't glare at me with such pity. Está bien, your Héctor . . . my Héctor, what's the difference, let's not argue, they have taken him from us, he is theirs now. But our love for him admits no satiety, that is good enough isn't it, good enough for this world, mi negro, that nearness . . . what else do we have? . . . those fingers that do not quite touch, those lips that just graze . . . *our* Héctor.

No, mi negro, gracias pero no, I cannot follow you back. What harmony is left in that world that compares to the harmony of those I will join? There is no remedy, no pardon. I am thrice an adulterer . . . to my husband, to my God, and to *our* Fidel . . . what holy one would convince them to put down their stones? It isn't his or yours or theirs or anyone's hell I am going to, but mine mine mine! Do not mock this stench-breathed abuelita! My bones can barely sustain my weight. What good is it to say to one on her deathbed that she may have lived if she had done this and not done that?

Sí, sí, cómo no, have some rum, help yourself, bundle up in your blankets, the cold rises from under the earth, perdóname, but I can't offer you a bath in the falcon-legged tub this time.

I could have told you stories like you told me, could have wiled away the day—if there were time, if you were not so tired. I could berate you for having fallen asleep without praying for me, mi negro, but I am not the type, I know it is much harder to crawl through holes than it is to swim. For a moment, I fooled myself into thinking it was you who came to escort me, though I knew all the time one always goes to the hour alone, it is the way this fatherless world is made. You have a great thirst for rum, mi negro, but at least you have found something, some method of forgetting. O how my bones ache, I will crawl towards you, since I have forgotten how to walk. I will kiss your breathing belly like I kissed his, aquí y aquí y aquí, adiós, I have lost that grooved vice to endure, adiós mi negro, mi bello, my darling of the wounded name, stay here, there will be those who will need to hear my story, draw your rum-laced breath and do without him a while longer. I cannot.

Una dos tres
que bella mi niña es . . .

I am an abuelita with four white legs, two of wood, two of crumbling bones. In the opening on the other side of the limestone wall, the side facing the rocky Caribbean shore, I found twin albino snakes asleep under the cleft of a rock. I commanded them to serve me and, mi negro, you should have seen how obsequiously they uncurled and petrified, as if I were already some dweller of the underworld. Canes! Two more legs to lead me to my hour! I'll take all the help I can get. I am a shorn-headed four-legged abuelita who never knew her grandchildren, wrapped in a muslin sheet like the dress of a guajiro bride, or a ready-made shroud, a veil through which not an inkling of shame can be hidden. My feet are wounded. What bloody dance is this? Thump-pa-clump, tatatap, thump-pa-clump. The white beaches are spotted crimson. Who dares put his dirty wings around this abuelita bride? Leave me alone, I am counting:

> *una dos tres,*
> *que bella mi niña es,*
> *cuatro cinco seis,*
> *quien no la queréis,*
> *siete ocho nueve,*
> *la tierra no se mueve . . .*

What desert is this shore? Does the rocky sand not know how to count, to read my steps? Carajo, why has la Revolución left the sand illiterate! We have *all* been jilted. I will teach it. I will teach the sand how to count. I will get on all fours and crawl backwards into the sea like a crab. Ahí, the abuelita without grandchildren throws one of her wooden white legs into the sunburnt air . . . and the other. Mira, mi negro, see how the serpents unpetrify, see how they wriggle in the air, thinking themselves acrobats, wingless birds and then, as they must, thump, thump: cursed are you among all wild creatures, on your belly you shall go and dust and rock you shall eat, há háha! you will want to count but you will have no fingers; but *I* can still count, he who condemns you cannot take everything, some knowledge, at least, some nonsense you keep:

> *una dos tres,*
> *que bella mi niña es,*
> *cuatro cinco seis,*
> *quien no la queréis,*
> *siete ocho nueve,*
> *la tierra no se mueve,*
> *diez once doce,*
> *la loca es la que cose.*

Like a crab, like a joyous crab I go. And I see them now, see them perched on the crags of the limestone walls, see them even though they are invisibly black, even though I am going from them, for the sun makes the glass in their rifle telescopes glimmer like diamonds. You are not surprised are you, mi negro? Did you think that they would not have some role to sing in this grand choral finale. I am going from them, like a crab, like a joyous crab, crawling back to the sands of my youth:

> *cose que la es loca la*
> *doce once diez . . .*

Há háha hahaharáha! What strangely familiar laugh is this? The sea tickles me with its foamy slippery fingers. It steals me. ¡Llegamos coño! Há háha hahaharáha hahaharáha háha Há. Take me, strangle me with your watery chords till you have purged me of this last illness, these laughing spasms. Out, out I go, my belly shall never crawl on dust and rock again. From this moment on, joy, joy. Há háha hahaharáha hahaharáha haha Há. Out, out I go.

But what's this? I float. My muslin sheet is as buoyant as a raft of truck tires. Traitors, traitors all! Will you not let a poor abuelita drown in peace? From whence came the order to poison your fabric with air? What yellow cable did you get from the capital? I float, I float, carajo. This gown is glued to me, I cannot anymore get out of it than I can get out of my own skin. Though I try. I try. What indignity! . . . I am a balsera floating on my shroud, I too am going to that blandest of hells, I am bobbing to Miami, coño. How the pale exiles will laugh when they see me!

Pero, mi negro, didn't I tell you to I stay awhile? Not to come after me. Then why does the sea shake its frothy hips to the drumbeat of the earth, as if a whole army were advancing on the shore? Why do the glittery glass eyes of the invisible black birds peel their gaze from me, this poor floating abuelita, and peer down below them, to the holes in the limestone wall, and then slowly lift them as they follow your hoof steps. Careful, these hunter eyes are more easily tempted by things in motion than by what not stirs. Careful, mi negro, slow down. What's the hurry? I am floating, floating like a cork, and here you are coming at full speed, as if you could save me. Careful, coño. What a beauty you are, mi negro, look at you rumbling towards me, coño. I see what our Héctor saw, look at all those rumbas hidden in your frame, your breath is a drum, your chest is a dancer, it leaps and then falls and bends at the knees and gathers all its mass low like a supplicant before it leaps again. What a gait, mi negro. Your skin is a jealous lover, it presses close to your body as if it owned it, as if it were not merely the sack that held it. It wraps all its arms around your hips. It dances. What music does it hear? What violent symphony? Is it joyous? Look at that! This is indeed what our bones were made for, not to hide the marrow, but as a rack for this suit of marvellous black flesh, you would make any god lonely in his fleshless heavens, scratching his airy bald pate, second-guessing himself, thinking perhaps it would have been the greater glory to have made man of flesh alone.

Leave me, you black pelican. What? Would you pouch a dead fish? I had imagined I was miles from the shore, around the nose of the Island, halfway to Miami, and yet, look, you waded to me, you didn't even need to swim! Good. What a sorry bride you hold in your arms. Only one groom for me. Much blacker than you, mi querido negro. The glass eyes are burning holes on your back. Turn, turn me towards them. Let not any holes be made in your lovely jealous skin. Only joy now. Do you hear it? Há háha hahaharáha hahaharáha háha Há. Turn, turn, let me face them, do not blindfold me with your black skin. And when the glass eyes have seen, when they have justified through both their gods and their demons the little pull of their invisible black-feathered fingers, when the bullets come, all seven of them (for la Revolución is very poetic in its justice), swim away, mi negro, do not try to alter the course of this my story, swim away and leave me here floating, exposed, so they will not miss their mark, aquí y aquí y aquí, and do not worry, I have been dressed for this hour, my muslin sheet is poisoned and penetrable, it has become one with my skin and I am far too wounded already, I will not feel the invisible bullets any more than a dead pigeon feels the cracking of its wings or a barefoot ghost the fire in a bed of coals.

Swim away, mi negro, there are so many worlds beyond their sea. Leave me here. I will not live to rest my cheek on any shore.

EPILOGUE

Two Dances

"Do me spiders."

And she would, before his coffee, as he murmured his morning prayers. She would do him spiders. First one and then two and then a few more and soon hundreds upon hundreds. (She was that good with spiders.) Up and down his back, up and down his hairless legs and especially around and around the hardened dried soles of his feet.

That terrible morning there was no joy in spiders.

He did not murmur his rosary as usual. He was restless as he had never been under the dance of the spiders. He shifted. He squirmed. He stifled his sobs with the pillow. The spiders that morning, so many years since the days of the hepatitis epidemic, seemed a sort of medieval torture, their spindly legs freshly dipped in hot lava, as if they had burrowed out from the holes of the netherworld and not dropped from the gardens of God, as if they wove for him a shroud of fire. There was nothing she could say, nothing she could do to ease his grief, except to do what she had always done, to sit by his bedside and do him spiders. Spiders had saved him then, and they would save him again.

"Do me spiders."

And she did, and the spiders danced on skinless flesh.

What does a pastor say when he has lost so many sheep? What does he do, besides trying to smuggle the survivors to some other meadow? And how dare *he* flee when the wolf still roams and so many are still vulnerable?

"Do me spiders."

And she did, as if she were doing it for the first time, as if she had never touched his old wrinkled spotted body, a body that she knew better than her own.

What could she do without him, or he without her, or they without spiders? If his tears were plentiful now, for his friend the old mother (the old mother more a sister than a friend), for the old mother and for the orphaned child—with their suitcases packed for over six years, waiting for permission—if his tears were plentiful now, for the woman coming home in a pine box on the six o'clock from Santiago from the land of her exile, where they had declared her death a swimming accident, black-garbed soldiers as pallbearers, who would make sure they would inter her without opening the box, but a least that, at least they would let her rest in the earth—for all of them, for all this ruined land—if his tears were plentiful now, what of the tears when the Lord decided to separate *them,* he from her and she from him, and they from this daily morning ritual that bound them closer than rings bind lovers?

"Do me spiders."

And she did, for all the witnesses had spoken and there were no words to add and no words to take away, and the woman whose own suitcase had been added to the stack by the door, next to the water-stained console of the black and white television, waiting for permission, was now returning, in a pine box, with six strangers in uniforms that mocked mourning, on the six o'clock from Santiago.

"Do me spiders."

And she did, for there was nothing else left to do.

The spiders have their dance.

The dead theirs.

ABOUT THE AUTHOR

Ernesto Mestre was born in Guantanamo, Cuba, in 1964. His family emigrated to Madrid, Spain, in 1972, and later that year to Miami, Florida. He graduated from Tulane University with a B.A. in English Literature and currently lives in Brooklyn, New York.